THE JUDGE

THE JUDGE

Rebecca West

Carroll & Graf Publishers, Inc.
New York

First published in Great Britain by Hutchinson & Co., Ltd.

This edition published by arrangement with
Virago Press Limited, London.

First Carroll & Graf edition 1995.

Carroll & Graf Publishers, Inc.
260 Fifth Avenue
New York, NY 10001

ISBN 0-7867-0287-7

Library of Congress Cataloging-in-Publication Data
is available.

Manufactured in the United States of America.

95 96 97 98 6 5 4 3 2 1

TO
THE MEMORY OF
MY MOTHER

THE JUDGE

CHAPTER I

(1)

IT was not because life was not good enough that Ellen Melville was crying as she sat by the window. The world, indeed, even so much of it as could be seen from her window, was extravagantly beautiful. The office of Mr. Mactavish James, Writer to the Signet, was in one of those decent grey streets that lie high on the northward slope of Edinburgh New Town, and Ellen was looking up the side-street that opened just opposite and revealed, menacing as the rattle of spears, the black rock and bastions of the Castle against the white beamless glare of the southern sky. And it was the hour of the clear Edinburgh twilight, that strange time when the world seems to have forgotten the sun though it keeps its colour ; it could still be seen that the moss between the cobblestones was a wet bright green, and that a red autumn had been busy with the wind-nipped trees, yet these things were not gay, but cold and remote as brightness might be on the bed of a deep stream, fathoms beneath the visitation of the sun. At this time all the town was ghostly, and she loved it so. She took her mind by the arm and marched it up and down among the sights of Edinburgh, telling it that to be weeping with discontent in such a place was a scandalous turning up of the nose at good mercies. Now the Castle Esplanade, that all day had proudly supported the harsh, virile sounds and colours of the drilling regiments, would show to the slums its blank surface, bleached bone-white by the winds that raced above the city smoke. Now the Cowgate and the Canongate would be given over to the drama of the disorderly night ; the slum-dwellers would foregather about the rotting doors of dead men's mansions and brawl among the not less brawling ghosts of a past that here never speaks of peace, but only of blood and argument. And Holyrood, under a black bank surmounted by a low bitten cliff, would lie like the camp of an invading and terrified army. . . . She stopped and said, " Yon

about Holyrood's a fine image for the institution of monarchy."
For she was a Suffragette, so far as it is possible to be a Suffragette
effectively when one is just seventeen, and she spent much of
her time composing speeches which she knew she would always
be too shy to deliver. "There is a sinister air about palaces.
Always they appear like the camp of an invading army that is
uneasy and keeps a good look-out lest they need shoot. Remember they are always ready to shoot. . . ." She interrupted
herself with a click of annoyance. "I see myself standing on
a herring-barrel and trying to hold the crowd with the like of
that. It's too literary. I always am. I doubt I'll never make
a speaker. Deed, I'll never be anything but the wee typist that
I am. . . ." And misery rushed in on her mind again. She
fell to watching the succession of little black figures that huddled
in their topcoats as they came down the side-street, bent suddenly at the waist as they came to the corner and met the full
force of the east wind, and then pulled themselves upright and
butted at it afresh with dour faces. The spectacle evoked a
certain local pride, for such inclemencies were just part of the
asperity of conditions which she reckoned as the price one had
to pay for the dignity of living in Edinburgh ; which indeed
gave it its dignity, since to survive anything so horrible proved
one good rough stuff fit to govern the rest of the world. But
chiefly it evoked desolation. For she knew none of these people.
In all the town there was nobody but her mother who was at all
aware of her. It was six months since she left John Thompson's
Ladies' College in John Square, so by this time the teachers
would barely remember that she had been strong in Latin and
mathematics but weak in French, and they were the only adult
people who had ever heard her name. She wanted to be tremendously known as strong in everything by personalities more
glittering than these. Less than that would do : just to see
people's faces doing something else than express resentment at
the east wind, to hear them say something else than "Twopence" to the tram-conductor. Perhaps if one once got people
going there might happen an adventure which, even if one had
no part in it, would be a spectacle. It was seventeen years
since she had first taken up her seat in the world's hall (and it
was none too comfortable a seat), but there was still no sign of
the concert beginning.

"Yet, Lord, I've a lot to be thankful for ! " breathed Ellen.
She had this rich consciousness of her surroundings, a fortuitous
possession, a mere congenital peculiarity like her red hair
or her white skin, which did the girl no credit. It kept

her happy even now, when from time to time she had to lick up a tear with the point of her tongue, on the thin joy of the twilight.

Really the world was very beautiful. She fell to thinking of those Saturdays that she and her mother, in the days when she was still at school, had spent on the Firth of Forth. Very often, after Mrs. Melville had done her shopping and Ellen had made the beds, they packed a basket with apples and sandwiches (for dinner out was a terrible price) and they took the tram down the south spurs to Leith or Grantown to find a steamer. Each port was the dwelling-place of romance. Leith was a squalid pack of black streets that debouched on a high brick wall delightfully surmounted by mast-tops, and from every door there flashed the cutlass gleam of the splendid sinister. Number 2, Sievering Street, was an opium den. It was a corner house with Nottingham lace curtains and a massive brown door that was always closed. You never would have known it, but that was what it was. And once Ellen and her mother had come back late and were taking a short cut through the alleys to the terminus of the Edinburgh trams (one saved twopence by not taking the Leith trams and had a sense of recovering the cost of the expedition), and were half-way down a silent street when they heard behind them flippety-flop, flippety-flop, stealthy and wicked as the human foot may be. They turned and saw a great black figure, humped but still high, keeping step with them a yard or so behind. Several times they turned, terrified by that tread, and could make nothing more of it, till the rays of a lamp showed them a tall Chinaman with a flat yellow face and a slimy pigtail drooping with a dreadful waggish schoolgirlishness over the shoulder of his blue nankin blouse; and long black eyes staring but unshining. They were between the high blank walls of warehouses closed for the night. They dared not run. Flippety-flop, flippety-flop, he came after them, always keeping step. Leith Walk was a yellow glow a long way off at the end of the street ; it clarified into naphtha jets and roaring salesmen and a crowd that slowly flocked up and down the roadway and was channelled now and then by lumbering lighted cars ; it became a protecting jostle about them. Ellen turned and saw the Chinaman's flat face creased with a grin. He had been savouring the women's terror under his tongue, sucking unimaginable sweetness and refreshment from it. Mrs. Melville was shedding angry tears and likening the Chinese to the Irish—a people of whom she had a low opinion —(Mr. Melville had been an Irishman)—but Ellen felt much sympathy as one might bestow upon some disappointed ogre in a fairy tale for this exiled Boxer who had tried to get a little homely pleasure. Ellen found it not altogether Grantown's gain that it was wholly uninhabited by horror, being an honest row of fishers' cottages set on a road beside the Firth to the west of Leith. Its wonder was its pier, a granite road driving its rough blocks out into the tumbling seas, the least urban thing in the world, that brought to the mind's eye men's bare chests and muscle-knotted arms, round-mouthed sea-chanteys, and great sound bodies caught to a wholesome death in the vicinity of upturned keels and foundered rust-red sails and the engulfing eternal sterilisation of the salt green waves.

From either of these places they sailed across the Firth : an arm of the sea that could achieve anything from an end-of-the-world desolation, when there was snow on the shores and the water rolled black shining mountains, to a South Seasish bland and tidy presentation of white and green islands enamelled on a blue channel under a smooth summer sky. Most often, for it was the cheapest trip, they crossed to Aberlady, where the tall trees stood at the sea's edge, and one could sit on seaweedy rocks in the shadow of green leaves. Last time they had gone it had been one of the " fairs," and men and women were dancing on the lawns that lay here and there among the wooded knolls. Ellen had sat with her feet in a pool and watched the dances over her shoulder. "Mummie," she had said, "we belong to a nation which keeps all its lightness in its feet," and Mrs. Melville had made a sharp remark like the ping of a mosquito about the Irish. Sometimes they would walk along a lane by the beach to Burntisland. There was nothing good about that except the name, and a queer resemblance to fortifications in the quays, which one felt might at any moment be manned by dripping mermen at war with the landfolk. There they would find a lurching, paintless, broad-bowed ferry, its funnel and metal work damascened by rust ; with the streamers of the sunset high to the north-west, and another tenderer sunset swimming before their prow, spilling oily trails of lemon and rose and lilac on waters white with the fading of the meridian skies, they would sail back to quays that mounted black from troughs of gold.

She thought of it, still smiling ; but the required ecstasy, that would reconcile her to her hopeless life, did not come. She waited for it with a canny look as she did at home when she held a match to the gas-ring to see if there was another shilling needed in the slot. The light did not come. By every evidence of her sense she was in the completest darkness. But she did not know what coin it was that would turn on the light again. Before there had been no fee demanded, but just appreciation of her surroundings, and that she had always had in hand ; even to an extent that made her feel ridiculous to those persons, sufficiently numerous in Edinburgh, who regarded their own lack of it as a sign of the wealth of inhibition known as common sense, and hardly at ease on a country walk with anybody except her mother or her schoolfellow Rachael Wing. She thought listlessly now of their day-long excited explorations of the Pentland Hills. Why had that walk on Christmas Eve, two years ago, kept them happy for a term ? They had just walked between the snow that lay white on the hills and the snow that hung black in the clouds, and had seen no living creature save the stray albatross that winged from peak to peak. She thought without more zest of their cycle-rides ; though there had been a certain grim pride in squeezing forty miles a day out of the cycle which, having been won in a girls' magazine competition, constantly reminded her of its gratuitous character by a wild capriciousness. And there were occasions too which had been sanctified by political passion. There had been one happy morning when Rachael and she had ridden past Prestonpans, where the fisher-folk sat mending their nets on the beach, and they had eaten their lunch among the wild rose thickets that tumbled down from the road to the sea. Rachael had raised it all to something on a much higher level than an outing by munching vegetarian sandwiches and talking subversively, for she too was a Suffragette and a Socialist, at the great nine-foot wall round Lord Wemyss's estate, by which they were to cycle for some miles. She pointed out how its perfect taste and avoidance of red brick and its hoggish swallowing of tracts of pleasant land symbolised the specious charm and the thieving greed which were well known to be the attributes of the aristocracy. Rachael was wonderful. She was an Atheist, too. When she was twelve she had decided to do without God for a year, and it had worked. Ellen had not got as far as that. She thought religion rather pretty and a great consolation if one was poor. Rachael was even poorer than Ellen, but she had an unbreakable spirit and seemed to mind nothing in the world, not even that she never had new clothes because she had two elder sisters. It had always seemed so strange that such a clever girl couldn't make things with paper patterns as Ellen could, as Ellen had frequently done in the past, as Ellen never wished to do again. She was filled with terror by the thought that she should ever again pin brown paper out of

Weldon's Fashions on to stuff that must not on any account run higher than a shilling the yard ; that she should slash with the big cutting-out scissors just as Mrs. Melville murmured over her shoulder, " I doubt you've read the instructions right. . . ." What was the good ? She was decaying. That was proven by the present current of her thoughts, which had passed from the countryside, towards which she had always previously directed her mind when she had desired it to be happy, as one moves for warmth into a southern-facing room, and were now dwelling on the mean life of hopeless thrift she and her mother lived in Hume Park Square. She recollected admiringly the radiance that had been hers when she was sixteen ; of the way she had not minded more than a wrinkle between the brows those Monday evenings when she had to dodge among the steamy wet clothes hanging on the kitchen pulleys as she cooked the supper, those Saturday nights when she and her mother had to wait for the cheap pieces at the butcher's among a crowd that hawked and spat and made jokes that were not geniality but merely a mental form of hawking and spitting ; of the way that in those days her attention used to leap like a lion on the shy beast Beauty hiding in the bush, the housewifely briskness with which her soul took this beauty and simmered it in the pot of meditation into a meal that nourished life for days. At the thought of the premature senility that had robbed her of these accomplishments now that she was seventeen she began again to weep. . . .

The door opened and Mr. Mactavish James lumbered in, treading bearishly on his soft slippers, and rubbing the gold frame of his spectacles against his nose to allay the irritation they had caused by their persistent pressure during the interview he had been holding with the representative of another firm : an interview in which he had disguised his sense of his client's moral instability by preserving the most impressive physical immobility. The air of the room struck cold on him, and he went to the fireplace and put on some coal, and sat down on a high stool where he could feel the warmth. He gloomed over it, pressing his hands on his thighs ; decidedly Todd was in the wrong over this right of way, and Menzies & Lawson knew it. He looked dotingly across at Ellen, breathed " Well, well ! "— that greeting by which Scot links himself to Scot in a mutual consciousness of a prudent despondency about life. Age permitted him, in spite of his type, to delight in her. In his youth he had turned his back on romance, lest it should dictate conduct that led away from prosperity, or should alter him in some manner that would prevent him from attaining that ungymnastic dignity which makes the respected townsman. He had meant from the first to end with a paunch. But now wealth was inalienably his and Beauty could beckon him on no strange pilgrimages, his soul retraced its steps and contemplated this bright thing as an earth creature might creep to the mouth of its lair and blink at the sun. And there was more than that to it. He loved her. He had never had enough to do with pitiful things (his wife Elizabeth had been a banker's daughter), and this child had come to him, that day in June, so white, so weak, so chilled to the bone, for all the summer heat, by her monstrous ill-usage. . . .

He said, " Nelly, will your mother be feared if you stop and take a few notes for Mr. Philip till eight ? There is a chemist body coming through from the cordite works at Aberfay who can't come in the day but Saturday mornings, and you ken Mr. Philip's away to London for the week-end by the 8.30, so he's seeing him the night. Mr. Philip would be thankful if you'd stop."

" I will so, Mr. James," said Ellen.

" You're sure your mother'll not be feared ? "

" What way would my mother be feared," said Ellen, " and me seventeen past ? "

" There's many a lassie who's found being seventeen no protection from a wicked world." He emitted some great Burns-night chuckles, and kicked the fire to a blaze.

She said sternly, " Take note, Mr. James, that I haven't done a hand's turn this hour or more, and that not for want of asking for work. Dear knows I have my hand on Mr. Morrison's door-knob half the day."

Mr. James got up to go. " You're a fierce hussy, and mean to be a partner in the firm before you've done with us."

" If I were a man I would be that."

" Better than that for you, lassie, better than that. Wait till a good man comes by."

She snorted at the closing door, but felt that he had come near to defining what she wanted. It was not a good man she needed, of course, but nice men, nice women. She had often thought that of late. Sometimes she would sit up in bed and stare through the darkness at an imaginary group of people whom she desired to be with—well-found people who would disclose themselves to one another with vivacity and beautiful results ; who in large lighted rooms would display a splendid social life that had been previously nurtured by separate tender intimacies at hearths that were more than grates and fenders, in private picture-galleries with wide spaces between the pictures, and libraries adorned with big-nosed marble busts. She knew that that environment existed for she had seen it Once she had gone to a Primrose League picnic in the grounds of an Edinburgh M.P.'s country home and the secretary had taken her up to the house. They had waited in a high, long room with crossed swords on the walls wherever there were not bookshelves or the portraits of men and women so proud that they had not minded being painted plain, and there were French windows opening to a flagged terrace where one could lean on an ornate balustrade and look over a declivity made sweet with many flowering trees to a wooded cliff laced by a waterfall that seemed, so broad the intervening valley, to spring silently to the bouldered river-bed below. On a white bearskin, in front of one of the few unnecessary fires she had ever seen, slept a boar-hound. It was a pity that the books lying on the great round table were mostly the drawings of Dana Gibson and that when the lady of the house came in to speak to them she proved to be a lisping Jewess, but that could not dull the pearl of the spectacle. She insisted on using the memory as a guarantee that there must exist, to occupy this environment, that imagined society of thin men without an Edinburgh accent, of women who were neither thin like her schoolmistresses nor fat like her schoolfellows' mothers and whose hair had no short ends round the neck.

But sometimes it seemed likely, and in this sad twilight it seemed specially likely, that though such people certainly existed they had chosen some other scene than Edinburgh, whose society was as poor and restricted as its Zoo, perhaps for the same climatic reason. It was the plain fact of the matter that the most prominent citizen of Edinburgh to-day was Mary Queen of Scots. Every time one walked in the Old Town she had just gone by, beautiful and pale as though in her veins there flowed exquisite blood that diffused radiance instead of ruddiness, clad in the black and white that must have been a more solemn challenge, a more comprehensive announcement of free dealings with good and evil, than the mere extravagance of scarlet could have been ; and wearing a string of pearls to salve the wound she doubtless always felt about her neck. Ellen glowed at the picture as girls do at womanly beauty. Nobody of a like intensity had lived here since. The Covenanters, the Jacobites, Sir Walter Scott and his fellows, had dropped nothing in the pool that could break the ripples started by that stone, that precious stone, flung there from France so long ago. The town had settled down into something that the tonic magic of the place prevented being decay, but it was though time still turned the hour-glass, but did it dreamingly, infatuated with the marvellous thing she had brought forth that now was not. So greatly had the play declined in plot and character since Mary's time that for the catastrophe of the present age there was nothing better than the snatching of the Church funds from the U.F.'s by the Wee Frees. It appeared to her an indication of the quality of the town's life that they spoke of their churches by initials just as the English, she had learned from the Socialist papers, spoke of their trade unions. And for personalities there were innumerable clergymen and Sir Thomas Gilzean, Edinburgh's romantic draper, who talked French with a facility that his fellow townsmen suspected of being a gift acquired on the brink of the pit, and who had a long wriggling waist which suggested that he was about to pick up the tails of his elegant frock-coat and dance. He was light indeed, but not enough to express the lightness of which life was capable ; while the darker side of destiny was as inadequately represented by Æneas Walkinshaw, the last Jacobite, whom at the very moment Ellen could see standing under the lamp-post at the corner, in the moulting haberdashery of his wind-draggled kilts and lace ruffles, cramming treasonable correspondence into a pillar-box marked G.R. . . . She wanted people to be as splendid as the countryside, as noble as the mountains, as variable within the limits of beauty as the Firth of Forth, and this was what they were really like. She wept undisguisedly.

(2)

" What ails you, Miss Melville ? " asked Mr. Philip James. He had lit the gas and seen that she was crying.

At first she said, " Nothing." But there grew out of her gratitude to this family a feeling that it was necessary, or at least decent, that she should always answer them with the cleanest candour. As one rewards the man who has restored a lost purse by giving him some of the coins in it, so she shared with them, by the most exact explanation of her motives whenever they were asked for, the self which they had saved. So she added, " It's just that I'm bored. Nothing ever happens to me ! "

Mr. Philip had hoped she was going to leave it at that

" Nothing," and bore her a grudge for her amplification at the same time that the way she looked when she made it swept him into sympathy. Indeed, he always felt about the lavish gratitude with which Ellen laid her personality at the disposal of the firm rather as the Englishman who finds the Chinaman whom he saved from death the day before sitting on his verandah in the expectation of being kept for the rest of his life that his rescuer has forced upon him. It was true that she was an excellent shorthand-typist, but she vexed the decent grey by her vividness. The sight of her through an open door, sitting at her typewriter in her blue linen overall, dispersed one's thoughts ; it was as if a wireless found its waves jammed by another instrument. Often he found himself compelled to abandon his train of ideas and apprehend her experiences : to feel a little tired himself if she drooped over her machine, to imagine, as she pinned on her tam-o'-shanter and ran down the stairs, how the cold air would presently prick her smooth skin. Yet these apprehensions were quite uncoloured by any emotional tone. It was simply that she was essentially conspicuous, that one had to watch her as one watches a very tall man going through a crowd. Even now, instead of registering disapproval at her moodiness, he was looking at her red hair and thinking how it radiated flame through the twilight of her dark corner, although in the sunlight it always held the softness of the dusk. That was characteristic of her tendency always to differ from the occasion. He had once seen her at a silly sort of picnic where everybody was making a great deal of noise and playing rounders, and she had sat alone under a tree. And once, as he was walking along Princes Street on a cruel day when there was an easterly ha'ar blowing off the Firth, she had stepped towards him out of the drizzle, not seeing him but smiling sleepily. It was strange how he remembered all these things, for he had never liked her very much.

He put his papers on the table and sat down by the fire. " Well, what should happen ? No news is good news, I've heard ! "

She continued to disclose herself to him without the impediment of shyness, for he was unattractive to her because he had an Edinburgh accent and always carried an umbrella. He was so like hundreds of young men in the town, dark and sleek-headed and sturdily under-sized, with an air of sagacity and consciously shrewd eyes under a projecting brow, that it seemed like uttering one's complaint before a jury or some other representative body. She believed, too, that he was not one of the impeccable and happy to whom one dare not disclose one's need for pity, for she was sure that the clipped speech that slid through his half-opened mouth was a sign that secretly he was timid and ashamed. So she cried honestly, " I'm so dull that I'll die. You and Mr. James are awfully good to me, and I can put up with Mr. Morrison, though he's a doited old thing, and I like my work, but coming here in the morning and going home at night, day in and day out, it drives me crazy. I don't know what's the matter with me, but I want to run away to new places and see new people. This morning I was running to catch the tram and I saw the old wife who lives in the wee house by the cycle shop had put a bit heather in a glass bottle at the window, and do you know, I was near turning my back and going off to the Pentlands and letting the work go hang ! "

They were both law-abiding people. They saw the gravity of her case.

" Not that I want the Pentlands. Dear knows I love the place, but I want something more than those old hills. I want to go somewhere right far away. The sight of a map makes me sick. And then I hear a band play—not the pipes, they make me think of Walter Scott's poetry, which I never could bear, but a band. I feel that if I followed it it would lead me somewhere that I would like to go. And the posters. There's one at the Waverley station—Venice. I could tear the thing down. Did you ever go to Italy, Mr. Philip ? "

" No. I go with the girls to Germany every summer."

" My patience ! " said Ellen bitterly. " The way the world is ! The people who can afford to go to Italy go to Germany. And I—I'll die if I don't get away."

" Och, I often feel like this," said Mr. Philip. " I just take a week-end off at a hydro."

" A hydro ! " snorted Ellen. " It's something more like the French Revolution I'm wanting. Something grand and coloured. Swords, and people being rescued, and things like that."

" There's nothing going on like that now," he said stolidly, " and we ought to be thankful for it."

" I know everything's over in Europe," she agreed sadly, " but there's revolutions in South America. I've read about them in Richard Harding Davis. Did ever you read him ? Mind you, I'm not saying he's an artist, but the man has force. He makes you long to go."

" A dirty place," said Mr. Philip.

" What does that matter, where there's life ? I feel—I feel "—she wrung her inky brown hands—" as if I should die if something didn't happen at once : something big, something that would bang out like the one o'clock gun up at the Castle. And nothing will. Nothing ever will!"

"Och, well," he comforted her, "you're young yet, you know."

"Young!" cried Ellen, and suddenly wept. If this was youth——!

He bent down and played with the fire-irons. It was odd how he didn't want to go away, although she was in distress. "Some that's been in South America don't find it to their taste," he said. "The fellow that's coming to-night wants to sell some property in Rio de Janeiro because he doesn't mean to go back."

"Ah, how can he do that?" asked Ellen unsteadily. The tears she was too proud to wipe away made her look like a fierce baby. "Property in Rio de Janeiro! It's like being related to someone in 'Treasure Island.'"

"'Treasure Island!' Imph!" He had seen his father draw Ellen often enough to know how to do it, though he himself would never have paid enough attention to her mental life to discover it. "You're struck on that Robert Louis Stevenson, but he wasn't so much. My Aunt Phemie was with him at Mr. Robert Thompson's school in Heriot Row, and she says he was an awful young blackguard, playing with the keelies all he could and gossiping with the cabmen on the rank. She wouldn't have a word to say to him, and grandfather would never ask him to the house, not even when all the English were licking his boots. I'm not much on these writing chaps myself." He made scornful noises and crossed his legs as though he had disposed of art.

"And who," asked Ellen, with temper, "might your Aunt Phemie be? There'll not be much in the papers when she's laid by in Trinity Cemetery, I'm thinking! The impairtinence of it! All these Edinburgh people ought to go on their knees and thank their Maker that just once, just once in that generation, He let something decent come out of Edinburgh!" She turned away from him and laid her cheek against the oak shutter.

Mr. Philip chuckled. When a woman did anything for itself, and not for its effect on the male, it seemed to him a proof of her incapacity to look after herself, and he found incapacity in women exciting and endearing. He watched her with a hard attention that was his kind of tenderness, as she sat humped schoolgirlishly in her shapeless blue overall, averting her face from the light but attempting a proud pose, and keeping her grief between her teeth as an ostler chews a straw.

"He had a good time, the way he travelled in France and the South Seas. But he deserved it. He wrote such lovely books. Ah," she said, listening to her own sombre interpretation of things as to sad music, "it isn't just chance that some people had adventures and others hadn't. One makes one's own fate. I have no fate because I'm too weak to make one." She looked down resentfully on her hands, that for all her present fierceness and the inkstains of her daily industry lay little things on her lap, and thought of Rachael Wing, who had so splendidly departed to London to go on the stage. "But it's hard to be punished just for what you are."

He wondered whether, although she was the typist, there was not something rare about her. He could not compare her in this moment with his sisters May and Gracie, who were always getting up French plays for bazaars, or Chrissie, who played the violin, for the earth held nothing to vex the sturdiness of these young women except the profligacy with which it offered its people attractions competitive with bazaars and violin solos. But he thought it unlikely that any occasion would have evoked from them this serene despair, which was no more irritable than that which is known by the nightingale. It was impossible that they could shed such tears as smudged her bright colours now, such exquisite distillations of innocent grief at the wasting of the youth of which she was so innocently proud, and generous rage at the decrying of a name that was neither relative nor friend nor employer but merely a maker of beauty. Without doubt she lived in a lonely world, where tears were shed for other things than the gift of gold, and where one could perform these simplicities before a witness without fear of contempt, because human intercourse went only to the tune of charity and pity. Suddenly he wanted to enter into this world ; not indeed with the intention of naturalising himself as its inhabitant nor with the intention of staying there for ever, but as a navvy might stop on his way to work and refresh his horny sweating body by a swim in a sunny pool. He felt a thirst, a thing that stopped the breath for her pity. And although his desire was but for participation in kindness, his instinct for conformity was so suspicious of her vividness that he felt furtive and red-eared while he searched in the purse of his experiences to find the coin that would admit him to her world. The search at first was vain, for most of them that he cared to remember were mere manifestations of the kind of qualities that are mentioned in testimonials. But presently he gripped the disappointment that would buy him her pity.

He said, " I'm right sorry for you, Miss Melville. But you
know . . . We all have our troubles."

She raised her eyebrows.

" I wanted to go into the Navy."

" You did ? Would your father not let you ? " She said
it in her red-headed " My-word-if-I'd-been-there " way.

" Aye, he would have liked it fine."

" What was it then ? " She leaned forward and almost
crooned at him. " What was it then ? "

His speech became more clipped. " My eyes."

" Your eyes ! " she breathed. He suddenly became a
person to her. " I never thought."

" I'm as short-sighted as a bat."

" They look all right." She frowned at them as though
they were traitors.

He basked in her pity. " They're not. I never could play
football at the University."

She rose and stood beside him at the table, so that he would
feel how sorry she was, and set one finger to her lips and murmured, " Well, well ! " and at the end of a warm, drowsy moment,
after which they seemed to know each other much better, she
said softly and irrelevantly, " I saw you capped."

" Did you so ? How did you notice me ? It was one of
the big graduations. "

" I went with my mother to see my cousin Jeanie capped
M.A., and we saw your name on the list. Philip Mactavish
James. And mother said, ' Yon'll be the son of Mactavish James.
Many's the time I've danced with him when I was Ellen Forbes.'
Funny to think of them dancing ! "

" Oh, father was a great man for the ladies." They both
laughed. He vacillated from the emotional business of the
moment. " Do you dance ? " he asked.

" I did at school—— "

" Don't you go to dances ? "

She shook her head. It was a shame, thought Mr. Philip.
With that long slender waist she should have danced so beautifully ; he could imagine how her head would droop back and
show her throat, how her brows would become grave with great
pleasure. He wished she could come to his mother's dances,
but he knew so well the rigid standards of his own bourgeoisie
that he felt displeased by his wish. It was impossible to ask a
Miss Melville to a dance unless one could say, ' She's the daughter
of old Mr. Melville in Moray Place. Do you not mind Melville
the wine merchant ? ' and specially impossible to ask this Miss

Melville unless one had some such certificate to attach to her vividness. But he wished he could dance with her.

Ellen recalled him to the business of pity. She had thought of dances for no more than a minute, though it had long been one of her dreams to enter a ballroom by a marble staircase (which she imagined of a size and steepness really more suited to a water-chute), carrying a black ostrich-feather fan such as she had seen Sarah Bernhardt pythoning about with in " La Dame aux Camélias." This hour she had dedicated to Mr. Philip, and he knew it. She was thinking of him with an intentness which was associated with an entire obliviousness of his personal presence, just as a church circle might pray fervently for some missionary without attempting to visualise his face ; and though he missed this quaint meaning of her abstraction, he was well content to watch it and nurse his private satisfaction. He was still aware that he was Mr. Philip of the firm, so he was not going to tell her that for two nights after he had heard the decision of the Medical Examiners he had cried himself to sleep, though he was fourteen past. But it was exquisite to know that if he had told her she would have been moved to some glorious gesture of pity. His imagination trembled at the thought of its glory as she turned to him with a benignity that was really good enough, and said diffidently, because her ambition was such a holy thing that she feared to speak of his : " Still, there are lots of things for you to do. I've heard . . ."

He was kindly and indulgent. " What have you heard ? "

Ellen had, as her mother used to say, a great notion of politics. " Why, that you're going to stand for Parliament."

" That's true enough," he said, swelling a little.

" Could anything be finer ? " she breathed. " What are you going to do ? "

" I'll have to contest two-three hopeless seats. Then they'll give me something safe."

" But what will you do ? "

He didn't follow.

" What'll you do after that ? " She towered above him, her cheeks flushed with intellectual passion. " In Parliament, I mean. There's so much to do. Will it be housing ? If it was me it would be housing. But what are you going to do ? "

" I'll sit as a Liberal," he said, with an air of quiet competence. " We've always been Liberals."

" Ach ! Liberal ! " she said, with the spirit of one who had cried, " Keep the Liberal out ! " at a Leith polling-booth and had been haled backwards by the hair from the person of Mr.

Winston Churchill. Mr. Philip laughed again and felt a kind
of glow. He never could get over a feeling that to discover a
woman excited about an intellectual thing was like coming on
her bathing ; her cast-off femininity affected him as a heap of
her clothes on the beach might have done. But the flash in
her eyes died to the homelier fires of a more personal quarrel.
" Is yon Mrs. Powell's heavy feet coming up the stair ? " she
enquired.

" It is so. I asked her to do a chop for me, so that I won't
need to dine on the train. . . ."

" Mercy me ! We'll see the fine cook she is ! " She ran
out to the landing (she had never known he was so nice). Mr.
Philip found that her absence acted curiously as a relief to an
excitement that was beginning to buzz in his head. Then she
came back with the tray, her cheeks bright and her mouth
pursed, for she and the caretaker had been sandpapering each
other's temperaments with a few words. " Be thankful she
thought to boil a potato. No greens. And I had to ask for a
bit bread. And the reason's not far to seek. She's had a drop
again. It staggers me how your father, who's so particular
with the rest of us, stands such a body in the place."

He did not answer her. The moment had become one of
pure enjoyment. There was no sense of strain in his appreciation
of her while she was putting down the tray, spreading out the
plates, and doing things that were all directed to giving him
comfort. Their relationship felt absolutely right.

" Will you have one of the bottles of Burgundy your father
keeps for when he lunches in ? " she said.

" I was just thinking I would," he answered, and went into
his father's room. As he stooped before the cupboard her
voice reached him, fortuitously uplifted in " The Flowers of
the Forest are a' wede away." Now how did she look when
she sang ? It improved some people. He knelt for a minute
in front of the dusty cupboard, frowning fiercely at the bottles
because it struck him that she would stop singing when he went
back, and he could think of no way of asking her to go on that
would not be, as he put it, *infra dig.* And sure enough, when
he entered the room a shy silence fell on her, which she broke
by saying, " If you've not got the corkscrew there's one on my
pocket-knife." He used it, telling himself that it spared turning
on the gas again in the other room, and she stood behind him
murmuring, " Yon's not a bad knite. Four blades and a thing
that takes stones out of a horse's hoof. . . ."

He sat down to his meal, and she remained by the fireplace

until he said, " Pray sit down, Miss Melville, I wish I could ask you to join me. . . ."

She obeyed because she was afraid she might be fretting him by standing there, and took the seat on the other side of the table. The gas-jet was behind her, so to him there was a gold halo about her head and her face was a dusky oval in which her eyes and the three-cornered patch of her mouth were points of ardour. She had an animal's faculty for keeping quite still. He felt a pricking appetite to force the moment on to something he could not quite previsage, and found himself saying, " Will you have some Burgundy ? "

She was shocked. " Oh no ! ".

He perceived that here was a matter of principle. But he felt, although principles were among his conventions, not the least impulse to defer to it. Instead, the project of persuading her to do something she felt she oughtn't to do flooded him with a tingling pleasure.

He said, " But it's so pretty ! " He could not imagine why he should have said that, and yet he knew when he had said it that he had hit on an argument that would weigh with her.

She sighed as who makes a concession. " Oh yes, it's pretty ! " And then, to his perplexity, her face fell into complete repose. She was absorbed in the red beauty in his glass.

It angered him, yet he still felt bland and coaxing. " You'll have a glass ? "

" No, thank you."

" You'll surely have a taste ? "

" Ah, no—— "

" Just a drop . . ."

Their eyes met. He was peering into her face so that he could be sure she was looking at him, and somehow the grimace seemed to be promising her infinite pleasure.

She muttered, " Well, just a drop ! " and found herself laughing unhappily.

He passed her his glass.

" But what," she asked in dismay, " will you drink from ? "

Almost irritably he clicked his tongue, though he still smiled. " Drink it up ! Drink it up ! "

She raised the glass to her lips and set her head back that the sin might have swift progress, expecting the loveliest thing, like an ice, but warm and very worldly ; and informed with solemn pleasure too, for such colours are spilt on marble floors when the sun sets behind cathedral windows, such colours come into the mind when great music is played or some deep voice speaks Shakespeare. . . .

" Ach ! " she screamed, and banged the glass down on the table. " It's horrid ! It draws the mouth ! " She started up and stood rubbing her knuckles into her cheeks and twisting her lips. She had never thought wine was like this. It was not so much a drink as a blow in the mouth. And yet somehow she felt ashamed of not liking it. " The matron at school used to give us something for toothache that was as bad as this ! " she said peevishly, and tears stood in her eyes.

Mr. Philip stood up laughing. The crisis of his pleasure in persuading her to do the thing which she hadn't wanted to do was his joy that she hadn't liked it when she had done it. And suddenly one of the walls of the neat mental chamber in which he customarily stood fell in ; by the light that streamed in upon him he perceived that his ecstasy was only just beginning. At last he knew what he wanted to do. With gusto he marked that Ellen too was conscious that the incident was not at its close, for she was still wringing her hands, though the taste of the wine must long have gone from her mouth, and was stammering miserably, " Well, if yon stuff's a temptation to any poor folk—— ! " Again he felt that their relationship was on a proper footing ; he moved towards her, walking masterfully. Oh, it was going to be ecstasy. . . .

There was a loud knocking at the outer door.

(3)

She forgot all about the wine at once, he was so very big. And he looked as though he had gold rings in his ears, although he hadn't ; it was just part of his sea-going air.

He looked at her very hard and said as though it hardly mattered, " I want to see Mr. James. My name's Yaverland."

" Will you step inside ? " said Ellen, with her best English accent. " Mr. Philip's expecting you." She was glad he had come, for he looked interesting, but she hoped he would not interrupt her warm comfortable occupation of mothering Mr. Philip. To keep that mood aglow in herself she stopped as they went along the passage and begged, " You'll not make him miss his train ? He's away to London to-night. He should leave here on the very clap of eight."

The stranger seemed, after a moment's silence, of which, since they stood in darkness, she could not read the cause, to lay aside a customary indifference for the sake of the gravity of the occasion. " Oh, certainly; he shall leave on the very clap of eight," he replied earnestly.

He spoke without an accent and was most romantically dark. Ellen wondered whether Mr. Philip would like him—she had noticed that Mr. Philip didn't seem to fancy people who were very tall. And she perceived with consternation as they entered the room that he had suddenly been overtaken by one of his moods. He had taken up the tray and was trying to slip it into the cupboard, which he might have seen would never hold it, and in any case was a queer place for a tray, and stood there with it in his hands, brick-red and glowering at them. She was going to take it from him when he dunted it down on the window-seat with a clatter. " What for can he not go on with his good chop ? " thought Ellen. " We're putting on grand company manners for this bit chemist body, surely," and she pulled forward a chair for the stranger and sat down in the corner with her note-book on her knee.

" You're Mr. Yaverland ? " said Mr. Philip, shooting his chin forward and squaring his shoulders, and looking as though his father were dead and he were the head of the firm.

" I'm Richard Yaverland. Mr. Frank Gibson said you might be good enough to see to my affairs for me. I've got a letter from him. . . ."

Decidedly the man had an air. He slid the letter across the table as if he did not care in the least whether anybody ever picked it up and retreated into a courteous inattention. She felt a little cross at Mr. Philip for not showing that Edinburgh too understands the art of arrogance, for opening the letter so clumsily and omitting to say the nice friendly thing. Well, if he was put about it was his own fault for not going on with the chop, it being well known to all educated persons that one cannot work on an empty stomach. If this man would go soon she would run down to Mrs. Powell and get her to heat up the chop again. She eyed him anxiously to see if he looked the kind of person who left when one wanted him to, and found herself liking him for the way he slouched in his chair, as though he wanted to mitigate as much as possible his terrifying strength and immensity. What for did a fine man like him help to make cordite, the material of militarism, which is the curse of the nations ? She wished he could have heard R. J. Campbell speak on peace the other night at the Synod Hall ; it was fine. But probably he was a Conservative, for these big men were often unprogressive. She examined him carefully out of the corner of her eye to estimate the chances of his being brought into the fold of reform by properly selected oratory. That at least was the character of contemplation she intended, but though she was so young that she believed the enjoyment of any sensory impression sheer waste unless it was popped into the mental stockpot and made the basis of some sustaining moral soup, she found herself just looking at him. His black hair lay in streaks and rings on his rain-wet forehead and gave him an abandoned and magical air, like the ghost of a drowned man risen for revelry; his dark gold skin told a traveller's tale of far-off pleasurable weather; and the bare hand that lay on his knee was patterned like a snake's belly with brown marks, doubtless the stains of his occupation; and his face was marked with an expression that it vexed her she could not put a name to, for if at her age she could not read human nature like a book she never would. It was not hunger, for it was serene, and it was not greed, for it was austere, and yet it certainly signified that he habitually made upon life some urgent demand that was not wholly intellectual and that had not been wholly satisfied. As she wondered a slight retraction of his chin and a drooping of his heavy eyelids warned her, by their likeness to the controlled but embarrassed movements of a highly-bred animal approached by a stranger, that he knew she was watching him, and she took her gaze away. But she had to look again, just to confirm her feeling that however fanciful she might be about him his appearance would always give some further food for her imagination; and presently, for though she was the least vain person in the world she was the most egotistical, began to compare the large correctness of his features with the less academic spontaneity of her own. "Lord! Why has everybody but me got a straight nose!" she exclaimed to herself. "But it's all blethers to think that an indented chin means character. How can a dunt in your bone have anything to do with your mind?" She rubbed her own chin, which was a little white ball, and pushed it forward, glowering at his great jaw. Then her examination ended. She noticed that all over his upper lip and chin there was a faint bluish bloom, as if he had shaved closely and recently but the strong hair was already pressing through again. That disgusted her, although she reminded herself that he could not help it, that that was the way he was made. "There's something awful like an animal about a man," she thought, and shivered.

"Och, aye!" said Mr. Philip, which was a sure sign that he was upset, for in business he reckoned to say "Yes, yes."

The two men began by exchange of politenesses about Mr. Frank Gibson, to whom they referred in the impersonal way of business conversations as though he were some well-known brand of integrity, and then proceeded to divest the property in Rio Janeiro of all interest in a like manner. It was a house, it appeared, and was at present let to an American named Capel on a five years' lease, which had nearly expired. There was no likelihood of Capel requiring any extension of this lease, for he was going back to the States. So now Yaverland wanted to sell it. There ought to be no trouble in finding a buyer, for it was a famous house. "Everybody in Rio knows the Villa Miraflores," he said. She gasped at the name and wrote it in longhand; to compress such deliciousness into shorthand would have been sacrilege. After that she listened more eagerly to his voice, which .she perceived was charged with suppressed magic as it might have been with suppressed laughter. The merry find no more difficulty in keeping a straight face than he found in using the flat phrase. And as she gleefully gazed at him, recognising in him her sort of person, his speech slipped the business leash. There were hedges of geranium and poinsettia about the villa, pergolas hung with bougainvillea, numberless palms, and a very pleasant orange grove in good bearing; in the courtyard a bronze Venus rode on a spouting whale, and there were many fountains; and within there was much white marble and pillars of precious stone, and horrible liverish Viennese mosaics, for the house was something of a prodigy, having been built in a trade boom by a *rastaqouère*. "Mhm," said Mr. Philip sagaciously, and from the funeral slide of respect in his voice Ellen guessed that he imagined *rastaqouère* to be a Brazilian variety of Lord Provost. She would have laughed had there not been the plainest intimation that he was still upset about something in his question whether Yaverland thought he would be well advised to sell the house, whether he had any reasonable expectation of recovering the capital he had sunk in it; for she had noticed that whenever Mr. Philip felt miserable he was wont to try and cheer himself by suggesting that somebody had been "done."

But that worry was dissolved by the enchantment of Yaverland's answer. He hadn't the slightest idea what he had paid for the villa. It happened this way. He had won a lot of money at poker ("Tchk! Tchk!" said Mr. Philip, half shocked, but showing by the way he put one thumb in his waistcoat armhole that he was so far sensible of the change in the atmosphere

that he felt the need of some romantic gesture), and had felt
no shame in pocketing it since it came from a man who was
gambling to try to show that he wasn't a Jew. Ellen hated
him for that. She believed in absolute racial equality, and sometimes intended to marry a Hindu as a propagandist measure.
And then he had remembered that a friend of his, de Cayagun
of the Villa Miraflores, was broke and wanted to move. Even
Rio was tired of poor de Cayagun, though he'd given it plenty
of fun. There had been great times at the villa. His phrases,
which seemed to have scent and colour as well as meaning,
made her see red pools of wine on the marble floor and rose
wreaths about the bronze whale's snout, and hear from the
orange grove the sound of harps, yet from a sullenness in his
faint smile she deduced there had been something dark in this
delight. Perhaps somebody had got drunk. But he was saying
now that that time had come to an end long before the night
when he had won this money from Demetrios. De Cayagun
had no more jewels to give away and even the servants had all
left him. . . . She saw night invading the villa like a sickness
of the light, the pools of wine lying black on marble that the
dusk had made blue like cold flesh ; and this stranger standing
white-faced in the stripped banquet-hall, with the broken body
of the Venus on a bier at his feet and above his head the creaking
wings of birds come to establish desolation under the shattered
roof. Why was he so sad because some people who were members
of the parasite class and were probably devoid of all political
idealism had had to stop having a good time ? It was, she
supposed, that ethereal abstract sorrow, undimmed by personal
misery and unconfined by the syllogisms of moral judgment, that
poets feel : that Milton had felt when he wrote " Comus " about
somebody for whom he probably wouldn't have mixed a toddy,
that she herself had often felt when the evening star shone its
small perfect crescent above the funeral flame of the day. People
would call it a piece of play-acting nonsense just because of its
purity and their inveterate peering liking for personal emotion,
which they seemed to honour according to its intensity even
if that intensity progressed towards the disagreeable. She
remembered how the neighbours had all respected Mrs. Ball in
the house next door for the terrific manifestations of her abandonment to the grief of widowhood. " Tits, tits, puir body ! "
they had said with zestful reverence, and yet the woman had
been behaving exactly as if she was seasick. She preferred
the impersonal pang. It was right. Right as the furniture in
the Chambers Museum was, as the clothes in Redfern's window

in Princes Street were, as this stranger was. And it had a high meaning too. It was evoked by the end of things, by sunsets, by death, by silence, following song ; by intimations that no motion is perpetual and that death is a part of the cosmic process. It had the sacred quality of any recognition of the truth. . . .

Well, he was telling them how he had gone up to de Cayagun, and they had knocked up a notary and made him draft a deed of sale, which he had posted to his agents without reading. He had only the vaguest idea how much money had changed hands. Mr. Philip shook his head and chuckled knowingly, "Well, Mr. Yaverland, that is not how we do business in Scotland," and suggested that it might be wise to retain some part of the property : the orange grove, for instance. At that Yaverland was silent for a moment, and then replied with an august, sweet-tempered insolence that he couldn't see why he should, since he wasn't a marmalade fancier. " Besides, that's an impossible proposition. It's like selling a suburban villa and retaining an interest in the geranium bed. . . ." In the warm, interesting atmosphere she detected an intimation of enmity between the two men ; and it was like catching a caraway seed under a tooth while one was eating a good cake. She was disturbed and wanted to intervene, to warn the stranger that he made Mr. Philip dizzy by talking like that. And the reflection came to her that it would be sweet, too, to tell him that he could talk like that to her for ever, that he could go on as he was doing, being much more what one expected of an opera than a client, and she would follow him all the way. But it struck her suddenly and chillingly that she had no reason to suppose that he would be interested. His talk was in the nature of a monologue. He showed no sign of desiring any human companionship.

Still, he was wonderful. She did not take it as warning of any coldness or unkindness in him that it was impossible to imagine him linked by a human relationship to any ordinary person like herself ; there are pictures too fine for private ownership. Just then he was being particularly fine in an exciting way. He sat up very straight, flung out his great arm with a gesture of abandonment, and said that he would have no more to do with this house. So might a conqueror speak of a city he was weary of looting. He wanted to sell it outright, and desired Mr. Philip to undertake the whole business of concluding the sale with the Rio agents. " It's all here," he said, and took from his pocket-book a packet of letters. " They hold the title-deeds and you'll see how things are getting on with the deal. But I suppose the language will be a difficulty. I can read you these, of course, but how will you carry on the correspondence ? "

" Och, we can send out to a translator—— "

A tingling ran through Ellen's veins. The men's words, uttered on one side in irritated languor and on the other with empty spruceness, had suddenly lifted her to the threshold of life. She had previsioned many moments in which she should disclose her unique value to a dazzled world, but most of them had seemed, even to herself, extremely unlikely to arrive. It was improbable that Mr. Asquith should fall into a river just as she was passing, and that he should be so helpless and the country-side so depopulated that she would be able to exact votes for women as the price of his rescue ; besides, she could not swim. It was improbable, too, that she should be in a South American republic just when a revolution was proclaimed, and that, the Latin attitude to women being what it is, she should be given a high military command. But there had been one triumph which she knew to be not impossible even in her obscurity. It might conceivably happen that by some exhibition of the prodigious bloom of her efficiency she would repay her debt to the firm and make the first steps towards becoming the pioneer business queen. For it was one of her dreams, perhaps the six hundred and seventy-ninth in the series, that one day she would sit at a desk answering innumerable telephone calls with projecting jaw, as millionaires do on the movies, and crushing rivals like blackbeetles in order that, after being reviled by the foolish as a heartless plutocrat, she might hand a gigantic Trust over to the Socialist State.

" Mr. Philip," she said.

Apparently he did not hear her, though the other man turned his dark glance on her.

" Mr. Philip," she said. He looked across at her with a blankness she took as part of the business. " I've been taking Commercial Spanish at Skerry's. I took a first-class certificate. Maybe I could manage the letters ? "

" Oh ! " exclaimed Yaverland explosively. He appeared to be about to make some objection, and then he bit back the speech that was already in his mouth. And as he tried to find other words the beauty of her body caught his attention. It was, as it happened, very visible at that moment. The fulness of her overall had fallen to one side as she sat on the high stool, and so that linen was tightly wrapped about her, disclosing that she was made like a delicate fleet beast ; in the valley between her high small breasts there lay a shadow, which grew greater when she breathed deeply. He looked at her with the dispassionateness which comes to men who have lived much in countries where nakedness offers itself unashamed to the sunlight, and said to himself, " I should like to see her run." He knew that a body like this must possess an infinite capacity for physical pleasure, that to her mere walking would give more joy than others find in dancing. And then he raised his eyes to her face and was sad. For sufficient reasons he was very sensitive to the tragedies of women, and he knew it was a tragedy that such a face should surmount such a body. For her body would imprison her in soft places : she would be allowed no adventures other than love, no achievements other than births. But her face was haggard, in spite of its youth, with appetite for travel in the hard places of the world, for the adventures and achievements that are the birthright of any man. " It's rotten luck to be a girl," he thought. " If she were a boy I could get her a job at Rio. . . . Lord, she has lovely hair ! " He perceived sharply that he was not likely to be of any more use to her than most men would. All he could do would be to avert the humiliation which the moment seemed likely to bring down on her.

" Oh, this is a wonderful country," he said aloud, " where you get people studying Spanish in their off-hours." Ellen thought it rather wonderful too, and looked at her toes with a priggish blankness. " You've got a marvellous educational system. . . ." He paused, conscious that he was too manifestly talking at random. " In two continents you've enjoyed the reputation of being able to talk the hind-leg off a donkey," he reminded himself. " It's the language to learn," he said aloud. " It's the language of the future. Ever been in Spain, Mr. James ? "

" No," said Mr. Philip, but I was thinking of going there— or mebbe Italy—ma Easter holidays." Ellen smiled brilliantly at him, for she knew that he had had no such thought till that evening's talk with her ; she had converted him to a romantic. He caught her eye, only to glare coldly into the centre of her smile.

It was Yaverland's opportunity, for he had spent two years as chemist at the Romanones mines in Andalusia ; and he had learned by now the art of talking to the Scotch, whom he had discovered to be as extravagantly literate as they were unsensuous. To them panpipes might play in vain, but almost any series of statistics or the more desiccated kind of social fact recited with a terrier-like air of sagacity would entrance them. "The mines are Baird's, you know—Sir Milne Baird; it's a Glasgow firm. . . ." "Mhm," said Mr. Philip, "I know who you mean." Detestable, thought Yaverland, this Scotch locution which implies that one has made a vague or incorrect description which only the phenomenal intelligence of one's listener has enabled him to penetrate, but he set himself suavely enough to describe the instability of Spanish labour, its disposition to call strikes that were really larks, and the greater willingness with which it keeps its saints' days rather than the commandments; the feckless incapacity of the Spanish to exploit their own minerals and the evangelic part played in the shameful shoes by Scotch engineers; and the depleted state of the country in general, which he was careful to ascribe not so much to the presence of Catholicism as to the absence of Presbyterianism. And he advised Mr. Philip that while a sojourn in the towns would reveal these sad political conditions, there were other deplorable aspects of the national decay which could only be witnessed if he took a few rides over the countryside. ("A horse or a bicycle?" asked Mr. Philip doubtfully.) Then he would have a pleasant holiday. The language presented few difficulties, although travelling off the tracks in Andalusia was sometimes impeded by the linguistic ingenuity of the peasants, who, though they didn't neigh and whinny like the Castilians, went one better by omitting the consonants. Why, there was a place which spelt itself Algodonales on the map and calls itself Aooae.

He watched her under his lids as she silently tried it over. It was a village of no importance, save for the road that close by forded the Guadalete, which was a pale icy mountain stream, snow-broth, as Shakespeare said. (Now what had he said to excite her so? Modesty and a sense of office discipline were restraining some eager cry of her mind, like white hands holding birds resolved on flight.) One passed through it on a ride that Mr. Philip must certainly take when he went to Spain. Yaverland himself had done it last February. He receded into a dream of that springtime, yet kept his consciousness of the girl's rapt attention, as one may clasp the warm hand of a friend while one thinks deeply, and he sent his voice out to Mr. Philip as into a void, describing how he had gone to Seville one saint's day and how the narrow decaying streets, choked with loveliness like stagnant ditches filled with a fair weed, had entertained him. For a time he had sat in the Moorish courts of the Alcazar; he had visited the House of Pontius Pilate and had watched through the carven windows the two stone women that pray for ever among the flowers in the courtyard; he had lingered by the market-stalls observing their exquisite, unprofitable trade. He was telling not half the beauty that he recollected, save in a phrase that he now and then dropped to the girl's manifest appetite for such things, and he took a malign pleasure in painting, so to speak, advertisement matter across the sky of his landscapes so that Mr. Philip could swallow them as being of potential commercial value and not mere foolish sensuous enjoyment. "There's so little real wealth in the country that they have to buy and sell mere pretty things for God knows what fraction of a farthing. On the stalls where you'd have cheap clocks and crockery and Austrian glass, they had stacks of violets and carnations—*violetas y claveles*. . . ." Then a chill and a dimness passed over the bright spectacle and a sunset flamed up half across the sky as though light had been driven out of the gates by the sword and had scaled the heaven that it might storm the city from above. The lanes became little runnels of darkness and night slowly silted up the broader streets. The incessant orgy of sound that by day had been but the tuneless rattling of healthy throats and the chatter of castanets became charged with tragedy by its passage through the grave twilight. The people pressed about him like vivacious ghosts, differentiating themselves from the dusk by wearing white flowers in their hair or cherishing the glow-worm tip of a cigarette between their lips.

He remembered it very well. For that was a night that the torment of loneliness had rushed in upon him, an experience of the pain that had revisited him so often that a little more and he would be reconciled to the idea of death. Even then he had been intelligent about the mood and had known that his was not a loneliness that could be exorcised by any of the beautiful brown bodies which here professed the arts of love and the dance and that drunkenness which would bring a physical misery to match his mental state. Though this was wisdom it added to his sense of being lost in black space like a wandering star. In the end he had gone into a café and drunk manzanilla, and with the limp complaisance of a wrecked sea-sick man whose raft has shivered and left him to the mercy of an octopus he had suffered adoption by a party of German engineers, who had made very merry with stories of tipsy priests and nuns who had not lived up to their position as the brides of Christ. Dismal night, forerunner of a hundred such. "Oh, God, what is the use of it all? I sit here yarning to this damned little dwarf of a solicitor and this girl who is sick to go to these countries from which I've come back cold and famined. . . ."

But he went on, since the occasion seemed to demand it, giving a gay account of the beauty which he remembered so intensely because it had framed his agony ; how the next day, under a sky that was temporarily pale and amiable because this was early spring, he had ridden down the long road between the brown heathy pastures to the blue barren downland that lies under the black mountains, and had come at last to a winding path that led not only through space but through time, for it ran nimbly in and out among the seasons. It travelled under the rosy eaves of a forest of blossoming almond up to a steep as haggard with weather as a Scotch moor, and dipped again to hedges of aloes and cactus and asphodel. At one moment a spindrift of orange blossom blew about him ; at another he had watched the peasants in their brown capes stripping their dark green orange-groves and piling the golden globes into the panniers of donkeys which were gay with magenta tassels. At one time there was trouble getting the horse up the icy trail, yet a little later it was treading down the irises and jonquils and bending its head to snuff the rosemary. So on, beauty all the way, and infinitely variable, all the many days' journey to the coast, where the mountain drops suddenly to the surf and reflects the Mediterranean sky as a purple glamour on its snowy crest. Ah, such a country !

He meant to go at that, for his listeners were now like honey-drugged bees : to toss his papers on the table, go out, and let the situation settle itself after his departure. But Mr. Philip said, " But surely they're crool. Bullfights and that—— "

He could not let that pass. " You don't understand. It's different over there."

" Surely right's right and wrong's wrong, wherever you are ? " said Mr. Philip.

" No. Spain's a place, as I said, where one travels in time as well as in space. . . ." He didn't himself agree that the bullfight was so much crueller than most organised activities of men. From the bull's point of view, indeed, it was a nobler way of becoming roast beef than any other and gave him the chance of drawing blood for blood ; and the toreador's life was good, as all dangerous lives are. But of course there were the horses ; he shuddered at his unspoken memory of a horse stumbling from the arena at Seville with a riven belly and hanging entrails that gleamed like mother-o'-pearl. Oh, yes, he admitted, it was cruel ; or, rather, would be if it were

committed by a people like ourselves. But it wasn't. That was
the point he wanted to make. When one travelled far back in
time. It was hard for us—" for you, especially," he amplified,
with a courteous, enthusiastic flinging out of his hand, " with
your unparalleled Scotch system of education "—to comprehend
the mentality of a people which had been prevented, by the
economic insanity of its governors and the determination of the
Church to sit on its intelligence till it stopped kicking, from
growing up. Among the things it hadn't attained to was the
easy anthropocentric attitude that is part of our civilisation.

Ellen thought him very wonderful, as he stood theorising
about the experiences he had described, like a lecturer in front
of his magic-lantern pictures ; for he was wholly given up to
speculation and yet was as substantial as any man of action.

Panic, he invited them to consider, was the habitual state
of mind of primitive peoples, the flood that submerged all but
the strongest swimmers. The savage spent his days suspecting
and exorcising evil. The echo in the cliff is an enemy, the
wind in the grass an approaching sickness, the new-born child
clad in mystery and defilement. But it wasn't for us to laugh
at the savage for, so to speak, not having found his earth-legs,
since our quite recent ancestors had held comets and eclipses
to be menacing gestures of the stars. Some primitive suspicions
were reasonable, and chief among these the fear that man's
ascendancy over the other animals might yet be disputed. Early
man sat by the camp fire gnawing his bone and sneered through
the dusk at the luminous, envious eyes of the wild beasts that
stood in the forest fringes, but he was not easy in his mind about
them. Their extreme immobility might be the sign of a tense
patience biding its time. Who was to say that some night
the position might not be reversed—that it would not be he
who stood naked save for his own pelt among the undergrowth
watching some happy firelit puma licking the grease of a good
meal from its paws ? That was the primitive doubt. It's an
attitude that one may understand even now, he said, when
one faces the spring of one of the larger carnivora ; and Ellen
thrilled to hear him refer to this as Edinburgh folk refer to a
wrestle with the east wind. It's an attitude that was bound
to persist, long after the rest of Europe had got going with more
modern history, in Spain ; where villages were subject on
winter's nights to the visitations of wolves and bears, and where
the Goths and the Arabs and the Christians and the Berbers
proved so extravagantly the wrangling lack of solidarity in the
human herd. There had from earliest times existed all round

the Mediterranean basin a ceremony by which primitive man gave a concrete ritual expression to this fear : the killing of the bull. They took the bull as the representative of the brutes which were the enemies of man and slew him by a priest's knife and with much decorative circumstances to show that this was no mere butchering of meat. Well, there in Spain it survived. . . . He had spoken confidently and dogmatically, but his eyes asked them appealingly whether they didn't see, as if in his course through the world he had been disappointed by the number of people who never saw.

"That's all very fine," said Mr. Philip, "but they've had time to get over their little fancies. We're in the twentieth century now."

Ah, the conception might never emerge into their consciousness, and perhaps they would laugh at it if it did ; but for all that it lies sunk in their minds and shapes their mental contour. When a dead city is buried by earth and no new city is built on its site the peasants tread out their paths on the terraces which show where the old streets ran. Something like that happened to a nation. Modern Spaniards hadn't, thanks to taxation and the Church, been able to build a mental life for themselves ; so, since the mind of man must have a little exercise, they repeated imitatively the actions by which their forefathers had responded to their quite real psychological imperatives. You couldn't perhaps find in the whole of the Peninsula a man or woman who felt this fear of the beast, but that didn't affect his case. It was enough that all men and women in the Peninsula had once felt it and had formed a national habit of attending bullfights, and as silly subalterns sometimes lay the toe of their boots to a Hindu for the glory of the British Empire— keeping the animal creation in its place by kicks and blows to mules and dogs.

It was incredible, he exclaimed, the interweaving of the old and the new that made up the fabric of life in Spain. He could give them another illustration of that. He had lodged for three weeks in Seville, in a flat at the Cathedral end of the Canovas de Castillo—"that's a street," he interjected towards Ellen, "called after a statesman they assassinated, they don't quite know why." In the flat there lodged a priest, the usual drunken Spanish priest ; and very early every morning, as the people first began to sing in the streets, a man drove up in an automobile and took him away for an hour. Presently he was told the story of this morning visitor by several people in the house, and he had listened to it as one didn't often listen to

twice-told tales, for it was amazing to observe how each of
the tellers, whether it was tipsy Fra Jeronimo or the triple-
chinned landlady, Donna Gloria, or Pepe, the Atheist medical
student who kept his skeletons in the washhouse on the roof,
accepted it as a quite commonplace episode. The man in the
automobile had lost his wife. He minded quite a lot, perhaps
because he had gone through a good deal to get her. When he
first met her she was another man's wife. He said nothing to
her then, but presently the way that he stared at her at the
bullfight and the opera and waited in the Paseo de la Delicias
for her carriage to come by made Seville talk, and her husband
called him out. The duel was fought on some sandy flat down
by the river, and the husband was killed. It was given out that
he had been gored by a bull, and within a year the widow married
the man who had killed him. In another year she was dead of
fever. Her husband gave great sums for Masses for her soul and
to charity, and shut up the house where they had entertained
Seville with the infantile, interminable gaieties that are loved
by the South, and went abroad. When he returned he went
back to live in that house, but now no one ever entered it except
the priest ; and he went not for any social purpose, but to say
Mass over the woman's bed, which her husband had turned into
an altar. Every day those two said Mass at that bed, though
it was five years since she had died. That was a queer enough
story for the present day, with its woman won by bloodshed
and the long unassuagable grief of the lover and the resort to
religion that struck us as irreverent because it was so utterly
believing ; it might have come out of the Decameron. But
the last touch of wildness was added by the identity of the man
in the automobile. For he was the Marquis d'Italica, the finest
Spanish aviator, a man not only of the mediæval courage one
might have guessed from the story, but also of the most modern
wit about machines. . . .

Yaverland bit his lip suddenly. He had told the story
without shame, for he knew well and counted it among the
heartening facts of life, like the bravery of seamen and the
sweetness of children, that to a man a woman's bed may sometimes be an altar. But Mr. Philip had ducked his head and
his ears were red. Shame was entering the room like a bad
smell.

For a minute Yaverland did not dare to look at Ellen. " I
had forgotten she was a girl," he thought miserably. " I thought
of nothing but how keen she is on Spain. I don't know how
girls feel about things. . . ." But she was sitting warm and

rosy in a happy dream, looking very solemnly at a picture she
was making in the darkness over his left shoulder. She had
liked the story, although the thought of men fighting over a
woman made her feel sick, as any conspicuous example of the
passivity common in her sex always did. But the rest she had
thought lovely. It was a beautiful idea of the Marquis's to turn
the bed into an altar. Probably he had often gone into his
wife's room to kiss her good-night. She saw a narrow iron
bedstead such as she herself slept in, a face half hidden by the
black hair flung wide across the pillow, a body bent like a bow
under the bedclothes, for she herself still curled up at nights as
dogs and children do ; and the Marquis, whom she pictured
as carrying a robin's egg blue enamelled candlestick like the
one she always carried up to her room, kneeling down and
kissing his wife very gently lest she should awake. Love must
be a great compensation to those who have not political ambitions. She became aware that Yaverland's eyes were upon her,
and she slowly smiled, reluctantly unveiling her good will to him.
It again appeared to him that the world was a place in which
one could be at one's ease without disgrace.

He stood up and brought a close to the business interview,
and was gripping Mr. Philip's hand, when a sudden recollection
reddened his face. "Ah, there's one thing," he said quite
lightly, though the vein down the middle of his forehead had
darkened. "You see from those letters that a Señor Vicente de
Rojas is making an offer for the house. He's not to have it.
Do you understand ? Not at any price."

The effect of this restriction, made obviously at the behest
of some deep passion, was to make him suddenly sinister. They
gazed at him as though he had revealed that he carried arms.
But Ellen remembered business again.

"Those letters," she reminded Mr. Philip, "had I not
better read them over before Mr. Yaverland goes ? "

Yaverland caught his breath, then spoke off-handedly.
"You're forgetting. They don't speak Spanish in Brazil, but
Portuguese." And added confidentially, "Of course you were
thinking of the Argentine."

She was as hurt by the revelation of this vast breach in her
omniscience as the bright twang of knowingness in her voice
had told him she would be.

"Yes," she said unsteadily, "I was thinking of the Argentine."

He shook hands with Mr. Philip, and she took him down the
corridor to the door. She blinked back her tears as he stood at

the head of the stair and put up his collar with those strange hands that were speckled like a snake's belly, for it seemed a waste, like staying indoors when the menagerie procession is going round the town, to let anything so unusual go away without seeing as much of it as possible. Then she remembered the thing that she had wanted to say in the other room, and wondered if it would be bold to speak, and finally remarked in a voice disagreeable with shyness, " The people up on the Pentland Hills use that word you said was in Shakespeare. Snowbroth. When the hill-streams run full after the melting of the snows, that's snow-broth."

He liked women who were interested in queer-shaped fragments of fact, for they reminded him of his mother. He took pains to become animated at her news.

" They do, they do ! " Ellen assured him, pleased by his response. " And they say ' hit ' for ' it,' which is Anglo-Saxon."

He noticed that her overall, which she was growing out of, fitted tightly on her over-thin shoulders and showed how their line was spoilt by the deep dip of the clavicle, and wondered why that imperfection should make her more real to him than she had been when he had thought her wholly beautiful. Again he became aware of her discontent with her surroundings, which had exerted on her personality nothing of the weakening effect of despair, since it sprang from such a rich content with the universe, such a confident faith that the supremest beauty she could imagine existed somewhere and would satisfy her if only she could get at it. He said, with no motive but to confirm her belief that the world was full of interest, " You must go on with your Spanish, you know. Don't just treat it as a commercial language. There's a lot of fine stuff in Spanish literature." He hesitated, feeling uncertain as to whether " Celestina " or Juan de Ruiz were really suitable for a young girl. " Saint Teresa, you know," he suggested, with the air of one who had landed on his feet.

" Oh, I can't do with religion," said Ellen positively.

He spluttered a laugh that seemed to her the first irrational flaw in something exquisitely reasonable, and ran down the dark stairs. She attended imaginatively to the sound of his footsteps ; as on her first excited night in country lodgings the summer before she had sat up in bed listening to horse's hooves beating through the moonlit village street, and had thought of the ghosts of highwaymen. But this was the ghost of an Elizabethan seaman. She could see him, bearded and with gold rings in her ears and the lustrousness of fever in his eyes, captaining with oaths and the rattle of arms a boat rowed by naked Indians along a yellow waterway between green cliffs of foliage. Yes, she could not imagine him consulting any map that was not gay with painted figures and long scrolls.

Dazed with the wonder of him, she went back into the room, and it was a second or two before she noticed that Mr. Philip was ramming his hat on his head and putting on his overcoat as though he had not a moment to lose. "You've no need to fash yourself," she told him happily. "It's not half-past seven yet. You've got a full hour. I can run down and heat up your chop, if you'll wait."

"Oh, spare yourself!" he begged her shortly.

She moved about the room, putting away papers and shutting drawers and winding up the eight-day clock on the mantelpiece a clear three days before it needed it, with a mixed motive of clearing up before her departure and making it clean and bare as befitted a place where heroes came to do business ; and she was more than unaware that Mr. Philip was watching her like an ambushed assassin ; she was confident in a conception of the world which excluded any such happening. He was standing by the mantelpiece fastening his furry storm-gloves, and though he found it teasing to adjust the straps in the shadow, he would not step into the light and look down on his hands. For his little eye was set on Ellen, and it was dull with speculation as to whether she knew what he had meant to do to her that moment when the knocking came at the door. Because the thing that he had meant to do seemed foul when he looked on her honourably held little head and her straight blue smock, he began to tamper with reality, so that he might believe himself not to have incurred the guilt of that intention. Surely it had been she that had planned that thing, not he ? Girls were nasty-minded and were always thinking about men. He began to remember the evening all over again, dusting with lasciviousness each of the gestures that had shone with such clear colours in his sight, dulling each of the sentences by which she had displayed to him her trimly-kept mental accoutrement until they became simpering babble, falsifying his minute memory of the scene until it became a record of her lust instead of his. Something deep in him stated quietly and glumly that he was now doing a wrong far worse than the thing that he had planned, and, though he would not listen, it was making him so sensible that the essence of the evening was his degradation that he felt very ill. If the palpitation of his heart and the shortness of his breath continued he would have to sit down and then she would be kind to him. He would never forgive her for all this trouble she had brought on him.

When she could no longer hold it in she exclaimed artlessly, " Yon Mr. Yaverland's a most interesting man."

He searched for an insult and felt resentful of the required effort, for his heart was making him very uncomfortable. He wished some crude gesture, some single ugly word, would do it. " You thought him an interesting man ? " he asked naggingly. " You don't surprise me. It was a bit too plain you thought so. I'll thank you not to be so forward with a client again. It'll give the office a bad name. And chatting at the door like that ! "

He looked for his umbrella, which was kept in this room and not in the hall-stand, lest its handsome cairngorm knob should tempt any of the needier visitors to the office, and removed its silk cover, which he placed in the pocket where he kept postage-stamps and, to provide for emergencies, a book of court plaster.

" I'm sure I'll not have to speak twice about this, Miss Melville," he said, with an appearance of forbearing kindliness, as he passed out of the door. " Good night."

(4)

She paused in the dark archway that led into Hume Park Square.

" It can't hurt me, what Mr. Philip said, because it isn't true." She wagged a pedagogic finger at herself. " See here ! Think of it in terms of Euclid. If you do a faulty proof by super-position and haven't remembered the theorem rightly, you can go on saying, ' Lay AB along DE ' till all's blue and you'll never make C coincide with F. In the same way Mr. Philip can blether to his silly heart's content and he'll never prove that I'm a bold girl. Me, Ellen Melville, who cares for nothing in the world except the enfranchisement of women and getting on. . . ."

She felt better. " There's nothing in life you can't get the better of by thinking about it," she said sententiously, and fell to dabbing her eyes with her handkerchief. She could easily pass off her tearstains as the marks of a bad cold. " It's a dreadful thing to rejoice in another body's affliction, but some-times I'm glad mother's so short-sighted.

" He wanted to make me unhappy, but he did not know

how," she thought, with a sudden renewal of rage. " Now I should have minded awful if he had noticed that slip I made about the Brazilians talking Spanish. It was a mercy yon man Yaverland thought I was thinking of the Argentine." But indeed the stranger would never have wanted to hurt her ; she felt sure that he was either very kind to people or very indifferent. She began to recall him delightedly, to see him standing in the villa garden against a hedge of scarlet flowers that marched as tall as soldiers beside a marble wall, to see him moving, dark and always a little fierce, through a world of beauty she was now too fatigued to imagine save as a kind of solidification of a sunset. Dreamily she moved to the little house in the corner. . . .

It was her habit to let herself in with the latchkey just as if she were the man of the house.

" Mercy, Ellen, you're late ! I was getting feared ! " cried her mother, who had gone to the kitchen to boil up the cocoa when she heard the key in the lock. She liked that sound. Ellen thought herself a wonderful new sort of woman who was going to be just like a man ; she would have been surprised if she had known how many of her stern-browed ambitions, how much of her virile swagger of life, were not the invention of her own soul, but had been suggested to her by an old woman who liked to pretend her daughter was a son.

" We had a great press of business and I had to stay," said Ellen with masculine nonchalance. " A most interesting client came in. . . ."

CHAPTER II

(1)

EVERY Saturday afternoon Ellen sold *Votes for Women* in Princes Street, and the next day found her as usual with a purple, white and green poster hung from her waist and a bundle of papers tucked under her arm. This street-selling had always been a martyrdom to her proud spirit, for it was one of the least of her demands upon the universe that she should be well thought of eternally and by everyone; but she had hitherto been sustained by the reflection that while there were women in jail, as there were always in those days, it ill became her to mind because Lady Cumnock (and everyone knew what she was, for all that she opened so many bazaars) laughed down her long nose as she went by. But now Ellen had lost all her moral stiffening, and as that had always been her speciality she was distressed by the lack; she felt like a dress-shirt that a careless washerwoman had forgotten to starch. The giggling of the passers-by and the manifest unpopularity of her opinions pricked her to tears, and she mournfully perceived that she had ceased to be a poet. For that the day was given over to a high melancholy of grey clouds, which did not let the least stain of weak autumn sunlight discolour the black majesty of the Castle Rock, and that a bold wind played with the dull clothes of the Edinburgh folk and swelled them out into fantastic shapes like cloaks carried by grandees, were as nothing to her because the hurricane tore the short ends of her hair from under her hat and made them straggle on her forehead. "I doubt if I'll be able to appreciate Keats if this goes on," she meditated gloomily. And the people that went by, instead of being as usual mere provocation for her silent laughter, had to-day somehow got power over her and tormented her by making her suspect the worthlessness of her errand. It seemed the height of folly to work for the race if the race was like this: men who, if they had dignity, looked cold and inaccessible to fine disastrous

45

causes; men who were without dignity and base as monkeys; mountainous old men who looked bland because the crevices of their expressions had been filled up with fat, but who showed in the glares they gave her and her papers an immense expertness in coarse malice; hen-like genteel women with small mouths and mean little figures that tried for personality with trimmings and feather boas and all other adornments irrelevant to the structure of the human body; flappers who swung scarlet bows on their plaits and otherwise assailed their Presbyterian environment by glad cries of the appearance; and on all these faces the smirk of superior sagacity that vulgar people give to the untriumphant ideal. " I must work out the ethics of suicide this evening," thought Ellen chokingly, " for if the world's like this it's the wisest thing to do. But not, of course, until mother's gone."

She mechanically offered a paper to a passing flapper, who rejected it with a scornful exclamation, " 'Deed no, Ellen Melville ! I think you're mad." Ellen recognised her as a despised schoolfellow and gnashed her teeth at being treated like this by a poor creature who habitually got thirty per cent. in her arithmetic examination. " Mad, am I ? Not so mad as you, my dear, thinking you look like Phyllis Dare with yon wee, wee pigtail. You evidently haven't realised that a Scotch girl can't help looking sensible. That graceful butterfly frivolity that comes so easy to the English, and, I've haird, the French, is not for us. I think it's something about our ankles that prevents us." She looked at the girl's feet, said " Ay ! " in a manner that hinted that they confirmed her theory, and turned away, remarking over her shoulder, " Mind you, I admire your spirit, setting out to look like one of these light English actresses when your name's Davidina Todd." The wind was trying to tear the poster from the cord that held it to her waist, the cold was making her sniff, and as she gave her back to this flimsy little fool she caught sight of a minister standing a yard or two away and giggling " Tee hee ! " at her. It was too much. She darted down on him. " Are you not Mr. Hunter of the Middleton Place United Free Church ? " she asked, making her voice sound soft and cuddly.

He wiped the facetiousness from his face and assented with a polite bob. Perhaps she was the daughter of an elder. Quite nice people were taking up this nonsense.

" I heard you preach last Sunday," she said, glowing with interest. He began to look coy. Then her voice changed to something colder than the wind. " The most lamentable sairmon

I ever listened to. Neither lairning nor inspiration. And a *read* sairmon, too."

As his black back threaded through the traffic remorse fell upon her. "Here's an opportunity for doing quiet, uncomplaining service to the Cause," she reproached herself, "and I'm turning it into a fair picnic for my tongue." Everyone was rubbish, and she herself was no exception. Her hair was nearly down. And she had to stay there for another hour.

But she determined to endure it ; and Richard Yaverland, who afar off had formed the intention of stopping and speaking to the girl with the poster because she had such hair, was suddenly reminded by the comic and romantic quality of her attitude that this was the typist he had met on the previous evening, whose manifest discontent and ambition had come into his mind more than once during his sleepless night and had distressed him until some recollected gesture or accent made him laugh. He slightly resented this recognition and the change it worked on his emotional tone. For he was compelled to think of her as a human being and be sorry because she was plainly cold and miserable ; and it was his desire to look on women with a magpie thievish eye and no concern for their souls. Considering the part that most of them played in life it was unwarrantable of them to have souls. The dinner that one eats does not presume to have a soul. But the happy freedom of the voluptuary was not for him ; against his will there lived in him something sombre and kind that was sensitive to spiritual things and despondent but powerfully vigilant about the happiness of other people. He said to himself, "That little girl is pretty well done up. She's nearly crying. Someone must have been rude to her." (He did not know his Ellen yet.) "I must give her a moment to get her poor little face straight." So until he drew level with her his dark eyes were fixed on the Castle Rock.

And Ellen thought, "Why, here is the big man who has been in Spain and South America and has the queer stains on his hands ! How big he is, and dark ! He looks like a king among these other people. And how wonderful his eyes are ! He is miles away from here, seeing some distant beautiful thing. Perhaps that mountainside he told us about where the reflection of the sky is like a purple shadow on the snow. A poet must look like that when he is thinking of a poem. But—but—if he keeps on staring up there he won't see me and buy a paper. I should like to interest him in the Cause. And I daren't speak to him." She flushed. Though Mr. Philip's claw had not done all the hurt it hoped, it had yet mauled its victim cruelly. " That would look bold."

But in the nick of time his eyes fell on her. He gave a start of surprise and said in his kind, insolent voice :

" Good morning. So you're a Suffragette."

She was pleased to be publicly recognised by such a splendid person, and answered shyly ; but caught a glint in his eyes which reminded her that she wasn't perfectly sure that he really had thought she was thinking of the Argentine when she had proposed writing to Brazil in Spanish. Was it possible that he was not being entirely respectful to her ? She would not have that, for she was splendid herself too, though the idiot world had given her no chance to show it. She pulled herself together, knitted her brows, and looked as much like Mr. Gladstone as could be managed with such a pliable profile.

" Sell me one of your papers," he said. " No, don't bother about the change. The Cause can let itself go on the odd elevenpence. Well, I think you're wonderful to stand out here in this awful weather with all these blighters going by."

" When one is wrapped up in a great Cause," replied Ellen superbly, " one hardly notices these minor discomforts. Will you not take a ticket for the meeting next Friday at the Synod Hall ? Mrs. Ormiston and Mrs. Mark Lyle are speaking. The tickets are half-a-crown and a shilling. But you'll find the shilling ones quite good, for they're both exceptionally clear and audible speakers. Women are."

"Next Friday? Yes, I can come up that night. Are you taking the chair, or seconding the resolution, or anything like that ? "

" Me ? Mercy, no ! " gasped Ellen. Had he really been taken in by her bluff that she was grown-up ? For she had a feeling, which she would never admit even to herself but which came to her nearly every day, that she was a truant child masquerading in long skirts, and that at any moment someone might come and with the bleak unanswerable authority of a schoolmistress order her back to her short frocks and the class-room. But this was nonsense, for she really was grown-up. She was seventeen past and earning. " No. I'll be stewarding and selling literature."

" Good." He handed her half-a-crown and took the ticket from her, folded it across, hesitated, and asked appealingly : " I say, hadn't you better write your name on this ? I once went to a Suffrage meeting in Glasgow and they wouldn't let me in because they thought I looked the sort of person who would interrupt. But if you wrote your name on my ticket they'll know I'm all right." He gave her a pencil-stump, and as she wrote reflected : " How do I come to be such a fluent liar ? I didn't get it from my mother. No, not from my mother. I suppose my father had that vice as well as the others. But why am I taking so much trouble to find out about this little girl—I who don't care a damn about anything or anybody ? "

He smiled when he took back the card, and with some difficulty, for she had tried to impart an impressive frenzy to her round hand, read her signature. Ellen Melville was a ridiculous name for one of the most beautiful people who have ever lived. It was like climbing to a towered castle on a high eagle-haunted cliff and finding that it was called " Seaview." She was amazingly beautiful now, burning against the grey weather with her private fire ; and she had been beautiful the night before, in that baggy blue overall that only the most artless female creature would have worn. But she had looked even younger then ; he remembered how, as she had opened the door, she had lifted a glowing and receptive face like a child who had been having a lovely time at a party. It occurred to him to question what the lovely time that she had been having in that dreary office could possibly be. And into the pretty print of the scene on his mind, like a humped marine beast rising through a summer sea, there obtruded the recollection of the little solicitor, the graceless embarrassment that he had shown at the beginning of the interview by purposeless rubbings of his hands and twisting of the ankles, the revelation of ugly sexual quality which he had given by his shame at the story of the bed that was made an altar. He looked at her sharply and said to himself : " I wonder . . ."

Oh, surely not ! The note of her face was pure expectancy. As yet she had come upon nothing fundamental of any kind. He had no prepossessions in favour of innocence, and he put people who did not make love in the same class as vegetarians, but he was immensely relieved. He would have hated this fine thing to have fallen into clumsy hands.

There was, he realised, not the smallest excuse for staying with her any longer. " Good-bye ; I hope I'll see you at the meeting," he said ; and then, since he remembered how keen she was on being businesslike, " and look after my villa for me."

" Yes, we'll do that," she said competently, and looked after him with smiling eyes. " Oh, he looks most adventurous ! " she thought. " I wonder, now, if he's ever killed a man ? "

(2)

"Is my frock hooked up all the way down?" wondered Ellen, as she stood with her back to a pillar in the Synod Hall. "Not that I care a button about it myself, but for the sake of the Cause . . ." But that small worry was just one dark leaf floating on the quick sunlit river of her mind, for she was very happy and excited at these Suffrage meetings. She had taken seven shillings and sixpence for pamphlets, the hall was filling up nicely, and Miss Traquair and Dr. Katherine Kennedy and Miss Mackenzie and several members of the local militant suffrage society had spoken to her as they went to their places just as if they counted her grown-up and one of themselves. And she was flushed with the sense of love and power that comes of comradeship. She looked back into the hideous square hall, with its rows of chattering anticipant people, and up to the gallery packed with faces dyed yellowish drab by the near unmitigated gas sunburst, and she smiled brilliantly. All these people were directing their attention and enthusiasm to the same end as herself : would feel no doubt the same tightness of throat as the heroic women came on the platform, and would sanctify the emotion as sane by sharing it ; and by their willingness to co-operate in rebellion were making her individual rebellious will seem less like a schoolgirl's penknife and more like a soldier's sword. "I'm being a politikon Zoon!" she boasted to herself. She had always liked the expression when she read it in *The Scotsman* leaders.

And here they were ! The audience made a tumult that was half applause and half exclamation at a prodigy, and the three women who made their way on the platform seemed to be moving through the noise as through a viscid element. The woman doctor, who was to be the chairman, lowered her curly grey head against it buttingly ; Mrs. Ormiston, the mother of the famous rebels Brynhild, Melissa, and Guendolen, and herself a heroine, lifted a pale face where defiance dwelt among the remains of dark loveliness like a beacon lit on a grey castle keep ; and Mrs. Mark Lyle, a white and golden wonder in a beautiful bright dress, moved swimmingly about and placed herself on a chair like a fastidious lily choosing its vase. Oh ! it was going to be lovely ! Wasn't it ridiculous of that man Yaverland to have stayed away and missed all this glory, to say nothing of wasting a good half-crown and a ticket which someone might have been glad of ? It just showed that men were hopeless and there was no doing anything for them.

But then suddenly she saw him. He was standing at one of the entrances on the other side of the hall, looking tremendous and strange in a peaked cap and raindashed oilskins, as though he had recenty stood on a heeling deck and shouted orders to cutlassed seamen, and he was staring at the tumult as if he regarded noise as a mutiny of inferiors against his preference for calm. By his side a short-sighted steward bent interminably over his ticket. "The silly gowk!" fumed Ellen. "Can the woman not read? It looks so inefficient, and I want him to think well of the movement." Presently, with a suave and unimpatient gesture, he took his ticket away from the peering woman and read her the number. "I like him!" said Ellen. "There's many would have snapped at her for that."

She liked, too, the way he got to his seat without disturbing his neighbours, and the neathandedness with which he took off his cap and oilskins and fell to wiping a pair of motor-goggles while his eyes maintained a dark glance, too intense to flash, on the women on the platform. "How long he is looking at them!" she said to herself presently. "No doubt he is taken up by Mrs. Mark Lyle. I believe such men are very susceptible to beautiful women. I hope," she continued with sudden bitterness, "he is as susceptible to spiritual beauty and will take heed of Mrs. Ormiston!" With that, she tried herself to look at Mrs. Ormiston, but found she could not help watching the clever way he went on cleaning the goggles while his eyes and attention were fixed otherwhere. There was something ill-tempered about his movements which made her want to go dancingly across and say teasing things to him. Yet when a smile at some private thought suggested by the speech broke his attention, and he began to look round the hall, she was filled with panic at the prospect of meeting his eyes. She did not permit herself irrational emotions, so she pretended that what she was feeling was not terror of this man, but the anger of a feminist against all men, and stared fiercely at the platform, crying out silently: "What have I to do with this man? I will have nothing to do with any man until I am great. Then I suppose I will have to use them as pawns in my political and financial intrigues."

Through this gaping at the client from Rio she had missed the chairman's speech. Dr. Munro had just sat down. Her sensible square face looked red and stern, as though she had just been obliged to smack someone, and from the tart brevity of the applause it was evident that that was what she had been doing. This rupture of the bright occasion struck Ellen, who found herself suddenly given over to irritations, as characteristic of the harshness of Edinburgh life. Here was a cause so beautiful in its affirmation of freedom that it should have been served only by the bravery of dignified women and speeches lucent with reason and untremulously spoken, by things that would require no change of quality but only rearrangement to be instantly commemorable by art ; and yet this Scotch woman, moving with that stiffness of the mental joints which nations which suffer from it call conscientiousness, had managed to turn a sacramental gathering of the faithful into a steamy short-tempered activity, like washing-day. " Think shame on yourself, Ellen Melville ! " she rebuked herself. " She's a better woman than ever you'll be, with the grand work she's done at the Miller's Wynd Dispensary." But that the doctor was a really fine woman made the horsehair texture of her manner all the more unpleasing, for it showed her sinisterly illustrative of a community which had reached an intellectual standard that could hardly be bettered and which possessed certain moral energy, and yet was content to be rude. Amongst these people Ellen felt herself, with her perpetual tearful desire that everybody should be nice, to be a tenuous and transparent thing. She doubted if she would ever be able to contend with such as they. " Maybe I shall not get on after all ! " she thought, and her heart turned over with fear.

But Mrs. Ormiston was speaking now. Oh, it was treason to complain against the world when it held anything so fine as this ! She stood very far forward on the platform, and it seemed as though she had no friends in the world but did not care. Beauty was hers, and her white face, with its delicate square jaw and rounded temples, recalled the pansy by its shape. She wore a dress of deep purple, that colour which is almost a sound, an emotion, which is seen by the mind's eye when one hears great music. Her hoarse, sweet North-country voice rushed forth like a wind bearing the sounds of a battle-field, the clash of arms, the curses hurled at an implacable and brutish enemy, the sights of the dying—for already some had died ; and with a passion that preserved her words from the common swift mortality of spoken things she told stories of her followers' brave deeds which seemed to remain in the air and deck the hall like war-tattered standards. She spoke of the women who were imprisoned at Birmingham for interrupting Mr. Asquith's meeting, and how they lay now day and night in the black subterranean prison cells, huddled on the tree-stumps that were the only seats, clad in nothing but coarse vests because

they would not wear the convict clothes, breathing the foul
sewage-tainted air for all but that hour when they were carried
up to the cell where the doctor and the wardresses waited to
bind and gag them and ram the long feeding-tube down into
their bodies. This they had endured for six weeks, and would
for six weeks more. She spoke with a proud reticence as to
her sufferings, about her recent sojourn in Holloway, from
which she had gained release by hunger-striking a fortnight
before.

" Ah, I could die for her ! " cried Ellen to herself, wet-
eyed with loyalty. " If only it weren't for mother I'd go to
prison to-morrow." Her love could hardly bear it when Mrs.
Ormiston went on, restrained rage freezing her words, to indict
the conspiracy of men that had driven her and her followers
to revolt : the refusal to women of a generous education, of a
living wage, of opportunities for professional distinction ; the
social habit of amused contempt at women's doings ; the meanness that used a woman's capacity for mating and motherhood
to bind her a slave either of the kitchen or of the streets. All
these things Ellen knew to be true, because she was poor and
had had to drink life with the chill on, but it did not sadden
her to have her reluctant views confirmed by the woman she
thought the wisest in the world, for she felt an exaltation that
she was afraid must make her eyes look wild. It had always
appeared to her that certain things which in the main were
sombre, such as deep symphonies of an orchestra, the black
range and white scaurs of the Pentland Hills against the south
horizon, the idea that at death one dies utterly and is buried
in the earth, were patterns cut from the stuff of reality. They
were relevant to fate, typical of life, in a way that gayer things,
like the song of girls or the field-checked pleasantness of plains
or the dream of a soul's holiday in eternity, were not. And in
the bitter eloquence of this pale woman she rapturously recognised that same authentic quality.

But what good was it if one woman had something of the
dignity of nature and art ? Everybody knew that the world
was beautiful. She sent her mind out from the hall to walk
in the night, which was not wet, yet had a bloom of rain in the
air, so that the lights shone with a plumy beam and all roads
seemed to run to a soft white cliff. Above, the Castle Rock was
invisible, but certainly cut strange beautiful shapes out of the
mist ; beneath it lay the Gardens, a moat of darkness, raising
to the lighted street beyond terraces planted with rough autumn
flowers that would now be close-curled balls curiously trimmed

with dew, and grass that would make placid squelching noises under the feet ; and at the end of the Gardens were the two Greek temples that held the town's pictures—the Tiepolo, which shows Pharaoh's daughter walking in a fardingale of gold with the negro page to find a bambino Moses kicking in Venetian sunlight ; the Raeburns, coarse and wholesome as a home-made loaf ; the lent Whistler collection like a hive of butterflies. And at the Music Hall Frederick Lamond was playing Beethoven. How his strong hands would beat out the music ! Oh, as to the beauty of the world there was no question !

But people weren't as nice as things. Humanity was no more than an ugly parasite infesting the earth. The vile quality of men and women could hardly be exaggerated. There was Miss Coates, the secretary of the Anti-Suffrage Society, who had come to this meeting from some obscure motive of self-torture and sat quite close by, jerking her pale face about in the shadow of a wide, expensive hat (it was always women like that, Ellen acidly remarked, who could afford good clothes) as she was seized by convulsions of contempt for the speaker and the audience. Ellen knew her very well, for every Saturday morning she used to stride up in an emerald green sports skirt, holding out a penny in a hand that shook with rage, and saying something indistinct about women biting policemen. On these occasions Ellen was physically afraid, for she could not overcome a fancy that the anklebones which projected in geological-looking knobs on each side of Miss Coates's large flat brogues were a natural offensive weapon like the spurs of a cock ; and she was afraid also in her soul. Miss Coates was plainly, from her yellow but animated pallor, from her habit of wearing her blouse open at the neck to show a triangle of chest over which the horizontal bones lay like the bars of a gridiron, a mature specimen of a type that Ellen had met in her school-days. There had been several girls at John Thompson's, usually bleached and ill-favoured victims of anæmia or spinal curvature, who had seemed to be compelled by something within themselves to spend their whole energies in trying, by extravagances of hair-ribbon and sidecombs and patent leather belts, the collection of actresses' postcards, and the completest abstention from study, to assert the femininity which their ill-health had obscured. Their efforts were never rewarded by the companionship of any but the most shambling kind of man or boy ; but they proceeded through life with a greater earnestness than other children of their age, intent on the business of establishing their sex. Miss Coates was plainly the adult of the type, who had found in Anti-Suffragism, that extreme gesture of political abasement before the male, a new way of calling attention to what otherwise only the person who was naturally noticing about clothes would detect. It was a fact of immense and dangerous significance that the Government and the majority of respectable citizens were on the side of this pale, sickly, mad young woman against the brave, beautiful Mrs. Ormiston. People were horrible.

And there was Mr. Philip.

Oh, why had she thought of him ? All the time that she had been in the hall she had forgotten him, but now he had come back to torture her untiringly, as he had done all that week. It had been all very well for her to run through the darkness so happily that evening, unvexed by the accusation of her boldness because she was not bold, for she had not then known the might of cruelty. Indeed, she had not believed that anybody had ever hurt anybody deliberately, except long-dead soldiers sent by mad kings to make what history books, to mark the unusual horror of the event, called massacres. She had begun to know better late last Monday afternoon. She had returned to her little room after taking down some shorthand notes from dictation, and, because there was a thick, ugly twilight and she had come dazzled by the crude light on Mr. Mactavish James's desk, had moved about for some seconds, with a freedom that seemed foolishness as soon as she knew she was observed, before she saw that Mr. Philip was standing at the hearth.

" Have you come straight off the train ? " it was in her mind to say. " Will I ask Mrs. Powell to get you some tea ? " But he looked strange. The driving flame of the fire cast flickering shadows and red lights on the shoulders and skirt of his great-coat, so he looked as though he was performing some evil incantatory dance of the body, while his face and hands and feet remained black and still. There was no sound of his breath. " Good mercy on us ! " she said to herself. " Is it his wraith, and has he come to harm in London ? " But the dark patch of his face moved, and he began his long demonstration to her that a man need not be dead to be dreadful. " Is there anything you want of me, Miss Melville ? " the clipped voice had asked. It was so plainly the cold answer to an ogle that she gazed about her for some person who deserved this reproach and whom he had called by her name in error. But of course there was no one, and she realised that he had come back from London her enemy, that this accusation of her boldness was to be the favourite weapon of his enmity, and that he found it the more serviceable way to accuse her of making advances to him as well as to the client from Rio.

"I want nothing," she said, and left him. Since there was nowhere else for her to go, she was obliged to wait in the lobby beside the umbrella-stand till he came out, quirked his head at her suspiciously, and went into his father's room. She perceived that there had been no need for him to go into her room save his desire to make this gesture of hate towards her. It came to her then that, although an accusation could not hurt one if it was false, the accuser could hurt by the evil spirit he discharged. If a man emptied a jug of water over you from a top window in the belief that you were a cat, the fact that you were not a cat would not prevent you from getting wet through. In the midst of her alarm she smiled at finding an apt image. There were still intellectual refuges. But very few. Every day Mr. Philip convinced her how few and ineffectual. He never now, when he had finished dictating, said, "That's all for the present, thank you," but let an awkward space of silence fall, and then enquired with an affectation of patience, "And what are you waiting on, Miss Melville?" He treated her infrequent errors in typing as if she was a simpering girl who was trying to buy idleness with her charm. And he was speaking ill of her. That she knew from Mr. Mactavish James's kindnesses, which brightened the moment but always made the estimate of her plight more dreary, since just so might a gaoler in a brigand's cave bring a prisoner scraps of sweeter food and drink when the talk of her death and the thought of her youth had made him feel tenderly. Only that morning he had padded up behind Ellen and set a white parcel by her typewriter. "Here's some taiblet for you, lassie," he had said, and had laid a loving, clumsy hand on her shoulder. What had Mr. Philip been saying now? And she did so want to be well spoken of. But there was worse than that—something so bad that she would not allow her mind to harbour any visual image of it, but thought of it in a harsh, short sentence. "*When Mr. Morrison went out of the room and we were left alone he got up and set the door ajar. . . .*" Something weak and little in her cried out, "Oh, God, stop Mr. Philip being so cruel to me or I shall die!" and something fiercer said, "I will kill him. . . ."

There was a roar of applause, and she found that Mrs. Ormiston had finished her speech. This was another iniquity to be charged against Mr. Philip. The thought of him had robbed her of heaven knows how much of the wisdom of her idol, and it might be a year or more before Mrs. Ormiston came

to Edinburgh again. She could have cried as she clapped, but
fortunately there was Mrs. Mark Lyle yet to speak. She watched
the advance to the edge of the platform of that tall, beautiful
figure in the shining dress which it would have been an under-
statement to call sky-blue, unless one predicated that the sky
was Italian, and rejoiced that nature had so appropriately given
such a saint a halo of gold hair. Then came the slow, clear voice
building a crystal bridge of argument between the platform
and the audience, and formulating with an indignation that was
fierce, yet left her marmoreal, an indictment against the double
standard of morality and the treatment of unmarried mothers.

Ellen clapped loudly, not because she had any great opinion
of unmarried mothers, whom she suspected of belonging to the
same type of woman who would start on a day's steamer ex-
cursion and then find that she had forgotten the sandwiches,
but because she was a neat-minded girl and could not abide the
State's pretence that an illegitimate baby had only one parent
when everybody knew that every baby had really two. And
she fell to wondering what this thing was that men did to women.
There was certainly some definite thing. Children, she was
sure, came into the world because of some kind of embrace ;
and she had learned lately, too, that women who were very poor
sometimes let men do this thing to them for money : such were
the women whom she saw in John Square, when she came back
late from a meeting or a concert, leaning against the garden-
railings, their backs to the lovely nocturnal mystery of groves
and moonlit lawns, and their faces turned to the line of rich
men's houses which mounted out of the night like a tall, impregnable fortress. Some were grey-haired. Such traffic was
perilous as it was ugly, for somehow there were babies who were
born blind because of it. That was the sum of her knowledge.
What followed the grave kisses shown in pictures, what secret
Romeo shared with Juliet, she did not know, she would not know.

Twice she had refused to learn the truth. Once a schoolfellow
named Anna McLellan, a minister's daughter, a pale girl with
straight, yellow hair and full, whitish lips, had tried to tell her
something queer about married people as they were walking
along Princes Street, and Ellen had broken away from her and
run into the Gardens. The trees and grass and daffodils had
seemed not only beautiful but pleasantly unsmirched by the
human story. And in the garret at home, in a pile of her father's
books, she had once found a medical volume which she knew
from the words on its cover would tell her all the things about
which she was wondering. She had laid her fingers between

its leaves, but a shivering had come upon her, and she ran downstairs very quickly and washed her hands. These memories
made her feel restless and unhappy, and she drove her attention
back to the platform and beautiful Mrs. Mark Lyle. But
there came upon her a fantasy that she was standing again in
the garret with that book in her hands, and that Mr. Philip was
leaning against the wall in that dark place beyond the window
laughing at her, partly because she was such a wee ninny not to
know, and partly because when she did know the truth there
would be something about it which would humiliate her. She
cast down her eyes and stared at the floor so that none might
see how close she was to tears. She was a silly weak thing
that would always feel like a bairn on its first day at school ;
she was being tormented by Mr. Philip. Even the very facts
of life had been planned to hurt her.

Oh, to be like that man from Rio ! It was his splendid fate
to be made tall and royal, to be the natural commander of all
men from the moment that he ceased to be a child. He could
captain his ship through the steepest seas and fight the pirate
frigate till there was nothing between him and the sunset but a
few men clinging to planks and a shot-torn black flag floating
on the waves like a rag of seaweed. For rest he would steer to
small islands, where singing birds would fly out of woods and
perch on the rigging, and brown men would come and run aloft
and wreathe the masts with flowers, and shy women with long,
loose, black hair would steal out and offer palm-wine in conches,
while he smiled aloofly and was gracious. It would not matter
where he sailed ; at no port in the world would sorrow wait
for him, and everywhere there would be pride and honour and
stars pinned to his rough coat by grateful kings. And if he
fell in love with a beautiful woman he would go away from her
at once and do splendid things for her sake. And when he
died there would be a lying-in-state in a great cathedral, where
emperors and princes would file past and shiver as they looked
on the white, stern face and the stiff hands clasped on the hilt
of his sword, because now they had lost their chief defender.
Oh, he was too grand to be known, of course, but it was a joy to
think of him.

She looked across the hall at him. Their eyes met.

(3)

There had mounted in him, as he rode through the damp night
on his motor-cycle, such an inexplicable and intense exhilaration,

that this ugly hall which was at the end of his journey, with its stone corridors in which a stream of people wearing mackintoshes and carrying umbrellas made sad noises with their feet, seemed an anti-climax. It was absurd that he should feel like that, for he had known quite well why he was coming into Edinburgh and what a Suffrage meeting would be like. But he was angry and discontented, and impatient that no deflecting adventure had crossed his path, until he arrived at the door which led to the half-crown seats and saw across the hall that girl called Ellen Melville. The coarse light deadened the brilliance of her hair, so that it might have been but a brightly coloured tam-o'-shanter she was wearing ; and now that that obvious beauty was not there to hypnotise the eye the subtler beauty of her face and body got its chance. " I had remembered her all wrong," he said to himself. " I was thinking of her as a little girl, but she's a beautiful and dignified woman." And yet her profile, which showed against the dark pillar at which she stood, was very round and young and surprised, and altogether much more infantile than the proud full face which she turned on the world. There was something about her, too, which he could not identify, which made him feel the sharp yet almost anguished delight that is caused by the spectacle of a sunset or a foam-patterned breaking wave, or any other beauty that is intense but on the point of dissolution.

The defile of some women on to the platform and a clamour of clapping reminded him that he had better be getting to his seat, and he found that the steward to whom he had given his ticket, a sallow young woman with projecting teeth, was holding it close to her eyes with one hand and using the other to fumble in a leather bag for some glasses which manifestly were not there. He felt sorry for her because she was not beautiful like Ellen Melville. Did she grieve at it, he wondered ; or had she, like most plain women, some scrap of comeliness, slender ankles or small hands, which she pathetically invested with a magic quality and believed to be more subtly and authentically beautiful than the specious pictorial quality of other women ? In any case she must often have been stung by the exasperation of those at whom she gawked. He took the ticket back from her and told her the number of his seat. It was far forward, and as he sat down and looked up at the platform he saw how vulgarly mistaken he had been in thinking—as just for the moment that the sallow woman with the teeth had stooped and fumbled beside him he certainly had thought—that the Suffrage movement was a fusion of the discontents of the unfit. These people on the platform were real women. The speaker who had risen to open the meeting was a jolly woman like a cook, with short grey curly hair ; and her red face was like the Scotch face—the face that he had looked on many a time in all parts of the world and had always been glad to see, since where it was there was sense and courage. She was the image of old Captain Guthrie of the *Gondomar*, and Dr. Macalister at the Port Said hospital, and that medical missionary who had come home on the *Celebes* on sick leave from Mukden. Harsh things she was saying— harsh things about the decent Scotch folks who were shocked by the arrest of Suffragettes in London for brawling, harsh suggestions that they would be better employed being shocked at the number of women who were arrested in Edinburgh for solicitation.

He chuckled to think that the Presbyterian woman had found out the Presbyterian man, for he did not believe, from his knowledge of the world, that any man was ever really as respectable as the Presbyterian man pretended to be. The woman who sat beside her, who was evidently the celebrated Mrs. Ormiston, was also a personage. She had not the same stamp of personal worth, but she had the indefinable historic quality. For no reason to be formulated by the mind, her face might become a flag to many thousands, a thing to die for, and, like a flag, she would be at their death a mere martial mark of the occasion, with no meaning of pity.

The third woman he detested. Presumably she was at this meeting because she was a loyal Suffragist and wanted to bring an end to the subjection of woman, yet all the time that the other woman was speaking her beautiful body practised fluid poses as if she were trying to draw the audience's attention to herself and give them facile romantic dreams in which the traditional relations of the sexes were rejoiced in rather than disturbed. And she wore a preposterous dress. There were two ways that women could dress. If they had work to do they could dress curtly and sensibly like men and let their looks stand or fall on their intrinsic merits ; or if they were among the women who are kept to fortify the will to live in men who are spent or exasperated by conflict with the world, the wives and daughters and courtesans of the rich, then they should wear soft lustrous dresses that were good to look at and touch and as carefully beautiful as pictures. But this blue thing was neither sturdy covering nor the brilliant fantasy it meant to be. It had the spurious glitter of an imitation jewel. He knew he felt this irritation about her partly because there was something base in him, half innate and half the abrasion his present circumstances had rubbed on his soul, which was willing to go on this stupid sexual journey suggested by such vain, passive women, and the saner part of him was vexed at this compliance ; he thought he had a real case against her. She was one of those beautiful women who are not only conscious of their beauty but have accepted it as their vocation. She was ensphered from the world of creative effort in the establishment of her own perfection. She was an end in herself as no human, save some old saint who has made a garden of his soul, had any right to be.

That little girl Ellen Melville was lovelier stuff because she was at grips with the world. This woman had magnificent smooth wolds of shoulders and a large blonde dignity ; but life was striking sparks of the flint of Ellen's being. There came before him the picture of her as she had been that day in Princes Street, with the hairs straggling under her hat and her fierce eyes holding back the tears, telling him haughtily that a great cause made one indifferent to discomfort ; and he nearly laughed aloud. He looked across the hall at her and just caught her switching her gaze from him to the platform. He felt a curious swaggering triumph at the flight of her eyes.

But Mrs. Ormiston had begun to speak, and he, too, turned his attention to the platform. He liked this old woman's invincible quality, the way she had turned to and made a battering-ram of her own meagre middle-aged body to level the walls of authority ; and she reminded him of his mother. There was no physical likeness, but plainly this woman also was one of those tragically serious mothers in whose souls perpetual concern for their children dwelt like a cloud. He thought of her as he had often thought of his mother, that it was impossible to imagine her visited by those morally blank moods of purely sensuous perception which were the chief joy he had found in life. Such women never stood upright, lifting their faces to the sunlight, smiling at the way of the wind in the tree-tops ; they seemed to be crouched down with ear to carth, listening to the footsteps of the events which were marching upon their beloved.

The resemblance went no further than this spiritual attitude, for this woman was second-rate stuff. Her beauty was somehow shoddy, her purple gown the kind of garment that a clairvoyant might have worn, her movements had the used quality of photographers' poses. Publicity had not been able to change the substance of the precious metal of her soul, but it had tarnished it beyond all remedy. She alluded presently to her preposterously-named daughters, Brynhild, Melissa and Guendolen, and he was reminded of a French family of musicians with whom he had travelled on the steamer betwen Rio and Sao Paulo, a double-chinned swarthy Madame and her three daughters, Céline, Roxane and Juliette, who sat about on deck nursing musical instruments tied with grubby scarlet ribbons, silent and dispirited, as though they were so addicted to public appearance that they found their private hours an embarrassment. But he remembered with a prick of compunction that they had made excellent music; and that, after all, was their business in life. So with the Ormistons. In the pursuit of liberty they had inadvertently become a troupe; but they had fought like lions. And they were giving the young that guarantee that life is really as fine as story-books say, which can only be given by contemporary heroism. Little Ellen Melville, on the other side of the hall, was lifting the most wonderful face all fierce and glowing with hero-worship. " That's how I used to feel about Old Man Guthrie of the *Gondomar* when I was seventeen," he thought. " It's a good age. . . ."

When he was seventeen. . . . He was not at all sure that those three years he had spent at sea were not the best time of his life. It came back to him, the salt enchantment of that time; the excitement in his heart, the ironic serenity of the surrounding world, on that dawn when he stood on the deck of his first ship as it sailed out of the Thames to the open sea. The mouth of the river was barred by a rosy, drowsy sunrise; the sky had lost its stars, and had blenched, and was being flooded by a brave daylight blue; the water was changing from a sad silver width to a sheet of white silk, creased with blue lines; the low hills on the southern bank and the flat spit between the estuary and the Medway were at first steamy shapes that might have drowned seamen's dreams of land, but they took on earthly colours as he watched; and to the north Kerith Island, that had been a blackness running weedy fingers out into the flood, showed its farms and elms standing up to their middles in mist. He went to the side and stared at the ridge of hills that lay behind the island, that this picture should be clear in his mind at the last if the storms should take him. There were the four crumbling grey towers of Roothing Castle; and eastward there was Roothing Church, with its squint spire and its sea-gnarled yews about it, and at its base the dazzling white speck which he knew to be his father's tomb. He hated that he should be able to see it even from here. All his life that mausoleum had enraged him. He counted it a kind of cowardice of his father to have died before his son was a man. He suspected him of creeping into his coffin as a refuge, of wearing its lead as armour, from fear of his son's revenges ; and the choice of so public a sanctuary as this massive tomb on the hillside was a last insolence.

Eastward, a few fields' length along the ridge, was the belvedere on his father's estate. He had not looked at it for years, but from here it was so little like itself that he could bear to let his eyes dwell on it. It was built at the fore of a crescent-shaped plantation on the brow of the hill, and the dark woods stretched away on each side of the temple like great green wings spread by a small white bird. And eastward yet a mile or so, at the end of a line of salt-stunted oaks, was the red block of Yaverland's End. Under that thatch was his mother. She would be asleep now. Nearly always now she dropped off to sleep before dawn. With a constriction of the heart he thought of her as she would be looking now, lying very straight in her narrow bed, one arm crooked behind the head and the other rigid by her side, the black drift of her hair drawn across her eyes like a mask and her uncovered mouth speaking very often. Many of her nights were spent in argument with the dead. At the picture he felt a rush of love that dizzied him, and he cursed himself for having left her, until the serenity of the white waters and the limpid sky imposed reason on his thoughts as it was imposing harmoniousness on the cries of the seagulls and the shouts of the sailors. Then he recognised the necessity of this adventure. It was his duty to her to go out into the world and do great things. He had said so very definitely to himself, and had turned back to his work with a scowl of resolution. So that boy, thirteen years before . . .

He shivered and wished he had not thought of the time when he meant to do great things, for this was one of the nights when he felt that he had done nothing and was nothing. He saw his soul as something detached from his body and inimical to it, an enveloping substance, thin as smoke and acrid to the smell, which segregated him from the participation in reality which he felt to be his due, and he changed his position, and cleared his throat, and stared hard at the people round him and at the woman on the platform in hopes that some arresting gesture might summon him from this shadowy prison. But the audience sat still in a sheeplike, grazing sort of attention, and Mrs. Ormiston continued to exercise her distinguished querulousness on the subject of male primogeniture. So he remained rooted in this oppressive sense of his own nothingness.

" Oh, come, I've had an hour or two ! " he reassured himself. There were those three days and nights when he stood at the wheel of the *Father Time,* because the captain and every man who was wise about navigation were dying in their bunks of New Guinea fever ; days that came up from the seas fresh as a girl from a bathe and turned to a torturing dome of fire ; nights when he looked up at the sky and could not tell which were the stars and which the lights which trouble the eyes of sleep-sick men. There was that week when he and Perez and the two French chemists and the handful of loyal workmen held the Romanones Works against the strikers. He was conscious that he had behaved well on these occasions and that they had been full of beauty, but they had not nourished him. They had ended when they ended. Such deeds gave a man nothing better than the exultation of the actor, who loses his value and becomes a suspended soul, unable to fulfil his function when the curtain falls. " But you are condemning the whole of human action ! " he expostulated with himself. " Yes, I am condemning the whole of human action," he replied tartly.

There remained, of course, his scientific work. That was indubitably good. He had done well, considering he had not gone to South Kensington till he was twenty and had broken the habit of study by a life of adventure, simply because the idea of explosiveness had captured his imagination. That rust is a slow explosion, that every movement is the result of a physical explosion, that explosives are capricious as women about the forces to which they yield, so that this one will only ignite with heat and that only with concussion—these facts had from his earliest knowledge of them been gilded with irrational delight, and it had been no effort to him to work at the subject with an austere diligence that had shown itself worth while in that last paper he had read at the Paris Conference. That was a pretty piece of research. But now for the first time he resented his chemistry work because it was of no service to his personal life. Before, it had always seemed to him the special dignity of his vocation that it could conduct its researches without resorting to the use of humanity and that he could present his results unsigned by his own personality. He had often pitied doctors, who, instead of dealing with exquisitely consistent chemicals, have to work on men and women, unselected specimens of the most variable of all species, which was singularly inept at variating in the direction of beauty ; and it seemed miraculous that he could turn the yeasty workings of his mind into cool, clear statements of hitherto unstated truth that would in no way betray to those that read them that their maker was lustful and hot-tempered and, about some things, melancholic. He had felt Science to be so gloriously above life ; to make the smallest discovery was like hearing the authentic voice of God who is no man but a Spirit.

But now none of these things mattered. He was caught in the net of life and nothing that was above it was of any use to him ; as well expect a man who lies through the night with his foot in a man-trap to be comforted by the beauty of the stars. The only God he could have any use for would be the kind the Salvationists talk about, who goes about giving drunken men an arm past the public-house and coming between the pickpocket and Black Maria with a well-timed text. There was nothing in Science that would life him out of this hell of loneliness, this conviction of impotence, this shame of achievementless maturity. He perceived that he had really known this for a long time, and that it was the meaning of the growing irritability which had of late changed his day in the laboratory from the rapt, swift office of the mind it used to be, to an interminable stretch of drudgery checkered with fits of rage at faulty apparatus, neurotic moods when he felt unable to perform fine movements, and desolating spaces when he stood at the window and stared at the high grassy embankment which ran round the hut, designed to break the outward force of any explosion that might occur, and thought grimly over the commercial uses that were to be made of his work. What was the use of sweating his brains so that one set of fools could blow another set of fools to glory ? Oh, this was hell ! . . .

The detestable blonde was now holding the platform in attitudes such as are ascribed to goddesses by British sculptors, and speaking with a slow, pure gusto of the horrors of immorality. For a moment her allusions to the wrongs of unmarried mothers made him think of the proud but defeated poise of his mother's head, and then the peculiar calm, gross qualities of her phrases came home to him. He wondered how long she had been going on like this, and he stared round to see how these people, who looked so very decent, whom it was impossible to imagine other than fully dressed, were taking it. Without anticipation his eyes fell on Ellen and found her looking very Scotch and clapping sturdily. Of course it must be all right, since everything about her was all right, but he searched this surprising gesture as though he were trying to read a signal, till with a quick delight he realised that this was just the final proof of how very much all right she was. Only a girl so innocent that these allusions to sex had called to her mind no physical presentations whatsoever could have stood there with perked head and made cymbals of her hands. Evidently she did nothing by halves ; her mind was white as her hair was red.

He felt less appalled by this speech now that he saw that it was powerless to wound simplicity, but he still hated it. It was doing no good, because it was a part of the evil it attacked ; for the spirit that makes people talk coarsely about sex is the same spirit that makes men act coarsely to women. It was not Puritanism at all that would put an end to this squalor and cruelty, but sensuality. If you taught that these encounters were degrading, then inevitably men treated the women whom they encountered as degraded ; but if you claimed that even the most casual love-making was beautiful, and that a woman who yields to a man's entreaty gave him some space of heaven, then you could insist that he was under an obligation of gratitude to her and must treat her honourably. That would not only change the character of immorality, but would also diminish it, for men have no taste for multiplying their responsibilities.

Besides, it was true. These things were very good. He had half forgotten how good they were. The meeting became a babble in his ears, a transparency of listening shapes before his eyes. . . . He was back in Rio ; back in youth. He was waiting with a fever in his blood at that dinner at old Hermes Pessôa's preposterous house, that was built like—so far as it was like anything else on earth—the Villa d'Este mingled with the Alhambra. The dinner, considered as a matter of food, had come to an end, and for some little time had been a matter of drink ; most of the guests had gathered in a circle at the head of the hall round fat old Pessôa, who had sent a servant upstairs for a pair of tartan socks so that he could dance the Highland fling. He had got up and strolled to the other end of the room, where the great black onyx fireplace climbed out of the light into the layer of gloom which lay beneath the ceiling that here and there dripped stalactites of ornament down into the brightness. Against the wall on each side of the fireplace there stood six great chairs of cypress wood, padded with red Spanish leather that smelt sweetly and because of its great age was giving off a soft red dust. These chairs pleased him ; they were the only old things in this mad new house, in this mad new society. He had pulled one out and lain back, feeling rather ill, because he had eaten nothing and his heart was beating violently. He hated being there, but he had to make sure. Much rather would he have been out in the gardens, standing beside one of those magnolias, watching the stars travel across the bay. "Then marriage is right," he said to himself. "Where there is real love one wants to go to church first."

Others who had wearied of the party drifted down to this recess of peace. An elderly Frenchman with a pointed black beard, and a slim, fair English boy with tears on his long eyelashes, sat themselves down in two of these great chairs, with a bottle of wine at their feet and one glass, from which they drank alternately with an effect of exchanging vows, while the boy whimpered some confession, sobbing that it would all never have happened if he had still been with Father Errington of the Sacred Heart in Liverpool, and the older man repeated paternally, mystically, and yet with a purring satisfaction, " Little one, do not grieve. It is always thus when one forgets the Church."

There came later another Frenchman, a fat and very drunken banker, who sat down at his right and complained from time to time of the lack of elegance in this debauchery. He wished that these people had left him alone, and stared at the wall in front of him, where curtains of crimson brocade and gold galoon hung undrawn between the lustred tiles and the high windows, black with the outer night but streaked and oiled with reflections of the inner feast. Opposite there hung a Bouguereau, which irritated him—nymphs ought not to look as if they had come newly unguented from a *cabinet de toilette*. Below it stood an immense Cloisonné vase, about the neck of which was tied a scarlet silk stocking. He remembered having seen it there on his last visit six months before. She must have been an exceptionally careless lady. Out here there were many ladies who were careless of their honour, but most of them were careful enough about tangible possessions like silk stockings. A fresh outburst in the babel at the other end of the room did not make him turn round, though the French banker had cried in an ecstasy, " *Tiens! c'est atroce!*" and had bounded up the hall. He sat on, hating this ugly place of his delay, while the Frenchman and the boy kept up an insincere, voluptuous whisper about God and the comfort of the Mass. . . .

At last he rose to his feet. It was a quarter to twelve, and time for him to go. He went up the hall, treading on lobster claws and someone's wig, and looking about him for a certain person. He could not see him among the group of revellers that stood in the space before the large folding-doors, and for a minute a hand closed over his heart as he feared that for once the person whom he sought had gone home before morning. But presently he saw a long chair by the wall, and on its cushions a blotched face and a gross, full body. He bent over the chair and whispered, "De Rojas, de Rojas!" But the fat man slept. Hatred gushed up in him, and a joy that the night was secure, and he passed on to the folding-doors. But from the little group that was gathered round the table, which before the dinner had supported the Winged Victory that now lay spread-eagled on the floor, there stepped Pessôa. He bade him good-night and thanked him for a riotous evening, but perceived that Pessôa was waving a cocked revolver at him and saying something about Léonore. What could he be saying? It appeared incredible, even to-night, that he should really be saying that every departing guest must kiss Léonore's back and swear that it was the most beautiful back in Brazil.

He looked along the avenue of revellers that had turned grinning to see how his English stiffness would meet the occasion, and saw poor Léonore. She was sitting on the table, one hand holding her pink wrapper to her breast and the other patting back a yawn, and her nightdress was pulled down to her waist so that her back was bare. Such a broad, honest back it was, for she was the thick type of Frenchwoman, and might have stood as a model for Millet's "Angelus." She looked over her shoulder and smiled at him benignantly, perplexedly, and he saw that she was unhappy. They had fetched her down from her warm bed, whither doubtless she had gone with hopes of having a good night's rest for once, since Hermes was giving a stag-dinner. They had not even given her time to wipe off all the cold cream, some of which lay in an ooze round her jaw and temples, or to take the curl-papers out of her hair, which still sported some white snippets of the *Jornal de Commercio*. She bore no malice, the good soul was saying to herself, but once a woman is in her bed she likes to stay there; still, men are men, and mad, so what can one expect?

He would not treat her lightly, nor spoil his sense of dedication to one woman. He flicked the revolver out of Pessôa's hand and flung it through the nearest window. The thick glass took a little time to fall.

"My friends will wait on you in the morning," Pessôa had spouted, and he had said the appropriate courteous things, and gone up to Léonore, and kissed her hand and said something chaffing in her ear, at which she smiled sleepily, and said in English, "Go on, you bad man!" She spoke so slowly and so meaninglessly, as stupid people do when they speak a foreign tongue, that the words seemed to be uttered by some lonely

ghost that had found a lodging in her broad mouth. Then
the men fell back to let him go out through the folding-doors,
and he went out into the Moorish arches of the entrance-hall,
where Indian flunkeys in purple livery gave him his coat and hat,
and he set his back to this queer mass of cupolas and towers,
that radiated from its uncurtained windows rays of light
which were pollutions of the moonlight. He thought of
that blotched face, that gross, full body. . . . It was a night
of strong moonlight. He was walking along a dazzling white
causeway edged, where the wall cast its shadow, with a ribbon
of blackness. Palms stood up glittering, touched by the
moon to something madder than their daylight fantasy of form.
The aluminium-painted railings in front of de Rojas' villa
gleamed like the spears of heroes. He stared between them at
the red façade ; if she was a coward she would still be somewhere in there. The thought struck him with terror. If she
were not waiting for him the moonlight would shatter and turn
to darkness, the violence of his heart-beat turn to stillness.

Now he had come to the Villa Miraflores. This was his house.
Yet he entered the gate like a thief, and crept along the shadow
of the wall that enclosed his own gardens. The magnolias
stood blazing white on the lawns, the stiff scarlet poinsettias
twitched resentfully under the poising fireflies' weight, and
from the dark geraniums scent rose like a smoke. He would
have liked to go to her with an armful of flowers, but he did
not dare to go out into the light. He passed the door that led
from his to de Rojas' garden, which had been made when a
father and son had been tenants of the two houses, and which
had never been blocked up because de Rojas and he were such
good neighbours. If it had not been unlocked to-night, if the
marble summerhouse were empty . . . He stood in the pillared
portico and did not dare go in. He thought of the temple,
not so very much unlike this, on a far-off Essex hillside, where
his mother used to meet his father ; and somehow this made
him feel that if Mariquita had failed him it would be a bitter
shame and dishonour to him. Very slowly, rehearsing cruel
things that he would say to her to-morrow, he opened the door
and let the moonbeams search the summerhouse. It showed a
huddled figure that wailed a little as it saw the light. He shut
the door and moved into the darkness, taking his woman in his
arms, finding her lips. . . .

It had all gone. He could remember nothing of it. He
could remember nothing of the joy that had thralled him for
two years, that by its ending had desolated him for two more

and alienated him from women. He knew as a matter of
historical fact that he had been her lover, but it meant no more
to him than his knowledge that Antony had once loved Cleo-
patra and Nelson Lady Hamilton ; of the quality of her kisses,
the magic that must have filled these hours, he could recollect
nothing. Perhaps it was not fair to blame her for that. Perhaps
it was not her fault but the fault of Nature, who is so determined that men shall go on love-making that she makes the
delights of love the least memorable of all. But it was her
fault that she had given him nothing spiritual to remember.
When he came to think of it, she had hardly ever said anything
that one could carry away with one. She was one of those
women who moan a lot, and one cannot get any solid satisfaction
out of repeating a moan to oneself. He grinned as he thought
of the alarm of his laboratory boy if he should ever try in some
cheerless stretch of his work to remind himself of Mariquita by
saying over to himself her characteristic moan. Nothing she
had ever said or done when they were lovers was half so real to
him as the tears she shed when she cast him off because the priest
had told her that she must ; when she broke the tie between
them with a blank dismissal which, if it had been given by a
man to a woman, these Suffragettes would have called a vile
betrayal.

   He could remember well enough his rage when he
took her to him in that last embrace and she would not give
him both her hands, because in one she held the ebony cross of
her rosary, to make her strong to do this unnatural thing. Well,
perhaps it was natural enough that that hour should seem most
real to him, for it was then that he had found out their real
relationship. To him it had seemed as if they were two children
wandering in the unfriendly desert that is life, comforting each
other with kisses, finding in their love a refuge from coldness
and unkindness. But in her fear he perceived that she had
never been his comrade. She had thought of him as an external
power, like the Church, who told her to do things, and in the
end the choice had been for her not between a dear and pitied
lover and a creed, but between two tyrants ; and since one
tyrant threatened damnation while the other only promised
love, a sensible woman knew which to choose. All he had
thought of her had been an illusion. The years he had given to
his love for her were as wasted as if he had spent them in drunkenness or in prison.

   Oh, women were the devil ! All except his mother. They
were the clumsiest of biological devices, and as they handed on

life they spoiled it. They stood at the edge of the primeval swamps and called the men down from the highlands of civilisation and certain cells determined upon immortality betrayed their victims to them. They served the seed of life, but to all the divine accretions that had gathered round it, the courage that adventures, the intellect that creates, the soul that questions how it came, they were hostile. They hated the complicated brains that men wear in their heads as men hated the complicated hats that women wear on their heads ; they hated men to look at the stars because they are sexless ; they hated men who loved them passionately because such love was tainted with the romantic and imaginative quality that spurs them to the folly of science and art and exploration. And yet surely there were other women. Surely there was a woman somewhere who, if one loved her, would prove not a mere possession who would either bore one or go and get lost just when one had grown accustomed to it, but would be an endless research. A woman who would not be a mere film of graceful submissiveness but real as a chemical substance, so that one could observe her reactions and find out her properties ; and like a chemical substance, irreducible to final terms, so that one never came to an end. A woman who would get excited about life as men do and could laugh and cheer. A woman whose beauty would be forever significant with speculation. He perceived with a shock that he was thinking of this woman not as one thinks of a hypothetical person, but with the glowing satisfaction which one feels in recounting the charms of a new friend. He was thinking of some real person. It was someone he had met quite lately, someone with red hair. He was thinking of that little Ellen Melville.

He looked across the hall at her. Their eyes met.

(4)

When he went over to her side at the end of the meeting she glowered at him and said, " Oh, it's you ! " as if it was the first time she had set eyes upon him that evening ; but he knew that that was just because she was shy, and he shook hands rather slowly and looked her full in the face as he said he had liked the speeches so that she might see she couldn't come it over *him*. And he asked if he might see her home.

She swallowed, and pushed up her chin, as if trying to rise to some tremendous occasion, and then pulled herself together, and with an air of having found a loophole of escape, enquired,

" But where are you stopping ? " and when he made answer
that he was staying at the Caledonian Hotel, she exclaimed in
a tone of relief, " Ah, but I live at Hume Park Square out by
the Meadows ! "

" I want to see you home," he said inflexibly.

" Oh, if you want the walk ! " she answered resignedly.
" Though you've a queer taste in walks, for the streets are
terrible underfoot. But I suppose you're shut up all day at
your work. You'll just have to sit down and wait till I've
checked the literature and handed in the takings. I doubt
yon stout body in plum-coloured velveteen who bought R. J.
Campbell on the Social Evil with such an air of condescension
has paid me with a bad threepenny-bit. Aren't folks the
limit ? " She was so full of bitterness against the fraudulent
body in plum-coloured velveteen that she forgot her shyness
and looked into his eyes to appeal for sympathy. " Ah, well ! "
she said, stiffening again, " I'll be back in a minute."

He leaned against a pillar and waited. The hall became
empty, became melancholy ; mysteriously and insultingly its
emptiness seemed to summarise the proceedings that had just
ended. It was as if the place were waiting till he and the few
darkly dressed women who still stood about chewing the speeches
were gone, and would then enact a satire on the evening ; the
rows of seats which turned their polished brown surfaces towards
the platform with an effect of mock attentiveness would jeeringly
imitate the audience, the chairs that had been left higgledy-
piggledy on the platform would parody the speakers. And
doubtless, if there is a beneficent Providence that really picks
the world over for opportunities of kindliness, halls which are
habitually let out for political meetings are allowed means of
relieving their feelings which are forbidden to other collections
of bricks and mortar. But he mustn't say that to Ellen. To
her political meetings were plainly sacred rituals, and in any
case he was not sure whether she laughed at things.

She called to him from the doorway, " I'm through, Mr.
Yaverland ! " She was wearing a tam-o'-shanter and a mackintosh, which she buttoned right up to her chin, and she looked
just a brown pipe with a black knob at the top, a mere piece
of plumbing. He thought it very probable that never before
in the history of the human race had a beautiful girl dressed
herself so unbecomingly. But that she had done so seemed so
peculiarly and deliciously amusing that as he walked by her
side he could hardly keep from looking at her smilingly in a
way that would have puzzled and annoyed her. And outside

the hall, when they found that the mist, like a sour man who will not give way to his temper but keeps on dropping disagreeable remarks, was letting down just enough of itself to soak Edinburgh without giving it the slightest hope that it would rain itself out by the morning, he caught again this queer flavour of her that in its sharpness and its freshness reminded him of the taste of fresh celery. He asked her if she hadn't an umbrella, and she replied, " I've no use for umbrellas ; I like the feel of the rain on my face, and I see no sense in paying three-and-eleven for avoiding a positive pleasure."

By that time Ellen was almost sure that he was smiling to himself in the darkness, and was miserable. It was a silly, homely thing to have said. " Ah, what for can he be wanting to see me home ? " she thought helplessly. " He is so wonderful. But then, so am I ! So am I ! " And as they went through the dark tangle of small streets she turned loose on him her enthusiasm for the meeting, so that he might see that women also have their serious splendours. " Hadn't it been a magnificent meeting ? Wasn't Mrs. Ormiston a grand speaker ? Could he possibly, if he cared anything for honesty, affirm that he had ever heard a man speaker who came within a hundred miles of her ? And wasn't Mrs. Mark Lyle beautiful, and didn't she remind him of the early Christian martyrs ? Didn't he think the women who were forcibly fed were heroines, and didn't he think the Liberal Governments were the most abominable bloodstained tyrants of our times ? " Though, mind you, I'd be with the Liberal Party myself if they'd only give us the vote." It was rather like going for a walk with a puppy barking at one's heels, but he liked it. Through her talk he noticed little things about her. She had had very little to do with men, perhaps she had never walked with a man before, for she did not naturally take the wall when they crossed the road. Her voice was soft and seemed to cling to her lips, as red-haired people's voices often do. Her heels did not click on the pavements ; she walked noiselessly, as though she trod on grass.

Suddenly she clapped her bare hands. " Ah, if you're a sympathiser you must join the Men's League for Women's Suffrage. You will ? Oh, that's fine ! I've never brought in a member yet. . . ." She paused, furious with herself, for she was so very young that she hated ever to own that she was doing anything for the first time. It was her aim to appear infinitely experienced. Usually, she thought, she succeeded.

To end the silence, so that she might say something to which he could listen, he said, " I was converted long before to-night, you know. My mother's keen on the movement."

" Is she ? " She searched her memory. " Yet I don't know the name. Does she speak, or organise ? "

" Oh, she doesn't do anything in public. She lives very quietly in a little Essex village," he answered, speaking with an involuntary gravity, an effect of referring to pain, that made her wonder if his mother was an invalid. She hoped it was not so, for if Mrs. Yaverland was anything like her son it was terrible to think of her lying in the stagnant air of ill-health among feeding-cups and medicine bottles and weak-tasting foods. The lot of the sick and the old, whom she conceived as exceptional people specially scourged, drew tears from her in the darkness, and she looked across the road at the tall wards which the infirmary thrust out like piers from its main corridor. " Ah, the poor souls in there ! " she breathed, looking up at the rows of windows which disclosed the dreadful pale wavering light that lives in sick-rooms. " It makes you feel guilty, being happy when those poor souls are lying there in pain." Yaverland did not seek to find out why she had said it, any more than he asked himself how this night's knowledge of her was to be continued, or what she meant the end of it to be, though he was aware that those questions existed. He simply noted that she was being happy. Yes, they were curiously happy for two people who hardly knew each other, going home in the rain.

They were passing down the Meadow Walk now, between trees that were like shapes drawn on blotting-paper and lamps that had the smallest scope. " Edinburgh's a fine place," he said. " It can handle even an asphalt track with dignity."

" Oh, a fine place," she answered pettishly, " if you could get away from it." He felt faintly hostile to her adventurousness. Why should a woman want to go wandering about the world ?

From a dream of foreign countries she asked suddenly, " How long were you a sailor ? "

" Three years. From the time I was seventeen till I was twenty."

Then it struck him : " How did you know I'd been a sailor ? "

" I just knew,"she said, with something of a sibylline air. Evidently he was thinking how clever it was of her to have guessed it, and indeed she thought it was a remarkable example of her instinctive understanding of men. And Yaverland, on his side, was letting his mind travel down a channel of feeling which he knew to be silly and sentimental, like a man who drinks yet another glass of wine though he knows it will make his head swim, and was wondering if this clairvoyance meant that there was a mystic tie between them. But it soon flashed over Ellen's mind that the reason why she thought that he had been a sailor was that he had looked like one when he came into the hall in his raindashed oilskins. She wondered if she ought to tell him so. An unhappy silence fell upon her, which he did not notice because he was thinking how strange it was that even in this black lane, between blank walls through which they were passing, when he could not see her, when she was not saying anything, when he could get no personal intimation of her at all except that softness of tread, it was pleasant to be with her. But he began to feel anxiety because of the squalor of the district. This must be a mews, for there were sodden shreds of straw on the cobblestones, and surely that was the thud of sleeping horses' hooves that sounded like the blows of soft hammers on soft anvils behind the high wooden doors. If she lived near here she must be very poor. But without embarrassment she turned to him in the shadow of a brick wall surmounted by broken hoarding and pointed down a paved entry to a dark archway pierced in what seemed, by the light that shone from a candle stuck in a bottle at an uncurtained window, to be a very mean little house. "The Square's through here," she said. "Come away in and I'll find you a membership form for the Men's League. . . ."

Beyond the archway lay the queerest place. It was a little box-like square, hardly forty paces across, on three sides of which small squat houses sat closely with a quarrelling air, as if each had to broaden its shoulders and press out its elbows for fear of being squeezed out by its neighbours and knocked backwards into the mews. They sent out in front of them the slimmest slices of garden which left room for nothing but a paved walk from the entry and a fenced bed in the middle, where a lamp-post stood among some leggy laurels, which the rain was shaking as a terrier shakes a rat. Huddled houses and winking lamp and agued bushes, all seemed alive and second cousins to the goblins. On the fourth side were railings that evidently gave upon some sort of public park, for beyond them very tall trees which had not been stunted by garden soil sent up interminable stains on the white darkness, and beneath their drippings paced a policeman, a black figure walking with that appearance of moping stoicism that policemen wear at night. He, too, participated in the fantasy of the place, for it seemed possible that he had never arrested anybody and never would; that his sole business was to keep away bad dreams from the little people who were sleeping in these little houses. They were probably poor little people, for poverty keeps early hours, and in all the square there was but one lighted window. And that he perceived, as he got his bearings, was in the house to which Ellen was leading him down the narrowest garden he had ever seen, a mere cheese straw of grass and gravel. It was a corner house, and of all the houses in the square it looked the most put upon, the most relentlessly squeezed by its neighbours; yet Ellen opened the door and invited him in with something of an air.

"It's very late," he objected, but she had cried into the darkness, "Mother, I've brought a visitor!" and an inner door opened and let out light, and a voice that was as if dusk had fallen on Ellen's voice said, "What's that you say, Ellen?"

"I've brought a visitor, mother," she repeated. "Go on in; I'll not be a minute finding the form. . . . Mother, this is Mr. Yaverland, the client from Rio. He says he'll join the Men's League and I'm just going to find him a membership form."

She went to a desk in the corner of the room and dashed it open, and fell to rummaging in a pile of papers with such noisy haste that he knew she was afraid she ought not to have asked him in and was trying to carry it off under a pretence of urgency; and he found himself facing a little woman who wore a shawl in the low-spirited Scotch way, as if it were a badge of despondency, and who was saying, "Good evening, Mr. Yaverland. Will you not sit down? I'm ashamed the hall gas wasn't lit." A very poor little woman, this mother of Ellen's. The hand that shook his was so very rough, and at the neck of her stuff gown she wore a large round onyx brooch, a piece of such ugly jewellery as is treasured by the poor, and the sum of her tentative expressions was surely that someone had rudely taken something from her and she was too gentle-spirited to make complaint. She was like some brown bird that had not migrated at the right season of the year, and had been surprised as well as draggled by the winter, chirping sweetly and sadly on a bare bough that she could not have believed such things of the weather. Yet once she must have been like Ellen; her hair was the ashes of such a fire as burned over Ellen's brows, and she had Ellen's short upper lip, though of course she had never been fierce nor a swift runner, and no present eye could guess if she had ever been a focus of romantic love. The aged are terrible—mere heaps of cinders on the grass from which none can tell how tall the flames once were or what company gathered round them.

She struck him as being very old to be Ellen's mother, for when he had been seventeen his mother had still been a creature of brilliant eyes and triumphant moments, but perhaps it was poverty that had made her so dusty and so meagre. " Yes, they are very poor," he groaned to himself. The room was so low, the fireplace so small a hutch of cast-iron, the wallpaper so yellow and so magnified a confusion of roses, and so unsuggestive of summer ; the fatigued brown surface of the leather upholstery was coming away in strips like curl-papers ; there were big steel engravings of Highland cattle enjoying domestic life under adverse climatic conditions, and Queen Victoria giving religion a leg up by signing things in the presence of bishops and handing niggers Bibles—engravings which they obviously didn't like, since here and there were little home-made pictures made out of quite good plates torn from art magazines, but which they had kept because no second-hand dealers would give any money for them, and the walls had to be covered somehow. And there was nothing pretty anywhere.

The little brown bird of a woman was asking in a kind, interested way if he were a stranger to Edinburgh, and he was telling her how long he had been in Broxburn and what he did there, and when he mentioned cordite she made the clucking, concerned noise that elderly ladies always made when they heard that his work lay among high explosives. And Ellen's rootings in the untidy desk culminated in a sudden sweep of mixed paper stuff on to the floor, at which Mrs. Melville remonstrated, " Ellen, it beats me how you can be so neat with your work and such a bad, untidy girl about the house ! " and Ellen exclaimed, " Och, drat the thing, it must be upstairs ! " and ran out of the room with her face turned away from them.

They heard a clatter on the staircase, followed by violent noises overhead as if a chest was being dashed open and the contents flung on the floor. " Dear, dear ! " ejaculated Mrs. Melville adoringly. She began to look him over with a maternal eye. " For all you've been six months in the North, you've not lost your tan," she said.

" Well, I had a good baking in Spain and South America," he answered. Their eyes met and they smiled. In effect she had said, " Well, you are a fine fellow," and he had answered, " Yes, perhaps I am."

" I like a man to travel," she went on, tossing her head

and looking altogether fierce Ellen's mother. " I never go into the bank without looking at the clerks and thinking what sumphs they are, sitting on their high stools." She seemed to have come to some conclusion to treat him as one of the family, for she retrieved her knitting from the mantelpiece and turned her armchair more cosily to the fire, and began a sauntering of the tongue that he knew meant that she liked him. "I hope you don't think Ellen a wild girl, running about to these meetings all alone. It's not what I would like, of course, but I say nothing, for this Suffrage business keeps the bairn amused. I'm not much of a companion to her. I'm getting on, you see. She was my youngest."

"The youngest!" he exclaimed. "I didn't know. I thought she was an only child." He flushed at this betrayal of the interest he felt in her.

"She's that now. But I had three others. They all died before Ellen was born. They sickened for influenza on a bad winter voyage my husband and I made from America." She mourned over some remote grievance as well as the sorrow "One was a boy. He was just turned five. That's a snapshot of Ronnie on the mantelpiece. A gentleman on board took it the day he was taken ill."

He stood up to look at it. "He must have been a jolly little chap."

" He was Ellen's build and colour, and he was wonderfully clever for his age. He would have been something out of the ordinary if he had lived. I knew it wasn't wise to sail just then. I said to wait till the New Year. . . ." Her voice changed, and he perceived that she was making use of the strange power to carry on disputes with the dead which is possessed by widows. The tone was a complete reconstruction of her marriage. There was a girn in it, as if she had learned to expect contradiction and disregard as the habitual response to all her remarks, and at the back of that a terror, far more dignified than the protest to which it gave birth, at the dreadful things she knew would happen because she was disregarded, and a small, weak, guilty sense that she had not made her protest loudly and, perhaps, cleverly enough. Life had behaved very meanly to this woman. When she was young and sweet her sweetness had been violated and crushed by something harsh and reckless ; and now she was not sweet any longer, but just a wisp of an old woman, and nobody would ever bother about her again ; and life gives one no second chances. Yaverland lamented, as Ellen had done, the fate of those exceptional people who are old or not perfectly happy.

" You're not Irish, are you ? " she enquired seriously ; and immediately he knew that her husband had been Irish, and that she held a naïve and touching belief that no one but a man of his race would have behaved as he had done, that all other men would have been kind. Particularly now that Ellen was growing such a big girl she didn't want any Irish coming into this little home, where at least there was peace and quiet.

" No," he said reassuringly, " I'm not Irish. My people have been in Essex for hundreds of years. I'm afraid," he added, for so evident was it that most of her fellow-creatures had dealt cheatingly with her that decent people felt a special obligation to treat her honestly, " my grandmother was an O'Connor, but she was half French. Lord, what's that ? "

It seemed as if a heavy sea was breaking on the back of the house as on a sea-wall. The gasolier trembled, the floor throbbed, the little goblin dwelling pulsated as if it were alarmed. Only the continued calm of Mrs. Melville at her knitting and the coarse threads of music running through the sound persuaded him that this riot was the result of some genial human activity.

" Oh, I suppose you notice it, being a stranger," said Mrs. Melville. " We hardly hear it now. You see, they've turned the Wesleyan Hall that backs on to the Square into a dancing-hall, and this is the grand noise they make with their feet. It's not a nice place. ' Gentlemen a shilling, ladies invited,' it says outside. Still, we don't complain, for the noise is nothing noticeable and it reduces the rent."

This was a masterpiece of circumstance. By nothing more than a thin wall which shook to music was this little home divided from a thick-aired place where ugly people lurched against each other lustfully ; and yet it had been made an impregnable fort of loveliness and decency by this virtuous ageing woman, whose slight silliness was but a holy abstinence, a refusal to side with common sense because that was so often concerned in cruel decisions, by this girl who was so young that it seemed at the sight of her as if time had turned back again and earth rolled unstained by history, and so beautiful that it seemed as if henceforth eternity could frame nothing but happiness. The smile of Ellen had made a faery ring where heavy-footed dancers could not enter ; her gravity had made a sanctuary as safe as any church crowned with a belfry and casketing the Host. And he, participating in the safety of the place, pitied the men behind the shaking wall, and all men over the world who had committed themselves to that search for pleasure which makes joy inaccessible. They had chosen frustration for their destiny. Because they desired some ecstasy that would lighten the leaden substance of life they turned to drunkenness, which did no more than jumble reality, steep the earth in aniline dyes, tinge the sunset with magenta. Because they desired love they sought out women who, although dedicated to sex, were sexually cancelled by repeated use, like postage-stamps on a much redirected letter, who efficiently went through the form of passion, yet presented it so empty of all exaltation that their lovers left them feeling as if they were victims of a practical joke.

And here, not half a dozen yards from some of these seekers, was one who could bring to these desires a lovelier death than they would meet on the dirty bed of gratification or the hard pallet of renunciation. Because the untouched truth about her could give ecstasy one would not lose the power of seeing things as they are, and she made one forget the usual sexual story. Although she was formed for love and the intention of being her lover was now a fundamental part of him, she was so busy with her voice and body in playing quaint variations on the theme of herself that he did not mind how long might be the journey to their marriage. She was more interesting than any other person or thing in the world. She was going to have more interesting experiences; because her unique simplicity comprehended a wild impatience with lies she would have a claim on reality that would give her unprecedented wisdom. Now he could understand why saints in their narrow cells despise sinners as dull stay-at-homes.

And when she burst into the room again he saw that all he had been thinking about her was true. It might be that everybody else on earth would see her as nothing but a red-haired girl in an ill-fitting blue serge dress with an appalling tartan silk vest, but still it was true.

"Here you are," she said, "you put your name *there*." She bent over him as he wrote and wished she could put something on the form to show how magnificent he was and what a catch she had made for the movement.

Well, there was no possible excuse for staying any longer, and the poor old lady was yawning behind her knitting. He rose and said good-bye, wondering as he spoke how he could make his entrance here again and how he could break it to these women, who were like hardy secular nuns, that he came for love. If this had been a Spanish or a Cariocan mother and daughter how easy it would have been ! The elder woman's eyes would have crackled brightly among her wrinkles and she would have looked at her daughter with the air of genial treachery which old women wear when they contrive a young girl's marriage, and she would have dropped some subtle hint at the next convenient assignation ; and the girl herself would have stood by like a dark living scythe in the Latin attitude of modesty, very straight from the waist to the feet, but the shoulders bent as if to hide the bosom and the head bowed, mysteriously intimating that she knew nothing and yet could promise to submit to everything. But here was Mrs. Melville saying something quite vague about hoping that he would drop in if he was passing, and Ellen lifting to him a stubborn face that warned him there would be a thousand resistances to overcome before she would own herself a being accessible to passion. Yet this harsh inexpertness about life was the essence that made these people delightful to him. It was unreasonable, but it was true, that he adored them because they were difficult.

"Ellen, run out and light the hall gas for Mr. Yaverland." And from the courtesy in the tone and something gracious in Ellen's obedience he saw that they were too poor to keep the gas burning in the hall all the evening, and so the lighting of it ranked as a ceremonial for an honoured guest. They were dear people.

As he buttoned his oilskins to the chin while Ellen stood ready to open the front door he did not dare look at her because his stare would have been so fixed and bright. He set his eyes instead on the engravings, which for the most part represented Robert Burns as the Scotch like to picture their national poet, with hair sleek and slightly waved like the coat of a retriever hanging round a face oval and blank and sweet like a tea-biscuit.

"You seem to admire Burns," he said.

"Me ? No, indeed. Those are my grandmother's pictures. I think nothing of the man. His intellectual content was miserably small."

"That's a proposition he never butted up against—— "

"What ? "

"A woman who said that his intellectual content was miserably small. You're one of Time's revenges. . . ."

She didn't follow his little joke, although she smiled faintly with pleasure at being called a woman, because she was distressfully wondering if her reluctance to let him go was a premonition of some disaster that lurked for him outside. She so strangely wanted him to stay. She could actually have wound her arms about him, which was a queer enough thing to want to do, as if the feelers of some nightmare-crawling horned beast were twitching for him in the darkness beyond the door. This inordinate emotion must have some meaning, and it could have none other than that Great Granny Macleod had really had second sight, and she had inherited it ; it was warning her that something dreadful was going to happen to him on his way to the hotel. "Well, if I see anything in the papers to-morrow morning about a big man being run down by a motor-car in the fog, I'll know there's something in the supernatural," said the cool elf that dwelt in her head. But agony transfixed her like an arrow because her thought reminded her that this glorious being whose eyes blazed with serenity as other people's eyes blaze only with rage, was susceptible to pain and would some day be subject to death.

"Good-night," he said. He did not know why her breath had failed and why she had raised her hand to her throat, but he knew that his presence was doing marvellous things to her, and he was sure that they were beautiful things, for everything that passed between from now on till the end of time would be flawlessly beautiful. "Good-night," he said again, and stopped when he had gone a yard or two down the path simply that they might speak to each other again. "You must shut the door. You're letting in the rain and cold."

"No," she said dreamily, sleepily, and slowly closed the door.

He went on in the impatient mood of a man who has been secretly married and must leave his wife in a poor lodging until he can disclose his marriage.

CHAPTER III

(1)

WHEN she opened the door with her latchkey on Monday evening, late from a class in Advanced Commercial Spanish at Skerry's College, and sat down in the hall to take her boots off, her mother cried out from the kitchen, "Ellen, I've got the grandest surprise for you!"

These fanciful women! "And what's that?" she cried back tolerantly, though the dark thoughts buzzed about her head like bees. She thought she could feel better if she could only tell someone how Mr. Philip had sat by her fire like a nasty wee black imp and said that awful thing. But she must not tell her mother, who would only be fretted by it and ask like a little anxious mouse, "You're sure you've not said anything, dear? You're sure you've been a careful girl with your work, dear?" and would brace herself with heartrending bravery to meet this culminating misfortune. "Ah, well, dear, if you do have to look round for a new post we must just manage." So she must keep silent and seem cheerful, though that memory was rolling round and round in her brain like a hot marble.

"Away into the dining-room and see what it is," said Mrs. Melville, coming out with the cocoa-jug in her hand. She had put on her brighter shawl, the tartan one.

"You look as we'd been left a fortune," said Ellen.

"No fear of that. If your grand-aunt Watson remembers you with a hundred pounds that's all we can expect. But there's something fine waiting for you. Finish taking off that muddy boot before you come. Now!"

She flung open the door.

"Roses!" breathed Ellen. "Mother—roses!"

On the table between the loaf and the syrup-tin there was a jug filled with red and white roses; on the mantelpiece three vases that had long held nothing but dust now held roses, and doubtless felt a resurrection joy; and on the book-cases

roses lifted stiff stems from two jam-jars. Ellen, being a
slave of the eye, grew so pale and so gay at the sight of the
flowers that almost everybody in the world except one man
would have jeered at her, and she put her arms round her
mother's neck and kissed her, though she knew the gift could
not have come from her. The flowers were beautiful in so
many ways. They were beautiful just as roses, because " roses "
is such a lovely word ; as clear patches of red and white because
red and white are such lovely colours ; and because a red rose
has so strange an air of complicity in human passion, and the
first white rose was surely grown from some phosphorescent
cutting that dropped through the starlight from the moon. And
these were the furled, attenuated blooms of winter, born out of
due season and nurtured in stoked warmth, like the delicate
children of kings, and emanating a faint reluctant scent like the
querulous sweet smile of an invalid. They looked hard and
cold, as if they had protected themselves against the cold
weather by imitating the substance of precious stones.

They were an orgy and a prophecy, these flowers. They
were an outburst of unnecessary loveliness in a house that did
not dare open its doors to anything but necessities ; and they
showed, since they blossomed here though the rain roared down
outside, that the world was not after all an immutably unpleasant place, and could be turned upside down very enjoyably
if one had the money to buy things. It really was worth while
struggling to get on. . . .

" Mother, where did they come from ? "

" Ah ! " said Mrs. Melville waggishly.

" Och, tell me ! I don't imagine you went out and pawned
the family jewels. Och, do tell me ! Come on ! "

" A boy brought them up from Gilbey the florist's this
morning. I could have fallen down when I opened the door.
And the wee brat of a boy tried to convey to me that he wasn't
used to coming to such a place. He wore a look like a missionary
in Darkest Africa. They were left for Miss Melville, mind you.
Not for your poor old mother. And they're from Mr. Yaverland.
Yon's his card sticking up against your grandmother on the
mantelpiece."

Ellen's hands, outspread over the roses, dropped to her
side.

" I would have thought he had more sense," she said sulkily.
" If he'd money to burn he should have sent this lot to the
infirmary."

" Och, Ellen, are you not pleased ? "

" What's the man thinking of to fill us up with flowers as if we were an Episcopal church on Easter Sunday ? "

" Ellen, you've no notion of manners. Gentlemen often send flowers to ladies they admire. When your Aunt Bessie and I were girls many's the fine present of flowers we got from officers at the Castle."

" I've neither time nor taste for such things. It makes me feel like a hospital. He'll be sending us new-laid eggs and lint bandages next. The man's mad."

" Ellen, you're a queer girl," complained Mrs. Melville. " If this argy-bargying about votes for women makes you turn up your nose at bonny flowers that a decent fellow sends you I'm sorry for you—it's just tempting Providence to scorn good mercies like this. I'll away and take the fish-pie out of the oven."

It was strange that as soon as her mother had left the room she began to feel differently about the roses. Of course they were very beautiful ; and they were contenting in a quite magic way, for besides satisfying her longing for pretty things, they seemed to have deprived of urgency all her other longings, even including her desire for a vote, for eminence of some severe sort, for an income of three hundred pounds a year (which was the most she believed a person with a social conscience could enjoy), for a perpetual ticket for the Paterson Concerts at the MacEwan Hall, and for perfect self-possession. She felt as if these things were already hers, or as if they were coming so certainly that she need not fret about them any more than one frets about a parcel that one knows has been posted, or concerning some desires, as if it did not matter so much as she had thought whether she got them or not. Especially that dream of being one of a company of men and women whose bodies should be grave as elms with dignity and whose words should be bright as butterflies with wit struck her as being foolish. It was as idle as wanting to be born in the days of Queen Elizabeth. What she really wanted was a friend. She had felt the need of one since Rachael Wing went to London. Surely Richard Yaverland meant to be her friend, since he sent flowers to her. But she wished the gift could have been made secretly, and if he came to pay a visit she should be quite alone. For no reason that she could formulate, the thought of even her mother setting eyes on them together seemed a threat of disgrace. She wished that they could be standing side by side at the fire in that five minutes when it is sheer extravagance to light the gas but so dark that one may stare as one cannot by day, so that she might look at what the driving flamelight showed of his black, sea-roughened magnificence. At her perfect memory of him she felt a rush of exhilaration which left her confused and glad and benevolent.

"Mother, dear," she said, for Mrs. Melville had come back with the fish-pie, and was bidding her with an offended briskness to sit forward and eat her meal while it was hot, "they're the loveliest things. I can't think what for I was so cross."

"Neither can I. There's so little bonny comes our way that I do think we might be grateful when we get a treat."

"I'm sorry. I can't think what came over me."

"Never mind. But, you know, you're sometimes terribly like your father. You must fight against it."

They sat down to supper, looking up from their food at the roses.

"Mother, the gas is awful bad for them. Carbonic acid is just murderous to flowers."

"I was thinking that myself. It was well known that gas was bad for flowers even when I was young, though we didn't talk about carbonic acid. But if you don't see them by gaslight you'll never see them, for it's dark by five. They must fall faster than they would have done."

"Och, no! I'd rather you had the pleasure of them by day, and let the poor things last. I must content myself with a look at them at breakfast."

"Nonsense! They're your flowers, lassie. But do you not think it would do if we brought in the two candles and turned out the gas? It'll be a bit dark, but it isn't as if there were many bones in the fish-pie."

And that is what they did. It was a satisfactory arrangement, for then there was a bright soft light on the red and white petals, and a drapery of darkness about the mean walls of the room, and a thickening of the atmosphere which hid the archness on the older woman's face, so that the girl dreamed untormented and without knowing that she dreamed.

"Ah, well!" sighed Mrs. Melville after a silence, with that air of irony which she was careful to impart to her sad remarks, as if she wanted to remove any impression that she respected the fate that had assailed her. "I don't know how many years it is since I sat down with roses on the table."

"I never have before," said Ellen.

(2)

It was indeed much more as the friend that Ellen wanted than as the declared lover he had intended to be that Yaverland came to Hume Park Square on Saturday in answer to the letter of thanks which, after the careful composition of eight drafts, she had sent him. All week he had meant to ask her to marry him at the first possible moment. By day, when the thought of her rushed in upon him like a sweet-smelling wind every time he lifted his mind from his work, and by night, when she stood red-gold and white on every wall of his room in the darkness it grew more and more incredible that he could meet her and not tell her that he wanted to spend all the rest of his life with her. He felt ashamed that he was not her husband, and at the back of his mind was a confused consciousness of inverted impropriety, as if continuance in his present course would bring upon him denunciations from the pulpit for living in open chastity apart from a woman to whom he was really married. There was, too, a strange sense of a severer guilt, as if by not letting his love for her have its way he was committing the crime a scientific man commits when he fails to communicate the result of a valuable research. Even when he went out to mount his motor-cycle for the ride to Edinburgh he meant to force on her at once as much knowledge of his love as her youth could hold.

But going down the garden he met the postman, who gave him a letter; and before he opened it it checked his enterprise. For the address was in his mother's handwriting, and though it was still black and exquisite, like the tracery of bare tree-boughs against the sky, it was larger than usual, and he had often before noticed that she wrote like that only when her eyes had been strained by one of her bouts of sleeplessness. "Why doesn't she go to a doctor and get him to give her something for it?" he asked himself impatiently, annoyed at the casting of this shadow on his afternoon; but it struck him what a lovely and characteristic thing it was that, though his mother had suffered great pain from sleeplessness for thirty years, she had never bought peace with a drug. Nothing would make her content to tamper with reality. He found, too, in her letter a phrase that bore out his suspicion, a complaint of the length of the winter, a confessed longing for his return in the New Year, which was a breach of her habitual pretence, which never took him in for an instant and which she kept up perhaps for that very reason, that she did not care when she saw him again.

" Oh, God, she must be going through it ! " he muttered.
He could see her as she would be at this hour, sitting at the
wide window in her room, which she kept uncurtained so that
the Thames estuary and the silver fingers it thrust into the
marshes should lie under her eye like a map. Her nightlong
contest with memory would not have destroyed her air of power
nor wiped from her lips and eyes that appearance of having
just finished smiling at a joke that was not quite good enough
to prolong her merriment, but being quite ready to smile at
another ; it would only have made her rather ugly. Her hair
would be straight and greasy, her skin leaden, the flesh of her
face heavy except when something in the scene she looked on
invoked that expression which he could not bear. Her face
would become girlish and alive, and after one moment of forgetfulness would settle into a mask of despair. Something on
the marshes had reminded her of her love. She had remembered
how one frosty morning she and her lover had walked with
linked arms through cold dancing air along the grassy terrace
that divided the pastures, the green bank to the east sloping
to a ditch whose bright water gave back the morning sky,
the bank to the west sloping white with rime to a ditch of
black ice ; or she had remembered how, one summer night when
the sky was a yellow clot of starshine, she had sat in the long
grass under the sea-wall with his head in her lap. And then
she had remembered the end.

It was strange that such things could hurt after
thirty years. Yet it seemed less strange to him to-day
than it had ever done before, because he could see
that the love that would happen if he was Ellen's lover would
be a living thing in thirty years' time. . . . It would be immutably glorious as his mother's love had been interminably grievous. Yet suddenly he did not want to think of
Ellen or the prospect of triumphant wooing any more. It
seemed disloyalty to be making happy love when his mother
was going through one of her bad times. He would have to go
to Hume Park Square, but he would talk coolly and stay only
a little time.

And before he had gone very far on his way to Edinburgh
something else happened to blanch his temper. A heavy motor-
van rumbled ahead of him with a lurching course that made
him wonder at the spirit of the Scotch that can get drunk on
the early afternoon of a clear grey day ; and ten minutes after
a turn of the road brought him to an overturned cart, its inside
wheels shattered like cracked biscuits and a horse struggling

wildly in the shafts, and a lad lying under the hedge with blood spattered on a curd-white face. Men and a hurdle had to be fetched from the farm that was in sight, the doctor had to be summoned from a village three miles away, and then he was asked to wait lest there should be need of a further errand to a cottage hospital. He was in a jarred mood by then, for the farm people had been inhumanly callous to the lad's suffering, but were just human enough to know that their behaviour was disgusting, and were disguising their reluctance to lift their little fingers to save a stranger's life as resentment against Yaverland himself for his peremptory way of requesting their help. They had known from his speech that he came from the south, so as he sat in the kitchen they exchanged comments on the incapacity of the English to understand the sturdy independence of the Scotch. He began to fret at this delay among these beastly people in their sour smoke, and to think greedily of how by this time he might have been with Ellen listening to the grave conversation that sat as quaintly on her loveliness as tortoiseshell spectacles on an elfin nose, and looking at that incomparable hair.

But it struck him that this impatience was a rotten thing to feel when it was a matter of helping a poor chap in pain. He rose and opened the door to see if the doctor was coming out of the room across the passage where the patient lay ; but he could hear nothing but the lad's moans. He shivered. They reminded him of the night when for the first time he had heard his mother make just such anguished sounds as these. He was twenty-one then, and a student at South Kensington, and it was on one of his week-ends at Yaverland's End. He had sat up late working, and as he was passing his mother's door on his way to bed he heard the sound of a lament sadder than any weeping, since it had no hint of a climax but went on and on, as if it knew the sorrow that inspired it would not fail all through eternity. It appalled him, and he felt shy of going in, so he went on to his room and sat on his bed. After an hour he went out into the passage and listened. She still was moaning. Without knocking, lest her pride should forbid him to come in, he went into her room.

She was sitting at the table by the window playing patience, and she stared over her shoulder at him with tearless eyes. But all the windows were flung open to let out misery, and she had lit several candles as well as the electric light ; and winged things that had risen from the marshes to visit this brightness died in those candle-flames without intervention from her who would at ordinary times try to prevent the death of anything. She wore nothing over her nightgown, and her lilac and gold kimono lay in the middle of the floor. Men who were lost in the bush stripped themselves, he had often heard it said ; and he had seen panic-stricken women on the deck of a foundering ship throw off their coats. She had turned back to her cards immediately, and he had not spoken, but in some way he knew that she fully understood. " Take those books off the armchair and sit down," she ordered in her rough, soft voice.

For some time he sat there, while over and over again she shuffled and dealt and played her game and started another at a speed which dazzled his eyes ; until she rose and said indifferently, " Let's go to bed. It must be past four." There was an upward inflection in her naming of the hour that showed she believed it later than she said, that she felt that this long agony must have brought her quite close to the dawn, but she had not dared to say so for fear of the disappointment which she knew followed always on her imagining of brighter things. But it was not yet three. " I can't think why we're sitting up like this," she continued scornfully, and her face crumpled suddenly as she fell sideways into his arms, crying, " Richard ! Richard ! " His heart seemed to break in two. He held her close and kissed her and comforted her, and carried her over to the bed, entreating her to lie quietly and try to forget and sleep. " But I have so many things to remember," she reminded him. Turning her face away from him, and drawing the bedclothes about her chin, she began to talk very rapidly about the intense memories that pricked her like a thousand thorns. But at the sound of Roothing Church clock striking, so far off and so feebly that it told no hour but merely sweetly reminded the ear of time, she rolled over again and looked at him, smilingly, glowingly, sadly. " Ah, darling ! " she said. " It is very late. Perhaps if you hold my hand I will drop off to sleep now." But it was he that had slept. . . .

And she was going through a bad time like that now.

When at last he was free to continue his ride to Edinburgh he did not greatly want to go. He would have turned back to Broxburn had he not reflected that, although Ellen and her mother had not named any particular day for his visit, they might perhaps expect him this afternoon. Indeed, he became quite certain that they were expecting him. But nothing seemed agreeable to him in his abandonment to this ritualist desire to live soberly for a little so that he might share the sorrow of the woman who was enduring pain because she had

given him life. He certainly would not make love to Ellen.
He hoped that she was not so wonderful as he had remembered
her.

But though his spirit doubled on his track it did not lead
him back to solitude. Perhaps when the sun falls over the edge
of polar-earth the Arctic fox laments that he must run through
the night alone, for in the white livery he must assume at the
year's death he feels himself beast of a different kind from the
brown mate with whom he sported all the summer-time ; and
hears a soft pad on the snow and finds her running by his side,
white like himself. So it was with Yaverland when he came
to Hume Park Square, for the Ellen he found was a dove, a
nun, a nurse. Up to the moment she opened the door to him
she had been a sturdy, rufous thing, a terrier-tiger, exasperated
because she had imperilled her immortal soul by coming off her
Princes Street pitch when a truly conscientious woman would
have gone on selling *Votes for Women* for at least five minutes
longer ; and because she had had to pretend to her mother all
through tea that she hadn't really expected him ; and because
after her mother had gone out she had begun to read the *Scotsman's* report of an anti-Suffrage meeting in London. " Yon
Lord Curzon's an impudent birkie," she said, with a rush of tears
to her eyes that seemed even to herself an excessive comment
on Lord Curzon; then the knock came. " It'll be my old boots
back from the mending," she had told herself bitterly, and went
to the door like a shrew. And because there had been some
secret diplomacy between their souls of which they knew nothing,
some mutual promises that each would attempt to give what
the other felt was lacking in the universe at the moment, the
first sight of him made her change herself from top to toe to a
quiet, kind thing.

The little sitting-room was drowsy as a church, its darkness
not so much lit as stained amber by candlelight, and her voice
was quiet and pattering and gentle, like castanets played softly.
She made him tea, though it was far too late, and he had politely
said he did not want any, and afterwards she sat by the fire,
listening without exclamation to the story of the accident,
making no demand on him for argument or cheerfulness, sometimes letting the conversation sag into silence, but always
showing a smile that such a time meant no failure of goodwill.
The unique quality of her smile, which was exquisitely gay
and comically irregular, lifting the left corner of her mouth a
little higher than the right, reminded Yaverland that of course
he loved her. It would make it all right if he wrote to his

mother about her at once. He reflected how he could word the letter to convey that this girl was the most glorious and desirable being on earth without lapsing into the exuberance of phrase which was the one thing that made her turn on him the speculative gaze, not so much expressive of contempt as admitting that the word contempt had certainly passed through her mind, which she habitually turned on the rest of the world. . . .

But Ellen was speaking now, apologising because she had made him eat by candlelight, offering to light the gas, explaining that she and her mother had burned candles all the week because they hurt his roses less. "But surely," he said, "these roses can't be the ones I sent you? That was five days ago. These look quite fresh." Her face became vivacious and passionate; she came to the table and bent over the vases with an excitement that would have struck most people as a little mad. "Of course these are your roses!" she exclaimed. "Five days indeed! They'll keep a fortnight the way mother and I do them. When they begin to droop you plunge the stalks into boiling water. . . ."

He watched her with quiet delight. In the course of his life he had given flowers to several women, but none of them had ever plunged their stalks into boiling water. Instead they had stood up very straight in their shiny gowns and lifted the flowers in a pretence of inhaling the fragrance which the strong scent they used must certainly have prevented them from smelling, and had sent out from their little mouths fluttering murmurs of gratitude that were somehow not references to the flowers at all, but declarations of femaleness. Surely both the woman who performed that conventional gesture and the man who witnessed it were very pathetic. It was as if the man brought the flowers as a symbol of the wonderful gifts he might have given her if they had been real lovers, and as if the woman answered by those female murmurings that if they had been real lovers she would have repaid him with such miracles of tenderness. The gesture was always followed, he remembered, by a period of silence when she laid the flowers aside for some servant's attention, which was surely a moment of flat ironic regret.

But the roses that he had brought Ellen were no symbol but a real gift. They satisfied one of her starvations. She was leaning over them wolfishly, and presently straightened herself and stared at a dark wall and told how early one spring she had gone to a Primrose League picnic ("Mother brought me up as a Consairvative. It's been a great grief to her the way

I've gone ") at Melville Castle. There had been lilac and laburnums. Lilac and laburnums! She had evidently been transported by those delicate mauve and yellow silk embroideries on the grey canvas of the Scottish countryside, and his roses had taken her the same journey into ecstasy, just as the fact of her had brought him back into the happiness away from which he had been travelling for years. They had a magical power to give each other the things they wanted.

But she was uneasy. The clock had struck seven, and she had seemed perturbed by its striking. "Do you want me to go?" he asked, with the frank bad manners of a man who is making love in a hurry.

"Och, no!" she answered reluctantly, "but there's the shopping."

"Can't I come and carry the things for you?"

She brought her hands together with a happy movement that at the last instant she checked. But indeed she was very glad. For nowadays if anybody was unkind, and on Saturday nights people were tired and busy and altogether disposed to be unkind, she immediately noted it as fresh evidence that there did indeed exist that human conspiracy of malevolence in which the sudden unprovoked unceasing cruelty of Mr. Philip had made her believe. But if the client from Rio were with her, things would not happen perversely and she would not think dark thoughts. "That'll be fine. You'll make a grand jumentum."

"Ju—— ?"

"Jumentum, jumenti, neuter, second. A beast of burden. It's a word that Cæsar was much addicted to."

When she came in again from the hall he saw with delight that she had put on her hat and coat in the dark, and, though she went to the mantelpiece, it was not to revise the rough draft of her dressing at the glass, but to fish some money out of a ginger-jar. She brought the coins over to the table and began to arrange them in little heaps, evidently making some calculation concerning the domestic finance, while her face assumed a curious expression of contemptuous thrift. It was as if she was making her reckoning with scrupulous accuracy and at the same time ridiculing her own penury and promising herself that there would come a time when she should make calculations concerning the treasures of emperors. She was deluding herself with dreams of the time when she should have crowned herself queen or made herself the hidden tyrant-saviour of an industry. He detested her ambition: he felt it to be a kind of spiritual adultery; he moved his clenched hand forward on the table till it almost touched her money. Immediately she ceased to add, slowly her gaze travelled from his fingers to his face, and she smiled a disturbed smile that expressed at first the greeting that one beautiful animal gives to another, and then poetic wonder at his beauty, and then happiness because they liked each other so, and at last it became a sheer grimace of courage because the happiness was turning into a slight physical misery because there was something she ought to do or say, and she did not know what it was. And he was smiling too, because he perfectly knew what she did not.

One of the candles had burnt to its socket, and at its guttering arms of shadow seemed to whirl about them, and at its death the darkness seemed to bend forward from the corners of the room and press them closer to each other. Very soon she would be in his arms, and there would be an exquisite, exciting contrast between the rough texture of the coat that his hands would grasp and the smooth skin that his lips would meet. But there would not. The passion that possessed him was so strong that it killed sensation. He desired her body ardently, but only because it was inhabited by her soul, for their flesh had become unreal. He felt an exaltation, an illusion that he was being interpenetrated with light, and the loveliness that he had thought of as Ellen seemed now only a richly coloured film blown round the fact of her. If he wanted to hold her close to him it was only that he might shatter these frail substances with a harsh embrace and let their liberated souls stream out like comets' hair. There followed a moment when wisdom seemed to crackle like a lit fire in his head. The plan of the universe lay set out among the coins on the table, and he looked down on it and said, " Of course ! " But immediately he had forgotten why he had said it. The world was the same again. And Ellen was sitting there on the other side of the table, and she seemed very real.

She murmured petulantly, " I can't remember a thing mother said. . . . I can't remember what I've got to buy," and swept the money into her pocket. She was fatigued and blinded, as though all day she had watched a procession of burnished armies passing in strong sunlight. " Let's go on," she said, and while he found his hat and coat in the lobby she went and stood in the garden, ringing her heels on the cold stone of the path, drinking in the iced air, abandoning herself to the chill of the evening as if it were a refuge from him.

But they were happy almost at once. Like all clever adolescents, she had a mind like a rag-bag full of scraps of silks and

satins and calicoes and old bits of ribbon which was constantly
bursting and scattering a trail of allusions that were irrelevant
to the occasion of their appearance, and so when he came to
her side she began talking about George Borrow. Didn't he
love ' Lavengro,' him being a traveller ? And had he ever seen
a prize-fight ? Oh, Yaverland had. He had even had the
privilege of crossing the Atlantic in the cattleboat *ss. Glory* with
Jim Corraway, since known to fame as Cardiff Jim. But he
broke it to her that now many of the best boxers were Jew
lads from the East End of London, and not a few came from
the special schools for the feeble-minded ; feeble-mindedness
often gave a man the uncloudable temper that makes a good
boxer.

So, chattering like that, they came to the business
of shopping. It was, he thought, an extravagantly charming
business. As well as any other place on earth did he like this
homely street, with its little low shops that sent into the frosty
air savoury smells of what they sold, and took the chill off the
moonlight with their yellow gas-jets. He liked its narrow
pavements thronged with shaggy terrier-like people who walked
briskly on short legs; he liked its cobbled roadway, along which
passed at intervals tramcars that lumbered along more slowly
than any other trams in the world, with an air of dignity which
intimated that their slowness was due to no mechanical defect,
but to a sagacity which was aware that in this simple town
nobody was doing anything more urgent than going home to
supper.

It seemed a courageous little city as it lay at the base
of the towering black and silver Northern night : a brave
kindling of comfort in the midst of the indifferent universe.
And Ellen's shopping manner, her east wind descent on salesmen, showed that she participated in the hardy quality of her
surroundings. In the first shop she was still too much aware of
him to get into her stride. It was a bakery—such a marvellously
stocked bakery as could be found only in the land of that re-
sourceful people, which, finding itself too poor to have bread
and circuses, set about to make a circus of its bread. She
bought a shepherd's bap, its pale smooth crust velvety with
white flour, and an iced cake that any other nation would have
thought prodigious save for a wedding or a christening, while
she smiled deprecatingly at him, as though he felt these were
mawkish foods to be buying in the company of a friend of
bruisers. But in the butcher's shop the Saturday night fever
seized her, and presently Yaverland, who had been staring at

a bullock's carcase and liking the lovely springing arch of the ribs, was startled to hear her cry, " Mr. Lawson, you surprise me ! " But it was only the price of a piece of a neck of mutton that had surprised her. After that he listened to the conversation that passed between her and the shopmen, and found it as different from the bland English chatter of such occasions as if it had been in a different tongue. It had the tweedy texture of Scotch talk, the characteristic lack of suavity and richness in sense, in casual informativeness, in appositeness. Here, it was plain, was a people almost demoniac with immense, unsensual, intellectual energy.

In the grocer's shop they had to wait their turn to be served. Ellen put in the time staring up at a Peter's milk chocolate advertisement that hung on the wall, a yodelling sort of landscape showing a mountain like a vanilla ice running down into a lake of Reckitt's blue ; she was under the illusion that it was superb because it was a foreign place. Yaverland watched the silver-haired grocer slicing breakfast sausage, for Ellen had told him that this was one of the city fathers, and it seemed to him that there was something noble about the old man in his white apron which reminded one of his civic dignity. Doubtless, however, in his civic robes he would remind one that he was a grocer, for it was the note of Edinburgh, of all lowland Scotland, to rise out of ordinary life to a more than ordinary magnificence, and then to qualify that magnificence by some cynical allusion to ordinary life. The old man seemed to like Ellen, though she was very rude about his ham and said, " If that's the best, then times have been hard for the pigs lately." Yaverland gave to their bickering amenities an attention that dwelt not so much on the words as the twanging, gibing intonations. But after they got into the streets again a question and answer began to tease his mind : " Would you be wanting your change in halfpence, Miss Melville ? "

" Och, no, thank you, Mr. Lindsay."

They had come to the end of Ellen's shopping list and she was taking him home through St. Patrick's Square. " Look at that lighted window, where they've got a blue blind ! That's where de Quincey stopped ! " she said excitedly, and he answered, " Oh, is it ? . . . I say, why did the old chap offer to give you change in halfpence ? "

" Well, to-morrow's Sunday, you see."

" I'm afraid I don't. I'm stupid. Why do you want halfpence more on Sunday than on any other day ? "

" Why, for the plate. For the collection. In church. But

we always put in threepenny-bits. Mother's picked up a lot of English ways. What's taken you?" She stared up in wonder at his laughter, until it broke on her that she had un-wittingly given him, an Englishman, food for the silly English taunt that the Scotch are mean. "Och, you don't under-stand," she began to stammer hastily. "I didn't mean that exactly."

And then a hot rage came on her. Why should she make excuses for her own people, because this stranger who was less than nothing to her chose to giggle? Wasn't he using his size, which was sheer luck, his experiences in foreign lands, of which she was bitterly jealous, and his maleness, which until she got a vote was a ground for hostility, to " come it over " her? She said acidly, " I'm glad you're amused. I suppose you don't do such things in England?" and at his laughing answer, "I don't know; I've never been to Church in England. But I shouldn't think so," her neatly-brushed and braided temper came down. She came to a sudden stop. They were on the unfrequented pavement of Buccleuch Place, a street of tall houses separated by so insanely wide a cobbled roadway that it had none of the human, close-pressed quality of a street, but was desolate with the natural desolation of a ravine, and under these windowed cliffs she danced with rage, a tiny figure of fury with a paper-bag flapping from each hand like a pendulous boxing-glove, while he stood in front of her in a humble, pinioned attitude, keeping his elbows close to his side lest he should drop any parcels.

He loved every word of it, from the moment she explosively told him that it was all very well to hee-haw up there like a doited giraffe, and his mind felt the same pleasure that the palate gets out of a good curry as she told him that the English were a miserable, decadent people who were held together only by the genius and application of the Scotch, that English industry was dependent for its existence on Scotch engineers, and that English education consisted solely of Uni-vairsities that were no more than genteel athletic clubs, and begged him to consider the implication of the fact that the Scotch, though a smaller people than the English, had defended a larger country. . . .

He woke up at that. He had been tranced in a pleasant reverie, for though she was angry he knew that she would not get too angry. She was running away from him, but in a circle.

"Scotland bigger than England!" he jeered. "Think of the map! Bigger than England!"

She thought of the map, and for a minute her mouth was a little round dismayed hole. But she was not to be beaten. " I was alluding to its surface," she said coldly. " It being such an elevated country, there must be many square miles standing practically on end, thus taking hardly any space on the map. Consequently I was correct in saying that Scotland is bigger than England." She drew breath to go on, but her lips began to twitch and her eyes to seek his half-ashamedly, and then she began to giggle at her own sophistry and was not angry when he joined her. They built a little bright vibrant cave in the night with their laughter, from which they did not wish to move. They were standing quite still on the broad pavement, staring intently at each other's faces, trying to remember the reality under the distortions painted by the strong moonlight. It was a precious moment of intimacy, and they did not quite know what to do with it. They did not even know whether to be grave or gay. It was as if they held between them a sheet of shot tissue and could not decide whether to hold it up to the light and show its merry rosy colour or let it sag and glow rich gold.

But indeed they had no choice. For he found himself saying huskily, " I didn't mean to be rude. I had forgotten you were Scotch. You're a person all by yourself. One doesn't think of you as belonging to any country."

" Well, of course," she murmured, " father was Irish ; but he was just an expense."

He choked back a laugh. But this sense that she was funny did not blur the romantic quality of his love for her any more than this last manifestation of her funniness spoiled the clear beauty of her face, which now, in this moonlight that painted black shadows under her high cheek-bones, was candid and alert like the face of a narcissus. " I didn't mean to be rude," he repeated. " I didn't think that what I said could possibly touch you. As if I could say anything about you that wasn't ..." His voice cracked like a boy's. He felt an agony of tenderness towards her, and a terrifying sense that love was not all delight. It was stripping him of the armour of hardness and self-possession that it had been the business of his adult years to acquire, and it was leaving him the raw and smarting substance, accessible and attractive to pain, that he had not been since he was a boy.

And it was all to no purpose. For nothing seemed more likely than that Ellen should look up at him fixedly and fully assume that expression of wisdom which sometimes intruded into the youth in her eyes ; that she should say in a new deep voice, "You are not good enough for me." And of course it would be true, it would be true. Then she would walk on and turn the corner to her home, and he would be left alone among these desolate tall houses, eternally hungry. He could imagine how she would look as she turned the corner, the forward slant of her body, the upward tilt of her head, the awful irrevocable quality of her movements, the ghostlike glamour the moonlight would lay on her as if to warn him that she was as separate from him as though she were dead. He would not be able to pursue her, for there was something about her which would prevent him from ever trying on her those ordinary compulsions which men are accustomed to apply to women ; quiet, menacing devotion, or persistent roaring importunities, or those forcible embraces, of which he thought with the disgust he now felt for the sexual processes of everybody in the world except himself and Ellen, which induce the body to betray the reluctant mind. Because he loved her he was obliged, in spite of himself, to acknowledge the sacredness of her will, even though that acknowledgement might frustrate every hope of his love. He greatly disliked that obligation.

She was abstractedly murmuring defensive things about the Scotch. "And Scotland is such a lovely place. Even round here. Dalmeny. Cramond Brig. Hawthornden. And oh, the Pentlands ! Have you not been to the Pentlands yet ? Oh, but they're the grandest place in the world. There are lochs hidden behind the range the way you'd never think. And waterfalls. The water comes down red with the peat. And miles and miles of heather."

"Take me there, Ellen."

"Would you like to come ? Let's go next Saturday. I've got the whole day off. Mr. James said it was my due, what with the overtime I've been doing. It'll be lovely. I've had nobody to go with since Rachael Wing went to London. But would you truly care to come ? It's just moors. You'll not turn up your nose at it ? "

"Anywhere I went with you I'd like."

She started and began to walk on. It was as if the sheet of tissue had grown too heavy for her young hand and she had dropped it. Although he went on talking about how much he liked Scotland, and how intelligent he found the workmen at the cordite factory at Broxburn, she hardly answered, but moved her head from side to side like a horse galled by its collar. "Had he thought her a bold girl, fixing up a walk with him so eagerly ? And ought he to have called her by her Christian name ? Of course he was so much older that perhaps he felt that he had a right to do it. When they passed through the arch into Hume Park Square she saw a light in the dining-room window and said, " Mother's home before us."

She did not know that in that minute she had decided the course of her life. For she did not know that just before she spoke she had sighed, and that Yaverland had heard her and perceived that she sighed because soon they would no longer be alone together. Perhaps something like fear would have come upon her if she had known how immense he felt with victory ; how he contemplated her willingness to love him in a passion of timeless wonder, watching her journey from heaven, stepping from star to star, all the way down the dark whirling earth of his heart ; and how even while he felt a solemn agony at his unworthiness he was busily contriving their immediate marriage. For there was a steely quality about his love that would have been more appropriate to some vindictive purpose.

It was apparent to him, when they went in, that Mrs. Melville understood what was going on, for she threw him a glance which was not quite a wink but which clearly suggested that had she been just a common body it was conceivable that she might have winked. As soon as they were alone he told her that he loved Ellen, that he wanted to marry her, that he had plenty of money, that he was all right, that they must marry at once. She did not seem to regard him as asking her permission, though he had tried to give his demand that flavour, but rather as acquainting her with an established fact at which she blinked in a curious confusion of moods. The demoniac music in the dancing-hall had begun to bludgeon the walls, and in the whirlpool of the physical vibrations of the noise and the spiritual vibrations of his passion the little woman seemed to bob like a cork. She was resigned and pleased, and plainly trusted him, but at the same time she was pitifully alarmed. " Mercy me ! you've not been long. . . . Well, you've caught a Tartar and no mistake. Never say I didn't warn you. . . . But you'll let the bairn bide for a wee bit longer ! She's but a bairn ! "

It was as if she quite saw that a husband was necessary for Ellen, and wanted her to have one, and at the same time believed that any husband would inevitably bring her pain. He set it down as one of the despondent misinterpretations of life that the old invent in the depression of their physical malaise, and answered, reassuringly, insincerely, " Yes, yes, I'll wait. . . ." But why should they wait? They were going to be radiantly and eternally happy. It might as well begin at once.

(3)

" Is it not beautiful ? Is it not just beautiful ? " cried
Ellen. And indeed at last it was beautiful, and warranted
that excited gait, that hopping from leg to leg and puppyish
kicking up of dead leaves with which she had come along the
road from Balerno station. It had seemed to Yaverland an
undistinguished pocket of the country, and there had been
nothing that caught his attention save the wreck of a ropeworks
close by the village, which had been gutted by fire two or three
nights before and now stood with that Jane Cakebread look
that burned buildings have by daylight, its white walls blotched
like a drunkard's skin with the smoke and water, and its charred
timbers sticking out under the ruins of the upper storey like
unkempt hair under a bonnet worn awry. There were men
working among the wreckage, directing each other with guttural
disparaging cries, moving efficiently yet slowly, as if the dire-
ness of the damage had made them lose all heart. Ellen stopped
to watch them, laying her neck over the top plank of the fence
as a foal might do ; there was nothing that did not interest her.
But after that it had seemed a very ordinary green-and-grey
piece of Scotland, and he thought tenderly of her love of it as
one of those happy delusions that come to the very young, who
see the world suffused with beauty even as a person who looks
out of half-opened eyes sees everything fringed with prismatic
hues.

But the road had lifted, a wildness had come on the hedge ;
where there had been bushes were slim wind-distorted trees,
and when the wall of the trim little estate on the right came to an
end they stood suddenly in face of a broad view. To the right
of the white road that drove forward was a wide moor of dark
moss-hags, flung like a crumpled cloth on a slope that stretched
as far as the eye could see to the base of black hills about which
clambered white mists. To the left were green fields, set with
tentative assemblies of firs, which finally, where the road dipped,
drew together in a long dark wood. These things were a
delicate frieze in front of a range of hills that rolled eastwards,
the colour of clouds and almost as formless as clouds, yet carving
such proud lines against the sky that they seemed to be crouched
in attitudes of pride and for all their low height had the austere
and magnificent quality of mountains. This was a country
he could like very well. Against its immensity human life
appeared as unimportant as he did not doubt that it was in

those periods when his own private affairs were not pressing, and it gave him such a sense of the personality of inanimate things as he had very rarely had except at sea. The fir copse by which they stood showed as much character as any ship in her behaviour under the weather, and these mountains and this moor showed by a sudden pale glow of response to a Jacob's ladder of sunlight that they changed in mood under changing skies even as the seas.

Two or three whaups rose from the moss-hags and then sailed pee-weeting towards the hills, as if despatched by the moor to warn them of the coming of these strangers ; and it was as if the range answered shortly, " Ay, I ken that, I ken that." The broad view was as solemn as eternity, and at the same time there was a dancing exhilaration in the air, which, when it was still, was sweet-flavoured with the sweetness of the firs and the bog-myrtle, and when it was disturbed by the diamond-hard wind was ice-cold and seemed to intoxicate the skin. There was a sound of wheels behind them, and they stepped aside to let a carriage pass down a track that turned aside from the road at this point and ran timorously between the moor and the white wall of the neat estate. In it sat an old lady, so very old that the flesh on the hand that was raised to her bonnet was a mere ivory web between the metacarpal bones, and her eyes had gone back to that indeterminate hue which is seen in the eyes of a new-born baby ; but she sat up straight in the open carriage and directed on the two strangers a keen belittling gaze that without doubt extracted everything essential in their appearance. He liked this harsh country, these harsh, infrangible people that it bred.

" Do you not think it's rather fine ? " asked Ellen, in so small and flat a voice that he perceived she was afraid that the climax she had worked up to hadn't come off and that he was sneering at her Pentlands. It seemed a little surprising to him that she didn't know what was in his mind without being told, and he hastened to tell her he thought it was glorious. The anxiety lifted from her face at that, and she gazed at the hills with such an exultant fixity that he was able to stare at her at his ease. She was looking very Scotch, and like a small boy, for her velvet tam-o'-shanter was stuck down on her head and she wore a muffler that nearly touched her rather pink little nose. Her jacket was too big for her and her skirt very short, showing her slender legs rising out of large cobbler-botched nailed boots like plant-stems rising out of flower-pots, and these extreme sartorial disproportions gave her a sort of " father's waistcoat " look. Yet at a change of the wind, at the slightest alteration of the calm content of their relationship, she would disclose herself indubitably romantic as the sickle moon, as music heard at dusk in a garden of red roses. He supposed that to every man of his horse-power there ultimately came a Juliet, but none but him in the whole world had a Juliet of so many merry disguises. He looked at the range and thought that somewhere behind them was the spot where he would tell her that he loved her. It gave him a foolish pleasure to imagine what manner of place it would be—whether there would be grass or heather underfoot and if the hill-birds would cry there also.

"Well, it's no use you and me seeing which of us can gape the longest if we mean to get to Glencorse before the light goes," said Ellen. "We'd best step forward. I'm glad you like the place. I love it. And this bit of the road's bonny. When Rachael Wing and I were stopping up in the ploughman's cottage at Kirktown over by Glencorse Pond we got up one day at sunrise and came over here before the stroke of four. And if you'll believe it, the road was thick with rabbits, running about as bold as brass and behaving as sensibly as Christians. The poor things ran like the wind when they saw us. I wish we could have explained we meant no harm, for I suppose it's the one time in the day when they count on having the world to themselves."

"I've felt like that about a jaguar," he said. "Came on it suddenly, on a clearing by a railway camp on the Leopoldina. It had been tidying up a monkey and was going home a bit stupid and sleepy. Lord, the sick fright in its eyes when it saw me. I'd have given anything to be able to stand it a drink and offer to see it home."

"Och!" she murmured abashed. "Me talking about rabbits, and you accustomed to jaguars. I suppose you never take notice of a rabbit except to look down your nose at it. But we can't rise to jaguars in Scotland. But I once saw a red deer running in the woods at Taynuilt."

"I've seen a red deer too," he said, "when I was motor-cycling up to Ross this summer." It flashed across his mind then as it had flashed across the road then, and a thought came to him which he felt shy to speak, and then said quickly and caught in his breath at the end, "The sunset was on it. It looked the colour of your hair."

"Well, if it did," she cried with sudden petulance, " pity me, that has to carry on a human head what looks natural on a wild beast's back. Och, come along! Let's run. I like

running. I'm cold. There's a bonny bridge where the road
dips, over the tail of Thriepmuir. Let's run." And for a
hundred yards or so she ran like the red deer by his side, and
then stopped for some reason that was not lack of breath. " I
don't like this," she said half laughingly. " I've a poor envious
nature. I'm used to running everybody else off their feet, and
here you're holding back to keep with me. I feel I'm being
an object of condescension. We'll walk, if you please."

Yaverland said, " Oh, what nonsense ! I was just thinking
how rippingly you ran."

" Havers ! " she replied. " You were thinking nothing of
the sort. You were wondering what for I carried an iron-
monger's shop in my pocket. But yon rattling's just a tin
with some coconuts I've in it that I made last night and slipped
in in case you'd like it, rubbing up against my protractor."

" But why in Heaven's name," Yaverland asked, " do you
carry a protractor about with you ? "

" Off and on I try and keep up my Euclid and do a rider
over my lunch, and I just keep a protractor handy."

Yaverland stopped. " Ellen," he said, " I haven't known
you very long." There was the faintest knitting of her brows,
and he added evenly, " I may call you Ellen, mayn't I ? This
modern comradeship between men and women . . ." " Och,
yes," beamed Ellen, fascinated by the talismanic catchword, and
he felt a little ashamed because he had used one of her pure en-
thusiasms for his own purposes. Sometimes he was conscious
of a detestable adroitness in his relations with women ; it was
not respectful ; it was half-brother to the carneying art of the
seducer, but he could not take back the insincerity. " As I
say, I haven't known you very long. But may I ask you a
favour ? "

" Surely," said Ellen.

" Turn out your pockets."

" But why ? "

" I want to see what's in 'em."

" Well," said Ellen resignedly, " there are worse vices than
inquisitiveness. Both pockets ? "

" We'll start with the one with the coconut ice and the
protractor, please."

" It's too cold to sit by the roadside and sort them, so you'll
have to take them from me as I get them out. Well, there's
the protractor, and there's the coconut ice. Have a bit ? Ah,
well, I notice that grown-up—that people older than me don't
seem to care for sweeties before their dinner. I wonder why.

And there's a magnetic compass I picked up on George the Fourth Bridge. There's a kind of pleasure in finding the north, don't you think? And—fancy this being here! I thought I'd lost it long ago. It's a wee garnet I found on the beach at Elie. I was set up all the afternoon with finding a precious stone. I would like fine to be a miner in the precious stone mines in Mexico. If I was a boy I would go. And the rest's just papers. Here's notes on a Geographical Society lecture on the geology of Yellowstone Park I went to last spring. Very instructive it was. And here's a diagram I did when I was working for the Bible examination on the Second Book of Kings—the lines of the House of Israel and the House of Judah drawn to scale on square paper, five years to a square and set parallel so that you can see which buddy was ruling on the one throne when another buddy was on the other. I came out fifth in all Scotland. And this is a poem I wrote. It's not a good poem. The subject was excellent—reflections of an absinthe-drinker condemned to death for the murder of his mistress—but I couldn't give it the treatment it desairved. No, you will *nut* see it. I'll just tear it up. There. It'll do the whaups no harm scattering over the moor, for they've no æsthetic sensibilities. But I shouldn't be surprised if you had, though I've heard that the English don't care much for art. I'm not much good at the poetry, but I have the grace to know it, and so I've just given it up. I make my own blouses, though I know I can't equal the professional product that's sold in the shops, because it comes cheaper. But with the Carnegie library handing out the professional product for nothing, I see no reason why I should write my own poems. That's all in this pocket. But I think there's more in the other. Oh, mercy, there's nothing at all except this pair of woollen gloves I had forgotten. Not another thing. And no wonder. There's a hole in it the size of an egg. Now, if that isn't vexatious. I had some real nice things in that pocket. A wee ammonite, I remember. Och, well, it can't be helped. I'm afraid you've seen nothing very thrilling after all."

"Oh yes, I have," said Yaverland.

"Indeed you've not. Yet certainly you're looking tickled to death. No wonder Scotch comedians have such a success when they go among the English if they're all as easily amused as you."

"Your pockets are like a boy's," he said. "In a way, you're awfully like a boy."

"I wish I was," she answered bitterly. "But I'm a girl,

and I've nothing before me. No going to sea for me as there was for you." But they were nearly at the bridge now, and she was changed to a gay child because she loved this spot. She ran forward, crying, " Is it not beautiful ? Look, you didn't think there was this grand loch stretching away there ! And look how the firs stand at the water's edge. The day Rachael and I came there was a clump of bell-heather just on that point of rock. A bonny pinky red it was. And look how Bavelaw Avenue marches up the hill ! Is it not just fine ? "

Her moment of desperate complaint had not moved him at all, nor did he perceive that her joy at the beauty of the place was more intense than anything a happy person would have felt, that her loud laughter bore as bitter a history of wretchedness as a starving man's grunt over a crust. He was not convinced that these sudden darkenings of her eyes and voice, and her flights from these moments into the first opportunity of gaiety, represented any real contest with pain. Life must be lovely and amusing for such a lovely and amusing person. These were but youth's moody fandangoes. He could look on them as calmly as on the soaring and swooping of a white seabird. So he stood on the bridge, leaving her soul to its own devices while he appreciated the view. Surely this country was not real, but an imagination of Ellen's mind. It was so like her. It was beautiful and solitary even as she was. The loch that stretched north-east from the narrow neck of water under the bridge was fretted to a majesty of rage by the winds that blew from the black hills around it ; but it ended in a dam that was pierced in the middle with some metallic spider's web of engineering ; even so would romantic and utilitarian Ellen have designed a loch. And the firs which formed a glade of gloom by the waterside, which by their soughing uttered the very song of melancholy's soul, were cut by the twirling wind into shapes like quips ; that too was like Ellen. And this magnificent avenue that began on the other side of the bridge, and solemnly ascended the hillside as if to a towered palace that certainly was not there, was not unfit walking for the princess that had no king for father.

But as the wonder of the place became familiar, that fever of discomfort which had been vexing Ellen all that day returned. There was, she felt, some remedy for it quite close at hand ; but she did not know what it could be. If she leapt from a height she might lift this curious burden from her heart. She scrambled up on the stone parapet of the bridge and jumped back to earth ; and he, because it was the kind of thing a boy might have done, took no notice. But she shivered because this tangible lump of misery was still within her. She must run about, or the beating of her heart would become an agony. "Rachael and I found a water-rat under the bridge," she cried; "preening its whiskers it was, quite the thing, till it saw us and ran off in a terrible fuff. Let's go and see if there's one now." She turned round, stared for a minute at the south-west, where ill weather discoloured the hills like a bruise, and said reproachfully, "Surely the rain will never come to spoil to-day." To-day was to be such a lovely holiday. And then she ran round the stone spur of the bridge and crouched down beside the arch on the damp turf.

There was no rat there now. The water was in spate with the autumn floods and the muddy ledge on which he had sat at his toilette was an invisible thing that sent up a smear of weed to tremble on the surface. But she continued to crouch down and watch the burn. Better than anything in nature she loved running water, and this was grey and icy and seemed to have a cold sweet smell, and she liked the slight squeaking noises her boots made on the quaggy turf when she shifted her balance. It was quiet here, and the gentle colours of the soft grey sky, the stern grey stream, the amber grasses that shook perpetually in the stream's violence, and the black stripped hawthorns that humped at the water's border made a medicine for her eyes, which had begun to ache.

There was always peace on the Pentlands. And such bonny things happened every minute. A bough of silver birch came floating along, doubtless a windfall from one of those trees that stood where Thriepmuir was but the Bavelaw burn, a furtive trickle among the moss-hags, a brown rushy confusion between two moors. It was as bright as any flower with its yellow leaves, and as fine as filigree ; and its preservation of this brightness and fineness through all the angry river's tumbling gave it an air of brave integrity. She watched it benignly, and peered beneath the bridge to see if it would have the clear course it deserved, and a kind of despair fell on her as she saw that it would not. The ill-will that creeps about the world is vigilant ; many are the branches that fall from the silver birch in autumn, and not one of them is forgotten by it. Doubtless the very leaves on the bough are numbered, lest one should sail bravely to the loch and make a good end. So there, where the shadow lay thickest under the arch, was a patch of still black water, confined in stagnancy by a sunk log on which alluvial mud had made a garden of whitish grasses like the beard of an unclean old man. The impact of the unchecked floods that rushed past made this black patch shake perpetually, and this irregular motion gave it a sort of personality. It suggested a dark man shaking with a suppressed passion of malice. It was like Mr. Philip. From some submerged rottenness caught in the log bubbles slowly floated up through the dark water, wavered a little under the glassy surface, and then popped up and made a dirty trail of spume. That was like the way Mr. Philip sat in the dark corner beyond the fireplace and showed by the way the whites of his eyes turned about that something bad had come into his mind, and let a space of silence fall so that one thought he was not going to say it after all, and then it would come out suddenly, cool and as mean as mean could be and somehow unanswerable.

With a twingeing hope that it would not be so, she watched the silver birch branch hesitate, yield to the under-ebb, and lie at last helpless on the black stagnancy, which continued to vibrate with an air of malice. Soon its pretty leaves were waterlogged, and it sank down to bed with the grassy rottenness beside the whitish grasses. It had had no chance, any more than she herself had when Mr. Philip contrived that although she should run away from him all day, there would come a time when they stood face to face in the little room where no one came, and stared and drawled until she said the silly bairn-like thing that gave him the chance to make a fool of her. It was all right to be here on the Pentlands enjoying herself, but on Monday she would have to go back and work under Mr. Philip. She could not go on like this. She would have to kill herself. She would jump over the Dean Bridge. Mother would just have to go and live with Aunt Bessie at Bournemouth.

Yaverland spoke behind her, indolently, because he felt he had all the rest of his life to be happy with her. " Where's this Rachael Wing you talk about ? Aren't you still pals ? "

Ellen swallowed her unshed tears. " 'Deed, yes," she said, " but she's gone to London to be an actress. I wish I knew how she was getting on. She's never written since the first month."

" Probably she's having hard luck."

" Not Rachael. She's not like me. I always was a poor creature beside her. Anybody could see that Rachael had a wonderful life before her. She's not a bit like me."

" But that's just what you look like."

" Havers ! " she said dully. " And me so pairfectly miserable ! " As soon as the words were out of her mouth she was

frozen with horror. In the presence of one who was both a
man and English she had admitted the disgraceful fact that
she was not an imperial creature insolent with success and well
pleased with the earth her footstool. She scrambled to her
feet and ran coltishly past him and over the bridge, hiding
her face and calling gaily, " Come on ! I want to get up on the
hills ! " And he followed slowly, thinking pretty things about
her.

When he drew abreast of her she had pulled off her tam-o'-
shanter and taken out her hairpins, and her hair was blowing
sideways across her breast and back. " It's good to feel the
wind through one's hair," she said. " I wish I had short hair
like a man's."

" Why don't you cut yours off then ? "

" I somehow feel it would be a shame when I have such a deal of
it," she answered innocently, and fell to chattering of the Spanish
military nun that de Quincey wrote about. She had passed
herself off as a man all right. Did he think a girl could go the
length of that anywhere nowadays ? No ? Surely there
was somewhere ? Oh, she was a child, a little child, and it
was not fair to talk to her of love for a little while yet. It
might be dangerous, for he had heard that sometimes, when a
girl was sought by men too soon, her girlhood tried to hold her
back from womanhood by raising obscure terrors that might
last as long as life. He would wait until she was eighteen.
Yet when the avenue bent at right angles half up the hillside,
and they drew together as an army of winds marched down
upon them from the mountains, she looked at him through her
scattered hair, and her face was wholly a woman's. So might
a woman smile who was drowning under a deep tide and loved
to drown so ; yet from a brave wisdom in her eyes it could be
seen that she was abandoning herself not to death but to life.
This, beyond all doubt, was adult love, though she herself was
not aware of it. He had only to admit it by some significant
speech or act, to rise spiritually to the occasion, and they would
be fused together as perpetual lovers.

He was conscious again as he had been when she sat with the
coins before her in the little dining-room in Hume Park Square, of
an involuntary austerity in his passion which, while he did not see
thesense of it, he recognised to be the authentic note of love. A moment ago, when she still seemed a child, he had been thinking what
fun it would be to kiss her suddenly on the very tip of that pink
little nose which moved when she talked as a rabbit's does when
it eats, to lay hold of her hands roughly and see how far those

ink-stained fingers, still pliable as children's are, would bend
back towards her wrist. But now that she was a woman the
passion between them was so strong that the delight of touching
her beloved flesh would have been too great for human nerves
to support, and it would have turned to pain. The mutual knowledge that they loved would be enough to work as many miracles
on the visible and invisible world as either of their hearts could
stand. " I love you," was what he had to say. . . .

It was the strangest thing in the world that he could not
say it. He could not even make a kind movement of his body,
a protective slackening of his step and overhanging of her spindrift delicacy with his great height, that might have intimated
to her that they were dear friends. He found himself walking
woodenly a pace away from her, and though his soul shouted
something hidden round the corner of his mind, it would not
let his lips articulate the desperate cry. He stared at the passing
moment as a castaway, gagged, and bound to a raft of pirates,
might wake from a delirious sleep, stare dumbly up at the steep
side of a galleon that rides slowly, and know that with it rides
away his chance of life because he cannot speak. Love of this
girl meant infinite joy and a relief such as nothing before had
ever promised him from the black regiment of moods that had
for long beleaguered him, self-hatred, doubt of the value of any
work on this damned earth, a recurrent tendency to brood on
his mother's wrongs until he was a little mad ; and if he did not
win her life would be more tormenting in its patent purposeless-
ness than even he, with his immense capacity for abstract rage,
had ever known. And yet it was utterly beyond him to speak
the necessary words. And the army of winds passed down to
the plains and there was stillness, the trunks of the trees ceased
to groan and the dead leaves did not race among their feet, and
she shook back her hair and was no longer a woman. She
leaned towards him and spoke rapidly, reverting to the subject
of women soldiers, and unquestionably the spirit of childhood
lodged upon her lips.

Granted that there was such a thing as future life,
though, mind you, she found the evidence in support of
it miserably weak, did he not think that the canonisation of
Joan of Arc must have been a terrible smack in the face for
St. Paul ? He made himself forget in laughter the priceless
moment that had passed, and he told himself, as sternly as once
in South America he had had to tell himself that he must stop
drinking, that her mother had been right, and he must not make
love to her because she was too young.

There was a curious colour of relief about this decision, and it was with a kind of gusto that he kept repeating it to himself all the long day that spread about before them after they passed Bavelaw Castle, the whitewashed farmhouse that was the anti-climax of the avenue. Two servant-girls were laying clothes on a bleaching-green within its dykes, the one taking them down from a clothes-line, the other laying them down on the grass, and they were exchanging cries that seemed at that distance wordless expressions of simple being like the calls of the whaups that circled above them. Here was a district remote from all human complexity, in which it was very sweet to walk with this young girl.

The road stopped, for this was no place where the marketing gig could spin along to any business, and two grassy tracks went forward, both marked by bare, un-inscribed posts, as if they led to destinations too unvisited to need a name. The one they did not take climbed over the grey shoulder of the range, and the other brought them into an eastward valley, where there was for the moment no wind and a serenity that was surely perpetual. The cries of the hill-birds did but drill little holes in the clear hemisphere of silence that lay over this place. The slopes on either side, thickly covered with mats of heather and bristling mountain herbage, and yet lean and rocky, were like the furry sides of emaciated animals, and up above bare black summits confronted the sky. It was the extremity of bleak beauty. And, unafraid of the grimness, Ellen ran on ahead, her arms crooked back funnily because she had her hands in her pocket to keep the coconut-ice tin from rattling against the protractor, her red hair streaming a yard behind. He absorbed the sight of her so greedily that it immediately seemed as if it were a recollected sight over which he had pondered and felt tenderness for many years, and he wondered if perhaps he had seen someone like her before. But of course he never had. There was no one in the world like her.

"Listen, we're coming to the waterfall! Do you not hear it!" she cried back to him; and they listened together, smiling because it was such fun to do anything together, to the risping, whistling sound of a wind-blown waterfall. "It comes down peat-red," she told him gloatingly, and with an air of showing off a private treasure she led him to the grey fold in the hills where the Logan Burn tumbled down a spiral staircase of dark polished rock. She ran about the pools at its feet, crying that this wee one was red as rust, that this big one was red as a red rose—

was it not, if you looked in the very middle ? But suddenly she looked up into his face and asked, " You'll have seen grand waterfalls out in Brazil ? "

" Yes," he said, " but I like this as well, and I would rather be here than anywhere else in the world."

" Tell me the names of some of the big waterfalls," she insisted, uninterested in the loving things that he had said.

" Well, the falls of Paulo Affonso are pretty good."

" Paulo Affonso ! " she repeated, her face avaricious with the desire for adventure, " I will go there some day. . . ."

That she should feel so intensely about something which did not concern himself roused his jealousy, and he set himself to interrupt her train of thought by saying boisterously, " This is a ripping place ! What's it like above the fall ?   Let's climb it." He strolled closer to the waterfall to see if there was an easy way up the rock, but was recalled by a ready, embarrassed murmur from her.

" I can't. . . ."

He imagined she was moved by shame at his greater strength, as she had been when they ran together, and he said encouragingly :

" Why not ?   You've got nailed boots."

But she continued to stand stiffly on a rock by the edge of the red pool, and stared over his head at the spray and repeated, " I can't. "

He wondered from her blush if in his ignorance of girls he had done something to offend her, and turned away ; but she misunderstood that, and cried fierily :

" Och, I'm not feared ! I've done it twenty times. But I took a vow.   Oh," she faltered, suddenly the youngest of all articulate things, " you'll laugh at me ! "

" I won't ! " he answered fiercely and gripped one of her hands.

" It was like this," she said, looking round-eyed and dewily solemn like a child in church. " Climbing up there used to be a great pleasure to me.   I used to come here a lot with Rachael Wing.   And then I heard Victor Grayson speak—oh, he is a wonderful man ; he seemed hardly airthly ; you felt you had to make some sacrifice. I made a vow I'd never climb it again till I had done something for the social revolution. And I've not done a thing yet."

They exchanged a long, confiding look, a mutual pressure of their souls ; but before he could say something reverently sympathetic she had uttered a sharp exclamation, and was looking past him at the waterfall, which a sudden gust of wind had blown out from the rock like a lady's skirt. " If we were climbing that now, yon spray would be on our faces, and I love the prick of cold water ! " she burst out. " Whatever for did I make that daft-like vow ? A lot of good it's like to do the social revolution ! I really am a fool sometimes ! "

Was there ever such a child, Yaverland asked himself triumphantly, as if he had proved a disputed point. He persuaded himself that the exquisite exhibition of her personality which delighted him all through the meal they presently shared on the rock beside this red pool was vouchsafed to him only because he had been wise enough not to treat her as a woman. She was as spontaneous as a little squirrel that plays unwatched in the early morning at the fringe of the wood. There was no movement of her beautiful bright-coloured person, no upward or downward singing of her soft Scotch voice, that did not precisely express some real action of her soul. But if he had spoken only one word of love it would not have been so. She would have blurred her clear gestures by traditional languors, she would have kept her mind busy draping her with the graces expected of a courted maiden instead of letting it run enquiringly about the marvels of the earth ; for the old wives and the artists have been so busy with this subject of love that they have made a figure of the lover, and the young woman who finds herself a bride can no more behave naturally than a young man who finds himself a poet. Oh, he was doing the sensible thing. There was no day in his life which he was more certain that he had spent wisely than this which he dawdled away playing with Ellen as a little boy might play with a little girl, on the edge of the two lochs to which this glen led. By the first, a dull enough stretch of water had it not been for its name, which she loved and made him love by repeating it, " Loganlee, Loganlee." She made him go on ahead for a few yards and then ran to him, clapping her hands, because he had come to a halt on the bridge that spanned a little tributary to the loch.

" There, I knew you'd stop ! There's no stranger ever gets across this bridge without stopping and looking over. They call it the Lazy Brig. The old folk say it's because there's a fairy sitting by the burn, a gossiping buddy who casts a spell on strangers so that he can have a good look at them and talk about them afterwards to the other fairies." But at the second loch, Glencorse Pond, she nearly quarrelled with him, though she was pleased with his evident awe at the place. Here black wild hills ran down to a half-moon of wind-fretted water, near a mile long, and dark trees stood on its banks with such a propriety of desolate beauty that it seemed as if it must be a conscious work of art ; one could believe that the scene had been wrought by some winged artist divine enough to mould mountains yet possessed by an ecstasy of human grief. There was a little island on the loch, a knoll of sward so thickly set with tall swaying firs that from this distance it looked like a bunch of draggled crow's feathers set in the water, and from this there ran to the northern shore a broad stone causeway, so useless that it provoked the imagination and made the mind's eye see a string of hatchet-faced men, wrapped in cloaks and swinging lanthorns, passing that way at midnight. It was, Ellen said, a reservoir ; but it was no ordinary reservoir, for under its waters lay an ancient chapel and its graveyard.

" Mrs. Bonar, the ploughman's wife who lives in the cottage up yonder on Bell's Hill—do you see it ?—told me she'd often seen the ghosts rising up through the water at night. And I said to her, ' That's most interesting. And what do the ghosts look like ? ' ' Och, the very dead spit of thon incandescent mantles my daughter has in her wee flat in Edinburgh.' Was that not a fine way for a ghost to look ? "

He laughed at that, but presently laughed at a private jest of his own, and so fell into disgrace. For in answer to her enquiring gaze he said, " A reservoir with a churchyard at the bottom of it. I wondered what cocktail Edinburgh took to keep itself so gay." To his surprise, tears came into her eyes. " Oh, you English ! " she snapped. " Cackling at the Scotch is your one accomplishment."

But they soon made friends. The skies intervened to patch it up between them, for presently there broke out a huge windy conflagration of a sunset, which was itself so fine a scarlet show and wrought such magical changes on the common colour of things that she had constantly to call his attention by little intimate cries and tuggings at the sleeve. This was not soft summer glow, no liquefaction of tints ; but the world became mineral as they looked. The field by the road was changed from a dull winter green to a greenish copper ; the bramble bushes cast long steel-blue shadows, and their scarlet and purple leaves looked like snips of painted tin ; and the Glencorse Burn on the other side of the field was overhung by bare trees of gold. Every window of the farmhouse across the valley was a loophole of flame ; and here it was evident, from the passing of a multitude of figures about the farm buildings and a babblement that drove in gusts across the valley, there was happening some event that matched the prodigiousness of the strange appearance lent it by the sunset.

" There's an awful argy-bargying at Little Vantage," said Ellen, " I wonder what's going on."

When they crossed over the burn and turned into the road that led back to the farmhouse they found the dykes plastered with intimations of a sale of live stock. " Ah, it's a roup! Old Mr. Gumley must be dead, poor soul!" And indeed the road was lined with farmers' gigs, paint and brass-work blazing with the evening light till they looked like fiery chariots that would presently lift to heaven. About the yard gate there was a great press of hale farmers, gilt and ruddy from the sunset they faced, and vomiting jests at each other out of their great bearded mouths ; and in the yard sheep with golden fleece and cattle as bright as dragons ran hither and thither before the sticks of boys who looked like demons with the orange glow on their faces, and who cursed and spat to show they would some-day be men. Richard and Ellen had to stand back for a moment while a horse was led out ; and as it passed a paunchy farmer jocularly struck it between the eyes and roared, " Ye're no for me, ye auld mare, wi' your braw be-ginnings of the ringbone ! " And there was so much glee at the mention of deformity in the thick voice, and so much patience in the movement of the mare's long unshapely head, that the incident was as unpleasing as if it had been an ill-favoured spinster who had been insulted. Yaverland was roused suddenly by the tiniest sound of a whimper from Ellen.

" What's the matter ? " he asked tenderly.

" Nothing," she quivered. " There's something awful sad about the evening sometimes. I've got an end of the world feeling." And indeed there was something awesome and unnatural about this quiet hour in which there was so much light and so little heat, in this furnace of the skies from which there flowed so glacial a wind. " Supposing the end of the world is like this," said Ellen, nearly crying. " A lot of beefy, red-faced angels buying us up and taking us off to their own places without a word to us of where we're to go to, and commenting most unfeelingly on all our failings. . . ."

" You funny person," he murmured, " you're tired. Probably hungry. Where's that cottage you talked about where they'll give us tea ? "

" Over yonder," she quavered, " but I'm not wanting any tea."

But just then a gig drew up beside them, driven

by an old man and laden with a couple of tin trunks and a cornucopia of a woman, who had snatched the reins out of the old man's hands. "What's this? A roup at Little Vantage! Feyther, what's happened?" The old man shook his head. "Feyther, ye niver ken onything." She raised a megaphonic voice. "Moggie! Moggie Gumley!" A fat young woman with a soap-shining face ran out of the farmhouse. "Wha's calling me? Och, it's you, Mistress Cairns!" "Ay, it's me. What's ta'en ye all here? I've been awa' for two months keepin' hoose for ma brither Jock while his wife's been in the Infirmary wi' her chumer. I didn't think I'd come back to find a roup at Little Vantage." "So ye've not haird?" gasped the fat young woman delightedly. "Feyther's deid o' his dropsy, and Alec and me's awa' to Canady this day fortnight." She panted it out with so honest a joy in the commotion, so innocent a disregard of the tragedy of death and emigration, that Yaverland and Ellen had to turn away and laugh; and he drew her across the road to the cottage.

The door was opened before they got there. "It's me, Mrs. Lawson!" said Ellen. "Indeed, I kenned that!" replied the housewife. "I was keeking out of the window when you came up the road, and I said to masel', 'There's Miss Melville, and she'll be wanting her tea,' so I awa' and popped the kettle on. Bring your gentleman in. He's a new face, but he's welcome. Ye'll pardon the parlour being a' of a reek wi' tobaccy, but Mr. Laidlaw and Mr. Borthwick cam' in and had a cup o' tea and a bit of a crack. They were both bidding at the roup and some business thegither. I think Mr. Laidlaw means to buy Cornhaven off Mr. Borthwick and give it to his son John, wha's married on a Glasca girl, a shelpit wee thing wi' a Glesca accent like skirling pipes played by a drunken piper." They watched her while she set the table with tea and scones and strawberry jam and cheese, and smiled rather vacantly at her stream of gossip, their natural liking for the woman struggling against their sense of the superfluity of everybody on earth except each other. When she left them they ate and drank almost without speech, soberly delighted by the mellowing of the world that followed the dwindling of the sunset fires. All things seemed to become more modest and reconciled; and farmers hawked out their last jests at one another, mounted their gigs and drove home; and the flocks of sheep and droves of cattle pattered by, bleating and lowing not so heartrendingly.

Ellen rose, went over to the mantelpiece and stroked the china dogs, and sat down in an armchair by the fire. " This has been a lovely day," she murmured. She joined her hands behind her head and crossed her knees and smiled blindishly into the shadow ; and his heart turned over in him. All his life he would remember her just as she was then : the lovely attitude of body that was at once angular and softly sensuous, like a blossom-laden branch ; the pure pearl colour of her skin, the pure bright colours of her hair and eyes and mouth ; the passionate and funny, shrewd and credulous pattern of her features ; and that dozing smile, that looked as if her soul had ceased to run up and down enquiringly and was resting awhile to enjoy the sweetness that was its own climate. He would never forget her as she was looking then. She might turn away from him, she might get old, she might die, but the memory of her as she was at that moment would endure for ever in his heart, an eternally living thing. He was aware, reluctantly enough, for he hated such mystical knowledge, and would have given the world to see life as a plain round of dicing and drinking and wenching, that real love was somehow a cruel thing for women ; that the hour when she became his wife would be as illimitably tragic as it would be illimitably glorious. But love was also very kind to women, since it enabled them to live always at their loveliest in their lover's memories, there perpetually exempt from the age and ugliness that even the bravest of them seemed pitifully to fear.

Yet, of course, love was not so kind to every woman. No one remembered his mother as he would remember Ellen. He began to ponder what his mother must have been like when she was that age, and it marked a certain difference between him and other men, that he was grudgingly surprised that the girl he meant to marry was as beautiful as his mother. Certainly, he reflected, with a bitter, gloating grief, Marion Yaverland must have been beautiful enough to deserve a lodging in some man's memory. She must have been brilliantly attractive in the obvious physical sense to have overcome the repulsion that her spirit and wit must certainly have aroused in such a man as his father ; and though he suppressed his earliest memories of her because they introduced that other who had shared his nursery, he had many pictures in his mind which showed her brown and red-lipped and subtle with youth, and not the dark, silent sledge-hammer of a woman that she had latterly become.

There came to him a memory of a distant winter afternoon, so far distant that he could not have been more than four or five, when they had come back from doing their Christmas shopping at Prittle-bay, and he had grizzled, as tired children do, at the steepness of the hill that climbed from Roothing station to Yaverland's End, always a stiff pull, and that day a brown muck of trodden snow. She had looked round with her hard proud stare to make sure that nobody was watching them, and then spread out her crimson cloak and danced backwards in front of him, and cried out loving little gibes at his heavy footedness, her own vitality flashing about her like lightning. When she was younger still, and had not wept so much, she must often have glowed very beautifully under her lover's eyes. It was a pity that she had chosen to love that thief, who stole the memories of her glorious moments as he had stolen her good repute and peace of mind, and crept away with the loot to the tomb on the hillside where his son could not pursue him. As he thought of the unmitigated quality of his mother's lot he hated other women for their cheerful lives; and Ellen, who had felt that his mood had turned from her, and was watching his face, said to herself: "He has some trouble that he is not telling me. Well, why should he? We are almost strangers." Suddenly she felt very weak and lonely, and put her hands over her face.

Mrs. Lawson put her head round the door. "You young people's letting the clock run on. Nae doot ye're douce and souple walkers, but if ye want to catch the Edinburgh bus ye'll hev none too much time."

Yaverland and Ellen both started forward, and their eyes met. "Oh, we must hurry!" she exclaimed, with a pale distress that puzzled him by its intensity. Yet she made him wait while she pinned up her hair; ane that almost made him suspect her as a minx, for she looked so pretty with her arms above her head and her white fingers shuttling in and out of her red hair. But when they got into the lane outside she hurried towards the high road as if she fled from something, catching her breath sobbingly when the darkness was so thick that she could not run, although he told her many times that there was no need for haste. "See," he said, as they took their stand at the cross-roads, "the bus isn't anywhere in sight yet." But she did not answer him, and he became aware that she was trembling. "Are you cold? Would you like my coat?" he asked, but she murmured a little broken mouseish refusal. Could it possibly be that she was frightened of being alone with him in the dark? He had to own to himself that she would have been afraid of him if she had known some of the things that he had done, although he did not admit that her fear would be anything more than a child's harsh judgment of matters it did not understand. But no rumours could have reached her ears, for he had always lived very secretly, even beyond the needs of discretion, since he knew that the passive sort of women with whom, for the most part, he had had dealings have an enormous power of self-deception, and could, as the years went on, if there were no witnesses to dispute it, pretend to themselves that what had happened with him was no reality but only a naughty dream that had come to them between sleeping and waking.

It came to him like a feeling of sickness that it was not absolutely impossible that those Christians, in spite of that personal ridiculousness which he had noticed in nearly all of them, were right. It might be that sin was sin and left a stain, and that those things which had appeared to him as innocently sweet as a bathe in a summer sea, and which he had believed to end utterly with dawn and the stealthy shutting of a door, had somehow left him loathsome to this girl. He perceived that there might have been a meaning adverse to him in the way she had delayed, in despite of her own wish to hurry, and pinned up her hair. Perhaps she had seen something in his face which made her shiver with apprehension that his hands might touch it ; not because it was her hair, but because they were his hands and had acquired a habit of fingering women's beauties. But indeed he was not like that. He sweated with panic, and raged silently against this streak of materialism in women that makes them so grossly dwell on the physical events in a man's life. This agony of tenderness he felt for her now, this passion of worship that kept half his mind inactive yet tense, like a devotee contemplating the altar, was more real than anything he had ever felt for those other women.

The bus came down the road to them and he stepped forward, shouting and lifting his stick. But it swept on, packed with soldiers in red coats, who sent out into the darkness behind them a fan of song. " It's the soldiers from the barracks at Glencorse, bother them," sighed Ellen. " And dear knows when there's a train." She spoke with such a flat extremity of despair that he peered at her through the darkness and found that her head had fallen back and her eyes were almost closed. Evidently she had been overcome by one of those sudden prostrations to which young people are liable when they have spilt out their strength too recklessly. He remembered how once, when the *Gondomar* had been scuttling for two days at the fringe of a cyclone, he had seen a cabin-boy lean back against a mast and become suddenly statuesque with inertia, with such a queer pinching of the mouth as hers. " It's all right," he said comfortingly. " There's a train in a quarter of an hour." She must have heard him, for she began to walk towards the station lights that twinkled up the road, but she answered in a tone that sounded as if her mind was inaccessible with somnolence, " I'm half asleep."

The train was in when they reached the station, and he told her to take a seat in it while he got the tickets. But she did not. Its carriages were not yet lit, and it looked black and cold and cheerless, like those burned buildings they had seen at Balerno ; and anyway, she did not want to take that train. She would have liked to turn back with him through the dark avenues into the Pentlands. The sunset, which had somehow been as vexing as it was beautiful, would by then have receded utterly before the kind, sleepy darkness, undisturbed there in the valley by the wee-est cottage light. It would be good to lie down for the night on the heather of some ledge on the hillside where one could hear the Logan Burn talking as it ran from the fall, and to look up and see Mr. Yaverland sitting in that nice slouching way he had, a great black shape against the stars. But that was a daft idea. She was annoyed for thinking of anything so foolish, and when he came out and chid her for standing about on the windy platform she found nothing on her lips but a cross murmur.

That did not really matter, for one could not hurt grown-up people. They were always happy. Everybody in the world was happy except her. Without doubt he would think her quite mad if he knew that she was in the grip of a depression that seemed to be wringing misery out of her body and brain as one wrings water out of a bathing-dress, so when they got into the train she turned away, muttered yawningly that she was very tired, and buried her face in the crook of her arm so that he might think she slept. It puzzled her that she felt so disappointed. What had she expected to happen to-day that hadn't happened ? Everything had been lovely. Mr. Yaverland had talked most interestingly, and the hills had been very beautiful. She was ashamed of all those tears that she shed more frequently than one would have expected from an intending rival of Pierpont Morgan, but these present tears filled her with terror because they were so utterly irrational. Irrational, too, was the sudden picture that flashed on her mind's eye of Mr. Philip sitting in the opposite corner of the carriage, screwing up his dark face with mocking laughter. " Mr. Philip is driving me mad," she thought to herself. " Some day soon I'll find myself in Morningside Asylum, sticking flowers in my hair and flattering myself I'm Queen Victoria. But I will not go mad. I am going to get on. I am going to be great. But am I ? I think I am not." Her face made a wet contorted mask against her sleeve, and a swallowed sob was as sharp in her throat as a fishbone ; and there struck through her like an impaling sword a certainty which she could not understand, but which was surely a certificate that there was to be no more happiness, that even if Mr. Philip ceased to persecute her she would still be hungry and tormented.

Perhaps if she could go to some new country she would escape from this misery. She saw a sky like stretched blue silk, stamped with the black monograms of palms ; a purple bay shaped like a shell and edged with a white embroidery of surf. Surely such fair weather killed with sweetness such coarse plants as her stupid gloom, as the foul weather here killed with its coarseness all sweet-flowering southern plants. She turned to Yaverland to ask him if he could help her to find work abroad, but she became aware that she was in the grip of an unreasonable emotion that prevented her from this. It was as horrible to her to see the coldly logical apparatus of her mind churning out these irrational conclusions as it would have been for her to find her mother babbling in drunkenness ; and this feeling that for Yaverland to know of her misery would be a culminating humiliation that she could not face seemed disgustingly mad. So she threw herself into a black drowse of misery unfeatured by specific ideas, until she began to think smilingly of the way his eyebrows grew ; they were very thick and dark and perfectly level save for a piratical twist in the middle. But she became conscious that he was standing over her, and her heart almost stopped. He said, "I think we're just coming into Edinburgh." There was no reason why she should feel chilled and desolate when he said that. She must be going out of her mind.

And he, since she had shown by the simplicity of her movements that she was not afraid of him, was quite happy.

He could see the picture of himself sitting beside the sleeping child as if it were printed in three colours on glossy paper. But he was a little troubled lest she had walked too far, and as they went up the stone steps from the station to Princes Street he bent over her and asked in a tone of tenderness that he enjoyed using, " Are you tired ? "

" Oh, very tired," said Ellen, drooping her head, and aping a fatigue greater than anything she had ever felt in all her young life.

CHAPTER IV

(1)

MR. PHILIP was crossing Princes Street when he saw them standing in the white circle under the electric standard by the station steps. The strong light fell on them like a criticism, and it seemed to him brazen the way they stood there being so handsome that the passers-by turned about to stare at them. Doubtless, since folks were such fools, they were whispering that the two made a fine pair. Surely it was the vilest indecency that there, under his very eyes, that great hulking chap from Rio bent his head and spoke to Ellen, and she answered him ?

"She's standing there making herself as conspicuous as if she were a street girl ! " he screamed to himself, and other shouts filled his ears, and he became aware that a cursing driver had pulled up his horse a foot away and that the loafers at the kerb were lifting jeering cries. He charged it one more offence to Ellen's account that she had caused him to make a fool of himself, and vowed he would never think of her again, and ran among the people to see where she had gone. Yaverland was leading her very quickly along towards the North Bridge, and she was now nothing but a dark shape that might, he thought with a glee that he did not understand, have belonged to some ageing woman with a bony body and a sallow face. But then he saw against the lit pavement her narrow feet treading that gait that was like a grave, slow dance, and he realised with agony that it was no use lying to himself and pretending that this was anybody but Ellen—Ellen, who was far different from every other woman in the world and more desirable. She slowly turned, as if her spirit had felt this rage at the fact of her running at her heels, and wished to have it out with him. He gripped his stick and raised a hand to hide his working mouth, and waited for the moment when she would see his face, but it did not come.

The man Yaverland had put out his great ham of a

hand and hailed a cab. When Mr. Philip tried to stop a cab he usually had to run alongside it, and often the driver was most impudent, but this swaggering bully checked the thing on the instant, and handed in Ellen and drove off in style as if he was a duke with his duchess in their own carriage. What did they want in a cab anyway? He followed the black trundling square on its spidery wheels as it turned round by the Register House to cross the North Bridge, and imagined the fine carryings on they were doubtless having in the dark in there. He called Ellen a name he had not thought of before.

There was nothing to be done about it. He stood for a while at the railing of that strange garden of concrete walks and raised parterres and ventilating-shafts that lies at this end of Princes Street, built on the roof of the sunk market. Its rectilinear aspect pleased him. It was not romantic, the gates were locked, and one could be sure that there were no lovers trysting there. Presently he moved along towards the West End, keeping still on the side of the street where there were no men and girls prancing about and grinning at each other like dirty apes under the lights, but only empty gardens with locked gates. What had those two been doing? They had come in by train. Unless they had travelled a very long journey it must have been dark before they started. They had been in the country alone together when it was quite dark. There came to him memories of sounds he had once heard when walking through a twilit wood, the crackling of twigs, a little happy cry of distress, and again the crackling of twigs; he had been compelled by something, which was not specially in him but was a part of the damned way life went, to stand and listen, though he knew it was not decent. He saw before him Ellen's face lying white on her spilt red hair, and it added to his anguish that he could not see it clearly, but had to peer at this enraging vision because he could not make out what her expression would be. He had seen her look a thousand ways during these last few weeks when she had kept on drawing his attention to her with her simpering girl's tricks, but he could not imagine how she would look then. It seemed as if she were defying his imagination as she defied him every day in the office, and he turned his mind away from the matter in a frenzy, but began soon to wonder what those two had been doing. They had come in by train. Unless they had travelled a very long journey it must have been dark before they started. . . .

He knew he must not go on like this, and looked round him. He had passed the classic portico of the Art Gallery and was walking now by the wilder section of the gardens, where the street lights shone back from the shining leaves of bushes and made them look like glazed paper, and with their glare made the trees behind seem such flat canvas trees as they set about the stage at theatres when there is need for a romantic glade for a lovers' meeting. How often had Ellen met Yaverland?

He ran across the road. It would be better among the people. It was not so bad if you did not watch them and see how happy they were. Everybody in the world was happy except him. No doubt Ellen and her Yaverland were just bursting with merriment in that cab. Would they be at home yet? She would be telling him all the office jokes. Well, she might, for all he cared. He knew fine that young Innes called him Mr. Philip Hop-o'-my-Thumb behind his back, and he didn't give a straw for it. He stopped in front of a picture-postcard shop that was hung from top to bottom of its window with strings of actresses' photographs, and stood there with a jaunty rising and falling of the heels, bestowing an exaggerated attention on the glossy black and white patterns that indicated the glittering façades of these charmers' smiles, the milky smoothness of their bean-fed femininity. Ah, these were the really fine women that it was worth troubling your head about, from whose satin slippers, it was well known, dukes and the like drank champagne. Who would bother about a wee typist when there were women like these in the world?

But as he looked at them he perceived that there was not one so beautiful as Ellen, and he walked waveringly on, wrathful at the way she insisted on being valuable when he wanted to despise her. A woman who had been watching him for some time, and who knew from a wide experience that he was in one of those aching miseries which make men turn to such as she, slipped from the shadows and murmured to him. She was taller than he, and had to bend her long slender neck that he might hear. He hated her for being a streetwalker and for being taller than he, and began to swear at her. But before he could get the words out of his mouth she had wiped the smile from her pale oval face with the adeptness of a proud woman who had long preserved her pride in the fields of contempt, and glided away with a dignity that denied what she was and what had happened. That struck him as a monstrous breach of the social contract, for surely if a woman was a bad woman she ought to stay still until one had finished swearing at her.

But all these women were vile. There was no measure to the vileness that Ellen had brought on him. For it was all her fault, since he never would have gone with that woman in London if it had not been for the way she had carried on the evening before. At the thought of that night in Piccadilly he began to hurry along the street, pushing in and out among the people as if he insanely hoped to lose the humiliating memory as one can lose a dog, until he remembered how he had had to hurry along beside the London woman because she was a great striding creature and he found it difficult to keep step, and then he walked slowly. It had all been so ugly, and it was a fraud too. It had been his belief that the advantage of prostitution was that it gave one command over women like Ellen without bringing on one the trouble that would certainly follow if one did ill to Ellen; for even if nobody ever found out, she would look at one with those eyes. But this woman was not in the least like Ellen. He had chosen her rather than the girl in the white boots at the other side of the pavement because he thought she had hair like Ellen, but when she took her hat off he saw that she had not. It was funny stuff, with an iridescence on it as if she had been rubbing it with furniture polish. Her flat, too, was not kept as Ellen would have kept it. And she had not been kind, as Ellen, when she moved softly as a cloud about the office fetching him things, or sat listening, with chin cupped in her hands and a hint of tears, to the story of his disappointment about the Navy; had fraudulently led him to believe what women were to men. She had been a cruel beast. For when she had got him to be so very wicked she might have spared him some of the nastiness, and not said those awful leering things so loud. Never would he forgive Ellen for dragging him down to those depths.

He was walking away from Princes Street to his own home now, and the decent grey vacuity of the streets soothed him. If he only had the sense to stay in the district of orderly houses where he belonged, and behaved accordingly, and did not go talking with people beneath him, he could not come to harm. But that would not alter the fact that he had once come to harm. As he passed the house at the corner of his street he saw that a " To Let " board had been put up since the morning. He wondered why the Allardyces were leaving it. He had been at school with the boys. He and Willie Allardyce had tied tenth in the mile race at the last school sports in which he had taken part before he left the Academy. He remembered how they had all stood at the starting-post in the windy sunshine, straight lads in their singlets and shorts, utterly uninvolved in anything but this clean thing of running a race ; the women were all behind the barriers, tolerated spectators, and one was too busy to see them ; his clothing had been stiff with sweat, and when he wriggled his body the cool air passed between his damp vest and his damp flesh, giving him a cold, pure feeling. Well, he was not a boy any longer. The Allardyces were moving ; everything was changing this way and that ; nothing would be the same again. . . .

The solidity of his father's house, the hall into which he let himself, with its olive green wallpaper, its aneroid barometer, and oil-painting of his mother's father, Mr. Laurie of the Bank of Scotland, made him feel better. He reminded himself that he belonged to one of the most respected families in Edinburgh, and that there was no use getting upset about things that nobody would ever find out, and he went into the dining-room and poured himself out a glass of whisky, looking round with deep satisfaction at his prosperous surroundings. There was a very handsome red wallpaper, and a blazing fire that chased the tawny lights and shadows on the leviathanic mahogany furniture and set a sparkle on the thick silver and fine glass on the spread table. "Mhm!" he sighed contentedly, and raised the tumbler to his lips. But the smell of the whisky recalled to him the flavour of that Piccadilly woman's kisses. The room seemed to contract and break out into soiled pink valances. He put down his glass, groaned, and made his mind blank, and was immediately revisited by the thought of Ellen's face on her spilt red hair. An ingenious thought struck him, and he hurried from the room. He met one of his sisters in the passage, and said, "Away, I want to speak to father." It was true that she was not preventing him from doing so, but the gesture of dominance over the female gave him satisfaction.

There was a little study at the back of the house which was lined from top to bottom with soberly bound and unrecent books, and dominated by a bust of Sir Walter Scott supported on a revolving bookcase which contained the Waverley Novels, Burns' Poems, and Chambers' Dictionary, which had an air of having been put there argumentatively, as a manifesto of the Scottish view that intellect is their local industry. Here, in a fog of tobacco smoke, Mr. Mactavish James reclined like a stranded whale, reading the London *Law Journal* and breathing disparagingly through both mouth and nose at once, as he always did when in contact with the English mind. He did not look up when Mr. Philip came in, but indicated by a " Humph ! " that he was fully aware of the entrance. There was an indefinable tone in this grunt which made Mr. Philip wonder whether he had not been overmuch influenced in seeking this interview by the conventional view of the parental relationship. He sometimes suspected that his father regarded him with accuracy, rather than with the indulgence that fathers habitually show to their only sons. But he went at it.

" Father, you'll have to speak to yon Melville girl."

Mr. Mactavish James did not raise his eyes, but enquired with the faintest threat of mockery, " What's she been doing to you, Philip ? "

" She's not been doing anything to me. What could she do ? But I've just seen her in Princes Street with yon fellow Yaverland, the client from Rio. They were coming out of the station and they took a cab."

" What for should they not ? "

" You can't have a typist prancing about with clients at this time of night."

" It's airly yet," said Mr. Mactavish James mildly, continuing to turn over the pages of the *Law Journal.* " We've not had our dinners yet. Though from the way the smell of victuals is roaring up the back stairs we shouldn't be long."

" Father, people were looking at them. They—they were holding hands." He forced himself to believe the lie. " You can't have her carrying on like that with clients. It'll give the office a bad name."

At last his father raised his eyes, which, though bleared with age, were still the windows of a sceptical soul, and let them fall. " Ellen is a good girl, Philip," he said.

The young man began a gesture of despair, which he restrained lest those inimical eyes should lift again. This was not a place, he well knew, where sentimental values held good, where the part of a young and unprotected girl would be taken against the son of the house out of any mawkish feeling that youth or weakness of womanhood deserved especial tenderness. It was the stronghold of his own views, its standards were his own. And even here it was insisted that Ellen was a person of value. There seemed nothing in the world that would give him any help in his urgent need to despise her, to think of her as dirt, to throw on her the onus of all the vileness that had happened to him. He broke out, " If she's a good girl she ought to behave as such ! You must speak to her, father. There'll be a scandal in the town ! "

Mr. Mactavish James seemed to have withdrawn his mind from the discussion, for he had taken out his appointment diary, which could surely have nothing to do with the case. But when

Mr. Philip had turned towards the door, the old man said, amiably enough, "Ay, I'll speak to Nelly. I'll speak to her on Monday afternoon. The morning I must be up at the Court of Session. But in the afternoon I'll give the girl a word."

It was on the tip of Mr. Philip's tongue to cry, "Thank you, father, thank you!" but he remembered that this was merely a matter of office discipline that was being settled, and no personal concern of his. So he said, "I think it would be wise, father," and went out of the room. He ran upstairs whistling. It would be a great come-down for her that had always been such a pet of his father's to be spoken to about her conduct. . . .

(2)

The door had swung ajar, so Mr. Mactavish James in his seat at his desk was able to look into the further room and keep an eye on Ellen, who was sitting with her back to him, supporting her bright head on her hand and staring fixedly down at something on the table. Her appearance entertained him, as it always did. He chuckled over the shapeless blue overall, just like a bairn's, that she wore on her neat wee figure, and the wild shining hair which resembled nothing so much as a tamarisk hedge in a high wind, though she would have barked like a terrier at anyone who suggested that it was not as neatly a done head as any in Edinburgh. But he was very anxious about her. For some moments now she had not moved, and this immobility was so unnatural in her that he knew she must be somehow deeply hurt, as one who sees a bird quite still knows that it is dead or dying. "Tuts, tuts," he sighed. "This must be looked to. She is the bonniest lassie that I've ever seen. Excepting Isabella Kingan." His right hand, which had been lying listlessly on the desk before him, palm upwards, turned over when he thought of Isabella Kingan. The fingers crooked, and it became an instrument of will, like the hand of a young man.

But he was really quite old, nearly seventy, and well on the way to lose the human obsession of the importance of humanity; so his attention began to note, as if they were not less significant than Ellen's agony, the motes that were dancing in the bar of pale autumn sunshine that lay athwart the room. "It is a queer thing," his mind droned on, "that when I came here when I was young I saw there was a peck of dust in every room, and I blamed old Mr. Logan for keeping on yon dirty old wife of a caretaker. I said to myself that when I was the master I would have it like a new pin and put a decent buddy in the basement. And now Mr. Logan is long dead, and the old wife is long dead, and I have had things my own way these many years, but the place is still foul as a lum, and I keep on yon slut of a Mrs. Powell. Ah well! Ah well!" He pondered, with a Scotch sort of enjoyment, on the frustration of youth's hopes and the progress of mortality in himself, until a movement of Ellen's bright head, such a jerk as might have been caused by a silent sob, brought his thoughts back to beauty and his small personal traffic with it.

"I do not know why she should mind me of Isabella Kingan. She is not like her. Isabella was black as a wee crow. It is just that they're both very bonny. I wonder what has happened to Isabella. She must be sixty-five. I saw her once in Glasgow, in Sauchiehall Street, after she was married, but she would not speak. Yet what else could I have done? I had my way to make, and it was known up and down the length of Edinburgh that her mother kept a sweetie shop in Leith Walk, and she had a cousin who was a policeman in the town. No, no, it would not have been a suitable marriage."

He moved restlessly in his chair, vexed by a sense of guilt, which although he immediately mitigated it into a suspicion that he might have behaved more wisely, made his memory maliciously busy opening doors which he had believed he had locked. But he was so expert in the gymnastic art of standing well with himself and the world that he could turn each recollected incident to a cause of self-approbation before he had begun to flush. For a few moments, using the idioms of Burns' love-lyrics, which were the only dignified and unobscene references to passion he had ever encountered, he thought of that night when he had persuaded little Isabella to linger in the fosse of shadow under the high wall in Canaan Lane and give up her mouth to his kisses, her tiny warm dove's body to his arms. Never in all the forty-five intervening years had he seen such a wall on such a night, its base in velvety darkness and its topmost half shining ghostly as plaster does in moonlight, without his hands remembering the queer pleasure it had been to crush crisp muslin, without his heart remembering the joy it had been to coax from primness its first consent to kisses. Before he could reproach himself for having turned that perfect hour into a shame to her who gave it by his later treachery, he began to reflect what a steady young fellow he had been to have known no other amorous incident in all his unmarried days than this innocent fondling on a summer's night.

But there pressed in on him the recollection of how she had dwined away when she realised that, though he had kissed her, he did not mean to marry her. He saw again the pale face she ever after wore; he remembered how, when he met her in the street, she used at first to droop her head and blush, until her will lifted her chin like a bearing-rein and she forced herself to a proud blank stare, while her small stature worked to make her crinoline an indignant spreading majesty behind her. Yet, after all, she was not the only person to be inconvenienced, for he had fashed himself a great deal over the business and had slept very badly for a time. He exhorted her reproachful ghost not to be selfish. Besides, she had somehow brought it on herself by looking what she did; for her dark eyes, very bright, yet with a kind of bloom on them, and her full though tiny underlip had always looked as if it would be very easy to make her cry, and she had had a preference for wearing grey and brown and such modest colours that made it plain she feared to be noticed. To display a capacity for pain so visibly was just to invite people to test it. If she had been a girl who could look after herself, doubtless she would have got him. He paid her the high compliment of wishing that she had, although he had done very well out of the marriages he had made, for his first wife, Annie Logan, had brought him his partnership in the firm, and his second, Christian Lawrie, had brought him a deal of money. But Isabella had been such a bonny wee thing.

His skin became alive again, and remembered the few responding kisses that he had wheedled from her, contacts so shy that they might have been the poisings of a moth. He shuddered, and said, " Ech ! Somebody's walking over my grave !" though, indeed, what had happened was that his youth had risen from its grave. He decided to be generous to Isabella and not bear her a grudge for causing him this revisiting heartache. With the softest pity that the lot of beauty in this world should be so hard, though quite without self-condemnation, he thought how very sure the poor girl must have been that he meant to marry her before she abandoned that proud physical reserve that was the protecting integument of her sensitive soul. That sensitiveness seemed fair ridiculous when things were going well with him ; but once or twice in his life, when he had been ill, it had appeared so dreadful that he had desired either to be young again and give a different twist to things, or to die utterly and know no after-life.

No, dealing unkindly with the lasses was an ill thing to do. It made one depressed afterwards even if it paid, just as cheating the widow and orphan did. His eyes went back to Ellen, who had moved again. " I must settle this business of Nelly's," he thought. " Of course, Philip is quite right. It would not be suitable. Besides, he is getting on nicely with Bob McLennan's girl, and that would be a capital match even for us. But I must put things straight for my Nelly, my poor wee Nelly." He rose, first feeling for his crutch, for he was fair dying on his legs with the gout, and padded slowly towards the open door.

And at the sound of that soft bearish tread Ellen felt as if she were going to die. There had arrived at last that moment for which she had waited with an increasing faintness all that day, since the moment when Mr. Philip had caught her in front of the mantelpiece mirror. She had gone to look at herself out of curiosity, to see whether she had in any way been changed by the extraordinary emotions that had lately visited her. For she had spent two horrible nights of hatred for Yaverland. She had begun to hate him quite suddenly when he brought her home to say good-night to her mother. There had broken out the usual tumult in the dancing-hall, and he had raised his head with an intent delighted look that at first she watched happily, because she loved to see his face, which too often wore gravity like a dark mask, grow brilliant with interest. But he quickly deleted that expression and shot a furtive glance at her, as if he feared she might have overheard his thoughts, and she saw that he was anxious that she should not share some imagination that had given him pleasure.

She went and sat on a low stool by the fire, turning her face away from him. So he was as little friendly as the rest of the world. Surely it was plain enough that she lived in the extremity of destitution. The only place that was hers was this drab little room with the shaking walls and peeling chairs: the only person that belonged to her was her mother, who was very dear but very old and grieving; and though everybody else on earth seemed to have acquired a paradise on easy terms, nobody would let her look in at theirs. It appeared that he was just like the others. She folded her arms across her breast to compress her swelling misery, while he sat there, cruelly not hurrying, and said courteous things that afterwards repeated themselves in her ear all night, each time a little louder, till by the dawn they had become ringing proclamations of indifference.

Yaverland had turned on the doorstep as he left and told her that, though he believed he had to motor-cycle to Glasgow the next day to see one of his directors there, it was just possible there might be a telephone message at his hotel telling him he need not do so ; and he had asked that if this were so might he spend the time with her instead. Because of this she had lived all Sunday in the dread of his coming. Yet very often she found herself arrested in the midst of some homely action, letting some tap run on to inordinate splashings, some pot boil to an explosion of flavoured fumes, because she was brooding with an infatuated smile on his rich colours and rich ways, on the slouch by which he dissembled the strength of his body, the slow speech by which he dissembled the violence of his soul. But there returned at once her hatred of him, and she would long to lay her hand in his confidingly as if in friendship, and then drive her nails suddenly into his flesh, so that she would make a fool of him as well as hurt him. At that she would draw her cold hands across her hot brow, and wonder why she should think so malignantly of one who had been so kind—so much kinder than anybody else had ever been to her, although she had no claim upon him. Yet she knew that no argument could alter the fixed opinion of her spirit that Yaverland's kingly progress through the world, which a short time ago she had watched with such a singing of the veins as she knew when she saw lightning, was an insult to her lesser height, her contemned sex, her obscurity. The chaos in herself amazed her. The glass showed her that she was very pale, and she wondered if such pallor was a sign of madness. " I will not go daft ! " she whimpered, and began rubbing her cheeks with her knuckles to bring back the colour ; and saw among the quiet reflected things the queer face, its features pulled every way with derision, of Mr. Philip.

He said twangingly, " Ten minutes past nine, Miss Melville ! "

Her heart was bursting with the thought of what made-up tales of vanity he would spin from this. " Later than that. Later than that," she told him wildly. " And I have been here since dear knows when, and there is nobody ready to give me work."

He shot out a finger. " What's that by your machine ? "

She noticed that his finger was shaking, and that he too was very pale, and she forgot to feel rage or anything but immeasurable despair that she should have to live in this world where everyone was either inscrutably cruel or mad. She murmured levelly, dreamily, " Why, papers that you have just put down. I will type them at once. I will type them at once."

For a time he stood behind her at the hearth, breathing

snortingly, and at times seeming to laugh ; said in a half-voice, " A fire fit to roast an ox ! " and for a space was busy moving lumps of coal down into the grate. A silence followed before he came to the other side of her table and said, " Stop that noise. I want to speak to you." The gesture was rude, but it was picoteed with a faint edge of pitifulness. The way he put his hand to his head suggested that he was in pain, so she shifted her hands from the keys and looked up vigilantly, prepared to be kind if he had need of it, for of course people in pain did not know what they were doing. But since there was no sense in letting people think they could just bite one's head off and nothing to pay, she said with spirit, " But it's ten minutes past nine, and what's this by my machine ? "

Mr. Philip bowed his head with an air of meekness ; he seemed to sway under the burden of his extreme humility, to be feeling sick under the strain of his extreme forbearance. He went on in a voice which implied that he was forgiving her freely for an orgy of impertinence. " Will you please take a note, Miss Melville, that Mr. Mactavish James wants to speak to you this afternoon ? "

" He usually does," replied Ellen.

" Ah, but this is a special occasion," said Mr. Philip, with so genial an expression that she stared up at him, her eyebrows knit and her mouth puckering back a smile, her deep hopeful prepossession, which she held in common with all young people, that things really happened prettily, making her ready to believe that it was all a mistake and he was about to announce a treat or a promotion. And he, reading this ridiculous sign of youth, bent over her, prolonging his kind beam and her response to it, so that afterwards, when he undeceived her, there should be no doubt at all that she had worn that silly air of expecting something nice to be given to her, and no doubt that he had seen and understood and jeered at it. Then the wave of his malice broke and soused her. " Things have come to a head, Miss Melville ! There's been a client complaining ! "

She drew herself up. " A client complaining ! " she cried, and he hated her still more, for she had again eluded him. She had forgotten him and the trap he had laid to make a fool of her in her suspicion that someone had dared to question her efficiency. " Well, what's that to do with me ? Whoever's been complaining—and no doubt if your clients once began at that game they wouldn't need to stop between now and the one o'clock gun—it's not likely I'm among his troubles. So far as my work goes I'm practically infallible."

"It's not your work that's been spoken of," said Mr. Philip, laughing. "Perhaps we might call it your play."

He had begun to speak, as he always did when they were alone, in a thick whisper, as if they were doing something unlawful together. He had drawn near to her, as he always did, and was hunching his shoulders and making wriggling recessive movements such as a man might make who stood in darkness among moving pollutions. But his glee had gone. It had grown indeed to a grey effervescence that set a tremor working over his features, made him speak in shaken phrases, and unsteadied everything about him except the gloating stare which he bent on her bowed head because he was eager to see her face, which surely would look plain with all her colour gone. "There's just a limit to everything, Miss Melville, a limit to everything. You seem to have come to it. Ay, long ago, I have been thinking ! You'd better know at once that you were seen late on Saturday night, hanging about with a man. It sounded like yon chemist chap from the description. You were seen entering a cab and driving away. I won't tell you "—he stepped backwards, swelled a little, and became the respectable man who has to hem a dry embarrassed cough before he speaks of evil —" what the client made of it all." And then he bent again in that contracted, loathing attitude, as if they were standing in an unspacious sewer and she had led him there, and with that viscous sibilance he said many things which she could not fully understand, but which seemed to mean that under decent life there was an oozy mud and she had somehow wallowed in it. "But doubtless you'll be able to give a satisfactory explanation of the incident," he finished ; and as she continued to bow her head, so that he could not see the effects of this misery which he had so adroitly thrust upon her, he leant over her crying out he hardly knew what, save that they were persecuting things.

But when she slowly raised her chin he saw with rage that though he had spoilt the colour of her skin with fear, and made her break up the serene pattern of her features with twitching efforts to hold back her tears, he had not been able to destroy the secondary meaning of her face. It had ceased to be pretty ; it no longer offered lovely untroubled surfaces to the lips. But it still proclaimed that she was indubitably precious as a diamond is indubitably hard ; it still calmly declared that if evil had come out of his meeting with her it had been contrived out of innocence by some dark alchemy of his own soul ; it still moved him to a madness of unprofitable loyalty and tenderness. In every way he was defeated. It seemed now the least of his miseries that he had failed to destroy his father's persuasion that Ellen was a person of value, for it was so much worse, it opened the door to so long a procession of noble and undesired desires, that he had not been able to destroy. That same persuasion in himself. He counted it a fresh grievance against her, and planned to pay it out with cruelty, that she had made him waste all his efforts. For though he had certainly made her cry, he could not count that any great triumph, since under the shower of her weeping her gaiety was dancing like a draggled elf. " Och me ! " she was saying. " You want me to give you an explanation ? But when I've got an appointment to talk the matter over with the head of the firrm, what for would I waste my time talking it over with the junior partner ? " And she began to type as if she was playing a jig.

He made a furious movement of the hands. She thought contemptuously, " The wee thing he is ! Even if he struck me I should not be afraid. Now, if it were Yaverland, I should be terrified. . . ." The idea struck through her like a pleasure, until there fell upon her as the completion of a misery that had seemed complete, like the last extreme darkness which falls on a dark night when the last star is found by the clouds, the recollection that Yaverland also was detestable. Ah, this was a piece of foolishness between Mr. Philip and herself. In a world where misery was the prevailing climate, where there were men like Yaverland, who could effortlessly deal out pain right and left by simply being themselves, it was so foolish that one who had surely had a natural turn for being nice, who had been so very nice that firelit evening when they had talked secrets, should put himself about to hurt her. Her eyes followed him imploringly as he went towards the door, and she cried out silently to him, begging him to be kind. But when he turned and looked over his shoulder she remembered his tyranny, and hardened her piteous gaze into a stare of loathing. It added to her sense of living in a deep cell of madness, fathoms below the rays of reason, that she had an illusion that in his eyes she saw just that same change from piteousness to loathing. For of course it could not be so.

Her quivering lips said gallantly to the banged door : " Well, there is my wurrk. I will forget my petty pairsonal troubles in my wurrk, just as men do ! " And she typed away, squeezing out such drops of pride of craftsmanship as can be found in that mechanical exercise, making no mistakes, and ending the lines so that they built up a well-proportioned page, so intently that she had almost finished before she noticed that it was funny stuff about a divorce such as Mr. Mactavish James always gave to one of the male clerks to copy. But that was all the work she had to do that morning, for Mr. Mactavish James was up at the Court of Session and Mr. Philip did not send for her. She was obliged to sit in her idleness as in a bare cell, with nothing to look at but her misery, which continued to spin like a top, moving perpetually without getting any further or changing into anything else. Presently she went and knelt in the window-seat, drawing patterns on the glass and looking up the side-street at the Castle Rock, which now glowed with a dark pyritic lustre under the queer autumn day of bright south sunshine and scudding bruise-coloured clouds, seeing the familiar scene strangely, through a lens of tears. She fell to thinking out peppered phrases to say of the client who had told on her. Surely she had as much right in Princes Street as he had ? And if it was too late for her to be there, then it was too late for him also. " It's just a case of one law for the man and another for the woman. Och, votes for women ! " she cried savagely, and flogged the window with the blindcord. Ten to one it was yon Mr. Grieve, the minister of West Braeburn, who fairly blew in your face with waggishness when you offered him a chair in the waiting-room, and tee-heed that " a lawyer's office must be a dull place for a young leddy like you ! " Well, she knew what Mr. Mactavish James thought of him for his dealings with his wife's money. . . .

But the peppered phrases would not come. One cannot do more than one thing at a time fairly well, and she was certainly crying magnificently. " Such a steady downpour I never did see since that week mother and I spent at Oban," she thought into her sodden handkerchief. " It was a shame the way it rained all the time, when we had had to save for months to pay for the trip. But life is like that. . . ." Ah, what did they think she had been doing with that man Yaverland ? The shocked dipping undertones of Mr. Philip's voice, the ashamed heat of his eyes, were just the same as grown-up people used when they told mother why they had had to turn the maid away, and that, so far as she could make out, though they always spoke softly so that she could not hear, was because the maid had let somebody kiss her. What was the use of having been a quiet decent girl all her days, of never stopping when students spoke to her, of never wearing emerald green, though the colour went fine with her hair, when people were ready to

believe this awful thing of her ? They must be mad not to
see that she would rather die than let any man on earth touch
her in any way, and least of all Yaverland, whom she hated.
There came before her eyes the memory of that bluish bloom on
his lips and jaw which she had noticed the first time she saw
him, and she rocked herself to and fro in a passion of tears at
the thought she was suspected of close contact with this loathsome maleness. She felt as if there was buried in her bosom a
harp with many strings, and each string was snapping separately.
   " Och, votes for women ! " she said wearily ; and tried to
make herself remember that after all there were some unstained,
noble things in the world by singing whisperingly a verse from
the Women's Marseillaise. " There's many singing that song
to-day in prison that would be glad to sit and breathe fresh air
and look at a fine view as you're doing, so you ought to be
thankful ! " And indeed the view of the Castle did just for
that moment distract her from the business of weeping, for
there had been a certain violent alteration of the weather.
The autumn sunshine, which had never been more than a sarcasm
on the part of a thoroughly unpleasant day, had failed altogether,
and Edinburgh had become a series of corridors through which
there rushed a trampling wind. It set the dead leaves rising
from the pavement in an exasperated, seditious way, and let
them ride dispersedly through the eddying air far above the
heads of the clambering figures that, up and down the side-
street, stood arrested and, it seemed, flattened, as if they had
been spatchcocked by the advancing wind and found great
difficulty in folding themselves up again. She looked at their
struggles with contempt. They were funny wee men. They
were not like Yaverland. Now, he was a fine man. She thought
proudly of the enormousness of his chest and shoulders, and
imagined the tremendous thudding thing the heartbeat must
be that infused with blood such hugeness. He must be one of
the most glorious men who ever lived. It surely was not often
that a man was perfect in every way physically and mentally.
   She turned away and hid her face against the shutters,
weeping bitterly. But her mind had to follow him in a kind of
dream, as he walked on, masterfully, as one who knows he has the
right to come and go, out of that wet grey street of which she was a
part, to wander as he chose in strange continents, in exotic
weathers, through time sequined with extravagant dawns and
sunsets, through space jewelled with towns running red with
blood of revolutions or multi-coloured with carnival. In every
way he was richer than she was, for he had more joy in travelling

than she would have had, since over the scenic world she saw there was cast for him a nexus of romance which she could not have perceived.

Everywhere he would meet men whom he had captained on desperate adventures, who over wine would point ringed fingers at mountain ranges and whisper of forgotten mines and tempt him to adventures that would take him away from her for ever so long. Everywhere he would meet women, hateful feminine women of the sort who are opposed to Woman Suffrage, who, because of some past courtesy of his, would throw him roses and try to make him watch their dancing feet. She sobbed with rage as she perceived how different from her the possession of this past made him. When he reached Rio he would not stand by the quiet bay as she would have stood, enraptured by the several noble darknesses of the sky, the mountains, and the ship-starred sea, but would go quickly to his house on the hill, not hurrying, but showing by a lightness in his walk, by a furtive vivacity of his body, that he was involved in some private system of exciting memories. He would open the wrought-iron gates with a key which she had not known he possessed, which had lain close to him in one of those innumerable pockets that men have in their clothes. With perfect knowledge of the path, he would step silently through the garden, where flowers run wild had lost their delicacy and grew as monstrous candelabra of coarsened blooms in soil greenly feculent with weeds ; she rejoiced in its devastation. He would enter the hall and pick his steps between the pools of wine that lay black on the marble floor; he would tread on the rosettes of corruption that had once been garlands of roses hung about the bronze whale's neck; he would look down on the white limbs of the shattered Venus, and look up and listen to the creaking flight of the birds of prey that were nesting under the broken roof ; and he would smile as if he shared a secret with the ruin and dissipation. His smile was the sun, but in it there was always a dark ray of secrecy. All his experience was a mockery of her inexperience. Her clenched fist beat her brow, which had become hot. . . .

All that day her mind had painfully enacted such fantasies of hatred or had waited blankly for this moment which the old man's shuffling step was now bringing towards her. She braced herself, though she did not look up from the table.

"Nelly, I've brought you a bit rock from Ferguson's."

She gazed cannily at the white paper parcel. It was the

largest box he had ever given her ; he always gave her sweeties when Mr. Philip had been talking against her. Ought she therefore to deduce from the unusual size that he had been saying something unusually cruel ? But, on the other hand, surely no one could ever give sweeties to a girl if they thought she had let herself be kissed. " You're just too kind, Mr. James," she said mournfully.

" Take out a stick and give me one. What for did I have false teeth put in at great expense if it was not that I might eat rock with my Nelly ? I'll take a bit of the peppermint. My wife is a leddy and will not let me eat peppermint in my ain hoose." He always spoke to Ellen, he did not know why, in the same rough, soft, broad Scots tongue that he had talked with his mother and father when he was a wee boy in the carter's cottage on the Lang Whang of the Old Lanark Road, that he still talked to his cat in his little study at the back of his square, decent residence. " Ay, that's right. But lassie, what ails ye ? You're looking at the box as though you'd taken a turn at the genteel and become an Episcopalian and it was Lent. If you've lost that fine sweet tooth of yours ye must be sickening for something."

" Och, me. I'm all right," said Ellen drearily, and picked a ginger stick, and bit it joylessly ; and laid it down again, and pressed her hand to her heart. She hearkened to the racing beat of her agony with eyes grown remote and lips drawn down at the corner with disgust, like a woman feeling the movements of an unwanted child. And Mr. Mactavish James was so wrung with pity for the wee thing, and the mature dignity with which she wore her misery, and the next moment so glowing with pleasure at himself for this generous emotion, that he beamed on her and purred silently, " Ech, the poor bairn ! I will go straight to the point and make her mind easy." He wriggled into an easier position in his chair, readjusted his glasses, and settled down to enjoy this pleasant occupation of lifting the lid off her distress, stirring it up, and distilling from it and the drying juices of his heart more of this creditable pity.

" Nelly," he said jocosely, " I've been hearing tales about you."

She answered, " I know it. Mr. Philip has told me."

" Ay, I thought he would," said Mr. Mactavish James comfortably. He could also make a pretty good guess at the temper his son Philip had put into the telling. For he was an old man, and knew that a young man in love may not be the quiet, religious lover pondering how a minute's kissing under the moon can

sanctify all the next day's daylight that the poets describe
him.   He may be inflamed out of youth's semblance by jealousy,
and decide that since he has no claws to tear the female flesh
as it deserves, he will do what he can with cruel words and
treachery.   It is just luck, the kind of man one happens to be
born.   Well, it was just luck. . . .

" He's tremendous excited about seeing you and Mr. Yaverland, Nelly."

Her eyes were blue fire.   " Och, 'twas him that saw me !
He said it was a client."

He covered his mouth with his hand, but decided to give his
son away.   All his life he had been rejecting the claims of
beauty and gentle things, and he could be sure that his well-
brought-up family would go on doing it after he was in his
grave.   Over this one little point, which did not really matter,
he could afford to be handsome.   " Aye, 'twas Mr. Philip that
saw you," he owned easily, and swerved his head before the
long look, pansy-soft with gratitude, that she now turned on him.
The girl was so inveterately inclined to dilate on the pleasant
things of life that his generosity in admitting that his son was a
liar, and thus assuring her that her shame had not been as
public as she had supposed, quite wiped out all her other emotions.   She fairly glowed about it ;   and at that the old man
felt curiously ashamed, as if he had gained a child's prattling
thanks by giving it a bad sixpence, although he could not see
what he had done that was not all right.   He rubbed his hands
and tried to kindle a jollity by crying, " Well, what would I do
but tell you ?   If I hadn't, ye'd have been running about distribut-
ing black eyes among my clients just on suspicion, ye fierce wee
randy ! "

" Och, you make fun of me—— ! " She smiled, palely, and
gnawed the ginger stick, her jaw being so impeded by her
desire to cry that she could not bite it.

" Poor bairn !   Poor bairn ! " he sighed, and his pity for the
little thing seemed to him so moving, so completely in the vein
of the best Scottish pathos, that he continued to gaze at her
and enjoy his own emotion, until a wryness of her mouth made
him fear that unless he hurried up and got to the point she
would rush from the room and leave him without this delicious
occupation.   So he went on, speaking cosily.   " I thought little
of it.   You are a good lassie, Nelly, and I can trust you.   I
know that fine.   Sometimes I think it is a great peety that
Philip was not born a wee girl, for he would have grown up
into a fine maiden aunt.   He is that particular about his sisters

you would not believe. Though losh ! he has no call for anxiety, for they're none of them bonny."

Ellen was pulling herself together, trying to take his lack of censure as a matter of course and choking back the tears of relief. " I'd not say that," she said in a strangled voice. " Miss Chrissie isn't so bad, though with those teeth I think she would be wiser to avoid looking arch. Och, Mr. James, what's come to you ? " For he was rolling with a great groundswell of merriment, and slapping his thigh and chuckling. " The things the simplest woman can say ! No need for practice in boodwars and draring-rooms ! It comes natural ! " She looked at him with wrinkled brows and smiling mouth, sure that he was not being unkind, but wondering why he laughed, and murmured, " Mr. James, Mr. James ! " It flashed on her suddenly what he meant, and she jumped up from her seat and cried through exasperated laughter, " Och, men are mean things ! I see what's in your mind ! But indeed I did not intend to be catty ! You must admit, though she's your own daughter, that Miss Chrissie's teeth are on the long side ! That's all I meant. Och, Mr. James, I wish you would not be such a tease ! " However, he continued to laugh bellyingly, and she started to run round the table as if to assail him with childish tuggings and shakings, but to leave her hands free she popped the ginger stick into her mouth like a cigarette, and was immediately distracted to gravity by important considerations. " What am I doing, eating ginger when I hate the stuff ? I'll nip off the end I've been at and put it back for mother. She just loves it, dear knows why, the nasty hot thing. I'll have one of the pink ones. They've no great flavour, but I like the colour. . . ."

While she bent over the box, her mind and fingers busy among the layers, the old man turned his bleared eyes upon her and wondered at her, and rejoiced in her variousness as he had not thought he would rejoice over a useless thing. For she had altered utterly in the last few seconds. When he had come into the room she had been a tiny cowering thing of soft piteous gazes and miserable silences, like a sick puppy, too sick to whimper ; now she was almost soulless in her beauty and well-being, and as little a matter for pity as a daffodil in sunshine. She was completely, absorbedly young and greedy and happy. The fear that life was really horrid had obscured her bright colours like a cobweb, but now she was radiant again ; it was as if a wind had blown through her hair, which always changed with her moods as a cat's coat changes with the weather, and had been lank since morning. He was not used to variable women. His two wives, Aggie and Christian, had always looked much the same. He remembered that when he went in to see Aggie as she lay in her coffin he had examined her face very carefully because he had heard that people's faces altered when they were dead and fell into expressions that revealed the truth about their inner lives ; but she did not seem to have changed at all, and was still looking sensible.

To keep the situation moving he drawled teasingly, " Och, you women, you women ! Born with the tongues of cats you are, every one of ye, and with the advawnce of ceevilisation ye're developing the claws ! There was a fine piece in the *Scotsman* this morning about one of your Suffragettes standing on the roof of a town hall and behaving as a wild cat would think shame to, skirling at Mr. Asquith through a skylight and throwing slates at the polis that came to fetch her. Aw, verra nice, verra ladylike, I'm sure."

" Well, why shouldn't she ? Yon miserable Asquith—— "

" Asquith's not miserable. He's a good man. He's an Englishman, but he sits for Fife."

" Anyway, it was Charlotte Marsh that did it. And if she's not a lady, who is ? Her photograph's given away with this week's *Votes for Women*. She's a beautiful girl."

" I doubt it, Nelly."

" I'll bring the photo then ! "

" Beautiful girls get married," said Mr. Mactavish James guilefully, watching for her temper to send up rockets. " What for is she not married if she is so beautiful ? "

" Because she's more particular than your wife was ! " barked Ellen, admitting reluctantly as he gasped and chuckled, " Yon's not my own. I heard Mary Gawthorpe say that at an open-air meeting. She is a wonder, yon wee thing. She has such a power of repartee that the interrupters have to be carried out on stretchers."

" Ah, ye're all impudent wee besoms thegither," said Mr. Mactavish James, and set his eyes wide on her face. From something throbbing in her speech he hoped that the spring of her distress had not yet run dry.

" Why are you not more respectful to the Suffragettes ? You're polite enough to the Covenanters, and yet they fought and killed people, while we haven't killed even a policeman, though there's a constable in the Grange district whose jugular vein I would like fine to sever with my teeth for what he said to me when I was chalking pavements. If you don't admire us you shouldn't admire the Covenanters."

"The Covenanters were fighting for religion," he murmured, keeping his eyes on her face.

"So's this religion, and it's of some practical use, moreover," she answered listlessly. She drew her hands down her face, threw up her arms, and breathed a fatigued, shuddering sigh. The conversation had begun to seem to her intolerably insipid because they were not talking of Yaverland.

She rose to her feet, moved distractedly about the room, and then, with a purposefulness that put into his stare that terrified cold enmity with which the sane look upon even the beloved mad, she swept two rulers off her desk on to the floor. But she knelt down and set them cross-wise, and then straightened herself and crooked her arms above her head, and began to dance a sword-dance. Even her filial relations to him hardly justified such a puncture of office discipline, and he sat blowing at it until he saw that this was a new phase of her so entertaining misery. It is always absurd when that pert and ferocious dance, invented by an unsensuous race inordinately and mistakenly vain of its knees, is performed by a graceful girl; and Ellen added to that incongruity by dancing languorously, passionately. It was like hearing the wrong words sung to a familiar tune. And her face was at discord with both the dance and her performance of it, for she was fixedly regarding someone who was not there. "She is fey!" he thought tolerantly, and gloated over this fresh display of her unhappiness and his pity, though a corner of his mind was busy hoping that Mr. Morrison would not come in. It was unusual in Edinburgh for a solicitor (at any rate in a sound firm) to sit and watch his typist dancing.

But soon she stopped dancing. Her need to speak of Yaverland took away her breath.

She slouched across the room to the window, laid her cheek to the glass, and said rapidly, "It is bad weather. It is bad weather here an awful lot of the time. Mr. Yaverland says there is a place in Peru where it is always spring. That would be bonny." She felt relieved and warmed as soon as she had mentioned his name, and sat down easily in the window-seat and smiled back at the old man.

"Ehem! So this Mr. Yaverland has surveyed mankind from China to Peru, as the great Dr. Johnson says."

But she could not speak of Yaverland again so soon. She tried to make time by wrangling. "Why do you call him the great Dr. Johnson? He was just a rude old thing."

"He was a man of sense, lassie, a man of sense."

"What's sense?" she cried, and flung wide her arms. Her

body pricked with a general emotion that was not relevant to the words she spoke, and indeed she was not quite aware what those were. "Sense isn't sitting in your chair all day and ruining the coats of your—of your digestion drinking too much tea and contradicting everybody and being rude to Mrs. Thrale when the poor body married again."

"It was a fule's marriage," said Mr. Mactavish James; "the widow of a substantial man taking up wi' an Italian fiddler."

"Marriage with one man's no worse than marriage with another, the way they all are," said Ellen darkly, and got back to her argument. "And hating the Scotch and democracy, and saying blunt foolish things as if they were blunt wise ones— that's not sense. And if it were, what's the good of living to be sensible ? It's like living to have five fingers on your hand. And life's so short ! Mr. James, does it never worry you dreadfully that life is so short ? I wonder how we all bear up about it. One ought to live for adventure. I want to go away, right away. There are such lots of lovely places where there are palms, and people get romantically shot, and there's a town somewhere where poppies grow on the roofs of mosques. I would like to see that. And queer people—masked Touaregs——"

"Lassie, you are blethering," said Mr. Mactavish James, "this is a pairfect salad of foreign pairts."

It had to come out. "Mr. Yaverland says Peru is lovely. He has been both sides of the Andes. He liked Peru. There are silver mines at Iquique and etairnal spring at the place whose name I have forgotten. Funny that I should forget the name of the one place on airth where there is eternal spring ! If I had all the money in the world I would not be able to go there because I have forgotten its name !" She laughed sobbingly, and went on. "And he's been in Brazil. He lived for a time in Rio de Janeiro." She stared fixedly at her mental image of the fateful house where there was a broken statue on a bier, shook herself, and went on. "And he's travelled in the forest. He's seen streams covered with the big leaves of Victoria Regia like they have it in the Botanical Gardens, and egrets standing on the bank, and better there than in ladies' hats. I wonder if I would be a fool if I had the money ?—if I would wear dead things on my head ? But indeed there are ways I think I would always be nice, however rich I was—ways that don't affect me very much, so that they're no sacrifice. And he's seen lots of things. Sloths, which I always thought were just metaphors. And ant-eaters, and alligators, and jaguars. And——"

"If you go to London," said Mr. Mactavish James, "you'll be losing your heart to a keeper at the Zoo."

"Who's losing their heart to anybody?" she asked peevishly. "And you needn't sneer. He's done lots else besides just seeing animals. Once he steered a ship in the South Seas for two days and two nights when the crew were down with the New Guinea fever. And another time he was working at a mine in Andalusia. The miners went on strike. He and some other men put up barricades and took guns. They defended the place. He is the first man I have ever known who did such things. And they come natural to him. He thinks no more of them than your son," she said nastily, "thinks of playing a round on the Gullane links."

"Imphm. I wonder what he's been doing traiking about like this. Rolling stones gather no moss, I've heard."

Her eyes blazed, then narrowed. "Oh, make no mistake! He earns a lot of money. He can beat you even at your own game."

Mr. Mactavish James tee-heed, but did not like it, for she was looking round the room as if it were a hated prison and all that was done in it contemptible; and these things were his life. "Well, you know best. And what's this paragon like? I've not seen the fellow."

"He's a lovely pairson," she said sullenly.

He began to loathe these two young people, who were all that he and his stock could not be, who were going to do the things his age could not do. "Ah, well! Ah, well!" he sighed, with a spurious shrewd melancholy. "He'll be like me when he's old, Ellen; all old men are alike."

She looked at him coldly and said, "He will not."

Her brows were heavy and the hand she held at her bosom was clenched. The rain was beating on the window-panes. The fire seemed diluted by the day's dampness; and there was a chill spreading through his mind as if they had been debating fundamental things and the argument had turned unanswerably to his disadvantage. He twisted in his seat and looked sharply at her, and though the mirror of his mind was apt to tilt away from the disagreeable, he perceived that she was regarding him and the prudent destiny he had chosen with a scorn more unappeasable than any appetite; and that the destiny she was choosing with this snarling intensity was so glorious that it justified her scorn. He felt a conviction, which had the vague quality of melancholy, that he was morally insolvent, and a suspicion, which had the acute quality of pain, that his financial solvency was not such a great thing after all. For Ellen looked like an angry queen as well as an angry angel. It seemed possible that these young people were not only going to have a mansion in heaven, but would have a large house on earth as well, and these two establishments made his single establishment in Moray Place seem not so satisfactory as he had always thought it. These people were going to take their fill of beauty and delight and all the unchafferable things he had denied himself that he might pursue success, and they were going to take their fill of success too! It was not fair. He thought of their good fortune in being born strong and triumphant as if it were a piece of rapacity, and tried to wriggle out of this moment which compelled him to regard them with respect by reversing the intentional, enjoyed purity of relationship with her and finding a lewd amusement in the fierceness which was so plainly an aspect of desire. But that meant moving outside the orbit of dignity; and he knew that when a man does that he gives himself for ever into the hands of those who behold him. So he worked back to the position of the rich, kind old man stooping to protect the little helpless working-girl.

He pushed the box of sweets across the table, and said in a tender and offended voice, " You're not eating your sweets, Nelly. I hoped to give you pleasure when I bought them."

One would always get her that way.

Someone was being hurt. Immediately she had the soft breast of the dove. " Oh, Mr. James! "

" I wish I could give you more pleasure," he went on. " But there! I've been able to do little enough for you. Well do I know it."

" You've done a lot for me. You've been so good."

" It's a pity we should have fallen out over a stranger. But I know I am too free with my tongue."

" Oh, Mr. James! "

" Never mind, lassie. I'm only an old man, and you're young; you must go your own way—— "

" Oh, Mr. James! " She rose and ran round the table to his side; and at the close sight of her, excited and yet muted with pity, brilliant as sunset but soft as light rain, the honest thing in him forgot the spurious scene he was carpentering. He exclaimed solemnly, " Nelly, you are very beautiful."

She was startled. " Me, beautiful? "

" Aye," he said, " beautiful."

For a moment she pondered over it almost stupidly. Then she put her hand on Mr. James's shoulder and shook him ; now that her sexual feelings were focussed on one man she treated all other men with a sexless familiarity that to those who did not understand might have seemed shameless and a little mad. " Am I beautiful ? " she asked searchingly.

" How many times do you want me to say it ? " he said.

" But how beautiful ? " she pursued. " Like a picture in the National Gallery ? Or like one of those actresses ? Now, isn't that a queer thing ? I'm all for art as a general thing, but I'd much rather be like an actress. Tell me, which am I like ? "

" You're like both. That's where you score."

She caught her breath with a sob. " You're not laughing at me ? "

" Get up on your chair and look in the glass over the mantel-piece."

She stepped up, and with a flush and a raising of the chin as if she were doing something much more radical than looking in a mirror, as if, indeed, she were stripping herself quite naked, she faced her image.

" You've never looked at yourself before," said the old man.

" 'Deed I have," she snapped. " How do you think I put my hat on straight ? "

" It never is," he retorted, and repeated grimly and exultingly, " You've never looked at yourself before."

She looked obliquely at her reflection and ran her hands ashamedly up and down her body, and tried for a word and failed.

" Are you not beautiful ? " he said.

" Imphm. There's no denying I'm effective," she admitted tartly, and stepped down and stood for a moment shivering as if she had done something distasteful. And then climbed on to the chair again. " In evening dress, like the one Sarah Bernhardt wore in La Dame aux Camélias, I dare say I could look all right with a fan—a big fan of ostrich feathers." This time she faced the image directly and almost gloatingly, as if it were food. " But considering my circumstances, that is a wild hypothesis. I suppose . . . I . . . am . . . all right. But I suppose I'm just good-looking for a private person. I'd look the plainest of the plain beside Zena or Phyllis Dare. Would I not ? Would I not ? "

" You'd look plain beside no one but Venus," said Mr. Mactavish James, " and her you'd better with your tongue."

" Ah ! " She breathed deeply, as if at last she drank. " So it doesn't matter my chin being so wee ? I've always hankered after a chin like Carson's. I think it makes one looked up to, irrespective of one's merits. But if what you say is true I've no call to worry. I'll do as I am." She shot an intense scowling glance at the old man. "You're sure I'll do?"

"Ay, lass, you'll do," he answered gravely.

She burst into a light peal of laughter, as different from her usual mirth as if she had been changed from gold to silver. "Oh dear! Oh dear!" she cried, her voice suddenly high-pitched and femininely gay. "What nonsense we're talking! Do—for what? It's all pairfectly ridiculous—as if looks mattered one way or another!" An animation of so physical a nature had come on her that her heart was beating almost too quickly for speech, and her body, being uncontrolled by her spirit, abandoned itself to entirely uncharacteristic gestures which were but abstract designs drawn by her womanhood. She lifted her face towards the mirror and pouted her lips mockingly, as if she knew that some spirit buried in its glassy depths desired to kiss them and could not. She stood on her toes on the hard wooden seat, so that it looked as if she were wearing high heels, and her hands, which were less like paws than they had ever been before, because she was holding them with consciousness of her fingers' extreme length, took the skirt of her frock and pulled it into panniers. She wished that she were clad in silk! But that lent no wistfulness to her face, which now glittered with a solemn and joyful rapacity, for her unconscious being had divined that there were before her many victories to be gained wholly without sweat of the will. "Ah!" she sighed, and wondered at her over-contentment; and then went on with her delicate shrill chatter, glowing and holding herself with a fine frivolity that made it seem almost as if she were clad in silk, and passing from flowerlike loveliness to loveliness.

"It's a pity Mr. Yaverland cannot see you now," said the old man, half from honest jocosity and half from an itch to bring the creature back to this interesting suffering of hers.

Gasping with laughter, though she kept her eyes gravely and steadily on her beauty, she answered, "Yes, it is a pity! It is a great pity! He's very handsome too, you know. We'd make a bonny pair! Oh dear, oh dear!"

Mr. James sat up. "What's that? What is it you're saying? Hec, you're talking of making a pair, are you?" Amusement always made his voice sound gross. "Has he asked you to marry him then, ye shy wee besom?"

She swung round on her toes, her face magic with passion and mischief. "Give me time, Mr. James, give me time!" she cried, and her head fell back on her long white throat, while her laughter jetted in shaking, shy, thin gusts like a blackbird's song. And then she ceased. Her head fell forward. Her gown dropped from her outstretched hands, which she pressed against her bosom. A second past she had filled with spring this office damp with autumn ; now she made it more asperous and grey than had November, for her season had changed to the extremest winter. She pressed her hands so hard against her breast and in a voice weak as if she were very cold she said, " Oh, God ! Oh, God ! "

" Eh ! " gaped Mr. James.

She had made a fool of herself. She had said dreadful things. She had boasted about something that could not come true, that would be horrible if it did. Her face became chalk white with such agony as only the young can feel.

Mr. James's gouty leg crackled out pains as he tried to rise, and he had to sink back in his chair and look up at her through the vibrating silence, whispering, " Nelly, my dear lass."

At that she shot at him such a cold sidelong glance as one might shoot at a stranger who has let one know that he has overheard an intimacy, and with movements at once clumsy and precise she got down from her chair and put it back at the table. She stood quite still, with her hands resting on it, her face assuming a mean and shrewish expression. She was remembering a woman who had been rude to her mother, a schoolfellow of Mrs. Melville's, who had married as well as she had married badly, and had allowed consciousness of that fact to colour her manner when they had run against each other in Princes Street. Ellen was trying to imitate the expression by which this bourgeoise had given her mother to understand that the interview need not long be continued. She caught it, she thought, but it did not really help. There was still this pressure of a flood of tears behind her eyes. She looked out of the window and exclaimed, " It's getting dark ! " She said it peevishly, as if the sun's descent was the last piece of carelessness on the part of a negligent universe. And as her eye explored the dusk and saw that the bright spheres round the lamps were infested by wandering ghosts of wind-blown humidity she thought of her walk home up the Mound and what it would be like on this night of gusts and damp. " That puts the lid on ! " her heart said bitterly, and the first tears oozed. Somehow she must go at once. She said thinly and quaveringly, " It's getting dark. Surely it's time I was away home ? "

There was a clock on the mantelpiece which told it was not yet half-past four, but they both looked away from it.

" Ay," said Mr. Mactavish James cheerfully, " you must run away home. I'll not have it said I drive a bairn to death with late hours. Good evening, lassie." He was so terrified by the intensity of her emotion that he had given up playing his fish. There stabbed a question through his heart. Had Isabella Kingan suffered thus ?

" Good evening, Mr. James," she said brightly, and went out into the hall letting the door swing to, and pulled on her coat and tam-o'-shanter in the darkness. Now that it did not matter if she cried, she did not feel nearly so much like crying. " That's the way things always are," she snorted, and began to hum the Marseillaise defiantly as she buttoned up her coat. But though she was not seen here, she was not alone. There pressed against her the unexpungeable fact of her disgrace. Her eyes, mad with distress, with too much weeping, printed on the blackness the figure of the man with whom she had associated herself in this awful way, by that idiot capering before the glass, by those maniac words. With rapture and horror she saw his dark-lidded eyes with their brilliant yet secretive gaze, the lips that were parted yet not loose, that his reserve would not permit to close lest by their setting strangers should see whether he were smiling or moody ; she remembered the bluish bloom that had been on his chin the first night she ever saw him. At that she brought her clenched fist down on her other palm and sobbed with hate. He had brought all this upon her.

And hearing that, Mr. Mactavish James hobbled towards the door, purring endearments. He was better now. That anguished melody of speculation as to Isabella Kingan's heart he had played over again with the *tempo rubato* and the pressed loud pedal of sentimentality, and it was now no more than agreeably affecting as a Scotch song . . . being kind to the wean for the sake of her who was my sweethairt in auld lang syne. . . .

She was so blind with hate of Yaverland that she was not aware of his presence till he bent over her, whinneying in the slow, complacent accents of Scottish sentiment, " Nelly, Nelly, what ails ye, lassie ? Nothing's happened ! I'll put it all right."

" Yes, of course nothing's happened ! " she snapped, her hand on the doorknob. " Who said it had ? " And then his words, " I'll put it all right," began to torment her. They threatened her that her disgrace was not to end here, that he might talk about it, that the thing might well be with her to her grave, that she had done for herself, that now and forever

she had made her life not worth living. " Och, away with it ! "
she almost screamed. " You've driven me so that I don't know
what I'm doing, you and your nasty wee black poodle of a son ! "

He had to laugh. " Nelly, Nelly, he's as God made him ! "

" Ye shelve your responsibility ! " she said, and breaking
immediately into the bitterest tears of this long day of
weeping, flung out of the door of this loathed place, to which
she remembered with agony as she ran down the stairs she
must return to-morrow to earn her living.

(3)

More than anything else she hated people to see her when
she had been crying, yet she was sorry that the little house was
dark. And though she had seen, as she came in through the
square, that there were no lights in any window, and though the
sitting-room door was ajar, and showed a cold hearth and furniture
looking huddled and low-spirited as furniture does when dusk
comes and there is no company, she stood in the hall and called,
" Mother ! Mother ! " She more than half remembered as
she called that her mother had that morning said something
about spending the afternoon with an old friend at Trinity.
But she cried out again, " Mother ! Mother ! " and lest the
cry should sound piteous sent it out angrily. There was no
answer but the complaining rattle of a window at the top of
the house, which, like all dwellings of the very poor, was perpetually ailing in its fitments ; and, letting her wet things fall
to her feet, she moved desolately into the kitchen. The gleam
of the caddies along the mantelpiece, the handles that protruded
like stiff tails over the saucepan-shelf above the sink, struck
her as looking queer and amusing in this twilight, and then
made her remember that she had had no lunch and was now
very hungry, so she briskly set a light to the gas-ring and put
on the kettle. She had the luck to find in the breadpan a loaf
far newer than it was their thrifty habit to eat, and carried it
back to the table, finding just such delicious pleasure in digging
her fingers into its sides as she found in standing on her heels
on new asphalt ; but turned her head sharply on an invisible
derider.

" I do mean to commit suicide, though I am getting
my tea ! " she snapped. " Indeed, I never meant to come
home at all ; I found myself running up the Mound from sheer
force of habit. Did you never hear that human beings are

creatures of habit ?   And now I'm here I might as well get myself
something to eat.   Besides, I'm not going shauchling down to
the Dean Bridge in wet shoes either." She kicked them off and
moved for a time with a certain conscious pomp, setting out
the butter and the milk and the sugar with something of a
sacramental air, and sometimes sobbing at the thought of how
far the journey through the air would be after she had let go
the Dean Bridge balustrade.   But as she put her head into the
larder to see if there was anything left in the pot of strawberry
jam her hand happened on a bowl full of eggs.   There was nothing,
she had always thought, nicer to touch than an egg.   It was cool
without being chill, and took the warmth of one's hand flatteringly
soon, as if it liked to do so, yet kept its freshness ; it was smooth
without being glossy, mat as a pearl, and as delightful to roll
in the hand; and of an exquisite, alarming frangibility that gave
it, in its small way, that flavour which belongs to pleasures that
are dogged by the danger of a violent end.   As elaborately as
this she had felt about it ; for she was silly, as poets are, and
believed it possible that things can be common and precious
too.

She held an egg against the vibrating place in her throat,
and, shaken with silent weeping, thought how full of delights
for the sight and the touch was this world she was going to
leave.   It also seemed to her that she could do very well with
it as an addition to her tea.   " Mother'll not grudge it me for
my last meal on earth," she muttered mournfully, putting it
in the kettle to save time.   " And I ought to keep up my
strength, for I must write a good-bye letter that will show
people what they've lost. . . ."

The egg was good ; and as she would never eat another she
cut her buttered bread into fingers and dipped them into the
yolk, though she knew grown-up people never did it.   The
bread was good too.   It was only because of all the things there
are to eat this was a dreadful world to leave.   She thought reluctantly of food ; the different delicate textures of the nuts of
meat that, lying in such snug unity within the crisp brown
skin, make up a saddle of mutton : yellow country cream,
whipped no more than makes it bland as forgiveness ; little
strawberries, red and moist as a pretty mouth ; Scotch bun,
dark and rich and romantic like the plays of Victor Hugo ; all
sorts of things nice to eat, and points of departure for the fancy.
Even a potato roasted in its skin, if it was the right floury sort,
had an entrancing, ethereal substance ; one could imagine that
thus a cirrus cloud might taste in the mouth.   If the name

were changed, angels might eat it. Potato plants were lovely, too.

Very vividly, for her mind's eye was staring wildly on the past rather than look on this present, which, with all the honesty of youth, she meant should have no future, there sprung up before her on the bare plastered wall a potato-field she and her mother had seen one day when they went to Cramond. Thousands and thousands of white flowers running up to a skyline in ruler-drawn lines. They had walked by the River Almond afterwards, linking arms, exclaiming together over the dark glassy water, which slid over small frequent weirs, the tents of green fire which the sun made of the overarching branches, the patches of moss that grew so symmetrically between the tree-trunks on the steep river-banks above the path that they might have been the dedicatory tablets of rustic altars. When the cool of the evening came they had sat and watched a wedding-party dance quadrilles on a lawn by the river, overhung by chestnut trees and severed by a clear and rapid channel, weedless as the air, from an island crowded by the weather-bleached ruins of a mill. The bride and bridegroom were not young, and the stiff movements with which they yet gladly led the dance, and the quiet, tired merriment of their middle-aged friends, gave the occasion a quality of its own ; with which the faded purples of the loosestrife and mallows leaning out above the water on the white walls on the island were somehow in harmony. That was a day most happily full of things to notice. Surely this was a world to stay in, not to leave before one need ! Ah, but it was now.

If to-morrow they started on such a walk the path by the river would be impassable by reason of the shadow of a tall, dark man that would fall across it, and she would not be able to sit and watch the dancers because in any moment of stillness she would be revisited by thoughts of the madness that had made her say those dreadful things, at the thought of which she laid her spread hand across her mouth, that had made her so rude to the good old man who was their only friend. Again she trembled with hate of Yaverland, a hate that seemed to swell out from her heart. She knew, as she would have known if a flame had destroyed her sight, that the turn life had taken had robbed her of the beauty of the world and was bringing her existence down to this ugly terminal focus, this moment when she sat in this cold kitchen, its cheap print and plaster the colour of uncleaned teeth, and tried to pluck up her energy to put on wet shoes and go through streets full of indifferent people and greased with foul weather to throw herself over a bridge on to rocks. She rose and felt for her shoes that she might go out . . .

Then at the door there came his knock. There was no doubt but that it was his knock. Who else in all the time that these two women had lived there had knocked so ? Two loud, slow knocks, expectant of an immediate opening yet without fuss : the way men ask for things. Peace and apprehension mingled in her. She crossed her hands on her breast, sighed deeply, and cast down her head. It seemed good, as she went to the door and reluctantly turned the handle, that she was in her stockinged feet ; her noiseless steps gave her a feeling of mischief and confidence as if there was to follow a game of pursuits and flights into a darkness.

His male breadth blocked the door. She smiled to see how huge he was, and stood obediently in the silence he evidently desired, for he neither greeted her nor made any movement to enter, but remained looking down into her face. His deep breath measured some long space of time. Her eyes wandered past him and to the little huddled houses, the laurels standing round the lamp, their leaves bobbing under the straight silver rake of the lamplit rain ; and she marvelled that these things looked as they had always looked on any night.

"Come out, I want to see you," he whispered at last, and his hand closing on her drew her out of the dark hall. She liked the wetness of the flags under her stockinged feet, the fall of the rain on her face.

"You little thing ! You little thing !" he muttered : and then, "I love you."

Her head drooped. She lifted it bravely.

"Ellen ! Ellen !" He repeated the name in a passion of wonder, till, feeling the raindrops on her head, he exclaimed urgently, "But you're getting wet ! Darling, let us go in."

When he had shut the front door and they were left alone in the dark, and she was free from the compulsion of his beauty and the intent gaze he had set on her face, she tried to seize her life's last chance of escape. She wrenched away her wrist and made a timid hostile noise. But he linked his arm in hers and whispered reassuringly, "I love you," and drew her, since there was a light there, into the kitchen. He put his hat down on the table beside her plate and cup and threw his wet coat across a chair, while she said querulously, sobbingly, "Why do you call me little ? I am not little !"

He took her hands in his ; her inky fingers were intertwined with his fingers, long and stained with strange stains, massive and powerful and yet tremulous. The sight and touch filled her with extraordinary joy and terror. At last things were beginning to happen to her, and she did not know if she had strength enough to support it. If she could have countermanded her destiny she would, although she knew from the rich colour that tinged this moment, in spite of her inadequacy, it was going to be of some high kind of glory.

He took her in his arms. His lips, brushing her ear, asked, "Do you love me? Tell me, tell me, do you love me?" Dreamily, incredulously, she listened to that strong heart-beat which she had imagined. But he pressed her. "Ellen, be kind! Tell me, do you love me?" That was cruel of him. She was not sure that she approved of love. The position of women being what it was. Men were tyrants, and they seemed to be able to make their wives ignoble. Married women were often anti-Suffragists; they were often fat; they never seemed to go out long walks in the hills or to write poetry. She laid her hands flat against his chest and pushed away from him. "No!" she whimpered. But he bent on her a face wolfish with a hunger that was nevertheless sweet-tempered, since it was beautifully written in the restraint which hung like a veil before his passion that he would argue only gently with her denial. And at the sight she knew his whisper, "Ellen, be kind, tell me that you love me," was such a call to her courage as the trumpet is to the soldier. She held up her head, and cried out, "I love you!" but was amazed to find that she too was whispering.

"Oh, you dear, giving thing!" he murmured. "It is such charity of you to love me!" A tremor ran through his body, his embrace became a gentle tyranny. He was going to kiss her. But this she could not bear. She loved to lay her hand on the blue shadowed side of marble, she loved to see gleaming blocks of ice going through the streets in lorries, she loved the wind as it blows in the face of the traveller as he breasts the pass, she loved swift running and all austerity; and she had confused intimations that this that he wanted to do would in some deep way make war on these preferences. "Ah, no!" she whimpered. "I have told you that I love you. Why need you touch me? I can love you without touching you. Please . . . please. . . ."

Oh, if he wanted it he must have it. As she let her head fall back on her throat it came to her that though she had not known that she had ever thought of love, although she would have sworn that she had never thought of anything but getting on, there had been many nights when, between sleeping and waking, she had dreamed of this moment. It was going to be (his deep slow breath, gentle with amorousness, assured her) as she had then prefigured it ; romantic as music heard across moonlit water, as a deep voice speaking Shakespeare, as, rich colours spilt on marble when the sun sets behind cathedral windows : but warm as summer, soft as the south wind. . . .

But this was pain. How could he call by the name of delight this hard, interminable, sucking pressure when it sent agony downwards from her mouth to the furthest cell of her body, changing her bones so that ever after they would be more brittle, her flesh so that it would be more subject to bruises ! She did not suspect him of cruelty, for his arms still held her kindly, but her eyes filled with tears at the strangeness, which she felt would somehow work out to her disadvantage, of the world where people held wine and kisses to be pleasant things. Yet when the long kiss came to an end she was glad that he set another on her lips, for she had heard his deep sigh of delight. She would always let him kiss her as much as he liked, although she could not quite see what pleasure he found in it. Yet, could she not ? Of course it was beautiful to be held close by Richard Yaverland ! His substance was so dear, that his very warmth excited her tenderness and the rhythm of his breathing made wetness dwell about her lashes ; it was most foolish that she should feel about this great oak-strong man as if he were a little helpless thing that could lie in the crook of her arm, like an ailing puppy ; or perhaps a baby.

A pervading weakness fell on her ; her arms, which had somehow become linked round his neck, were now as soft as garlands, her knees failed under her shivering body : but through her mind thundered grandiose convictions of new power. There was no sea, however black with chill and depth, in which she would not dive to save him, no desert whose unwatered sands she would not travel if so she served his need. It was as if already some brown arm had thrown a spear and she had flung herself before him and blissfully received the flying steel into her happy flesh. Love began to travel over her body, lighting here and there little fires of ecstasy, making her adore him with her skin as she had always adored him with her heart. And as the life of her nerves became more and more intense, her sensations more and more luminous, she became less conscious of her materiality. At the end she felt like a flash of lightning. From that moment she sank confused into the warm darkness of his embrace, while above her his voice muttered hesitant with solemnity : " Ellen. . . you are the answer . . . to everything. . . ."

They drew apart and stood far off, looking into each other's eyes. The clock, ticking away time, seemed a curious toy. " You. In this little room. Oh, Ellen, it is a miracle," he said.

Pressing her hands together beneath her chin, she smiled.

" Ah, you are so beautiful ! Your hair. Your eyes. The little white ball of your chin. As a matter of hard fact, you are more beautiful than I've ever imagined anybody else to be. The wildest lies I've ever told myself about the women I've wanted to love are true of you." For a moment he was still, thinking of Mariquita de Rojas as a swimmer might look down through fathoms of clear water on the face of a drowned woman. " But you . . . you are beautiful as . . . as an impersonal thing. . . ." He clenched his fists in exasperation. All his life the one gift he had exercised easily and indubitably, not losing it even when his besetting despair stood between him and the sun, was the power to talk. While he was speaking the dominoes lay untouched on the greasy café table ; men bent forward on their elbows that with his tongue he might make them companions of men who were half the world distant, maybe the whole world distant in their graves, that he might warm them with the beams of a sun long set on a horizon they would never see. That was vanity ; or, more justly, the filling in of dangerously empty hours, holes in existence through which it seemed likely the soul might run out. But now, when it was absolutely necessary that he should tell her what she was to him, he could not talk at all. He stuttered on to try to win in the way he knew her generous heart could be won by a statement of her new joy.

" Ellen—you know what I mean ? There's a particular kind of rapture that comes when you're looking at an impersonal thing. I mean a thing that doesn't amuse you, doesn't tickle up your greed or vanity, doesn't feed you. Like looking at the dawn. I feel like that when I look at you. And yet you are so sweet too. Oh, you dear Puritan, you will not like me to say you are like scent. But you are. Even at the feminine game you could beat all other women. You see, it is the loveliest thing in the world to watch women dancing ; but with other women, when their bodies stop it's all over. They stand beside you showing minds that have never moved, that have been paralysed since they were babies. But when you stopped dancing your soul would go on dancing. Your mind has as neat ankles as your body. You are the treasure of this earth! Ellen, do you know that I am a little frightened? I do believe that love is a real magic."

He had fallen into that lecturer's manner she had noticed on the first night at the office, when he had told them about bullfights. Her heart pricked with pride because she perceived that now she was his subject.

"I have been up and down the world and I have seen no other real magic. I do not believe that in this age God has altered anyone. People love God nowadays as much as the temperaments they were born with tell them to. He has grown too old for miracles. After two thousand years he has no longer the force to turn water into wine. Ellen, I love your dear prim smile. But always, everywhere, I have found the love of men and women doing that. Sometimes the love of places does something very like it. A man may land on a strange island, and abandon the journey on which he set out, and the home he set out from, to live there for ever. But there his soul has just sunk to sleep. It hasn't been changed. But love changes people. I've seen the dirtiest little greasers clean themselves up and become capable of decency and courage because there was some woman about. And oh, my darling! that happened with quite ordinary women. *Vin Ordinaire*. Pieces cut from the roll of ordinary female stuff. But how will the magic word act when you are part of the spell —you who are the most wonderful thing in the whole world, who are the flower of the earth's crop of beauty, who have such a genius for just being! Oh, it will be a tremendous thing."

He paused, marvelling at his own exultation, which marked, he knew, so great a change in him. For always before it had been his chief care that nothing at all should happen to him emotionally, and especially had he feared this alchemy of passion. He had been unable to pray for purity, since he felt it an ideal ridiculously not indigenous to this richly-coloured three-dimensional universe, and he had observed that it made men liable to infatuations in later life; but he had prayed for lust, which he knew to be the most drastic preventive of love. But it had evaded him as virtue evades other men. Never had he been able to look on women with the single eye of desire; always in the middle of his lust, like the dark stamen in a bright flower, there appeared his inveterate concern for people's souls. Every woman to whom he wanted to make love was certain to be engaged in some defensive struggle against fate, for that is the

condition of strong personality, and his quick sense would soon
detect its nature ; and since there is nothing more lovable than
the sight of a soul standing up against fate, looking so little
under the dome of the indifferent sky, he would find himself
nearly in love. And because that meant, as he had observed,
this magic change of the self, he would turn his back on the
adventure, for all his life he had disliked profound emotional
processes with exactly the same revulsion that a decent man
feels for some operation which, though within the law, is outside
the dictates of honesty. He knew there was no reason that
could be formulated why he should not become a real lover ;
but nevertheless he had always felt as if for him it would be an
act of disloyalty to some fair standard.

He quaked at his own oddness, until there struck home to his
heart, as an immense reassurance, the expression on Ellen's
face. It had been blank with the joy of being loved, a romantic
mask, lit steadily with a severe receptive passion ; but the
abstraction in his voice and an accompanying failure of invention in his compliments had not escaped unnoticed by her,
and there was playing about her dear obstinate mouth and fierce-
coloured eyebrows the most delicious look of shrewdness, as
if she had his secret by the coat-tail and would deliver it up to
justice ; and over all there was the sweetest, most playful smile,
which showed that she would make a jest of his negligence,
that she was one of those who exclude ugliness from their lives
by imposing beautiful interpretations on all that happened to
her ; and behind these lovely things she did shone the still
lovelier thing she was. It struck home to him the immense degree
to which brooding on so perfect and adventurous a thing would
change him, and once more he was not afraid. Taking her again
in his arms, he cried out : " Ellen ! Ellen ! You mean so much
to me ! I love you as a child loves its mother, partly for real,
disinterested love and partly for the thing you give me ! You
are going to do such a lot for me ! You will put an end to this
damned misery ! And just the sight of you about my home,
you slip of light, you dear miracle ! "

She put her hand across his mouth, blushing at the familiarity
of her gesture yet urgently impelled to it. " That'll do," she
said. " I know you think I'm nice. But what were you saying
about being miserable ? You're not miserable, are you ? "

" Sometimes. I have been lately."

" You miserable ! " she softly exclaimed. " You, so big
and strong—and victorious ! But why ? "

" Oh, no reason. It's a mood that comes on me."

"I have them myself. It's proof of our superior delicacy of organisation," she gravely told him.

"Oh, I don't know. The feeling that comes on you when you've taken particular care to turn up for an important appointment, and you get to the place ten minutes before the time, and find there's nobody there, and wait about, and suddenly find you've come a day late. And still you go on hanging round, feeling there must be something you can do, although you know you can't. It stays months sometimes. A sense of having missed some opportunity that won't come again. I don't know what it means. But it turns life sour. It seems to take the power out of one's fingers, to make one's brainstuff hot and thick and dark. It makes one's work seem not worth doing. But that's all over. It won't come again now I have you!" He sat down on the basket chair and drew her on to his knee, giving her light caresses to correct the heavy things he had just been saying. She received them abstractedly, as if she were thinking silent vows. "Ellen, I don't know what your eyes are like. The sea never looks kind like that, and they are wittier than flowers. You're not really like a flower at all, you know, though I believe that in our circumstances it's considered the proper thing for me to tell you that you are. You're too important, and you wouldn't like growing in a garden, which even wild flowers seem to want to do. I'll tell you what you're like. You're like an olive tree. They're slim like you, and their branches go up like arms, as if they were asking for a vote, and they grow dangerously (just as you would if you were a tree) on the very edge of cliffs ; and one looks past them at the blue sea, just as I look past you at the glorious life I'm going to have now I've got you. Dearest, when can we get married ? "

"Oh ! " exclaimed Ellen, greatly pleased. "Are you in a position to keep a wife ? "

He burst out laughing. "You darling ! Do you know, I believe I could keep two."

She did not laugh. "It's wicked to think that if you did I couldn't divorce you. You'd have to be cruel as well. I heard Brynhild Ormiston say so."

He went on laughing. "Well, don't let that hold you back. I dare say I could rise to being cruel as well. Let's look on the bright side of things. Tell me, darling, when will you marry me ? "

"Those iniquitous marriage-laws," she murmured. "It makes one think . . ." She looked down, weighing grave things.

"My dearest, you can forget the marriage-laws. I will adore you so, I will be so faithful, I will work my fingers to the bone so gladly to make you kind to me, that there is no divorce law in the world will let you get rid of me." Shy at his own sincerity, he kissed her hair, and whispered in her ear, "I mean it, Ellen."

She raised her head with that bravery he loved so much, and gave him her lips to kiss, but her eyes were still wide and set with reluctance.

"What can be worrying her?" he wondered. "Can it be that she isn't sure about my money? Of course she hasn't the least idea how much I've got. Wise little thing, if she dreads transplantation to some little hole worse than this." He looked distastefully at the age-cracked walls, stained with patches of damp that seemed like a material form of disgrace. That she should have grown to beauty in these infect surroundings made him feel, as he had often done before, that she was not all human and corruptible, but that her flesh was mixed with precious substance not subject to decay, her blood interpenetrated with the material of jewels. Perhaps some sorcerer had confusioned it of organic and inorganic beauty and chosen some ancestress of Ellen for his human ingredient; he remembered an African story of a woman fertilised by a sacred horn of ivory; an Indian story of a princess who had lain with her narrow brown body straight and still all night before the altar of a quiet temple, that the rays of a holy ruby might make her quick; surely their children had met and bred the stock that had at last, in the wise age of the world, made this thing of rubies and ivory that lay in his arms. He liked making fantasies about her that were stiff as brocade with fantastic imagery, that were more worshipful of her loveliness than anything he yet dared say to her. Absent-mindedly he went on reassuring her. "You know, I've got quite enough money. Fortunately the branch of chemistry I'm interested in is of great commercial use, so I get well paid. Iniquitously well paid, when one considers how badly pure scientific work is paid; and of course pure science ought to be rewarded a hundred times better than applied science. We ought to be able to manage quite decently. My mother's got her own money, so my income will be all ours. There's no reason of that sort why we shouldn't get married at once. We'll have to live in Essex at first. I've got to go and work on Kerith Island."

She wriggled on his lap. "What's that you were saying about science?" she asked, her voice dipping and soaring with affected interest. " Why isn't pure science to be rewarded better than applied science ? "

" Why is she trying to put me off ? " he speculated. " It isn't a matter of being sure of a decent home. In fact, she hated my talking about money. I wonder what it is." To let her do what she wanted with the conversation he said aloud, " Oh, because applied science is a mug's game. Pure science is a kind of marriage with knowledge—the same kind of marriage that ours is going to be, when you find out all about a person by being with them all the time and loving them very much. Applied science is the other sort of marriage. In it you go through the pockets of knowledge when he's asleep and take out what you want. But, dear, I don't want to talk of that. I want to know when you're going to marry me."

" I hope," she said quaveringly, " that all your people won't think I am marrying you for your money. But then . . . if they know you . . . they will know that you are so glorious . . . that any woman would marry you . . . if you were a beggar, or the ideal equivalent of that."

" Oh, you dear absurd thing ! " he cried, feeling intensely moved. " Haven't you the least idea how far beyond price you are, how worthless I am ! Anyway . . . I've no people, except my mother." He paused and wondered if he would tell her about his mother now ; but seeing that her brows were still knitted by her private trouble about their marriage, the nature of which he could not guess, he thought he would not do it just now. In any case, he did not want to. " And she will know how lucky I am to get you, how little I deserve you."

" I'd have married you," said Ellen, not without bitterness, " if you'd been an anti-Suffragist." The situation was so plainly presenting itself to her as being in some way dreadful that he anxiously held her with his eyes. She stammered, folding and refolding her hands. " It'll be queer, living in a house with you, won't it ? "

He had held her eyes, and thus forced her to tell him what was troubling her, on the assumption that he could deal with her answer. But this was outside his experience. He did not know anything about girls ; he had hardly believed in the positive reality of girlhood ; it had seemed to him rather a negative thing, the state of not being a woman. But in the light of her gentle, palpitant distress, he saw that it was indeed so real a state that passing from it to the state of womanhood would be as terrible as if she had to give birth to herself. . . . It was such a helpless state, too. She was, he said to himself again—

for he knew she did not like him to say it !—such a little thing. He remembered, with a sudden sweat of horror, the conversation in the lawyer's office that had sent him sweating up here, keeping himself so hot with curses at the human world that he had not felt the coldness of the weather. God, how he had hated that office from the moment he set foot in it ! He had hated Mr. Mactavish James at sight as much as he had hated his young son ; for the solicitor had surveyed him with that lewd look that old men sometimes give to strong young men. He had perceived at once, from the way Mr. James was sucking the occasion, that he had been sent for some special purpose, and he did not believe, from the repetition of that lewd look, that it related to his property in Rio or that it was clean. He was prepared for the drawled comment, " I hear ye've making fren's wi' our wee Nelly," and he was ready with a hard stare. It was enraging to see that the old man had expected his haughtiness and that it was evidently fuel for his lewd jest. " I am fond of wee Nelly. She's just a world's wonder. You sit there saying nothing, maybe it doesn't interest you, but you would feel as I do if you had seen her the way I did thon day a year ago in June. Ay ! " He threw his eyes up and exclaimed succulently, " The wee bairn ! " with an air of giving a handsome present.

Yaverland, who had not come much in contact with Scotch sentimentality, felt very sick, and increasingly so as the old man told how he had met her up at the Sheriff's Court. " Sixteen, and making her appearance in the Sheriff's Court ! " Yaverland had a vision of a court of obscure old men all gloating impotently and imaginatively on Ellen's red and white. " What was she doing there ? " he asked in exasperation, forgetting his vow to appear indifferent about Ellen, and was enraged to see Mr. Mactavish James chuckle at the perceived implications of his interested enquiry. " Well, it was this way. Her mither, who was Ellen Forbes, whom I knew well when I was young, had the wee house in Hume Park Square. You'll have been there ? Hev' ye not ? Imphm. I thought so. Well, they'd had thought difficulty in paying the rent. . . ." The story droned on perpetually, breaking off into croonings of sensual pity ; and Yaverland sat listening to it with such rage, that, as he soon knew from the narrator's waggish look, the vein in his forehead began to swell.

It appeared that the poor draggled bird that had in the summer of its days been known as Ellen Forbes had got into arrears with the rent; as some cheque had been greatly delayed, and that when the cheque had arrived she had been taken away to the fever hospital with typhoid fever, and that, since she had to lie on her back for three weeks, Ellen, who was left alone in that wee house—he rolled his tongue round the loneliness repellently—had neither sent the cheque on to her nor asked her to write a cheque for the rent. The landlord, " a man called Inglis, wi' offices up in Clark Street, who does a deal of that class of property "—it was evident that he admired such —saw a prospect of getting tenants to take on the house at a higher rental. So, " knowing well that Ellen was a wean and no' kenning what manner of wean she was," and hearing from some source that they were exceptionally friendless and alone, served her with a notice that he was about to apply for an eviction order. But Ellen had attended the court and told her story.

" By the greatest luck in the world I happened to be in court that day, looking after the interests of a client of mine, a most respectable unmarried lady, a pillar of St. Giles, who had been horrified to find out that her property was being used as a bad house. Hee hee." He was abashed to perceive that this young man was not overcome with mirth and geniality at the mention of a brothel. " The minute I saw the wee thing standing there in the well of the court, saying what was what— she called him ' the man Inglis,' she did !—I kenned there was not her like under the sun." She had won her case ; but Mr. James had intercepted her on the way out, and had stopped her to congratulate her, and had been amazed to find the tears running down her cheeks. " I took the wee thing aside." It turned out that to defend her home, and keep it ready for her mother coming out from the hospital, she had to come down to the court on the very day that she should have sat for the examination by which she had hoped to win a University scholarship. " The wee thing was that keen on her buiks ! " he said, with caressing contempt, " and she was like to cry her heart out. So I put it all right." " What did you do ? " Yaverland had asked, expecting to hear of some generous offer to pay her fees, and remembering that he had heard that the Scotch were passionate about affairs of education. " I offered her a situation as typist here, as my typist had just left," said Mr. Mactavish James, with an ineffable air of self-satisfaction. Yaverland had been about to burst into angry laughter, when the old man had gone on, " Ay, and I thought I had found a nest for the wee lassie. But a face as bonnie as hers brings its troubles with it ! Ay, ay ! I'm sorry to have to say it."

Oh ! it went slower and smoother like a dragged-out song at a ballad concert. "There's one in the office will not leave the puir lassie alone. . . ." Yaverland had fumed with rage at the idea ; and then had been overcome with a greater loathing of this false and theatrical old man. Inglis and the man who wanted her were at least slaves of some passion that was the fruit of their affairs. But this man was both of them. He had not wished this girl well. He had rejoiced in her poverty because it stimulated the flow of the juices of pity ; he had rejoiced in her disappointment ; he had rejoiced in Inglis's villainy because he could pity her ; he had rejoiced in the unknown man's lust because he could step protectively in front of Ellen ; and, worse than this, hadn't he savoured in the story vices that he himself had had to sacrifice for the sake of standing well with the world ? Had he not felt how lovely it must be to be Inglis and hunt little weak slips of girls and make more money ? Had he not felt himself revisited by the warm fires of lust in thinking of this unknown man's pursuit of Ellen and wallowed in it ? Yaverland had risen quickly, and said haltingly, trying to speak and not to strike because the man was old and his offence indefinite, " No doubt you've been very good to Miss Melville." Mr. Mactavish James had been amazed by the grim construction of the speech, the lack of any response matching his " crack " in floridity. He had expected comment on his generosity. Positive resentment had stolen into his face as Yaverland had turned his back on him and rushed up the wet streets to rescue Ellen from the world.

Alas, that it should turn out that he too was something from which her delicate little soul asked to be rescued ! He could not bear the thought of altering her. The prospect of taking her as his wife, of making her live in close contact with his masculinity, dangerous both in its primitive sense of something vast and rough, and also as something more experienced than her, seemed as iniquitous as the trampling of some fine white wild flower. But then, she was beautiful, not only lovely : destiny had marked her for a high career ; to leave her as she was would be to miscast one who deserved to play the great tragic part, which cannot be played without the actress's heart beating at the prospect of so great a rôle. Oh, there was no going back ! But he perceived he must be very clever about it. He must make it all as easy as possible for her. His heart contracted with tenderness as he took vows that could not have been more religious if they had been made concerning celibacy instead of concerning marriage.

He regretted he was an Atheist. He had felt this before in
moments of urgency, for blasphemy abhors a vacuum, but now
he wanted some white high thing to swear by ; something armed
with powers of eternal punishment to chastise him if he broke
his oath. He found that his eyes were swimming with tears.
Yes, tears ! Oh, she had extended life to limits he had not
dreamed of ! He had never thought he would laugh out loud
as he had done to-night. He had never thought his eyes would
grow wet as they were doing now. And it was good. He
looked at her in gratitude, and found her looking at him.

"Fancy you being miserable ! And me," she reproached
herself, " thinking that everybody was happy but myself !
Dear . . ." She rose to it, walking down to the cold water.
" Let's marry soon."

The sequence of thought was to be followed easily. She
was willing to take this step, which for reasons she did not understand made her flesh goose-grained with horror, because she
thought she could prevent him from being unhappy.
" Oh, Ellen ! " he cried out, and buried his head on her bosom.
" I want—I want to deserve you. I will work all my life to
be good enough for you." He felt the happiness of a man
who has found a religion.

They heard a key turning in the front door. Ellen slipped
off his knee and stood, first one foot behind the other, balanced
on the ball of one foot, a finger to her lips, in the attitude of a
frightened nymph. Then she recovered herself, and stood
sturdily on both feet with her hands behind her. How he
adored her, this nymph who wanted to look like Mr. Gladstone !

Mrs. Melville, pitifully blown about, a most ruffled little
bird, appeared at the door. She was amazed. " Mr. Yaverland ! In the kitchen ! And, Ellen, what are you doing in
your stocking feet ? Away and take Mr. Yaverland into the
parlour ! "

" He came in here himself," said Ellen. She had become
a little girl, a guilty little girl.

Yaverland caught Mrs. Melville's eye and held it for a fraction
of an instant. She mustn't know they had talked of it before.
That would never do, for a modern woman. " Mrs. Melville,"
he said, " I've asked Ellen to marry me."

Her eyes twinkled. " You never say so ! " she said, with
exquisite malice at the expense of her clever daughter. " I
am surprised ! " She sat down at the head of the kitchen table,
setting a string bag full of parcels on the table in front of her.
She was breathing heavily, and her voice, he noticed, was very

hoarse. Poor little thing! Yet she was glad. Wonderful to see her so glad about anything : pathetic to see how, though all her life had gone shipwrecked, she cheered her daughter to voyage. " She must live near us in Essex," he thought rapidly. " I must give her a decent allowance." " Well, well ! " she said happily.

Ellen, feeling that things were being taken too much for granted, so far as she was concerned, remarked suddenly, " And I think I'll take him."

Her eyes twinkled again at Yaverland. Wasn't there something very sweet about her ? She was, in effect, glad that he loved her daughter, because now she had somebody who could laugh at this wonderful daughter !

" Let me marry her soon," he said.

She became doubtful. Her face contracted, as it had done when she had said, " Let her bide ; she's only a bairn."

" We must live in Essex," he said, to get her past the moment.

She became tragic.

" You'd like, I think, to come and live near us ? If there isn't a house at Roothing, there are plenty at Prittlebay. It would be good for you. Obviously you can't stand this climate."

She looked up at him and said, the thought of them living together having obviously presented itself to her for the first time, " Ah, well. I hope you'll both be happy. Happier than I was." She receded back into memory, and found first of all that ancient loyalty that she had always practised in his life. " Not but what John Melville was a better man than anyone has allowed."

They didn't say anything, but stood silent, giving the moment its honour. Then Ellen stepped to her mother's side and said chidingly, " Mother, what's wrong with your throat ? You had a cold when you went out, but nothing like this. It's terrible."

" It's nothing, dear. Take Mr. Yaverland—maircy me, what shall I call you now ? "

" Richard. That's what my mother calls me."

" Oh," she cried flutteringly, " it's like having a son again. No one would think I was your mother, though, and you such a great thing ! Though Ronnie if he had lived would have been tall. As tall as you, I wouldn't wonder," she said, with a tinge of jealousy. " Well, Ellen, take Richard into the parlour and light the fire. I'll see to the supper."

" You will not," said Ellen, whom shyness was making deliciously surly. It was like seeing her in a false beard.

" R—Richard, will you take her into the parlour yourself ?
She's got a terrible throat. Can you not hear ? "

" Ellen dear ! "

" Away now ! "

" I will not away. Ellen, don't worry. You don't know
where I put the best tablecloth after the mending—and there's
nothing but cod-roes, and you know well that in cooking your
mother beats you. Run away, dear—you'll make Richard feel
awkward—— "

Ellen shrugged her shoulders. She knew that she ought
to insist, but she knew too that it would be lovely lighting the
fire for Richard.

(4)

He had not been able to see Ellen for three days. But he
had written to her three times.

" *I'm missing another day of you, Ellen. And I'm greedy for
every minute of you. There you are, away from me, and moving
about and doing all the sweet things you do, and saying all the things
you do say, and your red hair catching the light and your voice full of
exquisite sweet sounds, and I just have to get along seeing and hearing
nothing of it. I am the most insatiable of lovers. Life is thirst without you. I grudge every moment we have been alive on the same world
and not together. What a waste ! What a waste ! I've never wanted
an immortal soul before, but now I do—that I may go on with you
and go on with you, you darlingissima, you endlessly lovely human
thing. I'd go through all the ages with you ; we'd be like two children
reading a wonderful book together, and you'd light even the darkest
passage of time for me with your wit and your beauty. Tell me
everything you are doing, tell me every little thing, my lovely red-
haired Ellen. . . .*"

And she had written to him twice. . . .

" *And in the evening I went out shopping. I wish you would tell
me what you like to eat. It would give shopping an interest. Then
I went to the library and got a trashy novel for mother to read, as
I am still keeping her in bed. For myself, I wanted to read something about love, as hitherto I have not taken much interest in it and
have read practically nothing on the subject, so I got out the works
of Shelley and Byron. But their love poems are very superficial.*"

I do wish you were here. Please come soon. When mother is well I will be able to make cakes for you. Did you see the sunset yesterday? I am surprised to find how much feeling there is arising out of what is, after all, quite an ordinary event of life. For after all, this happens to nearly everybody. But I do not believe it can happen quite like this to other people. I am sure there must be something quite out of the ordinary about our feelings for one another. Do please come soon. . . ."

Well, he had come, his arms full of flowers and illustrated papers for the invalid, and neither his soft first knock, designed to spare Mrs. Melville's susceptibilities, nor his more vigorous second, had brought Ellen to the door. He stepped back some paces and looked up at the three dwarfish storeys of the silent little house, and alarm fell on him as he saw that all the windows were dark. The reasoning portion of his mind deliberated whether there could conceivably be any bedrooms looking out to the back, but with the crazed imagination of a lover he saw extravagant visions of the evils that might befall two fragile women living alone. He pictured Ellen sitting up in bed, blinking at the lanterns of masked men. Then it struck him as probable that Mrs. Melville's sore throat might have developed into diphtheria, and that Ellen had caught it, and the two women were even now lying helpless and unattended in the dark house, and he brought down the knocker on the door like a hammer. The little square, which a moment ago had seemed an amusing setting for Ellen's quaintness, now seemed like a malignant hunchback in its darkness and its leaning angles, and the branches of the trees in the park beyond the railings swayed in the easy wind of a fine night with that ironical air nature always assumes to persons convulsed by human passion. But presently he heard the crazy staircase creak under somebody's feet, and the next moment Ellen's face looked out at him. She held a candle in her hand, and in its light he saw that her face was marked with fatigue as by a blow and that her hair fell in lank, curved strands about her shoulders.

She nearly sobbed when she saw him, but opened the door no wider than a crack. " Oh, Richard ! It's lovely to see you, but you mustn't come in. They've taken poor mother away to the fever hospital with diphtheria."

" Diphtheria ! " he exclaimed. " That's rum ! It flashed through my mind as I knocked that it was diphtheria she had."

" Isn't that curious ! " she murmured, her eyes growing large and soft with wonder. But her rationalism asserted itself

and her glance grew shrewd again. "Of course that's all nonsense. What more likely for you to think, when you knew it
was her throat that ailed her?" Seeing that in her enthusiasm
for a materialist conception of the universe she loosed her grip
of the doorhandle, he pushed past her, and took her candlestick
away from her and set it down with his flowers and papers on
the staircase. "Oh, you mustn't, you mustn't!" she cried
under his kisses. "Do you not know it's catching? I may have
it on me now."

"Oh, God, I hope you haven't, you precious thing. . . ."

"I don't expect so. I've had an anti-diphtheritic serum
injected. Science is a wonderful thing. But you might get it."

"That be damned."

"Och, you great swearing thing!" she crooned delightedly,
and nuzzled into his chest. "Ah, how I like you to like kissing
me!" she whispered in a woman's voice. "More than I like
it myself. Is that not strange?" Then her face puckered,
and she was young again, hardly less young than any new-born
thing. "It's a mild case, the doctor said, but it hurt her so!
And oh, Richard, when the ambulance man carried her away she
looked so wee!"

"Why did you let her go?" he asked with sudden impatience. He loved her so much that her swimming eyes turned
a knife in his heart, and his maleness resented the pain her
female sensitiveness was bringing on him, and wanted to prove
that all this could have been avoided by the use of the male
attribute of common sense, and therefore she deserved no
sympathy at all. "I would have stood you nurses. I'm one
of the family now. You might have let me do that!"

"Dear, I thought of asking you for that," she said timidly,
"but, you see, nurses are ill to deal with in a wee house like this
where there's no servant. If I had sickened for it myself where
would we all have been? Worse than in the hospital." Of
course she had been wise; it was her constant quality. He shook
with rage at the thought of the extreme poverty of the poor,
whom the world pretends are robbed only of luxury but who
are denied such necessities as the right to watch beside the
beloved sick. "But I've been reckless!" she boasted with a
smile. "I've told them to put her in a private ward. She was
so pleased! She was six weeks in the general ward when she
had typhoid, and it was dreadful, all the women from the Canongate and the Pleasance. . . ." It brought painful tears to his
eyes to hear this queen, who ought to have had first call on
the world's riches, rejoicing because by a stroke of good fortune

her mother need not lie in her sickness side by side with women
of the slums. "Oh, my dear, I'm so glad I can look after
you!" he muttered, and gathered her closely to him.

"Oh dear, and me in my dressing-gown!" she breathed.

"You look very beautiful."

"I wasn't thinking of beauty; I was thinking of decency."

"Nobody would call a dressing-gown of grey flannel fastened
at the neck with a large horn button anything but decent."

"Yes, it's cairtainly sober," said Ellen placidly. "Beauty,
indeed! I'm past thinking of beauty, after having been up all
night giving mother her medicine and encouraging her, and
getting her ready in the morning for the ambulance, and going
away over to the doctor at Church Hill for my injection this
afternoon. I fear to think what I'm looking like, though doubtless it would do me good to know."

"You must be tired out. Run along to bed. I'll go away
now and come back the first thing in the moining."

"Who's talking of bed?" she complained with a smiling
peevishness. ("Ye've got—ye've got remarkable eyebrows.
The way they grow makes me feel all—all desperate.") "I've
had a lie-down since four. You woke me up with your knocking.
Dear, I've never been woken up so beautifully before. Now I
want my supper. I never lose my appetite even when the
Liberals win a by-election, which considering the way our
women work against them is one of those things that disprove
all idea of a just Providence. Dear, but it'll be such a poor
supper to set before you! There's not a thing in the house
but a tin of salmon. It is a mercy that mother isn't here,
for this is the kind of thing that upsets her terribly. She wakes
me up sometimes dreaming of the time the milk was sour when
Mr. Kelman came on his parish visit, though that's five years
ago now. Oh, Richard, mother is such a wee sensitive thing,
you cannot think! I cannot bear her to be ill! But indeed
she is not very ill. The doctor said she was not very ill. He
said I would be a fule to worry. She would be at me for letting
you stand out in the hall like this. You go into the parlour.
I'll light the fire, and then I'll away to the kitchen and get the
supper. We must just make the best of it, and I have heard
that some people prefer tinned salmon to fresh."

"It's the distinguishing mark of connoisseurs in all the
capitals of Europe," said Richard. "But darling, don't light
a fire for me. I'll go off as soon as you've had supper, so that
you can turn in."

"But as soon as supper's eaten I have to away out. Ah,

will you come with me? I like walking through the streets
with you. It's somehow like a procession. You're awful like
a king, Richard. Not the present Royal Family."

"But why must you go out?"

"To see how mother is. Do you not know? When the
ambulance men come they give you a number. Mother's is
ninety-three. Then every morning and every evening they put
a board in the window up at the Public Health Office in the High
Street, with headings on it: 'Very dangerously ill, friends
requested to come at once,' 'Very ill, but no immediate danger,'
'Getting on well,' and the numbers grouped against them.
She'll be amongst the 'Getting on wells.' The doctor said there
was no cause for worry at all. He is a splendid doctor."

"But, my God, can't you telephone?"

"No, of course not. They can't do that in these institutions.
They'd have to keep someone to do nothing but answer the
telephone all day. But it doesn't really matter. Hardly anybody dies of fevers, do they? I never heard of anybody dying
of diphtheria, did you? They used to in the old days, but it's
all different now. This serum's such a wonderful thing. But
they did hurt so when they injected it. She cried, although
she is awful brave as a usual thing. Oh, let's get on with this
supper!" She passed into the kitchen and began preparations
for a meal, banging down the saucepans, while he brought in
his gifts and laid them on the table. "I'm taking it for granted
that you like your cocoa done with milk. What's all this? Oh,
did you bring those flowers for her? Oh, that was kind of you!
Pink flowers, too, and she loves pink. It's her great grief that
all her life she wanted a pink dress, and what with one thing
and another, first having a younger sister so sallow that a pink
dress in the neighbourhood spoilt all her chances, and afterwards
father just wincing if there seemed any chance of her having
anything she liked, she never got one. Illustrated papers, too!
She likes a read, though nothing intellectual. Richard, I do
believe you're thoughtful. That'll be a great help in our married
life." She turned over the glossy pages, clicking her tongue
with disapproval. "Anti-Suffragists to a woman, I expect,"
adding honestly, "but pairfect teeth."

Her little face, seen now in repose, unlit by the light that
glowed in her eyes when she looked at him, was piteous with
fatigue. "Ellen, can't I go and look at this board?"

"No. I want to go myself."

"Then come and do it now, and then we'll go on and have
supper at some place in Princes Street."

"No. I want to leave it as late as possible. Then it'll seem like saying good-night to mother."

They ate but little. She tasted a few mouthfuls, and then clambered on to his knee and lay in his arms, burying her face against his shoulder. She might have been asleep but that she sometimes put up her hand and stroked his hair and traced his eyebrows and made a little purring noise ; and once she cried a little and exclaimed pettishly, "It's just lack of sleep. I'm not anxious. I'm not a bit anxious." And presently she looked up at the alarum clock and said, "That's never nine? We must go. Richard, you are great company!" She ran upstairs to dress, singing in the sweetest little voice, wild yet low and docile, such as a bird might have if it were christened. When she came down she faced him with gentle defiance and said, "I know I'm awful plain to-night. I suppose you'll not love me any more?" He answered, "Be downright ugly if you can. It won't matter to me. I love you anyhow." She lifted her hand to turn out the gas and smiled at him over her shoulder. "If that's not handsome!" she drawled mockingly, but in her glance, though she drooped her lids, there burned a flame of earnestness, and just as he was going to open the front door she slipped into his arms and rested there, shaken with some deep emotion, with words she felt too young to say.

"What is it? What is it you want to say? Tell me."

"Do you think we can do it, Richard? Love each other always. Now, it's easy. We're young. It's easier to be nice when you're young . . . But mother and father must have cared for each other once. She kept his letters. After everything she kept his letters. . . . It's when one gets old . . . old people quarrel and are mean. Ah, do you think we will be able to keep it up?"

She was remembering, he could see, the later married life of her parents, and conceiving it for the first time not with the harsh Puritan moral vision of the young, as the inevitable result of deliberate ill-conduct, but as the decay of an intention for which the persons involved were hardly more to blame than is an industrious gardener for the death of a plant whose habit he has not understood. It was, to one newly possessed of happiness, a terrifying conception.

He muttered, low-voiced and ashamed as those are who speak of things much more sacred than the common tenor of their lives . "Of course it'll be difficult after the first few years. But it's hard to be a saint. Yet there have been saints. All that they do for their religion I'll do for you. I will keep clear of evil things lest they spoil the feelings I have for you. I . . . There are thoughts like prayers . . . And, darling . . . I do not believe in God . . . yet I know that through you I shall find . . . something the same as God. . . ." He could not say it all. But it communicated itself in their long unpassionate kiss.

They crept out of the dark house that had heard them as out of a church. He was very happy as they went through the high, wide streets that to-night were broad rivers of slow wind. He was being of use to her; she was leaning on his arm and sometimes shutting her tired eyes and trusting to his guidance. The very coldness of the air he found pleasing, because it told him that he was in the North, the cruel-kind region of the world which sows seeds from the South in ice-bound earth in which it would seem that they must perish, yet rears them to such fruit and flower as in their own rich soil they never knew.

At the first, he reflected, it must have appeared that the faith they made in Rome would lose all its justifications of beauty when it travelled to those barren lands where the Holy Wafer and the images of Our Lord and Our Lady must be content with a lodging built not of coloured marble but of grey stone. Yet here the Northmen won. Since there were no quarries of coloured marble they had to quarry in their minds, and there they found the Gothic style, which made every church like the holiest moment of a holy soul's aspiration to God, and which is doubtless more pleasing to Him, if He exists to be pleased, than precious stones.

So was it with love. A man returning from the South, where all women are full of physical wisdom, might think as he looked on these Northern women, with their straight sexless eyes and their long limbs innocent of languor, that he had turned his back on love. But here again the North was victor. Since these women could not be wise about life with their bodies, they were wise about love with their souls. They can give such sacramental kisses as the one that still lay on his lips, committing him for ever to nobility. Ah, how much she had done for him by being so sweetly militarist! For it had always been his fear that the supreme passion of his life would be for some woman who, by her passivity, would provoke him to develop those tyrannous and brutish qualities which he had inherited from his father. He had seen that that might easily happen during his affair with Mariquita de Rojas; in those years he had been, he knew, more quarrelsome and less friendly to mild and civilising things than he was ordinarily. But henceforward he was safe, for Ellen would fiercely forbid him to be anything but gentle. Now that he realised how good their relationship was he wanted it to be perfect, and therefore he felt vexed that he had not yet made it perfectly honest by telling her about his mother. He resolved to do so there and then, for he felt that that kiss had sealed the evening to a serenity in which pain surely could not live.

" You're walking slower than you were," said Ellen sharply. " What was it you were thinking of saying ? "

He answered slowly, " I was thinking of something that I ought to tell you about myself."

She looked sideways at him as they passed under a lamp, and wrote in her heart, " When the vein stands out in the middle of his forehead I will know that he is worried," then said aloud, " Och, if it's anything disagreeable, don't bother to tell me. I'll just take it for granted that till you met me you were a bad character."

" It's nothing that I've done. It's something that was done to my mother and myself." He found that after all he could not bear to speak of it, and began to hurry on, saying loudly, " Oh, it doesn't matter ! You poor little thing, why should I bother you when you're dog-tired with an old story that can't affect us in the least ! It's all over ; it's done with. We've got our own lives to lead, thank God ! "

She would not let him hurry on. " What was it, Richard ? " she insisted, and added timidly, " I see I'm vexing you, but I know well it's something that you ought to tell me ! "

He walked on a pace or two, staring at the pavement. " Ellen, I'm illegitimate." She said nothing, and he exclaimed to himself, " Oh, God, it's ten to one that the poor child can't make head or tail of it ! She probably knows nothing, absolutely nothing about these things ! " Into his deep concern lest he had troubled the clear waters of her innocence there was creeping unaccountably a feeling of irritation, which made him want to shout at her. But he mumbled, " My father and mother weren't married to each other. . . ."

" Yes, I understand," she said rather indignantly ; and after a moment's silence remarked conversationally, " So that's all, is it ? " Then her hand gripped his and she cried, " Oh, Richard, when you were wee, did the others twit you with it ? "

Oh, God, was she going to take it sentimentally ? " No. At least, when they did I hammered them. But it was awful for my mother."

" Ah, poor thing," she murmured, " isn't it a shame ! Mrs.
Ormiston is always very strong on the unmarried mother in
her speeches."

He had a sudden furious vision of how glibly these women
at the Suffrage meeting would have talked of Marion's case
and how utterly incapable they would have been to conceive
its tragedy ; how that abominable woman in sky-blue would
have spoken gloatingly of man's sensuality while she herself
was bloomed over with the sensual passivity that provokes
men to cruel and extravagant demands. That nobody but
himself ever seemed to have one inkling of the cruelty of her
fate he took as evidence that everybody was tacitly in league
with the forces that had worked towards it, and he found himself
unable to exempt Ellen from this suspicion. If she began to
chatter about Marion, if she talked about her without that
solemnity which should visit the lips of those who talk of martyred
saints, there would begin a battle between his loves, the issue
of which was not known to him. He said with some exasperation : " I'm not talking of *the* unmarried mother; I am talking
of my mother, who was not married to my father. . . ."

But she did not hear him. The news, though it had roused
that high pitch of trembling apprehension which it now knew
at any mention of the sequel of love, had not shocked her. In
order to feel that quick reaction of physical loathing to the
story of an irregular relationship before hearing its details,
which is known as being shocked, one must be either not quite
innocent and have ugly associations with sex, or have had reason
to conceive woman's life as a market where there are few buyers,
and a woman who is willing to live with a lover outside marriage
as a merchant who undersells her competitors ; and Ellen was
innocent and undefeated. It seemed to her, indeed, just such
a story as she might have expected to hear about his birth. It
was natural that to find so wonderful a child one would have to
go to the end of the earth. There appeared before her mind's
eye a very bright and clean picture, perhaps the frontispiece
of some forgotten book read in her childhood, which represented
a peasant girl clambering on to a ledge half-way up a cliff and
holding back a thorny branch to look down on a baby that,
clad in a little shirt, lay crowing and kicking in a huge bird's
nest. She wondered what manner of woman it was that had
so recklessly gone forth and found this world's wonder. " What
is your mother like ? Tell me, what is she like ? "

" What is she like ? " he repeated stiffly. He was not quite
sure that she was asking in the right spirit, that she was not

moved by such curiosity as makes people study the photographs of murdered people in the Sunday papers. " She is very beautiful. . . ." But he should not have said that. Now when he brought Ellen to Marion he would hear her say to herself, as tourists do when they see a Leonardo da Vinci, " Well, that's not my idea of beauty, I must say ! " and he would stop loving her. But Ellen was saying, " I thought she would be. You know, Richard, you are quite uncommon-looking. But tell me, what is she like ? " Of course he might have known she was trying to get at the story. He had bet er tell her at once, so that he was not vexed by these anglings. He dragged it out of himself. " She was young, very young. My father was the squire of the Essex village that is our home. . . ." It was useless. He could not tell her of that tragedy. How black a tragedy it was ! How, it existing, he could be so crass as to eat and drink and be merry with love ? He turned his face away from Ellen and wished her arm was not in his, yet felt himself bound to go on with his story lest she might make a vulgar reading of the facts and imagine that his mother had given herself to his father without being married for sheer easiness. " They could not marry because he had a wife. They loved each other very much. At least, on her side it was love ! On his . . . on *his* . . ."

" Ah, hush ! " she said. She gripped his arm and he felt that she was trembling violently. " Dear, the way you're speaking of it . . . somehow it's making it happen all over again. . . ."

This was strange. He looked down on her with sudden respect. For she was using almost the same words that his mother had spoken often enough when he had sat beside her bed on those nights when she could not sleep for the argument of phantom passions in her room, and she opened her eyes suddenly after having lain with them closed for a time, and found him grieving for her. " Dear, you must not be so sorry for me. Hold my hand, but do not feel too sorry for me. It only makes it worse for me. Truly, I ask for my own sake, not for yours. Do you not see ? When all the ripples have gone from the pond I shall forget I ever threw that stone. . . ." Was it not strange that this girl, on whose mind the dew was not yet dry, should speak the same wise words that had been found fittest by a woman who had been educated by a tragic destiny ? But of course she was as wise as she was beautiful. His thought of Marion became fatigued and resentful because it had made him forget the marvel of his Ellen.

" Forgive me," he murmured.

" Of course I forgive you."

" What, before I have told you what it is I want forgiveness for ? "

" I have it in my mind I will always forgive you for anything you do."

" That's a brave undertaking ! "

They laughed into each other's faces through the dusk. " Well, I've always hankered after a chance to show I'm brave. When I was a wee thing I used to cry because I couldn't be a soldier. I had the finest collection of tin soldiers you can imagine. A pairfect army. Mother used to stint herself to buy them for me. . . . Oh, dear ! Oh, dear ! " He felt her tremble again. " Well, we've come to the end of George the Fourth Bridge. Is it not awful inappropriate to call a street after George the Fourth when it is nearly all bookshops ? "

She did not name the street which they were entering. Indeed, though her breathing was tense, lethargy seemed to have fallen on her, and she slackened her pace and made him halt with her at the kerb, where they were necessarily jostled by the press of squalid people, lurching with drink or merely with rough manners, that streamed up and down this street of topless houses whose visible lower storeys were blear-eyed with windows broken or hung with rags.

" Isn't this the High Street ? "

" Yes. And I wish we were here any time but this. Think if this was a fine Saturday morning now, and we were going up to the Castle to see the Highlanders drilling."

" Didn't you say the Public Health Office was opposite the Cathedral ? "

" I did so. But dear knows it was ridiculous of me to drag you here. Most likely her number will not be there at all. After all, she was only taken away this morning, and the doctor said there'd be no change. He said I would be just a fule to worry."

He guided her across the road and looked for the office among the shops that faced the dark shape of the Cathedral, while she hung on his arm. " You will be angry with me for dragging you for nothing out into this awful part."

" Is this it ? "

" Yes, you must look, my eyes ache," she said peevishly. " Besides, her number will not be there. Richard, did ever you see a white dog like yon in the gutter ? Is it not a most peculiar-looking animal ? "

After a moment's silence he said steadily, " What did you say your mother's number was ? "

" Ninety-three. I told you it would not be there. Richard, look at that white dog ! "

His arm slipped round her. " My little Ellen," he whispered, " Ellen l "

(5)

A turn of the long dark avenue brought them alongside the city of the sick, which till then had been only a stain of light on the sky, and they looked through the railings at the hospital blocks which lay spaced over the level ground like battleships in a harbour. She reproached her being as inadequate because no intuition told her in which block her mother was. After a further stretch of avenue they came to a sandstone arch with lit rooms on either side, which diffused a grudging brightness through half-frosted windows on some beds of laurel bushes and a gravel drive. These things were so ugly in such a familiar way, so much of a piece with the red suburban streets which she knew stretched from the gates of this place through Morningside past Blackford Hill to Newington, and which had always seemed to her to shelter only the residue of life, strained of all events, that she took them as good omens.

When they went into the room on the left, and found a little office with ink-spattered walls and a clerk sitting on a high stool, she told herself, while a quarter of her mind listened to Richard explaining their errand and thought how nice it was to have a man to speak for one, that it was impossible for such an ordinary place to be the setting of an event so extraordinary, so unprecedented as death. It was true that her father was dead, but it had happened when he was abroad, and so had seemed just his last extreme indulgence of his habit of staying away from home. But the clerk sprang to his feet and, thrusting his pen behind his ear as if he were shouldering arms, said in a loud consequential voice : " Ay, I sent a messenger along to your residence the same time I 'phoned up to the Head Office to hev' the patient put on the danger list ! Everything possible is done in the way of consideration for the feelings of friends and relations ! " Yes, this was a hospital, and of course people sometimes died in hospitals. But she pushed away that fact and set her eyes steadily on the clerk's face, her mind on the words he had just spoken, and nearly laughed aloud to see that here was that

happy and comic thing a Dogberry, a simple soul who gilds
employment in some mean and tedious capacity by conceiving
it as a position of power over great issues. He took a large key
down from a nail on the wall and exclaimed, " I'll take you
myself ! " and she perceived that he was going to do something
which he should have delegated to a porter, so that he might
continue to display himself and his office to these two strangers.

As they passed under the arch into the hospital grounds she
kept her arm in Richard's because the warmth of his body made
it seem impossible that the flesh could ever grow quite cold, and
fixed her attention on the little clerk, because he offered a proof
that the character of life was definitely comic. But these frail
assurances, that were but conceits made by the mind while it
marked time before charging the dreaded truth, were overcome
by the strangeness of this place. The paved corridor that
followed on and on was built with waist-high walls, and between
the pillars that held up the gabled wooden roof the light streamed
out on lawns of coarse grass pricking rain-gleaming sod ; at
intervals they passed the immense swing doors of the wards,
blaringly bright with brass and highly polished gravy-coloured
wood ; at times another corridor ran into it, and at their meeting-
place there blew a swift unnatural wind, private to this place
and laden with the scentless scent of damp stone ; down one
such they saw a group of women walking, wrapped in cloaks
of different colours, flushed and cheered from some night meal,
making among themselves the infantile merriment that nuns
and nurses know.

This was a city unlike any other. It was set apart for
the sick ; and some sick people died , and of course there
was no reason that people should not die merely because
they were greatly beloved. She sobbed ; and the clerk, who
was walking on ahead of them with the gait of one who carries
a standard, turned round and, waving the key, which there could
be no occasion for him to use, as all the doors were open, said
kindly : " You know you mustn't be downhearted. I've seen
folk who came down on the verra same errand as yourselves go
away in the morning with fine an' happy faces." But after half
a minute the intense intellectual honesty without which he
could not have been so marked a character reasserted itself, and
he turned again and added reluctantly, " But I've known more
that didn't." She laughed on to Richard's shoulder and
crammed the speeches greedily into her memory, that some
night soon by the hearth in the sitting-room at Hume Park
Square she might repeat them to her mother, whom she figured

sitting in the armchair, looking remarkably well and wearing the moiré blouse that she had given her for her birthday.

" She's here," said the clerk dramatically ; and they stared at a door that looked like all the others. It admitted them to a rectilinear place of white doors and distempered walls. " She's upstairs ! " said the clerk, and they followed him. But as he reached the top he bent double with a prodigiously respectful gesture, and cried to someone they could not see, " Good evening, sir, I've brought the friends of Ninety-three," and turned and left them with some haste, impelled, Ellen thought, as she still amusedly centred her imagination upon him, by a fear of being rebuked for officiousness. But as she came to the landing and saw the four people who were standing there, having evidently just come through the door, which one of them was softly closing, everything left her mind but the knowledge that mother was dying. They forced it on her by their appearance alone, for they said nothing. They stood quite still, looking at her and Richard as if in her red hair and his tall swarthiness they saw something that, like the rainbow, laid on the eye a duty of devout absorbent sight; and on them fell a stream of harsh electric light that displayed their individual characters and the common quality that now convinced her that mother was dying.

There were two men in white coats, one sprucely middle-aged, whose vitality was bubbling in him like a pot of soup—good soup made of meat and bones, with none of the gristle of the spirit in it ; the other tall and fair and young, who turned a stethoscope in his long hands and looked from the lines on his pale face to be a martyr to thought; there was a grey-haired sister with large earnest spectacles and a ninepin body ; there was a young nurse whose bare forearm, as she drew the door to, was not less destitute of signs of mental activity than her broad, comely face. And it was plain from their air of indifference and gravity, of uninterested yet strained attention, that they were newly come from a scene which, though almost tediously familiar to them, yet struck them as solemn. They were banishing their impression of it from their consciousness, since they would not be able to carry on their work if they began to be excited about such every-day events. They seemed to be practising a deliberate stockishness as if they were urging the flesh to resist its quickened pulses ; but their solemnity had fled down to that place beneath the consciousness where the soul debates of its being, and there, as could be seen from the droop of the shoulders and the nervous contraction of the hand that was common to all, was raising doubt and fear. The nature of this scene was disclosed as a nurse at the end of the passage passed through a swing door, and they looked for one moment into the long cavern of a ward, lit with the dreadful light which dwells in hospitals while the healthy lie in darkness, that dreadful light which throbs like a headache and frets like fever, the very colour of pain. This light is diffused all over the world in these inhuman parallelogrammic cities of the sick, and sometimes it comes to a focus. It had come to a focus now, in the room which they had just left, where mother was lying.

She ran forward to the middle-aged doctor, whom she knew would be the better one. " Can you do nothing for her ? " she stammered appealingly. She wrung her hands in what she knew to be a distortion of ordinary movement, because it seemed suitable that to draw attention to the extraordinary urgency of her plea she should do extraordinary things. " Mother —mother's a most remarkable woman. . . ."

The doctor pulled his moustache and said that there was always hope, in a tone that left none, and then, as if he were ashamed of his impotence and were trying to turn the moment into something else, spoke in medical terms of Mrs. Melville's case and translated them into ordinary language, so that he sounded like a construing schoolboy. " Pulmonary dyspnœa —settled on her chest—heart too weak to do a tracheotomy— run a tube down. . . ." They opened the door of the room and told her to go into it. She paused at the threshold and wept, though she could not see her mother, because the room was so like her mother's life. There was hardly anything in it at all. There were grey distempered walls, a large window covered by a black union blind, polished floors, two cane chairs, and a screen of an impure green colour. The roadside would have been a richer death-chamber, for among the grass there would have been several sorts of weed ; yet this was appropriate enough for a woman who had known neither the hazards of being a rogue's wife, which she would have rather enjoyed, nor the close-pressed society of extreme poverty, in which she would have triumphed, for her birdlike spirits would have made her popular in any alley, but had been locked by her husband's innumerable but never quite criminal failings into an existence just as decently and minimally furnished as this room.

Her daughter clenched her fists with anger at it. But hearing a sound of stertorous breathing, she tiptoed across the room and looked behind the screen. There Mrs. Melville was lying on her back in a narrow iron bedstead. Her head was turned away, so that nothing of it could be seen but a thin grey plait trailing across the pillow, but her body seemed to have shrunk, and hardly raised the bedclothes. Ellen went to the side of the bed and knelt so that she might look into the hidden face, and was for a second terrified to find herself caught in the wide beam of two glaring open eyes that seemed much larger than her mother's had ever been. All that dear face was changed. The skin was glazed and pink, and about the gaping mouth, out of which they had taken the false teeth, there was a wandering blueness which seemed to come and go with the slow, roaring breath. Ellen fell back in a sitting posture and looked for Richard, whom she had forgotten, and who was now standing at the end of the bed. She stretched out her hands to him and moaned ; and at that sound recognition stirred in the centre of Mrs. Melville's immense glazed gaze, like a small waking bird ruffling its feathers on some inmost branch of a large tree.

" Oh, mother dear !　Mother dear ! "

From that roaring throat came a tortured, happy noise ; and she tried to make her lips meet, and speak.

" My wee lamb, don't try to speak. Just lie quiet. It's heaven just to be with you. You needn't speak."

But Mrs. Melville fought to say it. Something had struck her as so remarkable that she was willing to spend one of her last breaths commenting on it. They both bent forward eagerly to hear it. She whispered : " Nice to have a room of one's own."

Richard made some slight exclamation, and she rolled those vast eyes towards him, and fixed him with what might have been an accusing stare. At first he covered his mouth with his hand and looked at her under his lids as if the accusation were just, and then he remembered it was not, and squared his shoulders, and went to the other side of the bed and knelt down. Her eyes followed him implacably, but there he met them. He said, " Truly . . . I am all right. I will look after her. She can't be poor, whatever happens. Trust me, mother, she'll be all right," and under the bedclothes he found her hand, and raised it to his lips. Instantly the taut stare slackened, her puckered lids fell, and she dozed. Tears ran down Ellen's face, because her mother was paying no attention to her during the last few moments they were ever to be together, and was spending them in talk she could not understand with Richard, whom she had thought loved her too well to play this trick upon her. She could have cried aloud at her mother's unkind way of dying. It struck her that there had always been a vein of selfishness and inconsiderateness running through her mother's character, which had come to a climax when she indulged in this preposterous death just when the stage was set for their complete happiness. She had almost succeeded in fleeing from her grief into an aggrieved feeling, when those poor loose wrinkled lids lifted again, and the fluttering knowledge in those great glazed eyes probed the room for her and leapt up when it found her.

There was a jerk of the head and a whisper, "I'm going!" It was, though attenuated by the frailty of the dying body, the exact movement, the exact gesture that she had used when, on her husband's death, she had greeted the news that she and her daughter had been left with seventy pounds a year. Just like she had said, "Well, we must just economise!" She was going to be just as brave about death as she had been about life, and this, considering the guarantees Time had given her concerning the nature of Eternity, was a high kind of faith. "Mother dear! Mother dear!" Ellen cried, and though she remembered that outside the door they had told her she must not, she kissed her mother on the lips. "Mother dear! . . . it's been so . . . enjoyable being with you!" Mrs. Melville made a pleased noise, and by a weary nod of the head made it understood that she would prefer not to speak again; but her hand, which was in Ellen's, patted it.

All through the night that followed they pressed each other's hands, and spoke. "Are you dead?" Ellen's quickened breath would ask; and the faint pressure would answer, "No. I have still a little life, and I am using it all to think of you, my darling." And sometimes that faint pressure would ask, "Are you thinking of me, Ellen? These last few moments I want all of you," and Ellen's fingers would say passionately, "I am all yours, mother." In these moments the forgotten wisdom of the body, freed from the tyranny of the mind and its continual running hither and thither at the call of speculation, told them consoling things. The mother's flesh, touching the daughter's, remembered a faint pulse felt long ago and marvelled at this splendid sequel, and lost fear. Since the past held such a miracle the future mattered nothing. Existence had justified itself. The watchers were surprised to hear her sigh of rapture. The daughter's flesh, touching the mother's, remembered life in the womb, that loving organ that by night and day does not cease to embrace its beloved, and was the stronger for tasting again that first best draught of love that the spirit has not yet excelled.

There were footsteps in the corridor, a scuffle and a freshet of giggling; the nurses were going downstairs after the early morning cup of tea in the ward kitchen. This laughter that

sounded so strange because it was so late reminded Ellen of
the first New Year's Eve that she and her mother had spent in
Edinburgh. They had had no friends to first foot them, but
they had kept it up very well. Mrs. Melville had played the
piano, and Ellen and she had sung half through the *Student's
Song Book*, and they had had several glasses of Stone's Ginger
Ale, and there really had been a glow of firelight and holly berry
brightness, for Mrs. Melville, birdlike in everything, had a
wonderful faculty for bursts of gaiety, pure in tone like a blackbird's song, which brought out whatever gladness might be
latent in any person or occasion. As twelve chimed out they
had stood in front of the chimneypiece mirror and raised their
glasses above their heads, singing "Auld Lang Syne" in time with
the dancers on the other side of the wall, who were making such
a night of it that several times the house had seemed likely to
fall in.

When they had given three cheers and were sipping from
their glasses, Mrs. Melville had said drolly: "Did ye happen
to notice my arm when I was lifting it? Ye did not, ye
vain wee thing, ye were looking at yourself all the time. But
I'll give ye one more chance." And she had held it up so that
her loose sleeve (she was wearing a very handsome mauve
tea-gown bought by Mr. Melville in the temporary delirium of
his honeymoon, from which he had so completely recovered
that she never got another) fell back to her shoulder. "Mother,
I never knew you had arms like that!" She had never before
seen them except when they were covered by an ill-fitting sleeve
or, if they had been bare to the elbow, uninvitingly terminating
in a pair of housemaid's gloves or hands steamy with dish-
washing. "Mother, they're bonny, bonny!" Mrs. Melville
had been greatly pleased, but had made light of it. "Och,
they're nothing. We all have them in our family. Ye have
them yourself. Ye must always remember ye got them from
your great-grandmother Jeanie Napier, who was so much admired by Sir Walter Scott at her first ball. And talking of
dancing . . ." and she had lifted up her skirts and set her feet
waggishly twinkling in a burlesque dance, which she followed up
with a travesty of an opera, a form of art she had met with in
her youth and about which, since she was the kind of woman who
could have written songs and ballads if she had lived in the age
when wood fires and general plenty made the hearth a home
for poetry, she could be passionately witty as artists are about
work that springs from æsthetic principles different from their
own. It had been a lovely performance. They had ended in a

tempest of laughter, which had been brought to a sudden check when they had looked at the clock and seen that it was actually twenty-five to one, which was somehow so much worse than half-past twelve ! It was that moment that had been recalled to Ellen by the sudden interruption of the pulses of the night by the nurses' laughter. That had been a beautiful party.

She would never be at another, and looked down lovingly on her mother's face, and was horrified by its extreme ugliness. There was no longer any gallant Tom Thumb wit strutting about her eyes and mouth, no little tender cheeping voice to distract the attention from the hideous ruin time had worked in her. Age diffused through her substance, spoiling every atom, attacking its contribution to the scheme of form and colour. It had pitted her skin with round pores and made lie from nose to mouth thick folds such as coarse and valueless material might fall into, and on her lids it was puckered like silk on the lid of a workbox ; but if she had opened them they would only have shown whites that had gone yellow and were reticulated with tiny veins. It had turned her nose into a beak and had set about the nostrils little red tendril-like lines. Her lips were fissured with purple cracks and showed a few tall, narrow teeth standing on the pale gleaming gum like sea-eroded rocks when the tide is out. The tendons of her neck were like thick, taut string, and the loose arras of flesh that hung between them would not be nice to kiss, even though one loved her so much.

Really she was very ugly, and it was dreadful, for she had been very beautiful. Always at those tea-parties to which people were invited whom Ellen had known all her life from her mother's anecdotes as spirited girls of her own age, but which nobody came to except middle-aged women in shabby mantles, though all the invitations were accepted, someone was sure to say : "You know, my dear, your mother was far the prettiest girl in Edinburgh. Oh, Christina, you were ! . . ." It was true, too, a French artist who had come to Scotland to decorate Lord Rosebery's ballroom at Dalmeny had pestered Mrs. Melville to sit to him, and had painted a portrait of her which had been bought by the Metropolitan Museum in New York. Ellen had never had a clear idea of what the picture was like, for though she had often asked her mother, she had never got anything more out of her than a vexed, deprecating murmur : "Och, it's me, and standing at a ballroom door as if I was swithering if I would go in, and no doubt I'd a funny look on my face, for when your grannie

and me went down to his studio we never thought he really meant
to do it. And I was wearing that dress that's hanging up in
the attic cupboard. Yes, ye can bring it down if ye put it
back as ye find it." It was a dress of white ribbed Lille silk,
with thick lace that ran in an upstanding frill round the tiny
bodice and fell in flounces, held here and there with very pink
roses, over a pert little scalloped bustle ; she visualised it as
she had often held it up for her mother to look at, who would
go on knitting and say, with an affectation of a coldly critical
air, " Mhm. You may laugh at those old fashions, but I say
yon's not a bad dress."

It was, Ellen reflected, just such a dress as the women
wore in those strange worldly and passionate and self-
controlled pictures of Alfred Stevens, the Belgian, of whose
works there had once been a loan collection in the National
Gallery. Her imagination, which was working with excited
power because of her grief and because her young body was
intoxicated with lack of sleep, assumed for a moment pictorial
genius, and set on the blank wall opposite the portrait of her
mother as Alfred Stevens would have painted it. Oh, she was
lovely standing there in the shadow, with her red-gold hair
and her white skin, on which there was a diffused radiance which
might have been a reflection of her hair, and her little body
springing slim and arched from the confusion of her skirts !
The sound of the " Blue Danube " was making her eyes bright and
setting her small head acock, and a proud but modest knowledge
of how more than one man was waiting for her in there and
would be pleased and confused by her kind mockery, twisted
her mouth with the crooked smile of the Campbells. Her innocence made her all sweet as a small, sound strawberry lying
unpicked in the leaves, and manifested itself in a way that
caused love and laughter in this absurd dress whose too thick silk,
too tangible lace, evidently proceeded from some theory of allure-
ment which one had thought all adults too sophisticated to hold.

Oh, she had been beautiful ! Ellen looked down in pity
on the snoring face, and in the clairvoyance of her intense
emotion she suddenly heard again the crisp rustle of the silk
and looked down on its yellowed but immaculate surface, and
perceived that its preservation disclosed a long grief of her
mother's. That dress had never been thrown, though they had
had to travel light when Mr. Melville was alive, and the bustled
skirt was a cumbrous thing to pack, because she had desired to
keep some relique of the days when she was so beautiful that
an artist, a professional, had wanted to paint her portrait. An

inspiration occurred to Ellen, and she bent down and said,
" Mother, Richard and me'll go to New York and see your
portrait in the Museum there." The dying woman jerked her
head in a faint shadow of a bridle and made a pleased, deprecating
noise, and pressed her daughter's hand more firmly than she had
done for the last hour. Ellen wept, for though these things
showed that her mother had been pleased by her present words,
they also showed that she had been conscious of her beauty and
the loss of it. She remembered that that New Year's Eve, seven
years before, before they had gone up to bed, her mother had
again held up her arm before the mirror and had sighed and
said : " They last longer than anything else about a woman,
you know. Long after all the rest of you's old ye can keep a
nice arm. Ah, well ! Be thankful you can keep that ! " and
she had gone upstairs singing a parody of the Ride of the Valkyries
(" Go to bed ! Go to bed ! ").

Of course she had hated growing old and ugly.
It must be like finding the fire going out and no more coal
in the house. And it had been done to her violently
by the brute force of decay, for her structure was unalterably
lovely, the bones of her face were little but perfect, the eye lay
in an exquisitely-vaulted socket ; and everything that could
be tended into seemliness was seemly, and the fine line of her
plait showed that she brushed her grey hair as if it were still
red gold. Age had simply come and passed ugliness over her,
like the people in Paris that she had read about in the paper
who threw vitriol over their enemies. This was a frightening
universe to live in, when the laws of nature behaved like very
lawless men. She was so young that till then she had thought
there were three fixed species of people—the young, the middle-
aged, and the old—and she had never before realised that young
people must become old, or stop living. She trembled with
rage at this arbitrary rule, and sobbed to think of her dear
mother undergoing this humiliation, while her free hand and a
small base fraction of her mind passed selfishly over her face,
asking incredulously if it must suffer the same fate. It seemed
marvellous that people could live so placidly when they knew
the dreadful terms of existence, and it almost seemed as if they
could not know and should be told at once so that they could arm
against Providence. She would have liked to run out into the
sleeping streets and call on the citizens to wake and hear the
disastrous news that beautiful women grow old and lose their
beauty, and that within her knowledge this had happened to
one who did not deserve it.

She raised her head and saw that the young nurse who had been coming in and out of the room all night was standing at the end of the bed and staring at her with lips pursed in disapproval. She was shocked, Ellen perceived, because she was not keeping her eyes steadfastly on her mother, but was turning this way and that a face mobile with speculation ; and for a moment she was convinced by the girl's reproach into being ashamed because her emotion was not quite simple. But that was nonsense ; she was thinking as well as feeling about her mother, because she had loved her with the head as well as with the heart.

Yet she knew, and knew it feverishly, because night emptied of sleep is to the young a vacuum, in which their minds stagger about, that in a way the nurse was right. If she had not been quite so clever she would never have made her mother cry, as she had done more than once by snapping at her when she had said stupid things. There rushed on her the recollection of how she had once missed her mother from the fireside and had thought nothing of it, but on going upstairs to wash her hands had found her sitting quite still on the wooden chair in her cold bedroom, with the tears rolling down her cheeks ; and how, when Ellen had thrown her arms round her neck and begged her to say what was the matter, she had quavered, " You took me up so sharply when I thought Joseph Chamberlain was a Liberal. And he *was* a Liberal once, dear, when your father and I were first married and he still talked to me. I'm *sure* Joseph Chamberlain was a Liberal then." At this memory Ellen put her head down on the pillow beside her mother's and sobbed bitterly ; and was horrified to find herself being pleased because she was thus giving the nurse proof of proper feelings.

She sat up with a jerk. She was not nearly nice enough to have been with her mother, who was so good that even now, when death was punishing her face like a brutal and victorious boxer, bringing out patches of pallor and inflamed redness, making the flesh fall away from the bone so that the features looked different from what they had been, it still did not look at all terrible, because the lines on it had been traced only by diffidence and generosity. With her ash-grey hair, her wrinkles, and the mild unrecriminating expression with which she supported her pain, she looked like a good child caught up by old age in the obedient performance of some task. That was what she had always been most like, all through life—a good child. She had always walked as if someone in authority, most likely an aunt, had just told her to mind and turn her toes out. It had given her, when she grew older and her shoulders had become bent, a peculiar tripping gait which Ellen hated to remember she had often been ashamed of when they went into tea-shops or crossed a road in front of a lot of people, but which she saw now to have been lovelier than any dance, with its implication that all her errands were innocent.

" Mother, mother ! " she moaned, and their hands pressed one another, and there was more intimate conversation between their flesh. Her exalted feelings, as she came out of them, reminded her of other shared occasions of ecstasy. She remembered Mrs. Melville clutching excitedly at her arm as she turned her face away from the west, where a winy darkness of banked clouds had succeeded flames, round which little rounded golden cloudlets thronged like Cupids round a celestial bonfire, and crying in a tone of gourmandise, " I would go anywhere for a good sunset ! "

There was that other time that she had been so happy, when they had watched the fish-wives of Dunbar sitting on tubs under great flaring torches set in sconces on the wall behind them, gutting herrings that slid silver under their quick knives and left blood on their fingers that shone like a fluid jewel, raw-coloured to suit its wearers' weathered rawness, and lay on the cobbles as a rich dark tesselation, The reflected sunset had lain within the high walls of the harbour as in a coffin, its fires made peaceful by being caught on oily waters, and above the tall roof-trees of the huddled houses behind the stars had winked like cold, clever eyes of the night. Mrs. Melville had circled about the scene, crying out at all its momentary shifts from key to key of beauty, murmuring that the supper would be spoiling and the landlady awful annoyed, but she must wait, she must wait. When the women had stopped gutting and had arisen, shaking a largesse of silver scales from their canvas aprons, and the dying torches had split and guttered and fallen from the sconces and been trodden out under the top-boots of bearded men, she had gone home with Ellen like a reveller conducted by a sober friend, exclaiming every now and then with a fearful joy in her own naughtiness, " It's nearly nine, but it's been worth it ! "

For this innocent passion for beauty the poor little thing (Ellen remembered how lightly her mother had weighed on her arm that night, though she was tired) had made many sacrifices. To see better the green glass of the unbroken

wave and hear the kiss the spray gives the sea on its return
she would sit in the bow of the steamer, though that did not
suit her natural timidity; and if passengers were landed at a
village that lay well on the shore she would go ashore, even if
there were no pier and she had to go in a small boat, though
these made her squeal with fright. And there was an absolute
purity about this passion. It was untainted by greed. She
loved most of all that unpossessable thing, the way the world
looks under the weather; and on the possessable things of
beauty that had lain under her eyes, in the jewellers'
windows in Princes Street or on the walls of the National
Gallery, she had gazed with no feelings but the most
generous, acclaiming response to their quality and gratitude for
the kindness on the part of the powers that be. She had been
a good child: she hadn't snatched.

But when one thinks of a good child faithfully adhering to
the nursery ethic the thought is not bearable unless it is understood that there is a kind nurse in the house who dresses her
up for her walk so that people smile on her in the streets, and
maybe buys her a coloured balloon, and when they come back to
tea spreads the jam thick and is not shocked at the idea of
cake. But mother was lying here in a hospital nightgown of
pink flannel, between greyish cotton sheets under horse-blankets,
in pain and about to die; utterly unrewarded. And she had
never been rewarded. Ellen's mind ran through the arcade
of their time together and could find no moment when her
mother's life had been decorated by any bright scrap of that
beauty she adored.

Ellen could see her rising in the morning, patting her
yawning mouth with her poor ugly hands, putting her flannel
dressing-gown about her, and treading clumsy with sleep
down the creaky stairs to put the kettle on the gas, on her
knees before the kitchen range, her head tied up in a handkerchief
to keep the ash out of her hair, sticking something into the fire
that made disagreeable grating noises which suggested it was
not being used as competently as it might be; standing timidly
in shops, trying to attract the notice of assistants who perceived
she was very poor: but she could never see her visited by
beauty. For her it had stayed in the sunset. It might have
abode with her in the form of love: indeed, Ellen thought
that would have been the best form it could have taken, for she
knew that she could be quite happy, even if her life were harder
than her mother's in the one point in which it could be harder
and there were not enough to eat, provided that she had Richard.

But she felt it impossible that her mother could have sipped any real joy from companionship with herself, whom she conceived as cold and vicious ; and pushing her memory back to the earliest period, where it hated to linger, she perceived innumerable heartrending intimations that the free expenditure of her mother's dearness had brought her no comfort of love.

She could remember no good of her father. It was his habit to wear the Irish manner of distraction, as he walked the streets with his chin projected and his eyes focussed in the middle distance to make them look wild, but his soul was an alert workman who sat tightening screws. By neat workmanship he could lift from negligences any reproach of negativeness and turn them into positive wounds. If he were going to send his wife too little money, and that too late, he would weeks before lead her to expect an especially large cheque so that she would dream of little extravagances, of new shoes for Ellen, of sweets and fruit, until they were as good as bought, and the loss of them added the last saltness to the tears that flowed when there had at last arrived not quite enough to pay the rent. He was indeed a specialist in disappointment. Ellen guessed that he had probably preluded this neglectful marriage by a very passionate courtship ; probably he had said to mother the very things that Richard said to her, but without meaning them. At that she shivered, and knew the nature of the sin of blasphemy.

How her mother had been betrayed ! It was as monstrous a story as anything people made a fuss about in literature. What had happened to Ophelia and Desdemona that had not happened to her mother ? Her heart had broken just as theirs did, and in the matter of death they had had the picturesque advantage. And her father, was he not as dreadful as Iago ? Thinking so much of him brought back the hated sense of his physical presence, and she saw again the long, handsome face, solemn with concentration on the task of self-esteem, surmounted by its high, narrow forehead, and heard the voice, which somehow was also high and narrow, repeating stories which invariably ran : " He came to me and asked me . . . and I said, ' My dear fellow . . .' " For, like all Irishmen, he was fond of telling stories of how people brought him their lives' problems, which he always found ridiculously easy to solve. Everything about him, the sawing gestures of his white, oblong hands, the cold self-conscious charm of his brogue, the seignorial contempt with which he spoke of all other human beings and of all forms of human activity save speculation on the Stock Exchange, seemed to have a secondary meaning of rejection of her mother's love and mockery of her warm, loyal spirit. There spoke, too, an earnest dedication to malignity in the accomplishment to which he had brought the art of telling unspoken, and therefore uncontradictable, lies about her mother. If, after helping him on with his coat in the hall and laying a loving hand on his sleeve because he looked such a fine man, she asked him for money to pay the always overdue household bills, or even to ask whether they would wait dinner for him, he would say something quite just about the untidiness of her hair, follow it up by a generalisation on her unworthiness, and then bang the door, but not too loudly, as if he had good-humouredly administered a sharp rap over the knuckles to a really justifiable piece of female imbecility.

Yet while she shook with hate at the memory of what her father was, she guessed what would please her mother most, and, leaning over her, she whispered, " Mother, do you hear me ? I believe father did care for you quite a lot in his own way." And the dying woman lifted her lids and showed eyes that at this lovely thought had relit the fires that had burned there when she was quite alive, and pressed her daughter's hands with a fierce, jubilant pressure.

How dared her father contemn her mother so ? Her father was not a fool. That she was quite submissive to life, that it was unthinkable that she could rebel against society or persons, was not because she was foolish, but because she was sweet. To question a law would be to cast imputations against those who made it and those who obeyed it, and that was a grave responsibility ; to question an act would perhaps be to give its doer occasion for remorse, and in a world of suffering how could she take upon herself to do that ? She had had dignity. She had had that real wildness which her husband had aped, for she was a true romantic. She had scorned the plain world where they talk prose more expensively than most professed romantics do.

Once on the top of a tram towards Craiglockhart she had pointed out to Ellen a big house of the prosperous, geometric sort, with greenhouses and a garage and a tennis-court, and said, " Yon's Johnny Fauld's house. He proposed to me once at a picnic on the Isle of May, and I promised him, but I took it back that very evening because he was that upset at losing his umbrella. I knew what would come to him from his father, but I could not fancy marrying a man who was upset at losing his umbrella." At the recollection Ellen laughed aloud, and cried out, " Mother, you are such a wee darling ! "

And she was more than a romantic : she was a poet. What was there in all Keats and Shelley but just this same passion for unpossessable things ? It was vulgar, like despising a man because he has not made money though it is well known that he has worked hard, to do her less honour than them because she was not able to set down in verse the things she undoubtedly felt. And she was good, so good—even divinely good. Life had given her so little beyond her meagre flesh and breakable bones that it might have seemed impossible that she should satisfy the exorbitant demands of her existence. But she had done that ; she had reared a child, and of the wet wood of poverty she had made a bright fire on her hearthstone. She had done more than that : she had given her child a love that was unstinted good living for the soul. And she had done more than that : to every human being with whom she came in contact she had made a little present of something over and above the ordinary decent feelings arising from the situation, something which was too sensible and often too roguish to be called tenderness, which was rather the handsomest possible agreement with the other person's idea of himself, and a taking of his side in his struggle with fate. This power of giving gifts was a miracle of the loaves and fishes kind. " Mother, I did not desairve you ! " she cried. " I do wish I had been better to you ! " And what had her mother got for being a romantic, a poet, and a saint who worked miracles ? Nothing. This snoring death in a hospital was life's final award to her. It could not possibly be so. She sat bolt upright, her mouth a round hole with horror, restating the problem. But it was so. A virtuous woman was being allowed to die without having been happy.

" Oh, mother, mother ! " Ellen wailed, wishing they had not embarked on the universe in such a leaky raft as this world, and was terrified to find that her mother's hand made no answer to her pressure. " Nurse ! " she cried, and was enraged that no answer came from behind the screen, until the door opened, and the nurse, looking pretentiously sensible, followed the two doctors to the bed. She found it detestable that this cold hireling should have detected her mother's plight before she did, and when they took her away for a moment she stumbled round the screen, whimpering, " Richard ! " trying to behave well, but wanting to make just enough fuss for him to realise how awful she was feeling.

Richard was sitting in front of the fire, rubbing the sleep out of his eyes, but he jumped up alertly and gathered her to his arms.

" Richard, she's going ! "

He could find no consolation to give her but a close, un-voluptuous embrace. They stood silent, looking at the fire. " Is it not strange," she whispered, " that people really die ? "

Richard did not in the least participate in this feeling. He merely looked at her with misted eyes, as if he found it touching that anyone should feel like that, and this reassured her. Perhaps he knew an answer to this problem. It might be possible that he knew it and yet could not tell it, for she had never been able to tell him how she loved him, though she knew quite well. She lifted her face to his that she might see if there were know-ledge in his eyes, and was disappointed that he merely bent to kiss her.

" No ! " she said fretfully, adding half honestly, half because he had disappointed her, " You mustn't. I've been kissing mother."

But he persisted ; and they exchanged a solemn kiss, the religious sister of their usual passionate kisses. Then she shook with a sudden access of anger, and clung to his coat lapels and stared into his eyes so that he should give her full attention, and poured out her tale of wrong in a spate of whispering. " Every night ever since I can remember I've seen mother kneeling by her bed to say her prayers, no matter how cold it was, though she never would buy herself good woollens, and never scamping them to less than five minutes. And what has she got for it ? What has she got for it ? " But they called for her behind the screen, and she dropped her hands and answered, pretending that her mother was so well that it might have been she who called, " I'm coming, darling."

The moustached doctor, when she had come to the foot of the bed, said gently, " I'm sorry; it's all over."

She bent a careful scrutiny on her mother. " Are you sure ? " she said wistfully.

" Quite sure."

" May I kiss her ? "

" Please don't. It isn't safe."

" Ah well ! " she sighed. " Then we'd best be going. Richard, are you ready ? "

As he came to her side she raised her head and breathed " Good night ! " to that ghostly essence which she conceived was floating vaporously in the upper air and slipped her arm in his. " Good night, and thank you for all you've done for her," she said to the people round the bed. As she went to the door a remembrance checked her. " What of the funeral ? "

" They'll tell you all that down at the office." This was a terrifying place, where there existed a routine to meet this strange contingency of death ; where one stepped from a room where drawn blinds cabined in electric light into a passage full with pale daylight ; and left a beloved in that untimely artificial brightness as in some separate and dangerous division of time ; where mother lay dead.

Yet after all, because terror existed here and had written itself across the night as intensely as beauty ever wrote itself across the sky in sunset, it need not be that terror is one of the forces which dictate the plot of the universe. This was a catchment area that drained the whole city of terror ; and how small it was ! Certainly terror was among the moods of the creative Person, whom for the sake of clear thinking they found it necessary to hold responsible for life, though being children of this age, and conscious of humanity's grievance, they thought of Him without love. But it was one of the least frequent and the most impermanent of His moods. All the people one does not know seem to be quite happy. Therefore it might be that though Fate had finally closed the story of Mrs. Melville's life, and had to the end shown her no mercy, there was no occasion for despair about the future. It might well be that no other life would ever be so grievous. Therefore it was with not the least selfish taint of sorrow, it was with tears that were provoked only by the vanishment of their beloved, that they passed out through the iron gates.

The scene did not endorse their hopeful reading of the situation. Before them stretched the avenue, confined on each side by palings with rounded tops which looked like slurs on a score of music ; to the right the hospital lay behind a flatness of grass, planted in places with shrubs , and to the left, on the slope of the hill on which the grey workhouse stood, painted the very grey colour of poverty itself, paupers in white overalls worked among bare trees. Through this grim landscape they stepped forward, silent and hand in hand, grieving because she had lived without glory, she who was so much loved by them, whose life was going to be so glorious.

BOOK II

BOOK II

CHAPTER I

Now that they had taken the tickets at Willesden, Ellen felt doubtful of the whole enterprise. It was very possible that Richard's mother would not want her. In fact, she had been sure that Richard's mother did not want her ever since they left Crewe. There a fat, pasty young man had got in and taken the seat opposite her, and had sat with his pale grey eyes dwelling on the flying landscape with a slightly sick, devotional expression, while his lips moved and his plump hands played with a small cross inscribed "All for Jesus" which hung from his watch-chain. Presently he had settled down to rest with his hands folded on his lap, but had shortly been visited with a distressing hiccup, which shook his waistcoat so violently that the little cross was sent flying up into the air. "Mother will laugh when I tell her about that," she said to herself, and did not remember for a second that her mother had been dead six weeks.

This sharp reminder of the way they had conspired together to cover the blank wall of daily life with a trellis of trivial laughter made her stare under knitted brows at the companionship that was to be hers henceforward. It could not be as good as that. Indeed, from such slender intimations as she had received, it was not going to be good at all. Her inflexibly honest æsthetic sense had made her lay by Mrs. Yaverland's letters with the few trinkets and papers she desired to keep for ever, because they were written in such an exquisite script, each black word written so finely and placed so fastidiously on the thick, rough, white paper, and she felt it a duty to do honour to all lovely things. But their contents had increased her sense of bereavement. They had come like a north wind blowing into a room that is already cold. She had not wished to find them so, for she disliked becoming so nearly the subject of a comic song as a woman who hates her mother-in-law. But it was really the fact that they had the air of letters written by someone who was sceptical of the very existence of the addressee and had sent them merely to humour some third person. And where the expressions were strong she felt that they were qualified by their own terseness. Old people, she felt, ought to write fluently kind things in a running Italian hand. She was annoyed too by the way Richard always spoke of her as Marion. Even the anecdotes he recounted to show how brave and wise his mother was left Ellen a little tight-lipped. He said she was in favour of Woman's Suffrage, but it was almost as bad as being against it to have such gifts and never to have done anything with them, and to have been economically dependent all the days of her life.

It became evident from the way that a kind of heated physical ill-breeding seemed to fall on everybody in the carriage, and the way they began to lurch against each other and pull packages off the rack and from under the seat with disregard for each other's comfort, that they were approaching the end of the journey ; and she began to think of Marion with terror and vindictiveness, and this abstinence from a career became a sinister manifestation of that lack of spiritual sinew which had made her succumb to a bad man and handicap Richard with illegitimacy. She prefigured her swarthy and obese.

She got out and stood quite still on the platform, as she had been told to do. The station was fine, with its immense windless vaults through which the engine smoke rose slowly through discoloured light and tarnished darkness. She liked the people, who all looked darkly dressed and meek as they hurried along into the layer of shadow that lay along the ground, and who seemed to be seeking so urgently for cabs and porters because their meagre lives had convinced them that here was never enough of anything to go round. If she and her mother had ever come to London on the trip they had always planned, she would have been swinging off now to look for a taxi, just like a man ; and when she came back her mother would have said, " Why, Ellen, I never would have thought you could have got one so quickly." Well, that would not happen now. She would have grieved over it ; but a train far down the line pulled out of the station and disclosed a knot of red and green signal lights that warmed the eye and thence the heart as jewels do, and at that she was as happy as if she were turning over private jewels that she could wear on her body and secrete in her own casket. She was absorbed in the sight when she heard a checked soft exclamation, and turning about had the illusion that she looked into Richard's eyes.

" I am Richard's mother. You are Richard's wife ? "

Ellen repeated, "I am Richard's wife," feeling distressed that she had said it, since they were not yet married, but aware that to correct it would be trivial.

It was strange to look down instead of up at those dark eyes, those brows which lay straight black bars save for that slight piratical twist, with no intervening arch between them and the dusky eyelids. It was strange to hear Richard's voice coming from a figure blurred with soft, rich, feminine clothes. It was strange to see her passing through just such a moment of impeded tenderness as Richard often underwent. Plainly she wanted to kiss Ellen, but was prevented by an intense physical reserve, and did not want to shake hands, since that was inadequate, and this conflict gave her for a minute a stiff queerness of attitude. She compromised by taking Ellen's left hand in her own left hand, and giving it what was evidently a sincere but not spontaneous pressure. Then, turning away, she asked, "What about your luggage?"

"I've just this suitcase. I sent the rest in advance. Do you not think that's the most sensible way?" said Ellen, in a tone intended to convey that she was not above taking advice from an older women.

Mrs. Yaverland made a vague, purring noise, which seemed to imply that she found material consideration too puzzling for discussion, and commanded the porter with one of those slow, imperative gestures that Richard made when he wanted people to do things. Walking down the platform, Ellen wondered why Richard always called her a little thing. His mother was far smaller than she was, and broad-shouldered too, which made her look dumpy. Her resemblance to Richard became marked again when they got into the taxi, and she dealt with the porter and the driver with just such quiet murmured commands and dippings into pockets of loose change as Richard on these occasions, but Ellen did not find it in the least endearing. She was angry that Richard was like that, not because he was himself, but because he was this woman's son. When Mrs. Yaverland asked in that beautiful voice which was annoyingly qualified by terseness as her letters had been, "And how's Richard?" she replied consequentially, with the air of a person describing his garden to a person who has not one. But Mrs. Yaverland was too distracting to allow her to pursue this line with any satisfaction. For she listened with murmurs that were surely contented; and, having drawn off her very thick, very soft leather gloves, she began to polish her nails, which were already brighter than any Ellen had ever seen, against the palms of her hands, staring meanwhile out of absent eyes at the sapphire London night about them, which Ellen was feeling far too upset to enjoy.

There was a tormenting incongruity about this woman : those lacquered nails shown on hands that were broad and strong like a man's ; and the head that rose from the specifically dark fur was massive and vigilant and serene, like the head of a great man. Moreover, she was not in the least what one expects an old person to be. Old persons ought to take up the position of audience. They ought, above all things, to give a rest to the minds of young people, who, goodness knows, have enough to worry them, by being easily comprehensible. With mother one knew exactly where one was ; one knew everything that had happened to her and how she had felt about it, and there was no question of anything fresh ever happening to her. But from the deep, slow breaths this woman drew, from the warmth that seemed to radiate from her, from those purring murmurs which were evidently the sounds of a powerful mental engine running slow, it was plain that she was still possessed of that vitality which makes people perform dramas. And everything about her threatened that her performances would be too strange.

She had a proof of that when the taxi turned out of a busy street into a brilliantly lit courtyard and halted behind another cab, suspending her in a scene that deserved to be gaped at because it was so definitely not Edinburgh. The air of the little quadrangle was fairly dense with the yellowed rays of extravagant light, and the walls were divided not into shops and houses, but into allegorical panels representing pleasure. They had stopped outside a florist's, in whose dismantled window a girl in black stretched out a long arm towards the last vase of chrysanthemums, which pressed against the glass great curled polls almost as large as her own head. It was impossible to imagine a Scotswoman practising so felinely elastic an attitude before the open street, or possessing a face so ecstatic with pertness, or finding herself inside a dress which, though black, disclaimed all intention of being mourning and sought rather, in its clinging economy, to be an occasion of public rejoicing.

Inconceivable, too, in Edinburgh, the place beside it, where behind plate glass walls, curtained with flimsy *brise-bises* that were as a ground mist, men and women ate and drank under strong lights with a divine shamelessness. It couldn't happen up there. There were simply not the people to do it. It might be tried at first ; but because middle-aged men would constantly

turn to middle-aged women and say, " Catch me bringing you
here again, Elspeth. It's a nice thing to have your dinner with
every Tom, Dick and Harry in the street watching every mouth-
ful you take," and because young men would as constantly
have turned to young women with the gasp, " I'm sure I saw
father passing," it would have been a failure. But here it was
a success. The sight was like loud, frivolous music. And on
the other side there was a theatre with steps leading up to a
glittering bow-front, and a dark wall spattered with the white
squares of playbills, under which a queue of people watched
with happy and indifferent faces a ragged reciter whose burlesque
extravagance of gesture showed that one was now in a
country more tolerant of nonsense than the North.

She wanted to sit there quietly, savouring the scene. But Mrs.
Yaverland said in her terse voice : " I've taken rooms at the Haps-
burg for to-night. I thought you'd like it. I do myself, because it's
near the river. You know, we're near the river at Roothing."
Ellen could no longer turn her attention to the spectacle for
wondering why Mrs. Yaverland should speak of the Thames as
if it were an interesting and important relative. It could not
possibly be that Mrs. Yaverland felt about the river as she felt
about the Pentlands, for elderly people did not feel things like
that. They liked a day's outing, but they always sat against
the breakwater with the newspaper and the sandwich-basket
while one went exploring ; at least, mother always did. Trying
to insert some sense into the conversation, she asked politely,
" Do you do much boating ? " and was again baffled by the
mutter, " No, it's too far away." Well, if it was too far away
it could not be near. She was tired by the long day's travel.

But the hotel, when they alighted, pleased her. The vast
entrance hall, with its prodigality of tender rosy light, the
people belonging to the very best families who sat about in
monstrously large armchairs set at vast intervals on the lawny
carpets, were not in the least embarrassed by the publicity of
their position and shone physically with well-being and the
expectation of pleasure ; the grandiose marble corridors, the
splendid version of a lift, and the number of storeys that flashed
past them, all very much the same, but justifying their monotony
by their stateliness, like modern blank verse, made her remember
solemnly her inner conviction that she would some day find
herself amid surroundings of luxury.

The necessity of looking as if she were used to and
even wearied by this sort of thing weighed heavily on
her, for she felt that it was almost dishonour not to express

the solemn joy this magnificence was giving her. So she stood in the fine room to which Mrs. Yaverland took her, and after having resolved that the minute she was left alone she would touch the magnificent crimson velvet roses that stood out in high relief all over the wallpaper, she felt that she could not graciously withhold praise from this which was to be her own special share of the splendour. She moved shyly towards Mrs. Yaverland, who had gone to the window and was looking down in the night, and said shyly, " This is a very fine room," but, she knew, too softly to reach such markedly inattentive ears. She stood there awkwardly, feeling herself suspended till this woman should take notice of her. If her mother had been with her they would have had a room with two beds, and would have talked before they went to sleep of the day and its wonderful ending in this grand place. She sighed. Mrs. Yaverland turned round.

" Come and look at your view," she said, and raised the sash so that they could lean out.

Beneath there was a deep drop of the windless, scentless darkness that night brings to modern cities ; then a narrow trench of unlit gardens obscured by the threadbare texture of leafless tree-tops, then a broad luminous channel of roadway, lined with trees whose natural substance was so changed by the unnatural light that they looked like toy trees made of some brittle composition, and traversed by tramcars glowing orange and twanging white sparks from invisible wires with their invisible arms ; at its further edge a long procession of lights stood with a certain pomp along a dark margin, beyond which were black flowing waters. To the left, from behind tall cliffs of masonry pierced with innumerable windows that were not lit yet gleamed, like the eyes of a blind dog, there jutted out the last spans of a bridge, set thickly with large lights whose images bobbed on the current beneath like vast yellow water-flowers. On another bridge to the right a train was casting down on the stream a redness that was fire rather than light. On the opposite bank of the river, at the base of black towers, barges softly dark like melancholy lay on the different harsher darkness of the water, and showed, so sparsely that they looked the richer, a few ruby and emerald lights. Above, stars crackled frostily, close to earth, as stars do in winter.

" That is the river," said Mrs. Yaverland.

She said it as if she desired to be out of this warmth, standing down there by the dark parapet marked by the line of lamps close to the flowing waters ; as if she would have liked all the beautiful bright lights to be extinguished, so that there would be nothing left but the dark waters.

Ellen went and sat down on the bed. There was a standard lamp beside it, whose light, curbed to a small rosy cloud by a silken shade like a fairy's frock, seemed much the best thing for her eyes in the room. She was sad that in this new life in England, which had seemed so promising, one still had to turn for comfort from persons to things. She was aware that wildness such as this, such preferences for walking abroad in the chill night rather than sitting in warm rooms, for sterile swift water rather than the solid earth that bears the crops and supports the cities, are the processes of poetry working in the soul. But it did not please her in an older woman. She felt that Mrs. Melville, who would have been trotting about crying out at the magnificence of the room, would have been behaving not only more conveniently, but more decently, than this woman who was now crossing the room and not bringing peace with her. Her open coat slipped backwards on her shoulders so that it stood out on each side like a cloak worn by a romantic actor striding across the stage to the play's climax. The ultimate meaning of her expression could be no other than insolence, for it gave sign of some preoccupation so strong that the only force which could hold her back from speaking of it could be contempt for her hearer. Her face was shadowed with a suggestion of strong feeling, which was as unsuitable on cheeks so worn as paint would have been.

Ellen drooped her head so that she need not look at her as she sat down on the bed beside her with neither word nor gesture that said it was a movement towards intimacy, and said, " I hope you're not very tired." When Ellen went into the bathroom she wept in her bath, because the words could not have been said more indifferently, and it was dreadful to suspect, as she had to later, that someone so like Richard was either affected or hypocritical. For if that wildness were sincere, and not some Southern affectation (and she had always heard that the English were very affected), then the nice but ordinary things she said when she was doing up Ellen's black taffeta frock must be all hypocrisy and condescension.

It was a pity that she was so very like Richard. When they had gone downstairs and taken a table in that same glittering room behind the plate glass walls, Ellen forgot her uncomfortable feeling that as she crossed the room everyone had stared at her feet in a nasty sort of way in her resentful recognition of that likeness. She was not, of course, so handsome as Richard, though she was certainly what people call "very striking-looking." Ellen felt pleased that the description should be at once so appropriate and so common. She did not allow herself to translate it from commonness and admit that it is a phrase that common people use when they want to say a woman's face is the point of departure for a fair journey of the imagination. It was true that a certain rough imperfection was as definitely a part of her quality as perfection was of his, and that there ran from her nose to her mouth certain heavy lines that could never at any age befall his flesh with its bias towards beauty. But everything that so wonderfully made its appearance a reference to romance was here also : that dark skin in which it seemed as if the customary pigment had been blended with mystery ; that extravagance of certain features, the largeness of the eye, the luxury of lashes ; that manner at once languid and alert, which might have been acquired by residence in some country where molten excess of fine weather was corrected by gales of adventure. But though so close in blood and in seeming to the most beloved, this woman could not be loved. She could not possibly be liked. But this was an irrational emotion, and Ellen hated such, and she watched her for signs of some quality that would justify it.

It was there. Strong intimations of a passion for the trivial were brought forth by movement. As she bent over the menu, and gave orders that trembled on the edge of audibility to a waiter whom she appeared not to see, she repeatedly raised her right hand and with a swift, automatic sweep of the forefinger, on which her pink nail flashed like a polished shell, she smoothed her thick eyebrows. It was evidently a habitual gesture and used for something more than its apparent purpose, for when she had finished and leaned back in her chair she repeated it, although the brows were still sleek. She did it, Ellen told herself with a tightening of her lips, as a person who would like to spend the afternoon playing the piano but is obliged to receive a visitor instead and strums on her knee. It was the only expression the occasion allowed for that passionate care for her own person which accounted for the inordinate beauty of her clothes. They were, she said to herself, using a phrase which she had always previously disliked, fair ridiculous for a woman of that age. They were, almost sinisterly, not accidental. The very dark brown hat on her head was just sufficiently like in shape to the crowns that Russian empresses wear in pictures to heighten the effect of majesty, which, Ellen supposed without approval, was what she was aiming at by her manner, and yet plain enough to heighten that effect in another way by suggesting that the wearer was a woman so conscious of advantage other than physical that she could afford to accept her middle age. And its colour was cunningly chosen to change her colour from mere swarthiness to something brown that holds the light like amber. Ellen felt pleased at her own acumen in discovering the various fraudulent designs of this hat, and at the back of her mind she wondered not unhopefully if this meant that she too would be clever about clothes. They must, moreover, have cost what, again using a phrase that had always before seemed quite horrid, she called to herself a pretty penny, for the materials had been made to satisfy some last refinement of exigence which demanded textures which should keep their own qualities yet ape their opposites, and the dark fur on her coat seemed a weightless softness like tulle, and the chestnut-coloured stuff of the coat and the dress beneath it was thick and rough like fur and yet as supple as the yellow silk of her fichu, which itself was sensually heavy with its own richness.

And as Ellen looked, the forefinger swept again the sleek eyebrows. Really, it was terrible that Richard's mother should be so deep in crime as to be guilty of offences that are denounced at two separate sorts of public meetings. She was a squaw who was all that men bitterly say women are, not loving life and the way of serving it, undesirous of power, content against all reason with her corruptible body and the clothing and adorning of it. She was an economic parasite, setting wage-slaves to produce luxuries for her to enjoy in idleness while millions of honest, hard-working people have to exist without the bare necessities of life. And now she was leaning forward, insolently untroubled by guilt, and saying in that voice that was too lazy to articulate :

" You won't like anchovies ; those things they're helping you to now."

Ellen made a confused noise as if she were committing an indiscretion, and was furious at having made it, and then furious that she had betrayed the fact that she did not know an anchovy when she saw it ; and then furious when the next moment Marion let the waiter put the limp bronze things on her own plate. Why shouldn't she like them if Marion did ? Did Marion think she was a child who liked nothing but sugar-cakes ? When another waiter came and Marion murmured tentatively, " Wine ? " she answered with passionate assumption of self-possession, " Yes, please." She almost wavered when Marion, not raising her eyes, asked, " Red or white ? " It brought her back to that night in the office when Mr. Philip had made her drink that Burgundy and then had come towards her, looking almost hump-back with strangeness, while all the shadows in the corners had seemed to leap a little and then stand still in expectation. Fear travelled through all her veins, weakening the blood ; she pressed her lips together and braced her shoulders, living the occasion over again till all the evil things dissolved at Richard's knock upon the door. Because of him, how immune from fear she had become ! She lifted her eyes to Marion and said confidently, " Red, please."

The blankness of the gaze that met her had, she felt sure, been substituted but the second before for a gaze richly complicated with observation and speculation. She scowled and remembered that she was disliking this woman on the highest grounds, and as she ate she sent her eyes round the restaurant, knowing quite well the line of the thought she expected it to arouse in her. She was not, in fact, seeing things with any acuteness. There was a woman at a table close by wearing a dress of a very beautiful blue, the colour of the lower flowers of the darkest delphiniums, but the sight of it gave her none of the pleasant physical sensations, the pricking of the skin, the desire to rub the palms of the hands together quickly that she usually experienced when she saw an intense, clear colour. But she saw, though all the images seemed to refuse to travel from her eyes to the nerves, many people in bright clothes, the women showing their arms and shoulders as she had always heard rich women do, the men with glossy faces which reminded her in their brilliance and their blankness of the nails on Marion's hands ; pretty food, like the things to eat in Keat's St. Agnes' Eve, being carried about on gleaming dishes by waiters whose bodies seemed deformed with obsequiousness ; jewel-coloured wines hanging suspended over the white cloths in glasses invisible save where they glittered ; bottles with gold necks lolling in pails among lumps of ice like tipsy gnomes overcome by sleep on some Alpine pass ; innumerable fairy frocks and vessels of alabaster patterned like a cloud invested strong lights with the colour of romance. It would have roused her fatigued imagination had she not remembered that she had other business in hand. She organised her face to look on the spectacle with innocent pleasure, and then to darken at some serious reflection, and finally to assume the expression which she had always thought Socialist leaders ought to wear, though at public meetings she had noticed they do not.

She coughed to attract attention, and then sighed. "It's tarrible," she declared, taking good care that her voice should travel across the table, "to see all these people being happy like this when there are millions in want."

Marion set down her wine-glass with a movement that, though her hands were clever, seemed clumsy, so indifferent was she to the thing she handled and the place she put it in, and looked round the restaurant with eyes that were very like Richard's, though they shone from bloodshot whites and were not so bright as his, nor so kind; nor so capable, Ellen felt sure, of losing all brilliance and becoming contemplative, passionate darkness. She said in her rapid, inarticulate murmur, "They don't strike me as being particularly happy."

Ellen was taken aback, and said in the tones of a popular preacher, "Then what are they doing here—feasting?"

"I suppose they're here because it's on the map and so are they," she answered almost querulously. "They'd go anywhere else if one told them it was where they ought to be. Good children, most people. Anxious to do the right thing. Don't you think?"

Ellen was unprepared for anything but agreement or reactionary argument from the old, and this was neither, but a subtlety that she felt matched in degree her own though it was probably unsound; and to cover her emotions she lifted her glass to her lips. But really wine was very horrid. Her young mouth was convulsed. And then she reminded herself that it could not be horrid, for all grown-up people like it, and that there had never been any occasion when it was more necessary for her to be grown-up, so she continued to drink. Even after several mouthfuls she did not like it, but she was then interrupted by a soft exclamation from Mrs. Yaverland.

"My dear, this wine is abominable. Don't you find it terribly sour?"

"Well, I was thinking so," said Ellen, "but I didn't like to say."

"It's dreadful. It must be corked."

"Yes, I think it must," said Ellen knowingly.

She called a waiter. "Would you like to try some other wine? I don't think I will. This has put me off for the night. No? Good. Two lemon squashes, one very sweet."

That was a good idea of Mrs. Yaverland's. The lemon squash was lovely when it came, and Ellen had time to drink it while they were eating the chicken, so that there was no competitive flavour to spoil the ice pudding. While they were waiting for that Mrs. Yaverland smoothed her eyebrows once again, and gave her nails one more perfunctory polish, and opened her mouth to speak, but caught her breath and shut it again ; and said, after a moment's silence, " I hope I've ordered the right sort of pudding. It's so hard to remember all these irrelevant French names. I wanted you to have the one with crystallised cherries. Richard used to be very fond of it." She looked round the restaurant more lovingly. " He liked this place when he was a boy. We used to come here once or twice every holiday and go to a theatre afterwards."

But Ellen knew what it meant when Richard did that :. when he opened his mouth and then shut it again and was silent, and then said very quickly, " Darling, I do love you." He had done it the very night before, in Grand-Aunt Jeannie's parlour at Liberton Brae, when he had wanted to tell her that his mother had been married to someone who was not his father before he was born. " It was not her fault. My father didn't stand by her. He was all right about money. But when he heard about the child, he was playing the fool as an aide-de-camp with a royal tour round the Colonies. And he didn't come back. So she lost her nerve " ; and that he had a younger stepbrother, but that the marriage had not been a success, and that she was always known as Mrs. Yaverland. She was dying to know what Richard was like in his schooldays, and she was willing to admit that Mrs. Yaverland, when she took him out for treats, had probably shown a better side of her nature that was not so bad, but because of this knowledge she leaned forward and asked penetratingly, " Now, what is it you are really wanting to say ? "

The older woman dropped her eyelids guiltily, and then raised them full of an extraordinary laughing light, as if she was beyond all reason delighted to have her secret thoughts discovered. " How you see through me, dear ! " she said in a voice that was rallying and affectionate, charged with an astringent form of love. " All that I wanted to say was simply that I am so very glad you have come. Perhaps for reasons that you'll consider tiresome of me. But Richard has been so much away, and even when he's at home he is out at the works laboratory so much of the time, that I've often wanted someone nice to come and live in the house, who'd talk to me occasionally and be a companion. Perhaps you'll think it is absurd of me to look on you as a companion, because I am much older. But then I reckon things concerning age in rather a curious way. You're eighteen, aren't you ? "

"Eighteen past," Ellen agreed, in a tone that implied she felt a certain compunction in leaving it like that, so near was she to nineteen. But her birthday had been a fortnight ago.

"And I was nineteen when Richard was born. So you see to me a girl of eighteen is a woman, capable of understanding everything and feeling everything. So I hope you won't mind if I treat you as an equal." She raised her wineglass and looked over its brim at the girl's proud, solemn gaze, limpid with intentions of being worthy of this honour, bright with the discovery that perhaps she did not dislike the other woman as much as she had thought, and she flushed deeply and set the wineglass down again, and, leaning forward, spoke in a forced, wooden tone. "I meant, you know, to say that to you, anyhow, whether I felt it or not. I knew you'd like it. You see, you get very evasive if you've ever been in a position like mine. You have to make servants like you so that they won't give notice when they hear the village gossip, because you must have a well-run house for your child. You have to make people like you so that they will let the children play with yours. So one gets into a habit of saying a thing that will be found pleasant, without particularly worrying whether it's sincere. But this I find I really mean."

As always, the suspicion that she was in the presence of somebody who had the singular bad luck to be unhappy changed Ellen on the instant to something soft as a kitten, incapable of resentment as an angel. "Well, I've got a habit of saying the things that will be found unpleasant," she said hopefully, in tones tremulous with kindness. "I'm just as likely to say something that'll rouse a person's dander as you are to say something that'll quiet it down. We ought to be awful good for one another."

Mrs. Yaverland turned on Ellen a glance which recognised her quality as queer and precious, yet was not endearing and helped her nothing in the girl's heart. For she was considering Ellen for what she would give Richard, what she would bring to satisfy that craving for living beauty which was so avid in him and because of his fastidiousness and his unwilling loyalty to the soul so unsatisfied. She wondered too whether Ellen could lighten those of his days which were sunless with doubt. And for that reason her appreciation brought her no nearer the girl than a courtier comes to the jewel he thinks fair enough to purchase as a present to his king. She became aware of the obstinate duration of their distance, and, trying to buy intimacy with honesty, because that was for her the highest price that could be paid, she said in the same forced voice, " You know, you're ever so much better than I thought you'd be."

" Am I now ? What way ? " Like all young people, she loved to talk about herself. " My looks, do you mean ? Now, I was sure Richard was funning me when he told me I was nice. He talks so much of my hair that I was afraid he thought little of the rest of me. I'm sure he told you that I'm plain. And I am. Am I not ? "

" No, you're beautiful. I expected you to be beautiful." There was a hint of coldness in her voice, as if she disliked the implication that her son might be lacking in taste. " It's the other things I'm surprised at : that you're clever, that you're reflective, that you feel deeply."

" As a matter of fact," said Ellen confidentially, leaning across the table, "since we're being honest, I don't mind saying that I think you're not over-stating it. But how do you know all that ? I'm sure I've been most petty and disagreeable ever since I arrived. I've just been hoping it's not the climate that's doing it, for that'd be hard on Richard and you."

The other woman became almost confused. " Oh, that was me ! That was me ! " she said earnestly. " I told you I was evasive. One form it takes is that when I meet people I'm very much interested in, I can't show my interest directly ; I take cover behind a pretence of abstraction. I polish my nails and do silly things like that, and people think I'm cold, and stupid about the particular point they want me to see, and they try to attract my attention by behaving wildly, and that usually means behaving badly. It was my fault, it was my fault ! "

" Indeed, it was my own ill nature," said Ellen stoutly. " But let us cease this moral babble, as Milton says. I wish you'd tell me why you're surprised that I should be clever, though you were quite cairtain that he would have chosen a good-looking gairl ? "

Mrs. Yaverland explained hesitantly, delicately. " Richard has tried to fall in love before, you know. And he has always chosen such stupid women."

Ellen was puzzled and displeased, though of course it was not the notion that he had tried to fall in love with stupid women that distressed her, and not merely the notion of his trying to fall in love with other women. Thank goodness she was modern and therefore without jealousy. " Why did he do that ? Why did he do that ? "

There appeared on Marion's face something that was like the ashes of archness. Her heart said jubilantly to itself :

"Why, because he loves me, his mother, so far beyond all reason! Because he thinks me perfect, the queen of all women who have brains and passions, and all other women who pretend to these things seem pretenders to my throne, on whom he can bestow no favour without suspicion of disloyalty to me. So he went to the other women, who plainly weren't competing with me; those who were specialising in those arts that turn them from women into birds with bright feathers and a cheeping song and lightness unweighted by the soul. He went to them more readily, I do believe, because he knew that their lack of all he loved in me would send him back to me the sooner. I will not believe that any son ever had for his mother a more absurd infatuation. I am the happiest woman in the world. And yet I know it was not right it should be so. What is to happen to him when I die? And he takes all my troubles on himself and feels as if they were his own. But I can see that you, my dear, are going to break the spell that, so much against my will, I've thrown over my son. And no other woman in the world could have done it. You have all the qualities he loves in me, but they are put together in such a different mode from mine that there cannot possibly be any question of competition between us. You are hardly more than a child, and I am an elderly woman; you are red and fiery, I am dark and slow; your passion grows out of your character like a flower out of the earth, while Heaven knows that I have hardly any character outside my capacity for feeling. So he feels free to love you. Oh, my dear, I am so grateful to you." But because for many years she had been sealed in reserve to all but Richard, she listened to free speech coming from her lips as amazedly as a man cured of muteness in late life might listen to his own first uncouth noises. So she said none of these things, but murmured, smiling coldly, "Oh, there's a reason. . . . I'll tell you some time. . . ."

The girl was hurt. Marion bit her lip while she watched her crossly pick up her spoon and eat her ice pudding as if it was a duty. "This is like old times," she essayed feebly. "I've so often watched Richard eat it. He went through various stages with this pudding. When he was quite small he used to leave the crystallised cherries to the very last, because they were nicest, arranged in a row along the rim of his plate, openly and shamelessly. When he went to school he began to be afraid that people would think that babyish if they noticed it, and he used to leave them among the ice, though somehow they always did get left to the last. Then later on he began to side with public opinion himself, and think that perhaps there was something soft and unmanly about caring so much for anything to eat, so he used to gobble them first of all, trying not to taste them very much. Then there came an awful holiday when he wouldn't have any at all. That was just before he insisted on going to sea. But then he came back—and ever since he's had it every time we come here, and now he always leaves the cherries to the last." She was now immersed in the story she told; she was seeing again the slow magical increase of the small thing she had brought into the world, and the variations through which it passed in the different seasons of its youth, changing from brown candid gracefulness to a time of sulky clumsiness and perpetually abraded knees, and back again to gracefulness and willingness to share all laughter, yet ever remaining the small thing she had brought into the world. With eyes cast down, trying to dissemble her pride, lest the gods should envy, she added harshly, " He was quite interesting . . . but I suppose all boys go through these phases . . . I've had no other experiences. . . ."

Ellen was longing to hear what Richard was like when he was a boy, but she had been stung by that insolent, smiling murmur, and she could do nothing with any statement made by this woman but snarl at her. " No other experience ? " she questioned peevishly. " I thought Richard said he had a half-brother."

There was no longer any pride in Marion's eyes to dissemble. She stared at Ellen, and said heavily, as one who speaks concerning the violation of a secret, " Did Richard tell you that ? " Before the girl had time to answer cruelly, " Yes, he tells me everything," she had remembered certain things which made her stiffen in her chair and keep her chin up and use her eyes as if there still flashed in them the pride which had utterly vanished. " Oh, yes," she asserted, in that forced voice, but very loudly and deliberately. " I have another son. He's a good boy. His name is Roger Peacey. You must meet him one day. I hope you will like him." She paused and recollected why they were speaking of this other son, and continued, " But, you see, I had nothing to do with him when he was a boy."

This struck Ellen as very strange. She went on eating her ice pudding, but she cogitated on this matter. Why had this second son been brought up away from his mother ? Surely that hardly ever happened except when there had been a divorce, and a husband whose wife had run away with another man was awarded by the courts " the custody of the child." Had she not talked of this son in the over-bluff tone in which people talk of those to whom they have done a wrong? She was possessed of the fierce monogamous passion which accompanies first and unachieved love, that loathing of all who are not content with the single sacramental draught which is the blood of God, but go heating the body with unblessed fermented wines ; and she glared sharply under her brows at this woman, who after losing Richard's father married another man and then, as it appeared, had loved yet another man, as she might at someone whom she suspected of being drunk. It was true that Richard adored her, but then no doubt this kind of woman knew well how to deceive men. Softly she made to herself the Scottish manifestation of incredulity, " Mhm. . . ." And Marion, for thirty years vigilant for sounds of scorn, heard and perfectly understood.

She remained, however, massively and unattractively immobile. There came to her neither word nor expression to remove the girl's dubiety. Since she had heard such sounds of scorn over so lengthy a period they no longer came to her as trumpet calls to action, but rather as imperatives to silence, for above all things she desired that evil things should come to an end, and she had learned that an ugly speech ricochetting from the hard wall of a just answer may fly further and do worse. She knew it was necessary that she should dispel Ellen's suspicion, because they must work together to make a serene home for Richard, and she desired to do so for her son's sake, because she herself was possessed by the far fiercer monogamous passion of achieved and final love, which is disillusioned concerning mystical draughts, but knows that to take the bread of the beloved and cast it to the dogs is sin. She had acquired that knowledge, which is the only valuable kind of chastity worth having, that night when she had been forced to commit that profanation. Shading her eyes while there rushed over her the recollection of a pallid face looking yellow as it bent over the lamp, she reflected that even if she conquered this life-long indisposition to reply, the story was too monstrous to be told. It would not be believed. This girl would look at her under her brows and make that Scotch noise again and think her a liar as well as loose. So she sat silent, letting Ellen dislike her.

She said at length, " Let's go and have coffee in the lounge." " I'm sure we don't need it," murmured Ellen, as a tribute to the magnificence of the meal.

Crossing the room was a terrible business. She hoped people were not staring at her because she was with a woman whom they could perhaps see had once been bad. No doubt there were signs by which experienced people could tell. Richard's presence seemed all at once to have set behind the rim of the earth.

They sat down at last on a kind of wide marble platform, which looked down on another restaurant where there dined even more glorious people, none of whom wore hats, who seemed indeed to have stripped for their fray with appetite. They were nice-looking, some of them, but not like Richard. She looked proudly round just for the pleasure of seeing that there was not his like anywhere here, and found herself under the gaze of Richard's eyes, set in Richard's mother's face. Doubt left her. Here was beauty and generosity and courage and brilliance. Here was the quality of life she loved. She found herself saying eagerly, that she might hear that adorable voice and hoping that it would speak such strong words as he used : " Yes, Marion ? "

" Ellen, when will you marry Richard ? "

" We've talked it over," said Ellen, with a certain solemn fear. " We think we'll wait. Six months. Out of respect for mother."

" But, my dear, your mother won't get any pleasure out of Richard being kept waiting. She'd like you to settle down and be happy."

Ellen looked before her with blue eyes that seemed as if she saw an altar, and as if Marion were insisting on talking loud in church. " I feel I'd like to wait," she murmured.

The older woman understood. In such fear of life had she once dallied, one night long before, at the edge of woods, looking across the clearing at the belvedere, and the light in the room behind its pediment, which sent a fan of coarse brightness out through the skylight into the pale clotted starshine. With one arm she clasped a sapling as if it were a lover, and she murmured, " He is there, he is waiting for me. But I will not go. Another night. . . ." She had been so glad that there was no moon, so that he would not see her from his window. She had forgotten that her white frock would gleam among the hazel thickets like a ghost ! So he had stepped suddenly from between the columns and come towards her across the clearing. It was strange that though she wanted to run away she could make no motion save with her hands, which fluttered about her like doves, and that when he took her in his arms her feet had moved with his towards the belvedere, though her lips had cried faintly but sincerely,

"No . . . no. . . ." Such a fear of life was of good augury
for her son. Those only feared life who were conscious of
powers within themselves that would make their living a tremendous thing. She was exhilarated by the conviction that this
girl was almost good enough for her son, but her sense of the
prevailing darkness of fate's climate caused her to desire to
make the promise of his happiness a certainty, and she exclaimed
urgently, "Oh, Ellen, marry Richard soon!"

Ellen turned a timid, obstinate face on this insistent woman,
who would not leave her alone with her delightful fears. "After
all, this is my life," she seemed to be saying, "and you have
had yours to do what you willed with. Let me have mine."

But there had come on Marion the tribulation that falls on
unhappy people when they see before them a gleam of happiness.
She had to lay hold of it. Although she knew that she was
irritating the girl, she said: "But, Ellen, really you ought to
marry Richard soon!" She forced herself to speak glibly and
without reserve, though it seemed to her that in doing so she
was somehow participating in the glittering vulgarity of the
place where they sat. "I want Richard's happiness to be
assured. I want to see him certainly, finally happy. I may
die soon. I'm fifty, and my heart is bad. I want him to be
so happy that when I die he won't grieve too much. For, you
see, he is far too fond of me—quite unreasonably fond. And
even if I live for quite a long time I still will be miserable if
he doesn't find happiness with someone else. You see, I've had
various troubles in my life. Some day I will tell you what they
are. I can't now. I don't mean in the least that I'm trying to
shut you out from our lives. But if I started talking about
them my throat would close. I suppose I've been quiet about
it for so many years that I've lost the way of speaking out
everything but small talk. But the point is that Richard frets
about these troubles far too much. He lives them all over
again every time he says they are worrying me. I want you
to give him a fresh, unspoiled life to look after, which will give
him pleasure to share as my life has given him pain. Do this
for him. Please do it. Forgive me if I'm being a nuisance to
you. But, you see, I feel so responsible for Richard." She
looked across the restaurant, as if on the great wall at its other
end there hung a vast mirror in which there was reflected the
reality behind all these appearances. She seemed, with her
contracted brows and compressed lips, to be watching its image
of her destiny and checking it with her reason's estimate of the
case. "Yes!" she sighed, and shivered and stiffened her back

as if there had fallen on her something magnificent and onerous. " I am twice as responsible for Richard as most mothers are for their sons."

She would have left it cryptically at that if she had not seen that Ellen would have disliked her as a mystificator. She drew her hand across her brow, and immediately perceived that the gesture had so evidently expressed dislike of this obligation to confide that the girl was again alienated, and in desperation she cried out all she meant. " I'm responsible for him in the usual way. By loving his father. Much more than the usual way, most people would tell me, because of course I knew it wasn't lawful. But there's something more than that. I was so very ill before he was born that the doctor wanted to operate and take him away from me long before there was any chance of his living. I knew he would be illegitimate and that there would be much trouble for us both, but I wanted him so much that I couldn't bear them to kill him. So I risked it, and struggled through till he was born. So you see it's twice instead of once that I have willed him into the world. I must see to it that now he is here he is happy."

Ellen said in a little voice, " That was very brave of you," and soared into an amazed exaltation from which she dipped suddenly to some practical consideration that she must settle at once. Her eyes hovered about Marion's and met them shyly, and she stammered softly, " Does having a baby hurt very much ? " She did not feel at all disturbed when Marion answered, " Yes," though that was the word she had been dreading, for the speech she added, " If the child is going to be worth while it always hurts, but one does not care," seemed to her one of those sombre and heartening things like " King Lear," or the black line of the Pentland Hills against the sky, which she felt took fear from life, since they showed it black and barren of comfort and yet more than ever beautiful. It settled her practical consideration : she had known that she would have to have children, because all married people did, but now she would look forward to it without cowardice and without regret. Now she could soar again to her amazed exaltation and contemplate the woman who had given her Richard.

Even yet she was not clear concerning the processes of birth. But in her mind's eye she saw Marion lying on a narrow bed, her body clenched under the blankets, and her face pale and concave at cheek and temple with sickness and persecuted resolution, holding at bay with her will a crowd of doctors pressing round her with scalpels in their hands, preserving by her tensity the miracle of life that was to be Richard. If she had relaxed, the world would not have been habitable, existence would have rolled through few and inferior phases. When she stood at the windows of Grand-Aunt's house on Liberton Brae every evening after mother's death she would have seen nothing but dark glass patterned with uncheering suns of reflecting gaslight, and beyond a white roadway climbed by anonymous travellers. She would have wept: not waited, as she did, for the sound of the motor-cycle that was driven with the dearest recklessness and would bring joy with it. She would never have had occasion to run to the door and open it impetuously to life. Her sensibility would have strayed on the dreary level of controlled grief. It would not have sank under her, deliciously ana dangerously, leaving her to stand quite paralysed while he flung off his cap and coat and gauntlets with those indolent, violent gestures, and whispered to her till his arms were free and he could stop her heart for a second with his long first kiss.

She would have sat all evening in the front parlour with Grand-Aunt and Miss McGinnis and helped with their sewing for the St. Giles's bazaar, instead of appearing among them for five minutes to let them have a look at her great splendid man, who had to bend to come in at the doorway and give Miss McGinnis an opportunity to cry, " Dear me, Mr. Yaverland, you mind me so extraordinary of my own cousin Hendry who was drowned at Prestonpans. He was just your height and he had the verra look of you," and to allow Grant-Aunt to declare, " Elspeth, I wonder at you. There was never a McGinnis stood more than five feet five, and I do not remember that Hendry escaped the family misfortune —mind you, I know it's not a fault—of a squint." There would not have been those hours in the dining-room when life was lifted to a strange and interesting plane where the flesh became as thoughtful as the spirit, and each meeting of lips was as inaividual as an idea and as much a comment on life, and the pressing of a finger across the skin could be watched like the unfolding of a theory.

But those were the fair-weather uses of love. It was in the foul weather she would have missed him most. If this woman had not given her Richard she would have walked home from the hospital alone and wept by the unmade bed whose pillow was still dented by mother's head ; she would have had to go to the cemetery with only Mr. Mactavish James and Uncle John Watson from Glasgow, who would have said " Hush ! " when she waved her hand at the coffin as it was lowered into the grave and cried, " Good-bye, my wee lamb ! " Life was so terrible it would not be supportable without love. She laid her hand on Marion's where it lay on the table, and stuttered, " Oh, it was brave of you ! "

The intimate contact was faintly disgusting to the other. She answered impatiently, " Not brave at all ; I loved him so much that I would have done anything rather than lose him."

" You loved him—even then ? "

" In a sense they are as much to one then as they ever are."

" Ah. . . ." Ellen continued to pat the other woman's hand and looked up wonderingly into her eyes, and was dismayed to see there that this fondling meant nothing to her. She was not ungrateful, but for such things her austerity had no use. All that she wanted was that assurance for which she had already asked. Ellen was proud, and she was a little hurt that the way in which she had proposed to pay the debt of gratitude was not acceptable, so she held up her hand and said coolly, " I'll marry your son when you like, Mrs. Yaverland."

The other said nothing more than " Thank you." Realising that she had said it even more than usually indifferently, she put out her hand towards Ellen in imitation of the girl's own movement, but did it with so marked a lack of spontaneity that it must, as she instantly perceived, give an impression of in- sincerity. " How I fail ! " she thought, but not too sadly, for at any rate she had got her son what he wanted. A man came and stood a little way behind her, looking here and there for someone whom he expected to find in the assembly, and she turned sharply to see if it were Richard ; for always when he was away, if the shadows fell across her path or there came a knock at the door, she hoped that it was him.

" I am stupid about him," she admitted, settling down in her chair, " but if he had come it would have been lovely. What would he think if he came now and found us two whom he loves most sitting here silent, almost sulky, because we have fixed the time of his marriage ? He would not understand, of course. When a man is in love marriage loses all importance. He thinks that he could wait for ever. He never realises, as women do, that it is not love that matters but what we do with it. Why do I say as women do ? Only women like me who have through making all possible mistakes found out the truth by the process of elimination. This girl is as unprovident as Richard is. So unprovident that I am afraid she is angry with me for insisting that she should put her capital of passion to good uses." And indeed Ellen was sitting there very stiffly, turning her hands together and looking down on them as if she despised them for

their cantrips. She wished her marriage had not been decided
quite like this. Of course she wanted to be married, because,
whatever the marriage-laws were like, there was no other way
by which she and Richard could tell everybody what they were
to each other. But she had wanted the ceremony as secret as
possible, as little overlooked by any other human being, and
she fancifully desired it to take place in some high mountain
chapel where there was no congregation but casqued marble
men and the faith professed was so mystical that the priest was
as inhuman as a prayer. Thus their vows would, though recorded, have had the sweet quality of unwritten melodies that are
sung only for the beloved who has inspired them. But now
this marriage was to be performed with the extremest publicity
before a crowd of issues, if not of persons. It was to be a sub-
ordinate episode in a pageant the plot of which she did not know.

Marion, watching her face, saw the faint twitches of resentment playing about her mouth and felt some remorse. " She
would be so happy just being Richard's sweetheart, if I did
the interfere," she thought. " Ah, how the old tyrannise over
not young. . . ." And there came on her a sudden chill as she
remembered of what character that tyranny could be. She
remembered one day, when she was nineteen, waking from sleep
to find old people round her. She had been having such a
lovely dream. On her lover's arm, she had been walking across
the fields in innocent sunshiny weather, and he had been laughing
and full of a far greater joy in impersonal things than she had
ever known him. When he saw gorse in life he would repeat
the country catch, " When the gorse is out of bloom then kissing's
out of fashion," but in her dream he laughed to see fire and water
meet where the gorse grew on the sheep-ponds broken lip. He
had liked the white cloths bleaching on the grass, and the song
the lark in the sky twirled like a lad throwing and catching a
coin, and the spinney on the field's slope's heights, where the
tide of spring broke in a green surf of budding undergrowth at
the feet of black bare trees.

During all the months her child was moving in her body she
was visited by dreams of spring. This was the best of dreams:
it was real. The lark's song and Harry's happy laughter
were loud in her ears ; and she rolled over in her bed and
opened her eyes on Grandmother and Aunt Alphonsine. She
looked away from them, but saw only things that reminded
her how ill she was ; the tumbler of milk she had not been
able to drink, set in a circle of its own wetness on a plate among
fingers of bread-and-butter left from the morning ; they had

been told to tempt her appetite, but they were betraying
that they felt she had had more than enough temptation
lately; the bottles of medicine ranged along the mantelpiece, high-shouldered like the façades of chapels and pasted
with labels that one desired to read as little as chapel
notice-boards, and with contents just as ineffectual at their
business of establishing the right; the jug filled with a bunch
of flowers left by some kindly neighbour who did not know what
was the matter with her.

That raised difficult issues. She turned her eyes back to
the old people. They looked terrible: Grandmother sitting
among her spreading skirts, her face trembling with a weak forgiving sweetness, her hands clasped on her stick-handle with a
strength which showed that if she was not allowed to forgive
she would be merciless; Aunt Alphonsine, covering her bosom
with those arms which looked so preternaturally and
rapaciously long in the tight sleeves that Frenchwomen
always love, and fingering now and then the scar that
crossed her oval face as if it were an amulet the touch of
which inspired her to be righteous and malign. Marion looked
away from them again at the flowers, and tried to forget that they
had been given by someone who would not have given them if
she had known the truth, and to perceive simply that they
were snapdragons, the velvet homes of elfs—reds and terra-
cottas and yellows that even in sunlight had the melting mystery,
the harmony with serious passion, that colours have commonly
only in twilight.

But the old people began to speak, and the flowers lost
their power over her. She had to listen while they proposed
that she should marry her lover's butler. He had made the
offer most handsomely, it appeared, and was willing to do it
at once and treat the child as if it were his own. "What,
Peacey?" she had cried, raising herself up on her elbow.
"Peacey? Ah, if Harry were here you would not dare to tell
me this!" And Aunt Alphonsine had said "Hush!" at the
squire's name, being to the core of her soul a *dame de compagnie*;
and Grandmother had said, with that use of the truth as an
offensive weapon which seems the highest form of truthfulness
to many, "Well, Sir Harry seems in no great haste to come
back to protect you. He could come back if he liked, you
know, dear."

That was, of course, quite true. He could have come back.
It was true that his return from the Royal tour would have
meant the end of his career at Court; but that consideration

should have seemed fatuous compared with his duty to stand beside his woman when she was going to have his child. She covered her face with the sheet and lay so still that they left her. Till the evening fell she remained so, keeping the linen close to her drawn about brow and chin like an integument for her agony which prevented it from breaking out into physical convulsions and shrieked lamentations. It seemed a symbol of her utter desolation that such a proposal should have been made to her when she should have been sacred to her child : but there was not the least fear in her heart that it would ever come to pass. She had not known how often the old people would come and sit by her bed, looking terrible.

Yes, they had looked terrible, but not, seen across the years, inexplicable. Grandmother had spent all her life being the good wife of Edward Yaverland, and she had not liked him, for in the days when she had ransacked her memory for pretty tales to tell her little grandchild she had never spoken of any place she had visited with him ; and indeed the daguerreotype on the parlour wall showed a man teased by developing prosperity as by an inward growth, whose eye would change pink apple-blossom to a computable promise of cider. It is not in the nature of any human being to admit that they have wasted their whole life, and since she had certainly gained no treasure of love from her forty years with her husband it was necessary that she should invent some good purpose which that tedious companionship had served. The theory of the sanctity of marriage came in handy ; it comforted her to believe that by merely being a wife she had fulfilled a function pleasing to God and necessary to the existence of society. But she had so often been assailed by moments when it had seemed that during all her living life had not begun, that she had to believe it passionately to quiet those doubts. To have asked her to stay away from the bedside would have been to ask her to admit that her life was useless, and that it would have been better if she had not been born. "Lord have mercy on us all !" thought Marion, and forgave her.

It was not so easy to forgive Aunt Alphonsine, for her voice had been as sharp as it could be without being honestly angry, like bad wine instead of good vinegar, and had run indefatigably up the switchbacks on which the voices of Frenchwomen travel eternally. She was the most responsible for the defeat of Marion's life. And yet Aunt Alphonsine too was not malignant of intent. The worst of illicit relationships

is the provocation they give to the minds that hear of them.
When it is said of a man and woman that they are married, the
imagination sees the public ceremony before the altar, the
shared house, the children, and all the sober external results of
marriage ; but when it is said of a man and woman that they
are lovers, the imagination is confronted with the fact of their
love. The thought of her niece night after night shut up with
love in the white belvedere all the long time the moon required
to rise from the open sea, fill all the creeks with silver, and drain
them dry again as she sunk westwards, must have been torment
to one whose left cheek, from the long pale ear to the inhibited
mouth, was one scar. That scar was an epitome of all that
was pathetic and mischievous about the poor faint woman, this
being formed to be a nun who had not been blessed with any
religion and so had to dedicate herself to the ridiculous god of
decorum. "Your aunt," Marion's mother had said to her,
" burned her face cleaning a pair of white shoes with benzine
for me to wear at my first Communion. It was a pity she did
it. And a pity for me too, since I have had to obey her ever
since in everything, though I wanted neither the white shoes
nor the Communion." In that speech were all the elements
of Alphonsine's tragedy, and therefore most of the causes of
Marion's. The French thrift that had made her clean the shoes
at home, and thereby maim herself into something that desired
to assassinate love whenever she saw it, made her terribly exercised at the possibility that the family might have to support a
fatherless baby. The affection for her sister Pamela which had made
her perform these services had enabled her to bring up that
lovely child through all the dangers of a poverty-stricken childhood in Paris, in spite of a certain wildness in her beauty which
might, if unchecked, have been a summons to disorder ; and her
triumph in that respect, had made it the most heartbreaking disappointment when the temptations she thought she had baulked
for ever in Paris twenty years before returned and claimed so
easily Pamela's child, whom she thought quite safe, since to her
French eyes Marion's dark brows, perpetually knit in preoccupation with the movements of her nature, were not likely to
be attractive to men.

That must have added to her bitterness. It must have seemed
very cruel to Alphonsine that she, with her smooth brown hair
whichshe coiffed perfectly, her long white hands, and her slender
body with its hour-glass waist, which had a strange air of having
been filleted of all grossness, could never know the joy that
could be obtained even by this black untidy girl. That would

account for the passion with which she forced Marion to do the
thing she did not want to ; and any suspicion that she was
actuated by a desire to punish the girl for her happiness she
would be able to dismiss by recollecting that certainly she had
served her little sister's welfare by crossing her will. Oh, there
was much to be said for Alphonsine. But all the same, it was
a pity that the old people had interfered. She had loved Richard
so much that it would not have mattered to her or to him that
he was fatherless, since from the inexhaustible treasure of her
passion for him she could give him far more than other children
receive from both parents. They might have been so happy
together if the old people had not made her marry Peacey.

"But this is different," she said to herself. "They compelled me to unhappiness. I am forcing happiness on Richard
and Ellen. It is quite different."

But she looked anxiously at the girl. They smiled at each
other with their eyes, as if they were friends in eternity. But
their lips smiled guardedly, for it might be that they were
enemies in time.

CHAPTER II

THE land, which from the time they left London had been so ugly as to be almost invisible, suddenly took form and colour. To the south, beyond a creek whose further bank was a raw edge of gleaming mud hummocks tufted with dark spriggy heaths and veined with waterways that shone white under the cold sky, there stretched a great quiet plain. It stretched illimitably, and though there were dotted over it red barns and grey houses and knots of trees growing in fellowship as they do round steadings, and though its colour was a deep wet fertile green, it did not seem as if it could be a human territory. It could be regarded only as a place for the feet of the clouds which, half as tall as the sky, stood on the far horizon. They passed a station, built high above the marsh on piles, and looked down on a ford that crossed the mud bed of the creek to a white road that drove southwards into the plain. A tongue of the creek ran inwards beside it for a hundred yards or so ; above its humpy mud banks the road protected itself by white wooden railings, and on its other side a line of telegraph poles ran towards the skyline.

This was the beauty of bleakness, but not as she had known it on the Pentlands. That was like tragedy. Storms broke on the hills, spread snow or filled the freshets as with tears, and then departed, leaving the curlews drilling holes with their cries in the sphere of catharised clear air ; and the people there, men resting on their staves, women at their but-and-ben doors, spoke with magnificent calm, as if they had exhausted all their violence on certain specific occasions. But this plain was like a realist mind with an intense consciousness of cause and effect. There would blow a warning wind before the storm. It would be visible afar off in its coming, as a darkness, a flaw on the horizon ; and when it had scourged the plain it would be seen for long travelling on towards the mainland. There would be no illusion that anything happens suddenly or that anything disappears. Here the long preparation of earth's

events and their endurance would be evident. It would breed
people like Marion, in whom a sense of the bearing of the past
on the present was so powerful that it was often difficult to know
of what she was speaking, and whether the tale she was telling
of Richard referred to yesterday or his boyhood ; that it was
impossible to say whether she smiled because of memory or
hope when she leaned forward and said, " This is Kerith Island."

"Mhm," said Ellen, since it was not her own country; "it's
verra flat."   And then, realising that she was belittling beauty,
she exclaimed, " I must have said that for the sake of being
disagreeable. I think it's fine, though very different from
Scotland.   But after all, why should everything be like Scotland?
There's no real reason. I don't see where Richard's going to
work, though."

" Three miles along the road and two to the right. You
can see the works from our windows."

" Of course you could," said Ellen sourly ; and explained,
" When I couldn't see the works I made up a sort of story for
myself, about the works being new ones, and the firm not being
able to get them finished in time for Richard to start work, so
that we had him hanging about the house all to ourselves. That
was silly. Of course. But I am silly about him. I suppose I
will soon get over it."

" I will hate you if you do," answered Marion, " for I never
have."

The island and its creek fell away to the south. The train
ran now across the marshes, flat and green, chequered with
dykes, confined to the right by the steep brim of a sea-wall.
To the left a line of little hills gained height. They fell back in
an amphitheatre, and a farmhouse turned to the sun a garden
more austere with the salt air than farmhouse gardens commonly are, and behind it, in the shelter of the curved green escarpment, some tall trees stood among the pastures. The hills rose
again to an overhanging steepness and broke down to a gap
full of the purples of bare woods, before which stood the cathedral-
esque ruins of a brick-kiln, with its tall tower and apse-like
ovens, on a green platform of levelled ground scored with the
red of rusted trolley-lines. The hill grew higher and stood sheer
like a turfed cliff, and was surmounted by four tall towers of
grey stone. It would have been impressive if the fall of the
cliff had not been disfigured by a large shed of pink corrugated
iron with " Hallelujah Army " painted on its roof, which was
built on a shelf where some hawthorn trees and bramble bushes
found a footing.

Then for a time, after an oblique valley had cleft the range, an elm-hedge ran along the crest, till there looked down a grey church with a squinting spire and grey-black yews set about it, and something white like a monument standing up on a mound beside it. Woods appeared and receded, leaving the hilltop bare, and returned ; there was a broken hedge of hawthorn ; a downward line of trees scored the gentler slope of the escarpment, and from a square red brick house on the skyline there fell an orchard.

"That is our house up there. That is Yaverland's End," said Marion ; "and look on the other window, that is Roothing Harbour." But all Ellen could see was a forest of slim straight poles leaning everywhere above the sea-wall. "Those are the masts of the fishing-boats," said Marion indifferently, even grumbling, as was her way when she spoke of the things she loved. "Don't laugh at this place, though it is all mud. I can tell you the Elizabethan adventures drew most of their seamen from here and Tilbury." The sea-wall stopped, and beyond a foreshore of coal-dust and soiled shingle and tarred huts, such as is found always where men go down to the sea in ships, lay a bare harbour basin in which fishing-boats lolled on their sides in silver mud. Further out, smaller boats lay tidily on a bar of coarse grass that ran out from a sea-walled island that lay alongside the marsh the train had just crossed, with a farm and its orchard lying at the end it thrust into the harbour.

Now the train ran slower, and it could be seen that the line had been driven violently through the high street with no decent clearance, for to its left it could be seen that it was overhung by the backs of cottages, and on its right was the cobbled roadway on which walked bearded men in jerseys and top boots and women with that look of brine rather than bloom which is characteristic of fishing-villages. It was a fairly continuous street of huddled houses and drysalters' shops, with their stock of thigh-long boots and lanthorns and sou'-westers heaped behind small dark panes, and here and there came quays, with whitened cottages and trim gardens facing dingy wharf-offices over paved squares set about the edge with capstans, and beyond a Thames barge showing its furled red sail against a vista of shining mud-flats and the vast sky that belonged to this district. This hard, bright, clouded day, which dwelt on the grey in all things, even in the rough grass, made all look brittle and trivial and, however old, still un-historic. It could be imagined that the people who lived under

this immense sky might come to lose the common human
sense of their own supreme importance, and to suspect themselves as being of no more account than the fishes which lie at
the bottom of the channel ; and might look up at the great
cloud galleons floating above and wonder if these had not for
ship's company beings that would be to them as men are to
fishes.   It was a place, Ellen saw, that might well have engendered such a curious vigorous lethargy as Marion's.   Its breezes
were clean enough to nourish strength, but there was something
about the proportions of the scene that would breed scepticism
concerning the value of all activities.

To see things in terms of Marion was weak, and a distraction
from delight.   She could neither behold things for their own
sake, as she had up till this autumn, nor for Richard's sake, as
she had till yesterday evening.   But she was forced to wonder
about this woman who had been able to be Richard's mother
and who was yet so little what one approved of, and who yet
again was so picturesque that one had to watch her with pleasant
intensity that was not usually associated with dislike.   Even
when she looked on the astonishing scene that lay before her
when they stepped on to the platform at Roothing station she
was distracted from her astonishment by a sense that she would
afterwards maintain an argument on the subject with Marion.
The surroundings were ignobly ugly, as eggshells and scraps
of newspaper trodden into waste ground are ugly.   She was
prepared to tell Marion so, though it was her own town.   There
had not been sufficient space to build a station with the up and
down platforms facing each other, so the up platform was further
back, facing the harbour, and this down platform was over-
shadowed on its landward side by smoke-grimed cottages and
tenements which rose on high ground in a peak of squalor.   Seawards one looked over a goods-siding, where there stood a few
wagons of cockle-shells and a cinderpath esplanade on to a vast
plain of mud.

It could not be beautiful.   A plain of mud could not be
beautiful.   Yet the mind could dwell contentedly on this new
and curious estate of nature, this substance that was neither
earth nor water, this place that was neither land nor sea.   It
had its own colours : in the shadow of the great couchant cloud
whose mane was brassy with sunshine that had lodged in the
upper air it was purple ; otherwise it was brown ; and where
the light lay it was as bright as polished steel, yet giving in its
brightness some indication of its sucking softness.   It had its
own strange scenery ; it had its undulations and its fissures,

and between deep, rounded, shining banks, a course marked
here and there by the stripped white ghosts of sapling trees,
a winding river flowed out to the far-off channel of the estuary
which lay a grey bar under the dark line of the Kentish hills.

It supported its own life ; hundreds of black fishing-boats and
some large vessels leaned this way and that, high and dry on
the mud, like flies stuck on a window-pane, and up on the river,
whose waters were now flowing from the sea to the land, men
came in dingeys, not rowing, but bending their bodies indolently
and without effort, because they were backwatering with the
tide, so that their swift advance looked as if it were made easy
by sorcery. They slackened speed before they came to the
wharf, which just here by the station jutted out in a grey bastion
surmounted by the minatory finger of a derrick, and some of
them climbed out and put round baskets full of shining fish upon
their heads, and, walking struttingly to brake their heavy boots
on the slippery mud, followed a wet track up to the cinderpath.
They looked stunted and fantastic like Oriental chessmen. It
was strange, but this place had the quality of beauty. It
laid a finger on the heart. Moreover, it had a solemn quality
of importance. It was as if this was the primeval ooze from
which the first life stirred and crawled landwards to begin to
make this a memorable star.

Again the place seemed curiously like Marion. It might
well have been that to make her a god had modelled a figure in
this estuary mud and breathed on it, so much, in her sallow
colouring and the heavy impassivity which was the equivalent
of the plain's monotony, did she partake of its qualities. Her
behaviour, too, was grand like the plain and yet composed of
material that, as stuff for grandeur, was almost as uncompromis-
ing as mud.

She took the girl to the railings and made her look out to the
sea, saying, "It is rather fine in a queer way, isn't it ? When
I was a girl I could run dryshod to the very end of the channel,
and I daresay Richard could still."

Ellen shivered. "Is it not terribly lonely out there, just
under the sky ? "

"Oh no, it's pleasant to be on innocent territory, with no human
beings living on it. There was a feeling, so far as I can remember it, of extraordinary freedom and lightness." She spoke
with a sincere cynicism, an easy grimness that appeared quite
dreadful to Ellen. The girl looked appealingly at her, asking her
not to give the sanction of her impressive personality to such
hopelessness about life, but had the ill luck to catch her in the

act of a practical demonstration of her dislike for her fellow-creatures. Now that the train had puffed out of the station the station-master, a silver-haired old man with a red face on which amiability clung like a lather, had come to Marion's side and was saying that he had not seen her for a long time, and asking how Richard was and when he was coming back. Ellen thought this was very kind of him, but Marion evidently found it tiresome, and hardly troubled to conceal the fact, walking rather more quickly along the platform than the old man could manage and giving no more answer to his questions than a vague smiling "Hum." Ellen hoped that the poor old man was not offended.

She found something dubious, too, about the lack of apology with which Marion led her into the squalor outside the station, over the level crossing, with its cobblestones veined with coal-dust, past the fish-shop hung with the horrid bleeding frills of skate, and the barber's shop that also sold journals, which stood with unreluctant posters at the exact point where newspapers and flypapers meet ; and up the winding road, which sent a trail of square red villas with broken prams standing in unplanted or unweeded gardens up the hill in the direction of the church and the castle they had passed in the train. But surely she ought to have apologised for bringing a girl reared in Edinburgh to a place like this. On one of the gates they passed was written "Hiemath," and there was something very characteristic of the jerry-built and decaying place in the cheap sentiment that had been too slovenly to spell its own name correctly. Yet to the left, over the housetops of foul black streets running upwards from the railway-lines, there shone the great silver plain, and afar off a channel set with white sailing-ships and steamers, and dark majestic hills. But because of the quality of the place, and perhaps of her guide, she did not want to recognise its beauty.

When they came to a cross-roads that followed westward along the crest of the hill she would hardly admit to herself that this was better, that this was indeed right in a unique way, and that the dignified houses of white marl and oak on one side of the road and the public lawns on the other were quite good for England. She was not softened by Marion's proud mutter: "It's jolly in spring, seeing the blue sea through the gap in the may hedge. And on the other side of the hedge there's one of those old grass roads. They used to say they were Roman, but they're far older. Older than Stonehenge. This used to run all the way to Canfleet—that's where Kerith Island touches the mainland—but it's all gone but this part here. . . ." She disliked the road when it took a disclaiming twist and left the houses out of sight and travelled between low oaks, because it was the road home, and she would never have chosen a home in this strange place, whose lack of meaning for herself could be measured by its plenitude of meaning for this woman who was so unlike her.

Certainly she would never have chosen this home. Very thick, trim hedges gave the long garden the look of a pound ; the standard rose-trees which grew in round flower-beds on the lawn, which was of that excessively deep green that grass takes on in gardens with a north aspect, had the air of being detained in custody, and the borders on each side of the broad gravel path showed that extreme neatness which is found in places of detention. The red brick farmhouse at its end was very small, and its windows such mere square peep-holes among a strong growth of ivy that one conceived its inhabitants as being able to see the light only by pressing their faces close against the glass.

"Oh, I know it's ugly !" muttered Marion, holding back the gate for her. "I should have had it pulled down when I built on the new rooms. But it's been here two hundred years, and there are some of the beams of the house that was here before in it, and we have lived here all the time, so it was too great a responsibility to destroy it." She looked sideways at the girl's clouded face, and explained desperately, "I couldn't, you know. When people don't understand why you did things, and say you did them because you had no respect for good old established decencies of life, you become most carefully conservative ! "

But confidence could not be maintained for long at this awkward pitch, and she went on to the front door. "You'll like our roses," she said hopefully, as they waited for it to open ; "they grow wonderfully on this Essex clay." But although there was evident in that an amiable desire to please, Ellen was again alienated by the cool smile with which Marion greeted the maid who opened the door, the uninterested " Good morning, Mabel." The girl looked so pleased to see them. Marion returned, too, to this curious idea of hers about not being able to destroy ugly things just because they are old, although of course it is one's plain duty to replace ugly things with beautiful whatever the circumstances, when they stepped in, through no intervening hall or passage, to a little dark room furnished, as farm parlours are, with a grandfather clock, an oak settle, a dresser, a gate-leg table with a patchwork cloth over it,

and samplers hanging on wallpaper of a trivial rosebud pattern.
" I hate this English farmhouse stuff," she said. " Heavy and
uninventive. The Yaverlands have been well-to-do for at least
four hundred years, and they never took the trouble to have a
single thing made with any particular appositeness to themselves. But I have left this room as it was. To have it disturbed would have been like turning my grandmother's ghost
out of doors, and I troubled her enough in her lifetime. But
look ! It's all right in the rooms I've built on." She held back
a door, and they looked into a shining room lined with white
panels and lit by wide windows that admitted much of the
vast sky. " But I'll take you to your room. It's in the old
part of the house. But I think you will like it. It's a room I'm
fond of. . . ."

They climbed a steep dark staircase and Marion opened a
low thatched door in which the light, obscured by drawn chintz
curtains, fell on cream walls and a bed, with its high headpiece
made of fine wood painted green, and a great press made of the
same. " There's a step down," she said, " and the floor rakes,
but I'm fond of the room. I slept here when I was a girl; but
all the things are new—I got them down from London; and I
had the walls done. So you have a fresh start." She went to
the chintz curtains and pulled them back, disclosing a very
large window that came down to within two feet of the floor and
looked on to a farmyard. " It's a good-sized window, isn't
it ? " she said. " There's a story about that. They say my
great-grandfather, William Yaverland, was as mean as he was
jealous, and as jealous as he was mean, and in middle life he
was crippled by a kick from a horse and bedridden ever after.
He'd a very pretty young wife, and a handsome overseer who
was a very capable chap and worth hundreds a year to the
farm, and it struck him that in his new state he'd probably not
be able to keep the one without losing the other. So he had
this window knocked out so that he could lie in his bed and
keep his eye on the dairy where his wife worked and see who
went in and came out. Well, now it'll let the morning sun in
on you."

She sat down on the windowseat, and with a sense of fulfilment watched the girl move delightedly among the new things,
touching the little white wreaths on the embroidered bedspread
and tracing the delicate grain with her forefinger, and coming to
a stop before the mirror and looking at her face with a solemn
respectful vanity because it had pleased her beloved. Marion
found this very right and fitting, because to her, in spite of the

story of this window, this room had always been sacred to the
spirit of young love.   She turned her head and looked out into
the farmyard.   When the land had been let out to neighbouring
cultivators the byres and outhouses had all been pulled down,
and the yard was now only a quadrangle of grey trodden earth,
having on its further side a wall-less shed in which there were
stacked all the billets that had been cut from the spinneys on
the land they retained, bound neatly with the black branches
fluting together and a fuzz of purple twigs at each end.

But she could remember another day, more than thirty years before, when it was brown and oozy underfoot and there was nothing
neat about it at all, and the mellow cry of well-fed cattle came
from the dark doors of tumble-down sheds, and she was standing
in the sunshine with two of the Berkshire piglets in her arms.
She had brought them out of the stye to have a better sight of
their pretty twitching noses and their silken bristles and their
playfulness, which was unclouded, as it is in the puppy by a
genuine fear of life, or in the kitten by a minxish affectation
of the same; and Goodtart, the cattleman, had drawn near with
a "Wunnerful, ain't they, Miss Marion?—and them not born at
four o'clock this morning," when she heard the clear voice
that was sweet and yet hard, like silver ringing on steel, calling
to the dogs out in the roadway, "Lesbia! Catullus! Come out
of it!"   The greyhounds had, as usual, got in among the sheep
on the glebe land opposite.   She ran forward into the darkness
of the stye and put down the two piglets among the sucking
tide of life that washed the flanks of the great old sow, but she
could not stay there for ever.   Goodtart, who, being in the sunlight,
could not see that she was looking out at him from the shadow,
turned an undisguised face towards the doorway, and she perceived that the dung-brown eyes under his forelocks were almost
alive and that his long upper lip was twitching from side to
side.

She walked stiffly out, hearing the voice still calling
"Catullus! Lesbia!" and went in to the house.   But Peggy
was baking in the kitchen and Grandmother was reading
the *Prittlebay Gazette* in the parlour, and she went upstairs
and threw herself on the bed.   She thought of nothing.
Her heart seemed by its slogging beat to be urging some argument upon her.   Presently she realised that he was no longer
calling to his dogs, and she turned on her pillow and looked
out of the big window into the farmyard.   He was there.   Cousin
Tom Stallybrass, who had been managing the farm ever since
Grandfather's death, had come out and was talking to him,

and from his gestures was evidently telling him of the recent collapse of the dairy wall, but he was not interested, for he did not point his stick at it, and in him almost every mental movement was immediately followed by some physical sign. There was something else he wanted. When the greyhounds licked up at him he thrust them away with the petulance of a baulked man, and whenever Tom turned his head away to point at the dairy he cast quick glances at the farm door, at the gate into the road, at the other gate into the fields. She could see his face, and it was dark, and the lips drawn down at the corners. What could it be that he wanted?

She rose from her bed and went to the window, and knelt down by it, pressing her face and the white bib of her apron close to the glass. Instantly he saw her, and his face was filled with worship and happiness as with light. At last she knew that she was loved, that the things he said when they met on the marshes were not said as they had been when she was a child, and that there had lately been solemnity throned in his eyes' levity. He made no motion for her to come down, nor when Tom turned his head again did he throw any furtive look at the window. It was enough for him to have seen her; and soon he went away with bent head followed by his forgotten dogs.

Well, now this girl should sleep here, and the place should be revisited by a love as sacred as that, and one which would not commit sacrilege upon itself. She gave a soft laugh, and in a haze of satisfaction that prevented her seeing that Ellen was beginning to tell her how much she liked the furniture she went out and passed to her own room. For a moment she stood at the side windows, looking out on the show of sky and sea and green islands that lay sealed in the embankments from the grey flood which was now running across the silver plain and trying at them treacherously through the creeks that lay loverlike beside them. Then she turned approvingly to the litter which betokened that this was a bedroom visited by insomnia more often than by sleep : the half-dozen boxes of different sorts of cigarettes, the plate of apples and figs, the pile of books, the portfolio of prints. It had been dreadful, that night at the hotel, with nothing to read. She was very glad to come home.

It would not have seemed credible to Ellen that anyone should feel like this about this house. The things in her room were very pretty, but it was spoiled for her by that large window, not because she was afraid that anyone would look in, but because Marion had told her that someone had once looked out.

Since that person had been kin to this woman who was dark with unspent energy, she figured him as being not quite extinguishable by death and therefore still a tenant of the apartment. The jealousy of one of his stock would probably have more dynamic power than her most exalted passions, so she would not be able to evict him. She thought these things quite passionately and desperately while at the same time she was placidly brushing her hair and thinking how nice everything was here. Her mind continued to perform this duet of emotions when they went downstairs and had lunch. It was very pretty, this white room with the few etchings set sparsely on the gleaming panels, each with a fair field of space for its black-and-white assertion; the deep, bright blue carpet, soft as sleep, on the mirror-shining parquet; the long low bookcases with their glass doors; the few perfect flowers, with their reflection floating on polished walnut surfaces as if drowned in sherry.

The meal itself pleased as being in some sense classical, though she could not see why that adjective should occur to her. There was no white cloth, and the bright silver and delicate wineglasses, and the little dishes of coloured glass piled with wet green olives, stood among their images on a gleaming table. The food was all either very hot or very cold. She had two helps of everything, but at the same time she was being appalled by the bareness of the room. Her intuition informed that if a violent soul became terrified lest its own violence should provoke disorder it would probably make a violent effort towards order by throwing nearly everything out of the window, and that its habitation would look very much like this. She knitted her brows and said "Imphm" to herself; and her doubts were confirmed by Marion's vehement exclamation, "Oh, when will Richard come! I wish he would come soon." Her perfect, her so rightly old mother would have said, "It'll be nice for you, dear, when Richard comes," and would not have clouded her dreams of his coming with the threat of passionate competition for his notice.

She said stiffly, looking down on her plate, "We're awful reactionary, letting our whole lives revolve round a man."

"Reactionary?" repeated Marion. It had always been Ellen's complaint that grown-up people took what the young say contemptuously, but to have her remarks treated with quite such earnest consideration filled her for some reason with uneasiness. "I don't think so. If I had a daughter who was as wonderful as Richard I would let my life revolve round her. But I don't know. Perhaps I'm reactionary. Because I don't

really believe that any woman could be as wonderful as Richard ;
do you ? ''

Ellen had always suspected that this woman was not quite
sound on the Feminist question. '' Maybe not as wonderful
as Richard is,'' she said stoutly, '' but as wonderful as any
other man.''

'' Do you really think so ? '' asked Marion. '' Women are
such dependent things. They're dependent on their weak frames
and their personal relationships. Illness can make a woman's
sun go out so easily. And then, since personal relationships are
the most imperfect things in the world, she is so liable to be
unhappy. These are handicaps most women don't get over.
And then, since men don't love us nearly as much as we love
them, that leaves them much more spare vitality to be wonderful
with.''

Ellen sat in a polite silence, not wishing to make this woman
who had failed in love feel small by telling her that she herself
was loved by Richard just as much as she loved him.

'' I don't know. I don't know. It's annoying the way
that one comes to the end of life knowing less than one did at
the beginning.'' She stood up petulantly. '' Let's go upstairs.''

Ellen followed Marion up to the big sitting-room with a
sense that, though she had not seen it, she would not like it.
She was as disquieted by hearing a middle-aged woman speak
about life with this agnostic despair as a child might if it was
out for a walk with its nurse and discovered this being whom
it had regarded as all-knowing and all-powerful was in tears
because she had lost the way. She had always hoped that
the old really did know best ; that one learned the meaning of
life as one lived it.

So she was shaken and distressed by the fine face,
which looked discontented with thinking as another face might
look flushed with drinking, and by the powerful yet inert body
which lay in the great armchair limply but uneasily, as if she desired
to ask a question but was restrained by a belief that nobody could
answer, but for lack of that answer was unable to commit herself
to any action. Her expression was not, as Ellen had at first
thought, blank. Nor was it trivial, though she still sometimes
raised those hands with the flashing nails and smoothed her
eyebrows. It showed plainly enough that doubt was wandering
from chamber to chamber of her being, blowing out such candles
of certitude as the hopefulness natural to all human beings had
enabled her to light. The fact of Richard streamed in like
sunshine through the windows of her soul, and when she spoke

of him she was evidently utterly happy; but there were some parts of her life with which he had nothing to do, as there are north rooms in a house which the sun cannot touch, and these the breath of doubt left to utter darkness. "You're imagining all this, Ellen," she said to herself; "how can you possibly know all this about her?" "It's true," herself answered. ": Well, it's not true in the sense that it's true that she's dark and her name's Mrs. Yaverland, is it?" "Ellen, have you nothing of an artist in you?" herself enquired with pain. "You might be a business body, or one of the mistresses in John Square, the crude way you're talking. It's not a fact that ye can look up in a directory. But it's perfectly true that this woman's queer and warselled and unhappy. But you're losing your head terribly on your first encounter with tragedy, and you fancying yourself a cut above the ordinary because you enjoyed a good read of 'King Lear' and 'Macbeth.'" "Well, I never said I wanted to take rooms with Lady Macbeth," she objected.

But Marion was asking her now if she liked this room, or if she found it, as many people did, more like a lighthouse than a home, and because she spoke with passionate concern lest the girl should not be at ease in the place where she was to spend her future life, Ellen immediately answered with a kind of secondary sincerity that she liked it very much. Yet the room was convincing her of something she was too young and too poor ever to have proved before, and that was the possibility of excess. All her delights had been so sparse and in character so simple that no cloying of after-taste had ever changed them from being finally and unquestionably delights; they stood like a knot of poplars on the edge of a large garden whose close resemblance to golden flame could be enjoyed quite without dubiety because there was no fear that the lawns or flowers would be robbed of sunlight by their spear-thin shadows. She did not know that one could eat too many ices, for she had never been able to afford more than one at a time; in rainy Edinburgh the stories of men whose minds became sick at dwelling under immutably blue skies had seemed one of the belittling lies about fair things that grown-up people like to tell; and since she had had hardly anybody to talk to till Richard came, and had never had enough books to read, it had seemed quite impossible that one could feel or think past the point where feeling and thinking were happy embarkations of the soul on bracing seas.

Yet here in this room the inconceivable had happened,

and she recognised that there was present an excess of beauty and an excess of being. For indeed the room was too like a lighthouse in the way that all who sat within were forced to look out on the windy firmament and see the earth spread far below as the pavement of the clouds on which their shadows trod like gliding feet. The walls it turned to the south and west were almost entirely composed of windows of extravagant dimensions, beginning below the cornice and stopping only a couple of feet above the floor, so that as the two women sat by the wood fire they looked over their shoulders at the leaning ships in the harbour and the tide that hurried to it over the silver plain, and the little house with its orchard at the island's end, not a stone's throw from the boats and nets, so marine in its situation that one could conceive it farmed by a merman and see him working his scaly tail up the straight path that drove through the garden to the door, a sheep-fish wriggling at his heels. They saw too the pastures of the rest of the island, of a rougher brine-qualified green, and the one black tree that stood against them like the ace of clubs; and past them lay the channel where the white sail of a frigate curtseyed to the rust-red rag of a barge, and the round dark hills beyond mothering a storm. And if they looked towards the window in the right-hand wall they saw a line of elms going down the escarpment to the marshes like women going down to a well; and between their slim purple statures, the green floor of Kerith Island stretched illimitably to the west. And everywhere there were colours, clear though unsunned, as if the lens of the air had been washed very clean by the sea winds.

She had never before been in a room so freely ventilated by beauty, and yet she knew that she would find living on the ledge of this view quite intolerable. All that existed within the room was dwarfed by the immensity that the glass let in upon it, like the private life of a man dominated by some great general idea. Because the clouds were grey with a load of rain and were running swiftly before an east wind the flesh became inattentive to the heat of the fire and participated in the chill of the open air, and though it is well to walk abroad on cold days, one wants to be warm when one sits by the hearth. Behind the glass doors of the bookcases were many books, with bindings that showed they were the inaccessible sort, modern and right, that one cannot get out of the public library. But one would never be able to sit and read with concentration here, where if the eye strayed ever so little over the margin it saw the river and the plain changing aspects at each change of the wind like

passionate people hearing news ; yet there are discoveries
made by humanity that are as fair as the passage of a cloud-
riving spot of sunlight from sea to marsh and from marsh to
creek, and more necessary for the human being to observe.
But when Ellen tried to rescue her mind from mersion into
this excess of beauty and to fix it on the small, warmly-coloured
pattern of the domestic life within the room it was lost as completely and disastrously, so far as following its own ends went,
in the not less excessive view of the spiritual world presented by
this woman's face.

Marion should not have lived in a room so full of light. The
tragic point of her was pressed home too well. The spectator
must forget his own fate in looking on this fine ravaged
landscape and wondering what extremities of weather had made
it what it was, and how such a noble atmosphere should hang
over conformations not of the simple kind associated with
nobility but subtle as villainy. Ellen knew that she would
never have a life of her own here. She would all the time be
trying to think out what had happened to Marion. She would
never be able to look at events for what they were in themselves
and in relation to the destiny she was going to make with Richard;
but would wonder, if they were delights, whether their delight-
fulness would not seem heartless as laughter in a house of mourning to this woman whose delight lay in a grave, and if they
were sorrows, whether coming to a woman who had wept so
much they would not extort some last secretion more agonising
than a common tear.

"But she is old ! She will die ! " she thought, aghast
at this tragic tyranny. " Mother died ! " she assured herself
hopefully. Instantly she was appalled at her thoughts.
She was ashamed at having had such an ill wish about
this middle-aged woman who was sitting there rather lumpishly
in an armchair and evidently, from her vague wandering
glance and the twist of her eyebrows and her mouth, trying
to think of something nice to say and regretting that she failed.
And as she looked at her and her repentance changed into a
marvel that this stunned and stubborn woman should be the
wonderful Marion of whom Richard spoke, she realised that
her death was the event that she had to fear above all others
possible in life. For she did not know what would happen to
Richard if his mother died. He cared for her inordinately.
When he spoke of her, black fire would burn in his eyes, and
after a few sentences he would fall silent and look away from
Ellen and, she was sure, forget her, for he would then stretch

out for her hand and give it an insincere and mechanical patting
which, though at any other time his touch refreshed her veins,
she found irritating. If his mother died his grief would of
course be as inordinate. He would turn on her a face hostile
with preoccupation and would go out to wander on some
stupendous mountain system of vast and complicated sorrows.
Not even death would stop this woman's habit of excessive
living.

Ellen shivered, and rose and looked at the bookcases. The
violent order characteristic of the household had polished the
glass doors so brightly that between her and the books there
floated those intrusive clouds, the aggressive marshes. She
went and stood by the fire.

"You look tired," said Marion timidly.

"Yes, I'm tired. Do you know, I'm feeling quite fanciful.
. . . It's just tiredness."

"You'd better go and lie down."

"Oh no, I would just lie and think. I feel awful restless."

"Then let's go for a walk." She shot a furtive, comprehend-
ing look at the girl. "This really isn't such a bad place," she
told her wistfully.

They separated to dress, smiling at each other kindly and
uneasily. Ellen went into her room, and stood about, thinking
how romantic it all was, but wondering what was the termination
of a romance where curtains do not fall at the act's end, until
her eyes fell upon her reflection in the mirror. She was standing
with her head bowed and her cheek resting on her clasped hands,
and she wished somebody would snapshot her like that, for
though of course it would be affected to take such a pose in
front of a camera, she would like Richard to have a photograph of her looking like that. Suddenly she remembered
how Richard delighted in her, and what pretty things he found
to say about her without putting himself out, and how he was
always sorry to leave her and sometimes came back for another
kiss, and she felt enormously proud of being the dispenser of
such satisfactions, and began to put on her hat and coat with
peacocking gestures and recklessly light-minded glances in the
mirror. The reflection of a crumpled face-towel thrown into
a wisp over the rail of the washstand reminded her in some way
of the white-faced wee thing Mr. Philip had been during the
last few days when she had gone back to the office, and this
added to her exhilaration, though she did not see why. She
was suddenly relieved from her fear of being dispossessed of
her own life.

CHAPTER III

THEY went out of the house by the French window of the dining-room, and crossed a garden whose swept lawns and grass walks and flower-beds, in which the golden aconite, January's sole floral dividend, was laid out to the thriftiest advantage. It showed, Ellen thought, the same wild orderliness as the house. Through a wicket-gate they passed into an orchard, and followed a downward path among the whitened trunks. " This is all the land I've kept of the old farm," said Marion. "The rest is let. I let it years ago. Richard never wanted to be a farmer. It was always science he was keen on, from the time he was a boy of ten."

" Then why did he go to sea ? " asked Ellen. The path they were following was so narrow that they had to walk singly, so when Marion did not answer Ellen's question she thought it must be because she had not spoken loudly enough. She repeated it. " Why did he go to sea, if he was so keen on science ? "

But Marion still took some seconds to reply, and then her words were patently edited by reserve. "Oh, he was sixteen . . . boys need adventure. . . ."

" I do not believe he needed adventure so much," disputed Ellen, moved half by interest in the point she was discussing and half by the desire to assert that she had as much right as anybody to talk about Richard, and maybe knew as much about him as anybody. " It's not possible that Richard could ever have been at his ease in a life of action. He'd be miserable if he wasn't always the leader, and he couldn't always be the leader when he was sixteen. And then he'd not be happy when he was the leader because he thinks so poorly of most people that he doesn't feel there's any point in leading them anywhere, so there couldn't have been any pleasure in it even when he was older. Isn't that so ? "

" I suppose so," muttered Marion uncommunicatively.

" Then why did he go to sea ? " persisted Ellen.

" I don't know, I don't know," murmured the other, but

244

her face, as she paused at a gate in the orchard hedge, was amused and meditative. She knew quite well.

It was one of those days of east wind that are clear and bright and yet at enmity with the appearances they so definitely disclose. The sea, which had now covered all the mud and had run into the harbour and was lifting the ships on to an even keel, was the colour of a sharpened pencil-point. The green of the grass was acid. Under the grey glare of the sky the soft purples of the bare trees and hedges became a rough darkness without quality. Yet as they walked down the fieldpath to the floor of the marshes Ellen was well content. This, like the Pentlands, was far more than a place. It was a mental state, a revisitable peace, a country on whose soil the people and passions of imagination lived more intensely than on other earth. There was a wind blowing that was as salt as sea-winds are, yet travelled more mildly over the estuary land than it would have over the waves, like some old captain who from old age had come to live ashore and keeps the roll and bluster of his calling though he does no more than tell children tales of storms.

And through this clear, unstagnant yet unturbulent air there rose the wild yet gentle cry of a multitude of birds. It was not the coarse brave cry of the gull that can breast tempests and dive deep for unfastidious food. It was not the austere cry of the curlew who dwells on moors when they are unvisitable by men. This was the voice of some bird appropriate to the place. It was unhurried. Whatever lived on the plain saw when the sun rose on its edge shadows as long as living things ever see them, and watched them shrink till noon, and lengthen out again till sundown ; and time must have seemed the slower for being so visible. It had the sound of water in it. Whatever lived here spent half its life expecting the running of waveless but briny tides up the creeks, through mud-paved culverts into the dykes that fed the wet marshes with fresh wetness; and the other half deploring their slow, sluggish sucking back to the sea. Sorrow or any other intemperance of feeling seemed a discourteous disturbance of an atmosphere filled with this resigned harmony.

Her mind, thus liberated from its own burdens, ran here and there over the landscape, inventing a romantic situation for each pictorial spot. Under the black tree on the island she said good-bye to a lover whom she made not in the least like Richard, because she thought it probable later in the story he would meet a violent death. A man fled over

the marsh before an avenger who, when the quarry tripped
on the dyke's edge, buried a knife between his shoulders ; and,
as he struck, a woman lit the lamp in the window of the island
farm, to tell the murdered man that it was safe to come.   Indeed,
that farm was a red rag to the imagination.   Perhaps a sailor's
widow with some sorceress blood had gone to live there, so that
the ghost of her drowned husband might have less far to travel
when he obeyed her nightly evocations.

"Who lives on that little house on the island ? " she called
out to Marion.

"The one on the Saltings ?   No one.   It has been empty for
forty years.   But when I was a child George Luck still lived
there.   George Luck, the last great wizard in England."

"A wizard forty years ago ! Well, I suppose parts of
England are very backward.   You've got such a miserable system
of education.   What sort of magic did he do ? "

"Oh, he gave charms to cure sick cattle, and sailors'
wives used to come to him for news of their absent husbands,
and he used to make them look in a full tub of water, and
they used to see little pictures of what the men were doing
at the time."   She laughed over her shoulder at Ellen.   "You
see, other women before us have been reactionary."

"Reactionary ? " repeated Ellen.

"They have let their lives revolve round men," said Marion
teasingly, and Ellen returned her laughter. They were both in high
spirits because of this wind that was salt and cold and yet not
savage.   Their glowing bodies reminded them that the prime necessities of life are earth and air, and the chance to eat well as they had
eaten, and that in being in love they were the victims of a classic
predicament, the current participators in the perpetual im-
broglio with spiritual things that makes man the most ridiculous
of animals.

They were walking on the level now, on a path beside the
railway-line, again in the great green platter of the marshes.
The sea-wall, which ran in wide crimps a field's width away on
the other side of the line, might have been the rim of the world
had it not been for the forest of masts showing above it.   The
clouds declared themselves the inhabitants of the sky and not
its stuff by casting separate shadows, and the space they moved
in seemed a reservoir of salt light, of fluid silence, under which
it was good to live.   Yet it was not silence, for there came
perpetually that leisurely, wet cry,

"What are those birds ?   They make a lovely sound,"
asked Ellen, dancing.

"Those are the redshanks. They're wading-birds. When Richard comes he will take you on the sea-wall and show you the redshanks in the little streams among the mud. They are such queer streams. Up towards Canfleet there's a waterfall in the mud, with a fall of several feet. It looks queer. These marshes are queer. And they're so lonely. Nobody ever comes here now except the men to see to the cattle. Even though the railway runs through, they're quite lonely. The trains carry clerks and shop-assistants down from their work in London to their houses at New Roothing and Bestcliffe and Prittlebay at night ; and they leave in the morning as soon as they've had breakfast. On Sundays they're too tired to do anything but sit on the cliff and listen to the band playing. During the week the children are all at school or too young to go further than the recreation grounds. There's nothing to bring these people here, and they never come."

She again struck Ellen as terrifying. She spoke of the gulf between these joyless lives and the beauty through which they hurled physically night and morning, to the conditions which debarred them from ever visiting it spiritually, with exhilaration and a will that it should continue to exist as long as she could help it. "But, Ellen, you like lonely country yourself," she addressed herself. "You liked the Pentlands for being so lonely. There's no difference between you really. . . . But indeed there was a difference. She had liked places to be destitute of any trace of human society because then a lovelier life of the imagination rushed in to fill the vacuum. Since the engineer had erred who built the reservoirs over by Carlops and had made them useless for that purpose, better things than water came along the stone waterways ; meadow-sweet choking the disused channel looked like a faery army defiling down to the plains, and locks were empty and dry and white, like chambers of a castle keep, or squares of dark green waters from which at any moment a knight would rise with a weed-hung harp in his arms and a tale of a hundred years in faeryland.

But to this woman the liked thing about loneliness was simply that nobody was there. Unpeopled earth seemed to her desirable as unadulterated food ; the speech of man among the cries of the redshanks would have been to her like sand in the sugar. They came presently to a knot of trees, round which some boys wrangled in some acting game in which a wigwam built between the shining roots that one of the trees lifted high out of earth evidently played an important part. Ellen would have liked to walk slowly as they passed them, so as to hear as much as possible of the game, for it looked rather nice, but Marion began to hurry, and broke her serene silence in an affectation of earnest and excited speech so that she need pay as little response to the boys' doffing of their caps. There was something at once absurd and menacing about the effect of her disinclination to return these children's greetings ; to Ellen, who was so young that all mature persons seemed to have a vast capital of self-possession, it was like seeing someone rich expressing serious indignation at having to give a beggar a penny.

To break the critical current of her thoughts she asked, " What's that church up there ? "

" It's Roothing Church. It's very old. It's a famous landmark."

" But what's that white thing beside it ? "

" Oh, that ! " said Marion, looking seawards. " That is the tomb of Richard's father."

" Indeed," breathed Ellen uncomfortably. " He must," she said, determined not to be daunted by an awkward situation, " have been well thought of in the neighbourhood."

" Why ? " asked Marion.

" It has the look of something raised by public subscription. Was it not ? "

" No, but you are right. It has the look of something raised by public subscription." She shot an appreciative glance at the girl, then flung back her head and looked at the monument and laughed. Really, Richard had chosen very well. Always before she had averted her eyes from that white public tomb, because she knew that it had been erected not so much to commemorate the dead as to establish the wifehood of the widow who seized this opportunity to prison him in marble as she had never been able to prison him in her arms. Now that this girl had expressed its architectural quality in a phrase, the sight of it would cause amusement and not, as it had done before, anger that a woman of such quality should have occupied the place that by right belonged to her. That secondary and injurious emotion would now disappear, and far from remembering what Ellen had said, and how young and pretty and funny she had looked when she said it, she would pass on to thoughts of the time when she was young like that, and how in those days she had lived for the love of the man who was under that marble ; and her mind would dwell on the beauty of those days and not on the long, the interminable horror that followed them. Even now she knew a more generous form of grief than hitherto, and was sorrowing because he who had liked nothing better than to walk on the marshes and listen to the cry of the marsh birds and smile into the blue marsh distances, lay deaf in darkness, and was not to be brought back to life by any sacrifice. Her love ran up the hillside and stood by his tomb, and in some way the fair thing that had been between them was recreated. She had turned smilingly to Ellen, and found the girl fixing a level but alarmed stare. She was facing the situation gallantly, but found it distasteful. "What is this?" Marion asked herself angrily, with the resentment of the elderly against the unnecessary excitements of the young. "What is this fuss? Ah, she thinks it is dreadful of me to look at Richard's father's tomb and laugh." There was nothing she could say to explain it, though for a moment she tried to find the clarifying word, and looked, she knew, disagreeable with the effort. "Let's come on. Round this bend of the bank there's a bed of young osiers. How fortunate that the sun has just come out! They'll look fine. . . . You know what osiers are like in the winter? Or don't they grow up North? . . ."

They came, when the path had run past a swelling of the bank, to the neck of a little valley that cleft the escarpment and ran obliquely inland for half a mile or so. The further slope was defaced by a geometric planting of fruit-trees, and ranged in such stiff lines, and even from that distance so evidently sickly, that they looked like orphan fruit-trees that were being brought up in a Poor Law orchard. Among them stood two or three raw-boned bungalows painted those colours which are liked by plumbers. But the floor of the valley was an osier-bed, and the burst of sunshine had set alight the coarse orange hair of the young plants.

"Oh, they are lovely!" cried Ellen; "but yon hillside is just an insult to them."

Marion replied, walking slowly and keeping her eye on the osiers with a look that was at once appreciative and furtive, as if she was afraid of letting the world know that she liked certain things in case it should go and defile them, that it was the Labour Colony of the Hallelujah Army, and that they had bought nearly all the land round Roothing and made it squalid with tin huts.

"But don't they do a lot of good?" asked Ellen, who hated people to laugh at any movement whose followers had stood up in the streets and had things thrown at them.

It was evident that Marion considered the question crude.

"They even own Roothing Castle, which is where we're going now, and at the entrance to it they've put up a notice, 'Visitors are requested to assist the Hallelujah Army in keeping the Castle select.' . . . Intolerable people. . . ."

"All the same," said Ellen sturdily, "they may do good."

But to that Marion replied, grumblingly and indistinctly, that style was the only test of value, and that the fools who put up that notice could never do any good to anybody, and then her eyes roved to the path that ran down the green shoulder of the escarpment on the other side of the valley's neck. "Ah, here's Mrs. Winter. Ellen, you are going to come in contact with the social life of Roothing. This is the vicar's wife."

"Is she our sort of pairson?" asked Ellen doubtfully.

"For the purpose of social intercourse we pretend that she is," answered Marion without enthusiasm.

They met her on the plank bridge that crossed the stream by which the osier beds were nourished, and Ellen liked her before they had come within hailing distance because she was such a little nosegay of an old lady. Though her colours were those of age they were bright as flowers. Her hair was white, but it shone like travellers' joy, and her peering old eyes were blue as speedwell, and her shrivelled cheeks were pink as apple-blossom. She bobbed when she walked like a ripe apple on its stem, and her voice when she called out to them was such a happy fluting as might come from some bird with a safe nest. "Why, it's Mrs. Yaverland. I heard that you'd gone up to town."

"I came back this morning. This is Miss Melville, whom I went to meet. She is going to marry Richard very soon." Marion did not, Ellen noticed with exasperation, make any adequate response to this generous little trill of greeting. The best she seemed able to do was to speak slowly, as if to disclaim any desire to hurry on.

"Oh, how do you do? I am pleased I met you on the very first day." The old lady smiled into Ellen's eyes and shook her hand as if she meant to lay at her disposal all this amiability that had been reared by tranquil years on the leeward side of life. "This will be a surprise for Roothing. We all thought Mr. Yaverland would never look at any woman but his mother. Such a son he is!" Ellen was annoyed that Marion smiled only vaguely in answer to this mention of her astonishing good fortune in being Richard's mother. "I hope Mr. Winter will have the pleasure of marrying you."

" I'm afraid not," said Ellen with concern. " I'm Presbyterian, and Episcopalianism does not attract me."

" Oh dear ! Oh dear ! That's a pity," said the old lady,
with a pretty flight of hilarity. " Still, I hope you'll ask us
to the wedding. I've known Richard since he was a week old.
Haven't I, Mrs. Yaverland ? He was the loveliest baby I've
ever seen, and later on I think the handsomest boy. Nobody
ever looked at my Billy or George when Richard was about.
And now—well, I needn't tell you, young lady, what he's like
now. I'm glad I've met you. I've just been up at Mrs. More's."

" Who is Mrs. More ? " asked Marion heavily.

" The new people who have the small-holding at Coltsfoot
the Brights had before. I think he used to be a clerk, and
came into a little money and bought the holding, and now they're
finding it very difficult to get along."

" This small-holding business ought to be stopped."

" Why ? " asked Ellen peevishly. Marion seemed to reject
everything, and she was sure that she had seen small-holdings
recommended in Labour Party literature. " I thought it was
sound."

" Not here. Speculators buy up big farms and cut them into
small-holdings and sell them to townspeople, who starve on them
or sell them at a loss. The land's wasted for good, and all
because it can't be farmed again once it's been cut up. To all
intents and purposes it's wiped off the map. It's a scandal."

" It is a shame," agreed the old lady. " I often say that
something ought to be done. Well, the poor woman's lost
her baby."

" Bad business," said Marion.

" Such a pretty little girl. Six months. I've been up seeing
them putting her in the coffin. The mother was so upset. I
was with her all day yesterday."

" I've seen the place," said Marion. " As ugly as one of
the Hallelujah Army shanties. What this bit of country's
coming to ! And Coltsfoot was a good farm when I was a girl."

" It isn't very nice now certainly. You see, now that the
other people have failed and gone away, it's difficult for them to
get loads taken down as there isn't a proper road. Before, they
did it co-operatively among themselves. But this winter they
say they've been without coal quite often, and the baby's been
ill all the time. I think Mrs. More's been terribly lonely. Poor
little woman, she's got no friends here. All her people live in
the Midlands, she tells me. I don't think they can afford a
holiday, so the next few months will be hard for her, I'm afraid."

"Incompetent people, I should think, from what you can see of the garden. Annoying to think that that used to be good wheat-land."

"They've never liked the place. They were terrified of losing the child because of the damp from the moment it came. She's quite broken by it all, poor thing."

Marion began to draw on the ground with the point of her stick.

"Ah, well, you'll be wanting to get on," said the old lady. "Now, do bring your future daughter-in-law to tea with us some day. I've got a daughter-in-law staying with me now. I should like you to meet Rose. She plays the violin very nicely. And we have a garden we're rather proud of, though of course this is the wrong time of the year to see it. Yet I'm sure things are looking very nice just now. Just look at it ! Could anything," she asked, looking round with happy eyes, "be prettier than this ? Look at the sunlight travelling over that hill ! " She cast a shy glance at Marion, who was continuing to watch the point of her stick, and bravery came into her soft gay glance. "It's passing over the earth," she said tremulously but distinctly, "like the kindness of God."

A silence fell. "The wee thing has courage," thought Ellen to herself. "It's plain to see what's happened. Marion's often sneered at her religion, and she's just letting her see that she doesn't mind. I like people who believe in something. Of course it might be something more useful than Christianity, but if she believes it . . ."

Marion lifted her head, stared at the hillside, and said, "Yes. And look. It is followed by the shadow, like His indifference."

Tears came into the old lady's eyes. "Good-bye. We must settle on an afternoon for tea. I'll send somebody round with a note. Good-bye." She pushed past them, a grieved and ruffled little figure, a peony-spot of shock on each cheek, and then she looked back at Ellen. "We'll all look forward to seeing you, my dear," she called kindly ; but feared, Ellen saw, to meet the hard eyes of this terrible woman, who was staring after her with a look of hostility that, directed on this little affirmation of love and amiability, was as barbarous as some ponderous snare laid for a small, precious bird.

"Let's get on," said Marion.

They climbed the hill and went along a path that followed the skyline of the ridge, over which the sea-borne wind slid like water over a sluice. To be here should have brought such a

stinging happiness as bathing. It should have been wonderful to walk in such comradeship with the clouds, and to mark
that those which rode above the estuary seemed on no higher
level than this path, while beneath stretched the farm-flecked
green pavement of Kerith Island, and ahead, where the ridge
mounted to a crouching summit, stood the four grey towers of
the Castle. But the quality of none of these things reached
Ellen because she was wrapped in fear of this unloving woman
who was walking on ahead of her, her stick dragging on the
ground. She was whistling through her teeth like an angry man ;
and once she laughed disagreeably to herself.

They came to a broken iron railing whose few standing divisions
ran askew alongside the footpath and down the hillside towards the marshes, rusted and prohibitive and futile.

" Look at them ! Look at them ! " exclaimed Marion in a
sudden space of fury. " The Hallelujah Army put them up.
It's like them. Some idea of raising money for the funds by
charging Bank Holiday trippers twopence to see the Castle.
It was a fool's idea. They know nothing. The East End
trippers that come here can't climb. They're too dog-tired.
They go straight from the railway-station to Prittlebay or
Bestcliffe sands and lie down with handkerchiefs over their
faces. Those that push as far as Roothing lie down on the
slope of the sea-wall and stay there for the day." She kicked a
fallen railing as she stepped over it into the enclosed land. " The
waste of good iron ! You're not a farmer's daughter, Ellen ;
you don't know how precious stuff like this is. And look at the
thistle and the couch-grass. This used to be a good sheep-feed.
The land going sick all round us, with these Hallelujah Armies
and small holdings and such-like. In ten years it'll be a scare-
crow of a countryside. I wish one could clear them up and burn
them in heaps as one does the dead leaves in autumn." Fatigue
fell upon her. She seemed exhausted by the manufacture of
so much malice. With an abrupt and listless gesture she pointed
her stick at the Castle. " It isn't much, you see," she said
apologetically. And indeed there was little enough. There
were just the two towers on the summit and the two on the
slope of the hill whose bases were set on grassy mounds so that
they stood level with the others, and these had been built of
such stockish material that they had not had features given them
by ruin. " I'm afraid it's not a fair exchange for Edinburgh
Castle, Ellen. But there's a good view up there between the
two upper towers. Where the fools have put a flagstaff. I
won't come. I'm tired. . . ."

She watched the girl walk off towards the towers and said to herself, " She is glad to go, half because she wants to see the view, and half because she wants to get away from me. I was a fool to frighten her by losing my temper with Mrs. Winter. But the blasphemy, the silly blasphemy of coming from a woman who has just lost her baby and talking of the kindness of God ! . . ." The tears she had held back since they had parted with the vicar's wife ran down her cheeks. It must, she thought, be the worst thing in the world to lose an only child. Surely there could be nothing worse in all the range of human experience than having to let them take away the thing that belongs to one's arms and put it in a coffin. There would be a pain of the body as unparalleled, as unlike any other physical feeling, as the pains of birth, and there would be tormenting fundamental miseries that would eat at the root of peace. A woman whose only child has died has failed for the time being in that work of giving life which is her only justification for existence, and so her unconscious mind would try to pretend that it had not happened and she would find herself unable to believe that the baby was really dead, and she would feel as if she had let them bury it alive. All this Marion knew, because for one instant she had tried to imagine what it would have been like if Richard had died when he was little ; and now this knowledge made her feel ashamed because she was the mother of a living and unsurpassable son and there existed so close at hand a woman who was having to spend the day in a house in one room of which lay a baby's coffin.

And it was such a horrid house too. Sorrow there would take a sickly and undignified form. For the Coltsfoot bungalow was unusually ugly even for an Essex small-holding. A broken balustrade round the verandah, heavy wooden gables, and an ingeniously large amount of inferior stained timbering gave it an air of having been built in order to find a last fraudulent use for a suite of furniture that had been worn out by a long succession of purchasers who failed to complete agreement under the hire system. There were Nottingham lace curtains in the windows, the gate was never latched and swung on its hinges, nagging the paint off the gate-post, at each gust of wind. If one passed in the rain there was always some tool lying out in the wet. Ugliness was the order of the day there, and it was impossible to believe that the owners were anything but weakeyed, plain people.

The baby had not really been pretty at all. Mrs. Winter's tribute to it had only been the automatic response to all aspects of child life which is cultivated by the wives of the clergy. And the parents would take the tragedy ungracefully. The woman would look out from her kitchen window at her husband as he pottered ineffectively with the goat and the fowls and all the gloomy fauna of the small-holding, which had, as one would not have thought that animals could have, the look of being underpaid. Perhaps he would kneel down among those glass bells which, when they are bogged in Essex clay on a winter afternoon, are grimly symbolical of the end that comes to the counter-meteorological hopes of the small-holder. The fairness and weedy slenderness which during their courtship she had frequently held out to her friends as proof of his unusual refinement, would now seem to her the outward and visible signs of the lack of pigment and substance which had left him at the mercy of a speculator's lying prospectus. When he came into the carelessly cooked meal there would be a quarrel. "Why did you ever bring me to this wretched place!" She would rise from the table and run towards the bedroom, but before she got to the door she would remember the coffin, and she would have to remain in the sitting-room to weep. She would not look pretty when she wept, for she was worn out by child-birth and nursing and grief and lean living on this damp and disappointing place. Presently he would go out, leaving the situation as it was, to potter once more among the glass bells, and she would sit and think ragingly of his futile occupation, while an inner region of her heart that kept the climate of her youth grieved because he had gone out to work after having eaten so small a meal.

Marion rose to her feet that she might start at once for these poor souls and tell them that they must not quarrel, and warn the woman that all human beings when they are hurt try to rid themselves of the pain by passing it on to another, and help her by comprehension of what she was feeling about the loss of the child. But immediately she laughed aloud at the thought of herself, of all women in the world, going on such an errand. If she went to Coltsfoot now the anticipation of meeting strangers would turn her to lead as soon as she saw the house, and the woman would wonder apprehensively who this sullen-faced stranger coming up the path might be ; when she gained admittance she would be able to speak only of trivial things and her voice would sound insolent, and they would take her for some kind of district visitor who intruded without even the justification of being a church worker and therefore having official intelligence about immortality. Her lips were sealed with inexpressiveness when she talked to anyone except Richard. She could not talk to strangers. She could not even talk to Ellen, with whom she ought to have been linked with intimacy by their common love for Richard, with whom she must become intimate if Richard's future was to be happy.

Her eyes sought for Ellen in the ruins, but she was not visible. Probably she had gone into one of the towers where her dreams could not be overseen and was imagining how lovely it would be to come here with Richard. It must be wonderful to be Richard's sweetheart. Marion had seen him often before as the lover of women, but he had never believed in his own passion for any of them, and therefore there had always been something desperate about his courtship of them, like the temper of a sermon against unbelief delivered by a priest who is haunted by sceptical arguments. But to a woman whom he really loved he would be as dignified as befitted one who came as an ambassador from life itself, and gay as was allowed to one who received guarantees that the fair outward show of the world is no lie; in all the trivialities of courtship he would show his perfect quality without embarrassment. She was angered that she would not be able to see him thus. There struck through her an insane regret that being his mother she could not also be his wife. But this was greed, for she had had her own good times, and Harry had been the most wonderful of sweethearts.

There had been a June day on this very hill. . . . She had been standing by the towers talking to Bob Girvan for a few minutes, and when she had left him she had felt so happy at the show of flowering hawthorn trees that stood red and white all the way down the inland slope of the ridge that she began to run and leap down the hill. But before she had gone far, Harry had walked out towards her from one of the hawthorns. She had felt confused because he had seen her running, and began to walk stiffly and to scowl. " Good morning, Marion," he had said. " Good morning," she had answered, feeling very grown-up because she had no longer bobbed to the squire. He told her, looking intently at her and speaking in a queer, strained voice, that he had found a great split in the trunk of the white hawthorn, and asked her if she would like to see it. She said, " Yes." It struck her that she had said it too loudly and in an inexpressibly foolish way. Indeed, she came to the conclusion as she followed him down the hillside that nobody since the world began had ever done anything so idiotic as saying " Yes " in that particular manner, and she became scarlet with shame.

When they came to the dazzling tree he advanced to it as if he cared nothing for its beauty, and showed her with a gruff and business-like air a split in the trunk. She could not understand how he had not seen it before, as it had been there for the last four months. Then he had pointed up to the towers with his stick. "Who's that you were talking to up there?" "Bob Girvan," she had answered; "did you want to speak to him, sir?" He seemed, she thought, cross about something. "No, no," he answered impatiently, "but he's a silly fellow. Why do you want to talk to him?" She told him that Bob had stopped to ask if his father could come over and look at the calf her grandmother wanted to sell, and that seemed to please him, and after that they had talked a little about how the farm had got on since Grandfather's death. Then he said suddenly, "I suppose that if you don't go about with Bob Girvan there's some boy who does take you out. Isn't there?" She whispered, "No." But he had gone on in a strange, insistent tone, "But you're getting quite a big girl now. Seventeen, aren't you, Marion? There'll be somebody soon."

At that, paralysis fell on her. She stared out of the scented shadow in which they stood together at the masts of Roothing Harbour far away, wavering like upright serpents in the heated air. Her heart seemed about to burst. Then she heard a creaking sound, and looked about for its cause. He had put up his arm and was shaking the branch which hung over her head so that the blossom was settling on her hair. When she looked at him he stopped and muttered, "Well, good-bye. It's time I was getting along," and walked away. From the shadow she had watched him with an inexplicable sense of victory rising in her heart, coupled with a disposition to run to someone old and familiar and of authority. A year later they had stood once more under that hawthorn tree, and again he had shaken the mayblossom down on her, but this time he had laughed. He murmured teasingly, "Maid Marion! Maid Marion!" and laughed, and she had looked up into his eyes. Like many rakes, he had bright, innocent grey eyes; and indeed, again like many rakes, he was in truth innocent. It was because he had remained as ignorant as a child of the nature of passion that he had experimented with it so recklessly.

With her he had delightedly discovered love. Indeed, she had had such a courtship that she need envy no other woman hers. For all about her days with Harry there had been the last quality the world would have believed it possible could pervade the seduction of a farmer's daughter of seventeen by a squire who was something of a rip: the quality of a fair dawn

seen through the windows of a church, of a generous spring-time
that synchronised with the beginning of some noble course of
action. She should have been well pleased. Yet she knew now
that the occasion would have been more beautiful if, standing
under that may-tree, she had looked up into Richard's eyes.
They would not have been innocent, they would not have
sparkled like waters running swiftly under sunshine. But
they would have told her that here was the genius who would
choose good with the vehemence with which wicked men choose
evil, who would follow the aims of virtue with the dynamic
power that sinners have, who would pour into faithfulness the
craft and virility that Don Juan spent on all his adventures.
Besides, Richard's eyes were so marvellously black. . . . She
reminded herself in vain that Harry had possessed far beyond
all other human beings the faculty of joy, that uninvited there
had dwelt about him always that spirit which men labour to
evoke in carnival, that there had been a confidence about his
gaiety as if the gods had told him that laughter was the
just final comment on life. But she knew quite well that
the woman who was chosen by Richard would be loved more
beautifully than she had ever been.

She started to her feet and looked urgently towards the
ruins to see if Ellen was returning, because she felt that if she
did not commit herself to affection by making some affectionate
demonstration from which she could not withdraw she might
find herself hating this unfortunate girl. Having once known
the bitterness of moral defeat, she dreaded base passions as
cripples dread pain, and she knew that this irrational hatred
would be especially base, a hunchback among the emotions.
It would be treason against Richard not to love anything he
loved; and besides, it would be most wrong to hate this girl,
who deserved it as little as a flower. Yet the emotion seemed
independent of her and now nearly immanent, and to escape
from it she hurried across the sloping broken ground, calling out,
" Ellen, Ellen ! "

She could see that there was no one on the level platform
by the flagstaff, so she took the footpath where it fell
below the two lower towers, and as soon as she had passed
the first and could look along the hillside to the second she
stopped. Now she could see Ellen. The girl was standing on
the very top of the grassy mound that supported the tower,
her back resting against the wall, her feet on a shelf that had
formed where the earth had been washed away from the masonry
foundations by the dripping from a ledge above. It was the

very place where Marion had been standing ever so long ago
at the moment where Richard had first moved within her. She
had dragged herself up the hill to escape from the bickerings at
Yaverland's End, and had been resting there, looking down on
the peace of the marshes and listening to the unargumentative
cry of the redshanks, and wishing that she might dwell during
this time among such quiet things ; and suddenly there came a
wind from the sea, and it was as if a little naked child had been
blown into her soul. All that she felt was a tremor feeble as
the first fluttering of some tiny bird, and yet it changed the
world. In that instant she conceived Richard's spirit as three
months before she had conceived his body, and her mind became
subject to the duty of awaiting him with adoration as her flesh
and blood were subject to the duty of nourishing him. Harry,
who had been lord of her life, receded rushingly to a place of
secondary importance, and she transferred her allegiance to
this invisible presence who was possessed of such power over
her that even now, when it could not be seen or touched or heard
or imagined, it could make itself loved. She had stood there
in an ecstasy of passion until the sun had fallen beyond Kerith
Island. Then her cold hands had told her that she must go
home for the child's sake ; and as if in recognition of this act of
cherishing there had come as she climbed the hill another
tremor that made her cry out with joy.

Ellen must not stand there, or she was bound to hate her.
It was intolerable that this girl who was going to be Richard's
wife should intrude into the sacred places of the woman who had
to be content with being his mother. " Ellen, Ellen ! " she
shouted, and waved her stick. The girl clambered down and
came towards her with steps that became slower as she came
nearer. She was, Marion saw, looking at her again under
faintly contracted brows, and she realised that because she wept
about the child at Coltsfoot her eyes were small and red, and
that had added to her face a last touch of ruin which made it
an unfavourable place for the struggles of an unspontaneous
expression of amiability. Of course the girl was alarmed at being
called down from her serene thoughts of Richard by grotesque
wavings of a woman whose face was such a queer mask. But there
was nothing to be said that would explain it all. She took
refuge in silence; and knew as they walked home that that also
was sinister.

CHAPTER IV

IT struck Marion that it was very beautiful in this room that night. The white walls were bloomed with shadows and reflections, and the curtains of gold and orange Florentine brocade were only partly drawn, so that at each window there showed between them an oblong of that mysterious blue which the night assumes to those who look on it from lit rooms. On the gleaming table, under the dim light of a shaded lacquer lamp, dark roses in a bowl had the air of brooding and passionate captives. Different from these soft richnesses as silk is from velvet, the clear flame of the wood fire danced again in the glass doors of one of the bookcases: and at the other, choosing a book in which to read herself to sleep, stood Ellen, her head a burning bush of beauty, her body exquisitely at odds with the constrictions of the product of the Liberton dressmaker. She held a volume in one hand and rested the other on her hip, so that there was visible the red patch on her elbow that bespeaks the recent schoolgirl, and all that could be seen of her face was her nose, which seemed to be refusing to be overawed by the reputation of the author whose work she studied. In the swinging glass door beside her there was a diffusion of reflected hues that made Marion able to imagine what she herself looked like, in her gown of copper-coloured velvet, sitting in the high-backed chair by the fire. She was glad that sometimes, by night, her beauty crawled out of the pit age had dug for it, and, orienting her thoughts as she always did, she rejoiced that Richard would find such an interior on his return.

" Have you found a book you like ? "

" No. There's lots of lovely ones. But none I just fancy. I'm inclined to be disagreeable and far too particular this evening. Are these your books or Richard's ? "

" Nearly all mine."

" You must be intellectual then. Now mother was different. No one could have called her an intellectual, though she could always take a point if you put it to her. Do you know, you're not like an elderly pairson at all. Usually one thinks of a lady of your age as just a buddy in a bonnet. But you've got such an active mind, not like a young pairson's. I'll take Froude's ' Life of Jane Welsh Carlyle.' That ought to do.''

" I shouldn't take it if I were you. It's too interesting. It'll keep you awake.''

" Oh, I'll not sleep in any case. I feel awful wakeful. But it'll be all right as soon as Richard comes.''

Her tone, betraying so unreproachfully that she quite expected that till then things would be all wrong, reminded Marion what evenings of aborted intimacies and passages of slow liking truncated by moments of swift dislike, had passed in this room whose appearance she had been watching with such satisfaction. She reflected on the inertia which inanimate matter preserves towards the fret that animate creatures conduct in its midst, the refusal of the world to grow grey at anybody's breath. Exhibited by nature in the benedictions of sunlight that fall through the court windows on the criminal in the dock, or the rain that falls on the flags and Venetian masts of the civic festival, it has an air of irony. But there is obstinacy about the way a chair keeps its high polish though its sitter cries her eyes red. . . . With alarm she perceived that she was showing a disposition to flee from a difficult situation into irrelevant thought, which she had always regarded as one of the most contemptible of male characteristics. She checked herself sharply. It was necessary that she should use the remaining moments of the evening in making Ellen like her.

" I think I'll wish you good-night, Mrs. Yaverland,'' said the girl.

" Let me come and see if you've got all you want.''

But there was nothing Ellen wanted. She passed into the room of bright new things and sat down on her bed and expressed complete satisfaction in dogged tones. " Indeed, that gas-fire's sheer luxury,'' she said, " for I'm strong as a horse. Really, I've everything, thank you. . . .''

" Let me brush your hair.''

As she took out the coarse black pins, her heart rejoiced because Richard would have all this beautiful hair to play with ; yet as she brushed it out she wished that his thirst for beauty could have been gratified by some inorganic gorgeousness, some strip of cloth of gold in whose folds there would not lie any white triangle of a face that had to be understood and conciliated. Her wish that it were so reminded her how much it was not so, and she bent forward and looked over the girl's shoulder at her reflection in the glass. " It is a face that believes there is no foe in the world with which one cannot fight it out," she thought. "Well, that is probably true for her. I, with my foes who are a part of myself, am unusually cursed. If these young people have ordinary luck they ought to make a fine thing of the world, and I will enjoy standing by and watching them. Oh, I must make friends with her. We have many things in common. I will talk to her about the Suffragettes. What shall I say about them ? I do honestly think that they are splendid women. I think there was never anything so fine as the way they go out into the streets knowing they will be stoned. . . ." A memory overcame her. "Ah ! " she cried out, and laid down the brush.

"What's the matter ? " exclaimed Ellen, standing up. There was a certain desperation in her tone, as if she thought the tragic life of a household ought to have a definite closing-time every night, after which people could go to bed in peace.

" I forgot—I forgot to take some medicine. I must go and take it now. And I don't think I'd better come back. I'm sure you'll brush your hair better yourself. I'm sure I tugged. You're so tired, you ought to go to bed at once. Good-night. Good-night." By the slow shutting of the door she tried to correct the queer impression of her sudden flight, but knew as she did so that it sounded merely furtive.

In her own room she undressed with frantic haste so that she could turn out the light and retreat into the darkness as into a burrow. But everywhere in the blackness, even on the inside of the sheet she drew over her face as she lay in bed, were pictures of the aspects of evil the world had turned to her that day : thirty years before, when she was stoned down the High Street of Roothing. She was in the grip of one of her recurrent madnesses of memory. There was no Richard to sit by her side and comfort her, not by what he said, for she had kept so much from him that he could say nothing that was really relevant, but by his beauty and his dearness, which convinced her that all was well since she had given birth to him ; so her agony must go on until the dawn.

She must get used to that, because when he was married to Ellen she would no longer be able to sit up in her bed and call "Richard, Richard ! " and strike the bell that rang in his room—that rang, as it seemed, in his mind, since no other sound but it ever wakened him in the night. Not again would he stand at the door, his dark hair damp and rumpled, his eyes blinking at the strong light, while his voice spoke hoarsely out of undispersed sleep. "Mother, darling mother, are you having bad dreams?" Not again would she answer moaningly, "Oh, Richard, yes!" and tremble with delight in the midst of her agony to see how, when this big man was dazed and half awake, he held his arms upwards to her as if he were still a little boy and she a tall overshadowing presence. In the future he must be left undisturbed to sleep in Ellen's arms. That thought caused her inexplicable desolation. Rather than think it she gave up the struggle and allowed herself to be possessed by memory, and to smart again under the humiliation of that afternoon when life had made a fool of her. For what had hurt her most was that she had gone out into the world, the afternoon it stoned her, in a mood of the tenderest love towards it.

She had risen late, she remembered, that day. All night long she had been ill, and had not slept until the first wrangling of the birds. Then suddenly she had opened her eyes, and after remembering, as she always did when she woke, that she was going to have a child, she had looked out of her wide window into the mature and undoubtful sunshine of a fine afternoon. She had felt wonderfully well and terribly hungry, and had hastened at her washing and dressing so that she could run downstairs and get something to eat. When she went into the kitchen she saw that dinner was over, for the plates were drying in the rack and Peggy, the maid, was not there. It was incredible that she had not known why Peggy had gone out, that she should fatuously have told herself that the girl was probably working in the dairy; but in those days her mind was often half asleep with love for the unborn.

She rejoiced that she had missed the family meal, for it was not easy to sit at the table with Grandmother and Cousin Tom and Aunt Alphonsine, unspoken comments on her position hanging from each face like stalactites. In the larder she found the cold roast beef, magnificently marbled with veins of fat, and the cherry pie, with its globes of imperial purple and its dark juice streaked on the surface with richness exuded from the broken vault of the pastry, and she ate largely, with the solemn greed of pregnancy. Afterwards she washed the dishes, in that state of bland, featureless contentment that comes to one whose being knows that it is perfectly fulfilling its function and that it is earning its keep in the universe without having to attempt any performance on that vexing instrument, the mind.

When she had finished, she wandered out cf the kitchen

aimlessly, benevolently wishing that her baby was born so that she could spend the afternoon playing with it.

The parlour door was ajar, and she peeped in and saw Grandmother sitting asleep in the high-backed chair, a shaft of sunlight blessing her bent head to silver and stretching a corridor for dancing motes to the bowl of mignonette. She saw the scene with the eye of an oleographer. In defiance of experience she considered her grandmother as a dear old lady, and the hum of a bee circling about the mignonette sounded like the peace that was in the room becoming articulate and praising God. Enjoyable tears stood in her eyes. Drying them and looking round the dear scene, so that she might remember it, she saw that the grandfather clock marked it as half-past two. Now was the time that she must go for her walk. The children would be back at school, the men would be at work, and the women still busy cleaning up after their midday meal. She was afraid now to walk on the Yaverland lands for fear of finding Goodtart, the cattleman, standing quite still in some shadowed place where she would not see him till it was too late to avoid touching him as she passed, and turning on her those dung-brown eyes in which thoughts about her and her state swam like dead cats in a canal; and though she desired to revisit the woods where she had walked with Harry, she had never gone there since that afternoon when Peacey had stepped out on her suddenly from behind one of the pillars of the belvedere. The marshes too she could not visit, for she could not now go so far. But there remained for her the wood across the lane, which ran from the glebe land opposite Yaverland's End and stretched towards the village High Street. No one ever went there at this time of day.

Her pink sunbonnet was lying on the dresser in the front parlour, and she put it on to save the trouble of going upstairs for a hat, though she knew it must look unsuitable with her dark, full gown. Stealing out very quietly so that she should not disturb Grandmother, she went down the garden, smiling at the robust scents and colours of the flowers. She had a feeling in those days that nature was on her side. The purplish cabbage roses seemed to be regarding her with clucking approval and reassurance that a group of matrons might give to a young wife. The Dolly Perkins looked at her like a young girl wondering. The Crimson Ramblers understood all that had happened to her. She loved to imagine it so, for thus would people have looked at her if she had been married, and she slightly resented for her child's sake that she was not receiving that homage.

Humming with contentment, she crossed the lane to the wood, whose sun-dappled vistas, framed by the noble aspirant oak-trunks, stretched before her like a promise of happiness made by some wise, far-sighted person.

It made Marion laugh angrily, as she lay there in the bed where she had slept so badly in the thirty years that had passed since that afternoon, to remember how she had walked in those woods in a passion of good-will to the world. She dreamed complimentary dreams of life, pretending that it was not always malign. She imagined that Harry would come back before the child was born and would cloak her in protective passion, and his pride in her would make him take her away somewhere so that everyone would see that he really loved her and that he did not think lightly of her. Freely and honestly she forgave him for his present failure to come to her. It was his mother's fault. She had made him marry when he was twenty-one, so that he had been led to commit a physical forgery of the spiritual fact of fatherhood by begetting children who, being born of a woman whom he did not love, were not the children of his soul. With aching tenderness she recalled the extreme poverty of the emotion that showed in his eyes when he spoke of his daughters, or when, as had happened once or twice, they had looked out of the belvedere window and seen the little girls running by on the brow of the hill, white leggy figures against the frieze of the distant shining waters.

It was indeed not so much emotion as a sense that in other circumstances these things might have aroused an emotion which, with his comprehensive greed of all that was lovely in the universe, he regretted being without. If he had only been with her now he would have been given that, and would have found, like her, that it is possible to be ardently in love with an unknown person. She was so sorry he was not here. But she knew that he would come soon, and then he would have the joy of seeing his true child, the child of his soul, and beyond the spiritual joy that must come of that relationship he would have the delight of the exquisite being she knew she was going to bring forth. For she knew then perfectly what Richard was going to be like. She knew she was going to have a son; she knew that he would have black, devout and sensitive eyes. She knew that he would be passionate and intractable and yet held to nobility by fastidiousness and love of her. She imagined how some day in a wood like this, but set in a kinder countryside, Harry would kneel in a sunlit clearing, his special quality of gaiety playing about him like another kind of sunshine, while there staggered towards him their beautiful dark child. He would miss nothing then, except this time of acquaintance with the unborn, and perhaps he would not even miss that, for no doubt he would make her the mother of other children.

At that thought she stood still and leaned back against the trunk of a tree and closed her eyes and smiled triumphantly, and ran her hands down her body, planning that it should perform this miracle again and again and people her world with lovely, glowing, disobedient sons and daughters. She felt her womb as an inexhaustible treasure. Slowly, swimmingly, in a golden drowse of exultation, she moved on among the trees till she came to the wood's end, and looked across the waste patch scattered with knots of bramble and gorse at the yellow brick backs of the houses in Roothing High Street and knew she must go no further. For the feeling against her was very high in the village. They had told the most foul stories of her ; it was as if they had been waiting anxiously for an excuse to talk of sexual things that they might let loose the unclean fantasies that they had kept tied up in the stables of their mind, that these might meet in the streets and breed, and take home litters filthier than themselves. Men and women told tales that they could not have believed simply that they might evoke before their minds, and strengthen by the vital force of the listeners' hot-eared excitement, pictures of a strong man and a fine girl living like beasts in the fields. Not only did they tell lies of how they had watched her and Harry among the bracken, they said she had been seduced by the young doctor who had been *locum tenens* here in February, and that they had seen her in the lanes with the two lads that were being tutored at the Vicarage. These things had been repeated to her by her grandmother in order that she might know what disgrace she had brought on her family, and in the night she had often lain in a sweat of rage, wanting to kill these liars. But that day, standing in the sunshine, she forgave them. She was glad that they had such brave yellow sunflowers in their little wood-fenced gardens : she hoped that all the women would sometimes be as happy as she was. She did not know that this was no day for her to venture forth and forgive her enemies, since it was the Lord's Day, when men ceased to do any manner of work, that they may keep it holy.

The first warning she was given was a sudden impact on a high branch of an oak-tree a yard or two from where she stood, and the falling to earth, delayed by the thick crepitant layers of green-gold, sun-soaked leaves, of a cricket ball. With the perversity of rolling things it dribbled along the broken ground and dropped at last into a mossy pit half filled with dead leaves which marked where a gale had once torn up a young tree by the roots ; and the next moment she heard, not distantly, the open-mouthed howl that comes from a cricket-field in a moment of crisis. Then she remembered that it was a habit of the young bloods of Roothing to evade their elders' feeling about Sabbath observance by going in the afternoon to an unover-looked wedge of ground that ran into the woods and playing some sort of bat-and-ball game. This must be Sunday. If she did not go home at once she would begin to meet the village lovers, who would not understand how well she wished them, and would look at her with the hostility that the lucky feel for the unlucky. But when she turned to follow the homeward path she heard from all over the wood scattered shouts. The lads were looking for their ball. One she could hear, from the breaking down of brushwood, was quite close to her. Her best plan was to hide. So she stood quite still under the low branches of an elder-tree, while George Postgate doubled by.

Poor George ! He was seventeen, and big for that, but his mind had stayed at twelve, and he was perpetually being ad-mitted in probation to the society of lads of his own age, and then for some act of thick-wittedness being expelled again. It was plain from the way that his great horny fingers were scratch-ing his head and his vast mouth was drooping at the corners that it was his fault that the ball crashed so disastrously out of bounds, and that he felt himself on the verge of another ex-pulsion. " Oh, ter dash with the thing ! " he exclaimed mourn-fully, and kicked a root, and lifted his face to the patch of blue sky above and snuffled. Marion's heart dissolved. She could not let this poor stupid thing suffer an ache which she was pre-vented from relieving only by a fear of rudeness which was probably quite unjustified. " George ! " she called softly, staying among the branches. He gaped about him. " George ! " she called a little louder. " The ball's in the pit, among the leaves." But he was transfixed by the wonder of the bodyless voice and would not pay any attention to her directions, but continued to gape. She saw that she would have to go and show him herself, and after only half a moment's reluctance she stepped forward. She did not really mind people seeing her, because she knew that it was only a convention that she was ugly because she was going to have a baby. For there was now a richer colour on her cheeks and lips than there had ever been before and her body was like a vase. It was only when they had awful thoughts about her that she hated meeting them, and George would not have awful thoughts about her if she did him a good turn. So she went over to him, pointing to the pit. " I saw it roll down there, George. Look ! There it is."

But he did not pick up the ball. He appeared to be petrified by the sight of her. " Make haste," she said, " they'll be waiting for you." At that he dropped his lids, and his lips thickened, and his face grew red. Then he raised his head again and looked at her with eyes that were not dull, as she had always seen them before, but hot and bright, and he began to shift his weight slowly backwards and forwards from one foot to the other. Her heart grew sick, because all the world was like this, and she turned again to the path home. But through the tree-trunks in that direction there came two other boys in search of the ball—Ned Turk, who to-day was the station-master at Roothing station, and Bobbie Wickes ; and at the sight of her they stood stock-still as George Postgate had done, and, like him, dropped their heads and flushed and lifted lewd faces. A horror came on her. It was as if they had assumed masks to warn her that they had some secret and sinister business with her. Then one pointed his hand at her and made an animal noise, and the other laughed with his mouth wide open. Neither said anything. Their minds were evidently engaged in pro-cesses beneath those which find expression in language. She stiffened herself to face them, though she felt frightened that these two boys, whom she had known all her life, with whom she had ridden on the hay-wains in summer and caught stickle-backs in the marsh dykes, should change to these speechless beings with red leering masks who meant her ill.

For the first time she felt herself too young for her destiny. " I am only nineteen," she cried silently. Tears might have disgraced her but that the child moved in her as if it had looked out at the frightening figures through her eyes, and she suddenly hated Harry for leaving her and his son unprotected from such brutes as people seemed to be, and was vivified by the hatred. She made to walk past the boys back towards Yaverland's End, but as she moved they sent up shrill wordless calls to their fellows who were still in the fields, which were immediately answered. She realised that any minute the woods would be full of lads whom the sight of her would change to obscene creatures, and that being consolidated in this undis-turbed place they would say and do things that would hurt her so much that they would hurt her child. There was nothing for it but to leave the cover of the wood and cross the waste

space and walk down Roothing High Street and go back to
Yaverland's End by the lane. Her mood of forgiving love for
the village, which the cricket-ball had interrupted, had been
so real that she felt as if a pact had been established between
it and her, and she was quite sure that she would be safe from
the boys there. If they were tiresome and followed her, no
doubt somebody like Mrs. Hobbs, who kept the general stores,
would take her in and let her rest till it was dark, and then
see her home. She turned round and walked out of the wood,
and because she could not, in her heavy-footed state, trample
through the undergrowth, she had to follow the path that led
her to within a yard or two of George Postgate. She could see
from the workings of his large face that he was forming some
plan of action. And sure enough, when she passed him, he cried
out " Dirty Marion ! " and twitched the sun-bonnet from her
head. The sudden movement made her start violently, for
though she had not known what fear was until she conceived,
she now knew a panic-terror at anything that threatened her
body. That made the boys shout with laughter and call to
their friends to hurry up and see the fun.

The sunshine that beat down on the unshaded field was hot
on her bare head. It would be awkward too, going into the
village hatless and with ruffled hair. But she must not be
angry with George Postgate, for indeed the incident had been
to him only a means of gaining that popularity with the fellows
that his poor stupid soul so longed for and had so often been
refused, and he could not know that the fright would make her
feel so ill. Since the first agonising months of her pregnancy,
when nausea and faintness had pervaded her days, she had
never felt as ill as this. A sweat had broken out on her face
and her hands ; she had to pant for breath and her limbs staggered under her. But she would be all right if she could sit
down for one moment. There was a hawthorn stump a little
way off, and to this she made her way, but as she sunk down on
it a clod of earth struck her in the shoulder. She spun round,
and another broke on her face. Grit filled her mouth, which
was open with amazement. She had been deaf with physical
distress, so she had not heard that the boys had gathered
together on the wood's edge and were now marching after her
in a shouting crowd. Something in her attitude when she turned
on them made them fall dumb and stock-still for a moment.
But as a gust of wind ruffled her hair and blew her skirts about
her body a roar of laughter went up from them, and earth and
dry dung flew through the air at her.

As she set her face towards the High Street again, which still seemed very far away, she sobbed with relief to see that old Mr. Goode, the carrier, had come down to the end of his garden to see what the noise meant, and that he had almost at once gone back into his house. Of course he would come out and save her. In the meantime she pushed on towards the houses, that because of her sickness and her fear rocked and wavered towards her flimsily like a breaking wave. A heavy clod struck her in the back, and she shrieked silently with terror. If they hurt her she might give birth to her baby and it would not live. She had not had it quite seven months yet, so it would not live. At that thought anguish pierced her like a jagged steel and she began to try to run, muttering little loving names to her adored and threatened child. She looked towards the road to see if old Mr. Goode was coming, and was surprised to see that he was standing at the gate of the field with two other men and a boy. And though they were all looking towards her, they made no movement to come to her help. Perhaps they did not see what was happening to her. It did not matter. She would be there in a few moments. One of the boys had found a tin can and was beating on it, and the sounds made her head feel bad. She staggered on, looking on the ground because of the sun's strong glare.

When she found that her feet had reached the patch of rutted ground that was around the gate, she sobbed with thankfulness. She threw out her hands to the multitude of people who had suddenly gathered there, and cried out imploringly, for if someone would only take her to a place where she could lie down she would be all right and she would keep her child. But none of them came to her, and her deafened ears caught a sound of roaring. She could not see who they were and what they were doing, for all things looked as if she saw them through flowing water. But she knew the tall figure by the gatepost must be Mr. Goode, so she stumbled to him and raised her head and tried to find his kind face. But, like the boys, he wore a mask. Veins that she had never noticed before stood out red on his forehead and his beard twitched, and the funny lines that darted about his eyes, which had become small and winking, made his face a palimpsest in which an affected disgust overlaid some deep enjoyment. He did not seem to be looking at her; indeed, he averted his eyes from her, but thoughts about her made him laugh and send out a jeering cry—wordless like the call of the boys. She realised that he and these people whom she could not see, but who must be people who had known

her all her life, had come out not to save but to see her ill-treated
and to rejoice. She stood stock-still and groaned. Her head
felt wet, and she put up her hand and found that a stone had
drawn blood behind her ear. The boys pressed close about her
and beat the tin can in her ears, and one stretched out a stick
and touched her, which made Mr. Goode and the unseen enemies
laugh. But at that she shrieked. She shrieked with such
terrible anger at those who insulted the mother of her child,
that all their jaws fell and they shrank back and let her pass.

But when she had gone a few paces up the road someone
shouted something after her, and there was a noise of laughter
and then of the shuffling of many feet behind her, and jeers
and cat-calls and the beating of the tin can. She went on,
looking to the right and the left for some old friend to come out
and take her to shelter, but now she knew that there would be
none. These people would drive her on and on. And when she
got home to Yaverland's End, if they would let her go there,
and did not trample her down on the roadside first, she would
lose her child. The core of her body and soul would be torn
out from her, and all promise of pleasure and all occasion of
pride. For there was no pleasure in the world save that to
which she had looked forward these seven months, of seeing
that perfect little body that she knew so well and kissing
its smooth skin and waiting for it to open those eyes—those
black eyes; and there could be no greater degradation than
to bring forth death, when for months the sole sustenance
against the world's contempt had been that she was going to
give birth to a king of life. There danced before her eyes all
the sons of whom she was to be bereft in the person of this son.
The staggering child, the lean, rough-headed boy of ten with
his bat, the glorious man.

Now her loss was certain. All the people were running out
into the gardens of the little houses on the right and throwing
up the windows over the shuttered shops on the left, and all wore
the flushed and amused masks that meant they were determined that she should lose her child. Mrs. Hobbs, who kept the
general store, the kind old woman whom she had thought would
take her in, and Mrs. Welch, the village drunkard, were leaning
over adjacent garden walls, holding back the tall, divine sunflowers that they might hobnob over this delight, and their faces
were indistinguishable because of those masks. Even Lily
Barnes, standing on the doorstep of the nice new Lily Villa
her husband, Job Barnes the builder, had built for their marriage,
with her six months old baby in her arms, was thus disguised,

and seeming, like Mr. Goode, to look through her old friend at some obscene and delicious fact, sent up that hooting wordless cry.

Marion was so appalled that a woman carrying her baby should connive at the death of another's that she stood quite still and stared at her, until the boys behind her thrust her with sticks. When she passed the alley between the post-office and the carrier's she saw the cattle-man, Goodtart, looking out at her from its shadows ; he did not move, but his dark brown eyes were more alive than she had ever seen them. A stranger stepped out of the inn and laughed so heartily that he had to loose his neckerchief. Of course she must look funny, walking bareheaded, with earth and blood caking her hair, and her skin sweaty and yellow with nausea and her burdened body, her face grimacing with anguish every time Ned Turk danced in front of her and beat the tin can in her ears.

"Oh, my baby, my baby !" she moaned. Ned Turk heard the cry and repeated it, screaming comically, "Oh, my baby, my baby !" All the crowd took it up, "Oh, my baby, my baby !" She shut her ears with her hands, and wished that wherever Harry was, he might fall dead for having left her and his child to this.

Then from the porch of the cottage at the angle of the High Street and the Thundersley Road, the cottage where Cliffe, the blind man, lived with his pretty wife, there stepped out Peacey. For a moment he shrank back into the shadow, holding a handkerchief in front of his face, but she had recognised the tall, full body that was compact and yet had no solidity, that suggested a lot of thick fleshy material rolled in itself like an umbrella. It was her last humiliation that he should see this thing happening to her. She lifted her chin and tried to walk proudly. But he had come forward out into the roadway and was coming towards her and her followers. He did not seem quite aware of what he was approaching. He walked delicately on the balls of his large and light feet, almost as though the occasion was joyful ; and he held his face obliquely and with an air of attention, as if he waited at some invisible table. There hung about him that threatening serial quality which made it seem that in his heart he was ridiculing those who tried to understand his actions before he disclosed their meaning in some remote last chapter. It struck her, even in the midst of her agony, that she disliked him even more than she disliked what was happening to her.

She had thought that he would smile gloatingly into her

sweaty face and pass on. But she saw swimming before her a fat, outstretched hand, and behind it a stout blackness of broadcloth, and heard her pursuers halt and cease the beating of their tin cans, and came to a swaying standstill, while above her there boomed, gently and persuasively, Peacey's rich voice. She could not pin her fluttering mind to what it said, because she felt sickish at the oil of service, the grease of butlerhood that floated on it, but phrases came to her. He was asking the village people what would happen when the squire came home and heard of this; and reminding them that they were all the squire's tenants. A silence fell on her pursuers. From the rear old Mr. Goode's kind voice said something about " A bit of boys' fun, Mr. Peacey"; Ned Turk piped, "We don't mean no 'arm," and the crowd dispersed. It shuffled its heels on the cobbles; it raised jeers which were mitigated and not sent in her direction, but were still jeers; it beat its tin cans in a disoriented way, as if it were trying to save its self-respect by pretending that Mr. Peacey had been so much mistaken in the object of their demonstration that there was no harm in going on with it.

She was left standing in the middle of the road, alone with Peacey. She realised that she was safe. If she could rest now she would keep her child. She knew relief but not exultation. It was as if life had been handed back to her, but not before some drop of vileness had been mixed with the cup. There was nothing to redeem the harm of that afternoon: the quality of her rescue had exactly matched the peril from which she had been rescued. When Peacey's voice had boomed out above her it had expressed agreeable and complete harmony with the minds of the crowd; it had betrayed that he, too, could imagine no pleasure more delightful than stoning a pregnant girl, that he had his position to think of, and he begged them to have similar prudence. He had risked nothing of his reputation as a just man in Roothing to save her. To this loathsome world Harry, who had been her lover for two years, had left her and her divine child. She looked up at Peacey and laughed.

His eyes dwelt on her with what might have been forgiveness. " You'd best come into Cliffe's cottage," he said, and went before her. It struck her, as she followed him, that to people watching them down the street it would look as if she was following him almost against his will or without his knowledge. Well, she must lie down, and this was the only door that was open to her. She must follow him.

Once they were within the porch he bent over her

solicitously, and through his loose-parted lips came the softest murmur: "Poor little girl!" Had he said that for her to hear, or had some real tenderness in his heart spoken to itself? Was he really a kind man? She looked at him searchingly, imploringly, but from his large, shallow-set grey eyes, which he kept fixedly on her face, she could learn nothing. In any case she must take his arm, or she would fall. She even found herself shrinking towards his pulpy body as he pushed open the door, because she was afraid the people inside might not welcome her. She did not know the Cliffes, for they were Canewdon people who had moved here four or five years back, when Grandmother was too old and she was too young to make friends with a young married woman. But its trim garden, where on golden summer evenings she had seen the blind man clipping the hedge, his clouded face shyly proud at such a victory over his affliction, while his wife stood by and smiled, half at his pleasure and half at her own loveliness, and the windows, lit rosily at night, had often set Marion wishing that Harry and she were properly married. Because she had received the impression that this was a happy home, she was uneasy, for of late she had learned that happy people hate the unhappy. But the shaft of sunlight that traversed the parlour into which they stepped was as thickly inhabited with dancing motes as if they were stepping into some vacated house given over to decay. There was dust everywhere, and the grandfather clock had stopped, and the peonies in the vase on the table had died yesterday; and the woman who stood in the middle of the room, looking down at her hands and turning her wedding ring on her finger, was not pretty or joyous. Her face was a smudge of sullenness under hair that was elaborately dressed yet was dull for lack of brushing, and her body drooped within the stiff tower of her thickly-boned Sunday-best dress. She looked at Marion without curiosity from an immense distance of preoccupation. There came from a room at the back of the house the strains of "Nearer, my God, to Thee," played on the harmonium, and at that she made a weak, abstracted gesture of irritation.

"Go and get a basin of water and a bit o' rag. The girl's head's bleeding," said Peacey, and she went out of the room obediently. He collected all the cushions in the room and piled them on the horsehair sofa, and helped her to lie comfortably down on them. Then he walked to the window, and stood there looking out until Mrs. Cliffe came back into the room. He took the basin without thanks, and set it down on a chair and began to bathe Marion's head, while Mrs. Cliffe stood by watching incuriously.

"Now then, Trixie," he said, not unpleasantly, "you'd best go into the back parlour and listen to your beloved husband playing hymns so trustfully."

She went away, still without speaking, and Marion, no longer feeling defensive before a stranger, closed her eyes. Really his fat hands were very gentle, very clever and quick. After a few moments he had finished, and she was able to turn her face to the wall and talk to her baby that had been saved to her, and to exult that after all she would see those eyes. She shivered to think how nearly she had lost him, and was transfixed by her hatred of Harry. She turned hastily and faced the room.

Peacey was watching her with his quiet eyes. He said in a silken voice, "This sort of thing wouldn't happen to you if you were married to me."

She lay quite still, looking at the ceiling. She knew that what he said was true.

"You've looked at me as if I were a pickpocket, you have," he went on, "just because I want to marry you. I don't hold it against you. You're young. That young, that it's a shame this has happened to you. But after to-day perhaps you'll judge me a bit fairer. You see, I'm older than you, and I've seen a bit of the world, and I know how things are. And I knew you'd have a nasty jar like you had to-day before you were through with it. And I don't doubt you'll have a few more before you're done. It ain't too good for the little one, if you'll excuse me mentioning it. You can't expect a man of any feelings to look on without trying to do what he can."

She looked up to scan his face for some sign of sincerity, and found herself for the first time wishing that she might find it and have reason to distrust her own dislike of him. But he was sitting sideways, with his head turned away from her, and she could see nothing of him but his hot black clothes and his fat hand slowly stroking the thigh of his crossed leg in its tight trouser. A sigh shook the dark bulk of his back.

"Me of all men," he said softly, "who had such a mother."

There was a long pause. She grew curious.

"Is she dead?" she asked.

"Died when I was ten. Not a soul's ever cared for me since then. I'm not sorry. It's made me remember her all the better. And she was one of God's saints."

His voice was husky. She muttered, "I am sorry," and was annoyed to find that she really was.

"Why need you be?" he asked. "There's those that haven't that much to look back on. All I want from you, Miss Marion, is to let me help you. Or at least not to think ill of me for wanting to help you."

He sat still for a moment and continued to stroke his thigh. "Marion," he began abruptly, and then paused as if to brace himself. "Marion, I hope you understand what I'm asking you to do. I'm asking you to marry me. But not to be my wife. I never wouldn't bother you for that. I'm getting on in life, you see, so that I can make the promise with some chance of keeping it. And besides, there's more than that to it. How," he asked, lifting his head and speaking mincingly, "should I presume to go where Sir Harry's been? I would never ask you to be a wife to me. Just to accept the protection of my name, that's all I ask of you."

They sat for a while in the embrowned sunshine of the dusty room.

He rose and stood over her, drooping his sleek head benevolently. "Ah, well," he said, "I'd best leave you alone. God knows I never meant to intrude on you. Perhaps you would take a little doze now, and after tea I'll take you home." He looked on her moistly, tenderly. "Think kindly of me if you dream." Some emotion coagulated his voice to a thick, slow flow. "You'll be the only woman who ever has thought of me in her dreams if you do. I've never had anything to do with women all my life. You see, I know I've got an ugly mug. I wouldn't dare to make love to any woman in case I saw—what I've seen in your face—what I saw in your face that night I came out on you from the belvedere. Oh, I don't blame you, Miss Marion. You're young—you're beautiful. You've had a real gentleman for your sweetheart. But I don't see why I shouldn't help you. Still, if you don't see it so . . ." He sighed, and brought his hands together and bowed over them. His eyes passed deliberately over her matronly body, as if he knew his thoughts about her were so delicate that no suspicion of indelicacy could arise out of his contact with her. "Poor little Miss Marion," he murmured in an undertone, and wheeled about and padded to the door. He turned there and stood, his body neckless and sloping like a seal's, and said softly, "And don't think it was me who put Lady Teresa up to coming down to Yaverland's End to-morrow morning. It is her ladyship's own idea. I said to her, 'Leave the poor girl alone.' I have always said to her, 'Leave the poor girl alone.'" His voice faded. He moved vaporously out of the room.

One is too harsh to one's dead self. One regards it as the executor and residuary legatee of a complicated will dealing with a small estate regards the testator. Marion shook with rage at the weak girl of thirty years ago who lay on the sofa and stared at the grained panels of the closed door and let the walls of her will fall in. Then it was that her life had been given its bias towards her misery. Then it was there was conceived the tragedy which would come to a birth at which all present should die. "What tragedy? What tragedy?" she said derisively, sitting up in bed. There spoke in her the voice of her deepest self. "The tragedy," it answered composedly. "The tragedy. Did you not know almost as soon as Richard stirred in you that he would have eyes like black fire? Were you not perfectly acquainted long before his birth with all the modes in which his body and soul were to move, so that nothing he has done has ever surprised you? Even so, you have always known that the end of you and yours will be tragedy." "What could happen to my Richard?" she argued. "He is well, he is prosperous, he has this lovely Ellen who will be a watchdog to his happiness. Tragedy cannot touch him unless the gods send down fire from heaven, and there are no gods. There are no gods, but there are men, and fire that comes from the will." She groaned, and lay back and wrapped the sheets round her closely like cerements, as if by shamming dead she could cast off the hot thoughtfulness of life. But indeed she gained some comfort from this dialogue with that uncomfortable self, for she knew again how wise it was, and its predictions seemed irrational only because it had remembered all that her consciousness had determined to forget for fear it threw so strong a light on her fate that she would lose the courage to live.

Her reasoning self was a light, irreligious thing, and thought about what she should eat and what she should drink and where she should sleep, but this other self had never awakened save to speak of Harry or Richard. She trusted it, and she could recall quite definitely that on that afternoon thirty years before it had sanctioned her decision to abandon conflict and do what people wished to do. It knew, what her consciousness had forgotten, of how she herself had felt when she was within her mother's womb, and it was able to warn her that her unborn baby was seriously thinking of revising its decision to live. While she had staggered under the stones, the child had quailed in the midst of her terror like a naked man above whom breaks a thunderstorm; her nerves had played round him like a shaft of lightning, her loud heart-beat had been the thunder. Now her fear-poisoned blood gave it sickly nourishment, at which the fœtal heart beat weakly, so that the embryo knew what the born know as faintness. The system of delicate mechanical adjustments by which it poises in the womb was for the moment dislocated, and at this violent warning of what life can be its will to live was overcast by doubt. If she could rest here now, and go home and have a long sleep, and sit all the next morning on the brow of the hill and watch the fishing-boats lie like black, fainting birds on the shining flats, the child would feel her like a peaceful fane around it and it would decide to live. But if Harry's mother came to see her next day it would forsake her.

She would come very early, for she was one of those people who suffer from a displaced day as others suffer from a displaced heart, and rose at six. Long before Marion had completed the long sleep that was necessary for the reassurance of her child she would be shaken, and look up into her grandmother's face, which she did not like, for though the expressions that passed over it were the same as they had always been, it was now overlaid with a patina of malice. She would smile now, as she dared to years ago, when she used to tell her little granddaughter that Lady Teresa had come to give her a present for reciting so nicely at the church school concert, but all her aspect would mean hatred of this girl who had been given the romantic love that she had been denied, and hope that its fruit might be destroyed. The room would be tidied; her drowsy head would be tormented by the banging of drawers and the rustling of paper. Out of consideration for Lady Teresa's feelings the photograph of Harry by her bed would be turned face downwards. That she would not really mind, for she would have liked to take it out of the frame and tear it to pieces; but she would have to pretend that she minded.

Then there would burst into her room the trailing and squawking personality of Lady Teresa. She would bring with her a quantity of warm black stuffs, for she was one of the most enthusiastic followers of Queen Victoria in the attempt to express the grief of widowhood by a profusion of dark dry goods, and she would sit close to the bed, so that Marion would lose nothing of the large face, with its beak nose and its bagging chin and its insulting expression of outraged common sense, or of the strangulated contralto in which she would urge that there was no reason why any sensible gel should not be proud to marry the butler at Torque House. By sheer noisiness she

would make Marion cry. The child would doubt again. . . .
Since these things would have happened she could not do other
than she did. Her surrender was the price she had to pay for
Richard's life.

How artfully, moreover, it was disguised from her that she
was going to pay any real price ! She looked back through the
past at Peacey's conduct of that matter as one might look
through the glass doors of a cabinet at some perfect and obscene
work of art. He had laid his hand so wonderfully across his
face while he was speaking of his ugliness, so that the drooping
fingers seemed to tell of humility and the renunciation of all
greeds. And that candid, reverent gaze which he turned upon
her to-day had been so well calculated to speak of purity to
one who had shivered under sidelong leers. He had indeed that
supreme mastery over vice which comes of a complete understanding and dilettante love of virtues. He knew how the
innocent hunger for love and pity, and, knowing well what these
things were, he could speak as one who came as their messenger.
Loathingly and yet giving homage to his workmanship, she
recalled that later scene by which he had added a grace note
to his melody of wickedness and made so sweet a song of it
that her will had failed utterly.

Mrs. Cliffe had come in with a cup of tea and some cake on
a tray. "You'll feel better for this," she said, and while Marion
had ate and drunk she had stood by the window and looked
at her. It seemed to Marion that she had greatly changed of
late. Before, she had belonged very definitely to the shop-
assistant class, which differentiated itself from the women-folk
of the village by keeping shapely and live-witted even after
marriage. But now she stood humpishly in her great apron
like any cottager's wife, and her hand, which she set akimbo,
looked red and raw and stupid. The way she stared at Marion's
figure too, was, indicative of a change from her pristine gentility.

"Funny I never heard of you being like this," she said at
last.

"It is. I thought everyone was talking about it."

"They may be. But there's times when one doesn't listen
to what people are saying." For a time she was silent. "Ah,
well," she meditated bitterly, "it doesn't pay to do wrong,
does it ?"

"I haven't done wrong," said Marion.

"So you say now," Mrs. Cliffe told her, "but there'll come a
day when you see you have." She drew in her breath with a
little gasp as Peacey put his head in at the door.

He looked sharply from one to the other, and then advanced
to Marion's couch, rubbing his hands genially. " Now then,
Trixy," he said teasingly, " you don't want me to talk too long
to your beloved husband, do you ? I might go telling him
things about you, mightn't I ? You run along and look after
him." Mrs. Cliffe retired quite taciturnly, nothing in her face
responding to this rallying, and he bent quickly over Marion.
" I hope she hasn't been worrying you ? " he asked. Concern
for her ?—it sounded just like concern for her—made his voice
tremble. " That's why I hurried back. Women are so narrow-
minded to their poor sisters who haven't been so fortunate.
I thought she might have been making you feel a bit
uncomfortable."

" Oh no," said Marion.

The mask of his poor ugly face, which had been grotesque with
pitying lines, became smooth. He sighed with relief, and sat
down by her side, very humbly.

" But she was beginning to talk rather strangely," the poor
fool Marion had continued. " I think she's altered very much
lately."

" Do you know, I was thinking so myself," Peacey had
answered reflectively. " I wonder if she's got anything on her
mind. I wish I could find out. One doesn't like a 'ome of
friends not to share its worries with you, without giving you a
fair chance to 'elp. I must see whether I can get it out of 'er."

Oh, he was a kind man. He was certainly very kind. She
put down her cup and braced her body and her soul, and said,
" Mr. Peacey . . ."

The world had deceived her utterly that day ; and yet there
was one in that cottage who had suffered more than she, for by
her suffering she had bought no Richard. Poor Mrs. Cliffe !
She was a woman of sixty now, white-haired, and fine-featured
with the anxious fineness of one who has for long lived out of
favour with herself and has laboured hard for re-establishment ;
but the fear still dwelt in her. Most times that Marion passed
down Roothing High Street, and saw the old woman sitting knitting in the garden while her old blind husband shuffled happily
here and there, they would but bow and smile and look away
very quickly. But every now and then, perhaps once a year,
she would put down her knitting so soon as Marion came in
sight and come into the road to meet her and would give her
nervous, absent-minded greetings. Then she would draw her
into the furthest edge of the pavement, because the blind have
such sharp hearing, and she would whisper ｅ

" Have you heard from *him* lately ? "

" No."

" He's still at Dawlish ? "

" They say so."

" Do you think he will ever come back ? "

" No. He will never come back."

" Ah." She would stand looking past Marion with her face cat's-pawed by memory and her fingers teasing the fringe of her shawl, till from the garden the blind old man would cry lovingly and querulously, "Trixy, where are you?" and she would answer, "Coming, dearie." As she turned away she would murmur : " I shouldn't like him to come back. . . ."

Poor Trixy Cliffe ! She should have known only the sorrow of pure femalehood, such sorrow as makes the eyes of heifers soft. Women like her should be harvested like corn in their time of ripening, stored in good homes as in sound barns, and ground in the mill of wifehood and motherhood into the flour that makes the bread by which the peoples live. But there must have been some beauty working in her soul, for Peacey went only where he saw some opportunity to cancel some movement towards the divine, being a missionary spirit. So she had been delivered over to that terror which survived for ever. Even in the exorcised blue territory of a good old woman's eyes. "Oh, poor Trixy, poor Trixy ! " moaned Marion, weeping. But it struck her that she was enjoying herself, and she sat up rigidly and searched her soul for the smuggled insincerity. " I must be lying," she said aloud with loathing. "I really cannot be pitying Trixy Cliffe because in my heart of hearts I care for no one but Richard. I would knead the flesh of anyone on earth and bake it in the oven if that were the only food I could give him. What am I doing this for? Ah, I see. I am hanging about this fictitious emotion simply because I do not wish to go on and remember Roger." She held out her hands into the blackness and cried out, " Oh, Roger, forgive me for shutting you out of my memory as I have shut you out of everything else. I will remember everything, I will ! " She lay down and let all pictures reappear before her eyes, but her mouth was drawn down at the corners.

CHAPTER V

IT was no use wondering now whether or not Peacey had really murmured " Good day, ma'am," as they parted at the door of the church after their furtive marriage. She had certainly thought she had heard this ironic respectfulness, and she had stared after him with a sudden dread that under the cream of benignity there might after all be a ferment of malign intention. But that gait, which was so light and brisk for such a heavy man, had already taken him some distance from her, and he was now entering the yew alley that was the private way from Torque Hall to the churchyard. The sunlight falling through the interstices of the dark mossy trees cast liver-coloured patches on his black coat. She had turned and looked down, as she always did when human complexities made her seek reassurance as to the worth of this world, on the shiny mud-flats, blue-veined with the running tides, and green marshes where the redshanks choired. Her misgiving had weakened at that beauty, for with the logic of the young she thought that if the universe was infinitely good it could not also be infinitely evil, and it had been utterly dispelled by his considerate conduct during the following weeks.

He did not try to see her at all until a day or two before the birth of her child was expected. Then he came at twilight. He would not let Grandmother put a match to the lamp in the parlour, and Marion knew from his quiet urgency that he was doing this so that she might continue to wear the dusk as a cloak. He sat down by the window, his shoulders black against the sunset, and his fat hands, with their appealing air of shame at their own fatness, laid on the little table beside him an old carved coral rattle and a baby's dress precious with embroideries. These he had bought, he said, up in London, where he had had to go for a day to do business with the wine merchants. He had not seemed to listen to her thanks. But his hunched shape against the primrose light and the gleaming of his thick white fingers playing nervously with the fragile gifts spoke of a passionate concern for her. No doubt that concern was sincere. They told her after her confinement that during the day and night through which her child was slowly torn from her he had not left the house, and at her cries a sweat had run down his face. That was not unnatural. An incomplete villainy would vex its designer as any unfinished work of art vexes the artist. But she interpreted it in the sense that he, knowing what delusions youth has regarding the human capacity for love, had foreseen that she would.

She let him see her before anyone else, and he had made the most of that ideal occasion when her being was so sensitive that it responded to everything, and so well pleased at having safely borne her son that she saw everything as evidence of creation's virtue. He had added stroke to stroke with the modest confused smile with which he entered the room, as if he felt his vast bulk ridiculous in this room of small rosebud patterns; the uneasy laughter with which he disguised his embarrassment when they could find no chair big enough for him; the shy wonder with which he put out his hand and hooded the tiny black head with it, and uncurled the little hand with his obese forefinger; the reticence with which he checked his remark that he had always wanted to have a child of his own. And he perfected the picture that he desired her to see by the assurance he gave murmurously from the darkness of the open door. " Get well soon. . . . You needn't be afraid of me. We made a bargain. I mean to stick to it." He had caught the very tune that dogged sincerity plays on the voice's chords. She lay happy after he had gone because she and her child had so true a friend.

It was, of course, from no malice against her that he set out to deceive her, but from the natural desire to protect his being from alterations hostile to its quality. Long after, sitting with Richard in a café in Rio de Janeiro, she had looked at the men who were taking the lovely painted women to themselves, and she detected behind the gross mask that the prospect of physical enjoyment set on the faces an expression of harsh spiritual defensiveness; and thenceforward she had understood why Peacey had practised this fraud on her. He had known, as all men know, that there is a beneficent magic in the relationship between men and women; the evil man, at war with all but himself, cannot but admit that for his supremest pleasure he depends on one other than himself, and by his gratitude to her is tainted with altruism and is no longer single-minded in his war on others. Such men uphold prostitution because it exorcises sex of that magic. It is not a device to save sensuality,

for love with a stranger is like gulping new spirit, and love with a
friend is drinking old wine.   Its purpose is indeed this very
imperfection of the embraces that it offers, for they leave the
soul as it was.

Peacey, she understood in the light of this discovery,
had desired her with a passion that, uncircumvented, would
have swept him on to love and a life on which his labori-
ously acquired technique of villainy would have been wasted,
so it had been the problem set his virtuosity to create a situation
which would let him fulfil his body's hunger for her and at the
same time kill for ever all possibility of love between them.
She could imagine him seated under the little window in the
butler's pantry, polishing a silver teapot with paste and his own
fingers, as old-fashioned butlers do, for he was scrupulous in all
matters of craftsmanship ; holding his fat face obliquely, so
that it seemed as unrelated to anything but space as a riding
moon, save when he looked down and smiled to see the blue
square of the window and the elm top shine upside down and
distorted in the bulbous silver : thinking his solution out to its
perfect issue.

It had been quite perfect.   By that visit, and by his abstention from any later visit, he had induced in her just that mood
of serenity and confidence which would be most shocked by the
irruption of his passion.   The evening when it all happened she
had been so utterly given up to happiness.   She had taken the
most preposterously long time to put Richard to bed.   He had
had a restless day, and had been so drowsy when she went to feed
him in the evening that she had put him back in his cradle in
his day clothes, but about half-past eight he had awakened and
called her, and she found him very lively and roguish.   She had
stripped him and then could not bear to put his night-clothes on,
he looked so lovely lying naked in her lap.   He was not one of
those babies who are pieces of flesh that slowly acquire animation
by feeding and sleeping ; from his birth he had seemed to be
charged with the whole vitality of a man.   He was minute as a
baby of three months is, he was helpless, he had not yet made the
amazing discovery that his hand belonged to him, but she knew
that when she held him she held a strong man.   This babyhood
was the playful disguise in which he came into the world in
order that they might get on easy terms with one another and
be perfect companions.   Never would he be able to feel tyrannous because of his greater strength, for he would remember
the time when she had lifted him in her weak arms, and that
same memory would prevent her from ever being depressed into

a sense of inferiority, so that they would ever move in the happy climate of a sense of equality. And every moment of this journey towards that perfect relationship was going to be a delight.

She bent over him, enravished by the brilliant bloom of his creamy skin and the black blaze of his eyes, which had been black from birth, as hardly any children's are; turned him over and kissed the delicate crook of his knees and the straight column of his spine and the little square wings of his shoulder-blades, and then she turned him back again and jeered at him because he wore the phlegmatic, pasha-like smile of an adored baby. She became vexed with love for him, and longed to clasp him, to crush him as she knew she must not. She put on his night-clothes, kissing him extravagantly and unsatedly, and when she finished he wailed and nuzzled to her breast. "Oh, no, you greedy little thing," she cried, for it was a quarter of an hour before he should have been fed again, but a wave of love passed through her and she took him to her. They were fused, they were utterly content with one another. He finished, smacking his lips like an old epicure. "Oh, my darling love!" she cried, and put him back into the cot and ran downstairs. If she stayed longer she would keep him awake with her kisses and play. She was brightened and full of silent laughter, like a girl who escapes from her sweetheart.

Grandmother sat very quietly at her sewing and soon went upstairs. Grandmother was getting very old. When she said "Good-night" she seemed to be speaking out of the cavern of some preoccupation, and when she went upstairs her shawl fell from her shoulders and trailed its corner on the ground. Marion hoped that the old lady had not worn herself out by worrying about her, and she pulled out the sewing that had been shut up in the work-basket and meditated finishing it, but she was too tired. Nowadays she knew a fatigue which she could yield to frankly, as it was honourable to her organism, and meant that her strength was going into her milk and not into her blood. She folded her arms on the table and laid her head on them and thought of Richard. It was his monthly birthday to-day. He was three months old. She grieved to think that she could feed him for only six months more. How could she endure to be quite separate from him? Sometimes even now she regretted that the time had gone when he was within her, so that each of her heartbeats was a caress to him, to which his little heart replied, and she would feel utterly desolate and hungry when she could no longer join him to her bosom. But she would always be able to kiss him. She imagined herself a few years ahead, calling him back when he was running off to play, holding his resistant sturdiness in her arms while he gave her hasty, smudged kisses and hugged his ball for more loving. But she reflected that, while the character of those kisses would amuse her, they would not satisfy her craving for contact so close that it was unity with his warm young body, and she must set herself to be the most alluring mother that ever lived, so that he would not struggle in her arms but would give her back kiss for kiss. She flung her head back, sighing triumphantly because she knew she could do it, but as her eyes met her image in the mirror over the mantelpiece she was horrified to see how little like a mother she was looking. Lips pursed with these long imaginary kisses were too oppressive for a child's mouth; she had lost utterly that sacred, radiating lethargy which hushes a house so that a child may sleep : on a child's path her emanations were beginning to cast not light but lightning.

She called out to herself: "You fool! If you really love Richard you will let him run out to his game when he wants to, that he shall grow strong and victorious, and if you call him back it must be to give him an orange and not a kiss!" But it seemed to her that this would be a sacrifice until, staring into the glass, she noticed that she was now more beautiful than she had ever been, and then she saw the way by which she could be satisfied. Harry must come back; she knew he was coming back, for they had inter-cepted his letter to her, and they would not have done that if it had been unloving. After she had weaned Richard she must conceive again and let another child lift from him the excessive burden of her love : then her mind and soul could go on in his company without vexing him with these demands that only the unborn or the nursling could satisfy. Then this second child would become separate from her, and she must conceive again and again until this intense life of the body failed in her and her flesh ceased to be a powerful artist exulting in the creation of masterpieces. It must be so. For Richard's sake it must be so. Her love would be too heavy a cloak for one child, for it was meant to be a tent under which many should dwell. Again as in the wood she laid her hand on her body and felt it as an inexhaustible treasure. Again she was instantly mocked.

There had come, then, a knock at the door. She had felt a little frightened, for since her stoning in Roothing High Street she had felt fear at any contact with the external world ; she knew now that rabies is endemic in human society, and that one can never tell when one may not be bitten by a frothing mouth. But it was not late, and it was as likely as not that this was Cousin Tom Stallybrass come to say how the Frisian calf had sold at Prittlebay market, so she opened it at once.

Peacey stood there. He stood quite still, his face held obliquely, his body stiff and jointless in his clothes, like a huge, fat doll. There was an appearance of ceremony about him. His skin shone with the white lacquer of a recent washing with coarse soap, he was dressed very neatly in his Sunday broadcloth, and he wore a black-and-white check tie which she had never seen him wear before, and his fingers looked like varnished bulging pods in tight black kid gloves.

He did not speak. He did not answer her reluctant invitation that he should enter. She would have thought him drunk had not the smell that clung about him been so definitely that of soap. From the garden behind him, which was quilted by a thick night fog, came noises as of roosting birds disturbed. His head turned on the thick hill of his neck, his lids, with their fringe of long but sparse black lashes, blinked once or twice. When the sound had passed, his face again grew blank and moonish and he stepped within. He laid his bowler hat on the table and began to strip off his gloves. His fleshy fingers, pink with constriction, terrified her, and she clapped her hands at him and cried out : " Why have you come ? "

But he answered nothing. Speech is human, and words might have fomented some human relationship between them, and he desired that they should know each other only as animals and enemies. He continued to take off his gloves, while round him fragments of fog that had come in with him hung in the warm air like his familiar spirits, and then bent over the lamp. She watched his face grow yellow in the diminishing glare, and moaned, knowing herself weak with motherhood. Then in the blackness his weight threshed down on her. Even his form was a deceit, for his vast bulk was not obesity but iron-hard strength. All consciousness soon left her, except only pain, and she wandered in the dark caverns of her mind. Her capacity for sexual love lay dead in her. She saw it as a lovely naked boy lying with blue lips and purple blood pouring from his side, where it had been jagged by the boar who still snuffled the fair body, sitting by with its haunches in a spring. She cried out to herself : " You can rise above this ! This is only a physical thing," but her own answer came : " Yes, but the other also was only a physical thing. Yet it was a sacrament and gave you life. There is white magic and black magic. This is a black sacrament, and it will give you death." Her soul fainted into utter nothingness.

She woke and heard Richard crying for her upstairs. She dragged herself up at once, but remembered and fell grovelling on the floor and wept. But Richard continued to call for her, and she struggled to her feet and made her way up the stairs, clinging to the banisters. She looked over her shoulder at the loathed room and was amazed to see that this mawkish early morning light showed it much tidier than it had been by the glow of the lamp the night before. It was evident that Peacey had set it in order before he let himself out, and had even neatly folded the sewing she had left crumpled on the table. At this manifestation of his peculiar quality she flung her arm across her face and fled to her son's room. But when she got there a sense of guilt overcame her and she was ashamed to go to him, though she knew he needed her, and staggered first to the window to look out at the sea and the shining plain, whose beauty had through all previous agonies reassured her. But the eastern sky was inflamed with such a livid scarlet dawn as she had never seen before, and the full tide was milk streaked with blood, and the sails of the barges that rode there were as rags that had been used to staunch wounds. Unreasonably she took this as confirmation that there had happened to her one of earth's ultimate evils, a thing that no thinking on could make good. But turning to her child to still his crying, she saw the tiny exquisite hands waving in rage and the dark down rumpled on the monkeyish little skull, and the black eyes in which all the beauty and high temper that were afterwards to be Richard were condensed, and she ran to him. She caught him up in her arms and laughed into the criminal face of the morning.

From that day on Marion and Richard lived together in the completest isolation. She had meals with her family, she moved among them doing what part of the household and dairy work that she had always done, but she never spoke to them unless it was necessary ; for she realised now why Grandmother had been so preoccupied that she let the tail of her shawl trail on the ground as she went upstairs that night, and why Cousin Tom Stallybrass had not come in to tell how the calf had gone at Prittlebay market. When one afternoon she came to the head of the stairs and saw Aunt Alphonsine gesticulating in her tight *dame de compagnie* black in the parlour below, stretching out her long lean neck like the spout of a coffee-pot to Grandmother's ear, she stood quite still, staring at the two women and hating them till they saw her and fell silent. She did not take her gaze from them until Aunt Alphonsine put up her hand to cover her scar. Then she knew that this wretched woman was at last afraid of her and would let her alone, and she turned contentedly to the room where Richard was.

But later on a misgiving seized her lest her aunt might have come as envoy from Peacey, and since she perceived that, her rage against the world was so visibly written on her that she inspired fear ; she thought it best to give her boy into the charge of Peggy and to go over to Torque Hall herself. She waited in the court-yard outside the servants' quarters while they fetched him, and stood with her head high, so that the faces peering at her from the windows should see nothing of her torment, at the corner of the gardens that was visible through the gracious Tudor archway. There was nothing showing save a few pale mauve clots of Michaelmas daisies standing flank-high in the slanting dusty shafts of evening sunshine, and the marble Triton, glowing gold in answer to the sunset, with gold autumn leaves scattered on his pedestal. But she knew very well how fair it all must be beyond, where she could not see—the broad grass walk stretching between the wide, formal flowerbeds, well tended but disordered with the lateness of the year, to the sundial and the chestnut grove. How could Harry, who had loved her, possess all this and not want to share it with her ? She could have sobbed like a child whose playmate is not kind, had not Peacey stood at her elbow. "I want to give you warning that if ever you come near me again I will kill you," she said. He looked sharply at her and she saw that he was convinced and discomfited. But suddenly he smiled. She went home, wondering uneasily why he should have smiled, but came to the conclusion that this was simply one of his mystifications and that he had simply been trying to cover his defeat. It was an extraordinary fact that there never once occurred to her that possibility, the thought of which, she after-wards realised, had made Peacey smile. The truth was that she never thought directly of that night's horror, but, perhaps because of that fantasy about the wounded youth which had vexed her delirium, she always disguised it in her mind as an encounter with a wild beast, and the expectation of human issue no more troubled her than it would a woman who had been gored by a boar.

It was partly for this reason, and partly because of a certain ominous peculiarity of her physical condition, that she did not know for some months that she was going to have Peacey's child. It was indeed a rainy December morning when she heard a knock at the door and knew it was little Jack Harken, because he was whistling " Good King Wenceslas," as he always did, and would not go to answer him, although she knew Grandmother and Peggy were both in the dairy, because she was distraught with her own degradation. Her encounter with Peacey had been like being shown some picture from a foul book and being obliged to stare at it till it was branded on her mind, so that whenever she looked at it she saw it also, stamped on the real image like the superscription on a palimpsest. But now she felt as if she herself had become a picture in a foul book. And she was quite insane with a sense of guilt towards Richard. This discovery had, of necessity, meant that she must wean him, and her obsession interpreted their conflict between them that had naturally followed as a wrangle between them as to her responsibility for this evil. Now he was lying in his cot screaming with rage, his clean frock and the sheets running with the rivulets of milk that he had spat out and struck from the teat of the bottle she was forcing on him, and she was sobbing, for this sort of thing had been going on for days, " I can't help it, darling, I can't help it."

Then Jackie began to thump rhythmically on the door below, and she ran down, maddened with so much noise, and snatched the letter he held out to her. At the writing on the envelope her heart stood still. She recanted all she had lately thought of Harry. Hatred and resentment fell from her. The promise of her lover's near presence came on her like a south wind blowing over flowers. At his message that he was waiting for her on the marshes under the hillside she remembered what love is—a shelter, a wing, a witty clemency that finds the perfect unguent for its mate's hurt as easily as a wit finds jests, a tender alchemy that changes the dark evil subsistence of the universe to bright, valuable gold. In her light shoes, and with her black hair loose about her shoulders, she ran out into the rainy yard, fled round the house quickly so that none might see her and spy on them, and plunged down the thaw-wet hillside, crying out with joy, even when she slipped and fell, because her lover's arms would so soon be round her.

She was amazed, for she had not yet had leisure or the heart to look out of the window, that beneath her the marshes crackled white with sunlit snow, and a blue sea stretched to the rosy horizon that girdles bright frosty days. Even as this beauty had lain unseen under her windows, so had her happiness waited unsuspected. She did not see him till she was close upon him, for he was striding up and down between the last two trees of the elm hedge. Her heart ached when she saw him standing, brilliantly lovely as the glistening snow-laden branches above him, for it was plain from the confident set of his shoulders and the loose grip of his hand on his stick that he was unaware that any situation existed which was not easily negotiable. They had evidently told him nothing at Torque Hall to destroy the impression she must have created by her last letter to him in which she had described her acceptance of Peacey's offer of a formal marriage. They had not dared, for they knew how terrible he would be when he moved to avenge her. But he lifted his eyes and ran to her and took her in his arms, and did not cease to kiss her till she sobbed out what they had done to her. Then it was as if a wind had blown and the snow had fallen from the branches, leaving them but dark, gnarled wood.

" But why did you marry him ? "

" The people stoned me in the street and I could get no peace at home."

" Couldn't you have tried to stand it ? "

" I was afraid for the boy."

" Then why couldn't you have gone away ? "

" How could I when I was so ill ? Why did not you come back ? "

" How could I leave the prince and princess ? "

She was aghast to find them quarrelling, and while he drew a shuddering breath between his teeth, she interrupted : " Oh, Richard is so lovely ! You must see him soon. Oh, such a boy ! "

But he had paid no heed and shakingly poured out words which seemed to weave a spell on her, changing her heart from young to old, her blood from that of a loved girl to a hating woman. He found the situation, she had thought at the time, and still thought after thirty years, far less negotiable than a high love would have done. It did not occur to him that he might take her away. He took it for granted that thereafter they must be lost to each other. But save for his desire to blame her for these mischances, which did not offend her, since it was so like the harmless spite of a child that beats his racquet because it has sent his ball into the next garden, he seemed not to be thinking of her part in that loss at all. It was his extreme sense of his own loss that was making him choke with tears. It appeared that love was not always a shelter, a wing, a witty clemency, a tender alchemy. She stood half asleep with shock until a sentence, said passionately in his delightful voice which made one see green water running swiftly, and at first refused admission to her mind by her incredulous love, confirmed itself by reiteration. " Damn it all," he was saying, " you were unique ! " At that she cried out, " Oh, you are Peacey too ! I will go back to Richard," and turned and stumbled up the wet hillside.

It is true that Harry's desertion nearly killed her—that there was a moment, as she breasted the hill-top and found herself facing the malevolent red house where they had always told her that he did not really love her, when she thought she was about to fall dead from excess of experience and would have chosen to die so, if Richard had not waited for her. Yet it was also true that for long she hardly ever thought of Harry. Such fierce and unimagined passions and perplexities now filled her, that the simple and normal emotions she felt for him became imperceptible, like tapers in strong sunlight.

The day after their meeting she had found Aunt Alphonsine all a dry frightened gibber, holding a whitefaced conference with Grandmother in the parlour, and they had asked her if she had known that Peacey had left Torque Hall that morning. She had shaken her head and given a dry-mouthed smile, for she saw how terrified they were lest all that had had a hand in her marriage were to be made to pay for it ; but because the child in her arms laughed, and the child in her womb had moved, she was so torn between delight and loathing that she had no time to speculate whether Harry had done this thing sweetly out of love for her or cruelly out of bodily jealousy of Peacey. Nor, when a few weeks later it was announced that for the first time in its history Torque Hall had been let furnished, and that the family was going to spend the next twelve months abroad and in London, did her heart ache to think he must be sad to leave the grey, salt Essex which he loved. She thought of it, indeed, but negligently. She could imagine well how he had walked with his dogs among the dripping woods and had set his face against a tree-trunk near some remembered place, and had wept (for like most very virile men, he wept in sorrow) ; and when he had gone home, thick-lipped and darkly flushed with misery, he had flung down his stick on the chest in the hall and muttered, while frightened people watched from the shadows of the armour or listened at doors held ajar, " I must get out of this." No doubt it was very sad, but it was simple ; it was brother to the grief of the yard dog when she lost her puppies. It was not like her agony. Nothing was simple there. Destiny had struck her being a blow that had shivered it to fragments, and now all warred so that there was confusion, and the best things were bad.

Her body was full of health and she was very beautiful.
Richard, who was beginning to take notice, took great pleasure
in her. He used to point his fingers at her great lustrous eyes
as he did at flowers, and he would roll his face against the smooth
skin of her neck and shoulders ; and when he was naked after
his bath he liked her to let down her hair so that it hung round
him like a dark, scented tent. But as she bent forward, watching
his little red gums shine in his laughing mouth, guilt constricted
her heart. For she knew that no woman who was going to have
a child had any right to be as well as she was. She knew that
it meant that she was giving nothing to the child, that the blood
was bright in her cheeks because she was denying every drop
she could to the child, that her flesh was nice for Richard to
kiss because she was electric with the force she should have
spent in making nerves for the child. She knew that she was
trying to kill the thing to which she had been ordered to give
life ; that the murder was being committed by a part of her
which was beyond the control of her will did not exonerate her.
In these matters, as she had learned in the moment when she
had discovered that her baby had conceived without the consent
of her soul, the soul cannot with honour disown the doings
of the body. The plain fact was that she was going to have a
child, and that she was trying to kill it. Remorse dragged
behind her like a brake on the swift movements of her happy
motherhood ; and at night she lay wide-eyed and whispered to
some judge to judge her and bring this matter to an end.

It was no wonder that even when a solicitor came to see her
and told her that Harry had settled on her and Richard a sum so
large that she knew he must be deeply concerned for her, since,
like many men of his type, he had such an abundant sense of the
pleasures which can be bought with money that to part with it
unnecessarily was a real sacrifice, she thought of him with only
such casual pity as she had felt when the yard-dog howled. Well,
that had all been set right, long afterwards on that day of which
she had told nobody.

But she had cheered herself in all those nights that she would
make up for her body's defection by loving the child very much
when it was born. She knew she would have no passion for
it as she had for Richard, but she foresaw herself being consciously
and slantingly tender over it, like a primitive Madonna over
the Holy Child. There was, of course, no such solution of the
problem. It became plain that there was not going to be in
that hour when she knew the unnatural horror of a painless
parturition. She had not been at all shocked by the violence

she had endured at Richard's birth. It had seemed magnificently consistent with the rest of nature, and she had been comforted as she lay moaning by a persistent vision of a harrow turning up rich earth. But contemplating herself as she performed this act of childbirth without a pang was like looking into eyes which are open but have no sight and realising that here is blindness, or listening to one who earnestly speaks words which have no meaning and realising that here is madness.

She was going through a process that should have produced life : but because of the lack of some essence which works through pain, but nevertheless is to the breeding womb what sight is to the eye or sanity to the brain, it was producing something that was as much at variance with life as death. The old women at her bedside chuckled and rubbed their hands because she was having such an easy time, but that was because they were old and had forgotten. If a young woman had been there she would have stood at the other side of the room between the windows, as far away from the bed as she could, and her lips would have pursed, as if she felt the presence of uncleanness. So were her own, when they showed her the pale child. She had indeed done an unclean and unnatural thing when she had brought forth a child that lived yet was unloved ; who was born of a mother that survived and looked at it, and who yet had no mother, since she felt no motion towards it, but a deep shiver of her blood away from it ; who aroused no interest in the whole universe save her own abhorrence ; who was, as was inevitable in one so begotten and so born, intrinsically disgusting in substance.

"Well, I have Richard to help me bear this," she said to herself, but her heart reminded her that though she had Richard, this child had no one. Pitifully she put out her arms and drew it to her breast, but detected for herself the fundamentally insincere kindness that a stranger will show to a child, confident that before long it will be claimed by its own kin.

She always remembered how good the little thing had been as it lay in her arms, and how distasteful. Those were always to remain its silent characteristics. It was so good. "As good," the nurses used to say, "as if he were a little girl." It hardly ever cried, and when it did it curiously showed its difference from Richard. He hated being a baby and subject to other people's wills, and would lie in a cot and roar with resentment ; but this child, when it felt a need that was not satisfied, did not rebel, but turned its face to the pillow and whined softly. That was a strange and disquieting thing to watch. She would

stand in the shadow looking at the back of its little head, so
repellently covered with hair that was like fluff off the floor,
and listening to the cry that trailed from its lips like a dirty
piece of string ; and she would wonder why it did this, partly
because she really wanted to know, and partly because it fended
off the moment when she had to take it in her arms. Perhaps,
she reflected, it muted its rage because it knew that it was
unlovable and must curry favour by not troubling people.
Indeed, it was as unlovable as a child could be. It was not
pleasant naked, for its bones looked at once fragile and coarse,
and its flesh was lax, and in its clothes it was squalid, for it was
always being sick or dribbling. Then her heart reproached her,
and she admitted that it cried softly because it had a gentle
spirit, and she would move forward quickly and do what it
desired, using, by an effort of will, those loving words that
fluttered to her lips when she was tending Richard. Time went
on, but her attitude to it never developed beyond this alternate
recognition of its hatefulness and its goodness.

She had called it Roger after her own father in a desperate
effort to bring it into the family, but the name, when she spoke
it, seemed infinitely remote, as if she were speaking of the child
of some servant in the house whom she had heard of but had
never seen. When he was out of her sight, she ejected the
thought of him from her mind, so that when her eyes fell on him
again it was a shock. He did not become more seemly to look
at. Indeed, he was worse when he grew out of frocks, for knicker-
bockers disclosed that he had very thin legs and large, knotty
knees. He had a dull stare, and there seemed always to be a
ring of food round his mouth. He had no pride. When she
took the children on a railway journey Richard would sit quite
still in his seat and would speak in a very low voice, and if any
of the other passengers offered him chocolates or sweets he would
draw back his chin as an animal does when it is offered food,
and would shake his head very gravely. But Roger would move
about, falling over people's legs, and would talk perpetually in
a voice that was given a whistling sound by air that passed
through the gap between his two front teeth, and when he got
tired he would whine. He was unexclusive and unadventurous.
He liked playing on the sands at Prittlebay in summer when
they were covered with trippers' children. He hated Richard's
passion for bringing the names of foreign places into the games.
When Richard was sitting on his engine and roaring, " I'm the
Trans-Andean express, and I don't half go at a pace!" Roger
would stand against the wall opposite and cry over and over

again in that whistling voice: "Make it the London, Tilbury and Prittlebay train ! Make it the London, Tilbury and Prittlebay train ! " When he felt happy he would repeatedly jump up in the air, bringing both his feet down on the ground at once, but a little distance apart, so that his thin legs looked horrible, and he would make loud, silly noises. At these times Richard would sit with his back to him and would take no notice. Always he was insolent to the other child. He would not share his toys with him, though sometimes he would pick out one of the best toys and give it to his brother as a master might give a present to a servant. He was of the substance of his mother, and he knew all that she knew, and he knew that this child was an intruder.

They clenched themselves against him. They were kind to him, but they would silently scheme to be alone together. If they were all three in the garden, she sitting with her needle-work, Richard playing with his engine and Roger making daisy-chains, there would come a time when she would arise and go into the house. She would not look at Richard before she went, for in externals she forced herself to be loyal to Roger. When she got into the house she would linger about the rooms at factitious operations, pouring out of the flower-glasses water that was not stale, or putting on the kettle far too soon, until she heard Richard coming to look for her, lightfootedly but violently, banging doors behind him, knocking into furniture. He would halt at the door and stand for a moment, twiddling the handle round and round, as if he had not really been so very keen to come to her, and she would go on indifferently with her occupation. But presently she would feel that she must steal a glance at the face that she knew would be looking so adorable now, peering obliquely round the edge of the door, the lips bright. with vitality as with wet paint and the eyes roguish as if he felt she were teasing life by enjoying it so, and the dear square head, browny-gold like the top of a bun, and the little bronze body standing so fresh and straight in the linen suit. So her glance would slide and slide, and their eyes would meet and he would run to her. If he had anything on his conscience he would choose this moment for confession. "Mother, I told a lie yesterday. But it wasn't about anything really important, so we won't talk about it, will we ? "

Then he would clamber over her, like a squirrel going up a tree-trunk, until she tumbled into some big chair and rated him for being so boisterous, and drew him close to her so that he revelled in her love for him as in long meadow-grass. Even as she imagined that night before Peacey came, he did not struggle in her arms but gave her kiss for kiss. They would be sphered in joy, until they heard a sniff and saw the other child standing at the open door, resting its flabby cheek on the handle, surveying them with wild eyes. There would be a moment of dislocation. Then she would cry, " Come along, Roger ! " and Richard would slip from her knee and the other child would come and very gratefully put its arms round her neck and kiss her. It would go on kissing and kissing her, as if it needed reassurance.

But she had always done her duty by Roger. That had not been so very difficult a matter at first, for Grandmother had made a great fuss of him and taken him off her hands for most of the day. Marion had never felt quite at ease about this, for she knew that he was receiving nothing, since the old woman was only affecting to find him lovable in order that it might seem that something good had come of the marriage which she had engineered. But the problem was settled when he was eighteen months old, for then Grandmother died. Marion did not feel either glad or sorry. God had dreamed her and her grandmother in different dreams. It was well that they should separate. But it had the immediate disadvantage of throwing her into perpetual contact with the other child. She looked after it assiduously, but she always felt when she had been with it for an hour or two that she wanted to go a great distance and breathe air that it had not breathed. Perpetually she marvelled at its contentedness and gentleness and unexigent hunger for love, and planted seeds of affection for it in her heart, but they would never mature.

The relationship became still more galling to her after yet another eighteen months, when Harry came back to live with his family at Torque Hall, who had returned there the year before. No communication passed between them, but sometimes by chance he met her in the lanes when she was out with the children. The first time he tried to speak to her, but she turned away, and Richard said, " Look here, you don't know us," so after that they only looked at one another. They would walk slowly past each other with their heads bent, and as they drew near she would lift her eyes and see him, beautiful and golden as a corn of wheat, and she would know from his eyes that, dark for his fair, she was as beautiful, and they would both look at Richard, who ran at her right side and was as beautiful as the essence of both their beauties. It seemed as if a band of light joined the bodies of these three, as if it were contracting and pulling them together, as if in a moment they would be pressed together and would dissolve in loving cries upon each other's breasts. But before that moment came, Harry's eyes would stray to the other child. Its socks would be coming down round its thin legs ; it would be making some silly noises in its squalid, whistling voice ; its features would be falling apart, unorganised into a coherent face by any expression, as common children's do. The situation was trodden into the mud. They would pass on—their hearts sunk deeper into dingy acquiescence in their separation.

Nevertheless she did not fail in her duty towards Roger. So far as externals went she was even a better mother to him than to Richard. Frequently she lost her temper with Richard when he ran out of the house into the fields at bedtime, or when he would not leave his tin soldiers to get ready for his walk, but she was always mild with Roger, though his habit of sniffing angered her more than Richard's worst piece of naughtiness. She took Richard's illnesses lightly and sensibly. But when Roger ailed—which was very often, for he caught colds easily and had a weak digestion—she would send for the doctor at once, and would nurse him with a strained impeccability, concentrating with unnecessary intensity on the minutiæ of his treatment and diet as if she were attempting to exclude from her mind some thought that insisted on presenting itself at these times. When they came to her on winter evenings and wet days and asked for a story, she would choose more often to tell them a fairy-tale, which only Roger liked, rather than to start one of the sagas which Richard loved, and would help to invent, concerning the adventures of the family in some previous animal existence, when they had all been rabbits and lived in a burrow in the park at Torque Hall, or crocodiles who slooshed about in the Thames mud, or lions and tigers with a lair on Kerith Island. She never gave any present to Richard without giving one to Roger too ; she dressed him as carefully in the same woollen and linen suits, although in nothing did he look well. Never had she lifted her hand against him.

As time went on she began to make light of her destiny and to declare that there was no horror in this house at all, but only a young woman living with her two children, one of whom was not so attractive as the other. It was true that sometimes, when she was sewing or washing dishes at the sink, she would find herself standing quite still, her fingers rigid, her mind shocked and vacant, as if some thought had strode into it and showed so monstrous a face that all other thoughts

had fled ; and she would realise that she had been thinking
of something about Roger, but she could not remember what.
Usually this happened after there had arrived—as there did
every six months—parcels of toys, addressed to him and stamped
with the Dawlish postmark and containing a piece of paper
scrawled "With love from father."

She would be troubled by such moments when they came,
for she was growing distantly fond of Roger. There was something touching about this pale child, whose hunger for love was
so strong that it survived and struggled through the clayey
substance of its general being which had smothered all other
movements of its soul ; who was so full of love itself that it
accepted the empty sham of feeling she gave it and breathed
on it, and filled it with its own love, and was so innocent that it
did not detect that nobody had really given it anything, and
went on rejoicing, thus redeeming her from guilt. He would
come and stand at the door of any room in which she was sitting,
and she would pretend not to know he was there, so that she
need caress him or say the forced loving word ; but when at
length, irritated by his repeated sniffs, she turned towards him,
she would find the grey marbles of his eyes bright with happiness, and he would cry out in his dreadful whistling voice,
" Ah, you didn't know I was watching you ! " and ran across
undoubtingly to her arms. There would be real gratitude in
the embrace she gave him. His trust in her had so changed
the moment that she need not feel remorse for it.

It had seemed quite possible that they could go on like this
for ever, until the very instant that all was betrayed. She had
had a terrible time with Richard, who was now seven years old.
After their midday meal he had asked permission to go and
spend the afternoon playing with some other boys on the marshes,
and she had given it to him with a kiss, under which she had
thought he seemed a little sullen. When Roger and she had
nearly finished their tea he had appeared at the door, had stood
there for a minute, and then, throwing up his head, had said
doggedly : " I've had a lovely time at the circus." She had
left the bread-knife sticking in midloaf and sat looking at him
in silence. This was real drama, for she had refused to take
them to the circus and forbidden him to go by himself because
there was a measles epidemic in the neighbourhood. It flashed
across her that by asking for permission to play with the boys
on the marshes when he meant to go to the circus he had told
her a lie. The foolish primitive maternal part of her was convulsed with horror at his fault. Because he was more important

than anybody else, it seemed the most tremendous fault that
anybody had ever committed, and because he was her son it
seemed quite unlike any other fault and far more excusable.
Her detached wisdom warned her that she must check all such
tendencies in him, since what would in other children be judged
a shortcoming natural to their age, would in him be ascribed
to the evil blood of his lawless begetting, and he would start life
under the powerful suggestion of a bad reputation.   She resolved
to punish him.   The core of her that was nothing but love
for Richard, that would have loved him utterly if they had not
been mother and son, but man and woman, or man and man,
or woman and woman, cried out with anguish that she should
have to hurt him to guard against the destiny which she herself
had thrust upon him.

She said in a strained voice : " How dare you tell a lie to
me and pretend that you were going to the marshes ? "
He answered, his eyebrows meeting and lying in straight,
sullen bars : " I had to do that so's you wouldn't worry
about me not coming home.   And I paid for myself with
the sixpence that was over from the five shillings Cousin Tom
gave me at Christmas.   And you know it doesn't really matter
about the measles, because I'm strong and don't always go
catching things like Roger does."

He made as if he were going to sit down at the table, but she
said : " No, you mustn't have any tea.   Go to your room and
undress.   You've lied and you've disobeyed.   I'll have to whip
you."   Her heart was thumping so that she thought she was
going to faint.   He lifted his chin a little higher and said :
" Very well, the circus was very good. . It was quite worf this."
He marched out of the room and left her sick and quivering at
her duty.   After she had heard him bang his door, she realised
that Roger was asking her again and again if he might have some
more cherry jam, and she answered, sighing deeply, " No, dear,
it's too rich.   If you have any more you'll be ill," and she rose
from the table and took the jar into the larder.   She decided
to clear away tea first, but that only meant carrying the tray
backwards and forwards twice, and after a few moments she
found herself standing in the middle of the kitchen, shaking with
terror, while the other child whined about her skirts and stretched
up its abhorrent little arms.   She pushed it aside, qualifying
the harsh movement with some insincere endearment, and
went to Richard's room and walked in blindly, saying : " I must
whip you—you've broken the law, and if you do that you must
be punished."   Out of the darkness before her came the voice

of the tiny desperado : " Very well. It was quite worf this. Mother, I'm ready. Come on and whip me." She pulled down the blinds and set herself to the horrid task, and kept at it hardly, unsparingly, until she felt she had really hurt him. Then she said, with what seemed to be the last breath in her heart-shattered body : " There, you see, whenever you break the law people will hurt you like this. So take notice." She moved about the room, leaving it as it should be left for the night, opening the windows and folding up the counterpane, while he lay face downwards on his pillow. Just as she was closing the door he called softly :

" Mummie ! "

She continued to close it, and he cried :

" Mummie ! "

But she remained quite quiet so that he thought she had gone. After a minute she heard him throw himself over in the bed and kick the clothes and sob fiercely, " Gah ! Why can't she come when I call her ? "

She was back by his bedside in a second, and his arms were round her neck and he was sobbing :

" Mummie, mummie, I know I've been naughty ! " And as he felt the wetness of her face he cried out, " Oh, mummie, have I made you cry ? I will be good. I will be good ! I'll never make you cry again ! I know I was a beast to go 'cos you really were frightened of us getting measles, but oh, mummie, I did so want to see a tiger ! "

They clung to each other, weeping, and he said things into her neck that were far more babyish than usual and yet fiercely manly, and they almost melted into each other in the hot flow of loving tears.

" You were quite right to whip me," he told her. " I wouldn't have believed you were really cross if you hadn't hurt me." Presently, when he was laying quietly in her arms, all sticky sweetness like toffee, he sighed, " Oh, darling, the circus was lovely ! There were such clever people. There was a Cossack horseman who picked up handkerchiefs off the ground when he was riding at full speed, and there was a most beautiful lady in pink satin. Mummie, you'd look lovely in pink satin !—and she'd bells on her legs and arms, and she waggled them and it made a tune. That was lovely, but I liked the animals best. Oh, darling, the lions ! "

She rebuked him for his continued enjoyment of an illicit spectacle that ought now to be regarded only as material for repentance, but he protested ; " Mummie, you are mean. Now

you've whipped me for going, surely I've a right to enjoy it."
But he lay back and just gave himself up to loving her. "Oh,
you beautiful mummie. You've such lots and lots of hair. If
there were two little men just as big as my fingers, they could
go into your hair, one at each ear, and walk about it like people
do in the African forests, couldn't they ? And they'd meet
in your parting, and one would say to the other, 'Mr. Livingstone,
I presume ? '" They both laughed and hugged each other, and
he presently fell asleep as suddenly as children do.

She lingered over him for long, peering at him through
the dusk to miss nothing of his bloomy brownness. He curled
up when he slept like a little animal, and his breath drove through
him deeply and more serenely than any adult's. At last she
felt compelled to kiss him, and, without waking up, he shook his
head about and said disgustedly, "Wugh !" as she rose and left
him.

Twilight was flooding the house, and peace also, and she
moved happily through the dear place where she lived with her
dear son, her heart wounded and yet light, because though she
had had to hurt him, she knew that henceforward he would obey
whatever laws she laid upon him. He had been subject to her
when he was a baby ; it was plain that he was going to be
subject to her now that he was a boy ; she might almost hope
that she would never lose him. "I must make myself good
enough to deserve this," she said prayingly. As she went
downstairs she looked through the open front door into the
crystalline young night, tinged with purple by some invisible red
moon and diluted by the daylight that had not yet all poured
down the sluice of the west, and resolved to go out and
meditate for a little on how she must live to be worthy of this
happy motherhood.

She walked quickly and skimmingly about the dark lawns,
exalted and humble. In a gesture of joy she threw out her
arms and struck a clump of nightstock, and the scent rushed
up at her. A nightingale sang in the woods across the lane.
These things seemed to her to be in some way touchingly
relevant to the beautiful destiny of her and her son, and
her eyes were filled with tears of gratitude for nature's
sympathy. She went round the house, walking softly, keeping
close to the wall, to eavesdrop on the lovely, drowsy, kindly
world. The silence of the farmyard was pulsed with the breath
of many sleeping beasts. The dark doors and windows of
the cattle-sheds looked out under the thick brows of their thatched
eaves at the strange fluctuating wine-like light as if they were

consciously preserving their occupants from the night's magic. As she walked to the garden's edge, the crickets chirped in the long grass and the ballet of the bats drove back and forwards in long streaks. The round red moon hung on the breast of a flawless night, whose feet were hidden in an amethystine haze that covered the marshes and the sea, and changed the lit liners going from Tilbury to floating opals ; and within the house was Richard. All was beauty.

Surely it would be given to her to deserve to be his mother ? She stood there in an ecstasy that was hardly at all excitement, until it blew cold and she remembered that she had left the fire unmended, and went back to the house.

She went in by the kitchen, and was amazed to see that the larder door was open and giving out a faint ray of light. She pulled it open and saw the other child standing on a chair and spooning cherry jam out of the jar into his mouth. A candle, which it had put on the shelf below it, threw on the ceiling an enormous shadow of its large, jerry-built skull. It turned on her a pale and filthy face and dropped the jar, so that gobs of jam fell on its pinafore, the paper-covered shelf, the chair, the floor. She lifted the child down and struck it. It gave her the most extraordinary pleasure to strike it. She struck it three times, and each time it was as good as drinking wine. Then she fell forward on her knees and covered her face with her hands. The child ceased to howl and put its jammy arms forgivingly about her while she wept, but its touch only reminded her how delicious it had been to beat it. Still, she submitted to its embrace, and muttered in abasement : " Oh, lovey, mummy shouldn't have done that ! "

The child was puzzled, for it knew it ought not to have stolen the jam, and as always, it was so full of love that it could not believe that anybody had behaved badly to it. There was nothing to do but to give it a kiss and take it off to bed. When she saw its horrid little body stripped for the bath, heat ran through her throat, and she remembered again how exquisite it had been to hurt him, and she speculated whether very much force would be needed to kill it. All the time it knelt at her knee saying its prayers she was wondering whether, when he was a little older, he would not get caught by the tide out on the flats. " You vile woman ! " she exclaimed in amazement. " You murderess ! " But that was merely conversation which did not alter the established fact that her profounder self still hated the child it had brought forth, as it had done before he was born, and now, as then, was plotting to kill it, and that some check which her consciousness had always exerted on that hatred had for some reason been damaged, and that he was in active danger from her.

All night she lay awake, and in the morning she went up to the bailiff's office at Torque Hall and asked them to send for Harry. She waited in an inner room, her heart quite calm with misery, and when Harry appeared in the doorway she did not care one way or another that he was white and shaken. Without delaying to greet him, she told him that she loathed Peacey's child so much that it must be taken away from her, at least for some time, and that she had wondered if she ought to give him a chance of finding affection with his father, who had, after all, never stopped sending him presents.

There was a silence, and she turned her eyes on him and found him looking disapproving. Plainly he thought it very unnatural of her to dislike her own child, and was daring to doubt if his own son was safe with her. He—he of all men—who by his disloyalty had brought on her this monstrous birth that had deformed her fate ! She clenched her fists and drew in a sharp breath and her eyes blazed. He moved forward suddenly in his chair, and she saw that this display of her quality had drawn him to her, as always the moon of her being had drawn the fluid tides of his, and that he wanted to touch her. Nearly he desired her. That also was insolence. Her acute hating glance recorded that whereas desire had used to make his face hard and splendid like a diamond, like a flashing sword, it now made it lax, and she realised with agony, though, of course, without surprise, that he had been unfaithful to their love times without number. But she looked into his eyes and found them bereaved as her heart was. She turned aside and sobbed once, drily. After that, they spoke softly, as if one they had both loved lay dead somewhere close at hand. He told her that Peacey had set up for himself in an inn, and that a widowed sister of his, named Susan Rodney, who also had been in the Torques' service, was keeping house for him. She was a really good sort, he declared, although she was Peacey's sister, and very motherly ; indeed, she had been terribly upset by the loss of her only child, a little boy of nine, so she would doubtless welcome the charge of Roger. At any rate, there would be no harm in letting the child go to her for a three months' visit.

" I'll settle the whole thing," he said. " You'd better not write ; he may want to meet you."

With distaste she perceived that although he had never

done anything useful for her, he was still capable of being jealous of her, and she abruptly rose to go. But she delayed for a moment to satisfy a curiosity that had vexed her for years.

" Tell me," she asked. " How did you get rid of Peacey? Was it money? "

He shrugged his shoulders. " Not altogether. You see, I found out something about him. . . ."

She walked home slowly, with her head bent, wondering what blood she had perpetuated.

So, a week later, Susan Rodney came. Her visit was a great humiliation. She was a woman of thirty-five, strangely and reassuringly unlike her brother, having a fair, sun-burned skin with a golden down on her upper lip, and slow-moving eyes, the colour of a blue sky reflected in shallow floods. She was as clean and useful as a scrubbed deal table. And because she was wholesome in her soul, she abhorred this woman who was sending away her own child. During the twenty-four hours she was at Yaverland's End she ate sparingly, plainly because she felt reluctance at accepting hospitality from Marion, and rose very early, as if she found sleeping difficult in the air of this house. This might have been in part due to the affection she evidently felt for her brother, which was shown in the proud and grudging responses to Marion's enquiries as to how he was getting on at Dawlish.

" He's doing ever so well, and he's made the place a picture," she would begin volubly, and then would toss her head slowly like a teased heifer, and decide that Marion did not deserve to hear tidings of the glorious man she had slighted. But the greater part of her loathing was that which a woman with a simple heart of nature must feel for one who hated her child, which the sound must feel for the leprous.

Marion could have mitigated that feeling in a great part, not by explaining, for that was impossible, but by simply showing that she had suffered, for Susan was a kind woman. Instead she did everything she could to encourage it. She told no lies, although by now her efforts to win over the neighbourhood, so that she could get a servant easily and be able to give her whole time to the children, had made her coldly sly in her dealings with humanity. She liked Susan too much for that. Merely she made no attempt to disguise her personality. After the children had gone to bed she sat by the hearth and held her head high under the other's ruminant stare, knowing that because of the times she had been subject to love and to lust her beauty was lip-marked as a well-read book is thumb-marked, and that

that would seem a mark of abomination to this woman in the salty climate of whose character passion could not bloom. She knew, too, that to Susan, who every Sunday since her babyhood had gone to church and prayed very hard, with her thick fair brows brought close together, to be helped to be good, the pride of her bearing would seem terribly wicked to a sinner who had broken one of the Ten Commandments.

Marion kept down her eyes so that the other should not see that the eyeballs were strained with agony, and should think that she was a loose and conscience-less woman. She hated doing this. She liked Susan so much, and she was terribly lonely. She would like to have thrown her arms round Susan's neck and cried and cried, and told her how terribly difficult she found life, and how she hated people being nasty to her, and asked her if sometimes she did not long for a man to look after her. But instead she sat there rigidly alienating her. For she had seen that because Susan disliked her she was precipitating herself much more impulsively than she would otherwise have done into affection for the child whom she suspected was being maltreated by this queer woman in this queer house. In any case she would have admitted Roger to her heart, for it was plainly very empty since the loss of her son, whom she had loved so dearly that she did not speak of him to Marion, but being slow of movement she might have taken her time over it ; and it was necessary that these two should love each other at once. At any moment Roger might understand his mummie hated him, and that would break his poor little heart, which she knew was golden, unless he had some other love to which to run. She was so glad when she found herself seeing them off at Paddington, although it was a horrible scene. Susan had primly, and with an air of refusing to partici-pate in the spoils of vice, declined to let Marion buy her a first-class ticket, so the parting had to take place in a crowded thirdclass compartment. Roger shrieked and kicked at leaving her, and leaned howling from the window, while Marion said over and over again, " Mummy's so sorry . . . it's only that just now she isn't well enough to look after you both . . . and Richard's the eldest, so he must stay . . . and you'll be back ever so soon. . . . And there's such lovely sands at Dawlish. . . ."

All the people in the corner-seats had looked with distaste at this plain, ill-behaved child and had cast commending glances on Richard, who stood by her side on the platform, absorbedly watching the porters wheeling their trucks along, but always keeping on the alert so that he never got in anyone's way.

She couldn't bear that. She wanted to scream out : " How dare
you look like that at this poor little soul who has been sinned
against from the moment of his begetting? Think of it, his
mother hates him ! "

She looked wildly at Susan for some comfort, but found her
pink with grave anger. Well, it was better for Roger that Susan
should feel thus about her. So she went on with these murmurs,
which she felt the child might detect as insincere at any moment,
until the green flag waved. She watched the diminishing train
with a criminally light heart. Richard began to jump up and
down. " Mummie ! Won't it be lovely—just us two ! "

It was lovely. It was iniquitously lovely. In the morning
Richard ran into her room and flung himself, all dewy after the
night's long sleep, into her bed and nuzzled into her and gave
her endless love which did not have to be interrupted because
the other child was standing at the head of the bed, its pale
eyes asking for its share of kisses. When he went to school,
she stood at the door and watched him run along the garden to
the gate, flinging out his arms and legs quite straight as a foal
does, and was exultantly proud of being a mother as she had not
been when there ran behind him Roger on weak, ambling limbs.
When he returned, they had their meal together to the tune of
happy laughter, for there was now no third to spill its food or say
it was feeling sick suddenly or babble silly things. In the
afternoon she had to drive him out to go and play games with
the other boys. Much rather would he have stayed with her,
and when she called him back for a last hug he did not struggle
in her arms but gave her back kiss for kiss. She always changed
her dress for tea, and arranged her hair loosely like a woman in a
picture, and went out into the garden to gather burning leaves
and put them in vases about the room, and when it fell dark she
set lighted candles on the table because they were kinder than
the lamp to her pain-flawed handsomeness and because they left
corners of dusk in which these leaves glowed like fire with the kind
of beauty that she and Richard liked. She would arrange all
this long before he came in, and sit waiting in a drowse of happiness, thinking that really she had lost nothing by being cut off
from the love of man, for this was much better than anything
she could have had from Harry. When Richard came in he
would hold his breath because it was so nice and forget to tell
her about the game from which he was still flushed ; and after
tea they would settle down to a lovely warm, close evening by the
fire, when they would tell each other all the animal stories that
Roger had not liked.

On Saturday afternoons they always went down to the marshes together, and they were glad that now was the ebbing of the year, for both found the beauty of bad weather somehow truer than the beauty of the sunshine. They loved to walk under high-backed clouds that the wind carried horizonwards in pursuance of some feud of the skies. They liked to see Roothing Castle standing up behind a salt mist, pale and flat as if it were cut out of paper. They liked to sit, too, at the point where there met together the three creeks that divided Roothing Marsh, the Saltings, and Kerith Island. That was good when the tide was out, and the sea-walls rose black from a silver plain of mud, valleyed with channels thin and dark as veins. They would wait until the winter sunset kindled and they had to return home quickly, looking over their shoulders at its flames.

Lovely it was to find that he liked all the things she did: loneliness and the sting of rain on the face and the cry of the redshanks; and lovely it was to find in watching his liking what a glorious being it was that she had borne. The eyes of his soul glowed like the eyes of his body. She had loved Harry's love for her because it made him quick and unhesitant and unmuddied by half-thought thoughts and half-felt feelings as ordinary people are, but this child was like that all the time. Pride ruled his life, so that she never had to feel anxious about his behaviour, knowing that he would pull himself up into uncriticisable conduct just as he always held his head high, and all the forces of his spirit were poured out into his passion for her. She had always known these things, and now the knowledge of them was not balanced by the knowledge that her faith held weight for weight of infamy and glory. For now that Roger was not here there was nothing to remind her that the man to whom she had given her virginity had not come to her help when she was going to have his child and had left her to be trodden into the mud by the fat man Peacey. Now she only knew that she was the beloved mother of this splendid son. What had happened to the man with whom, according to the indecent and ridiculous dispensation of nature, she had had to be enmeshed in a net of hot excitements and undignified physical impulses in order to obtain this child, mattered nothing at all. He had been so much less splendid than his son.

She grew well with happiness. She became plumper, and there was colour on her cheeks as well as in her lips. People ceased to treat her with the hostility that the happy feel for the unhappy. Presently she knew that she would soon regain complete self-control and would be able to keep shut the trap-

door of her hidden self, and that it would be quite safe for her
to have Roger back at the end of three months. She began to
speak of it to Richard. "Roger will be with us for Xmas," she
used to say. "We must think out some surprises for him. . . ."
To which Richard would answer tensely, "I s'pose so." That
always chilled her, and she would drop the subject, feeling that
after all there was no need to speak of it just yet. But once,
as the days passed into December, she tried to have it out with
him, and followed it up by saying : "You might try to be a
little more pleased about it. I do want you and Roger to be
nice to each other." He answered, looking curiously grown up,
"Oh, Roger will always be nice to me—you needn't worry about
that."

As she heard the tone, with its insolent allusion to Roger's
natural slavishness, she realised why the vicar and the teachers
in the village school, and many of the other people with whom
he came in contact, disliked him. There was something terrifying about this cold-tempered judgment coming from a child.
She had wondered, looking at the beauty of his contemptuous
little face and at the extraordinary skill with which his small
brown hands were whittling a block of wood into a figure, whether
it was not a sound instinct on the part of the race to persecute
illegitimate children. Either they were conceived more lethargi-
cally than other children, of women who yielded through feeble-
wittedness or need of money to men who did not love them
enough to marry them, and so were born below the average of
the race, dullards that made life ugly, or parasites that had to be
kept on honest people's money in prisons or workhouses. Or,
like Richard, they had been conceived more intensely than
other children, of love so passionate that it had drawn together
men and women separated by social prohibitions. So they were
born to rule like kings over the lawfully begotten, so that married
folk raged to see that, because they had known no more than
ordinary pleasure, their seed was to be penalised by servitude.
Richard would always be adored by all but the elderly and the
impotent.

Because vitality itself had been kneaded into his
flesh by his parents' passion he would not die until he was an
old, old man and needed rest after interminable victories ; and
because it played through his mind like lightning, he would
always have power over men and material, and even over himself. Since he had been begotten when beauty, like a strong
goddess, pressed together the bodies of his father and mother,
she would disclose more of her works to him than to other sons

of men with whose begetting she was not concerned. Even now, every time Marion let him take her to the turn of the road past Roothing, where he could show her the oak cut like a club on a playing-card and aflame with autumn that stood on the hill's edge, against the far grey desolation of Kerith Island and the sunless tides, he knew such joy as one would have thought beyond a child's achievement. He would get as much out of life as any man that ever lived. At the thought of the contrast between this heir to everything and the other child, that poor waif who all her life long would be sent round to the back door, tears rushed to her eyes, and she cried indignantly, " Oh, I do think you might be nice to Roger." Richard looked at her sharply. " What, do you really mind about it, mummie ? " The surprise in his tone told her the worst about her forced and mechanical kindnesses to Roger. " Oh, more than anything," she almost sobbed. " Very well, I'll be nice to him,"he answered shortly, adding after a minute, with a deliberate impishness as if he hated the moment and wanted to burlesque it, " After all, mums, I never do hit him. . . ." But for the rest of the evening the golden glow of his face was clouded with solemnity, and when she was tucking him up that night he said, in an off-hand way, " You know prob'ly Roger's got much older while he's been away, and I'll be able to play with him more when he comes back." She laughed happily. If he was going to help her to frustrate her unnatural hatred of Roger, she would succeed.

CHAPTER VI

THEN, a week later, Harry died. That might have meant grief wrecking and inexpressible, for she discovered that she was still his. Love lay in her, indestructible as an element. It was true that passion was gone from her for ever, but that had been merely an alloy added to it by nature when she desired to use it as currency to buy continuance, and love itself had survived. She might have lacerated herself with mourning for the fracture of their marriage and the separation of their later years had it not been for the beautiful thing that had happened the afternoon before he died. It was so beautiful that she hardly ever rehearsed its details to herself, preferring to guard it in her heart as one guards sacred things, preserving it immaculate even from her own thoughts. It had lifted the shame from her destiny. She perceived that the next day, when Richard came in and stood stumbling with the handle of the door, instead of running to the table, though she had arranged it specially, as if this were a birthday, with four candles instead of two, and had baked him a milk loaf for a treat, and had cut the last Michaelmas daisies from the garden and set them in blanched mauve clouds about the dark edges of the room.

"Mother, the squire's dead," he said at length. That she knew already. She had divined it early in the afternoon, when the village people began to go past the house in twos and threes, walking slowly and turning their faces towards her windows. "Yes, dear," she answered evenly. "Mother, is it true that the squire was my father? All the other boys say so." She had anticipated this moment for years with terror, because always before it had seemed to her that when it came she must break down and tell him how she had been shamed and abandoned and cast away to infamy, and she had dreaded that this might make him frightened of life. But because of what had happened the day before she was able to smile, as if they were talking of happy things, and say slowly and delightedly, "Yes, you are his son." He walked slowly across the room, knitting his brows and staring at her with eyes that were at once crafty and awed, as children's are when they perceive that grown-ups are concealing some important fact from them, and harbour at once a quick, indignant resolution to find out what it is as soon as possible, and a slow, acquiescent sense that the truth must be a very sacred thing if it has to be veiled. At her knee he halted, and shot sharp glances up at her. But the peace in her face made him feel foolish, and he said in an off-hand manner : " Mummie, Miss Lawrence says my map of the Severn is the best," and then turned to look at the tea-table. " Ooh, mums, milk-loaf ! " She could see as he continued that all was well with him. The squire had been his father : but it evidently was not anything to make a fuss about ; it seemed funny that he and mother hadn't lived together, but grown-ups were always doing funny things ; anyway, it seemed to be all right. . . .

As she sat and teased him for making such an enormous meal, and rejoicing silently because he had passed through this dangerous moment so calmly, it struck her that Roger also would participate in the benefits brought by the beautiful happening of the day before. Now that her past life had been made not humiliating, but only sad, she would no longer feel angry with him because he reminded her of it. That night she wrote to Susan Rodney and asked her to bring him back during the week before Christmas.

Marion, groaning, pressed the button of the electric clock that stood on the table by her bedside, and looked up at the monstrous white dial it threw on the ceiling. Half-past one. She rolled over and cried into the pillow, " Richard ! Richard ! " She had already been three hours in bed. There were six more hours till morning, six more hours in which to remember things, and memory was a hot torment, a fire lit in her brain-pan.

When, three days later, she received Peacey's letter saying that he would not allow the child to go back to her she felt nothing but relief. It was disgusting, of course, to get that letter, to have to read so many lines in that loathsome, large, neat, inflated handwriting, but she took it that it meant that those toys which he had sent Roger every six months were not, as she thought, mere attempts to torture her by reminding her of his existence, but signs that he had really wanted to be a father to his son, and that now that Harry was dead he was declaring his desire freely. That made her very happy, for she knew that love from the worst man on earth would be more nourishing for the boy than her insincerity. She did not tell Richard, because she could not have borne to see how pleased he would look, but she went about the house light-heartedly for winter days, bursting with song, and then penitently checking herself and planning to send Roger extravagant presents for Christmas, until Susan Rodney's letter came. She had sat with it open on her lap, feeling sick and wondering in whose care she could leave Richard while she went down to Dawlish and fetched the poor little thing away, for quite a long time, before it occurred to her that Harry had never told her the secret by which he held Peacey in subjection. Immediately she realised that Peacey knew this. Out of his cold, dilettante knowledge he had known that when she and Harry met they would not be able to speak his name for more than one minute. She wished she were the kind of woman who fainted from fear. The clock ticked, and not less steadily beat her heart, and nothing came to distract her from looking into the face of this fact that she had now no power over Peacey and he knew it.

Then she huddled forward towards the fire, which no longer seemed to heat her, and Susan's letter fell from her lap into the fender. She picked it up, crying, "Oh, my baby, how little I care for you!" and struck herself on the forehead as she reflected how many expedients would have suggested themselves to her if it had been Richard who was being maltreated down at Dawlish. She sat down and wrote a lying letter to Peacey, threatening him with the disclosure of the secret she did not know, and then, because the grandfather clock twanged out three and she knew the post was collected five minutes past, she ran out into the windy afternoon bareheaded. The last part of the distance, down the High Street, she ran, but she got into the grocer's shop too late and found Mr. Hemming just about to seal the bag. "Oh, Mr. Hemming!" she gasped. The three women in the shop turned round and looked at her curiously, and she perceived that if she betrayed her agony now she would lose all the ground she had gained during the past few years by her affectation of well-being. If it leaked out, as it certainly would, unless she at once lowered the present temperature of the moment, that a few days after Harry's death she had been excitedly sending a letter to Peacey, the village people would go through her story all over again to try to find out what this could possibly mean, and would remember that it was a tragedy, and once more she would be the victim of that hostility which the happy feel for the unhappy. Yet she found herself making a queer distraught mask of her face and saying theatrically, "Oh, Mr. Hemming, *please*, please let this letter go . . ." and, when he granted the favour, as she knew quite well he would have done to just half as much imploration, she went out of the shop breathing heavily and audibly.

"Why am I like this?" she asked herself. "Ah, I see! So that I can say afterwards that I did everything I could to get him back, even to the extent of turning people against me, and can settle down to being happy with Richard. Oh, Roger, I am a cold devil to you. . . ." She was indeed. For when she received Peacey's letter saying blandly that there was nothing in his life of which he need feel ashamed, and realised that the game was up and she was powerless, she was glad. She sat down and wrote her bluffing answer, a warning that if the child was not sent back within a week she would come down to Dawlish and fetch it, with an infamous fear lest it might be efficacious. And when Peacey wrote back, pointing out that Richard was legally his child, and that he would be taken out of her custody if she went on making this fuss about Roger, she chose immediately. She tore the letter into small pieces and dropped them into the heart of the fire, and knelt by the grate until the flame died. Though the boy was still out at school she lifted up her voice and cried out seductively, serenely, "Richard! Richard!"

What is this thing, the soul? It blows hot, it blows cold, it reels with the drunkenness of exaltation for some slight event no denser than a dream, it hoods itself with penitence for some act that the mind can hardly remember ; and yet its judgments are the voice of absolute wisdom. She did not care at all for Roger. When at nights she used to see in the blackness the little figure standing in his shirt, beating the dark air with his fists, as Susan told her he used to do when Peacey woke him suddenly out of his sleep to frighten him, her pity was flavourless and abstract. That she had unwittingly sent the child to its doom caused her no earthquake of remorse but a storm of annoyance. Yet she knew every hour of the day that her soul had taken a decision to mourn the child in some way that would hurt her.

One afternoon, a month or so after their happy, lonely Christmas, when she was playing balls in the garden with Richard, the postman came up and handed her another letter from Susan Rodney. Though Peacey had forbidden her to write to Susan Rodney, so that she had never been able to explain why she did not come and fetch Roger, he allowed

Susan to write· to her. Weekly Marion received letters cursing her cruelly in not coming, written in an honest writing that made them hurt the more. She took it and smiled in the postman's face. "Well, how is Mrs. Brown getting on with the new baby?" When he had gone she gave it to Richard and told him to go and drop it in the kitchen fire. While he was away she stood and stared down at the acid green of the winter grass, and wondered what she had missed by not reading the letter, what story of blows delivered cunningly here and there so that they did not mark, or of petting that skilfully led up to a sudden feint of terrifying temper; and suddenly she was conscious of a fret in the air, and said wonderingly, "It is far too early for the Spring. We are hardly into February yet." But the fret had been not in the air but in herself, and the change of season it had foreboded had been in her own soul.

That very night she had begun to have bad dreams. Twice before the dawn she was stoned down Roothing High Street, even as seven years before men looked at her from behind glazed, amused masks; and she had put up her hand to her head and found that a stone had drawn blood; and Mr. Goode's kind voice said something about, "A bit of boys' fun, Mr. Peacey," and she had stared before her at a black, broadclothed bulk. In the morning she woke sweating like an overdriven horse, and said to herself, "This is the worst night I have spent in all my life. Pray God I may never spend another like it."

But henceforward half her nights were to be like that. By day her soul walked like a peacock on its green lawn, proudly, pompously, struttingly, because she was the mother of this gorgeous son. There was no moment of her waking life that he did not gild, for either he had not long gone out and had turned at the gate to wave good-bye with a gesture so dear that when she thought of it she dug her nails into her palms in an agony of tenderness, or he was just coming back and she must get something ready for him. Even after he had gone to school he built her a bulwark against misery which endured till the night fell, for in the few hours that remained after she had finished the work she had now undertaken on the farm she read his letters over and over again. They were queer and disturbing and delicious letters, and they hinted that there was a content in their relationship which had never yet been put into words, for they were full of records of his successes in class and at games.

Now he had that complete lack of satisfaction in his

own performance which superficial people think to be modesty, though it springs instead from the sword-stiff extreme of pride ; when he made his century in a school match he was galled by the knowledge that he was not as good a player as Ranji, and when he was head of the science side his pleasure was mitigated to nearly nothing by his sense that still he did not know as much about these things as Lord Kelvin. That he gave her every detail of all his successes meant, she began to suspect, that he knew they were both under a ban, and that he was handing her these evidences of his superiority over the other people as an adjutant of a banished leader might hand him arrows to shoot down on the city that had exiled him. When he was home for the holidays he said nothing that confirmed this suspicion, but she noticed that only when he was with her was his mouth limpid and confident as a boy's should be ; in the presence of others he pressed his upper lip down on his lower so that it looked thin, which it was not, with an air of keeping a secret before enemies. She loved this sense of being entrenched quite alone with him in a fortress of love. She would not have chosen another destiny, for she did not think that she would ever have liked ordinary people even if they had been nice to her.

But that was only her daylight destiny. In the night she staggered down Roothing High Street under stones, or sat in the brown sunshine of the dusty room and watched Peacey stroking his fat thigh and talking of his dear dead mother ; or felt his weight thresh down on her like the end of the world ; or took into her arms for the first time the limp body of the other child. It did not avail her if she fought her way out of sleep, for then she would continue to re-endure the scene in a frenzy of memory, and either way she knew the agony that the experience had given her with its first prick, coupled with the woe that came of knowing that those things would go on and on, until in the end a little figure in a nightshirt beat the dark with its fists.

For a time she found solace in thinking that perhaps she was expiating her involuntary sin in hating her child, and indeed it seemed to her that when she evoked that little figure she felt something in her heart which, if she and the frozen substance of her were triturated a little more by torture, might grow into that proper loving pain which she coveted more than any pleasure. But that process, if it ever had begun, was stopped when Richard was fifteen.

It happened, two days after he had come home for the summer holidays, that in the early part of the night she had again been stoned and that she had started up, crying out, "Harry! Harry!" She heard the latch of the door lift, and someone stood on her threshold breathing angrily. Half asleep, she mumbled, "Harry, it can't be you? . . ." A voice answered haltingly, "No," and a match scratched, and Richard crossed the room and lit the candle by her bedside. She could not see him, for the light was too strong after the darkness, and she could not quite climb out of her dream, but she rocked her head from side to side and muttered, "Go to bed, I'm all right, all right." But he sat down on her bed and took her hand in his, and said sullenly, "You've been calling out for my father. Why are you doing that?" She whimpered, "Nothing. I was only dreaming." But he went on, terrifying her through her veil of sleep. "I know all about it, mother. The other boys told me about it. And Goodtart said something once." His hand tightened on hers. "You used to meet him up at that temple." For a minute he paused, and seemed to be shuddering, and then persisted, "What is it? Why do you cry almost every night? I've heard you ever so often. You've got to tell me what's the matter."

She stiffened under the fierce loving rage in his tone and stayed rigid for a moment. Through her drowsiness there was floating some idea that the salvation of her soul depended on keeping stiff and silent, but because she was still netted in the dream, and the beating of the tin cans distracted her, she could not follow it and grasp it, and soon she desired to tell him as much as she had always before feared it. In her long reticence she felt like a suspended wave forbidden to break on the shore by a magician's spell, and she lifted her hands imploringly to him so that he bent down and kissed her. It was as if the heat of his lips dissolved some seal upon her mouth, and she sobbed out: "It's when the boy touches me with a stick that I can't bear it!"

"What boy did that?"

"I think it was Ned Turk. When I was stoned down Roothing High Street."

"Mother, mother. Tell me about that."

She wailed out everything, while the hand that held hers gradually became wet with sweat. At the end of her telling she drew her hair across her face and looked up at him through it. "Have I lost him?" she wondered. "Harry did not like me so much after horrible things had happened to me." Then as she looked at him her heart leaped at the sight of his beauty and his young maleness and she cried out to herself, " Well, whether I have lost him or not, I have borne him ! "

But she had him always, for presently he bent forward and laid his face against her hand, and began to kiss it. Then he pulled himself up and sat hunched as if the story he had heard were a foe that might leap at him, and almost shouted in his queer voice, which was now breaking, " Mother, I would like to kill them all ! Oh, you poor little mother ! I love you so, I love you so. . . ." He buried his face in the clothes for one instant and seemed about to weep, and then, conscience of her tears, slipped his arm behind her and raised her up, and covered her with kisses, and muttered little loving, comforting things. She crooned with relief, and until the sky began to lighten and she had to send him back to bed, sobbed out all the misery she had so long kept to herself. He did not want to go. That she liked also ; and afterwards she slipped softly into dreamless sleep.

Yet strangely, for surely it was right that a mother should be solaced by her son ? There shot through her mind just before she slept a pang of guilt as if she had done some act as sensual as bruising ripe grapes against her mouth. How can one know what to do in this life ? Surely it is so natural to escape out of hell that it cannot be unlawful ; and by calling " Richard ! Richard ! " she could now bring her worst and longest dream to an end. Surely she had the right to make Richard love her ; and she knew that by the disclosure of her present and past agonies she was binding his manhood to her as she had bound his boyhood and her childhood. Yet after every time that she had called him to save her from a bad dream she had this conviction of guilt. She could not understand what it meant. It was partly born of her uneasy sense that in these nights she was unwillingly giving Richard a false impression of her destiny which laid the blame too heavily on poor Harry ; because she could not yet tell the boy of all Peacey's villainy, he was plainly concluding that what had broken her was Harry's desertion. But it was a profounder offence than this that she was in some way committing. She did not know what it was, but it robbed her torment of any expiatory quality that it might ever have had. For now, when she evoked the little figure in a nightshirt beating the dark with its fists, she felt nothing. There was not the smallest promise of pain in her heart. As much as ever Roger was an orphan.

But worst of all it was to have had the opportunity to settle this matter for once and for all and to expunge all evil, and to have missed it. For Roger came back. Richard was seventeen, and had gone to sea. How proud she had felt the other day when Ellen had asked why he had gone to sea! He might do many things for his wife, but nothing comparable to that irascible feat of forcing life's hand and leaping straight from boyhood into manhood by leaving school and becoming a sailor at sixteen so that he should be admirable to his mother. During the holidays, when he formed the intention, she had watched him well from under her lids and had guessed that his pride was disgusted at his adolescent clumsiness and moodiness and that he wanted to hide himself from her until he felt himself uncriticisable in his conduct of adult life. She had had to alter that opinion to include another movement of his soul when, as they travelled together to London the day he joined his ship, he turned to her and said : " My father never saw any fighting, did he ? " She had met his eyes with wonder, and he had pressed the point rather roughly. " He was in the army, wasn't he ? But he didn't see any fighting did he ? " She had stammered : " No, I don't think so." And he had turned away with a little stiff-lipped smile of satisfaction. That had distressed her, but she had a vague and selfish feeling that she would imperil something if she argued the point. But whatever his motives for going had been, she was glad that he went, for though she herself was not interested in anything outside her relationships, she knew that travel would afford him a thousand excitements that would evoke his magnificence.

The Spring day when he was expected to come home she had found her joy impossible to support under the eyes of the servant and the farm-men, for she had grown very sly about her fellow-men, and knew that it was best to hide happiness lest someone jealous should put out their hand to destroy it. So she had gone down to the orchard and sat in the crook of a tree, looking out at an opal estuary where a frail rainstorm spun like a top in the sunshine before the variable April gusts. She wondered how his dear brown face would look now he had outfaced danger and had been burned by strange suns. She had heard suddenly the sound of steps coming down the path, and she had turned in ecstasy ; but there was nobody there but a pale young man who looked like one of the East-End trippers who all through the summer months persistently trespassed on the farm lands. As he saw her he stopped, and she was about to order him to leave the orchard by the nearest gate when he flapped his very large hands and cried out, " Mummie ! Mummie ! " There was a whistling quality in the cry that instantly convinced her. She drew herself taut and prepared to deal with him as a spirited woman deals with a blackmailer, but as he ran towards her, piping exultantly, " Now I'm sixteen I can say who I want to live with—the vicar says so," she remembered that he was her son, and suffered herself to be folded in his arms, which embraced her closely but without suggestion of strength.

That day, at least, she had played her part according to her duty : she had corrected so far as possible the sin of her inner being. It had not been so very difficult, for Roger had shown himself just as goldenhearted as he had been as a child. He would not speak of the years of ill-treatment from which he had emerged, save to say tediously, over and over again, with a revolting, grateful whine in his voice, how hard Aunt Susan had worked to keep the peace when father had one of his bad turns. It appeared that for the last two years he had been an apprentice in a draper's shop at Exeter, and though there he had been underfed and overworked and imprisoned from the light and air, all that he complained of was that the " talk was bad." Tears came into his light eyes when he said that, and she perceived that there was nothing in his soul save sickly, deserving innocence, and of course this inexterminable love for her. There would never be any end to that. All through the midday meal he kept on putting down his fork with lumps of meat sticking on it and would say whistlingly : " Ooh, mummie, d'you know, I used to think it must be my imagination you had such a wonderful head of hair. I don't think I've ever seen such another head of hair."

But he was so good, so good. He said to her in the afternoon as they walked along the lanes to Roothing High Street, a scene the memory of which he had apparently cherished sentimentally, " You know, mummie, when I told Aunt Susan that I was going to run away and find you, she said that I had better try my luck, but I mustn't be disappointed if you didn't want me. But I knew you would, mummie. . . ."

Her heart was wrung, not so much by his faith in her, which was indeed a kind of idiocy, as by the sense that, if Susan thought he had better try his luck with her, his life with his father must have been a hell, and that he was not complaining of it. Flushing, she muttered, "I'm glad you knew how I felt, dear," and all day she did not flinch. When it was past eight, and Richard had not come, she cut for Roger the pastry that she had baked for the other, and laughed across the table at him as they ate ; and when the door opened and the son she loved moved silently into the room, looking sleepy and secret as he always did when he was greatly excited, she stood up smiling, and loyally cried, " Look who's

here, Richard ! " She thought as she said it how like she was
to a wife who defiantly faces her husband when one of her
relations whom he does not like has come to tea, and she tried
to be amused by the resemblance. But Richard's eyes moved
to the stranger's gaping, welcoming face, hardened with contempt, and returned to her face. He became very pale. It
evidently seemed to him the grossest indecency on her part to
allow a third person to be present at their meetings, and indeed she
herself felt faint, as she had used to do when she met Harry in
front of other people. But she pulled out of herself a clucking
cry that might have come from some happy mother without a
history : " Richard ! don't you see it's Roger ! "

Surely, after having been able to keep the secret of what she
felt for him through that torturing moment when she found
Richard's displeasure, she had the right to expect that all would
go well. It was loathsome having him in the house, and she
and Richard were hardly ever alone. But her bad dreams left
her. This was life simple as the Christians said it was, in which
one might hug serenity by the conscientious performance of a
disagreeable duty. Yet there came a day, about three weeks
after his coming, when Roger sat glumly at the midday meal
and did not talk, as he had ordinarily done, about the chaps at
Exeter, and how there was one chap who could imitate birds'
calls so that you couldn't hardly tell the difference, and how
another chap had an uncle who was a big grocer and used to
send him a box of crystallised fruit at Christmas ; and immediately the meal was finished he rose and left the room, instead of
waiting about and saying, " I s'pose you aren't going for a walk,
are you, mummie ? " Relieved by his departure, she had
leaned back in her chair and smiled up at Richard, saying, " How
brown you are still ! " when suddenly there had flashed across
her a recollection of how Roger's shoulders had looked as he went
out of the room, and she started up to run out and find him.
He was in one of the outhouses, clumsily trying to carpenter
something that was to be a surprise to somebody. He did not
look up when she came in, though he said with a funny lift in
his voice, " Hello, mummy ! " She stood over him, watching
his work till she could not bear to look at his warty hands any
longer, and then asked : " Roger, dear, is there anything the
matter ? " She spoke to him always without any character
in her phrases, like a mother in books. He mumbled, " Nothing,
mummie," but would not lift his head ; and after a gulping minute
whimpered : " I want to go back to the shop." " Back to the
shop, dear. But I thought you hated it. Darling, what is

the matter ? " He remained silent, so she took his face between her hands and looked into his eyes. Perhaps that had not been a very wise thing to do.

Marion had dropped her hands and gone back to Richard, and said with simulated fierceness : " You haven't done anything to Roger that would make him think that we don't like having him here ? " He glanced sharply at her and recognised that their destiny was turning ugly in their hands, and he answered : " Of course not. I wouldn't do anything to a chap who's been through such a rotten time." She thought, with shame, that if his face had become cruel at her question, and he had answered that he thought it was time the other went, she would have bowed to his decision, because he was her king, and she realised that it was no wonder that Roger had found out. That moment of which she was so proud because she had said heartily, " Richard, don't you see it's Roger ? " without showing by any wild yearning of the eye that she would have given anything to be alone with him, had been instantly followed by a betrayal. For when he had lifted his lips from her cheek and had turned to greet Roger with courtesy that was at once kind and insincere, he had left one hand resting on her shoulder as it had been when they embraced, and his thumb stretched out to press on the pulse that beat at the base of her throat. If she had been completely loyal she would have moved ; but she had stood quite still, letting him mark how she was not calm and rejoicing at all, but shaken as by a storm with her disgust at this loathsome presence. His hand had relaxed and he had passed it caressingly up her neck. She had let herself sigh deeply ; she might as well have said, " I am so glad you understand I hate him." That was the first of a thousand such betrayals. The words said between souls are not heard by the eavesdropping ear, but the soul also can eavesdrop, and tells in its time. That morning there must have come a moment to the poor pale boy, as he worked at his silly present in the little shed, when it was plain to him that the mother and the brother whom he had thought so kind were vulpine with love of each other, vulpine with hate of him.

There was no disputing his discovery, since it was true. The only thing to do was to try to arrange some way of life for him in which he would have a chance to become an independent person who could form new and unspoiled relationships. It was, of course, out of the question to send him back to the shop, but the problem of disposing of him was one that raised innumerable difficulties which Marion was the less able to face because her bad dreams had begun again. He had so little schooling that it was impossible to send him in for any profession. He, himself, who was touchingly grateful because they were not sending him back to the shop, chose to be trained as a veterinary surgeon, and he was apprenticed to old Mr. Taylor at Canewdon. But it turned out that though he had a passionate love for animals he had no power over them. After he had been chased round a field three times and severely bitten by a stallion with whom he had sat up for two nights, Mr. Taylor pronounced that it was hopeless and sent him home. They tried him as a chemist's assistant next, and he did well for ten months, until there was that awful trouble about the prescription. There had been nothing to do after that save to put him to work as a clerk and give him an allowance that with his wages would enable him to live in comfort and try to seem glad when he came home for his holidays.

For he was still not quite sure. His suspicion that his mother did not love him was so strong that, half because his sweetness of nature made him not want to bother her if his presence really gave her pain, and half because he could not bear to put the matter to a test, he would not take a situation anywhere near Roothing. But he liked to come home for his fortnight's holidays at Christmas, and sit by the hearth and look at his wonderful mother and comfort himself by thinking that if they were so kind he must have been wrong. Best of all, perhaps, he liked the Bank Holidays, when he travelled half the day in a packed carriage to get there and had only a few hours to spend with her ; it was easier to keep things going when he stayed such a short time, and there was less misgiving on his face when he waved good-bye from the carriage window than there was after any of his longer visits. But so far as she was concerned, all his visits were in essence the same, in that at the end of each of them she was left standing on the platform with her eyes following the retreating train and a fear coiling tighter round her heart. She had always known, of course, that this life for which she was responsible, and by whose fate she would be judged, would blunder to ruin, and as the years went on there came intimations, faint as everything connected with Roger, but nevertheless convincing, which confirmed her dread. He was always changing his situation and moving from suburb to suburb, for he would never take a job in the city, because the noise and crowds in the narrow streets frightened him.

From a bludgeoned look about him, which became more and more marked, she was sure that he was being constantly dismissed for incompetence, but he would never admit that. " I'm a funny chap, mummie," he would say bravely, " I can't bear being shut up in the same place for long." And she would nod understandingly and say, " Do as you like, dear, as long as you're happy," because he wanted her to believe him. But she would be sick with visions of this blanched, mis-begotten thing standing smiling and wriggling under the gibes of normal and brutal men throughout the inexorably long workday, and then creeping to some mean room where it would sit and snivel till the night fell across the small-paned window. And through the sallow mist of her unavailing and repugnant pity there flashed suddenly the lightning of certainty that some day the thing would happen. But what thing ? She would put her hand to her head, but she was never able to remember.

And when he was twenty-two and living at Watford some-thing did happen ; though it was not, she instantly recognised, the thing. She herself had never been angered by it, although she hated telling Richard about it, but had instantly perceived the pathos of the situation ; her mind had always done its duty by Roger. It told, of course, the most moving story of loneliness and humiliation and hunger for respect and love that he should have represented himself to the girl with whom he had been walking out as a man of wealth and that after a rapturous after-noon at a flower show he should have taken her to the best jeweller's in Watford and given her a diamond brooch and ear-rings, for which, even with his allowance, he could not possibly pay.

The visit to Watford she had to make to clear things up had seemed at first the happiest event of all her relationship with Roger. It had been unpleasant to find him grey with weeping and disgrace, but there had been victory in forcing herself to comfort him with an exact imitation of the note of love. It had been ridiculous to face the angry lady in the case, who wore nodding poppies in her hat and had an immense rectangular bust and hips like brackets, but it was pleasant to murmur, " Oh, but he was speaking the truth. I'm quite comfortably off. I've come to pay the jeweller," and watch the look of amazement on the hot, high-coloured face giving place to anger and regret as it penetrated into her that she had really had the chance of marrying a wealthy man, and that after the things she had said that chance would be hers no longer. Marion liked hurting the girl because she had hurt Roger. Marion felt with satisfaction that the pleasure was a feeling a mother ought to feel.

She liked, too, going into the jeweller's shop and sitting there under the goggling eyes of the tradesman and speaking in the right leisurely voice that she had learned from her lover: "Yes, but I don't want you to take them back. I want to pay for them. There seems to have been some misunderstanding. There is no difficulty about the money at all. My son only wanted you to wait till his quarter's allowance came. I have the money here in notes. If you would count it . . ." She was playing a mother's part well ; and she rejoiced because the jeweller's eyes were examining with approval and conviction her beautiful clothes. For she had begun lately to take great pains over her dressing, partly because it was pleasant for her who was so smirched with criticism both from within and without to be above reproach in any matter, but mostly because she liked to look well in Richard's eyes ; that this had served Roger's end seemed to lift from her a part of her guilt. She hurried back to give Roger the receipt, and took him in her arms and rocked him as he sobbed out his ridiculous story : " Oh, mummie, I never would have done it if I hadn't gone mad. You see, mummie, Queenie's such a glorious woman. . . ."

But the soul has the keenest ears of any eavesdropper. He sat up suddenly and lifted her arms off his shoulders and looked at her with pale, desperate eyes. She clapped her hand across her face and then took it away again, and said softly : "What is it, dear ? " But he had sunk into a stupor, and had dropped his protruding gaze on the pattern of the oilcloth on the floor, which he was tracing with the toe of his boot. She could get nothing out of him. He obviously did not want her to stay two or three days with him, as she had proposed to do, but, on the other hand, he said over and over again as they waited on the platform for her train, " Mummie, I do love you, mummie. I do love you. And thank you, mummie. . . ." But she knew that these alternations and inconsistencies of his mood did not matter to their lives any more than the pitch and roll of a steamer travelling through rough weather affects its course. For since that moment when he had stared into her eyes and seen she did not love him she had known that somewhere, far off, beyond time and space, there had been set a light to the fuse of that event which she had always feared . . . the event that would destroy them all. . . .

But had it ? For after all, nothing dreadful had happened. Roger had written to her the next day telling her that he would not take his allowance any more because he did not think he deserved it, and he must try and be a man and shift for himself, and saying that he was taking a situation in another town which he did not name. That was the last they heard of him for a long time, for he came no more to Roothing for his holidays. Presently, with an exultant sense of release, but with an increasing liability to bad dreams, she went abroad to join Richard, at first at the post he held at the Romanones Mines in Andalusia, and then in Rio de Janeiro. There she was happy. She was one of those Northerners to whom the South belongs far more truly than it does to any of its natives. For over those the sun has had power since their birth, consuming their marrows and evaporating their blood so that they become pithless things that have to fly indoors for half the day and leave the Southern sun blazing insolently on the receptive Southern earth. But with blood cooled and nerves stabilised by youth spent on the edge of the grey sea, she could outface all foreign seasons. She could walk across the silent plaza when its dust lay dazzling white under the heat-pale sky and the city slept ; the days of heavy rain and potent pervasive dampness pleased her by their prodigiousness ; and when the thunderstorm planted vast momentary trees of lightning in the night she was pleased, as if she was watching someone do easily what she had always impotently desired to do.

And Richard was so wonderful to watch in this new setting that matched his beauty, easily establishing his dominion over the world as he had established it over her being from the moment of his conception. There was a conflict raging in him which, since it never resulted in hesitancy, but in simultaneous snatchings at life by both of the warring forces, gave him the appearance of the calmest exultation. He loved riding and dancing and gambling so much that his face was cruel when he did those things, as if he would kill anybody who tried to interrupt him in his pleasure. But he gave the core of his passion to his work and disciplined all his days to the routine of the laboratory, so that he was always cool and remote like a priest. It gave him pleasure to be insolent as rich men are, but all his insolence was in the interests of fineness and humility. He was ambitious, so fastidious about the quality of his work that he rejected half the world's offers to him. And always he turned aside from his victories and smiled secretively at her, as if they were two exiles who had returned under false names to the country that had banished them and were earning great honours. She wished this life could go on for ever.

But one day Richard came to her as she sat in the dense sweetness of the flowering orange grove and tossed a letter into her lap. She did not open it for a little, but lay and looked

at Richard through her lashes. His swarthiness was burned
by the sun, and his body was slim like an Indian's in his
white suit, and his lips and his eyes were deceitful and satisfied,
as they always were when he had been with Mariquita de Rojas.
That did not arouse any moral feeling in her, because she did
not think of Richard's actions as being good or bad, but only as
being different in colour and lustre, like the various kinds of jewels ;
there are pearls, and there are emeralds. But it made her feel
lonely, and she turned soberly to opening her letter. It was
from Roger. He was in trouble ; he had been out of a job
for some months ; his savings were gone, and the woman was
bothering for her rent ; he asked for help. At first she did not
think that she would tell Richard, but recognising that that
was a subtle form of disloyalty to Roger, she said evenly :
" Richard, how can I cable money to Roger ? He wants
it quickly. And, Richard, I think I should go home and
look after him." Richard had set his eyes on the far heat-
throbbing seas and, after a moment's quivering silence, had
broken into curses. " Oh, don't speak of poor Roger like that ! "
she had cried out, and he had answered terribly : " I'm not
speaking of him ; I'm speaking of my father, who let you in for
all this." She had muttered protestingly, but because of the
hatred in his face she was not brave enough to tell him that she
had made her peace with his father before he died. Not even
for Harry's sake would she imperil the love between her and her
son.

She had gone home a few months later, but, of course, it had
been useless. Roger would never come back to live with her.
All she could do was to sit at Yaverland's End, ready to receive
him when he turned up, as he always did when he had got a new
post, to boast of how well he was going to do in the future.
Usually on these occasions he brought her a present, something
queer that wrung the heart because it revealed the humility of his
conception of the desirable ; perhaps a glass jar of preserved fruit
salad which had evidently impressed him as looking magnificent when he saw it in the grocer's shop. She would kiss
him gratefully for it, though every time he came back he was
more like the grey and hopeless men, cousins to the rats, who
hang round cab-ranks in cities.

A regular routine followed these visits. First he wrote
happy letters home every Sunday ; then he ceased to write so
often ; then there was silence ; and then he wrote asking
for help, because he had lost his job and owed money
to the landlady. Then she would seek him out, wherever

he was, and pay the landlady, who was usually well enough disposed towards Roger unless he had tried to win her affections by being handy about the house, in which case there were extra charges for the plumber and an irremovable feeling of exasperation. And she would ask him to come home with her, and not bother about working, but just be a companion to her. At that, however, he always slowly shook his small, mouse-coloured head. For he was still not quite sure . . . and he feared that he might become so if he went back and lived with her. As things were, he could interpret her prompt answer to his call as a sign of affection. Moreover, he had his poor little pride, which was not a negligible quality ; he never would have sent to her for money if he had not felt so sorry for his landladies. To admit that he could not earn a bare living when his brother was making himself one of the lords of the earth would have broken his spirit.

Knowing these things, she could not beg him over-much to come to her, but that left dreadfully little to say in the hours they had to spend together on these occasions. There fell increasingly moments of silence when, unreminded by his piteousness and her obligations by the good little pipe of her voice, she was aware of nothing but his unpleasantness. For he was becoming more and more physically horrible. As was natural when he lived in these mean lodgings, he was beginning to look, if not actually dirty, at least unwashed ; and there was something else about his appearance, something tarnished and disgraceful, which she could not understand till the landlady at Leicester said to her : "I do think it's such a pity that a nice young man like Mr. Peacey sometimes don't take more care of himself like he ought to." Drunkenness seemed to her worse than anything in the world, because it meant the surrender of dignity ; she would rather have had her son a murderer than a drunkard. She had wondered if the truth need ever reach Richard, and there had floated before her mind's eye a newspaper paragraph : "Roger Peacey, described as a clerk, fined forty shillings for being drunk and disorderly and obstructing the police in the course of their duty. . . ." She had asked quickly, "What is he like ? Does he get violent ? " The woman had answered : "Oh no, mum ; just silly-like," and had laughed, evidently at the recollection of some ridiculous scene.

Oh God, oh God ! When she struggled out of her bad dreams she awoke to something that, having had this confirmation, was now no longer fear, but a shudder under the breath of a stooping,

searching evil. She had always known that the existence of
Richard and herself and Roger was conditional upon their
maintenance of a flawless behaviour. There was somewhere
in the dark conspiring ether that wraps the world an intention to
destroy her for her presumption in being Richard's mother and
him for daring to be Richard—an intention that was vindictive
against beauty and yet was fettered by a harsh quality resembling
justice. It could not strike until they themselves became tainted
with unworthiness and fit for destruction. Now they had
become tainted. She knew that Roger's drunkenness would be
obscenely without dignity; she knew that she would side with her
triumphant son and against her son who needed her pity. They
would all be unworthy and they would all be destroyed. Nothingness would swallow up her Richard. To free herself from her fear
she leaped out of bed and ran to the window, and stared on the
white creeks that lay under the moonlight among the dark marsh
islands with a brightness that seemed like ecstasy, as if they were
receiving pleasure from it. Her thoughts ran along the hillside
to the man who lay high above and excluded from this glittering
world in his marble tomb. "Oh, Harry," she cried, "I'm not
blaming you, but if you'd stuck to me it would have been so
different. . . ."

If he had been loyal to her she would have awakened now in
a great house, with many rooms in which, breathing deeply and
evenly, there slept beautiful people who had begun their being
in her womb. Harry would not have died if he had been with
her. The procreative genius of her body would have kept him
in life to give her more. Her last-born child would still have been
quite young. It was to him she would have gone now; if she
had wakened she would have found him in the end room, a boy
fair as his father, and having the same look of integrity in joy,
of immunity from sorrow or profound thinking. She would
have watched his face, infantile and pugnacious with dreams
of the day's game, until she longed too strongly to touch him
and kiss him. Then she would have turned and went back
along the corridor, between the glorious young men and women
who lay restoring their might for the morrow, not one of them
threatened, not one of them doomed. . . .

Love could have made that of her life if it had not been
beaten away. The thought was bitter. She stared with thin
lips at the happy gleaming tides until it struck her suddenly
that love had come back into her house. It was here now,
attending on the red-haired girl, and it would not be beaten off;
it would be cherished, it would be given sacrifices. Surely if

it could have made beautiful her own life, which without it had been so hideous, it could exorcise Richard's destiny. She fixed her eyes on the high moon and said as if in prayer, " Ellen. . . . Ellen. . . ."

There sounded, in the recesses of the house, the ping of an electric bell.

She looked at the clock by her bedside. It was three o'clock. She said to herself, with that air of irony which people to whom many strange things have happened assume when they fear that yet another is approaching, so that they shall not flatter Fate by their perturbation, " It's late for anyone to call."

But the ping sounded again ; and then the thud of blows upon the door.

She cried out, " Ah, yes ! " She knew who it was. It was Roger, come in rags, come in an idiot hope of escaping justice, after some fatuous and squalid crime, to destroy Richard and herself. She hurried over to her wardrobe and drew out her warm dressing-gown and thrust her feet into slippers, while her lips practised saying lovingly, "Roger, Roger, Roger ! . . . Why, it's you, Roger ! . . . Come in. Come in, my boy. . . . What is it, my poor lad ? . . ."

She went down through the quiet house and laid her fingers on the handle of the door ; delayed for a moment, and raised her hand to her face and smoothed from it certain lines of loathing. Bowing her head, she murmured a remonstrance to some power.

But when she opened the door it was Richard who stood there.

CHAPTER VII

HE could not at once discern in the darkness who it was that opened the door, and he remained an aloof black shape against the moon-glare, lifting his cap and saying, " I am sorry to knock you up at this hour," so for a minute Marion had the amusing joy of seeing him as he appeared to other people, remote and vigilant and courteous and really more hidalgoesque than the occasion demanded. She laughed teasingly. The hard line of him softened, and he said "Mother," and stepped over the threshold and folded her in his arms, and kissed her on the lips and hair. She rested quietly within his groping, pressing love. This indoor darkness where they stood was striped with many lines of moonlight coming through cracks in doors and the margins of blinds, so that it seemed to have no more substance than a paper lanthorn, and outside the white boles and branches of the lit leafless trees were as luminous stencillings on the night. There was nothing solid in the world but their two bodies, nothing real but their two lives.

She did not ask him why he had come at this hour. There was indeed nothing so very unusual in it, for more than once when he was a sailor she had been wakened by the patter of pebbles on her window and had looked down through the darkness on the whitish oval of his face, marked like a mask with his eagerness to see her ; and later, in southern countries, he had often walked quietly into the dark, cool room where she lay having her siesta, though she had thought him a hundred miles away, and it had seemed as if nothing could move in the weighty heat outside save the writhing sea. It had always seemed appropriate to their relationship that he should come to her thus, suddenly and without warning and against the common custom. Thus had he come to be born.

She pushed him away from her. " Have you put your motor-cycle in the shed ? " she asked indifferently.

" No. It's outside the gate."

" Put it in. There may be frost by the morning."

331

He turned away to do it. To him it was always heaven, like the peace of dreamless sleep, to hand over to her the heavy sword of his will.

She watched him go out into the white ecstatic glare and pass behind the illuminated twiggy bareness of the hedge, which looked like the phosphorescent spine of some monstrous stranded fish. This was a strange night, crude as if some coarse but powerful human intelligence were co-operating with nature. She had a fancy that if she strained her ears she might hear the whirr of the great dynamo that served this huge electric moon. But however the night might be, this strange, dangerous son of hers was a match for it. She looked gloatingly after him as he passed out of her sight, and then turned and went into the kitchen. It was easy to prepare him a meal, for there was a gas-stove and the stores lay at her hand, each in its own place, since in her five minutes' visit to the cook every morning she imposed the same nervous neatness here and kept the rest of the house rectangular and black and white.

She heard the closing of the front door and his steps coming in search of her. She liked to think of him finding his way to her by the rays of light warmer than moonlight through half-open doors. If it had been anyone else in the world that was coming towards her she would have gathered up her thick plaits and pinned them about her head. But from him she need not hide the signs, which made all other people hate her, that she had been beautiful and had been destroyed.

When he came in she said, " Light the other gas-jets. Yes, both of them."

Now there was a lot of light. She could see the bird's-wing brilliance of his hair, the faint bluish bloom about his lips that showed he had not shaved since morning, the radiance of his eyes and the flush on his cheeks that had come of his enjoyed ride through the cold moony air. The queer things men were, with their useless, inordinate, disgusting yet somehow magnificent growth of hair on their faces, and their capacity for excitements that have nothing to do with emotion. . . .

He came and stood beside her and slipped his arm round her waist and murmured, " Well, Marion ? " and laughed. Always he had loved calling her that, ever since as a little boy he had found her full name written in an old book and had run to her, crying " Is that really your lovely name? " Even more than by the name itself had he been pleased by the way it was written, squintwise across the page and in a round hand, exactly as he himself was then writing his own name in his first school books. It made him see his mother as a little girl, and helped him to dream his favourite dream that he and she were just the same age and could go to school and play games together. It still gave him an inexplicable glow of pleasure, the memory of that brownish signature staggering across the fly-leaf of " Jessica's First Prayer."

She perceived that he was violently excited at coming back to her, but she took the toast from under the grill, buttered it, set it on the warm plate, and poured the eggs on it with an ironical air of absorption. These two went very carefully and mocked each other perpetually so that the gods should not overhear and be jealous. " Now, eat it while it's hot ! " she said, holding out the plate.

He put it down on the kitchen table and gathered her into his arms.

" Well, mother ? " he murmured, looking down at her, worshipping her.

" Oh, my boy," she whispered, " you've lost your brown, up there in Scotland."

" Oh, I'm all right. But you ? "

" As well as well can be."

" But, mother dear, you look as if you'd been having those bad dreams."

" No, I've had none, none at all."

" That means not too many. Does it ? "

They kissed, and he said tenderly yet harshly : " Roger hasn't been bothering you ? "

" Ah, the poor thing, don't speak of him like that," she said. " No, but I've not heard from him for six weeks. Not even at Christmas. I'm a little anxious. But it may be all right. You remember last Christmas there was a time when he didn't write. I expect it'll be all right." But with her eyes she abandoned herself to fear, so that he should soothe her and stroke her hands with his, which were trembling in spite of their strength because he was so glad to see her.

" Mother darling, I have hated leaving you alone. But it was necessary. I've done good work this winter." He made with one hand a stiff and sweeping movement that expressed his peculiar kind of arrogance, which stated that his was the victory, now and for ever, and yet took therefrom no pride for himself. " I've pulled it off," he said jeeringly, and smiled at her derisively but with tight lips, as if they must take this thing lightly or some danger would spring. " Where I get my brains from I don't know," he muttered teasingly, and put out his hand and traced the interweaving strands in one of her plaits. "What hair you've got!" he said. "I've never seen a woman with . . ." He started violently and was silent.

She cried out, "What is it?" But he answered, speaking clippedly, "Oh, nothing, nothing. . . ."

So evidently was he overcoming a moment of utter confusion that she turned away and busied herself with the coffee.

Behind her his voice spoke falsely, uplifted in a feint of the surprised recollection which at its first coming had struck him dumb the previous moment. "And Ellen! I'm a nice sort of lover to be five minutes in the house without asking for my Ellen! How is she? How have you been getting on together?"

"Oh, your dear Ellen!" she cried fervently. But her heart went cold within her. He was right. It was against nature that he should have forgotten the woman he loved when he came under the roof where she was sleeping her beautiful sleep. Could it be that Ellen was not the woman he loved and that his engagement to her was some new joke on the part of destiny? She whirled round to have a look at him, exclaiming to make time, "Oh, she is the most wonderful creature who ever lived." But he had forgotten his embarrassment now, and was standing with bent head, thinking intently, and on his face there was the dazzled and vulnerable look of a man who is truly in love. Well, if that were so, why could it not be pure and easy joy for them both, as it was for other sons and mothers when there were happy marriages afoot? Why must their life, even in such parts of it as escaped the shadow of Peacey or Roger, be so queer in climate? This time it was Richard's fault. She had been willing to be lightly, facilely happy over it like other people. Her spirit snarled at him, and she cried out impatiently, "Go and eat your eggs before they're cold." As Richard took his seat, moving slowly and trancedly, and began to eat his food with half indifference because of his dreams, she took the chair at the other end of the table, and, cupping her chin in her hands, stared at him petulantly.

"Why didn't you tell me in your letters how beautiful she was?" she demanded.

He answered mildly, "Didn't I?"

"No, you didn't," she told him curtly. "You said you thought her pretty. Thought her pretty, indeed, with that hair and that wonderful Scotch little face! . . ."

She caught her breath in irritation at the expression on his face, the uneasy movement from side to side of his eyes which warred with the smile on his lips. Why, when he thought of his love, need he have an air as if he listened to two voices and was distressed by the effort to follow their diverse musics? But she could not quarrel with him for long, for he was wearing the drenched and glittering look which was given him by triumph or hard physical exercise and which always overcame her heart like the advance of an army. His flesh and hair seemed to reflect the light as if they were wet, but neither with sweat nor with water. Rather was it as if he were newly risen from a brave dive into some pool of vitality whose whereabouts were the secret that made his mouth vigilant. Even he had the dazed, victorious look of a risen diver. Utterly melted, she cried out, " I am so glad you have come home."

He started, and came smiling out of his dream. " I am so glad to be here," he said. They laughed across the table ; the strong light showed them the dear lines they knew on one another's faces. " That's why," he cried brilliantly, " I've come at this ungodly hour. I had to be here. I got into London at nine o'clock and I went and had some dinner at the Station Hotel. But I felt wretched. Mother, I'm getting," he announced with a naïve triumph, " awfully domestic. I got the hump the minute Ellen left Edinburgh. I felt I must come down to you at once, so I went and got the cycle and started off straight away, and I would have been here by midnight if I hadn't had a smash at Upminster. No, I wasn't hurt. Not a scrap. It was at the beginning of that garden suburb. God, it must be beastly living in those new houses ; like beginning to colour a pipe. I'm glad we live in this old place. Well, a chap who'd bought some timber at an auction down in Surrey, and was taking it home to Laindon, dropped a log off his lorry, and I smashed into it and burst a tyre and broke half a dozen spokes in my front wheel, so I had to hunt round till I found a garage, and when I did I had to spend hours tinkering the machine up. The man who owned the place came down in his pyjamas and a dressing-gown and sat talking about his wife. She hadn't wanted to let him come down because it was so late. ' Is that a woman who'll help a man in his business, I ask you ? ' he kept on saying. Mustn't it be queer to have womenfolk with whom one doesn't feel identical ? " They exchanged a boastful look of happiness, the intensity of which, however, seemed the last effort he found possible. For his lids drooped, and he supported his head on his hand and took a deep drink, and said drowsily, " I'm glad to be here."

She went and stood beside him and stroked his hair. " I should have come to you at Aberfay," she grieved. " But I knew I couldn't stand the winter, and I would only have been a nuisance to you if I had been ill all the time. Did the woman feed you properly, dear ? "

He said, without looking up, " I wouldn't have let you come. It was a God-forsaken hole. I couldn't have stood it if it hadn't been for "—he gave it out with an odd hesitancy, almost as if he were boyishly shy—" Ellen. And I had to stand it, so that I could pull this thing off."

She asked, " What thing, my dear ? " though she was not so very greatly interested. By daylight her ambition for him was fanatic and without limit. But in this stolen hour, when no one knew that they were together, she let herself feel something like levity about his doings. It seemed enough, considering how glorious he was, that he should merely be.

He began to eat again and told the story tersely between mouthfuls. " You know the reason that I stayed up in Edinburgh after I'd sent off Ellen was that I thought I had to show the directors what I'd been doing at Aberfay next Thursday. They were to come on to me after they'd paid their visit to the Clyde works. Well, they came yesterday instead. Sir Vincent has to go to America sooner than he expected, so he wanted to get it over. When they saw what I'd been trying for during the last six months they got excited. As a matter of fact it is pretty good. I wish I could tell you about it, but you know I can't. Also I had told McDermott that Dynevors, the Birmingham people, had heard my contract was up in March, and wanted to buy me. So they got frightened, and offered me a new contract that they thought would keep me." He had finished his meal, and he pushed away his plate and stretched himself, looking up at her and smiling sleepily.

" Have you taken it ? "

" Rather. It couldn't have been better."

" What is it ? "

" They've doubled my screw and given me an interest in the business."

" How ? "

He shook his head, yawning. " A permanent agreement . . . percentages. . . . I'm too woolly-headed to tell you now."

" But what does it mean ? You don't care about money or position as a rule. You've always told me that your work was enough for you. Why are you so pleased ? " Though the moment before she had thought she cared nothing for the ways that his soul travelled, she was in an agony lest he had been changed by the love of woman and had become buyable.

He read her perfectly, and pulled himself out of his drowsiness to reassure her. " Now I'm not being glad because I'm pleasing them; I'm glad because now I can make them please me. It's what I've always been working for, and it's come two years before I expected it. I've got my footing in the biggest armament firm in England. I'm the youngest director. I've got "—again he made that stiff, sweeping gesture of arrogance that was not vanity—" the best brain of them all. In ten years I shall be someone in the firm. In twenty years I shall be nearly everybody. And think of what sport industry's going to be during the next half-century while this business of capital and labour is being fought out, particularly to a man like me, who's got no axe to grind, who's outside all interests, who, thanks to you, doesn't belong to any class. And you see I needn't be afraid of losing my power to work if I meddle in affairs. I'm definitely, finally, unalterably a scientific man. I've got that for good. That's thanks to you too."

" How could your stupid old mother do that ? " she murmured protestingly.

" You're not stupid," he said, and bending down he kissed her head where it lay on his shoulder. " Whatever good there is in me I've got from you. You gave me my brain. And I'm able to do scientific work because of the example you've been to me, though I'm rottenly unfit for it myself. Mother, look at my hands. Do you see how they're shaking ? They're steady enough when I'm doing anything, but often when there's nothing to be done they shake and shake. My mind's like that. When there's someone to impress or govern I'm all right. But when I'm alone it shakes—there's a kind of doubt. And there's such a lot of loneliness in scientific work, when even science isn't there. Then that comes. . . . Doubt. Not of what one's doing, but of what one is; or where one is. I never would have kept on with it if it hadn't been for your example. I couldn't have pushed on. I would have gone off and done adventurous things.

" Do you remember that French chap who wanted me to go with him into British Guiana ? I'd have liked that. There's nothing stops one thinking so well as being a blooming hero ; and it's such fun. And why should one go on doing this lonely work that's so hellishly hard ? Of course it's important. Mother, Science is the most wonderful thing in the world. It's a funny thing that if you think and talk about the spirit you only look into the mind of man, but if you cut out the spirit and study matter you look straight into the mind of God. But what good is that when you know that at the end you're going

to die and rot and there's not the slightest guarantee which
would satisfy anybody but a born fool that God had any need
of us afterwards ?   You can't even console yourself with the
thought that it's for the good of the race, because that will die
and rot too when the earth grows cold.   One has to stake everything on the flat improbability that service of the truth is a good
in itself, such a good that it's worth while sacrificing one's life
to it.

"That's where you've been such a help to me.   You had
no justification for supposing that life was worth living.   You'd
every reason to suppose that the whole business was foul, and
the only sensible thing to do was to get all the fun one could out
of it.   If you had determined to be as little a mother to me
as you could I would have understood it, considering of what I
must have reminded you.   You'd money, you were beautiful,
you've always been able to attract people.   You might so easily
have gone away from here and made a life of your own and just
kept me in the corner of your eye, as lots of unhappily married
women that one meets keep their children.   Instead you shut
yourself up here and gave yourself utterly to looking after me.
I sometimes feel that the reason I've grown up taller and less
liable to illness than other men is that you loved me so much
when I was a child.   You seemed to pour your life into me.   And
you didn't just take pleasure in me.   You trained me, and I must
have been a nasty little brute to train.   Do you remember
licking me because I went to that circus ?   You took it out of
yourself teaching me to be straight and decent.   If you'd been
an ordinary married woman who believed that you'd go to hell
if you didn't do your duty by your children, and who knew she'd
get public respect and the devotion of her husband as a reward
for doing it, the way you did it would have been magnificent.
But to do it like that when you knew that there was no such thing
as justice in heaven or earth—I tell you, mother, it's kept me
going to think of the sacrifice you made for me—— "

"Oh no," she cried.   "It wasn't a sacrifice at all, my dear,
to be with you."

"It must have been," he said harshly, as if he were piling
up a case against a malefactor, "for you of all women."   He
drew her alongside of him and stared up at her.   "Weren't
there bad times, when you hated being cheated of your youth ?
When you longed for a husband—for some man to adore you
and look after you ?   When you felt bitter because it had all
been over so soon ? "   She averted her face, but his arm gripped
her waist more closely, and he asked pleadingly, "Mother, let

me know everything about you. I'll be married soon. There'll be no more talking like this while the moon goes down after that. Let me know everything you've done for me, everything you've given me. Why shouldn't I know how wonderful you are? Tell me, weren't there bad times?"

Slowly and reluctantly she turned towards him a face that, wavering with grief, looked strangely childish between her two greying plaits. "I never went to a dance," she said unsteadily. "Isn't it silly of me I mind that? . . . Till a few years ago I couldn't bear to hear dance music. . . ."

"Oh, you poor darling!—and you would have danced so beautifully!" he cried in agony, and drew her into his arms. She tried to beat herself free and twisted her mouth away from his consoling kisses, so that she might sob, "But it wasn't a sacrifice, it wasn't a sacrifice! Those were only moods. I never really wanted anything except to be with you!" But her bliss in him had been too tightly strung by his sudden coming and by his open speech of that concerning which they spoke as seldom as the passionately religious speak of God, so for a little time she had to weep. But presently she stretched out her hand and pressed back his seeking mouth.

"Hush!" she said with a grave wildness. "We must not talk like this."

He lifted his face, which was convulsed with love and pain, and found her stern as a priestess who defends her mystery from violation. Meekly he let his arms fall from her body and turned away, resting his head on his hand and staring at a blank wall.

She saw that she had hurt him. She drew close to him again, and murmured lovingly, though still with defensive majesty: "Why should we talk of it, my boy? It's all over now, and you're a made man. This contract really does mean that, doesn't it?"

He answered, patting her hand to show that he submitted to her in everything, "Oh, in the end it means illimitable power."

To give him pleasure she exchanged with him a brilliant and triumphant glance, though at this moment she felt that her love for him concerned itself less with ambition than she had ever supposed. Incredulously she whispered to her harsh, sceptical mind that it almost seemed as if its sphere were not among temporal things. But it gave her a real rapture to perceive in his eyes the elder brother of the expression that had always dwelt there in his childish days when he announced to her his cricket-scores and his prizes; even so, she had thought then, the adjutant of a banished leader might hand him down arrows to shoot on the city that had exiled him. And indeed the success of their conspiracy had been marvellous. In old times they had looked out of this house under lowered and defiant brows, knowing there was none without who knew of them who did not despise them. But now they could smile tenderly and derisively out into this hushed moonlight that received the uncountable and fatuously peaceful breaths of the sleepers who had been their enemies and were to be their slaves. It was strange that at this of all instants she should for the space of a heartbeat lose her sense of the uniqueness of her fate and be confounded by amazement at the common lot in which they two and the vanquished sleepers alike partook. Was it possible that this could be? That this plethora of beings that coated the careless turning earth like grains of dust on a sleeping top were born—mysterious act!—and mated—act so much more mysterious than it seemed!—and died—act which was the essence of mystery! She was dizzied with astonishment, and to steady herself put out her hands and caught hold of those broad shoulders, which, her marvelling mind recalled to her, she had miraculously been able to make out of her so much less broad body. She felt guilty as she recovered, for the habit of thinking about subjects unconnected with her family had always seemed to her as unwomanly as a thin voice or a flat chest. Penitently she dropped a kiss on his forehead and muttered, "Richard, you're a good son. You've made up for everything I've been through many times over. . . ."

"Then stay up with me a little," he said. "Don't let's go to bed yet." He stretched out his arm and moved a wicker armchair that stood on the hearth till it faced the grate. "Sit down, dear, and I'll make you a fire. Dear, do sit down. This is the last night we shall have together." She obeyed, for he spoke with the sullenness which she knew to be in him a mask of intense desire. He busied himself with the fire and coal that the servants had left ready for the morning, and when he had made a blaze he squatted down on the rug and rested his head on her lap and seemed to sleep.

But he did not. Against the fine silk of her kimono she felt the sweep of his eyelashes. "Why is he doing this?" she wondered; and discovered happily, "Ah, he is going to tell me about Ellen." She waited serenely, while the clock ticked.

Presently he spoke, but did not lift his head. "Mother, I like being here. . . ."

She was not perturbed because he then fell silent. It was natural enough that he should be shy of speaking of his other love.

But he continued : "Mother, do you know why I would always have stuck to my people, no matter how they'd treated me ? I wonder if you'll think I'm mad ? I'd have stuck to them in any case—because they've got the works on Kerith Island, and I've always wanted to work there. Think of it ! I shall be able to sleep here at night and go out in the morning to a place I've seen all my life out of these windows. And all day long I'll be able to put my head out of my lab. door and look along the hill to our tree-tops. Mother, I do love this house," he said earnestly, raising his head and looking round the kitchen as if even it were dear to him, though he could not have been in it more than once or twice before. "It's a queer thing, but though you've altered this completely from what it was when I was a boy, it still seems the oldest and most familiar thing in the world. And though it's really rather exposed as houses go, hanging up here over the marshes, I feel when I come back to it as if I were creeping down into some hiding-place, into some warm, closed place where nothing horrible could ever find me. Do you feel like that, mother ? "

She nodded. "I might hate this house, considering all that's happened here. But I, too . . ." She spoke in the slightly disagreeable tone that a reticent nature assumes when it is obliged to confess to strong feeling. "Yes, I love it."

They looked solemnly into the crepitant blaze of the new fire. He grasped her hand ; but suddenly released it and asked querulously, as if he had remembered certain tedious obligations : "And Ellen, does she like the house ? "

She was appalled, "Yes, yes ! I think so," she stammered.

"Good," he said curtly, and buried his head in her lap again.

For as long as possible she endured her dismay ; then, bending forward and trying to twist his face round so that she could read it, she asked unsteadily, "Richard, you do love Ellen, don't you ? "

He sat up and met her eyes. "Of course I do. Have you been thirty-six hours with her without seeing that I must ? She—she's a lamp with a double burner. There's her beauty, and her dear, funny, young little soul. It's good to have someone that one can worship and befriend at the same time. Yes, we're going to be quite happy." His eyes slid away from hers evasively, then hardened and resolved to be honest, and returned again. "Mother, I tell you this is the end." After that his honesty faltered. He chose to take it that his mother was looking so fixedly at him because she had not understood the meaning of his words, so he repeated soberly, "I tell you, this is the end. The end of love making for me. I shall never love any other woman but Ellen as long as I live." And he turned to the fire, the set of his shoulders confessing what his lips would not—that though he loved Ellen, though he wanted Ellen, there was something imperfect in the condition of his love which made him leaden and uneager.

"That's right, that's right; you must be good to her," Marion murmured, and stroked his hair. "I don't think you could have done better than your Ellen if you'd searched the whole world," she said timidly, trying to give him a cue for praise of his love. "It's such astonishing luck to find a girl whose sense will be as much solid good to you as a fortune in the bank and who looks as pretty as a rose-tree at the same time."

He made no response. The words were strangled in her throat, and she fell to tapping her foot rhythmically against the fender. Her eyes were moist; this was so different from the talk she had expected.

Presently his shoulders twitched. "Don't do that, mother dear," he said impatiently.

"I'm sorry, darling," she answered wearily. She threw herself back in her chair and clenched her fists. Desperation fevered her, and she began to speak vindictively. "Of course it was a great relief to me when I saw the kind of girl Ellen is, considering how up till now you've sidled past women of any sort of character as if you'd heard that men got sent to prison for loving any but fools."

He laughed uneasily.

"Yes," she went on; "you always seemed to be looking carefully for anything you could find that was as insipid as a water-melon. You can't, you know, possibly count your love-affairs as amongst your successes." She jerked her head back, her lips retracted in a kind of grin. "Mariquita de Rojas!" she jeered.

He started, though not much. "I never knew you knew about that," he said mildly.

"Of course I did." She quivered with exaggerated humiliation. "To see my son spending himself on something so nearly nothing. And then the way you moped and raged at her when she threw you over. Seeing the poor woman was a fool, how else could you expect her to behave but like a fool ? It was undignified of you to put the burden of being the woman you loved on a poor thing like her—like overworking a servant girl." She perceived that she was hot and shaking, and that she was within an ace of betraying the secret that there sometimes rose in her heart a thirst to beat and hurt every woman that he had ever loved. Words would pour out that would expose her disgusting desire to strike and scratch if she did not substitute others. So she found herself crying in a voice that was thinner than hers: "And a married woman! To see you doing wrong!"

The moment she said it she was ashamed and drew an expunging hand across her lips. And as she had feared, he threw over his shoulder a glance that humorously recognised the truths which she had insincerely suppressed: that while she desired to hurt the women whom he had loved, she would gladly have murdered any woman who had refused to love him, whether married or single; and that she had never cared what he had done so long as he did not lose his physical and moral fastidiousness, and did not lust after flesh that, having rotted its nerves with delight unsanctioned by the spirit, knew corruption before death, and so long as he had not pretended to any woman that he wanted her soul when he wanted her body.

Seeing the tears in her eyes, he said kindly: "Well, I never thought Mariquita's marriage counted for much. Do you remember how you took her in one night when old de Rojas hid in a cloisonné vase on the verandah for cover and potted at the stars with his gun?" But in his voice she read wonder that for the first time in his life he should have found his honest mother forging a moral attitude.

It was dreadful that, on this of all nights, and so soon after a special illumination of their relationship, she should have set him making allowances for her to cover up her insincerity. She stammered miserably: "Well, Ellen's a dear, dear girl," and twisted her fingers in her lap, and cried out in a fresh access of fever: "It's strange: this is a cold night, and yet I feel hot and heavy and sticky as I did in Italy when the sirocco blew."

He slid his hand into hers again and altered his position so that he could smile up into her face. "Yes, she's a dear girl," he agreed comfortingly.

"Then marry her soon!" she begged. "You're thirty. It's time you had a life of your own. You must make the ties that will last when I am dead. Marry her soon."

"Yes," he said. "I will marry her soon."

"At once!" she urged. "You can be married in three

weeks, you know, if you set things going immediately. You'll see about it to-morrow, won't you?"

He said nothing, but stroked her hand.

"You will do that?" she almost shrieked.

He moistened his dry lips. "I hadn't thought . . . quite so soon. . . ."

"Why not? Why not?"

"She is so very young," he mumbled, and turned away his face.

"Why, Richard, Richard!" she exclaimed softly. "God knows I'm not in love with old-fashioned ideas. I've only to put up my hand behind my ear to feel a scar they gave me thirty years ago when I was hunted down Roothing High Street. But it seems to me that the new-fashioned ideas are as mawkish as the old ones were brutal. And worst of all is this idea about marriage being dreadful." She blushed deeply. "It's not. What you make of it may be, but the thing itself is not. If Ellen's old enough to love you, she's old enough to marry you. Oh, if you miscall—that, you throw dirt at everything." She paused; and it rushed in on her that he, too, had told a lie. To make an easy answer to her inconvenient question he had profaned his conviction that the life of the body was decorous and honourable. Why were they beginning to lie to each other, like other mothers and sons?

He liked his error as little as she liked hers. "It's all right, mother," he said drearily; and, after some seconds, added with false brightness: "I'm sorry in a way I didn't wait till to-morrow morning in town. I wanted to buy something for Ellen. I've never given her anything really good. It cost me next to nothing to live in Scotland. I've got lots of money by me. I thought a jade necklace. It would look jolly with her hair. Or, better still, malachite beads. But they're more difficult to get."

"Ah, jewellery," she said.

"Well, I suppose it's the best thing to give a girl," he assented, unconscious of her irony.

Now that she had heard him designing to give jewels to his little Ellen, that earnest child who thought only of laying up treasure in heaven and would say bravely to the present of a string of pearls, "Thank you, they're verra nice," and grieve silently because no one had thought to give her a really good dictionary of economic terms, she knew for certain that he had travelled far out of the orbit of his love. The heart is a universe, and has its dark, cold, outer space where there are no affections ; and there he had strayed and was lost. It was not well with him. Furtively she raised her handkerchief to her eyes. This was not the hour that she expected when she had opened the door and seen her son, and beyond him the gleaming night that had seemed to promise ecstasy to all that were about and doing in its span. Well, outside the house that perfect night must still endure, though it would be falling under the dominion of the dawn. The shadows of the trees would be lengthening on the lawn like slow farewells ; but the fields were still suffused with that light which proceeds from the chaste moon's misconceptions of human life and love. For the moon sees none but lovers, or those who stay awake by bedsides out of mercy, or those who sleep ; and men and women when they sleep look pitiful and innocent. So it sends down on earth this light that is as beautiful as love, and soft as mercy, and the very colour of innocence itself. It had seemed to Marion that often those who walked in those beams tried to justify the moon's faith in them. Harry had been the sweeter lover when the nights were not dark ; when there was this noble glory in the sky his passion had changed from greed for something as easily attainable as food, to hunger for something hardly to be attained by man. Perhaps his son, if he would walk in the moonlight, would remember that which he had forgotten. She said eagerly : " Richard, before you go to bed, let us go out into the garden, and look at the moon setting over Kerith Island."

"No," he said obstinately, and laid his head on her lap. She began to rock herself with misery, until he made a faint noise of irritation. There followed a long space when the clock ticked, and told her that there was no hope, things never went well on this earth. Then he exclaimed suddenly, " Marion."

" Yes ? "

She had hoped that there had come into his mind some special aspect of Ellen's magic which he loved and desired to share with her. But he muttered, " That box on the dresser. Up there on the top shelf."

She followed his eyes in amazement. " The scarlet one in the corner ? That belongs to cook. I think it's her workbox. What about it ? "

He stared at it with a drowsy smile. " You had a cloak that colour when I was a child," he murmured, and again buried his head in her lap.

" Why, so I had," she said softly, and thought proudly to herself, " How he loves me ! He speaks of trifling things about me as if they were good ale that he could drink. He speaks like a sweetheart. . . ." And then caught her breath. " But that," she went on, " is how he ought to speak of Ellen, not of me." A certain gaunt conviction stood up and stared into her face. She wriggled in her seat and looked down on her strong, competent hands, and said to herself uneasily : " I wish life could be settled by doing things and not by thinking. . . ." But the conviction had, by its truthfulness, rammed in the gates of her mind. She cried out to herself in anguish : " Of course ! Of course ! He cannot love Ellen because he loves me too much ! He has nothing left to love her with ! " A tide of exultation surged through her, but she knew that this was the movement within her of the pride that leads to death. For if Richard went on loving her over-much, the present would become hideous as she had never thought that the circumstances of her splendid son could do. The girl would grieve ; and she would as soon that Spring itself should have its heart hurt as dear little Ellen. And there would be no future. She would have no grandchildren. When she died he would be so lonely. . . . And it was her own fault. All her life long she had let him see how she wanted love and how she had been deprived of it by Harry's failure ; and so he had given her all he had, even that which he should have kept for his own needs. " What can I do to put this right ? " she asked herself. " What can I do ? "

She found that his eyes were staring up at her from her lap. " Mother, what's the matter ? "

" The matter ? "

" You were looking at me like a judge who's passing sentence."

" Well, perhaps I am," she said wearily. " Every mother is a judge who sentences the children for the sins of the father."

His face grew dark, as it always did when he thought of his father. " Well, if you had done that I should have had a pretty bad time."

It occurred to her that there was a way, an easy way, by which she could free Richard from his excessive love for her. He would not love her any more if she told him. . . . " But, oh, I couldn't tell him that," her spirit groaned. " It is against nature that anyone but me should know of that. It would spoil it to speak of it." But there was no other way. If she were to go away from him he would follow her. There was no other way.

She shivered and smiled down on him, into his answering eyes. It was strange to think that this was the last time they would ever look at each other quite like that. She prepared to bring herself down like a hammer on her own delicate reluctances.

"Hush, Richard," she said. "You shouldn't talk like that. Perhaps I ought to have told you long ago that your father and I made it up before he died."

He picked himself up and stood looking down on her.

"Yes, the day before he died we made it up," she began, but fell silent because of the beating of her heart.

Presently he broke out. "What do you mean? Tell me what you mean."

"Why, let's see, it was like this," she continued. "It was in the afternoon. Half-past two, I think. I was baking a cake for your tea. Of course that was in the old kitchen, on the other side of the house, which opened into the farmyard. Well, I looked up and saw your father standing in the doorway. I knew that meant that something strange was happening. From his coming at all, for one thing. And because he hadn't got the dogs with him. I knew that meant he'd wanted to be alone, which he hardly ever did. Those were the two greyhounds he had after Lesbia and Catullus died. How funny—how funny to think I never knew their names." This measure of how utterly she and her lover had been exiled from each other's lives filled her eyes with tears. She encouraged them, so that Richard might see them and be angry with her.

Something about his silence assured her that she had succeeded. She went on chokingly: "He said, 'Well, Marion?' I said, 'Well, Harry? Come in, if you wish to.' But I went on baking my cake. He came and stood quite close to me. There was a pile of sultanas on the table, and he helped himself to one or two. Then, all of a sudden, he said, 'Marion, I've got to have an operation, and they say I'm pretty bad. I did so want to come and see you.'"

Richard spoke in a voice as quiet as hers. "The whining cur! The snivelling cur! To come to you when he was afraid, after what he'd left you to for years."

"Oh, hush!" she prayed. "He is dead, and he was your father. Well, I took him into the other room and gave him a cup of tea, and he told me all about it. Poor Harry! He'd had a lot of pain. And dying is a dreadful thing, if you aren't old. I'm fifty, but I should be terribly frightened to die. And Harry was not much over forty. I remember him saying just like a child, 'I wonder, now, if there is another world, will it be as jolly as this?'"

"The brute! The beast! A jolly world he'd made for you!"

"Oh, Richard, don't be too hard on him. And don't you

see that he said that sort of thing because he really was like a child and didn't realise what life was, and consequently he hadn't ever had any idea what it had been like for me? Really, really he hadn't understood."

"Hadn't understood leaving you to Peacey? Mother—if I'd done that to a woman, what would you have said?"

"But, dear, of course one has a higher standard for one's son than for one's husband. One expects much more."

"Why?"

"Perhaps because one's sure of getting it." She tried to smile into his eyes and coquette with him as she had used to do. But he was like a house with shuttered windows. She trembled and went on : "Well, we talked. He asked a lot about you. Dear, you can't think what it meant to him not to have you with him. You don't care about children. I've been worried about that sometimes. But that'll come. I'm sure it will. But men like him ache for sons. If they haven't got them they feel like a mare that's missed her spring. Daughters don't matter. That's because a son's a happier thing than a daughter—there's something a little sad about women, don't you think, Richard? I suppose it's something to do with this business of having children—and men like that do so love happiness. He had coveted you most terribly when he saw you about the lanes. Truly he had. Then he said he felt tired, and he lay down on the couch. I covered him with a rug, and he had a little sleep. Then he woke up and said he must go because there was a solicitor coming at four, and he was going to settle everything so that it was all right for you and me. Then we said good-bye. And on the step he turned round and asked if I thought you would like a Sealyham pup. And I said I thought you would."

"Mother, it wasn't Punch?"

"Yes. It was Punch."

She noted the murderous gesture of his hands with bitter rapture. He had loved that dog, but now he wished he could hail it out of death so that he could send it back there cruelly. He was then capable of rooting up old affections. She was not permitted to hope for anything better.

She pretended anger. "You've taken more than a dog from him. You knew that it's his money that's made life so easy for us."

"I should have had that by right. And you should have been at Torque Hall."

The thought of what Torque Hall would have been at this

hour if he had, so full of lovely sleeping sons and daughters, made her sigh. She went on dully : " Well, that's all. He turned at the gate and waved good-bye. And the next day when you came in from school you told me he was dead." For a time she looked down into the depths of her old sorrow. When she raised her eyes, she was appalled by his harsh refusal to believe that there was any beauty in her story, and she forgot why she was telling it, and stammered out : " Richard, Richard, don't you understand ! Don't you feel about Ellen that there was a part of you that loved her long before you ever met ? It was like that with Harry and me. There was a part in each of us that loved the other long before we knew each other—and though Harry left me and I was bitter against him, it didn't matter. That part of us went on loving all the time, and making some-thing—something—— " Her hands fluttered before her ; she gasped for some image to express the high spiritual business that had been afoot, and her eyes rolled in ecstasy till they met his cold glance. " It is so ! " she cried defiantly.

The silence throbbed and was hot. She dropped her head on her hand and envied the quiet, moonlit marshes.

He shrugged his shoulders and moved towards the door. " I'm going to bed," he said.

" That's right," she agreed, and rose and began to clear the table. Uneasily he stood and watched her.

" Where does the Registrar live ? " he asked suddenly.

" The Registrar ? "

" Yes. I want to go to-morrow and put up the banns, or whatever it is one does."

" Of course, of course. Well, the registrar's named Wood-ham. He lives in the house next the school. ' Mizpah,' I think they call it. He's there only in the afternoon. Did you specially want to go to-morrow ? "

" Yes," he said. " Good-night."

When he had gone upstairs she lifted her skirts and waltzed round the table. " Surely I've earned the right to dance a little now," she thought grimly. But it was not very much fun to dance alone, so she went up to her room, shielding her eyes with her hand as she passed his door. She flung herself violently down on the bed, as if it were a well and there would be the splash of water and final peace. She had lost everything. She had lost Richard. When she had trodden on that loose board in the passage, that shut door might so easily have opened. She had lost the memory that had been the sustenance of her inmost, her most apprehensive and despairing soul. For it was the same memory now that she had spoken of it. Virtue had gone out of it. But she was too fatigued to grieve, and presently there stood by her bedside a phantom Harry, a pouting lad complaining of his own mortality. She put out her hand to him and crooned, "There, there!" and told herself she must not fidget if he were there, for the dead were used to quietness; and profound sleep covered her.

Suddenly she awoke and found herself staring towards panes exquisite with the frost's engravings, and beyond them a blue sky which made it seem that this earth was a flaw at the heart of a jewel. Words were on her lips. "Christ is risen, Christ is risen." It was something she had read in a book; she did not know why she was saying it. The clock said that it was half-past eight, so she leaped out of bed into the vibrant cold, and bathed and dressed. Her sense of ruin was like lead, but was somehow the cause of exultation in her heart as the clapper is the cause of the peal of a bell. She went and knocked on Ellen's door. There was no answer, so she stole in and stood at the end of the bed, and looked with laughter on the heap of bedclothes, the pair of unravelling plaits that were all that was to be seen of the girl.

"Ellen," she said.

The child woke up as children do, stretching and sulking. Marion loved her. She must suffice instead of the other child, the boy that should have slept in the room of the corridor in Torque Hall.

"Ellen, something wonderful has happened. Guess what it is."

Ellen lay on her back and speculated sleepily. Her little nose waggled like a rabbit's. Suddenly she shot up her head.

"I know. We've got the vote."

"Not quite as good as that. But Richard's come."

The girl sat up. "When did he come?"

"Last night."

"Last night? Would I have seen him if I'd stayed up longer?"

"No. He came very late indeed. It was really this morning."

Ellen sighed with relief. "Then the occasion's pairfect, for I've nothing to reproach myself with." She put her hand on one side and said shyly, "Please, I'd like to get up." Marion still hovered, till she noticed the girl's eyes were unhappy and that she was holding the sheet high up to the base of her white throat, and perceived that she was too modest to rise when anyone else was in the room. "How wise you are, my dear," she thought, and she left the room. "You are quite right; secrets lose their value when they are disclosed. . . ."

She went down and ate her breakfast before a long window that showed a glittering, rimy world and in the foreground a plump, strutting robin. Ordinarily she would not have been amused by his red-waisted convexity, for she regarded animals with an extreme form of that indifference she felt for all living beings who were not members of her family, but to-day she scattered it some crumbs. After that she walked to the end of the garden and looked down on the estuary's morning face. It was a silver plate on which there lay but a drop of deeply blue water, and the floating boats seemed like flies settled there to drink. The shining green marshes were neatly ruled with lines of unmelted frost that scored the unsunned westerly side of every bank, and the tiny grizzled trees and houses here and there might have been toys made of crockery, like the china cottages that stand on farmstead mantelpieces. From the chimneys above the rime-checkered slates of the harbour houses a hundred smoke-plumes stood tenuous and erect, like fastidious and honest souls, in the crystalline air. This was an undismayed world that had scoured itself cheerfully for the dawn, no matter what that might bring. She nodded her head, seeing the lesson that it read to her.

Ellen ran across the lawn to her, beetle-black in her mourning, but capering as foals do.

"I'll not have my breakfast till he does," she announced. "Is there anything I can do for him?"

"Nothing, my dear, I'm afraid. But look at the view. Isn't it lovely?"

The girl clapped her hands. "Oh, it's bonny. And it's neat. It's redded itself up for Richard's coming."

"'Redded itself up'? What does that mean?"

"Don't you use the word here? English seems to be a terribly poor language. Redding up means making everything tidy and neat, so that you're ready for anything."

That was what one must do: red oneself up. It was true that it was no use doing that for Richard any more, and that there was no one else in the world for whom she wished to be ready. But she must be schooled by the spectacle of the earth, for here it was shining fair, and yet it had nothing to expect; it was but the icing of a cake destined for some sun's swallowing.

"Is Richard a good riser?" asked Ellen, adopting a severe,

servant-engaging tone to disguise the truth that she was trembling with desire to see her lover.

" Usually, but he may be late to-day since he went to bed such a short time ago. He evidently isn't up yet, for his blind's still down. That's his room on the left."

But as they gazed the blind went up, and they saw him turning away from the window.

" Oh, why didn't he look at us ! " cried Ellen. " Why didn't he look at us ? "

" Because he is thinking of nothing but how soon he can get down to breakfast and meet you," said Marion ; but being aware of the quality of her blood, which was his, she knew that he had not seen his women and the glittering world because he had risen blind with sullenness.

" Will he be long, do you think ? " she pondered. " Not that I'd want him to miss his bath." She broke into a kind of Highland fling, looking down on the blue and silver estuary and chanting, " Lovely, lovely," but desisted suddenly and asked : " Mrs. Yaverland, do you think there's a future life ? "

Marion said lazily, " I shouldn't have thought you need to think out that problem yet awhile."

" Oh, I'm not worrying for myself. But on a fine day like this I just hate to think my mother's not getting the benefit of it somewhere. And seeing your age, I thought you might have begun to give the matter consideration."

Marion resolved to treasure that remark for repetition to Richard ; and was dashed to remember that it was probable in future they would not share their jokes. " Well, I don't think there's any evidence for it at all," she said aloud ; " but I don't think that proves that there isn't one. I don't think we would be allowed to know if there was one, for I'm sure that if most people knew for certain there was going to be another world they wouldn't make the best of this." But she saw, from the way that Ellen continued to stare down at her toes, that that abstract comfort had not been of any service, so she parted with yet another secret. " But I do know that when Richard's father died all the trees round the house seemed to know where he had gone."

Ellen raised wet but happier eyes. " Why, I felt like that when they brought mother's coffin out of the Fever Hospital. Only then it was the hills in the distance that knew—the Pentland Hills. But do you really think that was true ? "

" I knew it was then," said Marion. " If I am less certain now it is only because I have forgotten."

They nodded wisely. " After all, there must be something."
" Yes, there must be something. . . ."

Ellen began to dance again. Marion turned aside and tried
to lose the profound malaise that the reticent feel when they
have given up a secret in thinking how well worth while it had
been, since Ellen was such a dear, young, loving thing. She
found consolation in this frost-polished morning : the pale, bright
sky in which the light stood naked, her abandoned veil of clouds
floating above the horizon ; the swoop and dance over the
marshes of the dazzling specks that were seagulls ; the fur of
rime that the dead leaves on the hedgerow wore, and the fine
jewellery-work of the glistening grass tufts in its shadow. The
world had neglected nothing in its redding up.

At her elbow Ellen spoke shyly. " Richard's come down at
last. May I go in to him, Mrs. Yaverland ? "

" Of course you may. You can do anything you like. From
now onwards he's yours, not mine."

Ellen ran in and Richard came to the window to meet her.
As he drew her over the threshold by both hands he called
down the garden, " Good morning, mother." But Marion had
perceived that from the moment of seeing her his face had
worn the dark colour of estrangement. She turned and walked
blindly away, not noticing that Mabel had come out to bring
her the morning post, and was following at her heels, till the girl
coughed.

There were four letters. She opened them with avidity,
for they were certificates that there were other things in life as
well as Richard with which she could occupy herself. Two were
bills, the first from her dressmakers and the other from the
dealer who had sold her some coloured glass a few weeks before ;
and there was a dividend warrant for her to sign and send to her
bankers. Sweeping about the lawn as on a stage, she resolved
to buy clothes that would make her look like other untormented
women, and more hangings and pictures and vases to make her
house look gay. Then she observed that the fourth envelope
was addressed in the handwriting of the son whom she could
not love.

She looked towards the house and saw the son whom she loved,
but he did not see her. Ellen's red head was close to his shoulder.

It was horrible handwriting outside and inside the envelope :
a weak running of ink that sagged downwards in the second half
of every line and added feeble flourishes to every capital that
gave the whole an air of insincerity. It had the disgusting
appearance of a begging letter, and indeed that was what it was.

It begged for love, for condonation of the writer's loathsomeness. She held it far off as she read :

"DEAR MOTHER,
          "You will be wondering why I had not written to you. You will know soon that something you would not have expected has happened to me. I am not sure how you will take it. But I will be with you in two days, and then you will see for yourself. I hope you will not harden your heart against me, dear mother.
                                   "Your loving son,
                                             "ROGER."

There was no address, but the postmark was Chelmsford. No doubt he had written in the cells. For the letter could have no other meaning but that the disgrace she had foreseen had at last arrived.

She could not bear to be out there alone on that wide lawn, in the bright light, in the intense cold. She ran to the window, and not daring to look in lest they should be very close together, she called, "Richard, Roger is coming."

There was a noise of a chair being pushed back, and Richard stood over her, asking : "When ? Has he written ? "

She held out the letter.

There was the rustling of paper crushed in the hand, and she looked up into his burning and compassionate eyes. Her head dropped back on her throat ; she grew weak with happiness. He was her own once more, if she would but disclose in what great fear and misery she stood. But in the room behind there sounded the chink of china. Little Ellen was bending over the table, putting the tea-cosy over Richard's egg.

Marion said levelly : "Well, I shall be glad of Roger's company while you're occupied with Ellen." She added reprovingly, as if she were speaking to a child : "You mustn't be jealous of the poor thing. I saw last night that you can be jealous. . . ."

His eyes blazed at the indecency. He stepped back from the window.

CHAPTER VIII

ELLEN was very glad that Marion was going out for the whole of the afternoon, for then she would be alone with Richard; and though they had been out together all the morning, there had been that in the atmosphere which made a third. The whole time it had been apparent that the coming of this Roger, who must be an awful man, was upsetting him terribly. When he had taken her out into the garden after breakfast he had looked up into the vault of the morning and had put his hand to his head, making a sound of envy, as if he felt a contrast between its crystal quality and his own state of mind. He had liked standing with her at the edge of the garden and setting names to the facets of the landscape, which he plainly loved as he had never told her that he did. He really cared for the estuary as she did for the Pentlands; she need never be afraid of telling him anything that she felt, for it had always turned out that he felt something just like it. But that pleasure had not lasted long. He had shown her the gap where the Medway found its way among the low hills on the Kentish coast, and had told her that the golden filaments the sunlight discovered over the water were the masts and funnels of great ships, and he was pointing westward to the black gunpowder hulks that lay off Kerith Island, when his forefinger dropped. Something in the orchard below had waylaid his attention. Ellen looked down the steep bank to see what it was, and saw Marion sitting in the low crook of an apple-tree. She snatched at contemptuous notice of the way that the tail of the woman's gown, which anyway was far too good for any sensible person to wear just going about the house and garden in the morning, was lying in a patch of undispersed frost; but fear re-entered her heart. Marion was sitting quite still with her back to them, yet the distant view of her held the same terrifying quality of excess as her near presence. There could be no more looking at this brilliant and candid face of the

355

earth, because there was not anywhere so much force as in this squat, stubborn body, clayish with middle-age.

Richard said: "No, she isn't crying. She isn't moving. I should feel a fool if I went down and she didn't want me." And because his voice was thin and husky like a nervous child's, and because he was answering a question that she had not asked, Ellen was more afraid. This woman was throwing over them a net of events as excessive as herself. . . .

But these were only the things that one thought about life. As soon as one stopped thinking about them they ceased to be. The world was not really tragic. When he drew her back to the middle of the lawn where they could not see Marion she was happy again, and hoped for pleasure, and asked him if it were not possible to go boating on the estuary even now, since the water looked so smooth. He answered that winter boating was possible and had its own beauty, and told her, with an appreciation that she had to concede was touched with frenzy in its emphasis, but which she welcomed because it was an escape from worry, of a row he had had one late December afternoon. He spoke of finding his way among white oily creeks that wound among gleaming ebony mud-banks over which showed the summits of the distant hills that had been skeletonised by a thin snowfall ; and of icy air that was made glamorous as one had thought only warmth could be by the blended lights of the red sun on his left and the primrose moon on the right. She leaped for joy at that, and asked him to take her on the water soon, and he told her if she liked he would take her down to Prittlebay and show her his motor-boat which was lying up in the boat-house of the Thamesmouth Yacht Club there.

Their ambulations had brought them to the orchard gate again, but he turned on his heel and said, with what struck her as a curious abandonment of the languor by which he usually asserted to the world that he refused to hurry, " Go and put on your hat and we'll start at once." So they went out and hastened through the buoyant air down to the harbour and along the cinder-track to Prittle-bay esplanade, where she forgot everything in astonishment at the new, bright, arbitrary scene. There was what seemed to her, a citizen of Edinburgh, a comically unhistoric air about the place. The gaily-coloured rows of neat dwellings that debouched on the esplanade, and the line of hotels and boarding-houses that faced the sea, were as new as the pantomime songs of last Christmas or this year's slang. One might conceive them being designed by architects who knew as little of the past as children

know of death, and painted by fresh-faced people to match themselves, and there was a romping arbitrariness about the design
and decoration of the place which struck the same note of
innocence.

The town council who passed the plans for the
Byzantine shoulder the esplanade thrust out on to the sand on
the slender provocation of a bandstand, the man who had built
his hotel with a roof covered with cupolas and minarets and had
called it "Westward Ho!" must, Ellen thought, be lovely
people, like Shakespearean fools. She liked it, too, when they
came to the vulgarer part of the town and the place assumed
the strange ceremented air that a pleasure city wears in winter.
The houses had fallen back, and the esplanade was overhung now
by a steep green slope on which asphalt walks linked shelters,
in which no one sat, and wandered among brown and purple
congregations of bare trees, at its base were scattered wooden
chalets and bungalows, which offered to take the passer-by's
photograph or to sell ice-cream. The sea-salt in the air had
licked off the surface of the paint, so that they had a greyish,
spectral appearance. The photographs in the cracked show-
cases were brown and vaporous, and the announcements of
vanilla ice-cream were but breaths of lettering, blown on stained
walls. It seemed a place for the pleasuring of mild, unexigent
phantoms, no doubt the ghosts of the simple people who lived
in the other part of the town.

She was amused by it all, and was really sorry when
they came to the Thamesmouth Yacht Club, a bungalow
glossy with new paint which looked very opaque among the
phantasmic buildings. With its verandah, that was polished like
a deck, and its spotless life-belts and brilliant port-hole windows,
it had the air of a ship which had been exiled to land but
was trying to bear up ; and so, too, had the three old captains,
spruce little men, with sea-reflecting eyes and pointed, grizzled
beards, whom Richard brought out of the club after he had got
the boathouse keys. Ellen liked them very much indeed. She
had never before had any chance of seeing the beautiful and
generous emotion that old men who have lived bravely feel for
young men whom they see carrying on the tradition of brave
life, and it made her want to cry to see how crowsfeet of pleasure
came at the corners of their eyes when they looked at Richard,
and how they liked to slap his strong back with their rough
hands, which age was making delicate with filigree of veins and
wrinkles. And she could see, too, that they liked her. They
looked at her as if they thought she was pretty, and teased her

about the Votes-for-Women button she was wearing, but quite nicely.

When they were standing under the dark eaves of the boathouse, looking up at the gleaming tawny sides of the motor-launch, one of the old men pointed at the golden letters that spelt " Gwendolen " at the prow, and said, " Well, Yaverland, I suppose you'll have forgotten who she is these days." Another added : " He'd better, if he's going to marry a Suffragette." And all broke into clear, frosty laughter. She cried out in protest, and told them that Suffragettes were not really fierce at all, and that the newspapers just told a lot of lies about them, and that anyway it was only old-fashioned women who were jealous, and they listened with smiling, benevolent deference, which she enjoyed until her eyes lighted on Richard, and she saw that he was more absorbed in her effect on his friends than in herself.

For a moment she felt as lonely as she had been before she knew him, and she looked towards the boat and stared at the reflection of the group in the polished side and wished that one of the dim, featureless shapes she saw there had been her mother, or anyone who had had a part in her old life in Edinburgh. She turned back to the men and brought the conversation to an end with a little laughing shake of the head, giving them the present of an aspect of her beauty to induce them to let her mind go free. Again she felt something that her common-sense forbade to be quite fear when he did not notice for a minute that she was wistfully asking him to take her away. It was all right, of course.

When they had said good-bye to the happy old men and were walking along the promenade, he asked : " What was the matter, darling ? Didn't you like them ? They're really very good old sorts " ; and understood perfectly when she answered : " I know they are, but I don't want anybody but you." There was indeed vehemence in his reply : " Yes, dear, we don't want anybody but ourselves, do we ? " Undoubtedly there was a change in the nature of the attention he was giving her. Instead of concentrating in that steady delighted survey of herself to which she was accustomed, he alternated between an almost excessive interest in what she was saying and complete abstraction, during which he would turn suddenly aside and drive his stick through the ice on the little pools at the sagging outside edge of the promenade, his mouth contracting as if he really hated it. She hovered meekly by while he did that. If one went to see a dear friend, whose charm and pride it was to live in an exquisitely neat and polished home, and found him pacing hot-eyed through rooms given up to dirt and disorder, one would not rebuke him, but one would wait quietly and soothingly until he desired to tell what convulsion of his life explained the abandonment of old habit. But her eyes travelled to the luminous, snow-sugared hills that ran by the sea to the summit where Roothing Church, an evanescent tower of hazily-irradiated greyness, overhung the shining harbour ; and her thoughts travelled further to the hills hidden behind that point, and that orchard where there sat the squat woman who was so much darker and denser in substance than anything else in the glittering, brittle world around her.

Ellen drooped her head and closed her eyes ; the crackle of the ice under Richard's stick sounded like the noise of some damage done within herself. She found some consolation in the thought that people were always more moderate than the pictures she made of them in their absence, but she lost it when she went back into the high, white, view-invaded dining-room at Yaverland's End. For Marion stood by the hearth looking down into the fire, and as Richard and Ellen came in she turned an impassive face towards them, and asked indifferently, "Have you had a nice walk ? " and fell to polishing her nails with the palm of her hand with that trivial, fribbling gesture that was somehow more desperate than any other being's outflung arms. She was all that Ellen had remembered, and more. And she had infected the destiny of this house with her strangeness even to such small matters as the peace of the midday meal. For Mabel came in before they had finished the roast mutton, and said : " Please, ma'am, there's a man wanting to see you." And Marion asked, with that slightly disagreeable tone which Ellen had noticed always coloured her voice when she spoke to the girl : " Who is he ? " Mabel answered contemptuously : " He won't give his name. He's a very poor person, ma'am. His boots is right through, and his coat's half off his back. And he says that if he told you his name you mightn't see him. Shall I tell him to go away ? "

But Marion had started violently. Her eyes were looking into Richard's. She said, calmly : " Yes, I'll see him. Tell him I'll come through in a minute."

Mabel had left the room. Marion and Richard continued to stare at each other queerly.

She murmured indistinctly, casually : " It may be. Both Mabel and cook haven't been with me long. They never saw him here. They probably haven't seen him since he was a boy."

" It is the kind of thing," said Richard grimly, " that Roger would say at the back door to a servant just to make his arrival seem natural and unsuspicious."

Marion's head drooped far back on her throat ; her broad, dark face suffused with the bloom of kind, sad passion, and lifted towards her son's pitying eyes, made Ellen think of a pansy bending back under the rain. But her mouth, which had been a little open and appealing, as if she were asking Richard not to be bitter but to go on being pitiful, closed suddenly and smiled. She seemed to will and to achieve some hardening change of substance. An incomprehensible expression irradiated her face, and she seemed to be brooding sensuously on some private hoard of satisfaction. Lightly she rose, patting the hand Richard had stretched out to her as if it were a child's, and went out into the kitchen.

" Richard ! " breathed Ellen.

He went on eating.

" Richard," she insisted, " why did she look like that ? So happy. Does she want it to be Roger ? "

" God knows, God knows," he said in a cold, sharp-edged voice. " There are lots of things about her that I don't understand."

Some moments passed before Marion came back. Her face was easy, and she said placidly : " My purse, my purse. I want my purse."

" It's on the desk," said Richard, and rose and found it for her. He stood beside her as she opened it and began taking out the money slowly, coin by coin, while she hummed under her breath. " Mother ! " he burst out suddenly. " Who is it ? "

" A ten-shilling piece is what I want," she murmured. " Yes, a ten-shilling piece. I thought I had one. . . . Oh, who is it ? Oh, it's Henry Milford. Do you remember poor Milford ? He was the last cattleman but one in the old days when we ran the farm. I had to send him away because he drank so terribly. Since then he's gone down and down, and now he's on the road. I must give him something, poor creature. Such a nice wife he had—he says she's in Chelmsford workhouse. I'll send him on to old Dawkins at Dane End ; I'll get him to give the poor wretch a few days' work."

Ellen disliked her as she left the room. She looked thick and ordinary, and was apparently absorbed in the mildly gross satisfaction of a well-to-do woman at being bountiful. Moreover, she had in some way hurt Richard, for his face was dark when he came back to the table.

But an amazement struck Ellen as she thought over the scene. "Richard," she exclaimed excitedly, "is it not just wonderful that this man should come to your mother for help after she'd put him to the door ? I'm sure she'd make a body feel just dirt if she was putting them to the door. It would be a quiet affair, but awful uncomfortable. But she's such a good woman that, even seeing her like that, he knew she was the one to come to when he was really in trouble. Do you not think it's like that ? "

"Oh yes," he almost groaned. "Even when she's at her worst you know that she's still better than anyone else on this earth."

When Marion came back she sat down at the table without noticing what seemed to Ellen his obvious dejection, and began to talk about this man Milford, telling of the power he had over his beasts and how a prize heifer that they then had, by the name of Susan Caraway, had fretted for three weeks after he had left. She said that he gained this power over animals not by any real love for them, for he was indifferent to them except when he was actually touching them, and would always scamp his work without regard for their comfort, but simply by some physical magnetism, and pointed out that there it resembled the power some men have over women. It surprised Ellen that she laughed as she said that, and seemed to find pleasure in the thought of such a power. When the meal was over she sat for a moment, gathering together the breadcrumbs by her plate, and said pensively : "Yes, it might quite easily have been Roger." Ellen wondered how it was that Richard had always spoken of his mother as if she needed his protection, when her voice was so nearly coarse with the sense of being able to outface all encounterable events, and she felt a flash of contempt for his judgment. She wished, too, that when Marion rose from the table he had not followed her so closely upstairs and hovered round her as she took up her stand on the hearthrug, with her elbow on the mantelpiece and her foot in the fender, and kept his eyes on her face as she settled down in an armchair. It was just making himself cheap, dangling after a woman who was perched up on herself like a weathercock.

When she said, " I'm going to walk over to Friar's End. Old Butterworth wants me to do some repairs which I don't feel inclined to do, so I want to have a look at the place for myself," the announcement was so little tinged by any sense of the persons she was addressing that she might as well have held up a printed placard. Ellen thought he was a little abject to answer, " So far as I can remember, Butterworth's rather a rough specimen.

Wouldn't you like us to come with you ? " and almost deserved
that she did not hear. Such deafness argued complete abstraction ; and indeed, as she turned towards them and stood looking
out towards the river, her face again wore that incomprehensible
expression of secret and even furtive satisfaction. The sight
of it fell like a whip on Richard. He lowered his head and sat
staring at the floor. Ellen cried out to herself, " She's an aggravating woman if ever there was one. It's every bit as bad as
not saying what you feel, this not saying what you look," and
tried to pierce with her eyes the dreamy surface of this gloating.
But she could make nothing of it, and looked back at Richard ;
and shuddered and drew her hands across her eyes when she saw
that he had lifted his head and was turning towards her a face
that had become the mirror of his mother's expression. He,
too, was wrapped in some exquisite and contraband contentment.
She raised her brows in enquiry, and mockingly he whispered
back words which he knew she could not hear.

   " I think I'll go now," said Marion, from her detachment,
and left them. Ellen stretched out her arms above her head
and cried shudderingly ＄ " Why are you looking at me like that ? "
But he would not answer, and began to laugh quietly. " Tell
me ! " she begged, but still he kept silence, and seemed to be
fingering with his mind this pleasure that he knew of but would
not disclose. It struck her as another example of Marion's
dominion over the house that her expression should linger in
this room after she had left it and that it should blot out the
son's habitual splendid look, and she exclaimed sobbingly : " Oh,
very well, be a Cheshire cat if you feel called to it," and went
and pretended to look for a volume in the bookcase. It was
annoying that he did not come after her at once and try to comfort
her, but he made no move from his seat until there sounded
through the house the thud of the closing front door.

   She saw, a second after that, the reflection of his face gleaming
above the shoulder of her own image in the glass door of the
bookcase, and was at first pleased and waited delightfully for
reconciling kisses ; but because the brightness of its gleam
told her that he was still smiling, she wished again, as she had
that morning when she had stood beside the smooth, sherry-
coloured boat, that among the dim shapes of the mirrored world
might be one that was her mother. She knew that it was too
much to ask of this inelastic universe that she should ever see
her mother again in this world, standing, as she had lived, looking
like a brave little bird bearing up through a bad winter but could
not understand how God could ever have thought of anything

as cruel as snow. "And quite right too," she said to herself. " If there were ghosts we would spend all our time gaping for a sight of the dead, and we'd not do our duty by the living. But surely there'd be no harm just for once, when I'm so put about with this strange house, in letting me see in the glass just the outline of her wee head on her wee shoulders. . . ." But there was nothing. She sobbed and caught at Richard's hands, and was instantly reassured. For the hand is truer to the soul than the face : it has no moods, it borrows no expressions, and she read the Richard that she knew and loved in these long fingers, stained by his skeely trade and scored with cuts commemorative of adventure and bronzed with golden weather, and the broad knuckles that were hollowed between the bones as usually only frail hands are, just as his strong character was fissured by reserve and fastidiousness and all the delicacies that one does not expect to find in the robust. " You've got grand hands ! " she cried, and kissed them. But he wrested them away from her and closed them gently over her wrists, and forced her backwards towards the hearth, keeping his body close to her and shuffling his feet in a kind of dance. She was astonished that she should not like anything that he did to her, and felt she must be being stupid and not understanding, and submitted to him with nervous alacrity when he sat down in the armchair and drew her on to his knee and began to kiss her.

But she did not like it at all. For his face wore the rapt and vain expression of a man who is performing some complicated technical process which he knows to be beyond the powers of most other people, and she had a feeling that he was not thinking of her at all. That was absurd, of course, for he was holding her in his arms, and whispering her name over and over again, and pressing his mouth down on hers, and she told herself that she was being tiresome and pernickety like the worst kind of grown-up, and urged herself to lend him a hand in this business of love-making. But she could not help noticing that these were the poorest kisses he had ever given her. Each one was separate, and all were impotent to constrain the mind to thoughts of love ; between them she found herself thinking clearly of such irrelevancies as the bare, bright-coloured, inordinate order of the room and the excessive view of tides and flatlands behind the polished window-panes. The kisses had their beauty, of course, for it was Richard who was giving them, but it was the perishing and trivial beauty of cut flowers, whereas those that he gave her commonly had been strongly and enduringly beautiful like trees.

Always when he took her in his arms and she lifted her mouth to his it was like going into a wood, or, rather, creating a wood. For at first there was darkness, since one closed one's eyes when one kissed as when one prayed ; and then it seemed as if at each kiss they were being a tree, for their bodies were pressed close together like a tree-trunk, and their trembling, gripping arms were like branches, and their faces where love lived on their lips were like the core of foliage where the birds nest. She would see springing up in the darkness around her the grove of the trees that their kisses had created : the silver birches that were their delicate, unclinging kisses ; the sturdy elms that were their kisses when they loved robustly and thought of a home together ; the white-boled beeches with foliage of green fire that they were when they loved most intensely. But to-day they did not seem to be making anything ; he was simply moving his lips over her skin as a doctor moves his stethoscope over his patient's chest. And, like the doctor, he sometimes hurt her. She hated it when he kissed her throat, and was glad when he thought of something he wanted to say and stopped.

"Next time I go to London," he said, "I'm going to buy you a jade necklace, or malachite if I can get it. The green will look so good against your white, white skin."

"That's verra kind of you, but the money may as well lie by," she told him wisely, "for I couldn't go wearing a green necklace when I'm in mourning."

"But you won't be in mourning much longer."

"Six months in full mourning, six months half. That's as it should be for a mother."

"But what nonsense ! " he exclaimed irascibly. "When you're a young little thing you ought to be wearing pretty clothes. It doesn't do your mother any good, your going about in black."

"I know well it doesn't, but, remember, mother was old-fashioned Scotch, and she was most particular about having things just so. Specially on melancholy occasions. I remember she was most pernickety about her blacks after my father's death. And though she's entered into eternal life, we've no guarantee that that makes a body sensible all at once." She saw on his face an expression which reminded her that he had been careful never to acquiesce when she spoke of the possibility of a future life, and she cried out : "You needn't look so clever. I'm sure she's going on somewhere, and why you should grudge it to the poor woman I don't know. And your mother thinks

there's something after death, too. She told me this morning
in the garden that she was quite certain of it when your father
died. She said that all the trees round the house seemed to
know where he had gone."

" Oh, she said that, did she ? " His arms released her. He
stared into her face. " She said that, did she ? " he repeated in
an absent, faintly malevolent murmur ; and clasped her in his
arms again and kissed her so cruelly that her lips began to
bleed.

" Let me go, let me go ! " she cried. " You're not loving
me, you're just taking exercise on me ! "

He let her go, but not, she knew from the smile on his face,
from any kindness, but rather that he might better observe her
distress and gloat over it. She moved away from the heat of
the fire and from that other heat which had so strangely been
engendered by these contacts which always before engendered
light, and went to the window and laid her forehead against the
cold glass. The day had changed and lost its smile, for the sky
was hidden by a dirty quilt of rain-charged clouds and the frost
had seeped into the marshes and left them dark, acid winter green,
yet she longed to walk out there in that unsunned and waterlogged country, opening her coat to the cold wind brought by the
grey, invading tides, making little cold pools where she dug her
heels into the sodden ground, getting rid of her sense of inflamma-
tion, and being quite alone. That she should want not to be
with Richard, and that she should not be perfectly pleased with
what pleased him, seemed to her monstrous disloyalty, and she
turned and smiled at him. But there was really something
wrong with this room and this hour, for as she looked at him she
felt frightened and ashamed, as if he were drunk, though she knew
that he was sober ; and indeed his face was flushed and his eyes
wet and winking, as if smoke had blown in them. For some
reason that she could not understand he reminded her of Mr.
Philip.

She cried out imploringly. " Take me down to the marshes,
Richard ! "

He shook his head and laughed at some private joke. She
felt desolate, like a child at school whom other children shut out
from their secrets, and drooped her head ; and heard him say
presently : " We are going out this afternoon, but not on the
marshes."

" Where ? "

He was overcome with silent laughter when she stamped
because he would not answer. She ran over to him and began

to slap him, trying to make a game of it to cover her near approach to tears. Then he told her, not because he was concerned with her distress, but because her touch seemed to put him in a good humour. " We're going to the registrar, my dear, to fix up everything for our marriage in three weeks' time."

The sense of what he had said did not reach her, because she was gazing at him to try and find out why he was still reminding her of Mr. Philip. He was, for one thing, wearing an expression that would have been more suitable to a smaller man. Oh, he was terribly different to-day ! His eyes, whose wide stare had always worked on her like a spell, were narrow and glittering, and his lips looked full. She screamed " Oh, no ! Oh, no ! " without, for a second, thinking against what thing she was crying out.

He laughed and pulled her down on his knees. He was laughing more than she had ever known him laugh before. " Why, don't you want to, you little thing ? "

Her thoughts wandered about the world as she knew it, looking for some reason. But nothing came to her save the memory of the cold, wet, unargumentative cry of the redshanks that she had heard on the marshes. She said feebly, as one who asks for water : " Please, please take me down to the sea-wall."

His voice swooped resolutely down with tenderness. " But why don't you want to come and see about our marriage ? Are you frightened, dear ? "

Now, strangely enough, he was reminding her of Mr. Mactavish James, as he used to be in those long conversations when he seemed so kind, and said : " Nellie, ma wee lassie, dis onything ail ye ? " and yet left her with a suspicion that he had been asking her all the time out of curiosity and not because he really cared for her. She was dizzied. Whoever was speaking to her, it was not Richard. She muttered : " Yes, a little."

He pressed her closer to him, covering her with this tenderness as with a hot cloth rug, heavy and not fine. " Frightened of me, my darling ? "

She pulled herself off his knee. " I don't know, I don't know."

" Why ? Why ? "

She moved into the middle of the room and looked down on the sea and the flatlands with a feeling like thirst ; and turned loyally back to Richard, who was standing silently on the hearthrug watching her. The immobility of his body, and the indication in his flickering eyes and twitching mouth that, within his quietness, his soul was dancing madly because of some thought

of her, recalled to her the night when Mr. Philip had stood by
the fire in the office in Edinburgh. That man had hated her and
this one loved her, but the difference in their aspects was not so
great as she would have hoped. She could bear it no longer, and
screamed out : "Oh! Oh! That's how Mr. Philip looked?"

It took him a minute to remember who she meant. Then
his face shadowed. "Don't remind me of him, for God's sake!"
he said through his teeth. "Go and put on your things and
come out with me to the registrar."

She drew backwards from him and stood silent till she could
master her trembling He was very like Mr. Philip. Softly
she said : "You sounded awful, as if you were telling me."

"I was."

She began to want to cry. "I'll do nothing that I'm told."

He made a clicking noise of disgust in his throat. It struck
her as a mark of debasement that their bodies were moving more
swiftly than their minds, and that each time they spoke they
first gesticulated or made some wordless sound. He burst out,
more loudly than she had ever heard him before : "Go and put
on your things."

"Away yourself to the registrar," she cried more loudly
still, "and tell him he'll never marry you to me."

The ringing of her own voice and his answering clamour
recalled something to her that was dyed with a sunset light and
yet was horrible. She drew her hands across her face and tried
to remember what it was ; and found herself walking in memory
along a street in Edinburgh towards a sunset which patterned
the west with sweeping lines of little golden feathers as if some
vain angel, forbidden to peacock it in heaven, had come to show
his wings to earth. On the other side, turned to the colour of a
Gloire de Dijon rose, towered the height of the MacEwan Hall,
that Byzantine pile which she always thought had an air as if
it were remembering beautiful music that had been played
within it at so many concerts ; and at its base staggered a
quarrelling man and woman. The woman was not young and
wore a man's cloth cap and a full, long, filthy skirt. They were
moving sideways along the empty pavement about a yard apart,
facing one another, shouting and making threatening gestures
across the gap. At last they stopped, put their drink-ulcerated
faces close together, and vomited coarse cries at one another;
and she had looked up at the pale golden stone that was remembering music, and at the bright golden sky that was promising that
there was more than terrestrial music, as one might look at well-
bred friends after some boor had stained some pleasant occasion

with his ill manners. Then she had been sixteen. Now she was seventeen, and she and a man were shouting across a space. Could it be that vileness was not a state which one could choose or refuse to enter, but a phase through which, being human, one must pass? If that were so, life was too horrible. She cried out through his vehemence: "No, I'm not going to marry you."

"Don't be stupid. You're being exactly like all other women, silly and capricious. Go and put your things on."

"I will not. I'm going away."

"Don't talk nonsense! Where are you going?"

"Back to Edinburgh." She made a hard line of her trembling mouth. "My mind's made up."

He made a sound that expressed pure exasperation untouched with tenderness, and his eyes darted about her face in avaricious appraisement of this property that was trying to detach itself from him with a display of free will that might not be tolerated in property. She could see him resolving to take it lightly, and thought to herself: "Maybe it's just as well that it's to be broken off, for I doubt I'm too clever for marriage. I would read him like a book and, considering what's in him" —a convulsion of rage shook her—"he'd be annoyed at that."

He had been saying with deliberate flippancy: "Oh, you silly little Ellen," but at that convulsion a change came over him. Delight transfigured him. He jerked his head back as she had done, as if he would like to continue the violent rhythm of her movement through his own body, and blood and laughter rushed back to his face. Taking a step towards her, he called softly: "Oh, my Ellen, don't let us quarrel! Come here."

But she remembered then how that scene at the base of the golden stone had ended. The pair had swung apart and had staggered their several ways, shrieking over their shoulders; and had suddenly pivoted round and stood looking at each other in silence. Then they had run together and joined in a rocking embrace, a rubbing of their bodies, and had put their mouths to each other's faces so munchingly that it had looked as if they must turn aside some time and spit out the cores of their kisses. She would have no such reconciliation. "I won't! I tell you I hate you!" she cried, and escaped his arm.

Rage came into his face without displacing his intention to make love to her. That was against nature, unless nature was utterly perverse! She could not bear it. She struck him across the mouth and ran out of the room.

There was a moment of confusion on the landing when she could not tell which of the white doors on the right and left led into her bedroom. The first one she opened showed her a table piled with heavy books ; a vast wardrobe with glass doors showing a line of dresses coloured like autumn and of fabrics so exquisite that they might be imagined sentient ; under a shelf beneath it a long straight line, regular as the border plants in a parterre, of glossy wooden shoe-trees rising out of rather large shoes made from many kinds of leather and velvets and satins ; and in the carpets and the hangings a profound and vibrant blue. Accusingly she exclaimed into the emptiness, "Marion ! " and darted into her own room just as Richard burst out into the passage. She flung herself on the bed and lay quite still while he knocked on the door. Twice he called her name. Nothing in her desired to answer. That was both relief and the loss of all. Three times again he knocked, and there penetrated through the panels one of those wordless noises that had been disgusting her all the afternoon. After a moment's silence she heard him go downstairs. She leaped up and dragged her trunk from a corner into the middle of the room, but instead of beginning to pack she fell on her knees and wept on to the comfortingly cool and smooth black surface.

"I did so mean to be happy when I got among the English," she sobbed. "I thought England was a light-minded, cheerful kind of place. But I'll just go back to Edinburgh." She jumped up and went to the wardrobe and looked at her dresses hanging there, and cried : "It'll waste them terribly if I pack them without tissue paper, and I can't ring with my face in this pickle." There was not even a newspaper by to stuff into her shoes. Suddenly she wanted her mother, who had always packed and found things for her and who had been so very female, so completely guiltless of this excess of blood that was maleness. It would be dreadful to go back to Edinburgh and find no mother ; and it would be dreadful to leave Richard. The light of reason showed that as a necessary and noble journey towards economic and spiritual independence it somehow proved her, she felt, worthy of having a vote. But her flesh, which she curiously felt to be more in touch with her soul than was her mind, was appalled by her intention. It would be an unnatural flight. What had been between Richard and herself had mingled them in some real way, so that if she went back and lived without him she would be crippled, and that, too, in a real way : so real that she would suffer pain from it every day until she died, and that children would notice it and laugh at it when she got to be old and walked rusty and unmarried about the town.

Yet she could not stay here now when she had seen Richard red and glazed and like those wranglers in the street, and not pale and fine-grained and more splendid and deliberate than kings., She could not tell what her life might come to if she trusted it into the sweaty hands of this man whom, as it turned out, she did not know. Which of these horrid paths to disappointment must she tread? In her brooding she stared at her face in the glass which Marion had bought for her and noted how inappropriate the sad image was to the gay green and gold wood that framed it. It struck her how typical it was of Marion that the gaiety of a gift from her should, a day after the giving, become a wounding irony, and she was overwhelmed by a double hatred of this home and what had just happened to her in it.

She flung herself again on the bed and tried to lose herself in weeping, but had to see before her mind's eye the gorgeous seaworthy galleon that her love had been till this last hour. It seemed impossible that a vessel that had so proudly left the harbour could already have foundered. Hope freshened her whole body, till she remembered how the galleon of her mother's hopes had been wrecked and had sunk in as many fathoms as the full depth of misfortune. Certainly there were those who died God's creditors, and she had no reason to suppose she was not one of them.

She was lying with her face to the window, and it occurred to her that it was the plethora of light let in by that prodigious square of glass which was making her think and think and think. That the device of a dead Yaverland's spite against his contemporaries should work on the victim of a living Yaverland gave her a shuddering sense of the power of this family. She rolled over and covered her head with the quilt and wept and wept, until she fell asleep.

It was the slow turning of the doorhandle that woke her. Instantly she remembered the huge extent to which life had gone wrong during the past few hours, and rolled back to face the window, which was now admitting a light grown grave with the lateness of the afternoon. It might be that it was Richard who was coming into her room to say that he did not want to marry her either; or Marion, who would be quiet and kind, and yet terrifying as if she carried a naked sword; or one of those superior-looking maids to tell her that tea was ready. She lay and waited. Her heart opened and closed because these were Richard's steps that were crossing the room, and they were slow. They were more—they were shy. And when they paused

at the foot of the bed his deep sigh was the very voice of penitence. She shot up out of her pretence of sleep and sat staring
at him. Tears gushed out of her eyes, yet her singing heart knew
there was nothing more irrelevant to life than tears. For he was
pale again and fine-grained, and though he stood vast above her
he was pitiful as a child. She stretched out her arms and
cried: "Oh, you poor thing! Come away! Come close to
me!"

But he did not. He came slowly round to the side of the
bed and knelt down, and began to pick at the hem of the counterpane, turning his face from her. She was aware that she was
witnessing the masculine equivalent of weeping, and let him be,
keeping up a little stream of tender words and sometimes brushing
his tense, unhappy hands with faint kisses.

"Forgive me," he muttered painfully at last. "I was a
brute—oh, such a brute. Do, do forgive me."

"Yes, yes," she soothed. "Never heed. I knew you didn't
mean it."

"Oh, I was foul," he groaned, and turned his head away
again.

"But don't grieve so over it, darling; it's over now," she
said softly, and took his face between her hands and kissed it.
Its bronze beauty and the memory that she had struck it pierced
her, and she cried, "Oh, my love, say I didn't hurt you when
I hit you!"

He broke into anguished laughter. "No, you wee little
thing!" He strained her to him and faltered vehemently:
"You generous dear! When I've insulted and bullied you and
shouted at you, you ask me if you've hurt me! I wish you had.
It would have given me some of the punishment I deserve.
Oh, keep me, you wonderful, strong, forgiving dear! Keep me
from being a hound, keep me from forgetting—whatever it is
we've found out. You've seen what I'm like when I've forgotten
it. Oh, love me! Love me!"

"I will, I will!"

They clung together and spent themselves in reconciling
kisses.

"It was my fault, too," she whispered. "I was awful
hard on you. And maybe I took you up too quick."

"No, it was all my fault," he answered softly. "I was
worried and I lost my head."

"Worried? What are you worried about, my darling?
You never told me that."

"Oh, there's nothing to tell, really. It's not a definite

worry. It's to do "—his dark eyes left her and travelled among the gathering shadows of the room—" with my mother."

If he had kissed her now he would not have found her lips so soft. " Your mother ? " she repeated.

" Yes," he said petulantly. It struck her that there was something infantile about his tone, a shade of resentment much as a child might feel against its nurse. " She's been the centre of my whole life. And now . . . I don't know whether she cares for me at all. I don't believe she ever cared for anybody but my father. It's puzzling."

His eyes were fixed on the shadows. He had quite forgotten her. She leant back on the pillows, closing her eyes to try and master a feeling of faintness, and stretched out her hand towards his lips.

He dropped a kiss on it and went on : " So, you see, I fell back on you for consolation, and somehow at that moment love went out of me. It's funny the change it makes in everything. I became—so conventional. When you ran in here and slammed the door on me, I didn't follow you because I was conscious that I oughtn't to come into your room. Afterwards, when suddenly I loved you again and I wanted to come and be forgiven by you, I didn't care a damn for any rule." Their lips met again. She had to dissemble a faint surprise that at this moment he should think about anything so trivial as the rule that a man should not come into a woman's bedroom. " Ellen, it was beastly. Really, I didn't get any more fun out of it than you did. I lost my soul. I didn't feel anything for you that I've ever felt. I simply felt a sort of generalised emotion . . . that any man might have felt for any woman. . . . It wasn't us. . . ." The corners of his mouth were drawn down by self-disgust. " Perhaps I am like my father," he said loathingly. " He was a vile man." Again he forgot her, and again she laid her hand on his lips. When his thoughts came back to her he looked happier, though he had to think of her penitently. " I was a beast," he went on, " the coldest, cruellest beast. Do you know why I raged at you when you mentioned that little snipe you call Mr. Philip ? I knew it was the roughest luck on you to have gone through that time with him. But I wasn't sorry for you. I was jealous. I felt you might have protected yourself from being looked at by any other man in the world except me, though I knew perfectly you had to earn your living, and I ought to make it my business to see that you're specially happy to make up for those months you spent up in that office with those lustful old swine."

She checked him. He was speaking out of that special knowledge which she had not got and for lack of which she felt inferior and hoodwinked, and what he said to her suggested to her that a part of her life which she had thought she had perfectly understood was a mystery from which she was debarred by ignorance. "What do you mean?" she cried deridingly, as if there were no such knowledge. "Why do you call them lustful?"

In his excitement he spoke on. "Of course they both wanted you. I could see that little snipe Philip did. And everything you told me about them proves it. And the old man liked to think how he would have wanted you if he'd been young."

Ellen repeated wistfully, "They wanted me." She did not know what it meant, but accepted it.

A sudden hush fell on his vehemence. He turned away from her again, and began to pick at the hem of the counterpane. "Don't you know what that means?"

She shook her head.

"Oh, Lord!" he said. "I wasn't sure. How frightened you must be."

In the thinnest thread of sound, she murmured: "Sometimes. A little."

He was trembling. "You poor thing. You poor little thing. Yet I can't tell you."

She clapped her hands over her ears. "Ah, no. I couldn't bear to listen if you did." They sank into a trembling silence. Her black eyes, fixed on the opposite wall, saw the shape of mountains against the white evening of a dark sky; the dark red circle of a peat-stained pool lying under the shadow of a rock; the earth of a new-ploughed field over which seagulls ambled white in heavy air, under a cloud-felted sky; and other sombre appearances that moved the heart strangely, as if it discerned in them proofs that the core of life was darkness. There came on her suddenly a memory of that fierce initiatory pain which she had felt when she first drank wine, when she first was kissed by Richard. She remembered it with a singular lack of dismay. There ran through her on the instant a tingling sense of pride and ambition towards all new experience, and she leapt briskly from the bed, crying out in placid annoyance, as if it were the only care she had, because her hair had fallen down about her shoulders. They stood easily together in the light of the great window, she feeling for the strayed hairpins in her head, he looking down on the disordered glory.

"But what's that for ? " he asked, pointing at the open trunk in the middle of the floor.

Her eyes filled with tears. "I was packing to go back to Edinburgh."

"Oh, my dear, my dear!" he said solemnly. "I came near to imperilling a perfect thing." He took her face between his hands and was going to kiss her, but she started away from him.

"Oh, maircy! What cold hands!" she exclaimed.

"I've been out in the shed working at my motor-bicycle. It was freezing. And I made an awful mess of it too, because I was blind and shaking with rage."

"You poor silly thing!" she cried lovingly. "Give me yon bits of ice!" She took both his hands and pressed them against her warm throat.

For a little time they remained so, until her trembling became too great for him to bear, and he whispered : "This is all it is! This is all it is!"

"What do you mean?" she murmured.

"What you fear . . . is just like this. You will comfort my whole body as you are comforting my hands. . . ."

She drooped, she seemed about to fall, but joy was a bright light on her face, and she answered loudly, plangently : "Then I shall not be afraid!" They swayed together, and she told him in earnest ecstasy : "I will marry you any day you like." When he answered, "No, no, I will wait," she jerked at his coat-lapels like an impatient child, and cried : "But I want to be married to you!" Then their lips met in a long kiss, and they travelled far into a new sphere of love.

It amazed her when, in the midst of this happiness, he broke away from her. She felt sick and shaken, as if she had been sitting in an express train and the driver had suddenly put on the brakes, and it angered her that he once more made one of those wordless sounds that she detested. But her anger died when she saw that he was staring over her shoulder out of the window at some sight which had made his face white and pointed with that grave alertness which is the brave man's form of fear. She swung round to see what it was.

A man and a woman were standing in the farmyard looking up at them. Their attitude of surprise and absorbed interest made it evident that the width and depth of the window had enabled them to see clearly what was happening in the room ; and for a moment Ellen covered her face with her hands. But she was forced to look at them again by a sense that these people were strange in a way that was at once unpleasant and yet interesting and exciting. They were both clad in uniforms cut unskilfully out of poor cloth, the man in a short coat with brass buttons, braided trousers, and a circular cap like a sailor's, and the woman in an old-fashioned dress with a tight-fitting bodice and a gored skirt ; and round his cap and round the crown of her poke-bonnet were ribbons on which was printed : " Hallelujah Army."

The odd unshapeliness of their ill-built bodies in their ill-fitting clothes, the stained and streaky blue of the badly-dyed serge, and the shallow, vibrating magenta of the ribbon made it very fitting that they should stand in the foreground of the mean winter day which had coloured the farmyard and its buildings sour, soiled tones of grey. Their perfect harmony with their surroundings, even though it was only in disagreeableness that they matched them, gave Ellen a kind of pleasure. She felt clever because she had detected it, and she stared down into their faces, partly because she was annoyed by their steady inspection and wanted to stare them out, and partly because she wanted to discover what these people, who were behaving so oddly, were like in themselves. There was nothing very unusual about the woman, save that she united several qualities that one would not have thought could be found together. She was young, certainly still in her middle twenties, yet worn ; florid yet haggard ; exuberant and upstanding of body, yet bowed at the shoulders as if she were fragile. But the man was odd enough. He was pale and had a very long neck, and wore an expression of extreme foolishness. From the frown with which he was accompanying his gaping stare it was evident that his mind was so vague and wandering that he found it difficult to concentrate it ; she was reminded of an inexpert person she had once seen trying to put a white rabbit into a bag. She looked again at the girl, with that contempt she felt, now that she had Richard, for all women who let themselves mate with unworthy men, and found that her dark eyes were fixed sullenly, almost hungrily, on Richard. She laid her hand on Richard's arm and cried : " If it's not impudence, it's the next thing to it, staring like that into a pairson's room ! They're collecting, I suppose. Away and give them a penny."

" No," said Richard. " They are not collecting. That is Roger."

CHAPTER IX

ELLEN could not understand why Richard whispered explosively
as they turned away from the window: "Pin up your hair!
Quickly! We must go down at once!" or why he hurried her
downstairs without giving her time to use her brush and comb.
When they got down into the old parlour Richard went to the
side door that opened into the farmyard and flung it open,
beginning a sentence of greeting, but there was nothing to be
seen but the grey sheds, the wood-pile, and the puddle-pocked
ground. He uttered an exasperated exclamation, and drew it
to, saying to Ellen: "Open the front door! Please, dear."
She did so, but saw nothing save the dark and narrow garden
and the black trees against the white north sky. "What in
Christ's name are they doing?" Richard burst out, and flung
open the side door again. Both put their heads out over the
threshold to see if the two visitors were standing about anywhere, and a gust of wind that was making the trees beat their
arms darted down on the house and turned the draught between
the two open doors into a hurricane. Ellen squealed as her door
banged and struck her shoulder before she had time to steer
clear of it. "Oh, my poor darling!" said Richard, and he was
coming towards her, when they heard the glug-glug-glug of water
dripping from the table to the floor, and saw that the draught
had overturned a vase filled with silver boughs of honesty. He
picked it up and uttered another bark of exasperation, for it
had cracked across and he had cut his hand on the sharp edge
of the china.

"Oh, damn! oh, damn! oh, damn!" he cried, in a voice
that rage made high-pitched and childish, sucking his
finger in between the words. "What a filthy mess!" He
looked down on the wet tablecloth and the two halves of the
vase lying in the bedabbled leaves with an expression of distaste
so far out of proportion to its occasion that Ellen remembered
uneasily how several times that day she had noticed in him
traces of a desperate, nervous tidiness like Marion's. "If you

ring for one of the maids she'll soon clear it up," she said soothingly, and moved towards the bell. But he took his bleeding finger away from his lips and waved it at her, crying : "No! no! I don't want either of the servants round till I've found that fool and that woman! This is some new folly—probably I'll have to get him away before mother comes! Come on! Perhaps they're hanging about the garden, though God knows why!" After making a savage movement towards the broken vase, as if he could not bear to leave the disorder as it was, and checking it abruptly, jarringly, he rushed into the dining-room, and Ellen followed him.

The two were there, their faces pressed against the window-panes. Behind them the grey waste of stormy shallow waters and the salt-dimmed pastures, and the black range of the Kentish hills, hung with grape-purple rainclouds, made it apparent how much greater dignity belongs to the earth and sea than to those who people them. As Richard and Ellen halted at the door the faces receded from the glass. The woman stepped backwards and, looking as if she were being moved on by a policeman, passed suddenly out of sight beyond the window's edge. Richard crossed the room and opened the French window, but by the time he had unlocked it the man in uniform, who had been beckoning to his companion with long bony hands, had gone in search of her. As Richard put his head round the door to bid them enter, the wind, which was now rushing round the house, made itself felt as a chill commotion, an icy anger of the air, in which both he and Ellen shivered. Presently the pair in uniform appeared again, but at some distance across the lawn, and too intensely absorbed in argument to pay any attention to him.

"Oh, damn! oh, damn!" sobbed Richard. The wind was blowing earth-daubed leaves off the flowerbeds through the open door into the prim room. He stepped into the gale and shouted : "Roger! Roger! Come in!"

Roger waved his arms, which were too long for the sleeves of his coat, and from his mouthings it was evident that he was shouting back, but the wind took it all. In anger Richard stepped back into the room and made as if to close the doors, and at that the two on the lawn ran towards the house, with that look which common people have when they run for a train, as if their feet were buckling up under them. Richard held the door wide again, but when the couple reached the path in front of the house they were once more seized with a doubt about entering and came to a standstill.

" Come in," said Richard ; " come in."

The man took off his cap and ran his hands through his pale, long hair. " Is mother in ? " he demanded in a thin, whistling voice.

" Come in," said Richard ; " come in."

The man began : " Well, if mother's not in, I don't know——"

Richard fixed his eyes on the woman's face. " Come in," he said softly, brutally, loathingly. Ellen shivered to hear him speak thus to a woman and to see a woman take it thus, for at once the stranger moved forward to the window and stepped into the room. As she brushed by him she cringingly bowed her shoulders a little, and looked up at him as he stood a head and shoulders higher than herself. He looked back steadily and made no sign of seeing her save by a slight compression of the lips, until she passed on with dragging feet and stood listlessly in the middle of the room. It was evident that they completely understood one another, and yet their understanding sprung from no recollection of any previous encounter, for into the eyes of neither did there come any flash of recognition. There could be no doubt that Richard was feeling nothing but contempt for this woman, and her peaked yet rich-coloured face expressed only sick sullenness ; yet Ellen felt a rage like jealousy.

Richard turned again to the garden, and said : " Come in."

" Now don't be high-handed, old man," expostulated the stranger. But then he seemed to remember something, and stretched out both his arms, held them rigid, and opened his mouth wide as if to speak very loudly. But no sound came, and his arms dropped, and his long bony hands pawed the air. Then suddenly his arms shot out again, and he exclaimed very quickly in a high, strained voice : " Pride has always been your besetting sin, Richard. You aren't a bad chap in any way that I know of. But you're proud. And it doesn't become any of us to be proud "—his spirit was shaking the words out of his faltering flesh—" for we're all miserable sinners. You needn't order me "—he spoke more glibly now, the flesh and the spirit seemed in complete agreement—" to come out of the garden like that. I wish Poppy hadn't gone in." He caught his breath with something like a sob ; but the woman in uniform made no movement, and turned her eyes to Richard's face as if it were he that must give the order. " I've got a reason for staying out here. I know mother's not got Jesus. If she's ashamed of me now that I'm one of Jesus' soldiers, I won't come in. I'll go and wrestle on my knees for her soul, but I won't hurt her by coming in. So here I stay till she tells me to come in."

" But she's out," said Richard.

The man in uniform was discomfited. The light went out of his face and his mouth remained open. He shifted his weight from one foot to the other and muttered : " Ooh-er, is she ? "

" Yes," said Richard pleasantly. " She's gone over to Friar's End, but she'll be back any time now. I wish you'd come in. I haven't seen you for years, and I'd like to swap yarns with you about what we've been doing all the time."

" You'd have the most to tell," answered the other wistfully. " You've been here, there, and everywhere in foreign parts. And I haven't been doing nothing at all. Except— " he added, brightening up, " being saved."

" That's your own fault," Richard told him. " I've often wondered why you didn't try your luck abroad. You'd have been sure to hold your own. Well, anyway, come in and have some tea. I don't know what mother would say to me if she came in and found I'd let you stay out in the cold. She'd be awfully upset."

" Do you think she would ? " the man in uniform asked, and seemed to ponder. He looked up at the grey sky and shivered. " 'Tis getting coldish. And the cloth this uniform is made from isn't the sort that keeps out cold weather. God knows I don't want to grumble at the uniform I wear for Jesus' sake, but me having been in the drapery, I can't help noticing when a thing is cheap." He stared down at his toes for a time, lifting alternately his heels and pressing them down into the wet gravel ; then raised his head and said nonchalantly : " Well, old man, I think I will come in after all." But he halted yet again when he got one foot over the threshold. " Mind you, I'm not coming in just because it's cold," he began, but Richard, exclaimed, " Yes, yes ! Of course I know you're not ! " and gripped him by the arm and pulled him into the room. He did not seem to resent the rough treatment at all, and went over at once to the woman in uniform, and, looking happily about him, cried : " Isn't this a lovely home ? I always say there's nobody got such a nice home as my mother."

His voice whistled ; and Ellen in her mind's eye saw a vision of some clumsy, half-bestial creature wandering in primeval swamps, feeling joy and yet knowing no joyful word or song, and so plucking a reed and breathing down it, and in his ignorance being pleased at the poor noise. She felt pity and loathing, and looked across the room at Richard, meaning to tell him by a smile that she would help him to be kind to Roger. But Richard was still occupying himself with the window, examining with an air of irascibility a stain of blood which his cut finger had left on the white paint near the lock. His eyes travelled from it to the muddy footprints of the two who had come in from the garden and to the spatter of earth-daubed leaves on the polished floor, and his mouth drew down at the corners in a grimace of passion that made Ellen long to run to him and kiss him and bid him not give way to the madness of order so prevalent in this house. But he did not even look at her, so she could do nothing for him.

He went forward to Roger, determinedly sweetening his face, and shook his hand heartily. "It's good that you should have turned up just at this moment, for I'm going to be married before long to Miss Melville, whom I met in Scotland when I was working at Aberfay. Ellen, this is my brother, Roger."

Roger took Ellen's hand and then seemed to remember something. After exchanging a portentous glance with the woman in uniform, he looked steadfastly into her face and said sombrely: "I hope all's well with you, sister! I hope all's well with you!"

"Pairfectly," answered Ellen; and after a pause added, shyly: "And I'm pleased to meet you. I hope anyone that's dear to Richard will be friends with me."

He flung his head backwards and cried, in that whistling voice: "Yes, I'll be that! And I'm a friend worth having now I've got Jesus! And He's given me Poppy too! Aha, old man!" With a little difficulty he put both his thumbs inside the corded edge of his armholes and began to stride up and down, taking steps unnaturally long for thin legs. "You aren't the only man who's thought of getting married! Great minds think alike, they say!" With a flourish he stretched out his hand, and it was plain that he thought he would touch the woman in uniform, though he was some feet away. Richard's and Ellen's eyes met; it was repulsive to see a man dizzied by so small a draught of excitement. "Richard, Miss Melville, this is Lieutenant Poppy, who's going to be my wife."

It was difficult to know what to do, for the woman in uniform, although she made a murmuring noise, preserved that un-illumined aspect which conveyed, more fully than silence could have done, that her soul was glumly silent. But they went and greeted her, and looked into the matted darkness of her eyes.

"We're going to be married as soon as I've served my year of probation. That's a long time ahead, for I've only been at it a fortnight. I expect you'll be getting married much sooner. Things always went easier with you than me," he complained.

"But it'll be a happy day when it comes, and I get the two blessings at the same time, becoming a full soldier of Jesus and marrying Poppy. She's nearly a full soldier already. She joined the Army seven months ago."

"Do you preach in the streets?" asked Richard.

Roger's eyes filled with water. Ellen reflected that he must be curiously sensitive for one so dull-witted, for the rage and disgust behind the question had hardly shown their heads. "Yes, I do!" he said pettishly. "And if Jesus doesn't object, I don't see why you should."

"I don't object at all," Richard assured him amiably. "I only wondered what sort of work you did. I suppose you haven't come to work at the Hallelujah Colony here, have you?"

"That's just what I've done!" answered Roger joyfully. "I joined up at Margate and I've laboured there for three weeks. I didn't do so bad. Did I, Poppy? Not for a start? No one could exactly shine at street preaching at first, you know. They will laugh so. But I didn't do worse than other people when they begin, did I, Poppy? However, they've transferred me over here to the Colony, to do clerk work." He added with a touch of defiance: "And, of course, they'll want me to take services too, sometimes. In fact I'm going to take a service this evening."

"How long are you to be here?"

"Maybe always. They may feel I do the best work for Jesus here." He drew a deep, shuddering breath, and took his cap off and threw it on the table with a convulsive gesture. "If mother doesn't turn me away because I've given myself to Jesus," he said with that whistling note, "I'll be able to see her every day."

"She won't turn you away."

There was folly, there was innocence in Roger's failure to notice that Richard was speaking not in reassurance but in grimness, as one might speak who sees a doom fire or flood travelling down on to the place where he stood. "You ought to know, old chap," he murmured hopefully. "She's always shown her heart to you, like she never has to me. . . . I don't know. . . . Ooh, I've prayed. . . ."

"Well, you'll know for yourself in a minute," said Richard. "I heard the front door open and close a second ago."

Ellen felt a thrill of pride because he had such keen senses, for the sound had been so soft that she had not heard it, and yet it had reached him in the depth of his horrified absorption of his brother's being. She longed to smile at him and tell him how she loved him for this and all the other things, but again he

wouldn't pay attention to her.   Indeed, he could not, for, as she
saw from his white mask, he was wholly given up to pain and
apprehension.   Her heart was wrung for him, for she saw the
case against Roger.   He was sickening like something that has
been fried in insufficient fat ; and that his loathsomeness proceeded from no moral flaw made it all the more sinister.
If there was not vileness in his will to account for the
impression he made, then it must be kneaded into his general
substance, and meanness be the meaning of his pallor, and
treachery the secret of the darkness of his hair.   She looked at
him accusingly as he stood beside the buxom, sullen woman,
who in a slum version of the emotion of embarrassment was
sucking and gnawing one of her fingers, and she found shining in
his face the light of love ; true love that keeps faith and does
service even when it is used despitefully.   Perplexed, she
doubted all judgment.

The doorhandle turned, and Richard stepped in front of
Roger.   But when Marion slowly came into the room she did
not see him or anyone else, because she was looking down on a
piece of broken china which she held in her hand.

There was stillness till Richard whispered : " Mother."

She lifted her dark eyes and said, with inordinate melancholy,
" Oh, Richard, someone has broken the Lowestoft jug I used for
flowers in the parlour."

He answered softly : " No one broke it.   The wind blew it
down when I opened the door to Roger."

Her eyes did not move from his.   Her mouth was a round
hole.   He put out his hand to take the piece of china from her.
They both gazed down on it, as if it were a symbol, and
exchanged a long glance.   She gave it to him and, bracing
herself, looked around for Roger.   When she found him she
started, and stared at the braid on his coat, the brass buttons,
and the brass studs on his high collar.   Then she became aware
of the woman, and, with a faint, mild smile of distracted courtesy,
took stock of her uniform.   His cap, lying on the table, caught
her eye, and she picked it up and turned it round and round on
her hand, reading the black letters on the magenta ribbon.

" So you've joined the Hallelujah Army, Roger ? " she said,
in that muffled, indifferent tone.

" Yes," he murmured.

" Do you preach in the streets ? "   Her voice shook.

" Yes," he whispered.

She gave the cap another turn on her hand.   " Are you
happy ? " she asked, again indifferently.

"Yes," he whispered.

She flung the cap down on the table and stretched out her arms to him. "Oh, my boy!" she cried. "Oh, my boy, I am so glad you are happy at last!" Love itself seemed to have spread its strong wings in the room, and the others gazed astonished until they saw her flinch as Roger crumpled up and fell on her breast, and visibly force herself to be all soft, mothering curves to him.

Ellen cast down her eyes and stared at the floor. Roger's sobbing made a queer noise. Ahé . . . ahé . . . ahé. . . . It had an unmechanical sound, like the sewing-machine at home before it quite wore out, or Richard's motor-bicycle when something had gone wrong ; and this spectacle of a mother giving heaven to her son by forgery of an emotion was an unmechanical situation. It must break down soon. She looked across at Richard and found him digging his nails into the palms of his hands, but not so dejected as she might have feared. It struck her that he was finding an almost gross satisfaction in the very wrongness of the situation which was making her grieve—which must, she realised with a stab of pain, make everyone grieve who was not themselves tainted with that wrongness. He would rather have things as they were, and see his mother lacerating her soul by feigning an emotion that should have been natural to her, and his half-brother showing himself a dolt by believing her, than see them embracing happily as uncursed mothers and their children do. Uneasily she shifted her eyes from his absorbed face to the far view of the river and the marshes.

"Oh, mother!" spluttered Roger, coming up to the surface of his emotion. "I'm a rich man now! I've got Jesus, and you, and Poppy! Mother, this is Poppy, and I'm going to marry her as soon as I can."

The woman in uniform looked at the window when Marion turned to her, as if she would have liked to jump through it. One could imagine her alighting quite softly on the earth as if on pads, changing into some small animal with a shrew's stringy snout, and running home on short hindlegs into a drain. She moistened her lips and mumbled roughly and abjectly : "I didn't want to come."

Marion answered smoothly : "But now that you are here, how glad I am that you have," and took her two hands and patted them. Looking round benevolently at Ellen and back at Lieutenant Poppy, she exclaimed : "I'm a lucky woman to have two daughters given me in one week." She was behaving like an old mother in an advertisement, like the silver-haired old lady who leads the home circle in its orgy of eating Mackintosh's toffee or who reads the *Weekly Telegraph* in plaques at railway-stations. The rapidity from which she had changed from the brooding thing she generally was, with her heavy eyes and her twitching hands perpetually testifying that the chords of her life had not been resolved and she was on edge to hear their final music, and the perfection with which she had assumed this bland and glossy personality at a moment's notice, struck Ellen with wonder and admiration. She liked the way this family turned and doubled under the attack of fate. She was glad that she was going to become one of them, just as a boy might feel proud on joining a pirate crew. She went over and stood beside Richard and slipped her arm through his. Uneasily she was aware that now she, too, was enjoying the situation, and would not have had it other than it was. She drooped her head against Richard's shoulder, and hoped all might be well with all of them.

"You see, mother, since I saw you I've had trouble—I've had trouble——" Roger was stammering.

Marion turned from him to Richard. "Ring for tea," she said, "and turn on the lights. All the lights. Even the lights we don't generally use."

Roger clung to her. "I don't want to hide anything from you, mother," he began, but she cut him short. "Oh, what cold hands! Oh, what cold hands!" she cried playfully, and rubbed them for him. As the lights went up one by one, behind the cornice, in the candlesticks on the table, in the alabaster vases on the mantelpiece, they disclosed those hands as long and yellowish and covered with warts. The parlourmaid came in and, over her shoulder, Marion said easily: "Tea now, Mabel. There're five of us. And we'll have it down here at the table."

She waved her visitors towards chairs and herself moved over to an armchair at the hearth. All her movements were easy and her face wore a look of blandness as she settled back among the cushions, until it became evident that she was to be disappointed in her natural hope that Roger would see the necessity of stopping his babble while the servant was going in and out of the room. It was true that he did not speak when she was actually present, but he began again on his whistling intimacies the minute she closed the door, and when she returned cut himself short and relapsed into a breathy silence that made it seem as if he had been talking of something to the discredit of them all. Ellen felt disgust in watching him, and

more of this perverse pleasure in this situation, which she ought
to have whole-heartedly abhorred, when she watched Marion.
She was one of those women who wear distress like a rose in
their hair. Her eyes, which wandered between the two undesired
visitors, were star-bright and aerial-soft ; under her golden,
age-dusked pallor her blood rose crimson with surprise ; her
face was abandoned so amazedly to her peril that it lost all
its burden of reserve, and was upturned and candid as if she were
a girl receiving her first kiss ; her body, taut in case she had to
keep up and restrain Roger from some folly of attitude or
blubbering flight, recovered the animation of youth. It was no
wonder that Richard did not look at anybody but his mother.

"You see, mother, it was Poppy who brought me to Jesus,"
Roger said, a second before the door closed. "I . . . I'd had
a bit of trouble. I'd been very foolish. . . . I'll tell you about
that later. It isn't because I'm cowardly and unrepentant that
I won't tell it now. I've told it once on the Confession Bench
in front of lots of people, so I'm not a coward. And I don't
believe," he declared, casting a look of dislike at Richard and
Ellen, "that the Lord would want me to tell anybody but you
about it." The servant returned, and he fell silent ; with such
an effect that she looked contemptuously at her mistress as she
might have if bailiffs had been put into the house. When she
had gone he began again : "It was this way Poppy did it.
After my trouble I was walking down Margate Broadway—— "

The woman in uniform made so emphatic a noise of impatience
that they all turned and looked at her. "There isn't a Broadway
in Margate ! " she nearly snarled. "It's High Street, you mean.
The High Street. Broadways they call them some places. But
not at Margate, not at *Margate*."

"Neither it is," said Roger adoringly. "What a memory
you've got, Poppy ! "

Marion rose from the table, laying her hand on the woman's
braided shoulders as she passed. "Let's come to the table and
have some tea ; and take your hat off, dear. Yes, take it off.
That close bonnet can't be very comfortable when one's tired."

Ellen stared like a rude child as the woman slowly, with
shapeless red fingers, untied her bonnet-strings and revealed
herself as something at once agelessly primitive and most
modernly degenerate. The frizzed thicket of coarse hair which
broke into a line of tiny, quite circular curls round her low forehead made Ellen remember side-streets round Gorgie and Dalry,
which the midday hooters filled with factory girls horned under
their shawls with Hinde's curlers ; yet made her remember also

vases and friezes in museums where crimped, panoplied priest-
esses dispensed archaic rites. Her features were so closely
moulded to the bone, her temples so protuberant, and her eyes
sunk in such pits of sockets that one had to think of a skull, a
skull found in hot sand among ruins. The ruins of some lost Nubian
city, the mind ran on, for the fulness of her lips compared with
the thinness of her cheeks gave her a negroid look ; yet the smallness and poor design of her bones marked her as reared in an
English slum. But her rich colour declared that neither that
upbringing, nor any of the mean conditions which her bearing
showed had pressed in upon her since her birth, had been able
to destroy her inner resource of vitality. The final meaning of
her was, perhaps, primitive and strong. When she had stood
about the room there had been a kind of hieratic dignity about
her ; she had that sanctioned effect upon the eye which is given
by someone adequately imitating the pose of some famous
picture or statue. There flashed before Ellen's mind the tail
of some memory of an open place round which women stood
looking just like this ; but it was gone immediately.

"Well," said Roger, "I was telling you how I got Jesus.
I was going along Margate High Street, and I saw a crowd, and
I heard a band playing. I didn't take any particular notice of
it and I was going to pass it by—think of it, mother, I was going
to pass it by !—when the band stopped and a most beautiful
voice started singing. It was Poppy. Oh, mother, you must
hear Poppy sing some day. She has such a wonderful voice.
It's a very rich contralto. Before she was saved she sang on
a pier. Well, I got into the crowd, and presently I got close
and I saw her." A dreadful coyness came on him, and he turned
to Poppy and, it was plain to all of them, squeezed her hand under
the table. She looked straight in front of her with the dumb
malignity of a hobbled mule that is being teased. "Well, I
knew at once. I've often envied you and mother for going to
Spain and South America, and wondered if the ladies were really
like what you see in pictures. All big and dark and handsome,
but when Poppy came along I saw I didn't have to go abroad for
that ! And you know, mother, Poppy is Spanish—half. Her
name's Poppy Alicante. Her mother was English, but she
married a Spanish gentleman, of very good family he was.
In fact, he was a real don, wasn't he, Poppy ? But he died when
she was a baby, and as he'd been tricked out of his inheritance
by a wicked uncle, there wasn't much money about, so Poppy's
mother married again, to a gentleman connected with the Navy,
who lives just the other side of the river from over here. Funny,

isn't it ? But it was a very godless home, and they behaved
disgracefully to Poppy, when a rich man who saw her on the
road when he was riding along in his motor-car wanted to marry
her, and she refused because she didn't love him. They were so
cruel to her that she had to leave home and earn her living,
though she never expected to. But she didn't like mixing with
rough people, so as she'd always had Jesus she joined the Army.
And that's how we met."

After a pause Marion said, speaking fatuously in order to
avoid the appearance of irony : " You're quite a romantic bride,
Poppy."

The woman in uniform bit into her toast and swallowed it
unchewed.

" Well, I knew at once I'd met the one woman, as they say,
and I hung about just to see if I couldn't see more of her. And
that's how I got Jesus. She brought me to Him. Mother,
mother," he cried, in a sudden pale, febrile passion, "there's few
have such a blessed beginning to their marriage ! We ought
to be very happy, oughtn't we ? "

" Yes, Roger," she answered him. " You'll be very happy—
a husband that any woman would be proud of."

" Oh, I'm not nearly good enough for Poppy," he said
deprecatingly. He seemed used to Poppy's silence, and, indeed,
whenever her silent absence from speech was most marked, he
bent towards her in a tender attitude which showed a resolution
to regard it as maidenly bashfulness. " Well, to get back to
my story. I stood there peering through the crowd for another
look at her, and an officer began preaching. Captain Harris it
was. I didn't take any particular notice of him." He jerked
his whitish face about contemptuously. " He's a poor preacher,
isn't he, Poppy ? He never gets a grip on the crowd, does he ?
And they can't hear him beyond the first few rows. I don't
think I heard more than a few sentences that first evening. If
I'd had been in the Army as many years as he has, and I couldn't
preach any better than that, I'd find some other way of serving
Jesus. I would really.

" But after that "—he stopped, looked at some vision in
the air before him which filled his eyes with tears and fire,
and sighed deeply—" Captain Sampson preached the gospel.
It's Captain Sampson I've been working under since I joined
the Army. Oh, mother, mother, I wish you could hear him
preach. He would give you Jesus. That first evening
I heard him I saw Jesus as plain as I see you. I saw Him then
looking fierce like He was when He scourged the moneychangers

out of the temple. But when I'm alone, I see the other Jesus, the way he was most times." He put his head back and bleated : "'Gentle Jesus, meek and mild.' The One that loves us when we're weak and when we fall, and loves us all the better for it. Even you "—he looked at Richard with a faint, malign joyfulness—" must feel the want of Him sometimes. Life can't be a path of roses for any of us, however strong and clever we are. So I say it's not good preaching to go on always about fighting for Jesus and being a good soldier, and making it seem as if religion was just another trouble we had to face." His voice broke with petulance. " It's a shame not to show people Gentle Jesus."

He checked himself. Remorse ran red under his pale skin. " What am I saying ? " he cried out. " Captain Sampson is a holy man ! If he's harsh to those that work under him it's right he should be. God chasteneth whom He loveth, and it's the same way with Captain Sampson I expect. It's really a way of showing that he cares about you and is anxious about you. And anyway, he did give me Jesus that evening. Oh, mother, it was so wonderful ! " The words rushed out of him. " He made you feel all tingling like you do when the fire engine goes past. Oh, it's an evening to remember ! And it gave me Jesus ! Oh, mother, you don't know what it's like to find Jesus To know "—his voice whistled exultantly over the stricken tea-table—" that there's Somebody who really loves you ! "

For one second Marion covered her face with her hands.

Unseeingly he piped on : " I'm happy now. Always happy." He broke into thin, causeless laughter. " When I wake up in the middle of the night, instead of feeling miserable like I used to, and remembering things that happened at Dawlish when I was a kid, and wishing I hadn't ever been born as I wasn't any good for anything, I just think of Jesus and feel lovely and warm. And I've got earthly happiness as well. I've got Poppy. Oh, I'm a lucky man, lucky man ! And I've got a lifework instead of being an odd-come-short. I'll always have something to do now. They've had experience with all sorts of men for years and years turning them into soldiers for Jesus. Surely they'll be able to find some work for me, even if they don't want me to preach Look at what I'm going to do now. Even if I don't do anything but clerk work, it's helping the Labour Colony along—helping hundreds of poor souls to earn a decent living under Bible influence when, if they weren't, there they'd be, roaming about the streets hungry and in sin. I'll be doing my bit, won't I mother ? "

She smiled beneficently but speechlessly.

Ellen felt contemptuous. She had read about those Halle-lujah Army Colonies for the unemployed, and had heard them denounced at labour meetings, and they were, she knew, mere palliatives by using which the pious gave themselves the pleasure of feeling that they were dealing with the immense problem of poverty when they were merely taking a few hundred men and setting them to work in uneconomic conditions. The very consideration of them brought back the happy spasm in the throat, the flood of fire through the veins, the conviction that amidst the meadowsweet of some near field there lurked a dragon whose slaughter (which would not be difficult) would restore the earth its lost security ; and all the hot, hopeful mood which filled her when she heard talk of revolution. She hated the weak man for aggravating the offence of his unsightliness by allying himself with the reactionary powers that made this world as unsightly as himself. And it was like him to talk about teach-ing the Bible when everybody knew that there were lots of things that weren't true. The spectacle of this mean little intelligence refusing to take cognisance of the truths that men like Darwin and Huxley had worked all their lives to discover, and faced the common hatred to proclaim, seemed to her cruel ingratitude to the great and wanton contemning of the power of thought, which was the only tool man had been given to help him break this prison of disordered society. She leaned across the table and demanded in a heckling tone : " But you must know pairfectly well that these Labour Colonies are only tackling the fringe of the problem. There's no way of settling the question of un-employment until the capitalist system's overturned."

He looked at her with wide eyes and assumed an air of being engaged in desperate conflict. It was evident that his egotism was transforming this conversation into a monstrous wrestling with Apollyon. "Ah ! You're a Socialist. They only think of giving people money. But it isn't money people need. Oh, no. ' What shall it profit a man if he gain the whole world and lose his own soul ? ' It's Jesus they need. Give them the Bible and all their wants will be satisfied," he cried in a shrill peewit cry.

" But the Bible isn't final. There's lots of things we know more about than the people who wrote it. Look at all yon nonsense they put in about Adam and Eve because they didn't know about evolution. That alone shows it's absurd to rely solely on the Bible. . . ."

She looked round for signs of the others' approval. She

knew that Richard agreed with her, for among his Christmas presents to her had been Huxley's Essays, and when he had talked to her of science she had seen that research after that truth was to him a shining mystic way which he would have declared led to God had he not been more reverent than Church men are, and feared to use that name lest it were not sacred enough for the ultimate sacredness. But to her amazement he kept his eyes on the crumbs which he was picking up from the tablecloth, and through his parted lips there sounded the faintest click of exasperation. She looked in wonder at Marion, and found her eyes also downcast and her forefinger tapping on her chin as if she were seeking for some expedient to stop this dangerous chatter. Ellen despised them both. They had been terribly exercised at the thought that Roger was going to preach in the streets, but they did not care at all that he was delivered over to error. She looked at him sympathetically over the table, feeling that since these horrid people with whom she had got entangled did not like him, he might be quite nice, and found him exchanging a long, peculiar glance with Poppy, which was followed on both sides by a slow, meaning nod.

He looked in front of him again and his round eyes vacillated between Richard and Ellen, growing rounder at each roll. Presently he swallowed a lump in his throat and addressed himself to her. "Ah, you're an unbeliever," he said. "Well, Captain Sampson says there's always a reason for it if people can't believe." He moistened his lips and panted the words out at her. "If you've been doing anything that's wrong—— " A sob prevented him. "Oh, I can't go and spoil this lovely tea, even if I ought to for Jesus' sake !" he cried. "We're all so happy, I can't bear to break it up by telling you what it's my duty to do ! Poppy, doesn't mother have everything nice ? I've often thought of this tea-table when I've been eating at places where they did things roughish. Look at the flowers. Mother always has flowers on the table, even when it's winter. Jesus wouldn't expect me to break this up." His face became transfused with light. " I believe Jesus loves everything that's done nicely, whether it's a good deed or bread-and-butter cut nice and thin. That's why," he mourned, so wistfully that all of them save the impassive woman in uniform made a kind, friendly bending towards him, " I mind not to be able to do anything really well. But Jesus loves me all the same. He loves me whatever I'm like !" His brow clouded. "But because He loves me I owe Him a debt. I ought to preach Him wherever I am, in and out of season. But I can't spoil this.

Aren't we all happy, sitting here ? I'll tell you what. They've asked me to take the Saturday evening service to-night because the Commandant and the two under him are all down with influenza. If you'll come and hear me I'll tell you what Jesus wants you to hear. Oh, mother, Richard, do, do come ! "

" Yes, Roger dear, we'll come."

" You won't . . . make fun of it ? "

" Oh no ! Oh no ! " Her voice was hesitant, intimate, girlishly shy. " We haven't seen nearly as much of each other as a mother and son ought. There are lots of things about me you don't know. For all you know, what you said of Richard a moment ago . . . might be true of me. . . ."

" What I said about Richard ? . . ."

" About times when one feels life too difficult and wants Someone to help one. . . ."

She spoke seductively, mysteriously, as if she were promising him a pleasure ; and he answered in a voluptuous whining : " Oh, mother, if I could bring you to Jesus ! Oh, Jesus ! you are giving me everything I want ! " But in the midst of his rapture his face changed and he started to his feet, so violently that his chair nearly fell backwards. " Yes," he cried reproachfully, " Jesus gives me everything, and this is how I reward Him ! "

They all stared at him, except Poppy, who was gloomily reading the tea-leaves in her cup.

" I told a lie ! " he answered their common mute enquiry. " A silly, vain lie. I told you they'd asked me to take the Saturday evening service to-night. They didn't. I offered to take it. Nobody ever asks me to preach. They say I can't. Mind you, I don't think they're right. I think that if they would let me practise I wouldn't speak so badly. But that's not the point. I told a lie. I distinctly said they'd asked me to preach because I wanted to pretend that I was making a success of things like Richard always does. Oh, what a thing to do to Jesus ! "

" But, dear, that was only because you were speaking in a hurry. It wasn't a deliberate lie."

" Oh, mother, you don't understand," he fairly squealed. " You haven't been saved, you see, and you're still lax about these things. It does matter ! It was a lie ! I ought to wrestle this thing out on my knees. Mother, will it put anybody out if I go into the parlour and pray ? "

Marion answered tenderly : " My dear, of course you can," but Poppy clicked down her cup into its saucer and said in a tone of sluggish, considered exasperation : " You haven't time. We ought to be at the chapel half an hour before the meeting. It's a quarter to six now."

"Oh dear! oh dear! Is it as late as that? I wanted to write on a piece of paper what I'm going to say! Now I won't have time! Oh, and I did want to preach well! Oh, where's my cap?" He began to stumble about the room. Presently he caught his foot in one of the electric light cords and set an alabaster lamp on the mantelpiece rocking on its pedestal. Richard and Marion watched him and it with that set, horrified stare which the anticipation of disorder always provoked in them. "Tcha!" exclaimed Poppy contemptuously. "But it's there! On the armchair!" cried Ellen: she could not bear the look on Richard and Marion's faces. "Where?" asked Poppy. It was the first time she had spoken directly to Ellen. "There! There! Among the cushions," she answered, and rose and went round the table to pick it up herself. Richard came and helped her.

Roger seemed a little annoyed when Richard and Ellen found the cap for him among the cushions. Having to thank them spoiled, it could be seen, some valedictory effect which he had planned. He stood by while they shook hands with Poppy, who turned her head away as if to hide some scar, and when she had gone across to Marion tried to get in his designed tremendousness. By the working of his face, which made even his ears move a little, they knew they must endure something very characteristic of him. But into his weak eyes there bubbled a spring of joyful tenderness so bright, so clear, so intense that, though it would have seemed more fitting on the face of a child than of a man, it yet was dignified.

"You make a handsome couple, you two!" he said. "Richard, you're a whole lot taller than me. When I'm away from you I forget what a difference there is between us. And the young lady, she's fine, too."

"Come on! Come on!" said Poppy from the door.

He drew wistfully away from them. "I do hope you both come to Jesus," he murmured, and smiled sweetly over his shoulder. "Yes, Poppy, I'm quite ready. Why, you aren't cross with me over anything, are you, dear? Well, good-bye, mother."

"Good-bye, Roger. And we'll come to the meeting. I'll et you out myself, my dears."

Very pleased that she and Richard were at last alone together, Ellen sat down on one of the armchairs at the hearth and smiled up at him. But he would not come to her. He

smiled back through the closed visor of an overmastering preoccupation, and moved past her to the fireplace and stood with
his elbow on one end of the mantelpiece, listening to the sounds
that came in from the parlour through the half-open door:
Marion's urbane voice, thin and smooth like a stretched mem-
brane, the click of the front-door handle, the last mounting
squeal from Roger, which was cut short by a gruff whine from
Poppy, and, loudest of all, the silence that fell after the banging
of the door. They heard the turn of the electric switch. Marion
must be standing out there in the dark. But Ellen doubted that
even if he had been with her in soul as in body, and had spoken
to her the words she wished, she could have answered him as
she ought, for a part of her soul too was standing out there in
the dark with Marion. They were both of them tainted with
disloyalty to their own lives.

When Marion came in she halted at the door and turned out all
the lamps save the candlesticks on the table. She passed through
the amber, fire-shot twilight and sat down in the other armchair,
and began to polish her nails on the palm of her hands. They
were all of them lapped in dusk, veiled with it, featureless because
of it. Behind them the candlesticks cast a brilliant light on
the disordered table, on the four chairs where Richard and
Marion, Roger and Poppy had sat. Ellen's chair had been
pushed back against the wall when she rose ; one would not
have known that Ellen had been sitting there too.

Marion kept looking back at the illuminated table as if it
were a symbol of the situation that made them sit in the twilight without words. Suddenly she made a sound of distress.
"Oh dear ! Look at the cakes that have been left ! Ellen,
you can't have had anything to eat."

"I've just had too good a tea," said Ellen, using the classic
Edinburgh formula.

"But you must have an éclair or a cream bun. I got them
for you. I used to love them when I was your age." She rose
and began to move round the table, bending over the cake-
plates. Ellen was reminded of the way that her own mother
used to hover above the débris of the little tea-parties they sometimes gave in Hume Park Square, cheeping : "I think they
enjoyed their teas. Do you not think so, Ellen ? " and satisfying
an appetite which she had been too solicitous and interested a
hostess to more than whet in the presence of her friends.
That was how a mother ought to be, little, sweet, and moderate:

Marion brought her an éclair on a plate. She took it and
stood up, asking meekly : " Shall I take it and eat it somewhere

else ? You and Richard'll be wanting to talk things over."

" Ah, no ! " Marion was startled ; and Ellen, to her own distress, found herself exulting because this mature woman, who had dived so deeply into the tides of adult experience in which she herself had hardly been laved, was facing the situation so inadequately. She scorned her for the stiffness of the conciliatory gesture she attempted, for the queer notes which her voice made when she tried to alter it from her customary tone of indifference in saying : " But, Ellen dear, you're one of us now. We've no affairs that aren't yours too. We only wish they were a little gayer. . . ." She admired the facility of her own response for not more than a minute, for, giving her a kind, blindish smile, Marion walked draggingly across the hearthrug and took up her position at the disengaged side of the fireplace and rested her elbow on the mantelpiece, even as Richard was doing at its other end. They stood side by side, without speaking, their firelit faces glowing darkly like rubies in shadow, their eyes set on the brilliantly lit tea-table and its four chairs. They looked beautiful and unconquerable—this tall man who could assail all things with his outstretched strength, this broad-bodied woman whom nothing could assail because of her crouching strength.

Marion stretched out her hand to the fire. Her insanely polished nails glittered like jewels.

She said in that indifferent tone : " Well, it wasn't so bad."

Some passion shook him. " Mother ! Mother ! To think of him bringing that woman into this house—to meet you and Ellen ! "

" Hush, oh hush ! He does not know."

" But, mother ! He ought to ! Anyone could see—— "

" What she was. Yes, poor woman. But remember I made a bad job of Roger. I gave him no brains."

" Mother—it mustn't happen again. She can't come here again."

She grew stern. " Richard, you must say nothing to Roger. Nor to her. She's his love and pride. So far as he's concerned, she's a better woman than I am. I never put my love and pride in his life. If you speak to either of them you will . . . add to my already heavy guilt. Besides . . . how can she hurt Ellen and me ? She's very weak. We're very strong."

" But, mother, you saw what she was."

" More than you did. She's had a child not long since."

" A child ? " He stared at her curiously, reverently. " How do you know ? "

" Some people get a brown stain on their face when they're having a baby, and afterwards it lingers on. I had it with you. Not with Roger. She has it now." She slowly drew her fingers over her face, her eyes wide in wonder. " It's a queer thing, birth. . . ."

Ellen tingled with shame because such things were spoken of aloud, by someone old. But Richard muttered huskily : " I wonder what the story is. . . ."

" Something horrible. She's come from a good home. Her teeth were well looked after when she was a girl. That hair took some conscientious torturing to make it what it is. She was caught, I suppose, by her love of beauty. Did you ever hear anything more pathetic than her name—Poppy Alicante ? "

" I don't see anything more in it than it's an obvious lie."

" It was much more than that. Think of her as a little girl going with her mother into a greengrocer's and hearing about Alicante grapes, and asking what Alicante was, and being told it was in Spain, and making the most lovely pictures of it in her mind and keeping them there ever since. Oh, she's a poor, beauty-loving thing. That's how the handsome sailor picked her up in Chatham High Street on Saturday night."

" No doubt you're right," he said, looking into the fire.

" And she hated giving up the child. That's why she snarls at Roger. Until she gets another she'll be famished. It was taken over, I expect, by a married sister or brother who've got no children of their own. She's not allowed to see it now. Not since she left the nice place that was found for her after she'd got over her trouble. Twenty pounds a year—because of her lost character ; and for the same reason rather more work than the rest of the servants, who all found out about it. So she ran away."

He interrupted her : " Supposing all that's true. And I know it is. It's like you, mother, to read from a patch of brown skin on a woman's face things that other people would have found out only by searching registry records and asking the police. It's like the way you always turned your back on the barometer and read the sky for news of the weather. You're an old peasant woman under your skin, mother." His voice was hazed with delight. He had forgotten the moment in the timeless joy of his love for her. Ellen, in the shadows, stirred and coughed. He broke out again : " Well, supposing all that's true ! Are you going to be honest and be as clear-sighted about what happened after she ran away ? Mother, think of the things that have been done to her, think of the things she's seen ! "

The indifferent tone continued now, although she said :
" Think of the horrible things that have been done to me, think
of the horrible things I've seen ! Oh, you're right, of course.
Unhappy people are dangerous. They clutch at the happy
people round them and drag them down into the vortex of their
misery. But if you're going to hate anybody for doing that,
hate me. Look how I've dominated you with my misfortunes,
look how I've eaten up your life by making you feel it a duty to
compensate me for what I've endured. Hate me. But don't
hate Poppy. Oh, that poor, simple creature. Even now, after
all that's happened, she'd be pleased like a child if you took her
to a fair where there were merry-go-rounds. Oh, don't hate
her. And don't hate Roger." Wildness flashed through her
like lightning through a dense dark cloud. " Don't hate him,
Richard ! Take your mind off both of us. We're all right. I
can manage everything quite well. I'm hard. I haven't got
all those fine feelings you think I have. I'm quite hard. I can
arrange everything beautifully. Roger's happy in the Hallelujah Army. He's gone to Jesus for the love I ought to have
given him. I know they're thinking of turning him out. But
I'll see to it that they keep him. I'll pretend to have leanings
towards their religion, and I'll give them money from time to time
so that they won't dare get rid of him. It will be rather amusing
squaring them. I shall enjoy it. We will be all right. Leave
us alone. Don't think of us. Think of Ellen. Think of Ellen.
How you hold back from your happiness ! " she cried gibingly.
" I tell you, if I had had your chance of happiness when I was
young, neither my mother nor my father would have held me
back from it ! "

It was as if her soul had leapt, naked and raging, from out of
her mouth when she said that. Ellen stirred among the cushions,
feeling unformulated shame. She wondered how Richard
could endure hearing that hoarse vehemence from the lips of
one whom he must wish to be gentle and unpassionate. But
he was gazing at his mother trancedly and with slight movements
of his hands and feet, as if she were dancing and he desired to join
her in her spinning rhythm ; and she, mad, changeable woman,
shivered and pressed her fingers against her mouth to silence
herself, and looked down on her skirt, drawling lazily : " Well,
here I am, standing about in my outdoor clothes. If there's
anything I hate, it's wearing outdoor clothes in the house.
However, it'll save me changing, and I've none too much time
if I'm going to be punctual for Roger's meeting."

She moved towards the door. He followed softly, as her shadow, and held it open.

When he made to follow her out of the room she turned sharply. " You needn't come."

" I promised Roger," he said falsely.

" What nonsense ! " she blazed. " I'll tell him you had to stay here with Ellen."

She banged the door on him. He stood staring at its panels, which were rosy with firelight, and Ellen closed her eyes for weariness. After some seconds she heard his tread and felt him bend over her. " Ellen," he mumbled, " I must go with mother. That fool will be too awful on the platform. I must see her through."

From the dark fey shape he made against the firelight she knew that he was not thinking of her, that the life she had given him by her love no longer ran in his veins. She scratched one of her wrists. If she could have let the life he had given flow out of her veins she would have done it. " Ay, do," she said. " I like you to be good to your mother. You never know how long you may have her with you," she added piously and not without cheerfulness.

He left her with a kiss that was dry and spurious like a paper flower. She sank back into the chair and closed her eyes again, and listened for the closing of the front door which would leave her free to weep or rage or dance or do whatever would relieve the pressure of the moment on her brain. She filled in the throbbing tune by thinking of the visitors. It gave her a curious thrill, such as she might have felt if she had gratified her ambition to carry a heavy-plumed fan like Sarah Bernhardt's, to reflect that she had sat in the same room with a bad woman. A desire for unspecified adult things ran through her veins, as if she had just heard the strong initial blare of a band. Then she checked all thoughts, for from the hall she heard the sound of argument.

The door was flung open by Marion. She moved towards the hearth with a burly speed which marked this moment a crisis in the house of languid, inhibited movements, and cast herself down on a low stool by the fender. Richard followed and stood over her, the firelight driving over his face like the glow of excited blood, the shadows lying in his eye-sockets like blindness. She cried up at him : " No, I will not go if you come too. How can I go and sit listening to him, with you beside me hating him ! " He swayed slowly, but did not answer. She stripped herself of coat and furs and thrust them on him. " There·

Take them up to my room. I'm not going. I'll tell some lie.
Better than you hating him like this. And while you're up
you'll find some papers on my desk about the mortgage on White-
webbs. Attend to these. And don't come back just now. You
drive me mad when you hate Roger so."

When he had softly shut the door she put her hand to her
head and said : "Oh, Ellen, what has happened to me ? I have
lost all my strength."

But her voice was still level, and she was but a squat, crouching mass against the firelight. Ellen did not know whether she
was really moved, nor, if she were, whether she could feel com-
radely with such emotion, since she had seen the woman blench
at the thought of her son preaching in the street yet stay com-
placid at the prospect of him being lost in intellectual error.
So she did not answer.

"You must go for a long walk with Richard to-morrow,"
said Marion presently. "Over to Rochford, perhaps, where
Anne Boleyn lived. It's pretty there."

"That would be nice," Ellen answered. She liked it when
they talked as if they were merely strangers. "Do you think
it will be fine to-morrow ? Richard said you were awful clever
at telling the weather."

"I can't say. I only looked out for a moment. The clouds
are going and the moon's rising. But there's a queer feeling
in the air to-night. It's not like the winter or spring or summer
or autumn. It's as if we had come into some fifth season of the
year." She fell silent and sat tapping the floor with her foot ;
and asked more loudly but in the same tone : "What am I to
do, Ellen, to keep my sons from quarrelling over me ? "

Ellen was sure she was being mocked ; grown-up people
never asked one's advice. She muttered sullenly : "I don't
know " ; but as she spoke she heard from Marion's dark shape a
sound of discovery such as a searcher might make when his
groping fingers closed on the lost pearl. Its intensity convinced,
and she leaned forward, crying in full friendship : "You've
thought of something to settle them ? "

But Marion answered, with that indifference grown nearly
to a sneer : "Oh, no. . . . Oh, no. . . ."

Ellen leaned back, hating these adults that like to keep their
secrets from the young.

CHAPTER X

ELLEN was still on her knees fiddling with the lock of the French window in an effort to discover why Marion had found it so difficult to open and shut, when she saw through the lacquer of reflection which the lit room painted on the uncurtained glass that a dark mass had come to a halt just outside. It moved, and she perceived that it was a skirt. She stood up to face the intruder and looked through the glass into Marion's eyes. For a moment she stared back in undisguised anger. Of course, if the woman had had any sense she would never have formed this daft idea of going for a dander on the marshes at this hour of the night, whether her nerves were troubling her or not ; but she never ought to have pretended to be so set on it, and let a body feel sure of having the evening alone with Richard as soon as he had finished with those beastly papers, if she was going to turn back in five minutes. Then she remembered that this was Richard's mother, and that for some reason he set great store by her ; and she tried to smile, and laid her fingers on the doorknob to open it. But Marion shook her head and put out a prohibitory hand with so urgent a gesture that the unlit lantern which hung by a strap from her wrist bumped against the glass.

Yet she remained for some seconds longer with her face pressed close to the window. She was peering into the room with an expression of wanting to fix its contents and its appearance in her memory, which was odd in the owner of the house. Ellen moved aside in order not to impede her vision, and stood disliking her for her pervasive inexplicability and for her extreme plainness. She had been very ugly all that evening since she came down to dinner, and now the shining glass in front of her face was acting in its uncomeliness like a magnifying lens. Her hair had suddenly become greasy during the last few hours, and it showed in lank loops where her hat had been carelessly jammed down on her head. In the same short space of time her face seemed to have grown fatter, and her skin had taken on the pallor of unhealthy obesity. Against it the dark down on her upper lip looked like dirt. Her eyes were not magnificent to-night. After she had stared round the room she looked again at Ellen, and gave her a forced smile that looked the more unpleasant because the corners of her mouth were joined to her nose by deep creases. It so manifestly did not spring from any joy, that Ellen could not answer it save by just such another false grin. Her honesty hated this woman who had thus negotiated her into insincerity, and she turned away. When she looked back the face had gone.

She went back to the fire and sat thinking bitterly what a daft thing it was for a wife to go wandering round her own house in the night like a thief. But Marion was altogether an upsetting woman. She had kept the dinner waiting for nearly a quarter of an hour, and when she came down it was revealed that she had caused this delay, which must have inconvenienced the kitchen and was sheer cruelty to Richard, who had made next to nothing of a tea, by dressing herself up in a black and gold brocade affair that it was sheer madness to waste wearing when there was no company, and putting on jewels which made her stricken plainness look the more soiled and leaden. Then, once they sat down to the meal she had done her best to spoil, she had eaten so slowly that it dragged on interminably; and all the while had kept her great eyes fixed on Richard's face, so that though he sometimes turned aside and spoke to Ellen, he was always drawn away from her by his sense of that strong, exigent gaze. The minute they had finished, when there seemed a chance of their settling down in some more easy grouping by the fire, Marion had curtly and disagreeably asked him if he had gone through the papers about the mortgage; and when he answered that he had not been able to keep his mind on them she had told him to go upstairs and finish them just as if he were a child.

Ellen raised her upper lip over her teeth at the thought of Marion's subsequent awkwardness. There had not, when she announced her plan of taking Richard and Ellen up to town the next morning and spending the day shopping and going to a theatre, been the least real party-giving joy in her tone. Her will seemed to be holding her voice in its hands like a concertina and waving it to and fro and squeezing out of it all sorts of notes ; but the sound of generous happiness would not come. And when Ellen tried to tell her that it was very kind of her, but for herself she would rather stay quietly in the country and go for a walk with Richard, the woman had simply lifted her voice to a higher pitch and said : " Oh, but it'll be great fun. We must go before Sunday is on us." She was evidently one of those managing bodies who are accustomed to ride rough-shod over the whole world, and often do it under the pretence of kindness. It was most cunning the way she rang for the cook to try and make it seem that there was a pressing domestic reason for her taking this jaunt. But cook had let her down badly, staring in such ingenuous amazement, and blurting out : " Oh Lor', mum, I don't want no aluminium set now. All I said was I thought our copper saucepans would need re-coppering in a year or so, and that, considering the trouble and expense that meant, we might as well restock with aluminium.' There had been a hysterical stridency about the way in which Marion had flouted the woman's protests by repeating over and over again : " Yes, you shall have them now. There's not the smallest reason why you should wait for them. I shall go up to Harrod's to-morrow morning."

Indeed, Marion was a queer woman in all respects, from her broad face and squat body to her forced, timbreless voice and her unconvincing gestures. It was only her clumsiness that had prevented her from opening the French window ; the lock was all right. Ellen felt that she would die if she did not have an hour alone with Richard to relearn that life could be lived easily and with grace But it would be just like the creature's untimeliness and awkwardness to be still hanging about the garden in readiness and pop in just when everything was being lovely. Ellen crossed to one of the small leaded windows which were on each side of the French window and looked out of the open pane in its centre. It was as she feared. The light streaming from the room showed her Marion standing half-way across the lawn, looking up at the top storey of the house. As the ray found her she lowered her head and made a jerky, embarrassed movement in the direction of Ellen, who, feeling merciless, continued to hold back the curtain. Marion drew her cloak collar up about her ears and stepped aside into the darkness. Ellen went and sat down by the fire. From something in Marion's bearing, she knew that she would not be back for some time.

It would be beautiful when Richard came down to her. Now that the room was purged of its late occupant she felt herself becoming again the miracle that Richard's love had made her in the days before they left Edinburgh. Her heart beat quicker, she was sustained by a general mirth and needed no particular joke to make her smile. She felt the equal of the tall flame that was driving through the fire. It did not worry her that

Richard was not with her, for she knew that at each moment she was recovering more and more of that joy in life which had previously come to her every morning, though those were greyer than here : which had been a real possession, since Richard had often, when he was tired, found such restoration in reading its signs on her as a footsore man might find in throwing himself in long grass : which had been gradually going from her ever since the house had begun to draw her into its affairs. Now she was regaining it ; though, indeed, ever to have become conscious of it, as she had during the time of being without it, was to have lost the glad essence of it. She quailed and rejoiced like a convalescent who sets out to put his strength to the test, when she heard the slamming of a door overhead.

He did not come to her at once, but looked round the room and said : " Where's Marion ? "

It would be as well not to speak of the plain face pressed against the window, of the dark loiterer in the garden. Murmuring, " Oh, she'll be back in a minute," she opened her arms to him.

He swung her out of the chair and sat down himself, gathering her very close. " Oh, my Ellen, you are the very colour of that red deer I saw run across the road ! " he whispered in her ear. She knew immediately, from the peace that fell on his deep, driving breath, from the way that his lips lifted and let the splendour of his eyes shine out again, that he too was aware of her recovery of normal joy and was refreshing himself with it. She drooped down towards his mouth, but at the last minute he avoided her kiss and said irritably : " I wonder if Roger made an awful ass of himself preaching to-night ? "

" I've no doubt," answered Ellen, " that he made Jesus most dislikeable. But with all the attention Christianity gets, it can put up with a setback here and there."

" It's not that I'm worrying about," he told her. " I can't bear having mother's name bandied about again after the hell of a time she's had." He stared in front of him with obsessed eyes.

Ellen shifted uneasily on his knee. She would have liked to take his face between her hands and tilt it down till his eyes looked into hers ; but that was no use, for however she tilted it, his eyes would shift from her face to focus themselves on some blankness which he could fill with his obsession. She folded her arms round his neck and clung closer, closer. It would be all right if she could have a little time alone with him. The thudding of his heart made her think of the engine of a steamer ; and so

of the voyage which they had planned to make when they were
married, landing only where the sea beat on a shore as lovely as
itself. She sat forward on his knee and picked up a copy of
the *Times* which lay on a small table near them, and turned it
over till she found the mails and shipping columns ; and she
began to chant what her eye first saw.

"'Lamport and Holt. *Bruyère*, passed Fernando Noronha,
21st, Clyde, for Rosario. *Lalande*, left Santos 20th, Liverpool
for Rio Grande. *Leighton*, arrived Buenos Aires 20th from Liverpool. *Vestris*, left Pernambuco 17th for New Orleans.' Richard,
have you ever been to Pernambuco ? "

"Once," he said.

"What like is it ? " she said in her Scotch way.

"Oh, I don't know. . . . It's supposed to be like Venice."

"Like Venice ? Why ? "

"Oh, there are waterways . . . and all that sort of thing. . . ."

She looked at him as one might at a friend whom one had
supposed to be suffering from some mild ailment, but who mentioned casually some symptom which one knows the mark of a
disease which has no cure. If he had lost his pleasure in pro-
hibiting time to be a thief by recreating past days when the
earth had shown him its beauty, his mother's woes had made him
grievously sick in his soul. "Ah, well ! " she said ; and let the
silence settle.

After a while he asked impatiently : "Where is mother ? "

She put her hand to her head. Of course trouble would come
of this, as it did of all that Marion did or that was done to her.
"She's gone out," she said timorously.

"Gone out ! At this time of night ? Do you mean into the
garden ? "

"Yes, into the garden," she temporised. "She said her
head was bad and that she felt she'd be the better for a blow."

"Excuse me," he said curtly, and lifted her from his knee,
and went to the window and drew back the curtains. An
elm-tree in a grove to the east held the moon in its topmost
branches like a nest builded by a bird of light. It showed the
garden an empty silver square, trenched at the end by the soot-
black shadow of the hedge. "She's not there ! " he exclaimed.

"Well, she did say something about going down on the
marshes." Ellen felt a little sick as she saw his face whiten.
She had known when the woman announced her daft intention
that trouble would come of it. There was going to be more of
this Yaverland emotion, quiet and unhysteric and yet maddening,
like some of the lower notes on the organ.

"Going down on the marshes at nine o'clock on a freezing night!" He turned on her with a sharpness that she felt should have been incompatible with their relationship. "Why didn't you come and tell me she was doing this?"

Her temper spurted. "How should I know there was anything unusual in it? You are all strange in this house!" For a second they looked at each other in hatred; then eyes softened and they looked ashamed, like children who have quarrelled over a toy and have pulled it to pieces. She thought jealously of the woman who was the cause of all this trouble, walking down there in the quietness of the marshes, where all day she herself had longed to be. Despairingly, she moved close to him, slipping her hand inside his, and said, trying to hold back the thing that was drifting away: "I'm sorry. But she said she wanted to clear her head after the day she'd had. And I could never think she was a woman who'd be afraid of walking in the dark. And it seemed natural enough. Because it has been a day for her, hasn't it?"

He agreed grimly: "Yes, it's been a day," and looked over his shoulder at the quiet silvern garden, and shivered. "Tell me," he asked, with a timidity that filled her with fear, since it was the last quality she had ever expected to colour his tone to her, "what was she like, before she went out?"

"Oh, verra bright," said Ellen, with conscious acidity. "She was all for making arrangements for you and me to go up to town with her to-morrow and see a play, and I don't know all what. And she had the cook in to tell her about some aluminium saucepans that we're going to buy to-morrow if we go."

"Oh!" He was manifestly relieved. "Well, I suppose it's all right."

"Yes, it's all right," she told him pettishly; and then tried to make amends by speaking sympathetically of Marion. "I can understand why your mother thought it would do her good to go out. If you've lived all your life in a place I expect every field and tree gets a meaning for you. No doubt," she went on, unconscious of any feeling but contentment that she was so successfully taking cognisance of Marion's more pathetic aspect," the poor thing's gone for a walk to some place where she can get a bit of comfort by remembering the time when she was very young. Richard, Richard, what have I said?"

He looked at her coldly. "Nothing. What could you have said?" But he went to the window as if he had been told something that had made him hasten, and opened it and stepped outside. Against the moonlight he was only a silhouette; but from the hawkishness of the profile he turned to the west she knew that he was allowing himself to wear again that awful look of rage which had made her cry aloud. He stepped in again and said : " I'm sorry, Ellen, but I must go and look for her."

She might have known that she would not have her evening alone with him. " May I come with you ? " she asked through tears.

" No, no, it wouldn't be any fun for you," he answered fussily, " scrambling about these fields in the dark."

" Let me come with you ! " she begged ; and guilefully, seeing his brows knit sullenly, she waved her hand round the room, which she knew must be to him sombre with the day's events, and cried : " I shall feel afraid, waiting here."

" Very well. Go and put your things on. But be quick."

He had his hat and coat and stick when she came down ; and he had grudged the time spent in waiting for her. Wearily she followed him out of the window. From what her mother had told her about men, she had always known that even Richard, since he was male, might forget his habit of worship towards her and turn libellous as husbands are, and pretend that she was being tiresome when she was not. But she would never have believed that it could come so soon. And it was spoiling her. She no longer felt possessed of the perfect control of her actions, nor sure of her own nobility. Only a second or two ago she had betrayed her sex by pretending to be frightened by assuming one of the base qualities which tradition lyingly ascribed to women, because she had to be in his presence no matter at what price. There was no knowing where all this would end.

But in the inventive beauty of the night she found distraction, for it had wrought many fantastical changes in the dull world the day had handed it. The frost had made the soil that had been sodden metal-hard, while preserving its roughness, so that to tread the paths was like walking on beaten silver. Since its rising, the moon had sown and raised a harvest of new plants in the garden ; for the rose-trees, emaciated with leaflessness, had each a shadow that twisted on the earth like ground-ivy or climbed the wall like a creeper. Through an orchard piebald with moonbeams and shadow, and a gate, glaring as with new white paint, set in a lichen-grey hedge, they passed out on the grizzled hillside. He did not take her down the path by which she and Marion had gone on to the marshes the previous afternoon, but plunged forward into the short grey fur of the moonlit field, where there was no path, and led her up in a slanting course towards the top of the elm-hedge that striped the hill.

It was rough walking over the steep frozen hummocks, and she wished he would not walk so fast. But it was lovely going up like this, and with every step widening the wide, whitely-blazing view. The elm trees stood like chased toys made by silversmiths where the light struck them ; and in the darkness seemed like harsh twiggy nets hung on tall poles to catch the stars. Scattered over the polished harbour, the black boats squatted on their shadows and the tide licked towards them with an ebony and silver tongue. But far out in the fairway a liner and some lesser steamers carried their spilling cargo of orange brightness, and the further fringe of the night was spoiled by the comprehensive yellow wink of a lighthouse ; and these things tainted the black and white immaculacy of the hour. It was not on earth but overhead that the essence of the night displayed itself. Light rushed from the moon into the sky like a strong wind, carrying before it some shining vapours that might have been angels' clouts blown off a heavenly line. It was as if some horseplay was going on among the ethereal forces ; for the stars, dimmed by the violent brilliance of the moon, were like tapers seen through glass, and were held, perhaps, by invisible beings who had been drawn to their windows by the sound of carnival. To its zenith the night was packed with gaiety.

" Richard, Richard, is it not beautiful ? " she cried.

" Yes, yes," he answered.

They reached the topmost elm in the row, and opened a gate into a field which stretched inland from the hill's brow. Under the shadow of its seaward edge they still walked westerly, the ploughed earth looking like a patch of grey corduroy lying to their right. It struck her that he was moving now like a hunter stalking his quarry, as if the lightness of his feet were a weapon, as if he were looking forward to an exciting kill. At the corner of the field they stopped before a gap in the hedge. Triple barbed wire crossed a vista of close-cropped grass running to trees that lifted dark spires against the pale meridian starlight.

" Wait," said Richard.

He went forward and stamped down the long grasses at one side of the gap, and then bent nearly double and seemed to be pressing against something with his hands and his knee. The barbed wire began to hum, to buzz excitedly ; there was the groan of cracking wood and the grunt of his deep, straining breath. She found herself running her hands over her face and down her body and thinking, " Since he is like that, and I am like this, all will be well." That was quite meaningless ; it must be true that one of the moon's rays was unreason. The barbed wire danced and fell to the ground, singing angrily. Richard had broken in two the stake which supported it.

" Come on," he ordered her, and lifted her over the tangle of wires. They walked forward, again on the hilltop's unscreened edge. The harbour was hidden by the elms, but below lay the frosted marsh and islands, girdled by the glistening sea-walls and their coal black shadows, and great wide Kerith, its expanse jewelled here and there by the lights of homesteads. It was beautiful, but she did not say anything about it to Richard, who was walking on ahead, though there did not seem any reason why they should walk in single file, for the ground was level and the grass short. There was indeed a suavity about this place which was not to be found in fields or commons. The line of trees towards which they were going was only a spur of a dense wood that stretched inland, and light from some moonflooded place beyond outlined their winter-naked bodies and showed them beautiful with a formal afforested grace.

" Is this a park ? " she whispered, running forward to his side.

" Yes. My father's park."

" Oh ! " she breathed in surprise ; then, flaming up in loyalty, cried : " What a shame it isn't yours ! "

He made an exclamation of anger and disgust, and said coldly : " Can't you understand that I am glad that nothing which was his is mine ? "

Meekly she murmured : " That's natural, that's natural," and fell behind.

They passed the lacy clump of withered bracken, casting a shadow much more substantial than itself, which was the last dwindled outpost of the screen of trees ; and Richard hissed over his shoulder, " Hush ! " though she had not spoken. But nothing could spoil this. The silver forest waited in a half circle round a clearing that looked marshy with moonbeams ; and in the centre of the arc, set forward from the trees, shone a small temple, looking out to sea. It had four white pillars, which were vague with excessive light, columns of gleaming mist ; and these upheld a high pediment, covered with deep stone mouldings which cast such shadows and received such brightness that it looked like a rich casket chased by some giant jeweller. That it should last longer than a sigh did not seem possible.

But it endured, it endured ; until the urgent advocacy of romance which was somehow inherent in its beauty, and which was not likely to be fulfilled, caused an ache. She caught her breath in a sob.

"You think it beautiful?" asked Richard, close to her ear.

"Oh, yes! Oh, yes!"

"I had a summer-house in that villa of mine at Rio," he said, hotly and defiantly, "which was just like this, but much more beautiful."

He stepped forward and began to move towards the temple with that air of stalking a quarry. She followed him wearily, feeling that it was not right that they should have come here like this. They should have come in some different way. At each step the temple grew higher before them, more candid, more immaculate, but its beauty did not soften his inexorable aspect. When they could see the pale wedges which the moon drove in between the columns he paused and stared, and drew from his pocket something dark which lay easily in his hand. "What's that? What's that?" she asked in panic. "Only an electric torch," he muttered, without surprise at her suspicion, and went with springing, silent, detective gait up the three steps of the temple.

She remained without, drooping. Would he find his mother there? She hoped so, for then they could all go home and leave this place, which she felt despised her. The tall trees of the forest, lifting their bare branches like antlers against the stars, seemed to be holding their heads high in contempt of her defeat. For so to be forgotten was defeat.

No sounds came from the temple, and she timidly went up the steps and passed into the interior, which was cut by the colonnade into narrow chambers of shadows and broader chambers of light. At first she could not see him anywhere, and cried in alarm: "Richard!"

"I'm here," he answered. He was standing beside her, leaning against a pillar, but put out no hand to soothe her fear.

"Have you not found her?" she quavered.

He let the yellow circle of the electric torch travel over the cracked stucco-wall that faced them, the paintless door at its left extremity, the drift of dead leaves on the stone floor.

"What does that door open on to?" asked Ellen, forgetting the reason for their search in the queerness of the place.

"A staircase up to the room above."

"What a lovely place," she cried joyfully, trying to remind him of the existence of happiness, "to play in in the summer! Could one sleep up there, do you think?"

He switched off the light. " I daresay," he said gruffly in the darkness.

" And look ! " She pointed to a moonlit niche in the middle of the wall high and deep enough to hold a life-sized statue. " It would be fun if I stood up there, wouldn't it ? "

There was silence ; and then amazingly, his voice cracked out on her like a whip. " Why do you say that ? Did anybody tell you about this place ? Has she told you anything about it ? "

" Why, no ! " she stammered. " Nobody's told me a thing of it ! I just thought it would be fun if I were to stand up there like a statue. You take me up too quick."

His passion died suddenly. " No," he said weakly, exhaustedly. " Of course she wouldn't tell you. I was stupid. Yes, you're quite right. That's what a man would do with a woman, wouldn't he, if they were here together and they were lovers ? He'd make her stand up there." Insanely he switched on the electric torch and flashed it up and down the niche, though in the dazzling moonlight its rays were but a small circular soilure.

" But it's not summer now," she reminded him tenderly, laying her hand on his sleeve. " Since she's not here, let's go home. Think of those bonny fires burning away and nobody the better for them ! "

" That's what he'd do, he'd make her stand up there," he muttered, sending the light up and down the niche very slowly, as if in time to slow thoughts.

She turned and went down the steps and walked away, holding her hands close to her eyes like blinkers, so that she might be the less afflicted by the night, whose beauty was a reproach to her. A desire to look out towards the sea and the flatlands came on her. This temple set among the woods was a human place ; men had laid the stones, men had planted the trees, men had thought of it before it was. It was the stage for a scene in the human drama, which she had not been able to play. But the sea and the flatlands were not made by men ; they made humanity seem a little thing, and human success and failure not reasonable causes for loud laughter or loud weeping. At the hill's edge she leaned against a tree and gazed down on the moon-diluted waters, on the moon-powdered lands, and was jealous of the plain, disturbing woman who kept herself covered with the quietness of the marshes to the distress of others ; and saw suddenly, on the path at the foot of the slope, the far, weak ray of a dancing lantern.

She ran back to the temple. All she cared for really was pleasing him. " Richard, Richard ! I've found her ! She's down there on the marshes ! "

He was out beside her in a second. " Where ? How do you know ? "

" I saw her lantern down on the marshes ! "

When they got back to the hill's edge the light was still to be seen, bobbing along towards the elm brow. Richard clipped Ellen's waist to show her how well pleased he was with her. " Ah, that'll be Marion ! " he said. " Nobody else would be on the marshes at this hour." Then a little wind of anger blew over his voice. " Has she been to his tomb ? Can she have been to his tomb in the time ? It's a steep climb for her. I wonder. . . . I wonder. . . ."

The lantern bobbed out of sight behind the elm row. Feeling that they were again alone together, Ellen raised her lips to be kissed, but he had already turned away. " Let's go home now ! " he said urgently. " I want to know where she's been."

The place seemed far more beautiful to her than it had done before. " Oh ! Now you're sure she's quite safe, mayn't we stay here a little ? " she begged.

" No, no. Some other night. I'll bring you to-morrow night. But not now, not now."

She followed laggingly, looking about her with infatuation. There was something religious about the scene. Rites of some true form of worship might fitly be celebrated here. All appeared more majestic and more sacred than in the strained, bickering moments before she showed him the lantern. Now she perceived that it was the silver circle of trees which was the real temple, and that the marble belvedere was but a human offering laid before the shrine. It was in there, along the ebony paths which ran among the glistening thickets, that one would find the presence of the divinity.

" Oh, Richard ! It will never be so beautiful as this on any other night ! Let us stay ! "

" No. It will be just as good any moonlit night. I swear I'll bring you. But now I want to get back home."

He slipped her arm through his to make her come. She stumbled along, turning her face aside towards those mystic woods. At the end of those paths was another clearing, wide but smaller than this, and girdled all sides by the forest ; and there was something there. . . . Another temple ? A statue ? An event ? She did not know. But if they found it, they would be happy for ever. . . .

" Richard——— "

" No."

He swung her over the tangled wires, and they hurried through
the ploughed field. When they came to the gate at the top of
the elm-row they saw below them, on the path up from the
marshes to the orchard gate, the bobbing lantern.

" She's going fairly quickly," he said softly, speculatively.
" I wonder if she's been to his tomb ? Do you think she's had
time ? "

" I don't know," Ellen murmured, disquieted that he should
ask her when he must be aware she could not tell.

" Oh, well ! " he exclaimed, with a sudden change to loudness
and bluffness, switching on the electric torch and turning it on
the earth at their feet. " We'll find out when we get home.
Let's hurry back."

They ran across the hillside, Ellen following desperately,
with a dread that if she tripped and delayed him he might not
be able to behave quite nicely, the circle of light he cast on
the ground for her guidance. The humped and raw-edged
frozen earth hurt her feet. The speed they went at shook the
breath out of her lungs. At an easy, comfortable pace, the lantern
bobbed its way into the orchard and up towards the garden.
She was the lucky woman, Marion.

" Good," said Richard, as they passed through the gate.
" You did that in fine style."

" Why do you need to hurry so ? " she protested. " You
have all night now to ask her where she has been."

" I want to find out if she has been to his tomb," he repeated
with dull, drilling persistence.

When they came to the end of the garden he drew up sharply.
" Why is she standing by the servant's door ? Why the devil
is she always doing such extraordinary things ? "

Ellen saw in front of her, through a screen of bushes that ran
from the left-hand corner of the house to the left wall of the
garden, the steady rays of the lantern come to rest. " You'd
better go and ask her," she said pettishly.

He crossed the lawn quickly and halted before a trellis arch
which pierced this screen, and motioned her to go before him.
At that moment there came the sound of knocking near by. He
caught his breath, pressed on her heels impatiently, and when
they entered the tiled yard brushed past her and walked towards
the lantern, which was close to the door in the side of the house,
calling querulously : " Mother ! Mother ! "

The light swung and wavered. " What is the woman up to ? "

thought Ellen crossly. The strong yellow rays of the lantern dazzled before them and prevented them from seeing anything of its bearer, though the moonlight beams were still unclouded.

"Mother!" Richard cried irascibly, and levelled the torch on her like a revolver.

Its brightness showed the dewy roundness, towsled with perplexity, of a doe-eyed girl of Ellen's age.

"Ach!" said Richard, shouting with rage. "Who are you? Who are you?"

It struck Ellen that his refusal of any recognition of the girl's sweetness was unnatural; that it would have been more sane and wholesome, though it would have pricked her jealousy, if he had shown some flush of pleasure at this gentle, bucolic, nut-brown beauty.

"Please, sir," gabbled the girl with her wet, foolish, pretty lips, "I'm Annie Brickett, and your cook's my auntie, and I come over to say my married sister's had a little baby, and it's before her time, so would auntie give us the clothes she was making?"

The door opened, and aproned figures looked out of the kitchen brightness at them.

"Where is your mistress?" Richard asked them, cutting into the girl's sweet, silly speech. "Has she come back?"

The servants all started making twittering, consequential noises. "No, sir, she isn't." "We didn't know, any of us, you was out till the lady and gentleman come."

"What lady and gentleman?"

The two younger women shrunk back and left the cook to answer. "Mr. Roger Peacey, sir, and the lady." From the hindmost girl there came a giggle.

That was why they had not heard the knocking at the door. They had all been sitting laughing at his mother's other son and going over the family history. Ellen shrank back from the light. Marion's misfortunes made things very ill to deal with; they seemed to bring out the worst in everybody. And how the whole affair was hurting Richard! He turned on his heel and walked back to the trellis arch and went through it without waiting for her. By the time she had followed him round the corner of the house he was opening the French window into the dining-room. He found it quite easy to open; again she thought with rage and contempt of the way that Marion had fumbled with the handle. She had to run along the path lest in his forgetfulness he shut her out into the night.

She found him halted just within the room, pulling off his

gauntlets and forcing a white smile towards Roger, who was standing swaying on the hearthrug, his cheeks dribbled with tears. Poppy stood beside him, staring sullenly at a blank wall, her mouth a little open with distaste for him.

" So you're giving us another visit," said Richard, in that hollow conscientious tone of kindness he had used to them in the afternoon.

Roger opened his mouth but could not speak ; then flapped his hands to make it plain this was an occasion of importance, and cried bleatingly : " I've come to say that I forgive you all."

" Forgive us ! " exclaimed Richard, swept away to the bleak extremity of rage. Then checked himself. " Oh, for not coming to your meeting. We hoped you would. Ellen was tired."

" I couldn't bear to think of you p'raps going to bed and feeling that I was harbouring ill thoughts towards you, not realising that now I've got Jesus I'll forgive anything that any-body does against me ! " His voice wallowed rhapsodically. " So Poppy and I just nipped in here instead of going straight back to the Colony."

Poppy wriggled her body about in her clothes in an agony of desire to disassociate herself from him, from the situa-tion.

" That was good of you," said Richard.

" And now "—the whistling tone came back in his speech— " I want to tell mother ! "

" You can't do that. She isn't in."

" What, weren't you all out together ? Didn't she come home with you ? "

" No."

" Then, love o' goodness, where is she at this time of night ? "

" Down on the marshes," said Richard casually. " She had a headache. She thought a walk in the night air would do her good." Slowly and deliberately he smoothed out his gauntlets and laid them down on the table.

" Oh," murmured Roger, and was silent until Richard put out his hand and straightened the gloves, making them lie parallel with the grain of the wood. Then suddenly he ran round the table and looked up into his brother's face. " Here ! What's the matter with mother ? "

" Nothing ! Nothing ! " exclaimed Richard in exasperation. " She's down on the marshes, having a walk."

" Oh, but you can't take me in that way ! " the pallid creature cried, wringing his hands. " I can see you're frightened about mother ! "

" I'm not," said Richard vehemently.

" You needn't try to fool me. I'm stupid about everything else, but not about mother ! And I could always feel what was going on between you two. Many's the time I've had to leave the room because you two were loving each other so and I felt out of it. And now I know you're frightened about her ! You are ! You are ! "

" I'm not ! " shouted Richard.

Roger shrank back towards Poppy, who seemed to like the loud noise, and had raised eyes skimmed of their sullenness by delight. " If you'd got Jesus," he said tartly, " you'd learn to be gentle. Like He was." He recovered confidence by squeezing Poppy's hand, which she tendered him deceitfully, looking at Richard the while as if she were waiting for orders. " Now you'd better tell me what it is about mother that's making you frightened. She'd not be pleased, would she, if she came in and found you treating me like this, as if I hadn't a right to know anything about her, and me her own son just as much as you are ? "

That argument moved Richard, Ellen could see. He looked down at his white knuckles and unclenched his hands. " It's really nothing," he told Roger in that false, kind voice. " I went upstairs after dinner to look over some papers for mother and left her and Ellen down here. When I came back Ellen told me she'd gone out for a walk on the marshes. It struck me as rather an odd thing for her to do at this hour, so we went out and had a look round, but couldn't see her anywhere. There's not the slightest occasion for worry."

Roger stared at him, sucking his front teeth. " But you're frightened ! " he said explosively.

" I am not."

" You are. You think she's come to some harm down on the marshes." He slipped past him and flung open the French window, calling in a thin, whistling voice that could not have been heard fifty yards away : " Mummie ! Mummie ! "

A convulsion of rage ran through Richard. With one hand he jerked Roger back into the room by his coat-collar, with the other he slammed the French window. " Be quiet. I tell you she's all right. I know where she's gone."

" Where, then ? "

" Never mind."

" Where ? Where ? " His hands fumbled for the door-handle again.

" Oh, stop that ! " Richard loosed hold of him with the expression of one who had grasped what he thought to be soft grass and finds his palms scored by a fibrous stalk. He said, and Ellen could see that he liked saying it as little as anything that he had ever said all his life long : " If you must know, I think she's gone up to my father's tomb."

Roger shook his head solemnly. " No. You're wrong. She hasn't gone there. And she's come to harm."

" Why in God's name do you say that ? " burst out Richard.

" I know. I've known all the evening. That's really why I came back here after the service. That talk about forgiveness was just something I made up as an excuse. I knew quite well that something was wrong with mummie." His pale eyes sought first Richard and then Ellen. " Don't you believe a person might know if something happened to another person," he asked wistfully, " if they loved them enough ? "

There was indeed such an infinity of love in that weak gaze that Richard and Ellen exchanged the abashed look that passes between lovers when it is brought to their notice that they are not the sole practitioners of the spiritual art. Richard murmured, " Oh . . . perhaps . . . but really, Roger, she was quite bright before she went out. Ellen, tell Roger. . . ."

But Roger stared out at the empty silver garden and whimpered inattentively : " I can't help it. I want to go down to the marshes and look for her."

" Very well," agreed Richard, blinking. The sight of the love in those weak eyes made his voice authentically kind. " We'll go down. She ought to be easy to find as she's carrying a lantern. You're quite sure she has got a lantern with her, Ellen ? "

" Oh yes," said Ellen. " It bumped against the glass when she came back and looked through the window."

" When she came back and looked through the window ? What do you mean ? "

" Why," Ellen explained diffidently, not wanting to enlarge on his mother's eccentricity. " She said good-bye and went out and shut the door. Then in a minute or two I looked up and saw her face against the glass. . . . I offered to open the door, but she shook her head and went away."

" But, Ellen ! Didn't that strike you as very strange ? " She stared in amazement that his eyes could look into hers like this. He choked back a reproach. " Ellen . . . tell me everything . . . everything she said before she went out."

She passed her hand over her forehead, shading her face. It shamed her that he was going to be interested in what she told him and not at all in her manner of telling it. " I've told you. She was full of plans about us all going up to-morrow. To a theatre. And she sent for the cook and talked to her about saucepans."

" What saucepans ? "

" Aluminium saucepans."

" But what about them ? "

She laughed aloud in the face of his displeasure. An image of the temple in the wood mocked her mind's eye. Instead of standing in one of the narrow chambers of shadow that lay behind its pillars with his lips on hers, she was being cross-examined about saucepans. " She reckoned to get them in the forenoon before we went to the theatre."

For a second he pondered it ; then asked with an accent that pierced her because it was so infantine, so shamelessly mendicant of comfort : " She really was all right, Ellen ? "

" Cross my heart, Richard, she was that."

Their hands stole into one another's ; from the warm, fluttering pressure of his fingers she knew that his heart was feeling numberless adoring things about her. If everything had not happened as she wished, it was not because the dispensation of love had come to an end, but because it had not endured long enough. There was a golden age ahead. She leaned towards him, but was arrested by the change in his expression. His face, which had been a white mask of grief, became vulpine. " Yes, she will most probably be up there . . . at his tomb. . . ."

Roger, behind him at the window, fluted miserably: " Mummie ! Mummie ! " He turned on him with a gesture of irritation and opened the door. " Here, Roger, let's go now." The glance he shot backwards into the room was so preoccupied that it held no more intimate message for Ellen than for Poppy. " Well, I don't expect we'll be long. . . ."

They crossed the lawn, their short shadows treading it more gaily than their tall, striding selves. There seemed to be some mishap at the gate into the orchard. Apparently Roger squeezed his finger in the hinge ; but he was very brave. The two women stood at the window and watched him hop about, shaking the injured hand, while his shadow parodied him, and Richard waited with a stoop of the shoulders that meant patience and hatred. Then again the silver garden was empty.

Poppy and Ellen went and sat down at the hearth ; and

Poppy said with an extravagant bitterness : " Well, that's that. He knows as well as I do that the Army expects us officers to be in by eleven."

" No doubt Mr. Yaverland'll go round in the morning and explain the exceptional circumstances," murmured Ellen.

" I'm sure I don't care. I'm fed to the teeth with the Army, fed to the teeth. . . ." She stared into the fire as if she saw a picture there, and drew a little tin box from her pocket and offered it to Ellen, saying : " Take one. They're violet cachous." Sucking one, she sat forward with her feet in the fender and her head near her knees until, as if the flavour of the sweet in her mouth was reminding her of a time when life was less flavourless than now, she started up and began to walk restlessly about the room. She halted at the window and asked thickly : " That place over the other side of the river. Where there's a glow in the sky. Is that Chatham ? "

With awe, with the lifting of the hair, the chilling of the skin that those suffer who see the fulfilment of a prophecy, Ellen remembered what Marion had said that afternoon about the handsome young sailor in Chatham High Street. She murmured tremulously : " I think Richard said it was."

" Ah, Chatham's a nice place," said Poppy in a surly voice. She pressed her face against the glass like a beast looking out of its cage. It was quite certain, as the silence endured, that she wept.

Then Marion had been right. A wave of terror washed over Ellen. What chance had she of playing any part on a stage where there moved this woman of genius, who was so creative that she had made Richard, and so wise that she could see through the brick wall of this girl's brutishness ? She stammered, " Well, good-night, I'll away to my bed," and ran upstairs to her room and undressed furiously, letting her clothes fall here and there on the floor. In the first moments after she turned out the lights the darkness was brightly painted with pictures of the moonlit temple ; one everywhere she turned her eyes. And once, when she was far gone into drowsiness, she woke herself by sitting up in bed and crying acidly : " And do you think we will have to spend every night searching for your mother, Richard ? " But very soon she slept.

She woke suddenly and with her mind at attention, as if someone had whispered into her ear. She sat up and looked through the great window into that not quite full-bodied light of a day that was overcast and advanced past its dawn only by an hour or two. There was no one in the farmyard. Yet it came back to her that she had been called by the sound of men's voices ; of Richard's voice, she could be almost sure, for there was a filament of pleasure trailing across her consciousness. There was no reason why he should be out of doors at this hour, before the family had been called to breakfast, unless the search for Marion had been unsuccessful. She jumped out of bed and washed and dressed and ran downstairs, leaving her hair loose about her shoulders because she begrudged the time for pinning it when he needed her comfort. Mabel, the parlour-maid, was coming out of the dining-room with an empty tray in her hand. One corner of her apron-bib flapped loose and there was a smut on her face. Ellen knew that Marion had not been found, for if she had been in the house, alive or dead, the girl would not have dared to look like that. They passed in silence, but exchanged a look of horror.

There was no one in the dining-room but Roger and Poppy. Poppy was sitting in an armchair at the hearth, where she had evidently spent the night. Her uniform was unbuttoned half-way down her square bust ; and on the arms of the chair there rested two objects that looked like sections of dried viscera, but which Ellen remembered to have seen labelled as pads in hair-dressers' windows. Roger was kneeling before her, his head on her lap, and weeping bitterly. She was stroking his hair kindly enough, though her eyes were dwelling on the teapot and ham on the breakfast-table. The French window was swinging open, admitting air that had the chill of dawn upon it ; and out-side on the gravel path stood Richard, listening to a bearded old fisherman in oilskins. She hovered about the threshold and heard the old man saying : " 'Tes no question o' use you putting yourselves about to look for her now. Mostly you don't hear nothin' of them for three weeks, and then they comes out where they went in. Till the tide brings them back you can't fetch them." Richard said : " Yes, yes," and held out money to him. She saw he wanted to send the fisherman away, that he could not bear to hear these things ; but he was held rigid by the obsession, which he and Marion had followed as if it were a law, that one must not betray emotion. His inhibited hand became more and more talonlike, more and more incapable of making the gesture of dismissal. To aid him Ellen showed her-self at the open door in her wildness of loose hair and called : " Richard ! Richard ! "

That made the old man take his money and go away, and Richard stepped back into the room. He evaded her embrace. " This ghastly light ! " he muttered, and went to the corner of the room and turned on the electric switch. Then he let her take his old, grief-patterned face between her hands.

" My dear, my dear, what has happened ? "

" There's a place . . . there's a place . . . there's a place on the sea-wall. . . " He drew his hand across his forehead. " He is finding it difficult," her heart told her sadly, " to explain it to a stranger." " In the train, when you came, you must have seen a brick-kiln . . . on the right of the railway . . . deserted. . . . A trolley-line runs from there over a bridge to the sea-wall . . . to a jetty. It hasn't been used for years. The planks are half of them rotted away. The high tide runs right up among the piers. We found her lantern down there on the mud."

Her heart sickened. " Oh, poor, poor Marion ! " she wept, and asked foolishly, incredulously, as if in hopes of finding a flaw in the story, " But when did you find the lantern ? "

" An hour ago. We looked for her last night till two. We went all the way along to Canfleet. They took us in at the signal-box there. Then as soon as it was light we walked back along the sea-wall. And we found the lantern. Look, it's out on the lawn."

They gazed at the dark object on the edge of the grass as if at any moment it might move or speak.

" But, my dearest, she may not be in the water ! She may have dropped the light and been feared to go further without it, and gone into one of those wee byres on the marshes till the morning, and not have wakened yet ! "

He laughed sleepily, softly. " Yes, certainly she's not wakened yet."

" But, my own dear, it may be so ! She may be with us at any moment now ! "

He shook his head obstinately. " No. She's dead. I know she's dead. There's something like silence lying over everything. It means she's dead."

It was her impulse to throw her arms about his neck and bid him weep if he wished on her breast, but feeling his stillness, his nearly unbreathing immobility, she kept herself from him. To those who fall and hurt themselves one runs with comfort ; by those who lie dangerously stricken by a disease one sits and waits.

" Sit down and take a bit of breakfast," she bade him softly. He sank into a chair at the table, lumpishly, as if his limbs had grown thick and lithic, while she poured out a cup of tea and cut some ham. Her flesh was weeping for Marion, who had been

quick, who now was dead ; but the core of her was a void. She
cut him a nice feathery slice, unbroken all the way from the
bone to the outer rim of bread-crumb-freckled fat ; and through
the void there shot the thought, trivial yet tremendously exultant :
" Now that Marion is gone I shall always look after his food."
He drew his brows together and groaned softly. Hawkishly
she looked round to see what was distressing him. It was, of
course, Roger howling in Poppy's lap. . . . " Oh, my darling
mummie!" It must be stopped.

" Roger," she said kindly, " sit forward for your breakfast."
He raised a dispirited nose, red with weeping, and shook his
head mournfully. " No, thank you. It wouldn't be of any
use. I couldn't keep a thing on my stomach."

" But what about Miss Poppy ? " she asked guilefully.
" She must be wearying for her breakfast after the night she's
spent in that chair."

That brought him off his feet, as she had known it would.
" Oh, poor Poppy ! " he cried. " Oh, poor Poppy ! " and led
her to the table.

Richard ate and drank for some moments ; he seemed very
hungry. Then he laid down his knife and fork and said : " Ellen,
when your mother died did you feel like this ? As if . . . the
walls of your life had fallen in ? "

" Yes, yes, my love, so terribly alone."

" Alone, alone," he repeated. " I am so selfish. I can think
of nothing but my own loneliness. I can't think of her."

" Well, never heed, my dear, my own dear. She wouldn't
want you to worry."

" Oh, but I must think this out ! " he exclaimed in a shocked,
dreary tone. " It's so important. . . ." He looked up at
the electric light and grumbled : " Oh, that damned light makes
it worse ! " and rose to restore the room to the sallowness of
the morning.

When he sat down again he would not eat, but leaned his
head on his hands and his elbows on the table and watched the
other two. Poppy was saying in tones half-maternal, half-
disagreeable : " Eat up your 'am, you silly cuckoo. You know if
you don't you'll have one of your sick turns," and Roger was
obeying. Tears and the ham collided noisily in his throat.

Richard withdrew his eyes from them and looked secretively
at Ellen. " She killed herself, of course," he said in an undertone.

" Oh no ! " she cried. " Oh no ! "

But there sounded through the room a thunderclap of memory.

There had been words drawled there the night before that now detonated in Ellen's mind. . . . "What am I to do, Ellen, to keep my sons from quarrelling over me ?"

"Oh no !" she cried again, lest he should notice that she was deafened and dizzied and ask why. "Never think that of her, my dearie."

She had thought the woman strident and hysterical and thoughtless for persisting in her plans for the next day in face of her own faint, barely acquiescent smiles, and a poor, feckless, fashionless housewife for thrusting those unwanted saucepans on the cook. But these had been alibis she had sought to establish that she might clear her soul of a charge of lingering at the brink of dark waters, lest Richard should understand her sacrifice and grieve.

"Her heel may have caught in the rotting wood," she nearly shrieked, so that he should not overhear the thoughts that rushed in on her silence. "She wore high heels for her age. . . ."

That was why Marion had come back and looked in through the window. She was to shed one by one the shelters that protected her soul from the chill of the universe : her house, her clothes, her flesh, her skeleton. This first step had cost her so much that for one shuddering moment she had gone back on it.

"And things looked so strange last night. If there was a skin of ice on the wood it'd be hard to tell it from the moonlit water. . . ."

Oh, pitiful dark woman that had stood on the lawn looking up at the room where sat her son, whom she would never see again. "If I had not gone to the window then," thought Ellen to herself, "she might have looked much longer."

"She was very ugly last night," muttered Richard. "She was always ugly when she was unhappy."

His speculative tone made her perceive that, unlike herself, he did not know for certain that Marion had committed suicide. She must conceal her proofs, bury them under a heap of lying counterproofs. "My dear, you'd never think it if you'd seen her last night. . . ."

"Tell me everything. All she did after I went upstairs."

Grimly she remembered the former rich traffic of their minds. Henceforward he would do nothing but ask that question ; she would do nothing but answer it. It was the third time she had told this story in the twelve hours. "She was as bright as could be. Talked of going to a theatre, but said you cared for a good music-hall as much as anything. . . ." Her voice was thin, as liars' voices are. Surely he must notice it and feel distaste.

Oh, fatal Marion ! Even in her complete and final abnegation of her forcefulness she had used such an excess of force that the world about her was shattered. For Ellen perceived that never again would the relationship of Richard and herself be the perfect crystal sphere that it had been before they came here, but must always, till they died, be flawed with insincerity. She would never dare tell him how, thought over, those trivial plans for the next day's pleasuring were revealed, themselves, as devices of a tremendous hammering nobility ; how, seen with the intelligence of memory, the face at the window had been the greasy mask of a swimmer in the icy waters of the ultimate fear ; how there had stood on the lawn for a long time what had seemed a loiterer, but was in truth a pillar of love. If she let his inherited excessiveness learn this he would go mad ; and he would hate her for not reading these signs when they had been given her. All her life she would have to keep silence concerning something of which he would speak repeatedly. She would become queer and jerky with strained inhibitions . . . charmless. . . . Perhaps he would go from her to unburdened women. . . .

"Perhaps you're right," he said wearily when she had finished ; "maybe it was an accident." He began to eat again, but soon pushed away his plate and stood up looking down on the hearth. "Where did she sit ? Which chair ? "

"Yon, at your hand."

He drooped over it, caressing the velvet cover. "Will I ever get him out of this house, where everything will always remind him of her ? " she wondered savagely. Really Marion was magnificent, but she was very upsetting. She was like a cardinal in full robes falling downstairs. And for what inadequate reason she had caused all this commotion ! Just because her two sons quarrelled ! She could have prevented that easily enough if she had brought them up properly and skelped them when they needed it. Ellen curled her lip as she watched him stroking the soft velvet, laying his cheek against it.

"And the desk ? You say she sat there while she talked to cook ? "

"Yes."

She hated the way he sat down in front of it ; in a heap, like a tired navvy. By her death Marion had deprived her of her beautiful lightfooted lover. But she must wait. He would come back. She became aware that Roger was speaking to her. It appeared that he had sobbed in his cup and had sent jets of tea flying over the tablecloth, and he was now apologising.

"Never heed," she told him comfortingly ; " we'll have a clean one for lunch." " I didn't mean to," he quavered piteously, but she checked him. Richard had turned over his shoulder a white face.

"She sat here ? . . ."

"Yes. While the cook stood talking to her, she sat there."

"She . . . You didn't notice . . . when she was sitting there . . . if she was scribbling on the blotter ? "

" Yes, she did. I noticed that."

" Ah . . . ah. . . ."

She was beside him in the time of a breath. But he had not fainted, though his head had crashed down on the wood, for his fingers, buried in his hair, still laced and interlaced. She did not dare touch him ; but she grovelled for the blotter, which at the moment of his groan had fallen to the floor, and stood staring at it. For a second her attention was dispersed by a shudder of disgust, for she felt Roger's noisy mouth-breathing at her ears. Then the proof leapt to her eyes. There was a rim of plain paper round the calendar on the inside of the cover, and this was covered with words and phrases written in the exquisite small script of Marion. "This is the end. Death. Death. Death. This is the end. I must die. Give him to Ellen. I must die."

Roger tumbled back towards Poppy. "The awful sin of self-destruction ! " he wailed.

This proof struck through her with an awful, unifying grief. She had had evidence of Marion's intention which had convinced her mind, but it was all derived from ugliness : from the awkwardness of the woman's talk, the plainness of the face against the glass the intrusive loitering of a squat figure in the garden. The soul had hearkened to these ugly messengers from reality since it had desired to know the truth, but it had made them cry their message from as far off as possible and as briefly as might be. But this lovely black arabesque of letters had the power of beauty. It ran into the core of her soul and told its story at its leisure. Her flesh, which before had grieved as any that is living might grieve for any that is dead, now knew the sorrow appropriate to the destruction of Marion's wide, productive body. For what her spirit learned and admitted it had always known of that burning thing which had been Marion she looked round the room in reverence, since she had lived there. The light on the handle of the French window caught her eye, and she wept. She had been annoyed with Marion because she could not turn it. But who would not find it difficult to open a door if it was death on which it opened?

"Richard, I love your mother!" she sobbed. "I love your mother so!"

He muttered something. In case he was speaking to her she bent down and listened. But he was repeating over and over again in accents of irony: "Give him up to Ellen. Give him up to Ellen. Oh, mother, mother. . . ."

By the passion for Marion that was wringing her she could measure the flame that must be devouring him. There was a strong impulse in her to feel nothing but pity for him; to apprehend with resignation that there might be a period ahead during which he might feel hatred for her, loathing her for being alive when his mother, who deserved so well, was dead. She stepped backward from the desk so that he need not be vexed by any sense of her. Yet she had a feeling as she moved that she was taking a step infinitely rash, infinitely dangerous. . . .

She became aware that behind her Roger was shaking words out of his weeping body. "You ought to be on your knees, you two! You've killed my mummie with your wickedness!"

"What's that?" she murmured, turning on him. "What's that?" She was not quite attentive. A picture was forming in her consciousness which, when it was clear, would tell her why it was perilous to leave Richard to his grief. . . .

"Aw, shut up!" hissed Poppy, and tugged at his arm.

But he faced Ellen bravely and cried: "Yes, you've killed my mummie! She saw there was something wrong going on between you two. She found out what you'd been doing up there in the bedroom when Poppy and me caught you. It must have been an awful shock to her. It was to me," he said pathetically and with relish. "I could hardly believe it myself till Poppy said, 'Well, what would they be doing together in a bedroom if it wasn't that?' How could you do such filthiness. . . ."

Shame swept over Ellen's body, over Ellen's mind. It was not sexual shame, but shame that they should both be human, she and this. But when she turned her eyes away from him in loathing she came on something far worse in Poppy's florid and skull-like face. It would have been appalling if she had been quite attentive, but she was dreamy, because there was this picture forming in her consciousness which would explain the danger to her. . . . Round Poppy's eyes and mouth there was playing a thirsty look which she seemed to be trying to suppress, for she was glancing about the

room with an expression of prudence as if she were reminding
herself that not lightly must she run the risk of being evicted
from this comfort. But the thirst triumphed. She gave
herself the gratification she had desired, and turned on Ellen
eyes on whose dull darkness there floated like oil a glistening
look of lewd accusation. It took the form of a wet, twitching
smile. But behind it was every sort of beaten, desolate envy :
the envy of the happy which is felt by the unhappy : the envy
of the woman who has a strong and glorious man which is felt
by the woman who cannot disguise from herself that in her arms
lies weakness and ignobility : the envy of one to whom love has
come as love which is felt by one to whom it has come as a decep-
tion and a sentence to squalor. And she could not be pitied.
One cannot weep over the dead when they have begun to rot :
and she was rotten with resentments. Ellen stared at her in
anger and in misery that there should be one so sad and ill-used
whom she could not comfort ; and perceived why at seeing her
she had been reminded of an open space round which stood
figures. It was of nothing in art she had been thinking, but of
John Square in Edinburgh, where after nightfall women had leaned
against the garden railings, their backs to the lovely nocturnal
mystery of groves and lawns, their faces turned to the line of
rich men's houses which mounted into the night like tall, impregnable fortresses. If she had not been preoccupied with the
picture rising in her mind she would have felt fear, for the ultimate meaning of those women she had always suspected to be
danger. . . .

"Making me think evil of my poor mummie too ! " Roger
sobbed on. "I thought the reason she didn't come to my
meeting this evening was that she was ashamed to see her son
professing Jesus. I thought hardly of her for not bringing you
two along as she promised, because I didn't see you weren't
there, and I preached on the sin of impurity specially for you,
and it was a real sacrifice for me to do it, because the officers
thought it was a forward subject for me to choose, and it my first
service here. I had to wrestle to forgive her for it."

It was growing clearer in Ellen's mind, this picture which
would tell her why she must not allow Richard to abandon
himself to his grief, to his passion.

"But, of course, I see it all now. Oh, my darling, darling
mummie ! I suppose you two wouldn't come to my meeting
because you wanted to stay here and play your tricks, and she
saw through you and wouldn't leave you alone in the house.
To think I blamed my mummie ! "

Now she saw the picture. It was her own mother, her own old mother, shuffling about the kitchen in Hume Park Square in the dirty light of the unwarmed morning ; poking forward into the grate with hands on which housework had acted like a skin disease ; pulling her flannel dressing-gown about a body which poverty and neglect had made as ugly as the time, the place, the task. She was too tired to see it vividly, but she understood the message. That was what happened to women who allowed themselves to be disregarded ; who allowed any other than themselves to dwell in their men's attention.

"Richard ! Richard !" She beat on his shoulder to make him listen. "Hark what your brother's saying of us !"

He stirred. He sat up.

"He says we're bad."

He turned round and looked down on Roger. At the sight of his face, though it was still, Ellen wished she had not roused him.

"It's no use you looking at me like that," said Roger tearfully but resolutely. "I'm as good as you. In fact I'm better now that I've got Jesus. And I tell you straight, you've killed my mummie with your beastly lust. Mind you," he cried, in a tone of whistling exaltation inappropriate to his words, "I'm not pretending I'm without sin myself. I did evil once with a woman at Blackburn, but I saw the filthiness of my ways. Old man, I do understand your temptations !"

What was Richard's hand searching for on the breakfast-table ? She bent forward to see, so that she might give it to him.

Richard had found what he wanted. His fingers tightened on the handle of the breadknife.

"Let's put an end to this," he said.

He drove the knife into Roger's heart.

"Mummie !" breathed Roger. Meekly, but with no sign that he had any other quarrel with the proceedings save that they were peremptory, he sank down on the chair beside him and fell forward, his head lying untidily among the tea-cups. This, no doubt, was the disorder which Marion had always foreseen : to prevent which she had practised her insane tidiness.

He held the attention much less than one had thought a dead man could.

"God," said Poppy, "this is a copper's business. I'm off before they come. They think I know something about a thing that happened down in Strood last Easter, though God help me

I don't. They kind of mixed me up with someone else. Let me go."

" Right," said Richard, and put his hand into his pocket and brought out a fistful of coins. " Take this. Good luck."

She snatched it, and with no further look at any of the company, ran out by the French window.

They stood looking down on Roger. Death revealed no significance in him. The smallness of his head, the indefinite colour of his hair, palliated what had occurred and made them feel incredulous of their knowledge that presently much importance would be attached to it.

Richard breathed a deep sigh of relief. " Well, it's all cleared up now," he murmured. " It is as if she had never seen Peacey. . . ."

Ellen broke into sobs. " 'Tis I who made you do it. I thought of my poor mother and how she'd suffered through not making my father think of her first and last—and you were sitting there thinking of nothing but Marion—and I knew if you heard what Roger was saying about us you'd think of me, so I made you listen. If I hadn't given you yon dunts on your shoulders you never would have heard him and never would have killed him. Oh, my love, what I have done to you, and me that would have died rather than hurt you ! But I saw my mother plain—— "

" Oh, between our mothers . . . " he said wearily, and hushed her in his arms. Bitterly he broke out : '· If we could have lived our own lives ! "

" My love, my love, don't spoil our little time together. . . ."

" But there's nothing left."

" There's nothing left, Richard, so go on kissing me."

" Wait." He drew away from her and held up his fore-finger. " There's something still."

He looked, Ellen thought, very like Marion as he stood there, his eyes roving about her face. Because his shoulders were bowed his body looked thick like a tree-trunk ; his swarthiness had the darkness of earth in it and the gold of ripe corn ; and his gaze lay like a yoke on its object.

" There's something still," he whispered. A sudden joy flamed in him.

There came over him another aspect of Marion. He looked awkward and contemptuous, as she had done when she had told Ellen how in Richard's infancy she had been obliged to be nice to people whom she did not like for the sake of a placid social atmosphere. He muttered, " I'll go to the kitchen . . . tell the servants that Roger's fallen asleep . . . they're not to disturb him. . . . That'll . . . give us time . . ."

At the door he turned.

" You're not afraid ? " He pointed to the dead man.

She shook her head and he went on his errand. With a sense of leisure, as if she had strayed into a cul-de-sac of time, and since there is no going backwards must stay there for ever, she sat down and looked about her. Roger did not frighten her at all. If his spirit was in the room it was sickly and innocuous, like the smell of a peardrop. But the horror of all that had happened to her, and its refusal to be anything but horror, viewed from whatever aspect, had begun to be agony when there broke on her that which is the reward of tragedy. She perceived the miraculous beauty of the common lot. Men and women taking children home in trams . . . people on summer afternoons going into the country in brakes . . . that wedding-party she and her mother had seen long ago dancing by the River Almond, led by a bride and bridegroom middle-aged but gravely glad. . . . Ah, that wedding-party. . . She wept, she wept.

He had returned to the room, and was holding open the French window.

" Come," he said. " Come."

CHAPTER XI

SURELY, surely he was asking too much of her? . . .

Yet he had felt no doubt that she would comply. There had been indeed no tinge of supplication in his bearing when he had halted with her on the seaward slope of the sea-wall and pointed to the other wall on the further side of the creek, and he had told her that on the island it confined there was a hut which the cattlemen used when the herds pastured there ; where there would be a store of furze with which they could build a fire ; where they could be safe until the people came to take him. Rather had he spoken triumphantly, as if he had found a hidden staircase leading out of destiny. And when he left her to see if they could bribe the fishermen who were painting the keel of a boat on the grass two hundred yards away to hand over their waders, so that he and she might walk across dryshod to the island, he did not look over his shoulder, but walked straight ahead, utterly confident that she would be there when he returned.

But surely this was far too much to ask of her, who had learned what life was ; who knew that, though life at its beginning was lovely as a corn of wheat, it was ground down to flour that must make bitter bread between two human tendencies : the insane sexual caprice of men, the not less mad excessive steadfastness of women. Roger had died, Richard was about to die, because of the grinding together of these male and female faults— Harry and Marion . . . Poppy and her sailor . . . her own mother and father. . . . And love, which she had trusted to resolve all life's disharmonies, was either ineffectual or dangerous. Her love had not been able to reach Richard across the dark waters of his mother's love ; and how like a doom that love had lain on him. . . . Since life was like this, she would not do what Richard asked. She tried to rise that she might flee from him, from these marshes, back to the hills where the red roofs of safe human houses showed among the tended fields.

But she could not move. Although her mind was still arguing

the matter, all the rest of her being had consented. She was going to do this thing. In panic she looked along the wall at Richard, wishing he would come back to her. But he was going on talking to the fishermen, though he held their waders in his hand. She quite understood why he was doing that, and watched him through tears. This was the last time he would be able to exercise that charm of which he was a little vain, since on all his few future days his intercourse with his fellows would be strictly specialised ; so he was taking the opportunity. In watching him and the reflection of his magnificence in the fishermen's smiling subjugation, she was shot through by a pang of pride and exultation. Though the night should engulf Richard and Marion, the triumph was not with the night. In throwing in her lot with them and with the human race which is perpetually defeated, she was nevertheless choosing the side of victory. . . .

She leaned back against the slope and waited. This was a good place to wait. The call of the redshanks, the cloud shadows that moved over the marshes like the footprints of invisible presences, made her feel calm.

Nevertheless her heart could not help but beat quick with fear. She wished that he would come and comfort her. But though he had left the fishermen he was not coming straight to her. He had climbed the sea-wall and was looking out to the east, to the open sea, over the country of the mud. He was thinking of Marion, and wondering where the tide had carried her. The inexorable womb was continuing to claim its own. She wanted to start up and cry out to him and hail him noisily from his obsession ; but something in the place, in the call of the redshanks, in the procession of the shadows, reminded her that when she had cried out before she had brought death upon her lover. This quietness was the safer way. She would wait patiently until he came to make his exorbitant demand.

She sat and looked at the island, and wondered whether it was a son or daughter that waited for her there.

THE END